FORTUNE COOKIE

BRYCE COURTENAY

FORTUNE COOKIE

McArthur & Company
Toronto

First published in Canada in 2011 by
McArthur & Company
322 King Street West, Suite 402
Toronto, Ontario
M5V 1J2
www.mcarthur-co.com

Library and Archives Canada Cataloguing in Publication

Courtenay, Bryce, 1933-
Fortune cookie / Bryce Courtenay.

ISBN 978-1-55278-988-9

I. Title.

PR9619.3.C598F67 2011   823'.914   C2011-904300-9

Cover design by Cameron Midson © Penguin Group (Australia)
Text design by Tony Palmer © Penguin Group (Australia)
Cover photograph by Photolibrary
Author photograph by Graham McCarter
Typeset in 12pt Goudy Oldstyle

Printed and bound in Canada by Trigraphik LBF

10 9 8 7 6 5 4 3 2 1

For
Robbee Minicola

PART ONE

Singapore Sling

CHAPTER ONE

———

MY NAME IS SIMON KOO. I'm fourth-generation Australian. My great-great-grandfather, Koo Bing Fuk, came out from China in the late 1850s to the gold rush, got lucky (ha ha) working the tailings the white miners had abandoned, and by persistence and hard work made a few bob; enough to get a bit of a start, anyway.

Back then even a bit was considered a lot. Life wasn't easy. All the maxims of the time recommended caution, and nobody is more frugal than a Chinese peasant. *Never waste a grain of winter rice* is the Chinese equivalent of *A penny saved is a penny earned.* Ah Koo, as he would commonly be known, needed no such advice.

After removing the ore that could be won with a moderate amount of labour, many white prospectors quickly became discouraged – at least, that was true for much of the human detritus that had washed in from the four corners with their arses hanging out of their trousers. Most had dreamed of a quick and lazy fortune, but finding gold usually meant backbreaking work from dawn to dusk and a bit of luck besides. They deeply resented the idea of those dirty yellow bastards – the celestials, Mongolians, Chinks, as they were variously known – showing them up by working hard and striking paydirt in claims the white miners had abandoned out of idleness.

It soon became apparent to all the layabouts, drunks and no-hopers that the celestials were fair game, not officially welcome at the diggings, or anywhere else, for that matter. So when they were pissed they'd play 'Let's go get us a Chink'. Beating up a Mongolian was considered an almost honourable pastime and certainly not an incident that need trouble an indifferent officer of the law. The many incidents of Chinese beaten to death were simply recorded as mining accidents.

A favourite trick was for a group of whites to corner a Chinaman and throw him to the ground facedown. One would sit on his legs, while another would plant a boot on his shoulder and another on his wrist. Taking a bowie knife, the ringleader would run it around the circumference of the pigtail, then rip it off the back of his head. This was gleefully known among the white miners as 'hog-tailing', a term borrowed from the Californian gold rush.

Soon the cry went up in New South Wales and Victoria: 'The Chinamen are stealing our gold! No more celestials!' Both colonies quickly locked and chained the welcoming gate.

However, Ah Koo had arrived in the second wave of Chinese crammed into the holds of the three-masted barques from Shanghai that diverted to the tiny port of Robe in the free settlers' colony of South Australia, where no restrictions or landing fees applied. Robe was a great distance from the nearest goldfields, so Ah Koo, along with others, walked more than 700 miles overland to the Yass area of New South Wales, ignoring the shorter journey to the Victorian diggings.

When I was at uni I went to the archives and searched through some of the old newspapers. There were numerous reports of farmers and townspeople seeing long files of Chinese in conical hats, their pigtails flopping behind them, snaking across the black soil plains of New South Wales. They wore blue cotton smocks and calf-length blue trousers, and bore heavy loads balanced on long bamboo poles.

Not long after Ah Koo arrived at the Lambing Flat diggings, on a night with a full moon that was so bright you could almost thread a needle by it, he woke suddenly to see a group of white prospectors armed with pick handles approaching the area where he and several other Chinese had begun to work abandoned tailings. He'd been warned of such attacks and, hesitating only long enough to call a warning to his neighbour Wong Ka Leung, a man from north Shanghai, he ran and hid in the bush nearby.

His neighbour, exhausted from a long day's labour on the miners' sluice, failed to wake or hear his warning cry. Ah Koo watched helplessly as drunken white miners surrounded Ah Wong's tent, dragged him out, threw him to the ground and proceeded to hog-tail him then beat him to a pulp. The leader of the pack triumphantly looped the bloody pigtail through his belt, then, yelling and whooping like a pack of wild dogs, they moved on to find further celestial prey.

Ah Koo dragged his bleeding, unconscious countryman into his tent and, over a period of several weeks, nursed him back to health, undoubtedly saving his life. Moreover, on the morning after Ah Wong's brutal hog-tailing, Ah Koo prayed to the gods for forgiveness, then cut off his own pigtail.

He was a Chinese peasant and therefore accustomed to a world of hardship and injustice; sitting on your arse or complaining wasn't an option, and physical harm would not be a discouragement. He was beaten more than once, but each time he'd pick himself up, rub woodlock oil or *dit da jow* – the universal cure-all most Chinese miners carried – on his cuts and bruises and return to his sluice. 'It's better here than in China,' he would tell himself, although he was not always convinced.

Ah Koo had lost his entire family in the Taiping Rebellion, led by the psychopath general Hong Xiuquan, a converted Christian who improbably termed himself 'Younger Brother of Christ' and who, in the name of his crucified older brother, butchered an estimated twenty million of his countrymen, including three generations of Ah Koo's family.

In China the family is everything, both your identity and your reason for existence; without family you are simply a wandering ghost. Ah Koo decided he must ask for his ancestors' permission and, as the lone survivor of his ancient family, begin again elsewhere. Like others from southern China, he had heard rumours of the Australian gold rush or, as it was termed, New Yellow Gold Mountain – 'new' because California (the original Yellow Gold Mountain) had been depleted. How he got to Australia was never explained. Perhaps he worked his passage or had sufficient money to pay for the fare in steerage, because he wasn't recruited as indentured labour by one of the many unscrupulous Chinese or European profiteers.

Indentured labourers were virtual slaves, made to sleep on the ground in leaky tents or in crude huts infested with fleas and lice, given barely enough to eat, and usually cheated out of the pittance they earned by being charged for their accommodation and two bowls of rice each day. It was not why they had come to the New Yellow Gold Mountain. They too could dream of fortunes to be made. Even stupid men know that if they are going to endure hardship, then it should be for gain. At the first opportunity they would abscond and head straight for the goldfields. There they'd discover they were prevented from staking a claim by the bloody-minded white miners, and so would be forced to work the tailings of the *gwai-lo* prospectors who took the easy gold and discarded the rest.

Ah Koo knew he was on his own, that his life mattered to no one and that no family would grieve his passing or burn paper money to pay for a more comfortable existence for him in the hereafter. His seed was all that was left. It was up to him to start again. 'Just a little more,' he told himself, 'then I can buy a bit of land and send money home to China to buy a wife.' There was no point returning to China, where only his ancestral spirits resided. This new land would become his home.

He decided he'd order a strong peasant girl with child-bearing hips, who would cost him next to nothing in dowry money. Women were unwanted, considered a 'waste of rice', most of them not even worthy of a name but simply numbered according to the order of their birth. An ugly one would come even cheaper. One day, he promised himself, he'd revisit China to pray and pay homage to his ancestors, but for now he would put down roots here in New Yellow Gold Mountain.

And that's just what he did. After the Lambing Flat riots, Ah Koo headed north-east to Bathurst, to try his luck. Backbreaking work won him a little more gold, and he moved on, walking across much of New South Wales before he found a place where he believed he could make a living as a market gardener without being beaten or despised.

He bought ten acres of land that had recently been plundered for its cedar. It lay beside a permanently running creek in The Valley, one of several beautiful forested valleys nestling between the hills that roll up forty or so miles into the hinterland from the New South Wales Central Coast. All the other valleys had names, but this one was simply 'The Valley'. The lack of a name gave it a unique personality, as if it epitomised everything a valley should be. Even today, with the great forests gone and the hills bald except for the pastures the dairy farmers planted, people reckon it to be the most beautiful of them all.

Ah Koo's land was twenty-five miles inland – a long day's walk from the coast – and dirt cheap. Using a long-handled axe, he felled the native eucalypts remaining after the timber-getters had taken the red cedar from the virgin forest, then he hand-cleared the undergrowth and burned or dynamited the stumps. Finally he hauled the rich alluvial soil from the creek flats and mixed it with ash from the burnt stumps to nourish the soil. The market garden he established would supply vegetables to the timber-getters still logging the ancient forest for cedar.

The huge ancient cedar logs they took out were loaded onto timber jinkers and hauled by bullock team the forty or so miles to Tuggerah Lakes, to be sent by boat to Sydney, where this beautiful timber, prized elsewhere in the world for cabinet-making, was squandered as building timber for framing, basic carpentry and joinery.

Three years later, at the age of twenty-eight, with three of his ten acres under cultivation, Ah Koo walked to the coast and purchased a ticket to Sydney on a schooner plying the route along the Hawkesbury River and past coastal farms and settlements. In Chinatown, then situated just beyond the city area, near Surry Hills, he engaged the services of a scribe and sent a letter to the headman in his village with dowry money for a bride. He asked him to have her bring a supply of persimmon and pomegranate seeds as well as the seeds of numerous Chinese vegetables. He also requested a full set of carpenter's chisels, the best the village blacksmith could make, the cost of which he added to the money for her dowry, together with her food and passage in steerage on a three-masted barque from Shanghai. He stressed that looks were of no consequence, but that she should be strong and willing to work and must come from a lucky family with a reputation for predominantly male offspring.

Ah Koo knew that the wait for his bride to arrive would be a prolonged one, although now, with the gold rush waning, the panic over the arrival of the Chinese hordes had faded a little and shipping from Shanghai to Sydney was once again permitted. Along with the letter to the village headman in China, he'd included another for his bride to present to the Chinese scribe and general fixer in Chinatown upon her arrival in Sydney, which simply asked him to arrange to have her sent up the coast to Tuggerah Lakes. There was also a letter in English for her to give to the harbourmaster, requesting that she be sent to The Valley on a returning bullock wagon. Procuring a bride would take almost eighteen months.

Pushing his barrow towards his tool shed at the end of a bleak wintery Sunday, Ah Koo heard the sharp crack of a bullocky's whip from the wagon track above his property, its echo followed almost immediately by a piercing whistle. Leaving the barrow, he ran up to the track and waved to the bullocky.

'I brought your missus!' the bullock driver yelled, jerking his thumb over his shoulder towards the back of the wagon. Then, as Ah Koo drew closer, he added in a sympathetic voice, 'Jeez, mate, she ain't the best lookin' heifer in the flamin' paddock.'

Ah Koo glanced fleetingly at the solid shape huddled near the end of the long wagon and observed her broad, flat face, which was marked by smallpox scars. *It is nothing*, he told himself. *Progeny are not born with such scars.* Then he turned to the bullocky and withdrew a small leather pouch from his trouser pocket. Taking out half a crown, he held it between the forefingers and thumbs of both hands and proffered it with a stiff bow.

It was a generous payment, but the bullocky waved it away. 'Nah, keep yer money, mate. Got any spuds? Bag'a spuds'll do me fine.' He turned in his seat to watch the bride-to-be clamber down from the wagon and shook his head. 'Gawd help the miserable little buggers youse're gunna make between the two of yiz.'

The village headman in China had conscientiously complied with Ah Koo's brief and sent nineteen-year-old daughter number two from a family with five sons. As an indication of her good fortune in obtaining a husband from a well-remembered family, she had been officially honoured with a name, Xiu Ma Jiao – Little Sparrow. Whether this was meant as a joke Ah Koo didn't know or care. In fact, he was delighted with the choice; it had been money well spent. Looks had never been the prime consideration but strength was, and Little Sparrow was everything he'd hoped for in terms of her body. He was reminded of the proverb: *Women are all beautiful in the dark, but in the dawn not all can guide a plough.* She was also deeply respectful – a quality Ah Koo had long forgotten – quietly spoken, accustomed to hard work, and, he would discover, a good cook and thrifty housekeeper. All his needs were met when she allowed him to use her body whenever he wished, moving silently in compliant rhythm with his grunting thrusts.

With both of them working from dawn to sunset, the market garden prospered. Fresh produce, though of a specific kind, was locally in demand. Timber-getters and their gap-toothed wives liked plain food and were not all that keen on a plate piled high with green veggies. Their meals consisted of meat and spuds, carrots, cabbage and onions – all boiled to mush – with roast pumpkin on Sunday.

Ah Koo and Little Sparrow were able to cultivate a further two acres, and with permanent water from the creek for irrigation, regular rainfall and abundant sunshine, there was soon more than Ah Koo could sell. He purchased a pair of pigs to eat the excess, along with any spoiled vegetables and garden refuse, but as a peasant he abhorred the idea of feeding perfectly good produce to swine. He'd noted that in the timber camps where the single men lived, there was almost no call for vegetables other than potatoes and onions and the occasional bag of carrots. Discussing this with Little Sparrow, he asked for her opinion. Surprised, she suggested timidly, 'Honourable husband, I will cook them food and they will pay you.' Something had changed between them since she had delivered a fine strong son for him, the first of the large family he meant to create to replace all he had lost. He had named the baby Koo Li Chin, to bless it with strength and wealth, and secretly hoped that the second child now swelling Little Sparrow's belly would also be a boy.

So Little Sparrow started . . . well, I suppose you could call it a Chinese chophouse, but it was really just four bush poles and a tin roof with an open fire and a mud-brick oven in the middle. Even so, they were soon using up the extra produce and making an even better living, feeding the hungry men who, ravenous from a day in the forest or on the farm, sat on logs surrounding the open-air kitchen scoffing Chinese chow off chipped enamel plates. Little Sparrow was unknowingly one of the precursors of the Chinese restaurants responsible for the love affair Australians have with Chinese food to this day.

Ah Koo bought a Yorkshire–Berkshire crossbreed sow and boar from a Hawkesbury farmer and expanded the piggery. Soon Little Sparrow added pork dumplings, wantons, fluffy pork buns baked in the clay oven and other dishes from pigs grown fat on spoiled produce and kitchen peelings.

One of these recipes my mum still cooks when I'm home. It's called 'Ants crawling along a log'. As a kid I'd giggle about it – still do – but it's delicious. If you like, I'll give you the recipe. The dish is made with marinated minced pork, dried shiitake mushrooms, vermicelli, vegetables, soy sauce, sugar, vegetable oil, black bean sauce, ginger, garlic, shallots and rice wine. You stir-fry the pork mince in a couple of tablespoons of oil, stir in the chopped shallots, garlic (four large cloves) and ginger (a quarter of a small cup), then the mushrooms and other vegetables meanwhile adding the sauces to taste. When cooked, remove the pork and vegetables, leaving the sauces in the wok, to which you add the vermicelli and stir-fry until it is cooked. Return everything to the pan and stir-fry to heat, and the dish is ready to serve. I'm buggered if I know why it's called 'Ants crawling along a log'.

Ah Koo was clear-eyed about things. Life, in the sense of having a good or enjoyable existence, was something he didn't pause to contemplate. Life was about survival, taking it one day at a time. If you got through it, you were grateful. It didn't pay to dream. At least their lives weren't threatened by that rampaging madman who had claimed to be the brother of the Christian god.

After each day's work, the first two hours after sunset were taken up with mostly silent bowing and nodding as he helped serve food to an increasing number of illiterate and raucous larrikins, who seemed to delight in finding new racial insults. Ah Koo cared little that he was required to be subservient to even the lowest slobbering *gwai-lo*; it was a small price to pay for freedom and a measure of independence, even if only because he and Little Sparrow were essential to the white man's needs.

Like every Chinese, Ah Koo secretly longed for an extended family to give him an identity but accepted that the first tender roots of his new family tree had barely penetrated the topsoil. The first generation is always hard won in the face of sickness, accident and disaster, but Little Sparrow, sweating over a steaming wok, would prove to be fecund, a mewling baby constantly at her breast and a squall of snotty-nosed infants of various sizes crawling in the dust around her feet. He took a secret pride in the fact that he was to be the forefather of many in a new land, even though a Chinese heart always belongs to the motherland, where it hopes to rest in death. He was often taken by surprise when he realised there were already four additional mouths to feed. His heart swelled with gratitude at his good fortune that all were male progeny, a clear indication that the gods were smiling.

The years passed. As the timber-getters penetrated deeper into the cedar forest, he bought a donkey cart to transport his produce. Nothing much changed; he and Little Sparrow worked seven days a week, at least twelve hours a day – he in the garden, apart from the two hours after sunset, which were taken up with helping his wife serve food to an increasing number of oafish timber-getters, agricultural workers, bullock-wagon drivers and government timber inspectors.

Every February they'd celebrate Chinese New Year with one day of respite from their labour. In China, New Year is a spring festival, but in Australia, summer is at its height. The darling buds of promise and new life are long gone, green has burned to bleached brown, the creek is down to a sluggish trickle, and everything is struggling to survive the long, dry never-ending days of shimmering heat. However, traditions must be honoured, and so the chophouse closed for the day and, to the delight of the children, Ah Koo and Little Sparrow lit Chinese crackers to drive out evil spirits, burned incense and offered their thanks to the gods who had now blessed them with six sons in a row.

The house was thoroughly swept and every corner dusted and cleaned to oust any lingering evil and clear the way for good luck to enter in the year to follow. Doors and windows were decorated with red paper and charms – red to symbolise fire, to ward off bad luck, and the charms for wealth, happiness and longevity. The boys were given lucky money in red envelopes and wore red shirts. Chinese New Year celebrations traditionally end with the lantern festival, when the community gathers under the full moon to watch the dragon dance. As theirs was the only Chinese family in The Valley, they were forced to forgo this joyous gathering. It was Little Sparrow's greatest unspoken wish that some day she and her family might celebrate New Year properly with their own people.

Then, thirteen years after their firstborn son, came the double misfortune of twin girls. One girl is 'bad rice', twin girls are 'bitter rice'. Ah Koo stoically accepted Little Sparrow's lamentations and abject apologies and decided that he must have incurred the wrath of the gods. He couldn't think what he might have done, but then they were a notoriously fickle and cantankerous lot. It was clear they were telling him he had quite enough healthy sons to ensure comfort in his old age as well as to start a new dynasty. His good joss, at least in the matter of further male progeny, had been used up.

He burned incense at the family shrine, made a sacrifice of food and added a small bottle of brandy for good measure. Building the shrine was the only request Little Sparrow had ever made of him. It wasn't much larger than a birdcage and was set on a carved pedestal, but he'd made it from cedar. The shrine was Little Sparrow's most precious – in fact, her only – possession, and she prayed before it every day. Ah Koo promised the gods that he would never again enter his wife's exhausted body, a vow he kept and one for which she may or may not have been grateful, as she was still a comparatively young woman.

Not a great deal more is known about my great-great-grandmother other than a recurring dream that was instrumental in changing her husband's life. Only one studio daguerreotype exists of the entire family, taken when the twins were around sixteen. The oval-framed image shows Little Sparrow as a moon-faced woman with pockmarked skin, her eyes two dark lines that reflect no light under the narrow curves of her eyebrows, her mouth set hard. Silver-grey plaits hang almost to her waist, and she is wearing a *pao*, a black silk top, and a pair of black pants, a *ku*. On her feet are what appear to be white slippers.

She stands next to Ah Koo, her head not quite reaching the point of his thin shoulder. Her hands are held loosely at her sides, her body language impatient. It is as if she believes her hands have been idle too long in this pointless pose, which patently she feels her hands (and perhaps those of the twins) don't have the right to be. Nevertheless, she completely dominates the photograph. The rest of the serious family appear to be a pretty scrawny bunch, but what Little Sparrow lacks in height she more than makes up for in width: she is built like the proverbial brick shithouse.

Which pretty much describes my own body – five feet eight inches in height and 210 pounds, all chunk, no fat – I'm a definite throwback to my great-great-grandma. Think rugby union prop forward. I'm a dead ringer for Little Sparrow, the full tree-trunk torso and flat face. I was playing for the under-fourteen rugby team at Cranbrook when I first got the dumb nickname that has stuck to me ever since.

We were playing Scots College, just up the road from Cranbrook. The two private schools were deadly rivals: Cranbrook was smaller and prided itself on the individualism of its students, while Scots was the traditional model that produced future leaders, meaning the standard private-school product of wealth and privilege. Or so the theory went, anyway. The Scots' favourite taunt was a rhyme that went:

> *Tiddly-winks, young man*
> *Get a woman if you can*
> *If you can't get a woman*
> *Get a Cranbrook man!*

Scots, the larger school, usually gave Cranbrook a walloping at every sport and in particular on the football field. On this particular day, the Cranbrook under-fourteens were, by our usual standards, a pretty good side, and two fathers, both leading businessmen and mates, both wealthy and highly competitive, started a friendly argument about who would win. It seems this got somewhat out of hand, so that the bets on either side kept rising, to the amusement of the assembled dads and the disgust of the few mums who dutifully watched their sons playing in the first game on a wintry Saturday morning.

In a close game, Scots got a penalty with two minutes to go to full-time, which put them three points ahead, and it seemed to be all but over for the Cranbrook dad, who stood, by this time, to lose thirty quid. But at the restart after the penalty, I caught the ball and started to run with it; lumber is probably a better description, for, even at fourteen, my bulk was formidable. I managed to barge through and run half the length of the field to score under the posts. We converted the try and won by two points – a converted try in those days was only worth five points.

The final whistle went and the Cranbrook dad was jubilant. When we came off the field, he shouted at me, 'What's you name, son?'

'Koo, sir,' I replied in the accepted private-school manner, identifying myself by my surname alone.

'And your first name?' he called again.

I was still panting heavily and was perhaps over-excited at having scored the winning try. Had he asked for my Christian name I would have said Simon, but my first name in Chinese was Kee, so that's what I stupidly said.

He handed me two pound notes, shouting, 'Buy both teams a cream bun and a lemonade' – the accepted schoolboy treat at the time – 'and . . . thanks. You won me a fortune, Koo Kee.' He must have known that Chinese surnames come first. The team and the parents heard it, to much laughter, as, 'Thanks. You won me a fortune cookie.'

From that day I was forever after nicknamed Fortune Cookie. The under-fourteen blokes stayed together throughout our schooling, and in our final year most of us played for the first fifteen that would be unbeaten, something Cranbrook School had never previously managed. After that I was selected as one of the props for Australian Schoolboys, where my nickname, unfortunately, spread far and wide. When I played rugby for Sydney University, there were some who speculated about me getting a state or even eventually a Wallaby jersey, but it was not to be; this particular tree trunk was due to crash. I badly injured my knee and that was the end of my football career. But the nickname persisted.

I had always wanted to be an artist of some sort but my family believes in education of the kind that produces lawyers, doctors and businessmen. We're big in several businesses – coffin manufacture (Gold Chisel Caskets), funeral parlours (Blue Lotus Funerals) and restaurants (the Little Sparrow restaurant chain). Eating and dying are both inescapable and therefore good business, but art, in the family's opinion, is an occupation for dreamers who have little or no chance of earning an honest quid. Had it not been for Ah Koo four generations back, I'd have had Buckley's of becoming an artist. Even so, I was required to go to Sydney Uni where I did an honours degree in Commerce majoring in economics. Only then was I allowed to study graphic design at Sydney Technical College and finally move on to my present life in advertising, a compromise my folk find barely acceptable. If I know my mum, she'll probably attempt to buy the agency one day. Fortunately, it is a very large multinational with its head office in America, and therefore unlikely to come up for sale. Still, you never know with her.

I guess my parents are pretty disappointed that, as the oldest and only son, I haven't gone into one of the family's three areas of business. Pointing out that I've got three sisters who are not exactly intellectual slouches, and fifteen female cousins, most of them highly qualified, smart as whips and climbing the family corporate ladder in a competitive scramble, doesn't seem to help. We're pretty integrated as an extended Australian family (my grandfather was the last male Koo to grow up speaking Cantonese), and we've fought in every war, including the Boer War, but excluding Vietnam, where my name didn't come up in the lottery. But some Chinese customs persist, the privileges accorded the firstborn male being one of them.

When my three sisters and I were kids we would play a game called 'Hawks and Doves'. I would stand on a chair and be the hawk, while my sisters, squatting on the carpet, would be doves. 'Koo! Koo! Koo!' the doves would call, while I glared down at them ferociously, choosing my prey. If my mother caught me before I leapt, she would remind us sternly, 'Your name may sound like the call of a dove, but you will all be hawks, remember that.'

The eldest son of each generation of the Koo family has taken over as group chairman of the various family enterprises. Even though some of my dad's younger brothers, my uncles, were obviously smarter than he was, Dad still got the top job. If it hadn't been for my mum not so quietly taking the reins, the various businesses might not be where they are today. Not all Koos have proved to be happy little Vegemites. My dad has a problem with alcohol, *is* an alcoholic, which seems pretty rare among Sydney Chinese, but then perhaps it is simply kept well hidden, as things are in our family, or it's a gene picked up from one of his convict antecedents.

But that's the advantage of a large and varied family business: there's a place for everyone, be it chairman of the board or forklift driver in a warehouse. As an example, there are aspects of the death business that are better served by the exceedingly dull though trustworthy members of the family. Collecting the dead and dealing with the results of their bowels loosening and evacuating their contents at the moment of death is not for the squeamish. Preparing corpses, plugging orifices or babysitting the dead is not for the overly imaginative.

My dad's a pretty benign drunk and seldom creates a fuss, but my mum hates weakness of any sort. Her catchcry is 'Well, what can you expect? After five generations of intermarriage with convicts, your family is bound to have picked up a few bad habits.' Perhaps it's the intermarriage that has made him less obviously concerned with all things Chinese, whereas my mother, who came from Singapore at the age of three with her parents, is very proud of her Straits-Chinese heritage. Her dad was the youngest of four brothers in a family that was well placed in the palm-oil business. As number-four son he was last in the pecking order but was evidently pretty bright, so when he'd completed his matriculation at Raffles Institution in Singapore in 1910, he was sent to Cambridge and took a degree in organic chemistry.

Returning home just before the Great War, he was recruited by Levers to work in their new Malaya palm-oil plant, experimenting with industrial uses for palm oil, in particular, glycerine for explosives. He was considered a key man, his job essential to the war effort, and he was not permitted to join up. He married and my mum, Phyllis, was born in 1915. Four years later, with the war over, Levers offered him a position in Australia to establish a laboratory to produce refined glycerine. Levers had just signed a contract with the Nobel people, who had set up factories in Sydney and Melbourne to manufacture explosives in which nitroglycerine was a key component. While this wasn't a government initiative, Canberra nevertheless saw the local manufacture of explosives as important. Importing explosives during the war had proved both dangerous and costly. Australia was isolated from its allies, especially in the event of future hostilities. The fact that Albert Kwan, my grandfather's Europeanised name, was Chinese – and therefore subject to the White Australia Policy – was quietly overlooked, due to the importance of his work to Australia's future defence. In fact, he was given a token interview and made to translate a piece of writing into English, avoiding the usual dictation test in Russian, Hungarian or Scottish Gaelic, if necessary, which was used to deny entry to undesirables such as blacks and Asians.

Born in Singapore, my mother grew up in Australia and was educated at Presbyterian Ladies College in Pymble and is, to all intents and purposes, Australian. But that's not how she sees it. Her grandparents managed to flee Singapore just before the Japanese invasion of the island during the Second World War and hid out for its duration in one of their more remote palm-oil plantations in Malaya. But they lost two sons who'd joined up to fight the Japanese. After the war her grandparents returned to their large villa on Tanjong Katong (Turtle Bay) and resumed their place as an important Straits-Chinese family.

My mother's parents, Albert and Gloria Kwan, subsequently returned to Singapore island, where Albert joined his brother, Robert, in the family's palm-oil business. Both my mum's parents were tragically killed in an automobile accident in 1948.

So my mother regards herself as a well-born Chinese, who, in 1935 at the age of twenty, had the good fortune to marry into a very rich family, and the corresponding misfortune to blend her pure blood with that of a ratbag, mixed-up Chinese-Australian family with almost no sense of being Chinese. It didn't help either when my dad, leaving her with a two-year-old, joined up and was sent to New Guinea. Because of his experience in the coffin and funeral business, he was attached to the Army Graves Service as an officer and rose to the rank of captain, but in 1945 he returned to her a drunk.

Furthermore, my sisters, born after the war, don't look particularly

Chinese – well, perhaps if you take a hard look. Their hair, but not much else, shows their Asian heritage – so my pretty mother could take delight only in her first child, a throwback to my great-great-grandmother with a build like a tree stump and a flat Chinese peasant face that looks as if I were slammed very hard against a brick wall at birth.

With my great-great-grandfather producing six sons, all of whom survived childhood by some miracle, you'd think there'd be Koos aplenty, and, indeed, after four generations, my extended family runs to over two hundred members. But my father's generation must have offended the gods in a big way, because not one of my six Koo uncles has produced a male heir. I am the last of the male Koos. My recalcitrance in choosing not to join the family business empire (we also own a vast amount of real estate, known as First Nest Investments) has resulted in a fair amount of criticism from and disappointment amongst my extended family, and my failure to marry and produce a male heir hasn't helped my status much either. Despite our childhood game and my superior role in it, it seemed that I was the dove and my sisters were the hawks.

Anyway, enough of that Chinese dynastic nonsense. Ever since high school I've been called Fortune Cookie. I've grown so accustomed to the nickname that if any one of my friends were to call me Simon, I'd most likely do a double-take before responding.

However, I digress.

Great-great-grandfather Ah Koo was a philosophical sort of bloke, prepared to bide his time and cop what life brought him, good and bad. Like almost all Chinese peasants, he knew how to grow things, and the soil was his security, his guarantee of life, but it wasn't where his heart lay. He'd been trained as a carpenter and secretly longed to return to his vocation. He loved wood for itself and he was also, it seems, something of an artist.

In the Yass mining museum, there's a sluice made from ironbark rescued from a Lambing Flat creek bed that had once been a busy prospecting site. My grandfather claimed it once belonged to Ah Koo and that it carries his chop carved into one of the sluice planks.

A gold prospector's sluice is a pretty basic piece of field equipment: a few wooden posts and planks and, if you were lucky, a tin lining beaten out of kerosene cans. While I haven't seen it, this one is said to be practically a work of art, the ironbark sides decorated with dragons and birds, and the posts entwined with carved lotus blossoms.

The sluice boxes, or cradles, as they were sometimes called, contained thin timber bars known as riffles, placed at right angles to the flow of the creek. A shovel-load of gold-bearing alluvial gravel was dumped into the top of the sluice. The current then carried the muck down the length of the sluice box. The lighter 'tailings' would be held in suspension and flow over the top of the riffles, to be discharged back into the river or creek. At the same time, the tiny specks of gold, along with the heavy black sands, would drop to the bottom of the box and become trapped behind the riffles.

Ah Koo's riffles were carved in the shape of wriggling freshwater eels. But for me, anyway, as a fourth-generation member of his Australian family and also an art director in a Sydney advertising agency, it is an insight into how he viewed life. He worked like a dog from dawn to dusk in one of the world's toughest environments, surrounded by hard-eyed racists who often beat him up, yet he remained true to his artist's soul.

Working in advertising flogging things people probably don't need or even want, I wonder if I possess the same integrity and patience in this new and permissive world that Ah Koo possessed in his rigid, limited, racist and classist world.

He probably never expected the world to change. What he saw and experienced was all there ever was or could be for him. After all, continuity, not change, was what he craved. In the 1960s, more than a hundred years later, rapid change was something my generation took for granted. During my childhood and youth in the forties and fifties, the world seemed to settle into peace and order with a sigh of relief after the tumult of war, but in the next decade the winds of change that brought Vietnam and resulted in Kent State became a hurricane that roared through the sixties and ushered in a very different world. Rock 'n' roll, Elvis, the Beatles, the Rolling Stones and Bob Dylan musically represented the strident new voices of my generation.

I've always liked to think I've been involved in some of that change, which may even, perhaps, have been why I chose advertising as my career. But Ah Koo would have spent his life trying to occupy as small a space and make as little noise as possible: unseen, unheard, unobtrusive, unimportant, voicing no opinions, never rocking the boat – the heathen Chink bowing, smiling and nodding at everyone. *What's goin' on behind them slanty eyes? What's the yellow bastard really thinking?*

They had eight kids to feed, and Little Sparrow was worn and prematurely aged by hard work and repeated childbearing. They had no protest drums to beat, nor did they rattle the chains that society had placed around their ankles.

I sometimes imagine Ah Koo in his market garden, hearing the crack of a bullocky's whip and the creak of a wagon as he wipes his sweating brow on his sleeve, then leaning on a spade or mattock as he watches the bullock team pass, hauling the finest cedar in the world to be used for scaffolding and framing timber. A beautifully grained cabinet timber so wantonly squandered would be something he couldn't have understood. I'd like to think it would have deeply offended his craftsman's sensibilities.

Over the years he had expanded the original hut to accommodate his large family, and he'd also constructed a plain all-weather timber structure closer to the road as a kitchen and dining area for Little Sparrow's eatery. Known to the locals simply as 'The Chinks', it was virtually a compulsory stop for the bullock-drivers as well as for the timber-getters. Occasionally it was even used for weddings or Masonic celebrations. He'd made the tables and chairs and other fittings from practically indestructible ironbark rather than the splendid cedar. The chisels he used for joinery were made in Sheffield and Birmingham, and purchased from the new general merchant at The Entrance. The cheap homemade chisels he'd carried with him from China had been worn down by the hardness of the native timber on the goldfields and were beyond use before he reached The Valley.

Ah Koo was, above all things, a patient man. He waited until his two oldest sons could be put to work on the land. Then, with a hundred almost-mature persimmon and pomegranate trees bursting with early spring blossom to define the borders of his market garden, he opened the set of chisels Little Sparrow had brought with her from China all those years ago. My great-great-grandfather, it seems, used a chisel as if it were a natural extension of his hands. He removed each in turn from its grease-filled leather pouch, then appropriated a rare and precious hour cleaning them. Finally, he laid them, with their shiny blades and handles made from the heartwood of the persimmon tree, out along the length of the ironbark table. He sat and made a momentous decision: it was time to consult the gods. In order to propitiate them, he decided to offer them a roasted piglet, pomegranates and persimmons.

As always he was practical. If he was going to return to carpentry and, in particular, the self-indulgence of decorating using a chisel, there had to be a sound reason beyond the simple tugging at his heart, or the gods, seemingly pacified by his connubial abstinence, might revoke his prosperity. It never occurred to him that working with the chisels might be a hobby. The concept of time spent in pleasure was one he simply didn't comprehend, although he had been unable to keep his hands off Little Sparrow's shrine. Over the years, using a bowie knife, he had transformed it with elaborate carving. He'd chosen the American knife, purchased on the goldfields, because he had been too superstitious to open the set of chisels Little Sparrow had brought from China. 'It is not yet time,' he always told himself.

Now he duly attended the shrine, burning incense and making an offering before asking for guidance. Three days later, Little Sparrow, a vexed expression on her usually impassive face, approached him after he had taken his evening meal and asked permission to speak. Ah Koo nodded. 'Honourable husband, I have had a dream.' She paused. 'It has come three times.'

Ah Koo nodded again. He knew Little Sparrow would not have the temerity to mention her dreams if she didn't think they directly concerned him. 'You may tell me of these dreams,' he replied.

'One dream, always the same one. It concerns the chisels, a rocking cradle, a large box and a coffin. All have been carved by you. On the side of the cradle are carved birds of every kind, though none are birds of prey, no goshawk, no eagle and no kite. Also, on the board above where the infant would rest his head is a nest of four fledglings with a serpent hovering above it as if to strike. A fat dragon is carved on the lid of the large box. It is the only decoration and the wood is highly polished. The coffin stands on a tall marble plinth with three steps leading up to it. The lid leans against the side of the open coffin. It is too high for me to see inside, but on the centre of the lid are carved three lotus blossom buds. There are no open blooms.'

'And the chisels?'

'They are the ones I brought with me from China, the handles made from the heart of a persimmon tree. They lie in a neat row at the base of the white marble plinth in the same order as you laid them out on the table when you took them from their greased leather bags and cleaned them.' Little Sparrow hesitated, then said, 'Only they are different.'

'Different?'

'The blades are made of gold.'

Ah Koo smiled. 'This is a good omen!' But then, pausing to think, he added, 'But then again, not so good. Gold is too soft for a chisel blade.'

As if she hadn't heard him, Little Sparrow frowned and said, 'One of them is missing.'

'So?' Ah Koo suggested calmly, rather pleased with himself for puncturing this female dream with the male observation about the impractical nature of a gold chisel blade, but his remark was lost on Little Sparrow.

'It is the second largest,' she continued, 'the number-eight. It does not lie with the others. There is a gap where it ought to be.'

Ah Koo shrugged. 'It is missing. It is a dream. There is no need for an explanation.'

Little Sparrow drew back, a look of terror on her flat face. 'No! It is not missing!'

Ah Koo, somewhat surprised, felt a twinge of anxiety for the first time. Her obvious fear disconcerted him. Dreams, even women's dreams, must sometimes be taken seriously. He had asked for guidance from the gods, and while he doubted that they would reply through such a humble medium as Little Sparrow, her life had been blameless. Though roughly glazed and fired, she was a pure vessel. In an attempt to hide his concern, he demanded, 'Well, where is it?'

'In my dream I climb the three marble steps so that I am now able to see directly into the coffin,' she explained. 'Lying within it is an ancient and emaciated crone. She is naked and almost bald. Blood runs in a thin trickle from her left breast across her stomach.' Little Sparrow, her voice now barely above a whisper, began to sob. 'The handle of number-eight chisel protrudes from her heart.'

Ah Koo observed his tearful wife, making no attempt to console her. In fact, he had no idea how to do so. While there had been a hint of anxious tears when she had clambered down from the bullock wagon all those years ago to meet his eyes for the first time, he had never seen Little Sparrow cry.

In fact, the *gwai-lo* timber-getter's wife who acted as the local midwife remarked on her stoicism. Called to attend the birth of their first child, she had come from the bedchamber – a section of the hut curtained off with bleached rice sacks sewn together – shaking her head in apparent disbelief. Ah Koo, waiting anxiously at the front of the parted curtains, held both hands behind his back to conceal them. In his right was a pound note he had over-generously decided to pay the midwife if she had delivered him a son; in his left, a ten-shilling note, should it turn out to be a girl.

The midwife had drawled, 'A boy, no problems,' neglecting to add her congratulations. Delighted, Ah Koo had proffered the pound note.

She snatched it without saying thank you and pushed it quickly into her pinny pocket, glaring defiantly at him in case he expected change. Seeing the note was safe, with no protest coming from Ah Koo, she had proceeded to examine him. Starting from his bare mud-caked feet, her eyes had travelled slowly up his smooth brown legs, dirty shorts and shirt, coming to rest on his grinning, obsequious face. Her expression throughout had been one of silent contempt. Finally, she'd addressed him a second time. 'What are you people, anyway? Animals? Yellow monkeys?' She tossed her head in the direction of the bedroom door. 'T'ain't natural. She – Mrs Monkey – just give birth to a ten-pound bub and she never bawled, even the once.'

Now, seated at the table with her face buried in her arms, Little Sparrow wept. 'It is the gods!' she wailed. Then, looking pleadingly up at Ah Koo and choking back her sobs, she cried, 'They are speaking to you, honourable husband.'

Ah Koo's first instinct was to shout at her. Who was she, a woman, to suggest such a preposterous idea? But he was forced to admit to himself that her dream on three consecutive nights was filled with signs and perhaps even dangerous portents. Like all Chinese peasants he was deeply superstitious. To turn a deaf ear to the gods and, worse, his ancestors, and so provoke their anger was an extremely dangerous course of action. Not wishing her to sense his anxiety, he asked gruffly, 'Is that all?'

Little Sparrow looked up and fisted the tears from her dark swollen eyes. 'No, there is more,' she gulped. Ah Koo remained silent, waiting, his hands held below the surface of the table where he could feel them trembling on his knees. 'There is also a newborn child in the cradle. It has not yet been cleaned and there is nothing between its legs, male or female. The umbilical cord has not been cut and leads like a long twisted rope into the bloodstained birth gate of the old crone. In the dream I know I must cut it but have no means of doing so.' A loud sob escaped from Little Sparrow. 'Then I recall the chisel and withdraw it from the old crone's heart and cut the cord, then tie it off, but, like some live thing, it immediately attaches itself just beyond the knot.

I cut and tie it again but the same thing happens until the fourth knot is tied.

'Then the newborn infant suddenly begins to kick and cry. The birds carved into the side of the cradle come alive, and the four fledglings in the nest open their mouths, which are larger than their heads and shaped like open fire bellows. The lining of each mouth is a different colour: from the deepest yellow for the largest among them through to russet and then to white. The fourth fledging, the large yellow-mouthed one, suddenly drops out of the nest above the infant's head and into the baby's open bawling mouth and disappears. The birds from the cradle hover above the crying child's head and then start to sing. The newborn infant stops crying and kicking, and they alight one by one onto his tiny body, almost covering it. Finally, they begin to clean it with their beaks.

'The snake above the nestlings also comes to life and drops onto the belly of the child, where the birds – they are of every imaginable colour – hop aside unconcerned, allowing it a clear pathway across the chest and belly to the nothingness between its legs. The snake – a viper and iridescent blue – is not large.' Little Sparrow holds up her forefinger. 'Only three times the size of my finger, no more. It curls itself neatly between the infant's legs where its missing part should be, its head raised and swaying, its tongue flicking.'

'But you had the chisel. Did you not attempt to kill the snake?' Ah Koo asked, knowing almost immediately that so reasonable an action was unlikely in a dream.

'No, somehow I've lost the golden chisel or, rather, I discover I no longer hold it in my hand. Perhaps when I tied the umbilical cord I put it down. But now my attention is suddenly drawn to the coffin lid, and I watch as the carved lotus buds open fully and become real, and I can see that they exactly match the colour of the serpent. I turn just in time to see the baby's mouth stretch to the size of a large apple, and a yellow and brown fully feathered bird emerge from it, flap its wings and fly away out of the dream picture.'

'And the dragon? The fat dragon on the box? Is it . . . does it come alive?' Ah Koo asked anxiously.

Little Sparrow shook her head. 'No. It remains as it was, a beautiful wooden carving.' She looked up at him sorrowfully. 'Forgive me, honourable husband. In the dreams, when I turn back from the lotus blossoms to the dragon box I see the number-eight chisel again, but now it possesses its original steel blade. It has been firmly, perhaps even violently, driven into the place where the heart of the fat dragon would have been had it been alive and not merely a carving.'

Ah Koo's mind was besieged with symbols, omens and portents that he didn't begin to understand, except for one – the fat dragon. It was the sign of prosperity and it had remained inert, the chisel driven into the wooden heart. There was much too much in the dream to ignore. The embedded steel chisel in the fat dragon patently denoted disaster. 'We will go to Sydney to visit the *xun meng xing shang*, the fortune teller, for an interpretation,' he replied gruffly, hoping that, through her tears, Little Sparrow wouldn't see that his hands were shaking.

Taking the donkey cart, Ah Koo and Little Sparrow set off for Tuggerah Lakes to take the coastal schooner to Sydney. The driver's seat on the cart was only large enough for Ah Koo, so Little Sparrow had to sit cross-legged on the tray facing backwards, her squat frame absorbing every bump on the rutted wagon track. The children – even the youngest – capable and trustworthy, remained at home.

It was the first time since her arrival that Little Sparrow had been further than The Entrance, but her presence in Sydney was essential. Dreams must be told down to the smallest detail if the seer is to interpret them accurately. There was also the matter of mood, atmosphere, essence, a possible miasma around the old crone's coffin, the arrangements of the objects, all of which only Little Sparrow could describe. The process was expensive and they would have only one chance; they must give the dream to the soothsayer with every detail intact. It was even possible that he would send her back into the dream to find the answer to some question.

Little Sparrow was silently terrified. If the dream interpretation turned out badly, she might be accused of being a 'dream stealer': an impure and worthless vessel containing 'bitter rice' that had polluted her husband's dream and, in the process, destroyed his future. If this proved to be the case, he would have every reason to be rid of her.

However, it didn't occur to her that by remaining silent she could avoid any possible danger. Little Sparrow was convinced that the gods had answered her husband's need for guidance, and while a recalcitrant spirit might have misdirected their answer and sent it through her as a celestial joke, she could not possibly, even at the risk of her life, disobey their instructions.

The trip from The Entrance to Sydney by schooner wasn't pleasant. It was a brutally hot late November day and the deck was crowded. Ah Koo and Little Sparrow – 'the Chinks' – were, despite paying the full fare, ordered by the first mate below decks to a small space between a stack of empty wooden beer casks. They were forced to share with a fat, profusely sweating Aboriginal woman nursing a sick baby. The smell of stale hops mixed with the foetid air made it difficult to breathe, and Ah Koo's clean white starched shirt was soon soaked with sweat and clung to his skinny frame. The sea was choppy even before they sailed into a bad squall off Lion Island. All were seasick, the Aboriginal woman so violently that at one stage she helplessly dropped the baby onto the dirty planking, where it landed in a mess of vomit at Little Sparrow's feet. Despite her discomfort she impulsively picked up the child, then immediately perceived that the act of comforting this blackfella devil child might be yet another bad omen.

Arriving in Chinatown that evening, they paid to share a room with another couple, only to discover that there were also six children and an infant who was teething and cried most of the night. The following morning they visited the home of the scribe who, years earlier, had written Ah Koo's letter requesting a bride and arranged Little Sparrow's trip to The Valley. They discovered that he had recently died and they now had no one they could trust to help them.

There were dream interpreters, seers and soothsayers aplenty, it seemed. Almost everyone they asked knew one. Sydney was a raw new Chinese community, the seeds of traditional order and rank too recently sown. Anyone could be almost anything they wanted, and Ah Koo and Little Sparrow were easy to spot as a pair of country bumpkins ripe for the picking. They were not fools, yet they had no safe starting point. It seemed they could return home with the dream and Ah Koo's purse intact, or take a punt on someone who claimed to be a *xun meng xing shang* and looked and sounded trustworthy.

After three days Ah Koo was becoming increasingly morose and Little Sparrow blamed herself. If her dream were a message from the gods, then surely its interpreter should be awaiting their arrival. She was about to offer herself to her honourable husband for a severe beating when their luck changed. Coming down Wentworth Avenue towards them was a prosperous-looking Chinese man who seemed about to pass when he stopped suddenly and gave Ah Koo a quizzical look. 'Ah Koo?' he asked in a tentative voice.

Ah Koo nodded, but didn't recognise the stranger. The man slapped his chest and smiled fit to burst. 'Wong Ka Leung! You saved my life at the diggings!' he exclaimed.

There was much bowing and nodding and expressions of joy at the reunion, and Wong Ka Leung insisted they stay as his guests in a place he owned where they would have a room to themselves. 'We must celebrate!' he exclaimed. 'A banquet, tonight, and you will be the honoured guest.' He cast a glance at Little Sparrow. 'My wife will attend to your wife.' He clapped his hands together. 'I will invite the Dragon Master, Tang Wing Hung.'

Ah Koo was bewildered at the unexpected meeting and suddenly afraid. He had long since grown unaccustomed to his own kind or to being treated with honour and felt out of his depth. 'Ah Wong,' he protested, using the familiar form of Wong Ka Leung's name, 'I am unworthy, a grower of vegetables, no less a barefoot peasant than I was in China. Such a great honour is not for the likes of me. I do not possess the manners required or have the conversation for such a grand occasion, much less the temerity to address the head of the Triad.'

Ah Wong drew back. 'A brave man may sit in the company of the emperor,' he quoted. 'You will be the most worthy man at the banquet, Ah Koo.'

Ah Koo shook his head and indicated his shabby white cotton shirt and heavy boots. The collar of his shirt, washed and starched by Little Sparrow three days previously, was ringed with dirt from walking the dusty streets, and his suit was no better. 'I have one clean shirt, that is all. It is for visiting the *xun meng xing shang*,' he explained, then added lamely, 'We only expected to be here two days.' He shrugged, spread his hands and looked down at his thin torso. 'I have only this *gwai-lo* suit and no blacking for my boots.'

Ah Wong lightly touched the lapel of Ah Koo's jacket. 'We are the same size,' he said, then patted his stomach lightly and laughed. 'Perhaps I have a little more around the middle. I have lots of clothes and we will make a good fit.' His expression was suddenly serious. 'Ah Koo, you *must* allow me to repay my debt.'

Ah Koo shook his head slowly. 'I cannot accept your kindness, Ah Wong. What happened was many moons ago and is long forgotten. As there is no debt, there is no repayment necessary. I compliment you on your prosperity.'

Ah Wong sighed. 'With the help of the gods and the Dragon Master, yes, I have prospered. Now my greatest wish is to offer my gratitude in a tangible way.' He paused, thinking. 'But what is this about a soothsayer? Do you have a problem? Perhaps I can help.' He looked up and down the street, then turned back to them. 'It is hot standing here, and there is a tea-house.' He pointed across Wentworth Avenue. 'Let us take tea and talk.' He glanced at Little Sparrow. 'Do you wish your wife to accompany us? I can direct someone to take her to my house, where my wife will serve her tea.'

Ah Koo shook his head. 'No, she will stay,' he said, in a sudden panic at being left alone.

They crossed the street and entered a tiny room where there were two tables, both unoccupied. Ah Wong addressed an elderly woman who had been seated on a chair, a tray on her lap, shelling broad beans. Seeing them enter, she had risen and placed the tray on one of the tables. Clasping her hands, she bowed, silently greeting them.

Ah Wong indicated the tables. 'Both are now taken,' he instructed her. 'You will be paid twice the cost of what we order. Bring tea and *deem sum* then make yourself scarce. I will call if you are needed, old mother.'

The woman bowed and disappeared through a bead curtain to the back of the tea-house. The two men seated themselves and Ah Wong, smiling, turned to Ah Koo. 'Now, first you must tell me about yourself. I have thought of you often, and longed and prayed to the gods that you had prospered and that we should meet again. My prayers have been answered in this miraculous chance meeting.'

Little Sparrow, afraid that if she sat with Ah Koo he would lose face with his friend from the past, made to seat herself at the spare table. To her surprise, Ah Koo indicated for her to do otherwise and waited until she was seated before addressing the urbane Ah Wong. 'If you wish, I will tell you my unworthy story.' It was obvious he was uncomfortable at the prospect. 'Then, with your permission, Little Sparrow will tell you of the dream, the reason for our being here.' He paused, nervously clearing his throat. 'But before I do so, while I am grateful for your hospitality and we will accept your offer of a clean room, for which we will pay you, I must explain that I am no longer accustomed to the company of my own people, nor have I ever attended a banquet.'

Ah Wong interrupted, explaining, 'It is only a banquet in a manner of speaking, a few guests —'

'No, it is impossible!' Ah Koo threw up his hands in protest, then, fearing that he had spoken too forcefully, lowered his voice. 'I was seasick coming down the coast and my stomach has not yet adjusted.' As if to consolidate this untruth, he went on, 'I can eat only a little plain rice and so you will lose face with your guests. I cannot accept.' Ah Koo, thoroughly out of his depth, felt himself trembling and was afraid to meet the other man's eyes.

Little Sparrow, who had not felt his touch since the disastrous birth of the twins, now longed to comfort her distraught husband. While love was not a prerequisite for marriage and, indeed, she had no notion of what such an emotion might be, she deeply honoured this man who seldom castigated her and had never once taken the donkey whip to her unworthy hide.

Ah Koo finally summoned the courage to look up. 'If you can recommend a soothsayer of good reputation, it would be more than sufficient repayment where no payment was necessary. We would be most grateful,' he concluded.

It was clear to Ah Wong that his long-lost friend and saviour had made a final decision. 'Forget about the banquet,' he replied with a brush of his hand. 'I will see what I can do about a seer.' He grinned to indicate the subject of the banquet was closed and there were no hard feelings. He leaned forward, his elbows on the table. 'Now, tell me about yourself, Ah Koo,' he said again. 'It hardly seems possible. It is thirty years, even a little more perhaps, eh?'

The old woman, carrying a tray, entered the tiny room to the rattle of the bead curtain and placed on the table a large pot of green tea, three small ceramic bowls, a large tin plate of dim sims, chopsticks and three smaller tin plates, then bowed and departed.

Ah Koo nodded to Little Sparrow to pour the tea. He had missed breakfast and dinner the previous day and was ravenous, and the old lady's *deem sum* looked excellent, but then he realised that only minutes before he'd claimed to have an upset stomach. He took a sip of tea, then, clearing his throat, he attempted to explain his life in The Valley.

It was so long since he had talked about himself, even thought about his circumstances or compared them to those of other Chinese, that relating his life among the *gwai-lo* timber-getters came haltingly – the blessing of six sons, followed by the disaster of twin daughters was the main thrust. He mentioned the market garden and the humble eatery, the donkey cart, the pigs and the terrible waste of beautiful cedar, but skipped over the part where, after the birth of the twins, he promised the gods he would practise abstinence to appease their anger, aware that like almost all Chinese men, Ah Wong would cherish virility and potency above all things. He moved on to recent times, with his two eldest sons now sufficiently mature to manage the market garden and the remaining children able to help in the chophouse. He had decided to make an offering of a roasted piglet, pomegranates and persimmons to the gods and ask for their permission to use the chisels Little Sparrow had brought all those years ago from China. He looked over at her and then back at Ah Wong. 'She has since had a dream, three times, always exactly the same.' He shrugged. 'It is why we have come here, to find a good *xun meng xing shang* for a translation.'

Ah Wong nodded slowly and absent-mindedly indicated that Little Sparrow should fill his cup, even though he had barely sipped from it. 'The gods have been generous, Ah Koo. You have six sons to bring comfort to your old age.' Then, silently recognising the impossibility of twins finding someone who would be willing to marry one half of the same imperfect vessel, added in an encouraging voice, 'And two daughters who will be faithful and caring handmaidens to rub your feet and back and attend to your every need.' He paused and frowned, then nodded towards Little Sparrow. 'You say it is your wife who had this dream . . . dreams?' Clearly, as with Ah Koo's own initial response, his friend's first instinct was to discredit the dreams of a peasant woman.

Ah Koo, conscious of his scepticism, replied, 'She will tell it and you will decide for yourself.'

Little Sparrow was by nature a silent, self-effacing woman, who saw Ah Wong as far above her station in life. She accepted that he must harbour doubts that a mere ignorant peasant woman would be chosen by the gods as a vessel for transporting an important dream, and she was anxious not to let her husband down in front of this important stranger.

Ah Koo, still nervous and conscious of the fact that he had done a heavy-handed job of relating his past since the time the two men parted after leaving the diggings, didn't make things any easier by addressing her in a proprietary tone tinged with premature censure. 'You are my mouthpiece; speak *clearly* and do not under *any* circumstances leave anything out,' he instructed.

Little Sparrow was terrified, but she fervently believed the dream belonged to her honourable husband and was not her own. On pain of death, she must tell it well to this stranger who had promised to find a soothsayer they could trust. And so she began to speak. She related the dream, each sequence treated like a play and given its own weight and colour. Finally she completed the penultimate scene and glanced at Ah Koo for his approval. He nodded, whereupon she concluded with the image of the number-eight chisel, its original steel blade embedded in the wooden heart of the fat dragon.

Leaning forward for emphasis and holding three fingers above his head, buoyed by his wife's beautiful account of the dream, Ah Koo pronounced in an emphatic voice, 'It – the dream – has been repeated *three* times without a *single* change in detail!' He drew back and, with a jerk of the head, nodded his approval to Little Sparrow.

Despite himself, Ah Wong was impressed with the depth of content in this dream. It was so far beyond the imagination of a mere woman that he no longer doubted she had been used by the gods. Inexplicably, they had chosen to speak to his friend through his ugly, pockmarked wife. He was momentarily silent and seemed to be thinking. 'I have a plan,' he declared at last. 'The Dragon Master owns a chophouse, the best. There is a private room —'

Ah Koo interrupted. 'You promised, no banquet.'

'No banquet! Definitely no banquet! A quiet dinner, just you and me.' He grinned, conscious of the look of relief on his friend's face. 'There is a private room where we will eat alone.' He paused fractionally then added casually, almost as an afterthought, 'He will simply drop in for a few minutes to hear the dream. Whereupon I will ask him to help you.'

Ah Koo once again looked uncertain. The gesture from Ah

Wong – bringing in the Triad boss – was well beyond his personal merit and could be perilous. 'There is too much pork on my plate for the price of this dish,' he quoted.

Ah Wong attempted to reassure him. This message from the gods would require a great dream master and there was only one such in New Yellow Gold Mountain. He paused and then explained, 'Ah Koo, I am Hong Gun – Red Stick – second only to one other who serves Dragon Master Tang Wing Hung, who has at his exclusive disposal the most venerable soothsayer of all. If you come with me tonight, I will ask that he permit the great one – who even in our native land was revered as a master of celestial ways – to translate your dream.'

Little Sparrow gasped then clapped both hands over her mouth. It was an offer Ah Koo must not, could not, refuse.

It was indeed a monumental and generous offer, and Ah Koo suspected that even for the number three in the Triad, it was not going to be an easy request to make. But, unlike Little Sparrow, he was not sure it was such a good idea. He was aware that the gods had a pecking order and that an ignorant peasant such as he would never have a request answered by a member of the top celestial echelon, those gods who reserve their time for emperors, the well-born rich and dragon masters of special merit. Furthermore, an introduction to a *xun meng xing shang* as influential as the one Ah Wong proposed could be seen by them as a deliberate attempt at deception, one likely to result in further anger from the gods. By going over their heads, it might even cause a loss of face for those gods of a lesser order who created the dream in response to his request for guidance in the matter of putting the chisels to work. 'Ah Wong, a thousand thanks, but this honour is too great. Do you not know of a reliable seer you trust who deals with messages from the lesser gods?' Ah Koo asked.

'Of course, but he is not sufficient for this dream,' Ah Wong answered firmly. 'We *must* involve the Dragon Master.' He hesitated. 'But I cannot absolutely guarantee his cooperation. He will need to hear your dream before he decides.'

A look of undisguised relief crossed Ah Koo's face. 'Ah . . . but I cannot tell this dream sufficiently well. In my hands it is limp, dead weed that has no colour. It can only offend and waste the time of the venerable Tang Wing Hung.' Ah Koo glanced at Little Sparrow, knowing that she would not be permitted to dine with them or be allowed in the presence of the Dragon Master and that, at this moment, she would be utterly distraught that her husband had missed this once-in-a-lifetime opportunity.

Ah Wong had already demonstrated that he was a quick thinker and seemingly only paused for a moment. 'Aha, I see. Then I will arrange for a *ping fong* – a screen. She will tell the dream from behind it.' He turned to Little Sparrow. 'You shall wear servant's clothing. I will arrange for this and also for you to come through the rear entrance.' *How can a woman so ugly be chosen by the gods to carry a dream so filled with omens and portents?* he wondered.

Little Sparrow was not offended by this plan. In fact she was hard put to contain her delight. *I will tell his dream even better from behind a screen*, she said to herself.

Half an hour before the two men arrived at the chophouse, Little Sparrow was ensconced behind a double screen, the single one proving too narrow to hide her bulk. As with her great-great-grandson, this was not about fat; it was a peculiar build that was not often seen among Caucasians but was sometimes a characteristic of the Chinese peasant, where the requirement for strength was written in the genes. Anyway, there she was, seated uncomfortably on a small wooden stool, safely prevented from offending the eyes of the Dragon Master, should he deign to present himself.

Tang Wing Hung's chophouse was the best in Chinatown, which was simply another way of saying it was the best in Sydney. Not that the exterior was intended to impress. While there were a few Chinese who had prospered, none had prospered more than the Dragon Master, whose influence extended to every Chinese in the colony and, some said, in the entire country. Most Chinese were poor working men, and for a chophouse to prosper it had to provide cheap food of good quality served in abundance. The area serving the working population was pretty basic: sawdust-covered floors were crammed with as many long benches and tables as could be fitted into the space. For the Chinese worker who didn't cook at home, eating out was a necessity, not a luxury, and the quality of a chophouse was judged by the noise coming from it. No Chinese of that time would eat at a place he couldn't hear from a hundred yards away.

But the private room built at the back of the chophouse was clearly meant for the rich and important in the community. It was where the Dragon Master himself entertained and where business deals were struck, often with the *gwai-lo* population, respectable and otherwise, and it was intended to impress. While not large, the walls, three feet thick, were constructed of sandstone to keep out noise, while the door was covered in felt two inches thick. The décor was in the Shanghai Chinese tradition but with a touch of the Victorian salon. The heavy silk drapes were peacock blue, and red and gold wallpaper covered the walls. The black lacquer table and chairs seated six, and both were elaborately inlaid with mother of pearl featuring birds, dragons, carp and cherry blossoms. Ah Koo noted that the floor was of polished cedar covered in three silk carpets of elaborate design. Two screens of painted oyster-coloured silk featured a painting of vertiginous mountains, wind-blown trees and misty jagged rocks that appeared through clouds and rose out of dark lakes. It was framed in the traditional colours of black, red and gold.

Adjacent to the screens was an elaborate Chinese armchair featuring a large curled dragon carved into the headrest and two smaller dragons along the arms. The seat and part of the backrest were upholstered in plain yellow silk. It was a masterpiece of the wood-carver's art; for Ah Koo, already overwhelmed by the opulence surrounding him, it was the most beautiful object he had ever seen.

Ah Wong noticed his open admiration. 'It is the Three Dragon Chair. Only the Dragon Master may sit in it,' he explained.

Ah Koo longed to feel the carving but knew he dare not touch it. He felt intimidated just being in the same room as such a piece of furniture. And the thought of why the single chair faced the screen, where Little Sparrow sat hidden from view, made him want to run for his worthless life. But such a cowardly and unmannerly act would cause his host mortal offence.

Ah Koo silently prayed that the Dragon Master would think better of visiting someone so patently unworthy. He told himself for the umpteenth time that he would be more than satisfied with Ah Wong's second choice of *xun meng xing shang*, reasoning that a mere peasant's dream could not possibly need the personal attention of the greatest soothsayer in all the land.

Before the meal began, Ah Wong enquired solicitously about Ah Koo's stomach ailment and, now that the dinner was inevitable, was assured that a miraculous cure had taken place. Ah Koo's self-imposed fast meant he was starving.

The meal consisted of a great many dishes, all sumptuous, some extravagant, with a predominance of pork, to indicate Ah Wong's generosity as a host. Ah Koo had never tasted better. His host plied him with increasingly refined delicacies until he could not fit another grain of rice into his straining stomach. It was the most splendid repast he had ever eaten, and if it had not been a banquet for many, it had certainly been one for two old friends. In Ah Koo's opinion, he had been repaid a thousandfold for rescuing Ah Wong all those years ago.

He had, during the course of the dinner, graciously accepted two glasses of rice wine, and while the pork fat in his stomach prevented him being anything more than slightly tipsy, he was relaxed enough to overcome his jaw-chattering anxiety when a servant pushed open the heavy door and Tang Wing Hung, the Dragon Master himself, made a sudden appearance.

Both men kicked back their chairs and stood to rigid attention with their heads bowed in respect. Ah Koo was afraid to look up. No introductions were offered but the Triad boss was quick to put them at ease. 'Sit,' he said quietly and motioned them to resume their seats. Bowing deeply, they did as they were told. Tang Wing Hung moved over to the Three Dragon Chair and seated himself comfortably, with his hands resting on the dragon heads that terminated each of its arms. Ah Koo stole a quick glance at the seated Dragon Master. To his surprise, he saw that his face was as broad as any lowborn peasant's and as deeply pocked as Little Sparrow's, and that his legs were relaxed and crossed at the ankles.

Behind the screen, Little Sparrow had her hand tightly covering her mouth in case the Dragon Master should hear her rapid breathing.

Tang Wing Hung refused Ah Wong's offer of French brandy or food, then, slightly adjusting his position in the chair, he nodded and said quietly, 'You may proceed.'

Despite the effects of the rice wine, Ah Koo now found himself trembling uncontrollably, his knees knocking together under the table. He dared not raise his eyes as Little Sparrow began to talk. In fact, he kept them glued to the table for the entire dream recital.

Where she found the strength in her voice Little Sparrow would never know. She related the dream calmly, pausing, colouring in the background and placing the emphasis where it was needed. When her narration finally ended she had given a masterful performance.

Tang Wing Hung rose from the Three Dragon Chair, and the two men jumped from their seats and stood to attention, heads bowed. Ah Koo was momentarily terrified as he waited for a reaction to the dream. The Dragon Master gave them the briefest of nods, then glanced at the screen for a moment before looking down at Ah Koo. 'You may use the *xun meng xing shang*. There will be no charge for his services.' He nodded a second time and then, to the astonishment of the two men, turned and addressed the screen. 'Dream Mistress, it was a most worthy telling.' He turned and walked the few steps to the door, and before Ah Wong could rush to open it, it was swung open by a servant positioned on the other side who had had his eye glued to a tiny magnified glass peephole. Without turning to acknowledge them, the Dragon Master swept out.

Little Sparrow, seemingly riveted to the tiny three-legged stool, moved for the first time. Despite its undoubted chunkiness, she simply could not believe the extent of the pain in her unworthy arse.

CHAPTER TWO

I RECALL THE MOMENT when my life changed forever. The phone rang at my desk in the agency at exactly six minutes past one on a Monday at the start of the lunch hour. I know the exact time because Ross Quinlivan, our creative director, had popped his rusty, untidy, ginger-moustachioed Irish-Australian head around the door of my glass cubicle and said, 'Pub? Sango? Couple of beers?'

Ross always ordered a cheese and tomato sandwich with two middies to arrive on the bar together. The sango went untouched, save for a single bite. It was his make-believe lunch. The two beers, one fast, one slow, he regarded as an essential component of his diet. I once asked if he ever ate vegetables. 'That's a fucking tomato, isn't it?' he said, pointing to a red bit protruding from the bitten sandwich.

I knew the phone rang at six minutes past one o'clock because Ross's head always appeared at precisely five minutes past the beginning of lunch hour, just to demonstrate his self-discipline. He would have been thinking about the first two beers of the day since at least noon, but he always waited the additional five minutes to demonstrate to himself that he was a man with a will of steel.

'Not today, mate. Got a two o'clock Wills meeting. New fag. Gotta get this layout finished,' I'd replied. I heard his rubber-soled brogues squeak down the passage towards the distant *ding* of the lift arriving in the foyer of the creative department. So I reckon six minutes past the hour was spot-on.

I have no idea why when significant events occur the precise time is important to me. Maybe it's some sort of genetic throwback – the Chinese are obsessed with numbers. Or it may be like remembering where you were when you heard of President Kennedy's assassination. By the way, that was at exactly 12.30 p.m. on Friday, November 22nd, 1963, the exact time the first of Lee Harvey Oswald's rifle shots entered his upper back, penetrated his neck, slightly damaged a vertebra and the top of his right lung, then came out of his throat just below his Adam's apple and nicked the left side of his tie knot.

See? I can't bloody help myself.

Anyway, yeah, the phone rang. 'Hello, Cookie,' I said into the receiver.

'Koo?' a voice barked at the other end.

'Ah . . . yes?'

'My office, now, please!'

The 'please' was clearly insincere and the use of my surname alone wasn't a promising sign. The reference to my immediate presence in his office indicated it was someone in the agency, but I hadn't the foggiest idea who. I called the switchboard.

'Odette? Do you know who just called me?'

Odette had a reputation for being able to identify any voice in the world after hearing it only once. She was Maltese, but clearly had Spanish blood, and she'd been with the agency since just after the war, when she joined as a trainee on the switch at the age of seventeen. Having quickly been promoted, she was now senior switchboard operator and, at thirty-eight, still a great-looking sort with the figure of a flamenco dancer. Her dark flashing eyes could give you a hard-on at a glance or send you whimpering away like a kicked puppy. She was said to have been the chairman's mistress at one time, and while this may merely have been agency scuttlebutt (plenty of that around), anyone silly enough to think she didn't pack a punch in the agency would be wrong. She had the dirt on everyone, particularly the chairman, apparently. Fortunately, we got on very well.

'No call came through switch, Cookie,' she replied.

Whoever it was dialled direct. That can't be bad. No secretary or call through the switch. Then it hit me. The gravelly voice, almost a growl, the result of ten thousand fags too many. Jesus – the chairman of the board, Charles Brickman! He personally looked after the W.D. & H.O. Wills cigarette business – our biggest and oldest account. I flew into a panic. *The two o'clock Wills meeting? Christ, surely not! My layout for the new brand is no big deal. But he's dialled through himself, using his very own tobacco-stained forefinger!*

In five years he'd never attended a single client meeting. With him, it was strictly chairman to chairman. If it weren't for his portrait in the agency foyer, I'd have had trouble remembering what he looked like.

I'd never been in Brickman's office and had seen him only once, three years previously, the only time I'd heard his voice. He was a small, slight guy – shorter than me – in a trilby and with a pronounced limp. He was said to avoid the passenger lift, taking the goods lift from the car park in the basement to the tenth floor, where his office supposedly occupied the entire northern corner overlooking the harbour. It was also said that he never acknowledged staff. On the one occasion I heard him speak, senior staff had been summoned to the boardroom just before knock-off time at five o'clock. I must have only just made the cut, having been appointed a creative group head two weeks previously. Situated on the ninth floor and mostly used for client meetings, the boardroom wasn't all that big, so it was curious to see a microphone set up on a small temporary wooden platform near the door. The table had been removed, and the twenty or so senior staff were crammed together.

Our managing director, Paul Simons, suddenly called for silence from the doorway, then announced in a voice just short of senatorial, 'Lady and gentlemen, the chairman!'

Charles Brickman limped in and, mounting the platform, cleared his throat not once but twice. Enhanced by the microphone, it sounded like gravel moving down Ah Koo's gold sluice. Then he spoke. 'You will not be aware that I have just returned from America, where I sold Brickman & Crane to the Americans. We are henceforth to be known as Samuel Oswald Brickman.'

Crane had gone missing in the new name, though this was hardly a surprise. Nobody, not even Joy Young, the sole lady in Brickman's introduction and our radio manager, could remember when there had been a Crane, and she had joined the company a year after it started.

Rumour had it that before the war John Crane got six years in Long Bay for embezzling agency funds, dobbed in, it was said, by Charlie Baby himself. He then went to live on Norfolk Island, originally the most notorious convict settlement of them all. Anyway, he'd been rubbed out of the agency letterhead and history with this latest announcement; so had the corniest telephone joke in the industry. In response to Odette's standard phone greeting – 'Brickman and Crane!' – some smart-arse from a rival agency, fresh from a liquid lunch, would say, 'Oh, is that the construction company? I'd like to speak to the foreman.' Odette would famously respond in her delightful Maltese accent, 'Vamoose, wanker!' before she cut him off. Management had tried to stop her after a senior account man, attending an advertising convention, learned from a counterpart in another agency that they only did it to hear her famous rebuttal. But she had nevertheless continued and now John Crane was destined to become a forgotten part of agency history.

'There'll be a half-page advertisement announcing the sale in the financial section of tomorrow's *Sydney Morning Herald*,' Charles Brickman concluded hoarsely. He paused, glanced at his wristwatch and rasped, 'You can all go home now.' That was it, short and sweet, not a word more than necessary. A curt nod of the head and he limped from the boardroom.

'I guess he's not going to buy us a beer then?' Ross muttered out of the corner of his mouth.

I remember thinking the ad in the *Herald* the following morning announcing the sale must have been set at the newspaper. No art director in the creative department briefed on the announcement or, for that matter, anyone in the production department doing the finished art would have been foolish enough to keep it quiet. They'd know they'd blow the trust the rest of us had in them forever.

Later, over a beer in the pub where we'd all gathered to spread the news to the rest of the staff, Ross voiced my thoughts. 'Just goes to show what the bastards in management really think of creative, doesn't it? We'll be the first American agency to arrive in Australia since J. Walter Thompson in the late twenties, and it's left to an account executive to write the copy and some no-hoper *Herald* compositor, no doubt wearing boxing gloves, to finesse the job and do the actual layout for the announcement.'

'Mate, have you considered the acronym?' I asked.

'What?'

'S-O-B?' I pronounced each letter. This got a big laugh.

'Come to think of it, that's not too bad. *Sonofabitch* Advertising!'

I waited. 'Nah, Sob! We've gone from Brickman & Crane, the construction company, to Sob Advertising. I'm not so sure we're much better off. And just you wait – they'll send out a Yank creative director to kick arse.'

All-round murmurs and quaffing of beers followed while this thought was absorbed. We were all aware of the reformation in American advertising – the sixties' creative revolution coming out of New York. The winds of change had been blowing down Madison Avenue like everywhere else.

'Which is good,' we would reassure ourselves. 'About bloody time. Yeah, yeah . . . improve things . . . mumble, mumble, burp.'

But the cultural cringe was still a very real part of the Australian psyche and we secretly wondered if we were up to it. The print stuff coming out in the American *Art Directors Annual* was pretty piss-elegant, and we were conscious that we were not in the same league as the creative guys at Doyle Dane Bernbach, whose Volkswagen ads were among the very best of a thousand other mind-blowing print ads and

TV commercial reels coming out of New York agencies: Doyle Dane Bernbach, McCann Erickson, Ogilvy & Mather, Grey Advertising, Jack Tinker & Partners, BBDO and Ted Bates; and out of Chicago, Leo Burnett. New York's Madison Avenue was to the advertising business what Broadway was to theatre; it was where all the big American agencies were to be found and where these agencies' names were, so to speak, up in lights. In New York, the account executive prepared the brief and the creative department translated it into meaningful and exciting advertising. Here, the account executive called all the shots and decided with the client what they wanted, and the creative people simply did as they were told. Not surprisingly, the advertising was pretty dull. In creative terms, Australia was still in the dark ages.

My prophecy in the pub came true. New York sent out a creative director named Jonas Bold. (*Jonas!* Was this yet another portent?) But he proved to be a great darts player, all-round good guy and notorious 'muff-diver', as he called it. The secretaries and the girls in the media department must have been on the new contraceptive pill, because they all seemed to want a piece of the good-looking Yank. That was, until a lightly tanned leggy blonde junior copywriter named Sue Chipchase decided to exercise the second syllable in her surname and set out to get him. Six months later, he took Sue back to the Bronx to get his Jewish parents to agree to him marrying his blonde, blue-eyed, miniskirted Australian *shiksa*. Returning to Sydney, she marched Jonas down to Hardy Brothers, the jewellers who made the Melbourne Cup, and came back with a rock the size of a small agate.

Shortly after this, Jonas was promoted to creative director of the New York office and left Australia with his new bride, who, in the meantime, had given up copywriting (a clash of interests). She now had her own byline, working for *Vogue Magazine Australia* with a social-business-smart-girl-about-town magazine column, appropriately named 'Chip 'n' Chase'. Funnily, our New York agency held the *American Vogue* account.

But nobody really minded. Nepotism was, after all, the backbone of global advertising and we all liked Sue; she wasn't only long legs and big baby blues – there was a good brain in that pretty head. Besides, we owed Jonas heaps. He stood up to clients and account management and fought for our ideas. He'd taught us a heap, bolstered our confidence and fattened our egos, then left us to get on with it. Ross Quinlivan, a popular choice, was appointed creative director to replace him.

We were doing okay, in fact, pretty well. The previous year I got two print ads in the New York *Art Directors Annual*, and Ross got the first Logie for a TV ad for Coca-Cola. We were pretty chuffed with ourselves.

So here I was on the tenth floor, outside the chairman's office, being inspected by a dragon woman I judged to be in her late fifties, who had bobbed hennaed hair, the grey not entirely covered, who from her expression appeared very recently to have sucked a lemon. 'Mr Koo?'

'Yes.'

'You're late! The chairman doesn't like to be kept waiting.'

'I'm sorry . . . er, Mrs . . . ?'

'Miss!' A sharp reproof, no name proffered; then, a moment later, a forefinger stabbed at a button on the desk intercom. 'Mr Brickman, Mr Koo has *finally* arrived.'

'Yeah, righto.' The intercom's crackle added to his gravelled tones. He sounded three years closer to emphysema.

Miss Henna Head gave a dismissive toss of the head towards the inner office. 'You may go in.'

Charles Brickman was sitting at his desk, a huge, antique, early Georgian one – very nice. He was writing with a gold Parker pen and didn't look up when I entered. A thin blue spiral of cigarette smoke climbed into the air above his head from a large Lalique glass ashtray to his left, the beautiful object already filled with butts. The office was large and imposing, expensively furnished with carefully chosen antiques. It was in surprisingly good taste, which, sadly, hadn't extended to the rest of the agency, which consisted of wood and semi-opaque glass cubicles divided by long passages, each office equipped with a plain pine desk and plastic upholstered visitor's chair.

I'd designed the foyers and interview rooms for my family's eighteen Sydney funeral parlours and in the process learned a bit about antiques. I've always liked old furniture. It's another way of understanding history. While at art school I did a course in antique-furniture design, especially English and French. It was this that foolishly prompted my uncle John, who runs the family C&B – Coffins & Burials – to commission me to do the parlour interiors. Not that the average punter, known in the business as the 'Dearly Bereaved', would recognise a genuine antique from a fake as they negotiated the final send-off of a loved one, but what the hell. I was never going to get a second chance and so I figured I might as well do the job properly.

My uncle John damn near suffered a major heart attack when he got the final bill and lost no time bringing it up at the next board meeting. For once my mum stood up for me. My dad, probably pissed, was reported to have said, 'John, your class is up your arse! Leave the boy alone.' Needless to say, I wasn't given the job of doing the twenty-two parlours in the other states, even though sales had since jumped fifteen per cent in Sydney and a more affluent clientele had been attracted to the family death and dying business. Funnily, none of the other directors in charge of the eighty-eight Little Sparrow Chinese restaurants asked me to design their restaurant interiors.

Now, with my great flat feet planted on a handmade antique Aubusson silk rug spread in front of the desk, I stood opposite my chairman and was forced to revise the idea that Charles Brickman was a little guy. A surprising amount of his torso showed above the beautiful old desk, indicting a taller man than I remembered. He wasn't wearing a jacket, and his red striped American barbershop braces stood out against a plain white shirt. I wondered briefly if the chairman had received a sartorial tip from his well-known New York agency counterpart, the very British chairman of O&M, David Ogilvy, who famously wore red braces. But where did I get the notion that, like me, Charles Brickman was a short arse? Strange, I'm usually pretty observant and, like all vertically challenged men, I never failed to notice those who are shorter than me.

'Sit,' he growled, not looking up from his writing.

I glanced at the two chairs standing directly in front of the desk. They were Louis XV French medallion-back occasional chairs in gilded wood, upholstered in black velvet. The gold was suitably tarnished by age and, while this was a style of chair that was commonly reproduced, I hadn't the slightest doubt these two were genuine, the real McCoy. If I sound a bit precious, it's just that I'm into antiques and chose this exact style for the funeral-parlour interview rooms. They are known as SOS (Sales Opportunity Seats), where you settle the distraught Dearly Bereaved, ideally holding hands, their chairs always placed near a large vase of pungent white Easter lilies, and attempt to persuade them to upgrade to a more expensive casket. The death salesman is a peculiar breed, usually puny in stature, slightly hunched, convincing, sincere, sympathetic in manner, apparently guileless but utterly ruthless. Everyone is familiar with the representation of death – a skeleton in a monk's cowled robe carrying a sickle. But, according to my dad, if you look carefully into the dark shadow it casts, you'll find a coffin salesman gleefully rubbing his hands.

However, in the case of the funeral parlour's interview rooms, I was reluctantly forced to accept reproduction Louis XV chairs for the SOS because I couldn't find enough genuine antiques in Australia. Okay, I admit, that was not quite true. I didn't try very hard because the tarnished gilding, the 'don't touch' part of any genuine antique, would appear to your average mourner as a worn paint job, signifying a funeral parlour that was rundown and poorly managed. So I opted for reproduction chairs, precise copies handmade with immaculate gilded woodwork, and still expensive enough to cause Uncle John to have another major conniption.

But the problem was that the chairman's two chairs had arms and were not wide enough in the seat to accommodate my brick-shithouse build without damaging them.

'What?' Brickman asked, sensing me looming over him.

'The chair, sir, I could . . . damage it.'

Looking up for the first time, he reached for the blue-spiralling cigarette and took a puff. 'Bloody gaspers.' He managed several coughs before resting it on the lip of the French ashtray, then rasped, 'Miss Grace, bring the chair!' The shout came out as a strangled cough. Realising that his damaged voice wouldn't carry to her office, he jabbed at the intercom, repeating his demand.

'Shall I?' I nodded in the direction of her office.

'No, stay! She sits on her fat arse all day,' he growled.

So her surname was Grace – if ever there were a misnomer – and I would learn from Odette that her Christian name was Gertrude and that she was known among the female staff as Graceless Gertie. She was also said to share her boss's sunny disposition and ready smile.

Miss Grace, her sucked-lemon expression even more sour, was plainly not happy. She entered carrying a solid oak, straight-backed dining chair. I moved towards her to take it, but she rudely pushed past me. I jumped aside just in time to prevent a collision and caught a glimpse of the back of Brickman's desk out of the corner of my eye. The bugger had his chair set on a platform. *Jesus, the conceit.* Miss Grace plonked the chair down hard on the Aubusson rug as if hoping she might damage it. Then, without saying a word she turned and marched out. There was a ladder running down the calf of one of her nylon stockings. Her legs weren't bad. Funny, while some women cop varicose veins and puffy ankles as they age, with others the legs are the last to go. Miss Grace was one of the lucky ones.

Brickman watched her depart and then, shaking his head slowly, wheezed, 'You fuck 'em when they're young and sweet and you spend the rest of your life paying for it.' I was taken by surprise, not sure I'd heard correctly. This was not the sort of comment I'd expected. I couldn't believe the elevated seat either. Clearly there was something I didn't understand, about him, about her. I reminded myself to check if he wore built-up heels and to buy Odette a drink.

'Sit,' he said, nodding at the oak chair. 'And thanks, Koo. That frog chair cost a few bob.' Something resembling a grin momentarily revealed a sticky glimpse of tobacco-stained teeth.

I guess all this taken together meant that, in the chairman's eyes, we were off to a reasonable start. I sat down on the hard wooden chair. I still didn't know why I was here. Should I have brought the layout I was rendering for the two o'clock Wills meeting, I wondered. I couldn't think why – it was the usual research-inspired crap, a hand holding up the new pack, three cigs city-sky lining, poking from the top of a red packet at various heights. The subliminal message they were meant to convey was one for me, one for my mate and one to offer to someone as a friendly gesture – the holy trinity of the tobacco industry: personal satisfaction, mateship and new friends. One research report allowed that the third cigarette was for your lady friend.

The problem was that the client believed all this unadulterated research crap. Then there was the headline, the result of some independent research outfit flogging what they maintained the public *really* thinks. This deep probe into the public mind was invariably presented in a specially convened client meeting by some good-looking Economics graduate in a miniskirt, and wearing stilettos. Rather than seriously analysing the numbers her research company had crunched in a so-called 'five-state definitive survey', Miss Tits and Arse would be doing more work in the presentation with her eyes and body, crossing her legs, leaning forward to show her cleavage, turning to the slide screen to wiggle her cute little bum at the client product manager. It was show-and-tell in the adult world, and the client lapped it up, as it allowed him to stay safe and not to rock the boat with something that might resemble an original advertising idea. I was finalising the brilliant result for the meeting: *New Templeton – The Satisfaction of Full Flavoured Mildly Toasted Virginia Tobacco!* Every word in the headline was justified by the research gurus as 'deep and meaningful'. For fuck's sake! That ought to have the punters queuing up at the corner shop before dawn on the day of the launch.

W.D. & H.O. Wills hadn't yet caught up with the creative revolution in advertising. In fact, it hadn't even begun to penetrate the cloud of tobacco smoke fogging up the meeting room in their advertising department. In the five years I'd been with the agency Charles Brickman had never once asked to see a layout. As I mentioned before, he'd never even attended a client meeting. His part of the job was to smoke the product and massage the ego of Sir John Smith, the tobacco-company chairman. My job was to churn out endless shitty research-guided layouts and then spend hours discussing their subtle differences and how these would turn existing smokers on to the new brand. That was another tobacco industry shibboleth: *We don't cause people to take up smoking, we only try to influence them to switch brands.* The senior advertising manager responsible for that little gem, James Pudsworth, was promoted to the local company's board.

Brickman killed the fag, stabbing it into the ashtray, crushing it as if it were a deadly worm – unconscious malice in the gesture – then promptly lit another one. Earlier that year, the first warnings had appeared on cigarette packs in the US: *Cigarette smoking may be injurious to your health.* This got a bit of local publicity and Wills convened a special 'explanatory' meeting in the agency. They worked with the word 'may' in the message and pointed out that lots of things *may* be injurious to your health: coffee, sugar, alcohol, too much fat in your diet, even crossing the road. You can do a lot with an ambiguous word like *may*. If you heed every warning you get in life, you *may* not get out of bed in the morning. Then their tame medical researcher (nicotine-testing lab manager was a better description) stood up and said there were no definitive studies that showed tobacco was injurious to health. He pointed out that Europeans had been smoking tobacco since the Spanish introduced it in the early 1500s, along with potatoes, both, incidentally, from the same family as deadly nightshade. 'So there ought to be a warning on potatoes,' the so-called boffin concluded. This got the mandatory laugh. We knew he meant it as a joke, but we *wanted* to believe, *insisted* on believing him. The upshot of the meeting was that the operative word *may* won the day and we all left feeling safe. We should have recalled that the word *may* was also part of the cry uttered by those in deadly peril – mayday. The warnings on American packs were, in fact, the first mayday call about the physical harm done by smoking tobacco. Wills was, after all, the biggest account the agency had, our bread and butter; lose it and the agency would take a real belting in its financial billings.

'You're Chinese, Koo,' Charles Brickman said. It was a statement, not a question.

'No, sir, fourth-generation Australian.'

'Yes, but *still* Chinese. Your lot don't intermarry!'

'Well, no, sir, that's not strictly true. As a matter —'

'C'mon, cut the bullshit – take a look in the mirror next time you're in the toilet, son,' he interrupted.

I was almost at the first stage of really disliking this bloke. 'I'm a throwback, sir, to my great-great-grandmother. My sisters and several of my cousins look less Chinese than you do . . .' I remembered just in time to add 'sir'.

'Four generations, that's impressive,' he said, patronising me.

I ignored the tone. 'Not really, my great-great-grandfather came to Australia in the gold rush. I guess most people could trace their forebears back to convict times. After all, transportation to New South Wales only stopped fifteen years before the gold rush. I guess both our families were originally migrants in this land.' I was aware of overstepping the mark, but I was a little miffed. He obviously thought of the Chinese as intruders who didn't belong here. Or was that a chip on my own shoulder?

He didn't appear to notice. 'Yeah, you're right, I suppose, but it's always been easier for us British.' Then he added with a chuckle, 'Our throwbacks are not so noticeable.'

Jesus, this bloke's my chairman! What do I say next?

My Singaporean-born Chinese mother, desperately worried about the fact that I'm the last Koo unless I start producing sons – and the sooner the better – was extremely grateful that I was a throwback to Little Sparrow. Not that she didn't cherish my three distinctly Caucasian-looking sisters; she did. But my appearance was so intrinsically square, flat-faced peasant Chinese that, with her own ancestral genes coursing through my blood, she harboured a modest hope that a new oriental influence would permeate the next Koo generation, especially if I married a Chinese.

My mother had done a good deal of research into my dad's family and I had subsequently added to it with research of my own. She had passed all she knew on to us kids as faithfully as if it were about her own family. All this had produced an affinity with Little Sparrow so strong that she had developed a kind of ancestor worship, which meant that our great-great-grandmother had always been a strong presence in our childhood. Our growing years had been peppered with alleged Little Sparrow-isms. All of these were based on traditional wisdom and intended as guides to show us how we should behave. So that ignorant, silent, strong-minded peasant ancestor had become an iconic figure in our lives. One of her mythical sayings, transported telepathically all the way from the celestial realm to my mum, was: *When you are confused or angry, say nothing.* Or, put into my dad's lingo, 'Tell 'em bugger-all, son!'

Charles Brickman, his expression quizzical, said, 'You speak the language, of course.' It wasn't a question.

'What language is that?' I asked, knowing full well.

He clucked his tongue, a wet sound. 'Chinese! What else?'

I'd decided not to give the bastard an inch. He could fire me if he wanted to. With two ads in the New York *Art Directors Annual*, there wasn't an agency in town that wouldn't welcome me with open arms. 'I suppose you mean Mandarin, Hokkien or Cantonese. There are almost three hundred languages in China.' I paused meaningfully. 'I don't speak any of them.' This wasn't strictly true; my mum had taught us Cantonese when we were kids and she'd regularly converse with us, but this hadn't happened for ages and I wasn't sufficiently confident to claim it as a language I knew at street level.

His expression didn't change and, ignoring my less than subtle putdown, he asked, 'How would you like to go overseas, Koo?'

His question came as a surprise, though later I castigated myself that I should have seen it coming a mile off. 'Overseas?' My heart skipped a beat. *Shit! New York! Madison Avenue!*

'New York have asked us to send someone suitable from creative.'

Jesus! New York! Me! 'To the New York office, sir?' I asked, hurriedly reintroducing the 'sir'.

The chairman drew back in surprise and started to cough violently, then reached into his trouser pocket for a handkerchief, brought it up to his mouth and spat into it, albeit fairly politely, then spoiled it all with a final hoarse clearing of the throat. 'Have you not been listening to a single word I've said, Koo?' He took a deep breath. 'Singa-bloody-pore! *Ferchrissake!* They don't have Chinese working in the New York office!'

Despite myself, I drew back and repeated, 'Singapore?' as if it were a dirty word.

'What's that mean?' he spat.

'Well, it comes as a bit of a surprise. I didn't know we had a Singapore office.'

'We do now, son! What do you imagine we've been talking about?' He waved a hand, indicating the office and its furnishings. 'If you weren't so busy calculating the value of the stuff in my office, maybe you could concentrate for a minute or two!'

I felt my flat face burning. There was a Louis XV wall clock ticktocking away to his right, a receipt for which, if handed to Uncle John, would put him into one of our super-deluxe gold-handled caskets. 'May I think about it?'

'What? You're not going?' He stabbed at the intercom. 'Miss Grace, have Odette get me New York!'

I don't want to be a smart-arse, but as I said previously, I'm a time freak. Besides, Jonas called us from time to time. New York was fourteen hours behind Sydney, so it was after 11 p.m. yesterday, New York time. Only the cleaners would be at the agency that late. *I wonder if there are any Chinese cleaners in the New York office* – a wayward thought.

Miss Grace crackled through the intercom. 'It's 11 p.m. yesterday in New York. The office is closed!' Even through the intercom, her glee at one-upping him was palpable.

'Yeah, righto,' Brickman sniffed, not transmitting this back to her.

'Perhaps I can have a few more details?' I asked.

He snatched at a lone scrap of paper in a green felt-lined gold-embossed leather in-tray. 'Yeah, here somewhere,' he stopped and coughed. 'They've bought a Chinese . . . er, Singapore agency owned by . . .' he squinted at the paper, 'the Wing Brothers.' He looked up at me. 'Wing – that's Chinese, isn't it?' He didn't wait for my confirmation. 'Wing Brothers Advertising – the Americans are sending in a manager but the Chinese haven't got a creative department and they need a Western-trained creative director to start one.' He flashed me one of his stained smiles, then winked. 'Jesus, Koo, think of all that free Chinese pussy! At your age I'd have bloody jumped at it!'

There it was again. He was five feet five at the most, damn near a cripple, had half a dozen strands of grey hair pasted over his small pink head, obvious breathing problems, and when he opened his mouth it looked like he'd been eating shit. Like me, he was not exactly handsome and obviously never had been. Yet he gave the impression he was a veritable roué! I guess it went with the elevated chair. Poor old bugger. Miss Grace was probably it, his single amatory adventure. But then, in contrast, his office was in brilliant taste, not ostentatious but idiosyncratic and understated – he hadn't put a foot wrong, except, if you were being picky, for the painting. There was a single large painting on the wall behind me that I'd glimpsed when I turned around to try to help Miss Grace with the chair: a Sidney Nolan from his Ned Kelly series – ten grand, if it was worth a penny. Two walls were glass, looking out at a wide sweep of the harbour. I wondered to myself if the Ned Kelly was a bit of self-imaging.

'I'd like to think about it,' I said, realising suddenly I could have a bit of a personal problem at home with my mum, who might see the transfer as opportune. According to her, Singapore was three-quarters Chinese and therefore a much bigger marriage market than Australia. I was also most anxious to get out of the chairman's office and deliberately checked my watch. It was three minutes to two. 'Sir, I've got a Wills meeting at two o'clock.' I put on a concerned look. 'I really should be there. New brand, big budget.'

He took a drag and stood, making no pretence that he was six feet eight inches tall. He leaned over and crushed his cigarette, then reached for the pack and absent-mindedly took another. Standing on his dais, he glared down at me. 'You've got until Wednesday. Now don't you let me down, Koo. It was nice to be asked by the Americans, and they were pretty keen when I told them we had an art director in the office who was a Chinaman. Feather in our cap, what?'

I winced inwardly. *You'll keep, you racist bastard.* 'Sir, like I said, I'll have to think about it.'

'Think! Think about what? I'll tell you what to think, Koo, a red-blooded young bloke like you.' He winked again. 'Think pussy.' He reached down for the Ronson table lighter, lit up, inhaled deeply then exhaled, his head almost disappearing behind the smokescreen. 'Hop along now, Koo, can't keep the client waiting.'

I wanted to jump him, smash his nicotine-stained teeth down his scrawny turkey throat. Instead I turned and meekly left. I could hear him coughing as I nodded to Miss Grace, and before she could open her mouth I made a quick exit and headed towards the lifts.

'The chair! You forgot to bring back the chair!' she shouted after me.

I pretended not to hear, reached the lifts and pressed the button hard several times. The light above the door said it was on the ground floor. The three other lifts were all on different floors but none of them near the tenth. Miss Grace came flying out of her office and marched up to me. I jumped back as she glared down at me, ablaze with powder, rouge, mascara, cheap perfume and righteous indignation. 'You forgot the chair, Mr Koo!' she hissed through clenched teeth.

'Sorry.' I turned and sprinted back through her office and into the chairman's. 'Excuse me, sir,' I cried.

'That was quick. You've decided to take it,' he rasped.

'Yes, no, sir!' I pointed and said, 'The chair,' grabbed hold of it, then ran from his office and dropped it beside Miss Grace's desk.

She was standing at the door of her office. 'It doesn't go there!' she snapped.

'I'm late for a Wills meeting,' I gasped. I heard the lift finally arriving and the judder, then clunk of its doors opening. This time it was her turn to jump out of the way.

'Rude!' she shouted. I copped a second whiff of perfume as I tore down the passageway to the lift, arriving just in time to squeeze through the rapidly closing doors. *Kaboom!* Then the electric motor kicked in and whined as the lift descended. I was safe from the Dragon Lady. She was a good match for the chairman and I would henceforth think of them as 'the gruesome twosome'. It was six minutes past two o'clock. *Shit! Shit! Shit! Exactly an hour. The worst of my life!*

I skipped the Wills meeting and sent one of the guys in my group to attend and to present the layout. Fuck 'em. I'd had enough punishment for one day. Later, when I'd calmed down somewhat, I made a mental note. It was the 4th of July 1966, two days after the full moon, though it was still the 3rd in New York. Tomorrow would be Independence Day, a holiday in America. That little bastard upstairs knew all along it was well past business hours in New York. It was why he'd given me until Wednesday to make up my mind. The call to Miss Grace to get him the New York office was simply a ploy to put further pressure on me. I silently castigated myself. I'd done a bloody good job of underestimating Chairman Charles Brickman OBE.

The following day I bought Odette lunch (I needed more information from her than I'd get from a couple of drinks at the pub). She proved reluctant to talk about Graceless Gertie and the chairman, dismissing the subject with a sigh and sudden lift of her dark Spanish eyebrows – women's shorthand for 'I know but I'm not going to say'. It was plain that she and Gertie were not especially fond of each other. She also showed distinct ambivalence towards Charles Brickman, admitting he was an irascible bastard, but protesting that 'he has his good points'. She wouldn't elaborate.

I asked her – trying to put it carefully – how anyone so socially dysfunctional had succeeded in building a significant advertising agency even before the Yanks came along and added their international list of clients. She laughed. 'The war helped, contracts were awarded, he was a major in military supplies in Canberra. Then, after the war, he started out doing the political advertising for Bob Menzies' new Liberal Party who beat Ben Chifley in the 1949 election. A lot of people reckoned it was a brilliant campaign, but even Charlie, who wasn't shy about claiming credit, admitted it was probably Labor wanting to keep petrol rationing that really won the day. Then something blew up between him and Bob Menzies and he switched to Labor for the New South Wales state election in 1953. Everyone said Cahill, the Labor premier, hadn't a hope of staying in, but they won. The credit once again went to Charles, and his subsequent campaigns kept them in until Askin toppled them last year.' She giggled. 'Knowing him, if he'd had the chance he'd have switched to Askin and the Libs last year.' She leaned closer and said quietly, 'I took the phone calls. He very nearly pulled it off with Askin, but Frank Packer, who was supporting Askin's campaign, wouldn't have a bar of Charlie Brickman.'

'A man for all seasons, eh?'

'You can say that again. He can sniff a wind change long before it's a whiff of a breeze.' She laughed. 'In Canberra, among the Libs, his nickname was "Shit-a-Brick"; the Labor Feds call him "The Brickworks". If you need to destroy someone's reputation, he can build a solid foundation composed of lies and innuendo. He knows where the bodies are buried in both major parties, so should a company need a political favour, they know where to come.' She shrugged. 'The result is mutual back-scratching that leads to prosperity for all parties.' She glanced at her watch. 'Got to get back to the switch.' Reaching for her handbag, she added, 'Here's something to think about, Cookie. The chairman never does anything above the table.'

The previous night – Monday – I'd arrived home late from a darts game against another agency. We lost, mostly due to my lack of concentration. My mum was in bed, so thankfully I didn't have to front her. She only had to take one look to know something was wrong.

That Tuesday night, I had a vital decision to make: do I or don't I? 'Don't' was beginning to win. I should really have called Jonas and sussed him out, but the New York office was, of course, closed for the holiday. I even wondered if Brickman had worked that into the equation, then realised I was being paranoid. The big decision was whether or not to tell my mum. If I stayed *schtum* (a Yiddish word I'd picked up from Jonas), how could she find out? But then again, Phyllis Koo was not easily fooled. She often called me at the agency, and she and Odette had become very chatty on the phone. (Mum had sent flowers when Odette's mum died.)

I was thinking all this as I drove home to Vaucluse in the Vee Dub, bought as a sign of respect for the work coming out of DDB New York. My mum could react in a number of ways, none of them helpful. Should I or shouldn't I tell her? By the time I reached Double Bay, a Little Sparrow voice from somewhere deep down spoke to me (my mum's brainwashing from childhood). This was what she was saying (in perfect English, of course): *Cookie, honourable great-great-grandson, you are twenty-nine. You still live at home. Are you going to be a mummy's boy all your life? Your family is loaded. You're safe, comfortable, going nowhere fast. No hardship, no challenge in life. You're pure blancmange. Like it or not, you'll probably end up as chairman of the family companies. What about your big artistic career? At work you're stuck with tobacco as the major account in your group. The people at Wills insist you're their main man in creative. You got a whopping great rise to stay when you told management you wanted to opt out of tobacco. They're not going to let you go and jeopardise the biggest account in the agency. What will it be? You either put in your resignation and change jobs – go to another agency – or, paradoxically, Charles Brickman gets you off the Wills hook with this Singapore offer. How much longer are you going to go on drawing cigarettes poking out of packs? Accepting over-researched flaccid headlines and body copy that are an insult to your intelligence? Maybe this isn't such a bad idea after all? Time you left the nice cosy nest, anyway. Start your own creative department from scratch in Singapore. See if you're any good. Okay, if they don't have a creative department, it's probably a pretty primitive set-up, but is that such a bad thing? Your ideas, your way, you take all the credit!*

I changed into low gear to get round the final twist on Rose Bay hill, turned down Vaucluse Road at the convent and I was two minutes from home. *Shit, do I tell her or don't I?* My dad was probably stonkered in his study, watching the Tuesday night rugby league show on TV or at one of our restaurants in Dixon Street. It would be nice to talk to someone, get a second opinion, but I wasn't sure it should be my mother. I hadn't even mentioned it to Ross, who, as creative director, should have been the first to know of the offer. He'd want me to stay, anyway. I could hear him already: *Cookie, there's New York, London, us and then there's bugger-all. Zilch! Keep your powder dry. Don't disappear behind the bamboo curtain. Leave the Asians to fuck up in their own inimitable way. A great advertising idea has never come out of Hong Kong or Singapore, and the Brits have been there Christ knows how long.* I could see him grinning. *Besides, we need you in the darts team, mate.*

'Right then, Cookie!' I said to myself above the Vee Dub's frenetic engine whine. 'It's Tuesday. Tell her at dinner tonight.'

While I've mentioned Little Sparrow's influence on our childhood, I haven't mentioned the influence her dream had on us. You might be wondering how an illiterate Chinese peasant woman's dream could possibly have endured and remained intact for a hundred years. Well, as a matter of fact, it didn't. It was, as these things are in Australia, largely forgotten. Nothing endured intact, only bits and pieces, hanging on over the decades by a memory thread. These fragments were what inspired the company names: Gold Chisel Caskets, Blue Lotus Funerals, Valley Properties, although Little Sparrow, the name of the restaurant chain, went back to the founding Australian generation and Little Sparrow herself. Of the dream, nothing but these scraps of memory remained until my mum discovered a record of it among the family papers written in excellent copperplate. Having the obsession with signs and portents common to almost every Chinese, my mother immediately saw that the wealth the family had acquired over the generations could be attributed almost entirely to the dream.

I personally attributed the family's wealth to a degree of sagacity and good luck, but mostly to the qualities identified by Alfred Deakin in his warning to parliament in 1901: 'It is not the bad qualities but the good qualities of these alien races that make them dangerous to us. It is their inexhaustible energy, their power of applying themselves to new tasks, their endurance and low standard of living that make them such competitors.'

Yet another Little Sparrow-ism telepathically received by my mum across the ages concurs with part of Deakin's view: *Life is not about winning or losing, but about being the last one hanging on*. She would say that in business, tenacity was everything. Business was like an endless race to climb an impossibly steep cliff face; the winner was the last climber still hanging on when all the others had crashed to the valley below.

The endurance to which Deakin referred was still evident in my family, but the low standard of living was long past. The 28-roomed mansion built on an acre of private headland jutting out into Vaucluse Bay was a far cry from the mud-brick hut in The Valley, although, as a reminder of our humble beginnings, our present property has persimmon and pomegranate trees around its perimeter that bloom gloriously every spring. Porky Pimm, the head gardener, and his three assistants – referred to by my dad as Mow, Clip and Digger – spent a fair amount of their time protecting them from the salt air.

The main house was bigger than some luxury boutique hotels, and two-thirds of the rooms were now empty, but I didn't choose to live in it. I had my own private flat and art studio built above the eight-car garage, and I could come and go as I pleased, my only filial duty to dine with my mother once a week, usually on a Tuesday, and with my father if he was home or sober, which he rarely was. So when I said I still lived at home at twenty-nine, I did and I didn't.

Why hadn't I moved out? I'm aware that I was privileged, a little rich boy with indulgent parents, but I still hoped to make it as an artist someday and so I spent a good deal of time in my studio, which is not the kind of facility you can pick up in a rented property. Naturally, like Susan, the eldest of my three sisters, I would move away when I married.

The entrance to the flat is through a private gate that leads directly to the road, and it has a stairway through to the garage. My mum no doubt could tell when I was home, because she could see when the lights were on, but she knew better than to simply drop in without first phoning.

Yes, I did have female company quite often and, yes, they did stay the night. But when they woke in the morning and looked out into the garden over at the big house and out to the harbour, I could see they were gob-smacked. After that they're never the same again. I guess great wealth is a privilege, but, believe me, it can also be a pain in the bum.

Which brings me back to females, or rather, as they're known in the agency world, 'bunnies'. They were in plentiful supply, but I didn't kid myself it was because I was some Lothario. It was due to the advent of the pill. Suddenly women were free to have a good time, get drunk, go home with someone without fear of falling pregnant after a one-night stand. So I got my fair share – an ad agency was thought to be a glamorous environment and was loaded with good-looking sorts who regarded themselves as emancipated. Or, as Ross Quinlivan put it, 'Mate, we're living through the second bunny plague to hit Australia – it'd be a shame to waste it.'

This would come to sound pretty arrogant, if not plain offensive, by the 1980s but the feminist movement hadn't yet arrived on the scene. Betty Friedan had written her manifesto, *The Feminine Mystique*, three years earlier, but I knew of no women at the agency – or anywhere else, for that matter – who had read it, with the exception of Kathy, my middle sister, who was doing sociology at uni. She gave it to me to read after she'd quarrelled with my mum, who had referred to it as 'a load of rubbish'. I don't think it had ever occurred to my mother that she wasn't liberated.

To be fair, even the chicks used 'bunny', as in: 'He wanted me to be his bunny and party, but I said I had to go home, that it was my mum's birthday.' Or, 'No way I was going to bunny him!'

Despite the bunny plague, I didn't indulge as enthusiastically as did most of the single and a good few of the married blokes in the agency. While the reason was pretty self-revealing – even pathetic, I suppose – it was nevertheless very real to me, and I should perhaps shamefully confess it had nothing whatsoever to do with having a deeper respect for the opposite sex than the other men did. It had everything to do with my appearance. By Western standards – in fact, by any standards – I'm as ugly as sin, a peasant throwback, and almost certainly Li Chinese, although even they might disown me. I'm a hard worker, which the Li still value, but I'm also short, broad, flat-faced, slit-eyed, myopic, somewhat gap-toothed, with broad, flat feet like paddles. Ferchrissake, I'm five foot eight inches tall and take a size twelve shoe, great clodhoppers flapping like a clown's feet at the end of my thick legs. Most Australian girls towered over me. You could almost lip-read people saying, 'Look at that pretty girl with that short, ugly Chinese bloke.' Ross sometimes referred to me as the Toulouse-Lautrec of advertising. I only wished I had his talent.

There was another problem, one that rich little boys are constantly made aware of; me, in particular. My family was loaded, and there was a good chance much of the money would come to me, which meant that to a certain type of female I was a very worthwhile catch. They came on big-time and I knew, or I thought I knew, it was not me they wanted. They were after the lifestyle my family's money represented. Or that was what my mum had been saying for as long as I could remember. I knew this was pretty damn pathetic, but I really did want to marry a woman for love; I wanted to love her and know in return that she loved me. It was another reason why I drove a Beetle and bought cheap suits off the rack and wore outrageous ties in truly bad taste.

Now, if true romance was going to be hard to achieve with an Australian woman, it was going to be damn near impossible with a Chinese one – that is, with someone my mum would like me to marry.

In fairness to her, she made no bones about it: 'Simon, better the devil you know. Rather a gorgeous Chinese girl from a good family (she meant rich) than a white one who sees you as an unlimited bank account,' her point being that the Chinese don't marry for something as ridiculous as love. Two families simply try to match each other's wealth. Money marries money. While one family may have more than the other, the aggregated amount is what gives both families face. The conjoined are seen as a net gain for both families. Or, if you should choose (God forbid) a girl from a poor family, you're simply marrying her family, who hope to benefit from your wealth. Love seldom, if ever, enters into the equation.

So there you go. I was the proverbial poor little rich boy who was silly enough to believe in love – a very strange and unacceptable idea to the Chinese, and very probably a trap where some Western girls were involved.

I shouldn't have said that, I suppose. It was bloody pathetic.

If my Li Chinese looks were, in my own eyes, my greatest social drawback, to Phyllis Koo they were my strongest asset, given her ambition to reinvigorate the Chinese genes of the Koo family. My mum was very big on perseverance. She was frequently, though never to her face, referred to by my various uncles and cousins as 'Chairman Meow', which was not intended as a compliment. Never giving up was the single characteristic that most clearly defined her personality in both business and life.

In this matter of family she had been tenacious. Not only the Koo family genotype but also the Koo family history was in tatters before she came along. The memory threads would undoubtedly have frayed and failed during my generation had she not started digging into the past. Shortly after she married my thoroughly integrated, only slightly Chinese-looking Australian dad, she nominated herself as the family historian.

She claimed that if you looked hard enough, nothing ever completely disappeared. My mum insisted she could 'smell' the whereabouts of a family fact. While I might call it probability, or logic, or even lateral thinking, she trusted her instincts or, more precisely, like Little Sparrow, the ancestors. This was exacerbated by the visitations of Little Sparrow and her dreaded dream.

There's nothing a Chinese family likes more than a bunch of signs and portents of prosperity. In fact, these become a sort of treasure trove supervised by the ancestors. All Chinese are beholden to their ancestors and seek their advice, and such a treasure as Little Sparrow's dream is psychologically enormously powerful and motivating. Phyllis Koo, the young well-born Chinese bride, was no different. Her determination to search out every scrap of Chinese family history, along with all signs and portents, had become an obsession.

The fact that I must have been the plainest-looking newborn infant in the history of Crown Street Women's Hospital filled her with delight. I was healthy and, moreover, unmistakeably Chinese in appearance. She had the raw clay to work with and, as far as she was concerned, nothing else mattered.

After four generations in the cultural wilderness, tracing the family's fragmented history must have presented a formidable task to the would-be historian. In fact, it proved easier than she might have thought. My great-great-grandfather, like many Chinese peasants, had always been subject to some sort of authority, often bureaucratic and invariably punitive, and never threw away a piece of paper in case he might need it. All business correspondence, licences, certificates, approvals, receipts and documents, birth certificates, death certificates and mountains of accounts and ledgers were kept forever. Despite Ah Koo and Little Sparrow's offspring intermarrying with *gwai-lo*, this oriental instinct seems to have persisted through the generations.

Searching in my father's family archive – several tons of papers that filled two large sheds on the grounds of the Enmore casket factory – my mother dug out heaps of info. The patterns and trails left by buying and selling, the partnerships formed and dissolved, the political exigencies (otherwise known as bribes) and the commercial mistakes and triumphs produced a fairly clear picture of each generation. Carefully collated and looked at together, the result could be illuminating. She did a damn good job, and over a period of time a credible picture of the family's past emerged.

But she craved the magic, the myths, beliefs, ancestral directives, anxieties, daily struggles and triumphs, and these didn't come from receipts, account books or commercial records. Then, six months after I was born, she hit the jackpot. In an old tin trunk she found a manuscript consisting of fifty tightly written pages in a beautiful feminine copperplate, in total a hundred sides of that fine handwriting. The manuscript had been written by one of the twins, my great-great-aunty May, and ended shortly after her fortieth birthday. In those times good paper contained a large amount of cloth and so the document was perfectly preserved, although the ink was somewhat brown and faded. This journal proved to be the grand story of the first and second generations my mum had been looking for, and it included the entire Little Sparrow dream.

The manuscript – or journal, as it became known – told how Little Sparrow sent both her daughters off to The Valley School to learn the three Rs, despite twin girls being thought of as bitter rice. The twins were given similar-sounding English names, May and Mabel, although to Little Sparrow's Chinese ear this may not have been apparent. On the other hand, it may have seemed like the right *gwai-lo* thing to do with twins.

As they were mere daughters, Ah Koo didn't interfere with this altogether bizarre notion of educating girls, least of all twins with no prospects. They were notionally his wife's servants and what she decided for them was none of his business. The girls were Little Sparrow's but the boys were Ah Koo's, and they worked hard in the market garden and piggery, which produced veggies and pork for the chophouse as well as supplying the new local shop with bacon and some vegetables. The chophouse, in turn, supported the small business Ah Koo had established to make coffins and glory-boxes.

Unusually for a Chinese peasant family, Ah Koo allowed his first son, Koo Lee Chin, to join the mounted New South Wales Citizens' Bushmen. From the age of fifteen he'd worked briefly as a rouseabout and sometime drover further up north. Aunt May's journal didn't specifically deal with this anomaly. Firstborn males inherit and are not customarily expected to leave the family fold, but my mum reckons there must have been bad blood between father and son for this to have happened. Apart from the fact that Koo Lee Chin was fifteen when he left The Valley, no more is known about his relationship with Ah Koo.

Number-two son, Koo Sam Lee, was born with a harelip and had a great deal of trouble making himself understood. Remaining on the land, he was known as Silent Sam or Slow Sam by the local settlers who were buying up the cheap cleared land in The Valley. He took over the running of the veggie patch and piggery and was said to produce the best bacon on the Central Coast; in fact, his bacon would eventually end up contributing to the family fortunes. Today the six piggeries, all started by him with the help of Mabel, supply all the pork for the Little Sparrow restaurant chain.

My great-grandfather, by the way, was number-three son. He and a younger brother were trained by their father as carpenters so they could make the glory-boxes and coffins that he decorated with his fancy chisel work: the trademark open lotus flower on coffin lids and the fat dragon on glory-boxes. My great-grandfather married the daughter of a timber-getter, by no stretch of the imagination a rise in his social standing. The remaining two boys worked at getting, seasoning and milling the cedar wood for the family coffin- and box-making business.

All the boys left school at fourteen. With the exception of Silent Sam, who was said to be somewhat slow, all could read, write and count. None, however, particularly excelled at schoolwork.

The twins were different. The lone schoolteacher in The Valley, young Mr Thomas, an Englishman from Dorset, was a gifted and conscientious schoolmaster and a stickler for the three Rs; he encouraged good handwriting and a love of reading in the girls, and of arithmetic in the boys. Like all teachers in one-room schools, he taught children of all ages together. Bright youngsters could eavesdrop on the work of the more advanced students, and teachers could easily extend the more able students. So, even though the twins were withdrawn from school at the age of twelve to work in the chophouse, May and Mabel had developed far beyond what might have been expected of twelve-year-old girls. According to Mr Thomas, they had done the lessons he gave the few sixteen-year-olds who remained at the school. Moreover, regardless of age, the twins had long been his top two students.

May, in particular, seemed to have added the boys' third R and was more than competent at arithmetic. Though she was far too modest to say so in her journal, it was not hard to see that the two girls were the brightest of the Koo children. May seemed to have benefited the most from her basic education, though, obviously, from the way she wrote, she developed a great deal further intellectually. But we know more about her than we do about Mabel, who helped her mother establish what was to become the Little Sparrow restaurant chain.

Neither twin married, although several dubious suitors turned up on the chophouse doorstep, only to be sent packing with a flea in their ear by the girls' formidable brick-shaped mother. After years of feeding these roughneck timber-getters and bullock drivers, Little Sparrow had lost her awe of the dreaded male *gwai-lo*. Her twin daughters might be regarded as worthless back in China, but they were hard-working, clever, educated and obedient and she was not about to give them away to drunks and layabouts, the only whites prepared to marry a Chink. *What lies between your legs is better left untouched than ravaged by a drunken, dishonourable husband who will spawn a dozen unwanted children he has no ability or intention to feed.* This cogent advice appeared in Aunty May's Journal – the name by which it was always known in the family, even though May was my great-great-aunt.

Aunty May had a natural gift for storytelling, and her remarkable journal documented the first sixty years of Koo life in Australia, in fact, right up to two weeks before she died. Throughout the memoir, she claimed to be simply transcribing her mother's words, but the document was more than just a chronicle of events. This gifted daughter allowed us to see her mother and father very clearly as individuals: Little Sparrow, the shy, obedient and self-effacing peasant woman growing in confidence and business acumen over the years, and Ah Koo, the patient man of modest expectations who dreamt of carving beautiful wood but needed permission from the gods and his ancestors to do what he regarded as a self-indulgence.

Little Sparrow went on to open a restaurant known as Little Sparrow's Chinese Chophouse in Gosford on the Central Coast, which would prosper beyond her dreams. Ah Koo became renowned for his carving, and established the foundation for a business empire that was worth far in excess of the gold he had hoped to obtain from New Yellow Gold Mountain. It allowed him to earn a modest income.

May's description of Little Sparrow's dream was colourfully and masterfully described and, together with the interpretation in Chinese characters discovered by my mother, was a complete narrative. She told how her mother insisted on calling it 'The answer from the gods', because it finally allowed her husband to be granted his secret wish and led eventually to good fortune. In fact, my own earlier description of the visit of Ah Koo and Little Sparrow to Sydney for the dream interpretation simply does not do justice in tone or mood to her writing.

The family, we were told in the journal, moved in 1897 to the newly declared village of Gosford to meet the growing demand throughout the Central Coast for Ah Koo's handsome cedar coffins and glory-boxes. These cost very little more than the plain, fairly crudely made glory-boxes and coffins used by the common people at the time. Soon, every young girl dreaming of wedding bells simply had to have a fat-dragon glory-box at the foot of her bed as she prepared for married life, and the dead could now be buried with a modicum of family pride in a beautiful lotus-blossom cedar casket.

Ah Koo's fame soon spread even further and orders began arriving from Sydney funeral parlours, where more affluent customers sometimes requested a personal motif on the coffin lid or sides. This was usually a hastily dredged-up or invented coat of arms or some similar decoration, the Masonic emblem and a lodge number being the most common. According to Aunty May, this presented an obvious problem: while the coffin could be made in advance, the personal carving could not, unless notice was given a week before the recipient finally carked it. On the other hand, while a personalised casket involved very little additional work, Ah Koo could charge three or four times more for it. He was a Chinese peasant who instinctively grabbed every opportunity to make a penny, and he simply couldn't allow such an obvious one to pass. His sons were excellent carpenters but none of them possessed any talent with a chisel, so he decided he must make hay while the sun shone, never suspecting for a moment that he was beginning a dynastic enterprise that would eventually dominate the Australian funeral scene.

So, in 1901, the year of federation, at the ages of fifty-eight and forty-eight respectively, Ah Koo and Little Sparrow decided to move to Sydney. Unlike most of the population, for whom the making of a nation called Australia was a happy event, for my great-great-grandparents it was a time of sorrow. This was also the year of the culmination of the Boxer Rebellion, an uprising that had attempted to rid China of all foreigners and Christians. An eight-nation alliance involving Russia, Germany, Austria–Hungary, the United Kingdom, the United States, Japan, Italy and France was sent to quell it. Australia, eager to support the motherland's interests, sent a token force of three hundred from the New South Wales Citizens Bushmen's Contingent. In one of those instances where truth proves stranger than fiction, Koo Lee Chin, Ah Koo's number-one son, was part of the contingent. He died of typhoid near the Chinese forts at Pei Tang, which the Australians had been sent to capture.

When the family moved to Sydney, Mabel was left behind to run the Gosford chophouse, and Silent Sam remained in The Valley to run the piggery, along with number-four and number-six sons, who continued to supply the raw cedar for the rapidly expanding business. My great-grandfather had married hurriedly and my grandfather was a toddler when the family moved to Gosford and then, some time later, to Sydney. (May did not record the feelings of my Christian great-grandmother at moving twice and leaving behind her family and friends in almost as many years, but it seems that while she was illiterate, she was a good mother and caring wife.)

Little Sparrow opened what was termed a Chinese restaurant, as opposed to a chophouse. The usual strong Chinese family ties prevailed and everything concerning business was kept within the family. Aunty May became the bookkeeper and so was in an ideal position to know and record in her journal anything of historical interest, including the family fortunes as they grew.

Little Sparrow and Aunty May were the true business brains, or so it seems. As the coffin-manufacturing business prospered, they took it over and opened the first funeral parlour in Sydney, as well as three further restaurants. The rest is history. Over the next forty-five years, they bought real estate, opened more and more Little Sparrow restaurants, Gold Chisel Caskets became known Australia-wide, and the family opened several Blue Lotus Funeral Parlours in every state capital. Today there are forty altogether.

Ah Koo worked until the day he died at the age of eighty-three. There is a story told, one my mother loves to repeat as vindication of Little Sparrow's dream, that Ah Koo suffered a sudden heart attack while carving a fat dragon. As he fell to the floor of his carpentry shop, he inadvertently stabbed the number-eight chisel into the heart of the wooden carving in exactly the manner it had appeared in Little Sparrow's dream. Whether this is apocryphal I can't say, but Phyllis Koo – aka Chairman Meow, as my dad calls her when he's pissed – believes every word is true.

Ah Koo was taken by the first funeral car they owned from their first funeral parlour and cremated in the first New South Wales crematorium, built at Rookwood Cemetery, in a coffin he'd helped make. Aunty May notes in her journal that his ashes were placed in the miniature fat-dragon box he'd originally carved as a portable sample to be used for selling glory-boxes to hopeful maidens. This reminded her that her father had always felt guilty because he'd ceased making fat-dragon glory-boxes when they moved to Sydney. The coffins were in such demand that Ah Koo had no choice but to devote himself to them, despite being conscious that he was disobeying the instructions of the gods, who, according to the soothsayer, had commanded him to make both items, though, curiously, not children's cradles, the third carved item furnishing the dream. As a consequence, he would carve a fat dragon in the week before Chinese New Year to be used as a centrepiece at the family banquet. The dragon that ended with the chisel through its heart, if the story is true, would have been for Chinese New Year 1925, the year of the ox.

Ah Koo's ashes, snug in the little fat-dragon box, were sent back to his village in China. Little Sparrow, not one to miss an opportunity now that cremations were becoming popular, soon found a competent wood carver and began a line that continues to this very day. The funeral parlours supply a fat-dragon ashes casket or, as my dad puts it, a gone-to-glory-box.

There's not a lot more to know concerning the family, except that as there was a shortage of Chinese women in Australia, the boys, all teetotallers and good providers, married Caucasian girls from poor but respectable working-class families, and the genetic blending my mother was determined to reverse duly commenced.

Little Sparrow lived to the age of eighty-five, dying in 1937, the year I was born. By Chinese peasant standards of the time, she would have been regarded as an old crone. In fact, she outlived the twins as well as her first son: Mabel died at thirty-seven in the Spanish flu epidemic of 1919, and Aunty May died in 1932 of TB (tuberculosis) at the age of fifty. My mum, with the help of a live-in nurse, cared for the old woman during the first two years of her marriage to my dad, and to the very end Little Sparrow remained sharp as a tack. Mum formed a tremendous affection for her. Three days before she died of a stroke, she had promised my mum, 'I will send you messages after I go to my ancestors, granddaughter-in-law.' The subsequent telepathic messages from beyond the grave, received over the years from the old matriarch, were to be my mother's justification for a great deal of the Chinese-style hocus-pocus we were forced to endure as kids and, occasionally, as adults. In most other things, Chairman Meow appeared to be quite sane and very bright and was, as you might have guessed, the true chairman of the board.

There was a rather nice appendix to Aunty May's story. Rummaging through her papers, my mother came across a bundle of love letters between her and Mr Thomas, the schoolmaster. These were always addressed to 'My Beloved Darling Duncan', to which he responded 'My Darling Lotus Blossom'. The letters revealed that from the age of fifteen, when the family moved to Gosford, May had corresponded with him, first as a friend and later as a lover. He was fifteen years her senior, and they met twice a year when she visited The Valley to collate and reconcile Silent Sam's accounts. She wrote to him every week of her adult life. When he died, only two years before her own death, Aunty May had been careful to recover her letters. Nosy Mum read every one of them in sequence and, apart from uncovering a great deal more family minutiae, discovered that May's twice annual visits to The Valley were to do with somewhat more than sharing tea and scones with her old schoolmaster. Aunty May definitely didn't die physically unloved and unwanted by a good man, although why they never married remained a mystery.

Which just about wraps up the past and brings me to the point where, on the evening of the 5th of July 1966, I drove into the eight-car garage, where my pale-green Vee Dub was certainly the smallest and humblest vehicle. I noted that my dad's Roller was missing, which meant I wouldn't be spilling the beans to him, but my mum's Jaguar was in residence. She'd be waiting for dinner and the usual chat, which promised to be nothing but small talk about the day – hers and mine – typically followed by her update on family business matters, which normally began with dessert and concluded over coffee in the lounge. Persistent, persevering, never-give-up Phyllis Koo was determined that I would eventually take over the chairmanship of the board of companies and conscientiously briefed me whenever I was home for dinner.

Although I affected only polite interest, she secretly believed that by some sort of mental osmosis it was all being filed away in my brain for later use. Tonight, though, I guessed I'd be doing most of the talking. If I've given the impression it was usually all one-way chat with my mum and that she was a bit of a fruitcake, I've been misleading. She was an acute listener, who wore an expression of absolute concentration that made you choose your words very carefully – it was another reason why my uncles secretly feared her. She was a woman of remarkable business acuity, and knew when to remain silent.

By some instinct – to call it coincidence would be downplaying it – she'd had the cook prepare my favourite dinner – lamb shanks and mash followed by jam trifle, two dishes she usually dismissed as 'rubbish eating', maintaining that such food came from those first-generation marriages to working-class women whose parents had almost certainly been convicts. Now she smiled sweetly, sighed and said, 'So tell me about your yesterday and today. You were late home last night.'

'Yeah, darts,' I replied.

'What did you have for dinner?'

Why is this a vital piece of information for mothers?

'Lamb shanks,' I replied, joking.

'Oh no!' she exclaimed, bringing her hands to her lips.

'Only kidding, Mum. I can't remember . . . Oh yeah, chips and peanuts . . . beer . . .'

'That's awful! You'd think they'd supply something decent for you to eat.'

'They? Mum, it was at the pub. The pub doesn't do food at night.'

'The pub closes at ten o'clock; you got in after midnight,' she accused.

'Mum, ferchrissake! I'm twenty-nine years old! You don't have to wait up for me to come home!'

'I'm your mother, Simon,' she said, as if waiting up for your 29-year-old son was an essential part of motherhood. 'And please don't swear,' she added.

I sighed. 'Well, yeah, I parked at The Gap for a while. I had a few things on my mind.'

'The Gap!' It was a cry of consternation. She grabbed my hand, sending the shank and potato on my fork flying onto the damask. 'Simon, what's wrong?' She was plainly shocked and close to tears.

I'd momentarily forgotten that The Gap at South Head was Sydney's most popular suicide jump.

'Mum! Nothing like that.' I placed my knife and fork beside the barely touched shank and mash, knowing I'd probably eaten the last of my dinner, then wiped my lips on the starched damask table napkin, a material that may add formality but to me always removes the joy of eating. 'I had one or two things to think about.'

She was obviously relieved that I'd hesitated at the brink of death. 'Think about what, darling?' Her hand came to rest on my own, but this time it was a soft touch, all sympathy and understanding. Those hands were always beautiful and unblemished, the long painted nails perfectly manicured. I fleetingly wondered to myself what Little Sparrow's hands would have looked like at her age.

The time had come to open up the can of worms I'd been carrying about for two days. 'I've been offered a job in Singapore,' I said, looking directly at her.

'Singapore!'

I attempted to keep my voice casual. 'Yeah, our New York office has bought a Singapore advertising agency from three Chinese brothers and they want me to be the creative director, in fact, to build its creative department from scratch.'

The sympathetic mother, comforting a would-be suicide, transformed in an instant to Chairman Meow. 'What Chinese brothers?' she snapped, her dark eyes immediately suspicious.

'Wing, the Wing Brothers, Wing Brothers Advertising,' I answered, suddenly realising that Singapore was a small island and doubtless all the leading Chinese business families, of which my mum's was a notable example, would know each other. But then my grandfather had left in 1919, when she was four years old, so it was unlikely she'd recall the names of families. On the other hand, she had relatives among the Chinese upper crust.

'Names?'

'Mum, I just told you – Wing!'

'Most well-born Singapore Chinese have English names they use with *gwai-lo*.'

I shrugged. 'It didn't occur to me to ask.'

'I'll find out,' she announced.

'Does it matter?'

'Of course!'

'Why is that?'

She sighed. 'The Japanese murdered a number of the old Singapore families during the last war. Our relatives were lucky and got away in time to hide in one of our remote plantations in Malaya. After the war, a whole bunch of Chinese mercantile adventurers – business gangsters – came in from Hong Kong —'

'Mum!' I protested, 'I haven't even made up my mind whether I'll take the job.'

'Yes, I know. But you will.'

'Huh?' I gave her a quizzical look.

'The fourth fledgling, the big one with the yellow mouth,' she said, as if this explained everything.

'Mum, what on *earth* are you talking about?'

'The dream,' she explained. 'The fledgling that flew into and out of the baby's mouth.'

'Mum, are you feeling okay?' I asked. 'Not feeling a little Koo Koo?' (It was a childhood joke, but I truly had no idea what she meant.)

'Don't be rude, Simon!' she chided. 'I mean Little Sparrow's dream, of course. The baby. When the fledgling flies out of its mouth. That's *you* going to Singapore,' she explained, as if everything was perfectly clear and simple. I tried to recall the dream. It'd been a fair while since I'd had the benefit of one of Mum's telepathic messages from Little Sparrow. Nonetheless, I knew that it was pointless to protest. I took a mouthful of lamb and chewed. 'Okay, let's have it,' I said, resigned to listening.

'Simon, don't patronise me!'

'Well, fair go, Mum. The chairman of the agency called me up to his office yesterday —'

'You didn't tell me it was yesterday!' She looked genuinely astonished. 'Why, that's remarkable!'

I put up a hand to stop her in her tracks. 'Wait on, Mum, will ya? Lemme finish!' I took a breath before continuing. 'He, Charles Brickman, offered me a job in Singapore and suddenly it's an ancient prophecy come true, written in the stars, a message from the gods, ancestors, whatever? Jesus, Mum!' I brought my hands up as if I was protecting myself from a blow, then slapped them down hard on the table. 'That's total rubbish!'

She didn't react, but her mouth was the shape of a plucked duck's arsehole. Then, looking down into her lap, she said in a calm, somewhat hurt voice, 'Don't poke fun, Simon. You don't know *everything*.' She looked up at me. 'Now, when precisely did your chairman call?' Before I could answer, she went on, 'Just after one o'clock?'

'Yes, but you couldn't have known that.'

Her dark-brown eyes lit up. 'Ha! I didn't.'

I waited for the explanation that must follow.

'I was at the dressmaker's in Double Bay, Laura le Gay; you know, the jumped-up Hungarian migrant who pretends to be French. She always has the radio on in the background, very cheap,' she added. 'The music for the one o'clock ABC news came on five or so minutes after I arrived. Skirts are up this year, it's got something to do with Jean Shrimpton, that English model who came to the Melbourne Cup with her skirt up past her knees.'

'It was Derby Day,' I corrected. Wills were doing a promotion for Turf Cigarettes and I'd designed the point-of-sale artwork. Shrimpton was wearing a white A-line dress, and compared to the new miniskirts the girls in the agency were wearing, it was rather modest, and certainly not the big deal the press and TV made of it.

My mother dismissed my correction. 'Anyway, now we've all got to do the same thing and wear our skirts up around our bottoms.' I knew my mum was secretly very proud of her long, shapely legs, and Shrimpton's skirt length at Flemington Derby Day wouldn't be all bad news to her. 'Well, I wasn't going to throw out three perfectly good suits I'd bought in Paris last year, was I? I thought the skirts could come up just a little bit, perhaps to the middle of the knee. I trust Laura le Gay despite her silly carry-on; she's *such* a good seamstress.'

The mash and lamb were almost cold, but I had to eat something. 'Mum!' I protested, really growing impatient. 'What has this got to do with the time?'

'Why, everything, dear! I'm not the doubting Thomas around here! If I don't set the scene, you're not going to believe me. Anyway, I was standing there wearing the pale blue Chanel suit skirt, and Laura was on her haunches pinning the hem up when I began to shake. The poor woman pulled back in shock and fell onto her bottom – I mean, *really* onto her bottom, varicose stockings in the air. It was as if she'd had an electric shock!' Mum giggled at the recollection. 'Imagine! She was wearing those old-fashioned pink bloomers and she claims to be such a fashion fanatic. I knew it was coming. It's always like this when I start to shake involuntarily – not shake-shake, more a soft tremble. "I can't help it, Laura. I have to let it come through," I said to the poor woman.'

By this time, my mum had me. It was the way she told the story, not all mysterious and *sotto voce*, but as if it were perfectly normal, nothing to be upset about, just the daily message coming through loud and clear from Little Sparrow. At least she hadn't said it was at precisely six minutes past one o'clock on a Monday afternoon; then I'd have really freaked out.

I was familiar with her Little Sparrow messages. They came through pretty regularly throughout our childhood, usually in response to some new behavioural lesson we needed to learn, but also, occasionally, for no apparent reason – or, rather, for some reason of her own that had nothing to do with us, perhaps some business decision or problem with the board. As an adult I was aware that Little Sparrow's messages seemed to come at random. I'd even witnessed two of them and I have to admit they seemed to be spontaneous and uncontrolled, really quite weird. Moreover, there was simply no doubt that my mother believed in them. The Chinese are a contradiction: they can be highly intelligent and seemingly pragmatic, as my mother often was, clear, concise thinkers who don't suffer fools or bullshit gladly, but, at the same time, be deeply superstitious, happy to receive guidance from their ancestors in their daily life.

'So?' I said calmly. 'You had one of your Little Sparrow turns.'

'Yes, not turns, messages – just after one o'clock.'

I pulled myself together. *Okay, what did we have here? She's at the dressmakers just after one o'clock and has a Little Sparrow turn. Big deal, so what?* 'Mum, what has this to do with me going to Singapore?'

My mother closed her eyes for effect and lowered her voice. I guess she had to ham it up a little bit using her Little Sparrow voice. *'The yellow fledgling has grown. It has come out of the baby's mouth and flown out of the dream.'* She looked at me, the suggestion of a triumphant smile on her lips, her eyes almost shut. Chairman Meow was practically purring. 'Singapore,' she said quietly. 'It is flying to the land of my birth.'

'I need a coffee,' I said, furious with myself for falling into her trap.

'Oh, darling, I'm neglecting you!'

'No, you stay. I'll get it. Shall I get you one?'

'Simon, you know I *never* drink coffee at night.' She rose and asked, 'You wouldn't like a brandy to go with it, would you?' It was her way of saying she knew I was rattled.

CHAPTER THREE

———————

SO INSTEAD OF THE anticipated resistance from my mother to the Singapore job, I found only delight and encouragement. Despite what she said about Little Sparrow and her dream, I suspected there was quite another reason for her elation. Surrounded by her family and their friends, it was inevitable that I should find a Chinese wife.

While to Brickman I denied any knowledge of Cantonese, my ambitious and careful mother had seen to it that we children understood and had a fairly good grasp of one of China's four most popular languages. I was pretty rusty, since I now stubbornly refused to speak it at home. My dad barely understood a word, and I regarded speaking Cantonese as inappropriate and an affectation, since my mum had been in Australia from the age of four. The few ethnic Chinese I knew all preferred to speak English. Nevertheless, my sisters and I spoke Cantonese well enough to get by at a level that might be attained by a conscientious *gwai-lo*. My youngest sister, Helen, was the best linguist, but even she spoke it with an Australian accent. 'The rest you'll pick up in no time. Cantonese is an easy language. Besides, all the good families and big business people speak English,' my mum assured me.

I can't say I was thrilled by the thought of finding myself in the midst of her family: an ancient senile great-grandmother, a great-uncle and his wife, Fiona, their kids, my mother's cousins, who between them had two daughters and three sons, my second cousins. The girls, already married, had produced a pigeon pair each. My mother kept track of every birthday and on Chinese New Year everyone received generous red envelopes known as *hong bao*. I forget how many additional relatives there were but my mum kept in touch with one of her cousins, who had two sons, my second cousins, Patrick and Henry Kwan. One was in Chinese antiques and the other a sociologist who worked at the university.

Another second cousin, Bryan, lived in America. He never married, a fact that worried his grandmother, Fiona, no end. But whenever the subject came up, my mum would declare with a sniff that if she'd use the eyes in her head, she'd realise he was as camp as a row of tents. 'A Chinese man with a lisp, my goodness! I daily thank the gods we don't have to contend with *that*,' she'd say smugly, although I'm sure the possibility had crossed her mind more than once where I was concerned, and she might even have consulted the gods herself. I think it might have been the outrageous psychedelic neckties I wore. But the number of bunnies she'd witnessed coming and going must have reassured her. So the onus was on me to be the male supremo of my generation. My duty, besides becoming chairman of the family's businesses, was to spawn a squad of boys to carry on what my mum regarded as 'the honourable Koo surname' and appear as Chinese as possible.

'With my pure blood mixed in with your father's, no one will know they're not 100 per cent Chinese . . . A bit fair-skinned, maybe, but that's nice, that's good,' she'd sometimes say.

'It works both ways, Mum,' I'd reply. 'What if they're throwbacks and turn out tall, blonde and blue-eyed?'

'Impossible! It's not in Little Sparrow's dream,' she'd say, tight-lipped, although you could almost hear her heart skip a beat.

I sometimes wondered, considering how it all turned out, why, when I discovered my mother approved of me going to Singapore, I didn't reject the job offer. I doubt it would have affected my career. Charlie Baby wasn't a man to be crossed lightly, but he was a pragmatist and knew the value of biding his time. Also, the Wills advertising department would certainly have put the kibosh on the move. But none of this would now be tested. My acceptance might even give Charlie a certain amount of kudos in the New York office.

My several reasons for taking the Singapore position were complex. I'd been promised a one-man show at the Rudy Komon Gallery in Jersey Road, Woollahra, for which I would need at least sixteen paintings. After a year I'd completed six, and except for one, or maybe two, they were nothing to write home about. I was in a bit of a painting rut and couldn't see myself emerging from it in the near future. Too many cigarette packs too soon, I guess. So that was certainly one reason. Three years in Asia, I told myself, and I might see things differently or, at least, be reinvigorated.

Another reason was the chance to prove myself. I had resisted entering the family business, but I hadn't shown any real aptitude on my own. I'd huffed and I'd puffed and, while I may have loosened one or two roof tiles, I hadn't blown the house down. Sure, I could draw and paint a bit and had all the makings of a pretty good advertising man. I earned enough to run the Vee Dub, buy my own gear and generally pay my own way. But then of course I didn't pay rent. I'd mumble some excuse to myself about needing a studio for my painting, but really that was bullshit. At twenty-nine, I hadn't climbed to any dizzy heights or, for that matter, scaled the foothills of a personal achievement that might make my family sit up and take notice. I was simply a paid employee, and my executive supremo was an irascible semi-cripple with a rapidly advancing lung condition and thoroughly unpleasant manner.

It was high time I got away from everything I knew. I was kidding myself if I thought I was free and independent, or that I was unaffected by my family's major areas of business. When you grow up and just about every conversation in the home has something, directly or indirectly, to do with death, it gets under your skin like an itch. You find yourself watching a passing funeral procession to see if the hearse is being driven by one of your dimmer cousins, or if the deceased is being sent to their eternal rest in a Gold Chisel casket. I recall an incident when I was a six-year-old and one of the kids in my class announced that his grandma had died.

'Well, that's very sad,' Miss Bachelor replied, 'but, isn't it nice to know she's in heaven with all the angels?'

My hand shot up. 'No she isn't, Miss. She's in one of my daddy's coffins!'

My family has made a zillion dollars waiting at the end of the line to bathe and dress your ordinary bloke or sheila for the very last time: arranging the hair; applying pancake and filler to hide wrinkles, liver spots or burst capillaries; surgically collapsing beer guts so corpses fit into caskets; adding lippy, mascara and a little eye shadow. You'd think being in the funeral business we'd be in the thick of things. But the hoi polloi were still a mystery to me. I was, in truth, several steps removed from the lives of most of the people who went to their final rest under my family's expert ministrations.

Ordinary people (and I hated myself for thinking this) were almost a different species. The living, breathing, spitting, fighting, lonely desperate housewife or her jobless, alcohol-fuelled, frustrated husband; the suicidal teenagers; the abused kids out there on the streets; the ordinary Mr and Mrs Average with their 2.5 children in the 'burbs – all were strangers to me. The closest I ever got to any of them was listening to some pumped-up, sassy-arsed, horn-rimmed behavioural-psychology graduate-turned-researcher talking about the subliminal effects of three cigarettes sticking out of a hard pack or the phallic pleasure young women derived from all-white filter tips in a tactile soft pack.

I don't mean I was superior. God knows my family's social journey over four generations was as common as they come. I've honestly never seen myself as better or smarter, and in the looks department I'm way behind almost everyone. But, for instance, I couldn't imagine my mother having a crap, or even having the need for one. People in the street, yeah, that was easy, even the bunnies in the agency . . . but surely not my elegant mother? I simply could not envision her – feet in those

Charles Jourdan high-heeled courts nestling within her lacy knickers, the skirt of her navy Chanel suit rucked up around her waist – reaching for the gold-plated crap-paper holder with manicured fingers that carried a hundred grand's worth of gold and ice. See what I mean? It really was high time I jumped off the deep end and swam out into the real world.

Singapore was real, and I assured myself that I'd only be gone for three years – a change of scene, renewed inspiration for my painting, proof that I wasn't entirely worthless, and the chance to build the best advertising creative department in Asia. Moreover, I'd be rid of the W.D. & H.O. Wills account forever, and a lengthy plane flight away from the pervasive influence of my family and the death business. By this, I mainly meant Forceful Phyllis, aka Chairman Meow or Mother, who had never ceased to pry into my life, overseeing all I did even now. Much as I truly loved her, it was time to free myself from her influence. The only downside to Singapore was my mum's dreaded Chinese family. No doubt she would manage her network of relatives as effectively as any spymaster, but I told myself that if I showed sufficient reserve and was no more than politely dutiful, they'd be manageable.

And there was one more reason for going to Singapore: I longed for anonymity, to simply walk down a street and be just another face in the crowd. It wasn't the fact that I had a Chinese face – there were lots of those in Sydney – it was that mine seemed hard to ignore. People glanced at me for a little longer than they might look at any other person they'd pass in the street. They'd do the same to people in wheelchairs. While I wasn't a freak and had no physical deformities, my face was round and flat, with a button nose and fairly large mouth that turned up slightly at the corners. My mother would say, 'Simon was born with a smile on his face.' I recall that at art school when we were studying human features, using each other as models, a smart-arse student named Ken Done painted a portrait of me as a pale yellow dinner plate with two long black olives for my eyes, a tiny potato for my nose and a small, slightly bent cucumber for my mouth and called it Koocumber Salad. Somehow it bore an uncanny resemblance to the original, and everyone recognised me immediately and had a good laugh, including myself, until the bastard got a high distinction for it. But despite my face, to stick to the food analogy, I felt about as Chinese as Yorkshire pudding.

I dialled Graceless Gertie when I arrived at the agency at 8.45 a.m. on Wednesday, only to be ticked off sharply and told that she didn't expect to be called before 9 a.m., when the agency officially opened for business, and furthermore that the chairman arrived in his office around 11 a.m. and she'd call me when he felt disposed to see me.

Oops, off on the wrong foot yet again! Naturally I knew what time he arrived, but it had seemed advisable to be on the record as having called first thing. In fact I'd hoped Gertie might not have arrived yet, so I could later casually mention that I'd called previously and gather a few much-needed Brownie points.

I was aware that I'd been somewhat forward during our initial encounter, after Brickman, with a little help from his dragon lady, had ruffled my feathers. So I decided that this time I would keep my cool, no matter how irascible he, or they, proved to be. If he referred to Chinese pussy, I would attempt a conspiratorial grin. I would offer to carry the chair in with me in an attempt to make a good impression on both of them, having guessed that they worked as a team, a hunch Odette had confirmed at our lunch yesterday.

Despite the asinine little lecture from Her Grace (my future name for her), I remained upbeat. Besides, if I agreed to go to Singapore, surely they'd be pleased. My confidence was slightly shaken when, at ten minutes past nine, Her Grace called and said in a clipped voice, 'Mr Koo, under no circumstances are you to leave your office until the chairman calls you . . . whenever that might be.' For a moment I considered our relative rank in the agency and thought I probably didn't have to take her crap, but decided to let it pass. 'Kindly do not be late *this time*, Mr Koo.' Her sharp tongue was plainly the result of years of practising the art of being bloody difficult. I've noticed that some people take every opportunity to exercise their skill at getting under one's skin. *Not me, not today, no way, José. Today I'm bulletproof.*

I called Odette on the switch and asked her to give me a bell the moment the chairman arrived. She had previously told me he called her as soon as he removed his suit jacket. 'It's always the same routine, never so much as a good morning, just straight down to business. Always the same bark down the phone. He tells me who he doesn't want to speak to each day, who to keep waiting to the point of rudeness and who to put through immediately.' She giggled. 'Bob Menzies is mentioned as the number-one no-speak every morning, even though he hasn't called since they quarrelled after the election in 1949!' After a pause she had looked at me directly and said, 'By the way, be warned, Cookie. Charles Brickman never forgives and never forgets.'

Of course, with Bob Menzies at the top of the list, I didn't for a moment think that small-fry like me would qualify for even the lowest spot on the chairman's hate list. On the other hand, by ignoring her call to place the chair elsewhere, I may well have made it onto Her Grace's list.

I disregarded her instruction to stay put, until Odette called me to say the chairman had arrived just after 11 a.m.; then I thought I'd better stay put, which meant being stuck in my office for the remainder of the morning and through my lunch hour. By 2.30 I was feeling the effects of the four cups of coffee I'd consumed earlier and was busting for a slash. Of course, you guessed it, the chairman's call via Her Grace came while I was pointing at the porcelain. I returned to find the red light on my phone throbbing as if in pain, which meant call the switch.

'She's not happy, Cookie. Better skedaddle upstairs. Chairman's waiting,' Odette informed me.

I'd borrowed a blue and white polka-dot tie from my dad to replace Mickey Mouse playing the banjo on a bright pink background – the tie I'd worn to our previous meeting. As I recall, I'd even dabbed Brylcreem on my coarse, longish hair. Greasy Hippy – not a good look. 'Good afternoon, Miss Grace.' Her mouth was pulled into the characteristic duck's arsehole. 'Shall I take the chair in with me?'

'I see you make a habit of being late, Mr Koo.' She nodded towards the chair in the corner.

'Sorry, I was in the men's.' I kept my voice cheery as I retrieved the chair.

'You may go in,' she said with a terse nod.

Brickman sat at his desk, positively yelling down the phone at someone whom I took, after listening for a few moments, to be the gardener. 'Bring the Victoria Brickman camellias out of the bottom nursery! The ones you bagged and tied last week. I want them put down the driveway! Four foot apart. Use a tape measure. Take the Queen Elizabeth standards out and burn them. Should have done the same to the ex. I told the stupid woman roses weren't right for that location; nothing but mildew and black spot! Besides, they're pink. I fucking hate pink!'

Good thing I didn't wear the pink Mickey Mouse tie. I realised that the conversation might be going on for a while so I placed the chair carefully on the Aubusson and sat down to wait while the chairman continued his tirade.

'Josef, now you be bloody careful with those camellias! Check the pH of the soil first. I want the prize for new varietals at next year's show. If I don't get it, I'll have your miserable wop guts for garters.' He paused. 'Josef, I mean it. There's been a lot of work gone into creating that camellia. You should bloody know that! Oh, and tell Mrs Josef I'd like her spaghetti and meatballs for dinner tonight. Righto then.' He slammed down the phone. 'Bloody nurserymen, think they know everything!' he muttered. 'Yes, well, what's it to be, Koo?' His voice was only half a decibel or two below the tone used for the hapless Josef but he retained the impatience.

'I've decided to accept the job in Singapore, sir . . . Thank you,' I added hastily.

'Pussy, eh?' It was strange, a bloke like him being obsessed with a new camellia and then suddenly switching to the subject of sex. Or perhaps not, when you think of stamens, cross-pollination and the like.

I attempted a determined grin. 'No, sir . . . I'd like the opportunity to build my own creative department.'

'Umph!' But then he seemed to focus and in a fairly jovial voice said, 'Well, that's good, Koo. Three years, that's the contract. Don't let us down, son. Show 'em we Australians mean business.'

'Show who, sir – the Wing brothers?'

'Nah, they're bloody lucky to get you. I mean the Yanks. Feather in our cap sending someone like you who looks the part. You are Australian, aren't you, Koo? Oh, yes, I remember. Fourth-generation. Throwback.' He reached over and took a cigarette from an open silver box that hadn't been on his desk the last time I'd been in his office. I later learned from Odette that, in a fit of pique, he'd thrown it against the wall and it had only recently been returned from the jeweller. The top of the lid was facing me and I read the inscription:

To Charles Brickman
In appreciation
Bob Menzies
The New Liberal Party
1946

He tapped one end of the fag on the surface of the Georgian desk a couple of times, then absent-mindedly lit up, inhaled, exhaled and fanned the smoke away from his face. 'Bloody gaspers,' he said, placing the Ronson desk lighter back beside the box. 'Any questions?' Both remarks were made in the same flat voice, without a pause. He wasn't coughing as much this time, though each sentence was still punctuated with a small gasp and his voice was gravel shifting over tin.

'Yes, sir – when? When am I expected to arrive?'

Brickman stabbed the intercom. 'Miss Grace, when?'

'When what, Mr Brickman?' came the crackling reply.

Second stab at the intercom. 'When is Mr Koo needed in Singapore?'

Silence, then Miss Grace appeared and crossed to his desk to stand directly beside me. Reaching over, she removed several sheets of paper from his in-tray and I caught a whiff of her perfume. It evoked dead rose petals and violets in small muslin bags found in the underwear drawers of old ladies. 'The contract, it's all in there,' she said, placing it in front of him. 'Mr Koo has to sign it there,' she stabbed a freckled finger at the last line on the first page, 'and then initial the bottom of every page.'

'Yeah, righto,' Brickman said impatiently, 'every page.' Then he picked up the contract and began to read, cigarette held above his shoulder, smoke curling up to the ceiling. My eyes followed it and I noticed, to my surprise, that the white gloss ceiling directly above his head was stained a dirty brown with nicotine. Curiously, it suited the elegant room, made it seem more lived in, gave all the antiques a present tense, a current working life.

The document, I remember, was six pages in total, and either Charles Brickman was the world speed-reading champion or he was only pretending to read. Each page took him about ten seconds, his breathing punctuated with regular wheezy gasps and the occasional grunt. After a minute or so he looked up, slapped the contract down again, puffed, exhaled and said, 'Pretty straightforward. Don't seem to be any problems.'

'I'd like to read it, sir.'

'Yes, of course,' he pushed the contract across the desk. 'Go ahead, son.'

'Er . . . May I take it away with me?'

'What? Show it to a lawyer? This is white bread, Koo, nothing hidden. Slice it any way you want, it's plain and simple – snow white on the inside and brown crust on the outside.' I wondered briefly where he'd picked up this example of Madison Avenue jargon that was so patently out of character for a guy like him. 'Run it up the flagpole and let's see who salutes' was the most commonly used Hollywood-movie example. I confess I had heard very few people use any of these parody lines until I got to Singapore and met Ronnie Wing, the youngest of the three Wing brothers.

'Still, sir . . . I'd like to read it carefully.' I could hear my mum's shocked voice: 'What! You signed it without showing it to Uncle Herbert?'

Uncle Herbie is my dad's brother, the family lawyer and in Mum's opinion one of the few members of the family who commands respect. She would refer to him as being sharp as a tack, so he can't have been a fool. His hair was jet-black and his eyes almond-shaped, except that they were a pale, washed-out blue. On a girl they'd be spectacularly seductive, but on him they were disconcerting and weird, as if they were fading or slowly dying.

'Koo, what do you know about contracts?'

I grinned. Was he feeding me my next line? 'Enough to read them carefully before signing them, sir,' I responded predictably. Perhaps I should have mentioned that I have a Commerce degree.

'Hmm . . . Righto then, have it back in an hour.' He glanced at his watch. 'I'll still be here to witness it.'

'I'd like at least until morning, sir.'

His bushy eyebrows shot up. 'It's *only* six pages, Koo!'

'Still, I'd like to take it home, sir.' The whole thing was getting a little out of hand, but I must have had some of Chairman Meow's genes because I was not going to budge. Anyway, a six-page contract was bloody long.

Brickman sighed and stabbed his fag to death in the beautiful ashtray. 'Righto, son, good move,' he said, to my surprise. I recall he wore what might, conceivably, emerge as a smile, given enough time.

'Thank you, sir. What time shall I return it?'

'When your lawyer has looked it over, of course,' he said with a wave of the hand. He paused and the smile emerged in all its tobacco-stained splendour. 'Oh, and Koo, while you're about it, whatever salary package they offer, double it, and build in a new business bonus – 3 per cent of the gross total billing for the first three years based on media-placement billing and production costs. *Not* the net profit – there's never a net profit after the bloody accountants have made all their highly imaginative deductions. Then, after three years, for as long as the account and you stay with the agency, 2 per cent of the gross. I'm not sure who's paying, the Americans or the Chinese. Either way it's not us.' He grinned. 'Of course, there's also a hardship allowance.'

'Hardship?'

'Yes, mysterious East, malaria, dengue fever, dysentery, open drains, shit and piss in the *kampongs* and rivers, living away from home, missing loved ones – let's say that's an extra grand a year. Do you know anyone in Singapore?'

'Yes, sir, my mother has relatives there.'

'Business?'

'Yes, sir, palm oil. They're among the biggest exporters.'

'Good. Have them look at some suitable accommodation for you. It's a small island, a bit broken-down, but this bloke Lee Kuan Yew is changing things for the better. You see, Singapore is the ideal bridge between East and West. The international brands are becoming interested in the Asian market. That's why New York is buying into Wing Brothers.' He cleared his throat. 'Their clients can see the potential in an emerging market and want a piece of the action. Millions of potential new shoppers buying soap, detergent, tobacco, Coca-Cola, you name it. You can assume accommodation will be scarce and rents sky-high. If we're the first international agency in the market, you can bet your army boots that others will soon follow. Get someone in your family to work out the cost of what would be suitable for your needs in terms of size, prestige and location. Rent at the high end of the market. Put that in the contract. Spell it out, right down to the dishwasher – that's the housekeeper's salary. Remember, it's the level of his accommodation that makes a single senior executive look good.' He paused, threw his head back and blew smoke into the air. 'You must have the best, number-one pussy trap. Don't put that into the contract, but be sure to spell everything else out precisely. You're only going to get one go at it. It's all about being taken seriously by our Chinese agency partners.'

What he was talking about was 'face'. The Chinese are very big on face. My mum uses the word at least twenty times a day. To lose face is a fate worse than death to the Chinese.

'Thank you, sir, I'll do as you advise.' I couldn't quite believe the remarkable change in his demeanour.

'Good work, son. Can't have one of my lads disadvantaged. It's not the Australian way of doing business. You'll need more than tomorrow with that contract. See if you can get it back to us by next Wednesday – no, I'm with the Premier at the races then. It'll have to be Thursday – make it Thursday after lunch.'

I still couldn't quite believe my ears. This could only be the Charles Brickman Odette was hinting at when she'd protested that he had a good side to him.

'Will they buy that, sir? I mean all the extras?'

'Son, you'll never know unless you ask.' He dismissed me with a wave of his hand, but it wasn't an unfriendly gesture. I rose and picked up the chair and turned towards Her Grace's office. 'Ask and ye shall receive,' I heard him chuckle.

I entered her office and placed the chair in its former position. Suddenly she was all smiles. 'Why, thank you, Mr Koo. And when will we be seeing you again?' She positively oozed charm. 'I need to know so I can make sure the chairman is in.' She reached for a leather appointment book.

'Thursday afternoon, some time after lunch. Mr Brickman didn't say precisely.'

'Let's make it three-thirty then.' She wrote this in the book then glanced up with a smile. 'If there is any change in arrangements, I'll let you know in plenty of time, Mr Koo.'

Jesus! What's going on? I thought. 'Thank you, Miss Grace.' *Miracles will never cease.*

Well, between Chairman Meow getting on the telephone to Singapore, and the extras suggested by the chairman added in, and the whole caboodle being carefully scrutinised by Uncle Herbie, the contract I took back to the agency a week and a day later was tight as a squirrel's bum.

It was returned three weeks later from overseas, neatly retyped with a sentence or two changed, but to all intents and purposes intact. New York and Singapore accepted the deal with the proviso that either party could rescind the contract after a year. The New York office agreed to pick up my salary package for the trial year, and the Wing brothers, if all parties agreed that I should stay on, would foot the bill for the remaining two. I thanked the chairman and added that I greatly appreciated his help. Through a curtain of cigarette smoke, he replied, 'Just remember, Koo, only a fool prepares a contract where there's no room to move, and you want to know you'll not be working for a fool.'

'No, sir, thank you,' I replied, somewhat upbeat. We'd become . . . how shall I put it? Fellow conspirators? Jonas called it working buddies. It was fairly obvious Brickman didn't think much of the way the Americans were going about getting into Asia. And plainly he didn't trust the proprietors of the Chinese agency.

'Now, you look after yourself, Koo. Not everything is what it seems to be. The Chinese . . .' He left the final two words hanging in the air.

In addition to all the chairman's suggestions, Uncle Herbie had added four weeks' paid vacation (using the American word for annual holidays) outside Asia, with first-class airfares to and from anywhere in the world. Having a captive Koo as family lawyer had its advantages. Charles Brickman made one or two more calls to America, and a week later I signed the contract, now almost nine pages long, and passed it over the desk to Brickman.

He leaned back. 'Let me tell you something for nothing, son. While I've never met the Wing brothers, one of them is smart enough to have negotiated with New York to pay your first year's salary as well as all the trimmings, including the rent for your pussy trap. If it doesn't work out – clash of personalities, whatever – they've had the benefit of your work and the new business you'll no doubt attract, and it's cost them bugger-all. If it does work out, then better still – they pay you two years' salary for the price of three.' He looked at me directly then stabbed his tobacco-stained forefinger at me. 'Find out which Wing brother it is and keep your eye on him. Mark my words, he's going to try to screw you at every turn.'

My mum, who, as I previously mentioned, had been following the negotiations every step of the way, pronounced herself satisfied. She'd even taken a positive shine to Charles Brickman after I'd told her how he'd personally advised and cautioned me.

'I want to meet this man,' she said. 'I trust him intuitively.' I'd pointed out that this probably wasn't such a good idea. Unbeknownst to me she sent him three dozen Queen Elizabeth long-stemmed roses, accompanied by a thank-you note from the Koo family.

The phone rang in my office shortly after eleven o'clock the following day and, before I had a chance to speak, the chairman's gravel-sluice voice came roaring down the line. 'What's going on, Koo? I fucking hate pink roses!'

The 707 landed at Paya Lebar International Airport in the middle of a tropical downpour. As usual, the moment we touched down I checked my watch: 5.03 p.m. precisely on the 17th of September 1966. My mum, clapping her hands, would have exclaimed, 'Double lucky!' That's because $5 + 3 = 8$ and $1 + 7 = 8$, which, to the Chinese, is doubly lucky because the number eight is the luckiest of all numbers. I'd be lying if I said this thought hadn't occurred to me.

A uniformed airport attendant stood under a red and white striped beach umbrella at the bottom of the canvas-covered gangway, which was anchored by several sandbags against the effects of the storm. He was dispensing brollies for the short walk across the tarmac to the terminal, expertly snapping the brolly open, timing it so that not a drop of the driving rain touched an emerging first-class passenger.

I accepted mine as I glanced back to see that no such assistance was afforded those who travelled economy, neither a covered gangway nor free brollies. It was my first lesson in Asia – not all are born equal. I was to learn that the primary means of judging your social status was money, and there was no secondary means. For instance, you might be well-born but poor, or highly educated and broke, and you would be regarded as a nobody. The genteel poor were not an accepted category in Asia.

Everything in Chinese society is dictated by visible wealth; face dominates everything. It is the primary cause of suicide and the reason for every ostentatious and vulgar display. In effect, the first-class passengers gained face by being issued umbrellas and those in economy were accordingly deprived of it by entering the terminal soaked to the skin.

God help the neophyte I undoubtedly was at the time. When I think about it now, the Chinese dragon must have been salivating – no, positively slavering – at the prospect of my arrival. I might have achieved the physical anonymity I had always craved, as I was soon to discover, but it was accompanied by a staggering naïvety.

I had been on Singaporean soil for less than a minute when the first incident occurred. Through the sheets of water pelting down I saw a Chinese mother coming out of economy clutching a swaddled baby to her breast with one hand and carrying a piled-up basket in the other. The poor woman was obviously struggling, but none of the other economy passengers attempted to help her. Heavy drops thudded into my nylon umbrella and bounced off as I rushed over, grabbed the basket from her and handed her my umbrella.

She gave me a look of shocked surprise that turned in an instant to fury. Gripping the infant even more tightly to her breast, she collapsed the brolly into a lethal weapon and began to whack me over the head, neck and shoulders, shouting what were undoubtedly curses.

In desperation, I dropped the basket onto the tarmac and brought my arms up to protect my head, stumbled backwards in an attempt to escape her furious onslaught and tripped over a tarmac cone, landing hard on my bum in a puddle. The rain pelted down on my unprotected skull like warm sharp needles as the woman retrieved the basket she must have assumed I was highjacking and stood over me to deliver another explosion of invective, while the rain beat down on her head and poured from her hair into the face of the bawling infant. Throwing the offending umbrella at my feet, she turned and marched off towards the airport terminal, stamping furiously through the silver puddles.

Most of the economy passengers, regardless of the downpour, paused to stare, and while no one attempted to help me to my feet, they must have been pissing themselves. Such an hilarious incident was a welcome reward at the end of a long, uncomfortable trip.

By the time the bewildered airport attendant, waiting for the last first-class passenger to disembark, arrived to help me to my feet, I had lost enough face to last for the remainder of my time in Asia, with some to spare, but I had also learned my first lesson: kind gestures to strangers were simply not on.

While we may all have been born equal in the sight of God, He clearly hadn't told the Chinese or they obviously didn't believe Him. The chivalrous gesture I'd attempted would have been unthinkable for a wealthy Chinese, and must have been seen as a deliberate provocation. But to everyone's amusement and perhaps satisfaction, I'd come off second-best, a nabob in first class getting his comeuppance from a woman in steerage.

It struck me then that my wish had been granted: nobody, including the woman with the baby, had seen me as a *gwai-lo* but as a fellow Chinese. Even so, my outside still belied my inside, and I realised with some consternation that nothing had in fact changed. Whether in Australia or Singapore, I was a European in a Chinese body – wholeness still eluded me.

I had left strict instructions that my mum's relatives were not to meet me at the airport. My contract stipulated a room at Raffles Hotel for the first two weeks of my stay so that I could get my bearings and find permanent accommodation. Pleading that I would be exhausted from the trip, I had planned to take a taxi to the hotel and contact the family two days later. Now, drenched to my underpants, I was grateful for this precaution. I wouldn't need to explain myself and no relatives had lost face by witnessing my umbrella incident.

Several wet people standing at the luggage carousel in the customs hall had a go at me in what I recognised as Cantonese, but it was spoken too fast for me to understand. Their meaning was unmistakeable, though, the words delivered in an angry, remonstrating tone accompanied by much finger-wagging in my face. They'd obviously witnessed my vicious, unprovoked attack on the poor woman and her baby. Anxious to beat a retreat, I retrieved my suitcases without bothering to look for a luggage trolley and carried them into customs, where the officers spied the two smart-looking leather Harrods suitcases being lugged about by a short, broad Chinese peasant who was soaked to the skin, and I was done like a dinner. Anonymity was already giving me the shits.

Three-quarters of an hour later, with every carefully wrapped and beribboned family gift from my mum opened and examined, I eventually staggered into the reception hall, where I was immediately importuned by two porters anxious to help me with my suitcases. I told them in no uncertain terms to bugger off, but they persisted, jabbering and pointing at my two cases. I was deeply into my second bout of serious loss of face. In Asia, you don't even carry your own toothbrush.

I'd read those Somerset Maugham books where, following the afternoon tropical shower, the rain-washed air carries the perfume of frangipani blossom. The rain had ceased all right, and the sky was certainly clear and clean, but the air carried some sort of cooking smell, although not one I'd ever noticed at any of our restaurants. It smelt something like rancid palm oil and garlic.

I headed down the hall for the taxi rank with the two persistent porters at my heels. I would later learn that their livelihood depended on their strong backs and whatever tips they could collect. The introduction of the personal luggage trolley had severely reduced their earnings, and I must have seemed one of the few hopeful prospects.

Right, kid, how does it feel to be an anonymous face in the crowd, alone, confused, soaked to the skin, cut and bruised about the face, carrying two heavy suitcases and conscious that you've fucked up big-time within two minutes of landing on foreign soil? Our hero had landed in the real world at last. I told myself firmly that it couldn't get any worse and I should snap out of my misery. After a shower, a change of clothes and a beer in the bar at my hotel, I'd be right as rain.

But I was wrong. Halfway to the taxi rank I was accosted by two police officers, who placed themselves on either side of me in case I made a run for it. One of them, a sergeant, said something in Cantonese, the gist of which I understood although I pretended not to. What I thought he was saying was that I was wanted for questioning. I placed the suitcases at my feet. They had barely touched the ground before the two porters made a grab for them. 'I don't speak Chinese,' I said firmly in English.

There followed a moment's pause and then the sergeant said, 'You come.' There was no polite 'please' or 'sir' attached to the demand. Sandwiched between them, I was led away, with the porters following with my suitcases and jabbering happily.

It was at that moment that I saw an extremely attractive young woman in a Mary Quant miniskirt and a Vidal Sassoon five-point haircut, holding up a slate that read 'Mr Simon Koo'. *There is a God in heaven after all*, I thought. I simply couldn't believe my luck. It was unlikely that there would be another Simon Koo at the airport at this precise moment.

'Hello. I think you're looking for me,' I called, stopping abruptly.

The two policemen glanced at the young woman, then the sergeant asked, 'This one you know?' pointing at her rudely.

'It is someone come to meet me from Raffles Hotel,' I replied, hoping this was correct.

Whoever she was, she seemed to sum up the situation immediately and ran over to where we stood. 'What is happening, Mr Koo?'

'I'm not sure I know, Miss. But am I glad to see you.'

She gave me the briefest of smiles, then launched into a rapid conversation in Cantonese with the two policemen, which seemed interminable. She held herself very erect, but her voice was emphatic, whereas the police sergeant kept pointing at my face, which I would later discover sported a cut and a darkening bruise on the left cheekbone. I had been too preoccupied with customs and the like to realise that one of my eyes was almost shut and a line of dried blood showed on the left side of my neck where I'd been whacked under the ear with the brolly. Little wonder customs had hauled me in.

'We must go with the policemen to the station. It is here in the airport,' she said at last, then added, 'I will talk to them.'

In a large office that passed for a police station, I was given a chair while the sergeant made a phone call. The young lady introduced herself as Mercy B. Lord. This didn't seem like the right moment to quiz her about her somewhat surprising name. 'Can you tell me, please, what happened, Mr Koo?' It was clear Miss Lord spoke and understood English very well. A police lieutenant arrived, possibly summoned by the sergeant's call, and I then began to tell the whole sad, pathetic story, feeling more stupid by the minute. The lieutenant appeared to understand and kept nodding his head, but every minute or so Mercy B. Lord would hold up her hand while she translated what I'd told her for the policemen. This continued for half an hour. An incident in the rain that had lasted no more than two or three minutes was taking an eternity to explain. Seated in my soaked trousers with my underpants pulling against my crotch, I noticed that my eye and cheekbone were beginning to throb. No notes were taken, and at the end of my account, the lieutenant said in almost perfect English, 'I am satisfied there has been a misunderstanding, sir. You are free to go.'

To my surprise, the two porters were waiting, standing beside my suitcases outside the door. 'Will you make sure they are generously tipped?' I asked Mercy B. Lord. 'I have no local currency. I'll settle with you later.'

She gave me a brilliant smile. 'They are much too heavy. You must *not* carry them, sir.' She smiled. 'Welcome to Singapore.' She extended her hand, head tilted, dark eyes amused. 'Now we will start again. I am Mercy B. Lord – how do you do? You are still wet and you have cuts and bruises I must attend to.'

'Thank you, Miss Lord, for everything. I don't know that I could have managed without you.' Later, thinking about it, I had held her hand far too long, my round face no doubt set in an expression of pathetic gratitude.

She shrugged. 'It is my job, Mr Koo. Come, I have a car waiting.'

After paying the two porters what I hoped was a generous gratuity, she waited for the chauffeur to load my bags into the boot before joining me in the back of the limo, a big black Buick. We pulled away from the scene of my multiple humiliations and Mercy B. Lord handed me her business card, holding it formally in both hands, forefingers beneath and thumbs on top. I accepted it using both hands as Phyllis Koo, mother and now Chinese mentor, had instructed me to do.

I'd never carried a card in Australia but my canny mother had given me a box printed in the correct manner, where, on the flip side, I saw my name for the first time printed in Chinese characters. I'd taken half a dozen out of the box and placed them in the outside top pocket of my suit. I now reached in to retrieve one and pulled out a small soggy square of card, which I handed to Mercy B. with the same due ceremony.

'At five o'clock it rains in Singapore,' she said, accepting the wet card.

I glanced at her own card and saw how her improbable name was represented in print.

Miss Mercy B. Lord

Snr. Residential Settlement,

City Guide & Co-ordination

The Beatrice Fong Agency

200 Orchard Road, 1st Fl. Kwan Fok Building.

Tel: Sing. 86 222

'Please call me Simon or, if you like, Cookie, which is what my friends in Australia call me,' I offered.

Mercy B. Lord put her hand up to her lips to stifle a giggle that still managed to sneak through her fingers. 'Cookie? That is not nice for a man, is it?'

I grinned. 'You mean if I use it here I'll lose face?'

She nodded her head vigorously. 'I think so.'

'Yes, so I've been told. It's Simon, then, although when you're angry with me you may call me Cookie.'

Her eyes widened. 'I will not be angry with you, Simon. It is not permitted.'

'Permission granted, Miss Lord. I'm surprised you're not angry already. I've made a fool of myself and lost more face in my first hour in Singapore than I can possibly regain if I spend a lifetime in Asia.'

She clucked her tongue dismissively. 'You will not see those people again. It will be okay. I will teach you the customs.'

'Do I have the pleasure of your company until later in the evening? I'd very much like it if you'd have dinner with me. But first I need a clean-up, a shower and a change of clothes.'

'No, first we go to the doctor, then we will go to the hotel, and if you are not so tired we can have dinner.'

'Will you make a booking?'

She laughed. 'There is no need, Simon. All the restaurants give Beatrice Fong squeeze. We will be welcome.'

I was surprised. While I didn't know much, I knew from my mother that the Chinese seldom show affection in public, much less hug each other. 'They hug her?' I said as a polite, roundabout way of correcting her grammar. 'They must really like her . . .'

Mercy B. Lord threw back her head and laughed. 'I think I will explain later when you are feeling much better, Simon.'

If face is everything to the Chinese, nothing happens without 'squeeze' – that is to say, without a bribe or a percentage of every deal struck going to someone else. Mercy B. Lord's employer, as the head of a foreign visitors agency, was in a position to bring in customers and, in return, received her percentage in the better Chinese restaurants.

If I'd made an unpropitious start in Singapore, the one piece of truly good joss was Mercy B. Lord. I should point out that she was always referred to by her full name, never as just plain Mercy or even Mercy B., although I never heard her insist on it. Now somewhat more in control and driving to the doctor or to Raffles Hotel, I said, 'Mercy B. Lord, you well and truly saved me from a fate worse than death, but I hadn't been told to expect you.'

She looked surprised. 'But I have a telegram from Mr Arthur Grinds in New York. We know him here. He has visited many, many times when he was looking for an advertising agency. He is,' she paused as if she wanted to be sure she got it right, 'Senior Vice President International, Asia and South America. I have it here, the telegram.' She retrieved it from her bag and handed it to me to read:

ATT BEATRICE FONG AGENCY STOP

SIMON KOO ARRIVING QANTAS FLIGHT 8 STOP

17TH SEPT STOP

PLEASE FACILITATE AS IF US CITIZEN STOP

ALL FACILITIES GRANTED STOP

ARTHUR GRINDS SNR VP INT A&SA STOP

NY OFFICE

I recalled that Arthur Grinds had been one of the signatories, along with the Wing brothers, on my contract. But there had been no mention of my being met at the airport. Charles Brickman may have had a low opinion of how the Americans operated in Asia but they'd just effectively saved my pseudo-Chinese backside in the very welcome and pretty form of Miss Mercy B. Lord.

'What does "all facilities granted" entail, Mercy B. Lord?' I asked mischievously.

Her quick glance told me that she understood but wasn't going to go there. 'I will be available for the next two weeks to familiarise you with Singapore and to find you suitable accommodation. That is, if you wish . . .'

'Yes, yes, of course, thank you. When shall we meet, at night? I will be expected in the agency during the day.'

'No, not at night,' she said quickly. 'It is only during the day. It is called familiarisation; I think you will need it.'

'I agree, but I'm not sure the Wing brothers will approve.'

'They have approved. It is the custom for American *gwai-lo* who come to work in Singapore. Now also you, Simon. We have the correct notification from New York. It is not easy if you do not know your way around. I will show you everything.'

I doubted that Mercy B. Lord's 'everything' was the same everything I had been told about in the pub back home when everyone knew I was coming here. It seemed that three or four guys' fathers each had a story about places such as the notorious Bugis Street with its transvestites, sleazy bars, nightclubs and brothels. Nevertheless, I was delighted to discover she would be my guide for my first fortnight in Singapore, though I couldn't help wondering what the Wing brothers would think privately about the American initiative. But then again, they weren't paying for it or me.

There isn't a lot more to say about my first late afternoon and evening. Mercy B. Lord insisted on my seeing a doctor, who pronounced each wound 'superficial', dabbed a little iodine on my neck and cheek and told me to expect a very black eye for the next few days. My room at Raffles was small and, although not airconditioned, was perfectly adequate. I showered and changed while Mercy B. Lord waited downstairs, and then I joined her for a cold beer in the famous Long Bar while she had a martini. Then she took me to a Chinese restaurant where we had dinner. I'd declared myself, after my flow of excess adrenalin at the airport, to be positively starving and she'd insisted on a small banquet with all the trimmings. Faced with a different dish seemingly every few minutes, I tried to imagine that first banquet for Ah Koo in Sydney in the late nineteenth century, although things had changed. For example, a beautiful woman was sharing this one with me, while the closest Little Sparrow got to being present at a banquet was to earn an exceedingly sore bum while crouched behind the screen interpreting her dream for the Dragon Master. Now, eighty years later, I wondered to myself how much had *really* changed – they were country bumpkins in a strange city, and I had already demonstrated that I was no more sophisticated here in an equally strange Singapore.

My learning curve would need to be a bloody steep one. They'd managed theirs well enough to create a dynasty. I wondered just what lay ahead for me. Would I make a cock-up of things or be a success? But at least for the moment I had the pretty and charming Mercy B. Lord to smooth my path. I told myself things couldn't be all bad over the next two weeks.

Tired from the long flight and with several more beers in me than I customarily consumed, I was forward enough to ask Mercy B. Lord about her, as I put it, 'simply wonderful name'. When she hesitated I added, 'If you don't tell me, it's going to drive me crazy all night and I won't get any sleep. It will be your fault if I arrive at Samuel Oswald Wing a broken and battered man.' I pointed to my eye, now virtually closed. 'I'm already looking pretty crook.'

'Crook? I hope you are not a crook, Simon,' she exclaimed.

'It's an Australian word; it means feeling poorly, sick, in bad shape, hung-over, unwell.'

Mercy B. Lord giggled. 'You have a funny English language, Simon. Like Americans, you say things that mean other things. How will I learn this?'

'Don't worry, I'll teach you Australian, but first you have to explain your name.'

'It was given to me by Sister Charity at the St Thomas Aquinas Catholic Mission Orphanage. You see I am an orphan.'

Mercy B. Lord then went on to tell me how, as a day-old baby, she had been left on the doorstep of the orphanage. Sister Charity, the oldest Irish nun, had discovered her, almost tripping over the tiny bundle on the kitchen doorstep. 'Mercy be, Lord!' she'd exclaimed. 'What have You sent us?' It was as easy as that. She had always been known, not as Mercy, but as Mercy B. Lord, there being, predictably enough, an orphan named Mercy already. She'd never been given any other identity, such as a Chinese name. But later in life when she'd sought to have it translated, it came out as Child of Guanshiyin – the one who hears the cries of the world.

'I was born in March 1946 and was lucky my mother took me to the nuns, who had just returned to the orphanage after the Japanese occupation.' She paused. 'There were a lot of Chinese murdered by the Japanese, so if I was Chinese pure-blood, she would have kept me. To be a Chinese child then, so soon after the war, was good, even a girl child with an unmarried mother, so the nuns knew I was a half-caste.'

'But you don't seem to have any pronounced European features; your dad's genes must have been swamped,' I laughed. 'I should know. My family are all half-castes; I just happen to be a throwback, a return of the irrepressible Chinese genes. I have cousins and an uncle with fair skin and blue eyes. That's okay in Australia but not growing up amongst the Chinese, I guess.'

Mercy B. Lord looked down at her plate. 'Not European, Simon – Japanese. My mother would have been raped by a Japanese soldier. It was common and is the only reason she would have given me up. The people in her *kampong* would have known this and killed me at birth. Bad rice.'

'But how would you know that?'

'Almost all the children in the orphanage were one of two things. If they were above the age of four, then they were orphans, whose parents had been killed by the Japanese. If they were babies, then their mothers had been raped by Japanese soldiers. My mother, the nuns explained, wanted to confess her shame, to explain why she would give up her baby and leave me at the orphanage, so she swaddled me in a Japanese soldier's shirt. The nuns kept the shirt and I have it now; one of the sleeves has been cut off.'

I was silent for a few moments then said quietly, 'That's tough.'

'No, nobody could really tell once I got a little older, and people have forgotten.' She paused before continuing. 'But sometimes, I don't know why, I just feel different.'

'Yeah, I know what you mean, only with me the outside contradicts the inside.'

'I know it's ridiculous, but walking down the street I sometimes think people look at me in a different way, that somehow they realise.'

'I know the feeling well. But in your case you are misinterpreting their looks. What they are staring at is – as we would say in Australia – a grouse-looking sheila with the latest in Mary Quant clothes and a Vidal Sassoon five-point hairstyle.'

She looked briefly taken aback. 'Simon, I don't understand. A grouse is a bird, is it not, but who is Sheila?'

'No, "grouse" means really good, terrific – in your case extremely beautiful – and "sheila" is Australian for a girl or woman.'

Mercy B. Lord laughed. 'That is a very strange language, Simon.'

The following day, I put on the second of my three suits, a light tropical-weight khaki gabardine. I had two like this and a lightweight wool, 'for more formal occasions when you meet the prime minister', my mother, who'd had them tailor-made, had said with a laugh. So, suited, brushed and polished and looking the part of a hot new creative director in a light blue Brooks Brothers shirt with a button-down collar, one of three I'd ordered through Jonas from America, and the tie I had never returned to my dad, I entered the premises of Samuel Oswald Wing. I had taken the precaution of phoning at five minutes past nine to make an appointment. I felt sure they knew of my arrival but I didn't want to lob in unexpectedly.

'My name is Simon Koo. May I speak with Mr Wing, please?' I asked when the switch answered.

'Which Mr Wing do you want?' a pleasant voice answered.

'Mr Sidney Wing?'

'One moment, I'll put you through to his secretary.'

Sidney Wing's secretary offered only her first name. 'Sally, hello?'

'Hello, Sally, this is Simon Koo.'

'Yes, Mr Koo, what can we do for you?' It was friendly enough, but not the reaction I'd expected.

'Simon Koo from Australia . . . I think I'm expected. I'm the new creative director.'

There was a moment's awkward silence. 'Creative director? I do not understand, sir.'

'From Australia. I was with Samuel Oswald Brickman. New York has sent me.' I tried to sound cheery. 'I am to be your new creative director.'

'Oh, I see.' More silence, then, 'New creative director?' It was obviously an unfamiliar term that she was struggling to understand.

Sidney Wing was one of the signatories on my contract and I was dumbfounded that his secretary didn't even know that the biggest change about to happen to the agency was to its creative component. This, I was to learn, was very Chinese, where if a personal secretary isn't a family member, she doesn't always know what's going on, especially if something is confidential, although it was hard to think of my appointment as confidential. Perhaps it just wasn't considered sufficiently important for her to know about. It wasn't a good beginning, but then perhaps I was being paranoid as usual.

'Do you have a department that produces the newspaper advertisements, with people who draw the pictures?' I'd been told that creative was pretty primitive, and it would be my job to change all that, so I shouldn't have been surprised. I guess the word 'creative' was a new one for Sally. But then she suddenly came alive.

'Oh, yes, Mr Koo, you got the wrong Mister Wing, you want Mr Ronnie Wing. When you come he will be your boss. I will put you back to switch and they will put you through.'

I felt a sudden frisson of anger. It's weird how your mind can suddenly do an about-turn. *I've got news for you, lady. Mr Ronnie Wing will not be running creative. What's more, it will be an honest operation, no more corruption. What was it Mercy B. Lord called it? 'Squeeze.' There will be no more squeeze.*

As I waited for the phone to be answered, I recalled dinner the previous night when Mercy B. Lord had explained 'squeeze' to me: the all-pervading system of bribery, inducements, cuts and percentages that was so endemic in Asia it wasn't even questioned. 'Simon, nothing among the Chinese or in Chinese business is done without squeeze; advertising could not be the exception.' (Charles Brickman had also warned me never to accept things at face value.) She'd leaned forward across the restaurant table for emphasis. 'There are no exceptions!' She sat back in her chair and added, 'It's not a part of the system. It *is* the system.'

'Ah, things may be changing,' I replied confidently. 'Asia is being invaded by the West.'

'What, capitalism?'

'Well, business; big business, anyway.'

Mercy B. Lord laughed. 'The Chinese have been capitalists for thousands of years, Simon. The action all happens under the table; above the table everyone nods and agrees and is very polite.'

I'd done my mental arithmetic: if she was born in 1946, then she was twenty, and she worked as a guide for a business agency, which was hardly at the cutting edge of business action. 'How do you know all this?' I asked. I thought of my sisters, all within a couple of years of her age. Although they were all bright, they were still largely preoccupied with how short a miniskirt could be without being indecent, so as to pass the Phyllis Koo test. This also went for the bunnies in the agency, where I suspected that the subject of nail polish could take up half the lunch hour. The blokes weren't any better. If I hadn't majored in economics, I'd probably have been the same.

Mercy B. Lord gave me a straight look. 'To the Chinese, squeeze is like breathing; you don't think about it, you just do it to stay alive. I'm a Catholic,' she said quietly. 'I have been taught that bribery and corruption are both sins.' She spread her hands, her nails long and perfectly manicured. 'But I also know that it is not a sin in the eyes of a different god, and the Chinese have a god for everything, as you would know.'

'*Ch'ao Kung-ming*, the god of wealth. My mum told us as kids that he rode a black tiger and used pearls as hand grenades.'

Mercy B. Lord laughed. 'Yes, we know him, but the wealth god around here is *Ts'ai Shen Yeh*. His shrine is to be found in nearly every home. I was forgetting you're Chinese.'

It must have been the first time ever that my Chinese face had been overlooked in favour of my European mind. 'Be careful, remember what happened at the airport. I told you it's only skin-deep. Inside I'm a dumb *gwai-lo*. Okay, this dinner is on me. When I pay the bill, does Miss Beatrice Fong get squeeze?'

Mercy B. Lord thought for a moment. 'We have two problems here, Mr Koo. You have invited me to dinner. If I offer to pay, then you will lose face. This must never happen. Please remember that.'

'But it's out of the question – of course I'll pay.'

Mercy B. Lord brought her fingers to her lips, but again the giggle managed to slip through. 'That is the second problem. You see, this banquet *is* squeeze.'

The phone had rung for some time in what I hoped was the production department. Then, at last, a male voice answered. 'Hello?'

'Mr Wing . . . Ronnie Wing?'

'I fetch him. Who you, sir? I tell him.'

'Simon Koo from Australia.'

'You call from Australia?'

'No, no, I'm at Raffles Hotel, here in Singapore.' I was getting decidedly irritable, but told myself it was a reasonable mistake – bad phrasing on my part.

'Yes, I know this hotel, sir. But I am not going there, not once. Only I am going past when I am going Beach Road. I will tell him, sir. You wait, please.'

What seemed like another interminable wait followed, in the middle of which came a knock on my hotel-room door. 'I'm on the phone. Please come in,' I called. It was the hotel *dhobi*, or laundry man. Overnight, my suit had been cleaned and pressed, my shirt starched, my socks and underpants washed, and each delivered on a separate hanger covered in clear plastic. I pointed to the wardrobe, reached for my wallet and extracted an overly generous tip, but was forced to hold it out using only one hand. He thanked me with a large smile and a nod, accepting it with both hands then backing away towards the door.

'Hello, Ronnie Wing here. Welcome to Singapore, Simon. I'm greatly looking forward to meeting you. When can we press the flesh?'

I was to learn that Ronnie Wing was in love with the advertising business, the 'run it up the flagpole and see if it salutes' Hollywood clichéd version. He'd bought the whole package. He talked, praised and encouraged using the jargon, invented his own metaphors and probably knew more about the sleazy side of Singapore nightlife than anyone else on the island. He walked the walk and talked the talk as if born to meet, greet and treat. He was the original glad-hander, joker, and brothel or bargirl negotiator. He never forgot a name and laughed uproariously at anyone's corny jokes. He wanted more than anything in the world to be a creative hotshot, and collected all the art-director annuals and 'how to make effective advertising' books, and was the first in the office every month to read *Advertising Age*, the magazine that reported on the American ad scene. Ronnie read it from cover to cover and knew more current New York, Chicago and West Coast gossip than its editor. He seemed to believe that the big American names in advertising, such as David Ogilvy and Bill Bernbach, were the new free-enterprise celestial gods. Ronnie was a complete walking, talking and cavorting parody of a sixties American ad man. He even wore blue seersucker suits for official occasions when a jacket might be required. In Singapore he was accepted as a member of the expat advertising group that came mostly from Jackson Wain, an Australian-owned ad agency, and Cathay Advertising, a Hong Kong outfit with agencies throughout the region and owned by a woman named Elma Kelly, where they would gossip, drink and play liar dice. Unfortunately, Ronnie didn't have a creative bone in his body and I was to be stuck with him.

I recall almost every word of that first telephone call to Samuel Oswald Wing, the day after I arrived in Singapore. I was bright and bushy-tailed in my new khaki gabardine suit, blue shirt and shiny shoes, and ready to start my brilliant new career. Ronnie was the first Wing I spoke to and the first I was to meet face to face, but 'spoke to' is not really accurate, because before I had time to say anything, he was off again. 'Congratulations, you are the star on the top of the Christmas tree, Simon.'

'Oh,' I said, surprised. 'Star billing even before I start?'

'Absolutely! Your two ads in the New York *Art Directors Annual* are 100 per cent shrink-proof, double-stitched ant's pants. Yes, sir! Singapore gets the show pony that's hot to trot, the best of the lot!'

'Mr Wing,' I laughed, 'we have yet to meet. I'm almost as broad as I am tall and if I was a pony I'd have trouble raising a trot – I have a black eye and a bruised cheekbone – but I was hoping I might come into the agency. You know, meet you all, see my office, familiarise myself with the location, all the usual stuff . . .'

'No, no, no, I *must* come to you first, Simon! It is the Chinese way. Lunch at the Town Club, a hotel limo will take you. I will call them now. Does twelve o'clock suit? We will chew the creative fat.'

I confess I winced. The idea of this maker of bad metaphors holding me captive in his club for the afternoon didn't appeal one bit. I hesitated, then asked, 'Would it be appropriate to invite Miss Mercy B. Lord?'

'Jesus Christ, *no!*' Ronnie Wing was obviously taken completely by surprise, then quickly recovering, he said, 'No women allowed, old chap, it is the Chinese way.'

'Mr Wing, how will I recognise you?' I was to learn that 'the Chinese way' was anything Ronnie wanted it to be at the time; it was his major ethnic weapon.

'Just tell the doorman you're Ronnie Wing's guest. I will have signed you in.' There was a moment's pause. 'Oh, and, Simon, it's Ronnie. We are going to be close creative buddies, collaborators, fellow conspirators, in fact – two peas in a very exciting creative pod.' He laughed. 'The cart horse and the show pony. I'll pull and you can run ahead, a two-horse show, eh?'

CHAPTER FOUR

———

THE TAXI DROPPED ME off at the Town Club in Battery Road at the mouth of the Singapore River. It was not without some trepidation that I entered the bar just a minute or so before noon on my first full day in Singapore. If the phone call was any indication, I was about to meet a Chinese bloke who appeared to have introduced ad-speak into Asia, and I wasn't sure I was quite up to the task of participating in a luncheon conversation littered with clichés. My busted cheek, bunged-up eye and the large patch of white surgical plaster just under my ear did nothing for my confidence either. *Pull yourself together, Simon*, I thought. *Pretend you're down at the pub listening to Ross Quinlivan delivering his one-liners: 'The only thing less substantial than the smoke in this morning's Wills meeting was the client, who, as usual, left all the hard decisions up in the air.'* Hopefully Ronnie Wing would talk about what needed to be done to build a creative department. That is, if he realised the need for one in the first place.

Lunch obviously began early in the tropics. The bar was already one-deep and all the stools seemed to be occupied. All were expats, I noted with some surprise. All wore lightweight tropical suits, white shirts and conservative, nondescript ties. Most were distinguished by being overweight, from pot-bellied to grossly fat. I'd imagined that, with the federation of Malaysia, independence would have put an end to colonialism, but this mob looked every inch the part, and I was soon to learn that the narrow-minded, bigoted archetype was still very much alive and well in Singaporean society.

Then I saw that one stool was vacant at the far end of the bar next to a tall, thin Chinese wearing a blue striped seersucker suit and a pink shirt with a brightly coloured psychedelic tie, similar to one I owned. Perhaps it was not as 'look-at-me' as the Mickey-Mouse-with-banjo tie, nonetheless it was out there attempting to make some sort of statement. Resting precariously on the padded leather stool was a martini, the green olive clear to see in the elegant glass. From his voice over the phone, I'd expected a short chubby guy, not a beanpole. Ronnie Wing was really very tall for a Chinese – six foot and then some – his black hair worn long in a very un-Chinese haircut that was especially noticeable among the short-back-and-siders lining the bar.

Truly tall Chinese are not that common in Australia, and I realised that I'd subconsciously hoped for a shortarse like myself. Ronnie Wing was hunched over the bar, both hands loosely encircling his own martini glass, staring into space or, rather, at the spirits bottles against the mirrored wall behind the bar.

Several of the men glanced over at me as I entered and I couldn't say their looks were overly welcoming or even neutral, as one might expect on entering a bar, even at a private club. I thought my somewhat battered face might be the reason, although I didn't exactly look prepossessing at the best of times.

Walking up to the Chinese guy, I said, 'Ronnie? Ronnie Wing?'

He jumped at the sound of his name, as if he'd been deep in thought. 'Jesus, you're Chinese,' he said, turning to face me.

'Yeah, fourth-generation throwback,' I laughed.

'You should have told me,' he said, recovering. 'We could have gone somewhere else.'

'Why?' I said, looking around. 'This seems okay.'

'As a general rule, no Asians are allowed.'

'Well, that's okay. I'm Australian, but you're Chinese, I take it?'

'Well, yes, Straits-Chinese, not entirely the same thing.'

'The same as my mother. Nevertheless, Asian . . .'

'Of course, but only half a dozen or so families – the males, of course – are members here: Long Me Saw, one of the movie magnate brothers; the Sultan of Brunei; a couple of billionaires whose families, like ours, go back two or three generations. Some were heroes, or served the British somewhere along the line, and were rewarded with honorary membership in perpetuity.'

I was hard put to see his point and realised I shouldn't pursue the subject, but I couldn't resist one last question. 'Ronnie, how is Straits-Chinese different? As I said, my mum is Straits-Chinese like you, but she's obsessed with the Chinese aspect.'

'You mean how do Straits-Chinese differ in culture from the Chinese somewhere else? Like, say, Hong Kong?'

'Yeah, I guess.'

'Well, it's quite different here in Singapore, where mixed marriages with the Javanese and Malays are not unusual. I look very Chinese because my father, like his father before him, went back to China to find his wife. But whether we're racially mixed – that is, Peranakan – or not, we still think of ourselves as Chinese unless we marry Caucasians; then our offspring are Eurasian.'

'But your culture, do you follow traditional Chinese customs?' It seemed I couldn't stop myself asking dumb questions. My nerves were getting the better of me.

Ronnie Wing nodded politely, no doubt wondering when this crap would end. 'Yes, a lot of stuff comes from the old culture – attitudes, religion, beliefs, festivals, superstitions – these things die hard for the Chinese. It's our way to hang on through thick and thin. Even though we are ethnically integrated here in Singapore, we still hark back to China. It's an old culture and a strong one. Our ethnic group makes up 75 per cent of Singapore's population.'

I nodded my head briefly towards the men at the bar. 'And this happy little gin-and-tonic lot think of themselves as the supremos.'

My host laughed. 'Nothing quite like the English middle class abroad – a place in the sun for shady people.'

'Well, speaking in plain English, if it's awkward with me in here, why don't we go elsewhere?'

Ronnie Wing's expression changed. 'No, fuck them. We're staying.'

That one familiar well-worn expletive broke the ice. I laughed. 'Mate, good on ya, but it's not going to upset me in the least if we leave.'

Ronnie Wing shook his head then suddenly jumped up. 'God, what am I doing? Keeping you standing, prattling on like this.' He indicated the vacant bar stool. 'Here, sit. I hope you don't mind, I got you a martini, very dry, Bombay gin.'

I laughed, extended my hand, and he took it. 'Thank you for inviting me,' I said. Unlike most Chinese, who barely touch your hand, he had a good firm grip. Okay so far. I placed the glass on the bar and seated myself beside him.

'Welcome to Singapore, Simon.' He extended his glass. 'And chin chin.' He spoke with just a hint of an American accent.

'Thanks, Ronnie. Nice to be here.' We clinked. 'I better come clean. I've never tasted a martini. What makes it dry as opposed to wet?'

'Martini and Rossi – the dry vermouth – and I personally believe the gin you choose dictates how dry a martini is.' He chuckled. 'Never heard of a wet martini. Only degrees of dry.'

I nodded and took a cautious sniff. 'If this is what the juniper berry smells like, I'm not sure, but there's always a first time, I guess.'

'Okay, that's enough of the small talk. What the fuck happened to your face?'

I was beginning to like this guy. 'Do you mean the face I was born with or the face I have now after being beaten up by a savage Chinese female assailant?'

He indicated my wounds and said, 'Are you telling me that happened here . . . in Singapore?'

I nodded.

'You're kidding, aren't you? You only got in last night! What, did you go straight to Bugis Street?'

I kept my expression serious and shook my head. 'Nah, it happened within a minute of landing in the middle of a tropical rainstorm, when I was viciously attacked by a furious, baby-wielding woman with an umbrella who knocked me down. The police were involved. I was finally rescued by Miss Mercy B. Lord, who cleared things with the cops, took me to the doctor and then out to dinner.' I could contain myself no longer and started to laugh. 'Ronnie, you might as well know up front what a drongo I am.'

'Drongo?'

'Fool. Actually, the term comes from the word for a dud racehorse, but drongos are really birds. Miss Mercy B. Lord has promised to teach me the customs so I can stay out of trouble.'

'I hope you prove to be a fast learner, Simon,' Ronnie Wing said laconically.

'I'll drink to that.' I picked up the martini and took a fairly generous slug. My mouth exploded and I sprayed gin and vermouth onto the tiled floor at my feet. 'Jeezus!' I said, wiping my mouth. The men at the bar turned as one to observe me. I had 'done an airport' within a couple of minutes of arriving, but this time I was not the only one who lost face.

'I see what Mercy B. Lord means,' Ronnie said nonchalantly. He wasn't buckling to the fuckwits who'd turned to stare. 'Your first martini always tastes like an old crone's piss.' This got a laugh from most of the expat eavesdroppers and I could see Ronnie had recovered effortlessly from an awkward situation. The men at the bar resumed their conversations and Ronnie said quietly, 'Would you like a Carlsberg instead?'

'Yes, please, any beer will do.' I was to learn that Ronnie only talked brand names. The beer was set before me as, almost simultaneously, a servant in a starched white uniform with large, highly polished brass buttons arrived with a mop and bucket.

I reached for my wallet to give him a tip but Ronnie gripped my arm.

'My club, old chap. You can't use your money here, you'll get me into trouble.'

'But I —'

'Not the Chinese way,' he said, then added with a grin, 'I'll lose face.'

'You mean, again,' I said. Over the beer I told him the details of my humiliation and loss of face at the airport. 'So if it hadn't been for Miss Mercy B. Lord,' I concluded, 'I would probably have had to use my one telephone call to get you to bail me out after a cold, wet night in a police cell.'

'She's the best in the business,' Ronnie said, 'and Beatrice Fong is one of the few people Sidney doesn't resent paying for her services.'

'Oh, I thought the Americans were picking up the tab.'

'They are, but Sidney uses Beatrice in various ways.' Ronnie didn't choose to elaborate. 'We want you to spend the next two weeks with Mercy B. Lord getting your bearings. It will give us time to build your office,' he added.

'What? I'm not to come in for two weeks?' I asked, surprised.

He shrugged. 'No point, no office. I don't have one, so you can't share mine. Besides, you'll be flat-out finding a place to live and learning your way around.' He paused, sipping at his second martini. 'Oh, and, Simon, take my advice, she's a real doll – but then you know that already – just don't try to sleep with her.' He paused momentarily. 'It doesn't make Aunt Beatrice happy when you shit on her office doorstep. And Beatrice Fong's displeasure is not to be taken lightly.'

'Of course,' I exclaimed. 'I wouldn't dream —'

'Oh, yes you would,' he assured me. 'Comfort yourself that this town is crawling with girls, most of them excellent, obliging and cheap. Anything you could possibly want is yours for the asking, except Miss Mercy B. Lord.'

'As I said, no problem. I understand the doorstep rule, but is that because she's already taken?'

'No, she's unattached,' he said, not explaining further. Then, lifting his martini, he downed it in a single gulp, reached over and bottomed what was left of mine. 'Come, finish your Carlsberg and let's have a bite to eat, and then we'll go out to play and possibly get gloriously drunk.'

I chug-a-lugged my beer and we set off for the club dining room. 'The chow's not bad – the curry's excellent,' he informed me on the way. We were seated, with a fair bit of fuss from the maître d', at a table covered in heavily starched damask with table napkins of the same persuasion and monogrammed cutlery. Chairman Meow would have approved. Ronnie ordered a brand of gewürztraminer, and while he was quite specific about it, I don't remember the particular label. 'Ronnie, not for me, mate.' I held up my hand. Table wine, as opposed to plonk – cheap sherry and port – was just beginning to become popular in Australia. But, to use an advertising term, I was not among the early adopters, those few in any population who start a trend, although some blokes testified that Porphyry Pearl was a guaranteed leg-opener. Some years later I would recall Ronnie's choice as indicative of the Chinese preference for sweet wines, but at the time I knew nothing about the subject.

'No wine?' Ronnie said. 'I always thought you Aussies drank anything containing alcohol.'

I grinned a little sheepishly. 'I might as well come clean on this as well. I'm not big on the grog, Ronnie, not much of a drinker. A few beers when it's hot, that's about it, with the emphasis on a few, two or three max.'

Ronnie Wing gave me a serious look. 'Simon, I guess this is a personal question but I need to ask it. You see, what we do this afternoon and tonight will be fairly typical of the Singaporean entertainment given to an important visitor.' He hesitated as the wine waiter brought the wine and poured a taster into his glass, then sipped and nodded approval. 'Not for my guest, Napoleon,' he instructed in the local patois I was to learn was called Singlish, and was a pidgin that combined English, Malay, Chinese and Tamil as well as words borrowed from everywhere else. Napoleon filled Ronnie's glass to the halfway point and took the bottle away, no doubt to keep it chilled elsewhere. 'Now, where was I? Oh yes.

Simon, I guess we're going to be partners in crime, so I need to ask you a question. Are you a modest drinker because you're a bad drunk?'

It was a pretty direct question and perhaps I should have taken exception; I probably would have done back home. 'You mean lose the plot, fight, throw up on the carpet, abuse birds . . . ?'

Ronnie grinned. 'You Aussies have a certain turn of phrase that seldom leaves any doubt as to your meaning, but abuse birds? I don't understand . . .'

'Give the lady you're with a hard time,' I explained.

He laughed. 'Oh, I see. For a moment there my imagination conjured up all sort of possibilities. But only a large goose would have been big enough for the activity that sprang to mind.'

We both laughed. 'No, as a matter of fact I'm a pretty easygoing drunk. I have a dad who gives his elbow a fair workout,' I said by way of explaining without explaining. In fact, on the few occasions I had been stonkered, after a rugby grand-final win or when the agency had pitched and won a big account over several other ad agencies, I'd always been the last man standing among my legless mates. It may have had something to do with my tree-stump physique. I was fairly firmly planted.

A waiter wheeled up a trolley that contained at least a dozen covered silver dishes of curries and condiments. 'Know your curries, Simon?'

'Alas, my ignorance knows no bounds,' I admitted. 'But I think I can take it fairly hot.' Despite my apparent candour, we were still feeling each other out. So far, I was someone who couldn't be trusted to act without losing face in public, allowed myself to be beaten up by the weaker sex, was a near wowser, had disgraced myself in front of the expat, all-white, all-male members of his racist club, was potentially a sexual predator on an important doorstep and, finally, knew nothing, or very little, about the world's second-most popular cuisine. If we were, say, five rounds into a boxing match, then they'd all have gone overwhelmingly to Ronnie Wing. His jabs, straight lefts and right crosses had all landed. The next punch was going to be obvious and I was ready for it; talk of food follows talk of drink as sunset eventually follows sunrise. Ronnie

Wing was, perhaps not intentionally, being just a tad condescending. I was the redneck Australian and he the Singaporean sophisticate.

'So you're not really a gourmet, Simon?' he asked right on cue, indicating a number of dishes to the waiter.

'By no means. The only cuisine I know a bit about is Chinese.'

'Your mother is a good Chinese cook?'

'Not particularly.' I tried to imagine Chairman Meow in a kitchen but failed. 'Most Australians eat Chinese once a month or so. We've had local Chinese restaurants since the gold rush in the nineteenth century.' I realised that I could have delivered an unexpected knockout blow right there and then by telling him about the almost ninety-strong Little Sparrow Chinese restaurants.

'Chinese? But as you know, I'm sure, there are many more than one style of Chinese food. I believe most of the gold-rush Chinese were Cantonese, and men – not the greatest of cooks. Besides, I understand very few were allowed to stay unless they'd married a local white woman. The White Australia Policy . . .'

'Yeah, very regrettable.' Ronnie was still quietly putting me in my place. Another left jab followed by a right uppercut. I suspected that, despite his sophistication, Ronnie Wing measured people in the traditional Chinese way – by the extent of their wealth. Had I chosen to do so, I could have lifted myself from being the fool on the airport tarmac to the son of a wealthy family, got myself renewed face and respect simply by telling him of the Little Sparrow restaurants. But I wasn't going to kowtow to a bloke who knew the price of everything and the value of nothing and judged everything by its brand name, nor was I going to ride on my family's coat-tails any longer. I reckoned what respect I might gain in Singapore had to be of my own making.

Ronnie, having gained the upper hand, now said, 'Well, what do you think? Shall we kick on after lunch, Simon? With your eye and cheekbone you can't have had a lot of rest after the long flight from Sydney. Would you rather . . . ?' He left the afternoon choice of activity hanging in the air.

I realised he was testing me and that if I wished to save face, I would be obliged to go along with whatever he had in mind. The only way I could think to do this was to match him, drink for drink and deed for deed, and hope that I'd be the last man standing. Stupid, I know; little boy stuff, but it was the traditional Australian male way to restore what, to my mind, needed to be a relationship of mutual respect and, if I could pull it off, it just might work with the Chinese. In boxing parlance I could choose to retire hurt and live to fight another day, or go another few rounds. But if I couldn't stay the distance, I realised, Ronnie would have the knockout blow he was hoping for.

My dad seldom if ever lost the plot when he was pissed and I'd never seen him falling-down drunk. With luck I'd inherited this characteristic. Chairman Meow would often say, 'Your father is fooling nobody but himself when he pretends to be sober!' But I knew for a fact that in big-business circles he was admired for his equanimity. As Kipling said, 'If you can keep your head when all about you are losing theirs . . .' Though I doubt that Rudyard, who may well have had a very active elbow himself, had such meaning in mind when he penned 'If —', the greatest coming-of-age poem ever written.

'What the hell, let's go. This is a chance to get to know each other. C'mon, let's paint the town red, eh? By the way, it's bloody good of you to do this.'

'One rule, Simon – you don't pay.'

'Wait on, mate. I'd like to pay my way. I'd feel better.'

Ronnie laughed. 'What happened last night with Mercy B. Lord? Did you pay?'

'No, I offered, but I was told it was . . .' I hesitated, 'something called "squeeze".'

'You got it in one, son. We've had dozens of Yanks visiting over the last year and they're all on big expense accounts, which they're keen to use, so we're about to take advantage of some of the accumulated squeeze.'

'What, with restaurants?' I asked, wondering how many meals you could eat in one afternoon and evening.

'Everything: bars, brothels, places of interest – not all of them sex destinations – and, yes, restaurants. They all owe us a large amount of goodwill or, if you like, squeeze. Americans are generous, uncomplicated people, and they like to spend.'

'You mean all those count for squeeze purposes?' I fear my voice was rather sharp.

Ronnie Wing decided to ignore my tone. 'See, you're already learning to tap-dance to the Singapore beat, Brother Simon,' he drawled, exaggerating his vowels to accentuate his American accent.

'And then we can expect repayment in kind for their patronage?'

'In this instance, yes, repayment of one kind or another. Squeeze isn't bribery. It's a mutually understood but unspoken part of Chinese business. The seeming generosity of the Chinese is really a short or long-term investment.'

'And I'm expected to participate?'

Ronnie shrugged, his mouth puckered. 'Entertainment is an essential part of business; you do it in the West, we do it here.'

'So with the overseas visitors, I'll be taking them not just to bars but also to brothels? Mate, I'm not sure that doesn't make me a pimp.'

'Pimp?' He could no longer ignore what I was saying and was momentarily silent, head to one side, eyes narrowed, his expression quizzical. When he spoke I could see he was serious, although perhaps also trying to keep things light. 'You look more Chinese than me, Simon, but you really *are* a Caucasian on the inside. Pimp?' he repeated. 'That's a thought that could never occur to a Chinese man. Let me explain. Our attitude to women is more than two thousand years old. Females are born inferior to males – it's a natural law in Chinese society. The only occasional exception is a very rich widow or spinster – and I mean *very* rich.'

'Nobody told my mother she was inferior,' I said, trying for a lighter tone as I realised that perhaps I'd gone too far with the pimp thing. But Ronnie wasn't finished yet.

'There are four – no, five categories of women, excluding royalty. Excluding ancestors, who are worshipped, the first category is mother and grandmother. The second is wife and daughter, although in a peasant society a daughter is bitter rice and only tolerated as a glorified servant. The third, in a rich man's house, is the concubine, then servant or peasant and, finally, whore. The West sees it differently, of course. They are taught that paid sex is sinful, dirty, clandestine, that the urges all men feel must be curbed by going for a long run, taking a cold shower, thinking pure thoughts or, as a last resort —'

'Masturbating?' I suggested, still trying to keep it light.

Despite himself, Ronnie laughed. 'No, I was going to say praying for guidance. A Texan executive from Mobil Oil told me that, during his first "man-to-man" with his father at thirteen, he was advised to pray if he had any uncontrollable urges. He was six foot four inches, two hundred and thirty pounds, an ex-college football quarterback and he was still obeying his daddy.'

'So when you showed him Singapore at night, I guess all his prayers were answered,' I laughed.

'Something like that. It took the East to liberate him, though he'll probably go home to his wife and teenage son and tell the kid the same crap, or the modern equivalent. Probably suggest the boy has a good workout with weights in the gym. Unfortunately nothing is going to help. Men are men, and as long as they have a rampant cock, white guys will be secretly on the lookout for an Alice to take them into Wonderland. To the Chinese man, it's all just bullshit. Sex is there for the taking, as long as we do it with a woman who is from a subservient class.'

'A bar girl or a pro?'

'We don't see it as anything strange. The first sexual experience I had was when I was thirteen. It was arranged through the correct channels by my father. The Chinese version of the birds and the bees is very different.'

'I can see that would work. But what about love? That doesn't ever come into it?'

Ronnie sighed, feigning impatience. 'There you go again, Simon. Well, perhaps in today's society and in some rare instances, yes, you may be right. The idea of love has been introduced, probably by Hollywood, but it is not necessarily an improvement. Chinese marriage partnerships are essentially based on wealth. Among the wealthy and would-be wealthy, which is just about every Chinese alive, marriage has two purposes: procreation and asset accumulation. Two fortunes working together are better than one; love simply isn't necessary or useful, and comes a very poor third.'

'But you Chinese are smart enough to know what's going on in Western men's heads . . .'

Ronnie grinned, serving himself seconds from one of the curry dishes, although, curiously, he had barely touched his plate. Perhaps it was the oriental equivalent of Ross Quinlivan's cheese and tomato sandwich. 'Absolutely! And like everything else we'll exploit it. In Asia, bar girls are a part of doing business with the prurient West. It isn't Wonderland and Suzie Wong isn't Alice, but after half a dozen martinis or beers it can seem that way to a horny business associate. He is confronted with a beautiful young woman who is happy to satisfy his every desire . . . even the darkest, most shameful of them – shameful in his own mind, I mean.' He spread his hands. 'So, there you have it in a nutshell, it has nothing whatsoever to do with pimping. It's just doing what's natural and it's yet another opportunity to influence your client favourably.'

You will have gathered by now that Ronnie Wing was highly articulate, and he certainly had a better command of English than I did. But why shouldn't he be more articulate? Such a thought was racist, I silently reminded myself, and resolved to look up the word 'iconoclastic' when I had a moment and a dictionary. (I discovered much later that an iconoclast is someone who attacks traditional beliefs and values, just in case, like me at the time, you don't know what it means either.) The Texan had possibly rejected his childhood faith and was no longer a god-botherer, but had been left with all the hang-ups from his early indoctrination. I guess I was, and possibly still am, no different, influenced by the Koo background, Little Sparrow's dream, and my mum's ambitions to bring us all closer to our Chinese origins.

'I think I get the idea. I will be expected to entertain . . .' I hesitated then grinned, '. . . in the local tradition.'

Ronnie abruptly changed the subject. 'Simon, you levelled with me about the airport incident and that was good, very good. This isn't a big city – well, not in the sense of the businesspeople who make it hum – so the story would have reached me or Sidney hopelessly distorted and as a far from amusing incident that would not have been to your ultimate advantage. The Chinese don't do business with anyone who has been publicly shamed.'

'You mean Miss Mercy B. Lord will talk?'

'No, she's Beatrice Fong-trained and completely discreet. You can depend on her to ride shotgun for you, as she did at the airport. But there will have been others watching, first-class passengers. You weren't the last off the plane, were you?'

'No, there were only a few passengers ahead of me.'

'I can hear the gossip going on in the Meyer Road mansions from here. All Chinese, even the very rich, are acute observers. Their lives have always depended on being one jump ahead of ever-present danger, having a big stick to use against a potential enemy. We are a people overwhelmed by paranoia. It starts with the peasant, knee-deep in a rice paddy pushing a wooden plough behind a buffalo, and ends with the emperor . . . or his modern counterpart, Chairman Mao.' He smiled. 'I'm glad you told me about the airport incident because it's going to affect things, the way we manage things in the office.'

'I'm not sure I understand.'

'Well, at the moment I'm run off my feet coping with entertainment. We've recently had planeloads of look-see Americans sent from the New York office, and Yanks looking for new business opportunities in Asia are landing in increasing numbers – but you know that; it's why New York bought Wing and sent you here in the first place. I've also had several Germans involved with the engineering plants out at Jurong. They relish the local fleshpots, and the Yanks, while they pretend to play it straight, are just as bent as anyone else. There'll be heaps more Westerners with manufacturing or marketing partnerships in mind coming to check out the territory. It's why you're here, and Dansford Drocker is due to arrive soon.' He seemed to be thinking aloud. 'And you will both have your first day in the office —'

'You mean when I'm allowed into the office.'

Ronnie ignored the barb. 'The day the builders complete your office and his. Anyhow, what I'm trying to say is you'll both have to help me with entertaining foreign visitors. I'm kept pretty busy as it is with the locals, our old clients, mostly Chinese and Krauts. My older brother, Sidney, as chairman, only takes care of the very top Chinese honchos. Johnny never comes near clients. What with all the work of running the advertising for our old accounts as well, as I said, I need some help.'

'But I can handle, *will* handle, all your local work, at least the creative component, for all your existing clients.'

'Well, no, it doesn't work that way.'

'Because the Chinese don't do business with anyone who has been publicly shamed?' I couldn't believe what I was hearing.

'No, we don't know that yet. It just might take a while to gain their trust. Which brings me to the point. Putting it plainly, if you don't drink and fuck, it's going to make things difficult.'

'Who said anything about the second activity?' I grinned. 'Do they have to go together?'

'Well, in Singapore, when it comes to entertaining businessmen and their clients, they usually go hand in hand. Certainly, if the client is too senior for the girlie bars and brothels, occasionally he will hear a discreet knock on his hotel door and discover a beautiful Asian woman who announces that she has been sent for his delectation. She's an expensive gift from Sidney, and whether the bigwig client sends her away or accepts her, nothing will ever be mentioned afterwards. But for the most part, your average Westerner – Wasp, Catholic or Jew – can't be taken directly to a brothel and left to his own devices. That, in his mind, would be wrong. Besides it would appear cynical. And, as you suggested, he could well think of me, us, as pimps, especially if we had suggested it. He has first to get gloriously drunk. Then whatever follows can be blamed on the demon drink. He is accountable for what he does sober, but what he does when he's pissed is entirely excusable. Besides, he can always claim, as he inevitably does the first time, that he was too pissed to recall what happened.' Ronnie shrugged and opened his arms. 'That's showbiz.'

I guess it wasn't quite what I'd expected from my first day in the exotic East. In my mind I was going to build the best creative department in Asia, the oriental equivalent of DDB (Doyle Dane Bernbach) in New York, and be an advertising trendsetter, with my award-winning campaigns used in Hong Kong, Malaysia, Thailand and the Philippines. It'd be good stuff, mentioned in the West whenever Asian advertising was being discussed. Now, with my creative brilliance largely ignored, I was expected to be a barfly. With my build, no doubt it would be a big, fat bluebottle!

'Ronnie, thanks for being honest with me, although I must say I thought that kind of action was largely left to account service.'

'It's management here, Simon. We *are* the account managers. The remainder of the staff do as they're told and don't have these privileges.'

Some privilege, I thought. 'How often am I expected to be out to lunch until midnight?'

Ronnie looked sympathetic. 'It's not often that bad, Simon. The Americans, most of them, have a work ethic, so it's usually after five or six in the evening. The Germans and the French are the bad guys. They want lunch and then they can play on into the early hours. The Japs are sniffing around, wanting to get into the market too, with the results of their postwar economic miracle. But don't worry. I'll handle most of the non-American traffic. How often will we need to play host? In the busy season, three or four times a week, but between the three of us, maybe once or perhaps twice each. Hopefully Dansford Drocker will do his share.'

'With my luck he'll probably turn out to be a Baptist lay preacher,' I laughed. 'I guess I can manage once, or even occasionally twice, a week if I have to, particularly if it doesn't include lunch. I'm here to build a creative department, remember?'

'And I'm personally delighted that you are.'

'Ronnie, I have an unrelated question. Two, actually.'

'I'm listening.'

'Well, why would you belong to a club with a bunch of fat foreigners? Surely that's a classic case of losing face?'

Ronnie threw back his head and laughed. 'On the contrary, I gain face by belonging.'

'Huh? Excuse me, how?'

'To the Chinese, belonging to something that is exclusive or difficult to attain but that represents status is the highest achievement of wealth and position. This club has only six Chinese members, after almost a hundred years under British colonial rule. In the eyes of other wealthy Chinese, it is exclusivity that money simply can't buy, it is ultimate face – there can be no better kind.'

'Jesus, most of the blokes in the bar probably come from lower middle-class families in Britain. In terms of class and sophistication you're miles ahead. It doesn't make sense.'

Ronnie Wing emptied the contents of his wine glass before he responded, then signalled to Napoleon to refill it. Perhaps he needed time to compose an answer. 'It's the Chinese way, Simon. Sense, even commonsense, has nothing to do with it. For instance, five years ago this club was in the old GPO building when the Singapore Development Board summarily decided to kick us out. "This is a government-owned building. All-white clubs don't belong anymore," was the unspoken message given to us.'

'I can't say I disagree with that,' I said.

'Ah, no, no, you don't see it from the Chinese perspective. We moved here to Battery Road and the eviction made us even more exclusive. To Chinese, the way we are perceived by our peers – what we refer to as face – that is everything. Exclusivity is important, even if it means being a member of the Triads. Being one of a privileged few is seen as the gold standard. Now, Simon, your second question?'

'Yes, you mentioned the Japanese and their economic miracle. The war memories are still pretty fresh in Australia – Changi Prison here in Singapore, the Burma Railway – we're still coming to terms with doing business with the Japanese. But as long as there's a quid or, now that we've changed to decimal currency, a buck in it, I guess we'll find a way. But you blokes, the Chinese, in particular here on this island, doesn't it . . . you know, isn't it bloody hard to be civil to a Nip?'

'Yeah, sometimes, when you hear the stories from your parents, read about the Sino–Japanese War. But in the end we're Chinese; one way or another, shit has been happening to us for a long time.'

I thought about Ah Koo who had lost his entire family to the warlord Hong Xiuquan, who had bizarrely assumed the name 'Younger Brother of Christ'. It was the reason why I was an Australian, and had it not happened, I guess I'd be a Chinese peasant in a rice paddy guiding a wooden plough behind a buffalo.

Ronnie shrugged. 'The trick with the Japs is to turn the shit into pure gold.' He laughed, adding, 'Turds into eighteen-carat ingots.'

'Yeah, my Chinese great-great-grandfather did precisely that,' I acknowledged. 'Only it was we Australians who gave him shit.'

It was approaching three o'clock and we were the last in the dining room when Napoleon returned to say the bottle of gewürztraminer was empty. Lunch was, I presumed, close to over. I'd eaten, even had seconds – the curry was really something – but Ronnie hadn't added to his initial mouthful of food and, despite the martinis and wine, didn't seem any the worse for wear. Apart from the beer at the bar, I'd stuck to water. I reckoned that no matter how good he was at holding his grog, I now had a chance of staying with him if we kicked on.

Ronnie leaned back in his chair. 'Well, what's it to be, Simon?' He touched his face. 'Home to nurse your wounds, or shall I show you the ropes? But first, one for the road at the bar, eh?' He signed the chit Napoleon brought him and we left the club dining room and entered the bar, though a different one, this time a large, comfortable-looking lounge.

Ronnie's question in the dining room – 'What's it to be?' – had been intentionally ambiguous. He was giving me a second chance. Was I going to be a piker and go back to the hotel, or would I play? Earlier on he'd been solicitous, now he was just a tad sarcastic. The drink was finally showing.

He indicated a table for two placed beside a large picture window. 'The view of the river is splendid from here,' he announced as we sat in a couple of big, well-cushioned wicker chairs.

'No, no, by all means, let's kick on. I'm feeling fine. The sooner the better, I guess. Though I can't promise to match you in the drinks department.' I looked about the large room. A dozen or so patrons were lying on planter chairs with the backs down so they could stretch out full length, and appeared to be asleep, with their arms folded across their chests. One had his face and chest covered with a copy of the *Straits Times*. Another expat, who had only just adjusted his chair and stretched out, summoned a waiter, who promptly produced a piece of chalk and wrote on the sole of the man's shoe.

'Wait on, why are they numbering his shoe?' I whispered to Ronnie.

'Look around at the others,' he suggested, indicating the sleeping men. And indeed they all carried a chalked number on the sole of one shoe. 'It's the time they wish to be awakened with a cup of tea.'

Looking down at the river five storeys below, I saw that both the surrounding roads and waterway were teeming with traffic of every description. Small boats of every commercial configuration, floating rafts and punts with outboard motors crowded the river, and the roads were packed with trucks, rickshaws, bicycles loaded to the sky and men pulling handcarts. In the fly-buzzing afternoon calm of the Town Club lounge bar, I had to remind myself I was in the exotic East; that down there at street and river level it would be a bloody hard place to earn a living. I ordered another beer for Ronnie's peace of mind, nominating a Carlsberg, and he ordered a Scotch over ice.

'Well, where was I?' Ronnie asked. 'Oh yes, I'm afraid the downside is that if you don't get pissed it could be a long evening. We rely on our clients getting a little drunk, but I'll try to make it interesting for you anyhow. The upside is if you enjoy yourself with everything on offer, at least you'll remember the experience in the morning.'

I laughed nervously. 'The "everything" – is that expected?'

Ronnie Wing looked at me hard then smiled. 'What, getting laid?' He hesitated. 'You're not . . . ?'

'A queen? No, of course not!' I protested, feeling both indignant and foolish at the same time. I felt myself blushing.

My host ignored my protest. 'If you are, that isn't a problem, Simon. In this ambisextrous candy shop of a town, the problem isn't what your sexual proclivity may be,' (big Ronnie Wing words) 'it's that you can't possibly taste everything that's available and openly on display.'

'No, perhaps I didn't make myself clear. I meant in a habitual sense. If, in the hopefully unlikely event you're out with four different clients on four different nights, does that mean you're in the saddle four times that week with four different bar girls or . . .' I paused because I hated the word, 'whores?'

'No, of course not! Those terms, by the way, are interchangeable. It's a matter of location. Bars have bar girls and brothels have whores. It's a definition of place, not activity. The answer to your question is no, you only make it look that way. It's essential to look like the stud you aren't. If you don't appear to be complicit, your client gets nervous, particularly the following morning.'

'When, incidentally, he can't remember a thing that happened?' I added, aiming for a wry tone. 'So, what's the drill? What do *you* do, Ronnie?'

'I select someone, a bar girl or pro I've previously taken a shine to, someone you have when you actually want to indulge yourself, someone you like, trust and enjoy as your permanent Suzie Wong. Then, whether you do or don't use her, you pay her anyhow. It's a great opportunity for a couple of hours of shut-eye. If you're lucky and the client passes out or decides he wants to prolong the experience, you may even get a good night's sleep. At any rate, your regular wakes you with a hot towel, a massage and a cup of *chai*, then tells you when the client has had enough and wants to go back to his hotel. By Asian standards, Singapore is a pretty safe city, even in the red-light district. If you choose the right Suzie Wong, you can often go home after the client has been dispatched with his choice, and she'll see to it that he gets safely to his hotel. If it's a brothel, the *mama-san* will do the same. You'll soon get the hang of it.'

'Mate, why don't we just do shit-hot advertising so the Americans, Brits and Germans select us because we're the obvious choice to make them lots of money?'

Ronnie Wing looked at me. God knows what he was thinking. But he kept his cool. 'That's a novel idea. I don't think Sidney has ever thought of it quite like that. I guess it just isn't the Chinese way.' He thought for a moment. 'Besides, it's not the same thing.'

'Oh, why's that?'

'Well, the money we'd be making for them doesn't go to them as individuals, you see? They mostly work for international companies and the profit goes to London, Stuttgart, New York or Chicago. Money's one thing, living the fantasy is quite another.'

'At the risk of sounding like a prig, what if we forgot about squeeze and simply entertained clients in a good restaurant? Then, if they wanted to play afterwards, we could drop them off at their hotel, and they could get a callgirl the way it's done everywhere else in the world – by asking the doorman.'

Ronnie laughed. 'God, we couldn't do that! What, and miss the opportunity for squeeze? You don't seem to understand, Simon, the Chinese don't do business without squeeze.' He laughed again. 'I'm only kidding. But I still don't think you understand the psychology involved. As I said before, it's a way to bond with a client, the traditional extra dimension of doing business in Asia. Sex just *isn't* a big deal here; it's a way to be employed if you're pretty and have no education, and it's the way we've always done business – us, the Brits, everyone in South-East Asia.'

'What? Prostitution is a tradition . . . er, I mean, an accepted way to be employed? Poor young Chinese women simply accept it as a job?'

'Ah, now you're beginning to understand, Simon. It's a perfectly legitimate and generally accepted way of earning a living. As I said, it's also a traditional way for us to do business. If we didn't do it, and you may find this hard to believe, half the accounts in the agency would go to the opposition who do. It works for us, always has, and it works for the girls. In the end it harms no one!'

'That's hard to believe. You mean the girls *choose* to be prostitutes? Is that what you're saying?'

Ronnie sighed. 'There you go again. Choice is the prerogative of very few; it comes with wealth. The Chinese peasant doesn't think in terms of choice. Women in our society, the ones at the bottom of the heap, don't choose, they survive, not only as prostitutes, but as charladies, servants, streetsweepers, labourers, peasants. But with a pretty young girl, the gods put a purse between her legs and she's not ashamed to fill it with foreigners' cash. Some few have risen to great wealth by getting their start in a whorehouse. When you're unwanted in the first instance why would you be granted the luxury of choice? That's both a ridiculous notion and not one that's going to change in a hurry. Mind you, we have a relatively young prime minister in Lee Kuan Yew, who says his People's Action Party is going to make it all happen. Abracadabra and we'll all be equal, the maid and the millionaire. Now that we're out of the Federation and back on our own, he has ambitions for Singapore.'

'Oh?'

'He's already talking about hippies as long-haired drug peddlers and smugglers – "human detritus", he called them at a private dinner I attended recently. In fact, there are rumours that he's going to standardise haircuts – short back and sides for all.'

I grinned and nodded towards the bar. 'This mob will be happy. But how will that stop drug peddlers?'

Ronnie shook his head. 'Beats me. The Chinese have been smuggling and peddling drugs ever since the end of the Opium Wars. We all know who the real culprits are in Singapore and it's not the hippies; rather, it's one or two well-known Hong Kong Chinese millionaires. All this is prime-ministerial window dressing, meant to impress the

American industrialists – the new Yank investors in South-East Asia he hopes to attract. With the Vietnam War still on, Lyndon B. Johnson has discovered the real potential of South-East Asia. Win or lose, the Yankees are coming into Asia to trade.'

'And your PM wants Singapore's share by cleaning up your act?'

He nodded. 'Yes, something like that. Which is the problem with an education at the London School of Economics and Cambridge – it doesn't exactly keep one in touch with the man in the street. He recently described Bugis Street and its bars, brothels and transvestites as a place of institutionalised moral turpitude as well as an eyesore – everything that's wrong with South-East Asia.' Ronnie looked at me. 'The man simply doesn't comprehend. It's what brings in the tourists and helps drive our economy. It *is* Singapore. He wants us industrially mean and squeaky clean. Next thing he'll have us picking up cigarette butts from the pavements or he'll ban smoking in public altogether!'

I grinned. 'You'd better have a haircut, mate, and so had I. What do you think? Will he succeed?'

'What, clean up the sex industry? Not a snowball's hope in hell. It's not the Singaporean way or the Chinese way, hasn't ever been, never will be.'

'What about China, Mao's communist revolution?' I suggested. 'They appear to have changed things.'

Ronnie Wing looked at me and shook his head. 'Yes, well . . . you will have noted how many Chinese from Hong Kong or here in Singapore are pushing down the fence on the Chinese border in a desperate scramble to get back into the motherland. Shit, Simon, communism is just another method devised to dominate and exploit the peasant. For all the rhetoric, Chairman Mao is no less an emperor than Puyi. The only equality between the communist elite and the Chinese proletariat is that they both wear denim. You can't close down commercial pussy even if it is against the law. It's Asia's way of entertaining foreigners, has been since the Brits arrived here, in China and India. Girlie bars and brothels are an institution our PM meddles with at his peril.'

'Oldest profession, eh? I guess it's universal.'

'Universal maybe, but not equally enjoyable. Have you ever been to a brothel on your own in a strange city?'

'I confess not. Have you?'

'Yes, on one occasion in Stuttgart. The Germans love Asia's "tight" little almond-eyed girls. I was visiting an engineering company client and wanted to see if the Brunhilde archetype turned me on to the same degree. The brothel was full of blonde Polish whores with thighs like tree trunks and breasts the size of melons. I never got to find out because they were all frightened of fucking Genghis Khan, a six-foot two-inch Chinaman. I use the word Chinaman advisedly, because that's what the German madam called me in English. "Nein, they don't vont to fok a Chinaman, for zem it is very bod luck!"' Ronnie mimicked. 'Believe me, there is nothing worse than solitary sex in a strange city.'

'Yeah, okay, fine, I get it, but if it's liberating and fun Boy's-own stuff for visiting clients, what is it for us? Once in a while it might be fun, but not as a regular part of my job. No way! I came here to build a creative department, not to hold my client's dick! Surely that's not our responsibility? It isn't built into the new business proposition or the agency agreement.'

Ronnie Wing threw back his head and laughed. 'Now he tells me!' He paused. 'Simon . . . I wish! Look carefully at the last line in the agreement, it's written in invisible ink and plain for all to see if they want to keep the account safe. If it's an agreement with an advertising agency here, Jakarta, Bangkok, Hong Kong, Kuala Lumpur or Manila, it's there, all right, in three European languages, English, German and French, and soon, I dare say, in Japanese. *"The visiting client shall get laid by a beautiful young Asian nymphette, facilitated by agency management who will be in attendance at all times to encourage, abet, excuse and forget."'*

'Wait on. This is supposed to keep the account *safe?* I don't think so. Here's a not-unlikely scenario. You set out to paint the town red, you both get pissed, the client says something you won't cop from anybody, you abuse him and consequently lose the account.' I raised my eyebrows. 'It's been known to happen in Australia.'

Ronnie smiled broadly. 'Got it in one, Brother Simon. Admittedly, it's a thin line to tread and if you can't hold your liquor, you're right, it can be dangerous, even disastrous. Nevertheless, the mandatory night on the town for foreign visitors is still required; it's still part of the fucking job.'

'Or vice versa,' I added. 'So who does the actual work in the agency?'

'Ah, that's just it, rain or shine, with or without a hangover that has you walking into the agency with your chin down near your kneecaps, you're in the agency by 9 a.m. to organise your staff, go to a client meeting, answer the phone, see a supplier's rep, write a piece of copy, whatever.'

'And pretend you're on top of things?'

'Well, yes, with the help of your Suzie Wong, you'll learn soon enough how to do that, Simon.' He downed his Scotch. 'Last Scotch, first brandy coming up.'

'Oh, why the switch? First a martini, then wine, Scotch and now brandy?'

'Only when the evening shift begins.'

'How's that? What's so special about brandy?'

'Take my advice, Simon, brandy is the only spirit that keeps the mood buoyant.'

'You mean doesn't depress?'

'I didn't say that. But if you mean below the belt, yes, no brewer's droop.'

'I'm not big on spirits, mate.'

Ronnie Wing looked deliberately grim-faced. 'You're going to learn to stay out of Asian toilets as much as possible, and you know what beer does to the bladder. The only dependable "flush" in this part of the world is to be found in a game of poker. Plumbing isn't our forté – especially in the girlie bars.'

'Oh, nice,' I laughed. 'Perhaps Lee Kuan Yew will fix that as well.'

Ronnie gave me a sardonic smile. 'Well, he's certainly good at stirring up shit. We'll have to wait and see if he's any good at cleaning it up.'

As it transpired, Ronnie's warning about toilets in South-East Asia, and not only in the girlie bars, possessed a great deal of truth.

'Well, shall we be off? The first lesson from the Gospel of Asian Advertising is about to begin.'

'Thank you for the lesson and the *spirit* in which it is given,' I said, standing, silently pleased with the pun. 'Lead on, McDuff.'

'I think you'll find it's "Lay on, McDuff",' said Ronnie with a grin, landing the final verbal punch.

CHAPTER FIVE

———

MY FIRST MEETING WITH Sidney and Johnny Wing was at a cocktail party to meet the staff at a modest hotel across the road from the agency, although neither was present when I arrived. Ronnie, I quickly learned, was a true enthusiast and it was simply impossible not to like him. He was a lovely bloke and the only Wing I grew to trust – that is, when he wasn't conveying explicit messages from his oldest brother or making judgements on creative work. He was the director in charge of print production and, as a shareholder, was technically senior to me. This was, of course, a matter of face and I accepted that things had to appear to work that way, even though in practice, as the creative director appointed by New York, I called the creative shots.

Sidney Wing was the ringmaster in the Three Wing Circus; middle brother, Johnny, was the animal trainer who acted as staff manager and media director; while Ronnie, for want of a better description, was the clown. Johnny Wing kept a very low profile and affected a permanent scowl and an irascible manner to ensure that he had as little contact as possible with anyone. I never really got to know what was going on in his head. Whatever it was, it had arrived there via a detour to Sidney's desk. According to Ronnie, his middle brother never made a move without Sidney's consent.

Sidney Wing was, I was later to learn, 'Mr Squeeze'. If Ronnie cared enormously about advertising, Sidney only had one motive and that was to make money any way he could. Samuel Oswald Wing existed to make Mr Squeeze rich and powerful, and I often wondered if it ever occurred to him that the company made a product called advertising.

As soon as we arrived at the party, Ronnie busied himself by introducing me to the staff. Their obvious ambivalence and divided loyalties made it a mostly awkward experience. Was I to be their superior or did they still answer to the Wings, who were free to order, rebuke or fire them at a moment's notice? Consequently, they laughed nervously at everything I said and nodded even when it was fairly obvious they had no idea what I was talking about.

This was especially true of those from the production department who made the print advertisements: the Chinese language copywriter and layout man (there were no women), who had never for one moment thought of themselves as creative. For example, I attempted to describe the independence and integrity of a good creative department, but soon realised that it had never occurred to them that their point of view had any value. It was the wrong choice of subject, introduced at the wrong time and in the wrong manner. I was displaying Australian and American attitudes that were completely alien to them. I was to learn that these people had no independence and that integrity wasn't a word in the lexicon of the Chinese office worker. They obeyed orders and did what it took to keep their jobs. It wasn't that they licked arse, there simply wasn't any other way to behave. What we might regard as sycophancy was simply normal behaviour. What we considered personal initiative they considered reckless.

I began my time at Samuel Oswald Wing by asserting myself when I should have been tiptoeing through the proverbial tulips. It proved to be my first mistake in a disastrous evening, a bull-in-the-china-shop preface to perhaps the worst two hours in my professional career. I can't imagine what they must have said to each other the following morning at work, but the consensus would probably have been that a mad foreigner had arrived in the agency and was about to cause chaos and threaten their jobs and their livelihoods.

Most people fear change, but the Chinese have learned from bitter experience that anything that disturbs the status quo inevitably leads to further suffering. Persecution was a frequent visitor, while restitution seldom if ever knocked on the door. My arrival wasn't an occasion for celebration. Their rice bowls were reasonably full and if they didn't rock the *sampan*, their jobs were comparatively safe. The changes I talked about so enthusiastically would have filled them with dread. 'Fools rush in where angels fear to tread' was never more appropriate an axiom.

And then, half an hour or so into the welcoming drinks, Ronnie tapped me on the shoulder. 'Time to meet my brothers, Simon – a short meeting in Sidney's office.'

'Right.' I excused myself and followed him out of the hotel and across the road. Singaporean buildings at the time were low-rise rococo Victorian or more austere Edwardian red brick, and the Samuel Oswald Wing building was typical of the latter. The foyer looked as though it had recently been renovated or, rather, tizzied-up. High-gloss maroon paint on the walls picked up every tiny fault in the plaster, and two chrome and black leather couches bracketed a glass coffee table on which rested a neatly folded copy of the *Straits Times*, which seemed more like a prop than something meant to be opened and read. In lieu of the usual bowl of flowers, a large and perfectly splendid aspidistra that would have done justice to a Noël Coward set rested on a stand in a blue and white porcelain bowl. With its carefully polished leaves it was quite the most handsome object in the foyer. The wall-to-wall carpet was chocolate brown and just beginning to wear near the base of the reception desk. Across the entire maroon wall behind reception, polished chrome letters almost a foot high announced:

Samuel Oswald Wing

The letters were much too large for the proportions of the foyer, and Braggadocio, the name of the typeface, was fat, lazy and complacent. Its original Art Deco style was redolent of a different era and these days it was more commonly found on cheap chocolates or fake Cuban cigars. An advertising agency in a sense tells you who it is – modern, traditional, professional, young, established – by the typeface it chooses. Braggadocio sent all the wrong messages. It was the fat boy eating his lunch alone in a corner of the schoolyard and not the kid dancing around his mates with a soccer ball at his toes in the playground.

On the left-hand wall as you entered the foyer were two truly bad oil paintings in identical ornate gilded frames: the first of Lee Kuan Yew, the second of President Lyndon B. Johnson with rather more hair than he really had. Sidney Wing was making his bilateral loyalties known to the world without any subtlety at all.

In retrospect I can see that this first reaction to the agency sounds a bit precious. My advertising training had taught me that every object and product has a personality, and so first impressions are important; what you see is what you can expect. For instance, if you see a grossly fat man waddling towards you, you reach a whole set of conclusions that are quite different from those associated with a trim, upright man striding purposefully. I'd barely set foot in the agency and already I had a sinking feeling in my gut.

I now realise I had jumped to a conclusion that was quite wrong and simply unfair. There were very few advertising agencies, in any meaningful sense of the term in Singapore at the time. Most were simply a couple of scruffy back rooms along dirty corridors in old buildings. Chinese-owned advertising agencies were seen simply as an opportunity to make a little easy money.

For the most part a business, if British owned, wrote its own copy and sent it off to the printer for typesetting and layout. The resulting stereotype plate was then sent to the various newspapers for printing. Some of the larger organisations, such as Jardine Matheson, the great British shipping and trading house, and Robinsons, the department store,

Singapore's equivalent of Harrods and established in 1856, maintained their own advertising departments, with a manager to buy space and a layout artist with more versatility than talent, a jack-of-all-trades – or more rarely a jill – who could do a bit of everything.

Significant British accounts were serviced by Cathay Advertising, owned by Elma Kelly, a legendary female figure who held most, if not all, of the big accounts for British industry and business in post-war Singapore and the rest of South-East Asia. She, or rather Cathay, together with recent entry Jackson Wain and, of course, Wing Brothers Advertising, were the only decent-sized agencies in town.

Then there were the mostly Chinese-owned ad agencies in narrow, rat-infested, garbage-choked lanes, up dank, dirty stairs in old buildings that smelled of bad toilets. These looked after the Chinese businesses, producing small print ads for the newspapers and magazines in languages other than English. Incidentally, I was to discover that plumbing was not high on the list of priorities for most businesses run by the Chinese and was, with few exceptions, one of the worst aspects of being in Singapore and South-East Asia. The stench of faecal matter and urine from toilets that were almost invariably blocked invaded most stairways – often, perniciously, entire floors. This fundamental public-health issue seemed to be the one most neglected. I was to learn that, among employers, staff welfare was of little or no significance.

In advertising, Sidney Wing was to the Straits-Chinese what Elma Kelly was to the British. He'd attended the Raffles Institution, a posh private school for the sons and daughters of elite families, and inherited generations of good connections, or *guanxi* (pronounced *guan-she*), going back a hundred years or more to China, which allowed him to exert enormous influence. There is a Chinese proverb that covers obligation and the matter of associations: *'When drinking water from a well, one should never forget who dug it.'* While this appears to refer to anyone who has been helpful, gratuitous help is rarely forthcoming from a stranger. The Chinese help each other not so much as a matter of goodwill or kindness but as an acknowledgement of mutual obligation in an association that can reach into both the past and the future. This means you are a part of their *guanxi*.

Advertising wasn't Sidney's main game but simply a convenient front for investments and associations that were, it seemed, widespread and extended into most aspects of Singapore and Hong Kong's financial worlds, both legitimate and dodgy.

Of course, I was still oblivious to all this, charged as I was by my American masters with building an effective creative department. I was single-minded and naïve, but I should have paid more attention to the ad world around me. Mercy B. Lord helped me get an idea of the social environment in the two weeks of show and tell I spent with her, but I assumed that the advertising business was much the same in Singapore as in Australia. I'd forgotten one of the most important rules: know your competitors in the business.

As it turned out, Samuel Oswald Wing was a veritable palace compared to most of the other ad agencies, and despite my high-handed criticism, the Wing brothers had every reason to be proud of it. They'd deliberately created it in the image of a Western advertising agency to appeal to potential international partners and had succeeded. To criticise this makeover in even the smallest way was unwarranted, except for criticism of the staff toilets, which were atrocious shit holes. Fortunately, the one reserved for management had been upgraded and was kept under lock and key. But of all the staff battles that lay ahead, and they were many, the one that caused me the most anxiety was the simple matter of preventing the staff toilets from breaking down. Sidney Wing, who owned the building, would simply refuse to replace the ancient and inadequate plumbing.

But all this lay ahead, with the agency décor currently the least of my problems. Now, with Ronnie leading, I proceeded up a short flight of brown-carpeted stairs to Sidney's office on the first floor.

Ronnie ushered me into the ringmaster's office. Well, what can I say? I had been expecting Chinese décor – stout, heavily carved, bandy-legged dragon chairs upholstered in yellow silk brocade surrounding a coffee table with similar dragon-clawed legs. Sidney Wing would work from a large and grotesque glass-topped ebony desk with, again, the same fat dragon legs. I'd even pictured a beautiful Chinese silk carpet on the polished teak floor. I'd imagined the entire wall behind Sidney Wing's desk would be occupied by a gigantic aquarium containing five enormous golden carp, a vivid aquascape of living coral and gently waving weed set in motion by belches of bright bubbles. The fish would be grandly suspended, their tails and fins barely moving, their scales glinting gold and silver, the colours of wealth, their bulging jet-black eyes staring, each seeming to say, 'No, you could not afford me.'

This wonderfully detailed vision evaporated in the face of the unbridled bad taste of Sidney's large office, which took its inspiration from the foyer, except that the foyer had been done on the cheap whereas this décor was ugliness done with an open and bulging purse.

The furnishing was Scandinavian modern, the desk made of yellow polished pine with a smoked-glass top, behind which Sidney sat in a very large high-backed chrome and black leather swivel chair. In front of the desk were four bright-yellow leather and chrome chairs. The wall-to-wall carpet was brown, the wallpaper a deep green with gold fleur-de-lis, which picked up or exacerbated the yellow theme of the décor so that the room throbbed with chocolate and yellow, accentuated by the high-gloss yellow of the ceiling, venetian blinds, window frames, doorframe and skirting boards.

During Mercy B. Lord's familiarisation program, she had taken me to several backyard furniture-makers with a view to furnishing my flat before we finally settled on one. What struck me about them was the craftsmanship. While some of the furniture wasn't to my taste, it was all beautifully made and you could commission just about anything you desired from cabinet-makers as good as any in the West. Why, I asked myself, would Sidney Wing pay through the nose for Scandinavian furniture when such beautiful stuff was so readily available locally? I later questioned Mercy B. Lord.

'Ah, Simon, there is a saying among wealthy Chinese: *"Local chilli – not very hot."* It means anything Chinese is by definition inferior, unless it is antique, rare and expensive. By contrast, expensive imported Scandinavian furniture is about as far from Chinese as it is possible to be, so it would be seen as the epitome of fashion and good taste.'

Instead of the aquarium I had imagined on the wall behind Sidney Wing's desk, there was a large painting of Sidney wearing an Arnold Palmer cap, white monogrammed open-necked golf shirt, red windcheater and black trousers with white golf shoes. His hand rested on the top of a leather golf bag with a full set of Dunlop clubs, the logo carefully painted on a putter. Over his left shoulder was the artist's impression of a fairway with a sand bunker and putting green, the flag in the far distance. Sidney wore a heroic expression, his eyes narrowed as if he were looking into the distance. Like Ronnie, Sidney Wing was a tall, good-looking man and the artist, unmistakeably the one responsible for the paintings downstairs, hadn't done him justice. The portrait was larger than life size and perhaps twice the size of the two downstairs, with an identical gilded frame. I could only think the paintings and the frames must have come as a job lot.

Against the wall beside the window was a lighted display cabinet with a glass front, made from the same yellow wood as the desk, in which were displayed numerous silver golf trophies, most of them small silver eggcups with handles, of the kind you get for playing in a tournament rather than winning it.

But then, in this citrus and chocolate Mixmaster mess, I found a pleasant surprise: a Victorian walnut cabinet with a softly lit interior stood against the far wall, filled with exquisite pieces of jade and antique porcelain. On top of this superb cabinet squatted a 'happy Buddha' wearing a smile of merry contentment like a happy bullfrog with a stomach full of dragonflies. He was carved from moss-green jade, his earlobes falling to his shoulders, his chubby legs tucked under his enormous belly.

This cabinet and its contents, rather than the fish tank I had imagined, were the ancestors' guarantee that not everything had gone to hell in a handbasket and that life and the pursuit of wealth was on course for the eldest Wing. The antique porcelain within the cabinet covered dynastic periods spanning 1400 years and was beyond anything I could value. I even saw one or two pieces that appeared to be from the Tang dynasty. I would learn that very few of Singapore's wealthy Chinese could have afforded such a collection. To a knowledgeable observer, the contents of this cabinet would be sufficient to establish Sidney's position in the big league. I was also not to know at the time that he owned the golf course and that it was in Miami.

Every Chinese, rich or poor, my mother included, believes with unshakeable conviction that their ancestors watch every move they make, most of the time with grim disapproval. The pacification of ancestors preoccupies the Chinese mind well beyond any religious zealotry we might exhibit in the West. No matter how switched-on or 'Western' a Chinese individual may be, he or she fears one thing more than any other: ancestors. The religion of the Peranakan – that is, the Straits-Chinese – is founded on the belief that gods and ancestor spirits exist and can influence people's affairs. While a person's fate is fixed, luck can be controlled with their help. Neglect your ancestors and you're headed for big trouble.

A further pleasant surprise awaited me in Sidney Wing's office. I turned towards the source of a loud ticking and saw a large eighteenth- or nineteenth-century grandfather clock with a break-front panel revealing its swinging brass pendulum. Black Roman numerals etched and outlined in red enamel adorned the brass face, and directly within were two fat dragons, their noses meeting below the XII and the tips of their tails joining above the VI. It had probably been made in China from a British design and was a truly splendid and valuable timepiece. Whether this was also an ancestor pacifier I couldn't say, although it would reassure them that Sidney had certainly provided amply for the next generation. I was later to learn that the clock's face was in fact solid gold and the pendulum was gold-plated. Sidney Wing considered that if ever the pendulum stopped it would be extremely bad joss. He would wind the clock himself every morning, even though a single complete winding lasted for a week, and when he was overseas or away from the office he would phone each morning to ensure it had been wound.

Sidney's expensively furnished Westernised office was, I guessed, designed to give its owner appropriate face. Perhaps the clock, with its mixture of European design and Chinese manufacture, represented a link between China and the West, or perhaps it symbolised immortality. Ancestor-worship and the interpretation of signs and portents preoccupies most Chinese. I knew from my mother that the world's most superstitious people are undoubtedly the Chinese, who see and read meanings, both good and bad, into almost everything – hence her preoccupation with Little Sparrow's dream. These mysterious links between the future and dreams, events or symbols, which defy Western logic, enhance the inscrutable nature of oriental and, in particular, Chinese culture.

I questioned Mercy B. Lord about Chinese superstitions, and while she agreed that I was right, she reminded me that superstition wasn't unique to the Chinese and that we all share it in one way or another. Even rational people may feel a twinge on Friday the thirteenth, especially if they walk under a ladder, then see a black cat crossing the road. 'In the orphanage one of the kids found a natural stain on a river stone that resembled the Virgin Mary. It was around Easter and the nuns immediately saw it as a miracle and reported it to the bishop in Hong Kong. Now every Easter hundreds of pilgrims arrive to pray to the Singapore Virgin who resides in the Hong Kong cathedral.' She paused and looked directly at me. 'Several miraculous cures are attributed to her.'

'Aha, ecumenical superstition!'

'Very funny, Simon.' But I could see she wasn't amused.

'And you believe it's an authentic sign? A miracle?' I asked.

Her eyes widened. 'Of course!'

Sidney and Johnny Wing, the elder brother seated behind his desk, the middle brother in one of the chrome and yellow leather jobs, looked up at us as Ronnie entered with me in tow. Sidney managed the semblance of a welcoming smile, but Johnny immediately looked away, as if my arrival was of little or no importance.

Johnny Wing, I was to learn, was greatly feared by the mostly Straits-Chinese employees, and his silent, morose demeanour didn't help endear him to me, either. I was to discover that he wasn't regarded as a bundle of joy by the newspaper, magazine and radio reps calling into the agency. He never accumulated squeeze, because he never entertained or accepted an invitation.

Neither of the two brothers stood as I reached down to shake Johnny's hand and then stretched across the desk to reach Sidney. Both had limp grips, the fingers only barely responding to my touch, but this was simply the Chinese male handshake, more an acknowledgement of someone's presence than an indication of character or a sign of welcome.

Ronnie introduced me formally as Koo Kee, adding my Christian name, Simon, almost as an afterthought.

Sidney said something in Cantonese to Johnny, who nodded and replied without changing his expression. Then the elder Wing leaned back to take a good look at me. 'Welcome, Kee, please sit,' he said, pointing to one of the yellow and chrome Scandinavian atrocities.

'Thank you.' I smiled and seated myself.

'So, Kee, you look Chinese but, hey, man, you're Australian?' This was said with a smile and I took it as a playful comment.

'Yes, fourth-generation. My great-great-grandfather left Shanghai in the mid-1850s for the gold rush in Australia. I'm afraid his was the last marriage to a Chinese woman until my dad married my mum.' I was conscious of being too voluble, but couldn't stop. 'I guess my looks are a throwback, because I'm a dead ringer for my great-great-grandmother.' I hesitated a moment then said with a grin, 'In Australia my friends call me Fortune Cookie, but I'd be happy if you called me Simon.' As replies go, it was overkill.

Sidney didn't smile at the mention of my nickname and Johnny showed no reaction whatsoever. 'The fortune cookie is not Chinese. We do not have such a thing,' Sidney remarked.

'No, I know, it's American.' I grinned again. 'Most Australians wouldn't know that.'

'When we print your Chinese name card, Fortune Koo Kee is a very good name. You must use it. It will look good in Chinese characters,' Sidney said, pleased with his observation. I was to learn that Chinese in business with the West quite often adopted an English name, one that was usually intended to add an impression of power; Hercules, Napoleon, Samson, Churchill and Atlas were common, and Fortune not unusual.

'And how should I address you? By your Chinese names?'

Stabbing his chest with his forefinger, he said, 'Sidney,' then pointed to his brother and said, 'Johnny.' Johnny grunted and nodded his head but didn't smile or even glance at me.

While outwardly friendly enough, the brothers were beginning to make me feel distinctly awkward. 'Thank you for the welcoming party over the road,' I said in an attempt to conceal my lack of composure.

'You look Chinese,' Sidney persisted. 'You say your mother is Chinese?'

'Yes, Straits-Chinese.'

'But you can't speak Cantonese.' It was a statement, an indictment, not a question. Then, before I could reply, he said, 'You are half-Chinese and you do not have your mother's language.'

There are times in all of our lives when we inexplicably lose the plot, do or say the wrong thing at the wrong time in the wrong place. It was at that precise moment that I fucked up big-time. Why then I will never know. Perhaps I was already feeling the burden of the job I'd been given by the Yanks and was realising that it wasn't going to be easy. Maybe it was an overreaction to the premises or to the fear I sensed amongst the production staff of the change I represented. But in retrospect it was unforgiveable, and I can only think that it was an attempt to establish myself as an independent and consequential future creative director of the agency. I simply don't know, but whatever the reason, I most certainly should have known better and kept my big mouth well and truly shut. I had already overcome the temptation to tell Ronnie about the family restaurant chain, which would have been both unnecessary and decidedly unwise. It wasn't as if I didn't know any better. When we were kids, my mother had drummed into us a maxim apparently derived from Little Sparrow: *When you are confused or angry, say nothing.* I was both confused and angry about the observation Sidney had made to Johnny in Cantonese when we'd entered Sidney's office, and that I'd understood perfectly.

I smiled, looking first at Sidney and then at Johnny. 'I speak and understand Cantonese well enough to know that you insulted me when we entered.'

It was the first time I heard the infamous Sidney Wing giggle, just two high-pitched notes in a girlish voice.

Ronnie jumped up. 'Simon, hey, you must have misunderstood,' he protested.

It was my last chance to backpedal but I didn't take it. Instead, I maintained my slightly superior smile and added the insult of a shrug. 'What is there to misunderstand? You said plainly, "He looks like a Chinese peasant," and Johnny here replied, "And that's the way we'll treat him!" Shall I repeat it for you in Cantonese?'

Sidney, his face expressionless, stood up. 'We will go to the cocktail party now.' Johnny rose with a grunt and both walked to the door, leaving Ronnie standing and me seated. Moments later their footsteps could be heard crossing the landing to the stairs.

Ronnie frowned deeply. 'Shit! What now? This is bad, Simon. They have lost face.'

'And I haven't? What's with you guys? Sidney giggled like a fucking schoolgirl when he realised I knew what he'd said.'

'No, no, you don't understand. He's always had the giggle, it's spontaneous, some sort of affliction he can't control. It can be terribly embarrassing. Once it occurred during an after-dinner speech by the Prime Minister. Fortunately, they were at school together, so he didn't end up getting a tap on the shoulder from a government goon.' Ronnie grinned, trying to calm me. 'If St Vitus's Dance was a sound, it would be my brother Sidney's giggle.'

Ronnie's lengthy reply gave me time to recover from my anger. 'So you think I should have taken it on the chin? Said nothing?' I was growing increasingly mortified by my enormous gaffe, but felt stupidly compelled to defend myself.

Ronnie thought for a moment. 'You must find a way to apologise.'

'You're kidding. Apologise! Me? No way!' *Jesus, Simon Koo, get real, back down!*

'*Shi mianzi* – causing someone to lose face – can have very serious ramifications, Simon. In Chinese society what may appear a minor indiscretion to a Westerner can sometimes create an enemy for life. You must think about this carefully and we *must* find a way to repair the damage.'

'But shit, Ronnie, this wasn't of my making. Why doesn't Sidney find a way to apologise to me?' It was a final pathetic attempt at justification.

'Because it is you who are at fault!'

'Eh?'

'You should have kept your mouth shut. It would have given you the moral advantage – now you have handed it to them.'

'C'mon, Ronnie, I was appointed by New York, not by Sidney.'

Ronnie laughed. 'Sidney holds the purse strings. It was never going to be easy to get the budget to hire the right people to build your creative department, but now it will be impossible.'

I shrugged, trying to look unconcerned. 'My contract stipulates I become a director after three months and Dansford Drocker, when he arrives as managing director, will support me, and with you on side . . .'

Ronnie shook his head. '*Guanxi*, my friend – I will support my brother. I have no choice.' He placed a hand on my shoulder. 'I will do my best to repair this damage, but listen to me carefully, Simon. In future, when dealing with the Chinese, always leave them a way out of any face-losing situation. Get this into your head once and for all: if it is a contest between face and the truth, then face will win every time. If you do not apologise to Sidney and Johnny, then prepare yourself for future acts of revenge, which I seriously doubt you can survive.' He looked at me steadily. 'Simon, despite that face of yours, this is not your culture. This is not something you can win. Morality, justice, integrity, call it what you may, none of them play a part in this.'

I remained silent for quite some time, knowing I was between a rock and a hard place. 'Okay, so how do I go about this?'

'Simple. We retranslate,' Ronnie said, obviously relieved.

'What the hell does that mean?'

'Well, you were mistaken about what you heard. Your knowledge of Cantonese unfortunately let you down, a common enough occurrence with foreigners who do not speak it as their mother tongue. Now, with my help in translation, what was said is entirely the opposite to the unfortunate meaning you placed on what they *in fact* said.'

'Tell me more.'

'One word, that's all you need to change, and not the word, just the inflection. You heard Sidney say, "He looks like a Chinese peasant."'

'Yeah, that's what he *did* say.'

'No, no, you're quite wrong! You think the word *peasant* was an insult. In our society a peasant can become rich and powerful and enjoy every privilege. We do not have a class structure the way you do in the West. What Sidney *really* said was, "He looks like a Chinese," and Johnny then replied, "And that's the way we'll treat him," meaning that you will be treated like one of us.' Ronnie spread his hands. 'See how easy it is to get the wrong end of the stick when you're not absolutely fluent in a foreign language?'

It was clever, very clever, and I almost believed Ronnie's off-the-cuff explanation, but more importantly I knew I must accept it. I grimaced. 'I asked you to be honest with me and you have been. Now, how do we go about this so that I don't have to eat crow?'

'Eat crow?'

I grinned, 'It's Australian for losing face.'

'You must stay here and I will fetch them and explain how the mistake was made and that you wish to most humbly apologise and appear genuinely contrite. Then we will all return together and mix with the staff, and Sidney will welcome you and tell the staff how fortunate we are to have you join the agency.'

'Simple as that – I just cop it sweet?'

'More Australian idioms?'

'Yes, it means I just have to accept what's coming to me, that I am going to lose face. Will that be enough?'

'I hope so. When aroused, my brother can be a vengeful bastard.'

'Okay, go ahead. I'll wait here and practise looking abject and truly humble.' I grinned. 'Oh, and by the way, I know I'm a dead ringer for a Chinese peasant.'

Ronnie turned and took a step towards the door, then he half-turned and gave me a serious look. Ignoring my self-deprecating attempt to lighten the mood, he said, 'I am confident you get the idea, so make it look good, Simon.'

'I'll try, mate, but I don't know if I'll ever understand your mob.'

'You won't, so don't try too hard. When in doubt, say nothing or ask me.'

'Yeah, that's what my mum says. I should have remembered.'

He paused, looking down at his shoes. 'Never trust a Chinese in business, not even me. Forget about such nice Christian concepts as conscience or guilt. Anything is permitted as long as you don't get caught or it directly compromises your *guanxi*.'

'Ronnie, why are you doing this? I mean helping me? For instance, how do you know *you* can trust *me*?'

'When I was no longer capable of standing after our tour of Bugis Street, you carried me to a taxi, took me home, put me to bed and haven't mentioned it since. You allowed me to save face.'

I laughed. 'Mate, you've got it wrong! I don't recall a thing about that day.'

He smiled. 'Stay there, I'll be back in fifteen minutes.'

Ronnie must have done a great job on his two elder brothers because when they returned Sidney smiled and Johnny almost did. Looking humble, eyes downcast, I explained my inadequacy with Cantonese and begged for their forgiveness, which was duly and seemingly generously granted. I promised fervently to become more proficient at the language.

'Now you are one of us,' Sidney said finally and then let out his girly giggle. Ronnie's previous warning about causing him to lose face meant that I'd probably not been forgiven, and I had a distinct feeling Sidney had made up his mind about me. Perhaps it was simply the position I was going to occupy in the agency that he disliked – making creative decisions where previously he had been the sole arbiter of everything.

Returning to the cocktail party, Sidney, with Johnny nodding all the while, dutifully jumped through the welcoming hoops, but the overall atmosphere in the hotel room remained edgy and tense, in particular when members of the staff were addressed by either of the two older brothers. It was fairly obvious that both Wings felt something verging on disdain for the general run of employees, who, not surprisingly, were extremely uneasy and overly attentive (we would say 'sycophantic') in their presence. I'm certain I wasn't the only person in the room who was hugely relieved when, at eight o'clock, this social misery was finally over.

Fortunately, I wasn't required to go to dinner with the Wings. I had, amazingly, delightfully, and at her suggestion, a dinner date with Mercy B. Lord. Under normal circumstances I would probably have gone back to the hotel to lick my wounds and attempt to assuage my mortification with a few beers, but I'd been looking forward to this dinner for the past two days. Her invitation had been delightfully couched. 'Simon, I have been to a Wing cocktail party. Ronnie works the crowd as best he can, but he can't compete with the deathly miasma produced by the other two brothers. You're going to need cheering up afterwards, and so I give you permission to take me to dinner. Besides, I have just had a new cheongsam made and I'm anxious to get your opinion on it.'

'My opinion?' I'd asked, surprised.

'Of course. You knew about Mary Quant and greatly surprised me by remarking on my Vidal Sassoon hairstyle. Not too many men could do that.'

She wasn't to know, but I'd learnt everything I knew from Sue Chipchase, who'd been an early adopter of the Mary Quant miniskirt – hardly surprising, with her legs. She wore her blonde hair in what she'd once described to me as the famous five-point geometric cut by Vidal Sassoon. I distinctly recall her casting scorn on the beehive fashion most of the bunnies had affected. 'It looks like a nice place for all sorts of nasties to live, darling,' she'd said in a very *Vogue* voice with one eyebrow arched.

In fact, Sue Chipchase and Mercy B. Lord could have been the Snow White and Rose Red of style, each with similar fashion sense, glorious legs and the same helmet-style haircut worn close to the head with five geometric points lying against their cheeks and necks, the pure gold Chipchase sheen replaced by the polished anthracite of Miss Mercy B. Lord. I asked myself whether I had fallen in love-lust with an oriental Chipchase, who, like the golden version, was also forbidden fruit.

And now this peach had asked me to invite her to dinner after what she correctly surmised would be a disastrous welcoming party – quite how disastrous I decided on my return to the hotel not to mention.

I was greatly looking forward to the dinner and even more so because she was allowing it to be my treat. I'd longed for just such an occasion but had been reluctant to ask. Mercy B. Lord was with me from 10 a.m. to 5 p.m. every day except Thursday, when she was needed in the office. The problem I faced was that I knew if I asked her to dinner she would be obliged to accept. Ronnie's cryptic warning and my own battered looks were both discouraging, but now, to my enormous delight, she'd taken the initiative. After ten days my bruised jaw had recovered, the cut to my neck had healed and only a smudge of purple and yellow showed below my eyebrow; I was almost back to being just plain old unprepossessing Simon, who, you will recall, was hardly God's gift to womankind.

'I insist on taking you to a posh restaurant where the Beatrice Fong Agency isn't owed squeeze,' I'd said at the time.

'I've picked the restaurant,' Mercy B. Lord replied, then grinned. 'Not a hint of squeeze in sight.'

'Good, but expensive, I trust.'

She laughed merrily. 'One goes there to be seen and that's always expensive.'

'Shall I pick you up or send a limo?' On the two or three occasions when we'd been out all day and I'd suggested I drop her home she'd refused, her excuse being that she needed to check in at the office.

'No, I'll meet you in reception at eight-thirty. We're dining at the Palm Court Grill.'

'But it is patronised mainly by Europeans . . .'

'Precisely,' she replied.

The Palm Court Grill was where overseas visitors staying at Raffles were able to repay some of the hospitality they'd received from their local hosts and was Singapore's most expensive eatery.

'Then allow me to send a limo to pick you up.'

'Already arranged.' She laughed. 'Squeeze. Big Black Buick.'

I arrived back at Raffles Hotel fifteen minutes late because Ronnie wanted me to cross the road to the agency and inspect the area intended for my office. It was two days before my two weeks with Mercy B. Lord were up and they'd only just marked the area out on the floor. 'Will it be ready in time?'

'Of course!' he'd replied, 'It'll only take a day to install – the top half is glass and the varnish on the wooden part will take perhaps another day to dry.' So much for the two weeks he'd originally required. It was also obvious that Sidney had chosen to spend the absolute minimum on what could be laughingly called an office. Certainly it was not one that would give the occupant any sense of importance or reflect his seniority. It was so small that it would need to be built around the desk – either that or the desk would have to be lowered over the wooden and glass partitions that were to form the walls. I couldn't complain. Ronnie sat in the open with the staff, and as a director and partner was in theory senior to me. But my American appointment carried with it unspoken but clear seniority, especially regarding decisions about creative product for foreign clients or those gained through business submissions initiated by Dansford Drocker or myself.

Mercy B. Lord was seated in a large peacock-tail wicker chair, one beautiful leg stretched deliciously and provocatively from the black silk cheongsam, when I arrived. Now, I'd like to hear a convincing argument for why a full-length, black, figure-hugging, mandarin-collared cheongsam split halfway up the thigh on a beautiful woman in stilettos isn't the single most sexy way imaginable to present the female body. Almost everything except the elegance of bared arms and the occasional flash of leg is hidden from the eye, yet the promise of what lies beneath this glorious casing is enough to send any red-blooded male crazy.

I felt that this was simply the most beautiful visual and emotional experience I would ever have. I know that's saying a lot – the world is full of beautiful women, and what we see often belies what lies within. Beauty may only be skin-deep, but superficial as it often is, it can be a shattering experience, a single moment or event so powerfully fixed in our subconscious that the edges never blur and the image never fades. I promise you that, on my deathbed, when I review for the last time the sights and sounds, the places I've been and races I've seen, people I've known and things I've been shown, when the grand kaleidoscope of everything I've done passes through my mind's eye and I'm about to step off this mortal coil, Mercy B. Lord in a black cheongsam will be there at the forefront of my visual memory.

She rose as I approached and unconsciously assumed a graceful pose, her weight on one hip, the exposed leg in high heels slightly forward, her right hand holding a small black-velvet evening bag that accentuated her long crimson nails. Most cheongsam carry some embroidered motif, a bright spray of flowers or a golden dragon design, on the front, but hers, apart from what appeared to be a tiny gold toggle that closed the mandarin collar, was completely without any such artifice, her own superb figure all the decoration one could possibly require. The simplicity added to her elegance.

'Holy macaroni!' I exclaimed. 'Is this all for me?'

'Count yourself lucky, Mr Koo. I've been here half an hour and have been propositioned four times.'

'I'm not surprised. You look simply amazing. Too wonderful for words.'

'Thank you.' She laughed happily.

'I apologise for being late. Ronnie Wing wanted to show me what is laughingly known as my future office. I've been inside bigger domestic toilets. Shall we have a drink at the bar?'

I moved closer to take her arm then saw it. I couldn't quite believe my eyes. The mandarin collar of the beautiful gown had a dragon motif embroidered around it, also in black – in effect, black on black. The tiny gold toggle looked like a gold chisel embedded in the dragon's body. It was Little Sparrow's dream made flesh.

'No, if you don't mind, let's go straight in,' Mercy B. Lord urged as I dragged my eyes away from that golden shaft. 'The restaurant is full and I've booked for eight-thirty, the only time I could get. The booking clerk let me know he was doing me a favour fitting us in and somewhat sternly cautioned me about being late. I'm afraid it isn't the greatest table, Simon. This is Raffles, after all – snooty and still very British.' She smiled. 'Besides, if we go to the bar they'll think the fifth proposition, from one Simon Koo, was an offer too good for me to refuse.'

'I'm delighted to be the one you've accepted,' I joked as she took my arm and we made our way to the restaurant.

'Don't think I wasn't tempted,' she teased as we walked. 'The first was a Frenchman, who said with an exquisite accent and manners that he was dining alone and would I care to join him. Then I had two separate Americans, both of whom invited me for a drink, and then a German, who came right out and asked me how much.'

'The first three were easy but what did you say to the crass Kraut?'

Mercy B. Lord laughed. 'I told him he couldn't afford me.'

'Good answer.'

'No, he then said, "Try me."'

'Oh, that's tricky.'

'I named an outrageous sum, five thousand dollars, then just for fun added, "US, of course."'

I laughed. 'And?'

Mercy B. Lord giggled. '"Is that for a short time or for the whole night?" he asked.'

'A German with a sense of humour – how unusual.'

'Oh? You don't think I'm worth five thousand US dollars, Simon?'

'Sweetheart, you're priceless,' I answered, feeling myself colouring.

'Well, of course I'm not. We have three of Singapore's most expensive, experienced and desirable *ah ku* on the Beatrice Fong Agency books and they charge US$250 for the night. Five thousand would buy one of them for weeks. He, the German, said that if I agreed to meet him tomorrow night he'd have the money.'

It was an awkward moment. I mean, what does one say? But for once in my life I got it right and sidestepped more or less neatly. 'Mercy B. Lord, let me tell you, the German is right in only one respect – you are simply the most beautiful woman I have ever seen and probably ever will see, but your value cannot possibly be estimated in mere dollars.'

'Thank you, Simon, you're sweet.'

She wore nothing other than the cheongsam and black high-heel courts, not a single piece of jewellery. Chairman Meow possessed a diamond choker and pendant earrings, the choker half an inch wide with God knows how many carats in the set. I tried to imagine it and the earrings on Mercy B. Lord. Why do diamonds so often end up displayed on necks and ears, wrists and fingers that are past their best? My dad once told me that young women should be given diamonds and older women should be told often that they are loved. But glitter can add little to perfection, and as we reached the restaurant door, I knew I was escorting a woman very close to perfection.

But I was entirely unprepared for the effect our entrance had on the busy restaurant. In seconds it went from babble to silence. Then an elegant-looking European woman who looked to be in her sixties, wearing a pearl-coloured satin evening gown and a diamond necklace that appeared to contain half the annual produce of an African diamond mine, started to clap, the sound sharp in the silent restaurant. Then a stout bloke, a whisky-nosed, sanguine Colonel Blimp type, scraped back his chair and stood. Holding up his glass, he called out, 'Bravo!'

I can only assume the almost exclusively European diners must have thought Mercy B. Lord was an Asian film star because all the men then stood, most of them holding up their wine glasses. When the clapping ceased, a distinctly Australian voice from the far end of the restaurant shouted out, 'You lucky bastard!' He was probably pissed, but this brought a sudden gale of appreciative laughter.

All I could do was to try to control an inane grin. Had I been Noël Coward, or someone like him, I'd have said something people would have remembered for years. Mercy B. Lord clung to my arm and managed somehow to smile brilliantly, hopefully giving the impression that we were an item, even lovers, although I could feel her entire body trembling against mine.

The maître d' now started to fuss – he was obviously surprised at the reception and thought he'd been caught napping and should have known who we were. 'A very nice table has just become available, sir, madam.' He glanced down at his booking list. 'Mr Koo, may I offer you both a glass of champagne?'

'Thank you,' I said, while Mercy B. Lord gave him the courtesy of another brilliant smile.

Seated with a glass of French champagne, I raised it. 'Well, here's to a black cheongsam on a beautiful woman,' I said.

'Phew! I had no idea it would cause such a disturbance. I'm very sorry if I embarrassed you, Simon.'

'I was mortified,' I teased. 'But I'll manage to live it down . . . eventually. But, of course, you understand, I've lost a great deal of face.'

'I'll make it up to you, I promise,' she said, half-seriously.

I lifted my champagne glass again. 'Mercy B. Lord, your entrance will go down as one of the best moments of my life, and as for you, it's a long way from the orphanage, kid.'

We clinked our champagne glasses, but she said only 'Hmm', then brought her glass to her lips. The little rich boy had got it wrong again. I guess it's never a long way from the orphanage.

'I can't believe it's almost two weeks since I arrived. I'm going to miss you as my daily companion more than I can say.' The idea of not having Mercy B. Lord in my life each day, looking morning fresh and beautiful, waiting for me in the tea-house, didn't bear thinking about.

'I have good news,' she said, neatly avoiding a mawkish moment.

'Uh-huh? Tell me.'

'I think I've found your flat. Exactly what we've been looking for. It will give you great prestige.'

I couldn't help reacting to the 'we', even though I knew she had no intention of moving in with me. No chance of that happening. But apart from a spare room with good light where I could paint, I hadn't a clue what I wanted and so I'd simply given her my painting-room brief and then said she must find something unfurnished she'd personally love to live in.

The flat above the garage at home had been designed by my mum, with the exception of the room in which I painted, and seemed to have everything I needed with none of the gold taps, Persian rugs, French antiques, Chippendale furniture, and the rest of the conspicuous crap that filled the big house.

While I knew a bit about antiques and enjoyed discovering their history, I had no desire to surround myself with them. I suppose I wasn't really into things; I liked to look at them and think about their past but I didn't need to own them to enjoy them. Browsing through an antique shop was a pleasant pastime but didn't leave me lusting after any of the items. By asking Mercy B. Lord to find me an unfurnished flat, I was trying to keep my surroundings simple, comfortable and welcoming, but not much more.

'If you like it, that'll do me fine, as long as it has a view,' I'd concluded.

My mum's Singapore family had done their homework and my rental allowance was extremely generous. This meant Mercy B. Lord had a bit of scope. She assured me there was quite a lot of good rental real estate within my price bracket. I knew I'd end up with more than I needed, a pad that made me seem more important than I really was, but what the hell. This was how things worked in the East – you were what you seemed to be and were accepted at face value. Perhaps that's where the expression originated. Face had to be constantly maintained; it had to be a major preoccupation.

'Can we have a house-warming party after I've moved in? I need to invite my relatives, my mum's people. If we include the kids, there could be about twenty altogether.'

Mercy looked thoughtful, so I took a deep breath and said, 'You wouldn't consider being the hostess, would you?' Then I added quickly, 'Just that, no suggestion of anything else, just . . . well, I don't think I could organise something like that. We could have it catered for, hire maids, a waiter, whatever it takes, I could book it through your agency, if you wish . . .' I was babbling.

Mercy B. Lord sidestepped this neatly. 'It would be cheaper and better if you went to a restaurant, Simon.'

'But doesn't that, you know, defeat the purpose? House-warming, new flat and all that?'

'No, no, not at all! The outside is what matters.'

'Outside?'

'Where it is, the location, street, the building. The rest must be private.'

'Why would that be?'

'Face.'

'You know, Mercy B. Lord, I have been here less than two weeks and already I'm sick and tired of bloody face.'

'Then you must go back to Australia at once, Simon,' she said simply. 'It is not usual to be invited into a Chinese home unless you want to impress someone who you definitely know has less wealth than you.'

'By "outside" do you mean splashing fountains, peacocks in the gardens, carp in the pond, that sort of thing?'

She nodded. 'You see, people are afraid you may be critical of the *kampong* where they live, the look of the street, the house, the building. You may discover that they're not as wealthy as they wish to appear and so they lose a great deal of face. That is why you will always be invited to a restaurant. In that way people can gain face by the choice of the place or the expense of the meal. They will often spend much more than they can afford, even put themselves into debt to do this.' She smiled. 'If you want to know where you stand in someone's estimation, check the prices on the menu of the restaurant they select. But, of course, there won't be a menu on the night, because it will be a banquet. You can tell from the number and quality of dishes what your standing is and how they hope to influence your opinion of their own status.'

'You mean if I invite someone home – my relatives, for instance – they'll think I'm rubbing their noses in my good fortune?'

'Certainly, especially those who are less fortunate than you.'

'And those who are more fortunate?'

She laughed. 'The Chinese are very careful to make sure you don't lose face but equally careful that you don't gain it at their expense. If you gain, then they may lose. It is essential that people be left to imagine your wealth, status and good fortune. Later they will sort things out, but initially I recommend the neutrality of a good restaurant and a truly splendid banquet.'

'Okay, I give you permission to pick a restaurant where the squeeze factor benefits you personally.'

Mercy B. Lord said seriously, 'I will book you a good restaurant and be your hostess,' then she smiled. 'And thank you, Simon, I am honoured.'

There wasn't much more to say. It explained why, on my third night in town, I had been the guest of my mother's cousin and the rest of my Singapore relations at an elaborate banquet held in a posh Chinese restaurant.

'Did you tell them we'd take it, the flat?' I now asked.

'No, no, you must see it first, I insist. I think you will like it. You will gain face,' she said again, happy for me.

'Please, not that word again. And it's unfurnished and within my budget?'

'Well, it's furnished at the moment, but the owner is happy to remove the furniture. And yes, of course, I have kept it within your rental allowance. But if you like it, and since you want it unfurnished, I will bargain for a better deal.'

'I'm quite sure I'll like it. Phone them in the morning and tell them it's a deal.'

Mercy B. Lord hesitated. 'No, Simon, I cannot accept that responsibility. You *must* see it first.'

'Right, Miss Lord,' I laughed, saluting her. 'Then as soon as you can arrange it.'

In the two weeks I was with Mercy B. Lord I had learned that she wasn't simply a walking Singapore encyclopaedia, capable, beautiful and excellent company. She had a mind and a will of her own. She was not unlike a young version of Chairman Meow, and perhaps this was why I was tentative. I sensed Mercy B. Lord had a side to her I didn't wish to animate.

It is often said that men fall in love with versions of their mother, but the thought that this might be true didn't occur to me at the time. Nor did I realise that Mercy may have banked on the spontaneous reception we'd received as we'd entered the restaurant. She may well have selected the Palm Court Grill because it was almost entirely patronised by foreigners where she knew she would be noticed in her new gear, whereas a roomful of Chinese male diners may have admired her looks but were less likely to react publicly. In the course of business Mercy B. Lord had been in the company of many foreigners, most of them men in senior positions who wouldn't have been backward in remarking on her looks. She undoubtedly knew she was attractive to men, even sexy, but she carried this knowledge with modesty and a sense of decorum. It was only natural that, once in a while, like many beautiful women, she felt the need to strut her stuff. And while she'd rejected the guys who had approached her in the hotel foyer, she had nonetheless seemed to enjoy the experience and felt quite comfortable telling me about these encounters, almost as if she was prompting me to react. She was as far from a cockteaser as you could get, but she was a beautiful woman who, on this occasion, was flirting with me. I told myself it was nothing, the new gown, looking gorgeous, the unacknowledged need to be admired. After all, given my looks, I was the perfect foil for her beauty. Yet I'd felt her tremble at the reception we received as we entered. Now I asked myself, was it nervous tension or the excitement of having triumphed? For a woman with no family or normal social support, her looks were all the power she possessed.

The session in Sidney's office had affected me. My own mother was Chinese, yet my chances of understanding the complexities of her race seemed remote. Those generations of isolation from Chinese culture, not to mention the influence of my occidental ancestors and compatriots, had reprogrammed my mind and decidedly altered my genes. All I felt was a sense of alienation. Curiously, my unprepossessing appearance didn't seem to ruin my chances with women, where I was as successful as most of my mates at bunny-hopping. In other words, in the glorious early years of the pill, I got my fair share. For the first time, women were sexually liberated and could decide to go to bed with you without fear of pregnancy, which had often surfaced in the sober morning light. But now, in Singapore, where I more or less blended naturally with the surrounding populace, I was overcome with apprehension. Ronnie's warning had certainly contributed to my caution, but I knew that even without it, I might still have found myself inhibited by my looks, telling myself that I was unworthy of her, the one woman I longed for more than any other woman I had ever met.

I was besotted with Mercy B. Lord and spent nights alone in my hotel room trying to unravel her personality, figuring her out, trying to analyse what it was that made her tick. She had been raised a Catholic but within the local community, and was therefore potentially a bridge between the Christian and Buddhist–Taoist cultures. She'd told me more than once that she was constantly aware of the misfortune of her Sino-Japanese blood. All these things must have contributed to who she was. I wondered if I had fallen in love with someone psychologically stuck between cultures, with the need to keep her Japanese heritage secret. I had yet to discover which influence – the Catholic, Japanese, Chinese or Peranakan – was dominant in her.

Now, in the restaurant, tormented by jealousy, I fretted about the German who was willing to buy what he wanted. Surely Mercy would not consider such an exchange? But then, I asked myself, was she the good Catholic she seemed, full of the moral rectitude firmly inculcated in her by the nuns? Or would Chinese pragmatism and yearning for wealth persuade her to take up the German's proposed assignation the following night? Five grand American was probably close to six months' salary in her present position, a temptation that might require a fair dollop of Christian ethics to overcome. Counting rosary beads and saying several hundred Hail Marys might seem a small price to pay for such a highly profitable night.

Our reception, rather *her* reception, when we'd entered the Palm Court Grill proved that she was a bombshell, beautiful, sexy and desirable to every man in the room who would, like me, fantasise about her in bed that night. Perhaps the handsome *grande dame* in the diamond necklace would also do so – you never knew with the upper class. I even conjured up the image of a fat Kraut, now definitely ex-Hitler youth turned rich industrialist, masturbating in the shower in anticipation of tomorrow night with Mercy B. Lord – a disgusting and unworthy thought but nevertheless ashamedly mine.

These were my confused and not very pleasant musings in the salubrious surroundings of the Palm Court Grill as I ate grilled lobster tail in a ginger, chive, garlic and butter sauce and shared a bottle of champagne with this astonishingly beautiful and charming young woman whose motives or morals I had not the slightest reason to doubt. Moreover, I told myself she was her own woman and free to do anything she wished and I was simply one of the many foreign escorts with whom she would have dined. I knew almost nothing about her personal life and it had been strongly suggested by Ronnie that I not attempt to pry into it.

Although she was being paid to chaperone me for two weeks, I still felt I owed her much more than a posh meal to thank her for the fortune fortnight she'd given me. She had gone out of her way to show me every aspect of life in Singapore, unpeeling each social layer so that I had, if not an expert's knowledge, at least a working one of how it functioned and what I would need to know if ever I was to appeal to the hearts and minds of the various segments of society likely to use consumer products. For example, I knew that Dansford Drocker was to bring with him an international soap-powder brand as a new account, which he would personally supervise. Thinking I would get a head start, I'd asked Mercy, 'What brand of washing powder do people most commonly use in their machines in Singapore?'

'It's a local brand called Hands On,' she said, deadpan.

Trying to be funny, I said, 'Shouldn't that be "Hands Off"?'

She burst out laughing, but not at my joke. 'Oh, Simon, the average wash is done by hand, fingers and knuckles against a washboard. Most people can only dream of owning a washing machine.'

So as you can see, there was a whole heap I had to learn not only about Mercy B. Lord, but also about my market. Fortunately, I had impressed her with my enthusiasm.

'It's as if you're *really* interested, Simon. I like that. I like that a lot,' she'd admitted. 'Most of my foreign clients are only interested in what they can take from Singapore, and haven't the slightest interest in the locals, whom they see as merely factory fodder, cheap labour. It's funny how the poor are not expected to have brains, hearts, feelings or sensitivity, only arms, legs and strong backs, and ears only for receiving instructions.'

We'd been everywhere, from the obscenely rich streets with unbelievable displays of pure ostentation to the poorest *kampongs* with rutted, muddy and puddled dirt roads; chooks; ribbed, flea-bitten, mangy mongrel dogs; garbage; and the pervading stench of garlic, rancid cooking oil, open drains and sewage. Mercy B. Lord told me I was fortunate to have missed the season for durian, a delicious-tasting fruit much favoured by the locals with a smell like a bad latrine that pervaded the island's atmosphere. We'd been up the river in a dinghy equipped with an outboard belching smoke and out to sea on ferries to some of the surrounding islands, big and small – Pedra Branca, Pulau Ubin and Sentosa among others. We'd eaten well: satay from bicycle carts or street stalls and countless delicacies in holes in the wall where we were served food of incredible variety – Malay, Indonesian, Chinese, Indian and a mixture of every one of these cuisines, hot, spicy and invariably delicious.

We'd met hundreds of people, some of whom spoke Cantonese or Hokkien, though most of the poorer people seemed to speak either Malay or Indonesian. The local Indians spoke either Hindi or Tamil, and in all cases Mercy B. Lord acted as interpreter. Children, emboldened by my smile and the gift of a lolly, would take me by the hand and turn it over and examine my palm. 'They say they know you're a foreigner even though you look like a Chinese because the palm of your hand is pink,' she'd explained on one occasion.

I'd asked her what she thought of the present one-party government and she'd hesitated for a moment and then said quietly, 'It is not a subject I can discuss, Simon.' Then she'd added, 'For the poor, food on the table and a regular wage is more important than the freedoms permitted in a democracy where they starve.' In all other things she had been entirely open, as well as a constant, courteous and utterly professional companion and guide.

But the sum total of Mercy B. Lord was more than all her parts. I longed for every bit of her, on almost any terms, although I couldn't think of any terms – emotional or otherwise – I had the right or the courage to put to her. I was like a child taken into a lolly shop with money in his pocket but with his hands tied behind his back and his mouth taped. Ronnie's warning produced fanciful explanations as I lay in bed at night in my hotel room conjuring up a rich and powerful Chinese 'Ming the Merciless' billionaire who, for some reason or another, couldn't openly accept her as his concubine but to whom she was beholden because of some kind of nefarious blackmail. My febrile imagination even considered the word 'enslaved'. Or perhaps some all-powerful politician leading an outwardly blameless life kept Mercy B. Lord tucked away for his private delectation.

My addled mind was an indication of the emotional mess I was becoming. In an effort to put myself out of my misery, I'd asked Ronnie to tell me more, to explain why Mercy B. Lord was untouchable. 'Is it simply professional? Is it her job with the Beatrice Fong Agency, or what?' I'd demanded.

His reply rocked me back on my feet. 'Simon, I beg you, don't take it any further. I can't and I won't tell you more, other than to say that the formidable Beatrice Fong has powerful connections, *guanxi*. You sleep with Mercy B. Lord – that is even if she would consider you – and they'll throw you out of this country so fast you won't even bounce. Forget her – she's out of bounds.'

I had mixed feelings about the fact that Mercy B. Lord had polished off half a bottle of French champagne as well as the complimentary glass and still seemed perfectly in control. It was a vastly more expensive leg-opener than the legendary Australian Porphyry Pearl. While I hadn't intended the bottle of champagne to be a means of seduction, I was nevertheless impressed by her demeanour; outwardly nothing appeared to have altered; she was flirtatious and engaging, amusing and considerate of my gastronomic needs, but no more so than when we'd first been seated. My admiration for her expanded commensurably.

I'd passed the Ronnie grog test on our trial client-entertainment night in Bugis Street, but the hangover I experienced the next morning would, had I shared it equally amongst my premiership-winning Sydney university rugby team, have left them in a parlous state. I vowed never again. I'd made my statement, earned my stripes, and in future it would be a few beers of any brand Ronnie cared to nominate, as long as they were cold. Ronnie could hold his booze, and so it seemed could Mercy B. Lord, and I guess, at great cost to my wellbeing, could I. Five glasses of champagne would have seen most bunnies well on their way to an indiscretion, although I sensed no loosening of any moral resolve Mercy B. Lord may have brought to the evening.

I could feel the warm glow of the champagne, the first small signs of impending inebriation. Not reckless abandon by any means, but certainly a lessening of inhibitions. *Be careful, mate,* the voice within my head cautioned. But if Mercy B. Lord felt any such inner glow, she showed no outward signs of it and seemed to be functioning perfectly normally.

We completed the meal with very 'English' fresh strawberries and cream, a pot of fragrant jasmine tea for Mercy B. Lord and coffee and Drambuie for me. She excused herself to go to the ladies and I sat dreading the moment when she must leave me. If only I smoked I could have lit up a good Havana cigar and appeared to any casual observers to be completely at ease, taking my beautiful escort for granted as I blew the aromatic Cuban smoke into the air above my head.

Mercy B. Lord returned, struggling to suppress a giggle. 'Lady Townsend invited me to afternoon tea tomorrow,' she laughed. Looking up at me wide-eyed, she said, 'It was rather disconcerting. She said that she'd like to get to know me.'

'Lady Townsend?'

'Yes, the lady with the diamond necklace who clapped when we entered.'

My mind immediately leapt to an outrageous conclusion: another Mercy B. Lord assignation. Holy shit! Things were rapidly getting out of hand – in my overheated imagination, at least. Fortuitously, my flat, bland peasant face is good at concealing emotion. 'Well, I guess the meaning of that sentence very much depends on inflection,' I grinned.

'Oh, I'm glad you said that, Simon. I thought it might just be my imagination. Anyway, I told her I was unavailable tomorrow.'

'And she said . . . ?'

'She handed me her card. "Do call me soon," she said, "I'm sure I can be helpful," then she added, "Your beauty deserves to be enhanced with diamonds, a subject I know rather well, my dear. But not gold, gold is for when, alas, your skin is somewhat older." Whatever do you think she meant, Simon?'

I shrugged. 'Who can say?' The evening was effectively over; it was big black Buick time. 'Your driver will be waiting,' I said. 'May I escort you to your limousine, mademoiselle?'

'Oh no, we're taking a taxi, Simon.'

'We?'

'Yes, tomorrow is Thursday, so I can't show you the flat, can I?' She opened the velvet purse and, reaching into it, produced a set of keys. 'I have the keys so why don't I show you tonight?' She hesitated. 'Unless you'd rather not, of course . . .'

I swallowed hard. 'Great idea. I'll get the maître d' to call a cab.'

By the time the taxi dropped us at a location beside the river I was a mess. Just the thought of being alone with Mercy B. Lord – I mean completely alone at night in a private place where no other person could possibly know we were together – was both tremendously exhilarating and bloody scary. I told myself this was no different from coaxing a bunny to bed, something I'd done several times. You ended up somewhere – her place, yours, an anonymous hotel room – but somewhere private, anyway . . . What was the difference?

The difference was that Mercy B. Lord was no bunny and, according to Ronnie, had powerful connections. If we began a relationship and it was discovered, I would be kicked out of Singapore 'so fast you won't even bounce', as he'd put it. Beatrice Fong and Sidney Wing, her boss and my boss, were both somehow implicated in the mystery, and were no doubt friends or more likely shared *guanxi*. Beatrice was powerfully connected and influential and also, for some reason, guardian of Mercy B. Lord's love life, which was a conundrum that ended with the word 'forbidden' no matter which way you looked at it. It was, I told myself, reason enough to be very careful indeed.

'It is a short walk from here, Simon, perhaps half a mile. In this way even the taxi driver won't know the location.'

I didn't ask her why she thought to take such a precaution. 'A walk would be nice – the river, a little fresh air – great. Look, it's a three-quarter moon and light enough to see the neighbourhood. Very clever of you to arrange the moonlight,' I smiled. 'But why don't you go barefoot? Half a mile in six-inch heels on a tarred road isn't going to be much fun.' I paused. 'You can see where you're going, and you can wash your feet at the flat.'

'My God, a man who understands.' She stopped and kissed me lightly on the cheek. 'Thank you, Simon.' Then, holding onto my arm for balance, she removed her shoes.

'Here – let me carry them,' I offered.

'Ah, the tar is still warm,' she murmured, handing me her shoes. 'Oh dear, what a lovely relief!' Then she took my arm and pecked me on the cheek again. 'Thank you, you're a very sweet man, Simon,' she said softly.

How can a peck so soft it barely brushes the skin leave your heart pounding like a schoolboy's? And why does the word 'sweet', an indication of nothing beyond simple gratitude, create such a flare of hope? It might even have been a gentle and courteous deterrent, a premature warning. *Ferchrissake* – I was twenty-nine years old! I had lost my virginity at twenty, at a time when girls had to be careful about going 'the whole way'. But a few years later, with the emancipation brought by the pill, they had been generous with their favours and I wasn't exactly a novice. Even so, I was no Don Juan, but I genuinely loved women. I mean, I loved the gender, not simply as sex objects but for their complex, funny, caring, wild, generous, intelligent, unpredictable, raunchy, loving, gossiping and even sometimes bitchy natures. I loved the way they smelled, the make-up they used, their skin, hair, everything. But I also loved to make love and never thought, as some guys did, that I'd conquered them in some sort of primordial battle, or that the morning after they became the sexual equivalent of a notch in your rifle butt or a casual boast in the pub.

Making love was a mutual joy, or so it seemed to me. I'm not suggesting I was a good lover, but I liked to think I was better, perhaps more caring, than average, and those bunnies who chose to sleep with me, I'm happy to say, would invariably do so more than once and seemed to enjoy the way they were treated. Mornings after were nice, too: coffee and toast, freshly squeezed orange juice in the kitchen, the girl perched on my kitchen stool after a shower with a towel wrapped like a maharajah's turban around her head and wearing my dressing-gown, listening to the radio . . .

But this time I had no idea what the next step might be. Mercy B. Lord, apart from being extraordinarily pleasant, helpful, patient with my ignorance and always obliging, had never given me a reason to feel that she was physically attracted to me. Perhaps because she had grown up in an orphanage, she didn't touch spontaneously as most women do, and I sensed a reserve, a no-go zone she had marked out. I asked myself what the invitation to inspect the flat could mean. Was it simply because tomorrow was Thursday and she was not available, that my time with her was running short and we needed to make a decision? Or had she planned it for when she was at her most ravishing?

Anyway, at last the champagne seemed to kick in, and Mercy B. Lord became delightfully animated on the walk, often running a few steps ahead like a child, turning to point something out – the moon reflected on the surface of the river, an elaborate wrought-iron gate painted gold, a red post box with the royal coat of arms, a lingering reminder of the colonial past. We talked nostalgically in a light-hearted way of the past week or so and reminded each other of some of the things we'd seen or enjoyed. She teased me about my silly washing-machine question, then noted that the flat didn't have a washing machine. Hire a maid to do the cleaning, washing and ironing, she advised. 'She gets a job and a wage and, besides, a couple of years' wages won't cost you a lot more than a washing machine, a dryer and a vacuum cleaner,' she explained.

With about a hundred yards to go she pointed out a new-looking multi-storeyed apartment block, imposing only in the sense that the houses surrounding it were traditional Singapore bungalows. High-rise architecture in the mid-sixties still suffered from post-war pragmatism, even though there was no longer a shortage of building materials. Multi-storeyed buildings were square blocks of concrete that made very little attempt to look good, except perhaps for a bit of moulded cement tizz around the window frames and an imposing front door that distinguished them only slightly from a 1950s municipal housing block. The heavy hand of government pragmatism in town planning was everywhere and size was thought to give sufficient prestige. In Singapore at that time, location was the most important factor.

Mercy B. Lord pointed upwards. 'See the bigger windows? That's the penthouse, that's the one. Your painting room has a view across the river and you can see across the harbour and out to sea.'

'Looks great.'

I was even more impressed once I was inside the flat. The large windows had shutters to keep out the heat and ceiling fans everywhere, and while it was furnished in an over-elaborate Chinese style, this turned out to be purely for display purposes. The penthouse was brand-new.

'I think it will make a nice home for you, Simon.' Mercy B. Lord then proceeded to show me around, turning on and testing every tap, even the shower, and every light, including the bedside lamps. 'See, everything works!' she exclaimed. Then she jumped impulsively onto the double bed, bouncing several times on her knees at the centre of the elaborately embroidered multi-coloured floral silk bedspread. 'What do you think?' she cried. Then, before I could answer, she fell backwards so that she now lay at the centre of the bed, her hands behind her head, grinning happily.

'Think? I think you are the most beautiful woman in dirty bare feet I have ever seen, Miss Mercy B. Lord.'

She shot bolt upright. 'Oh my God! I'm so sorry, Simon. I've shown you over the flat in my bare feet. I have been too familiar. I must wash my feet and put on my shoes!'

'Whoa! That's not what I meant. Now, as you were, please, I have something to say.'

'But still, it is not right, not professional.'

'Oh dear, I shall have to report you to Miss Beatrice Fong.' I grinned.

It was a clumsy mistake. At the mention of her employer's name, Mercy B. Lord looked up sharply then immediately down at her hands folded in her lap. She remained seated in the centre of the bed with her feet now tucked under her. 'What is it, Simon?' she said quietly. It was one of those images you snap and have forever in your mind; the soft light from the bedside lamp gleaming on a beautiful woman in a black cheongsam sitting on a brilliantly coloured bed of flowers.

I sat on the edge of the bed, trying to seem casual, looking directly at her and attempting to keep my voice calm, the beginning of a grin on my face that would either widen with acceptance or disappear with rejection. 'Mercy B. Lord, I'm awfully afraid I've fallen head over heels in love with you.'

She remained silent, eyes downcast, then slowly looked up. 'You are not like the others, Simon. They all try; most expect I will, that it is part of my job. I have not felt that with you; you are different.' She paused. 'This is very dangerous, because I feel the same way and know I must not – cannot.'

'But why?' I asked. 'Is there someone else?'

'No, no.'

'Then?'

Mercy B. Lord's dark eyes welled with tears and I thought for a moment she was going to cry in earnest. 'I cannot say,' she whispered. Then, brushing away her tears, she said, 'Simon, if you wish you can kiss me, but that is all. You *must* promise.'

'Forever?'

'I cannot say,' she repeated. Then she moved towards me and I took her in my arms.

Oh God, I couldn't bear it if this is all it is ever going to be. I held her tight, wanting to be able to recall the feeling of her body against mine. 'I promise,' I said, then lowered my head to kiss her.

The thought of possibly not seeing her again was too awful to contemplate, and as she was preparing to leave and I was about to accompany her downstairs to see her into a taxi, I said, 'Mercy B. Lord, I am regarded as a passably good painter. Would you allow me to do your portrait? Sit for me? Just the way you are tonight?'

She smiled. 'Simon, I'd like that. I'd be honoured.'

CHAPTER SIX

———

AND SO TO THE arrival of Dansford Drocker, chief executive and senior vice president, or managing director as the position was called in Singapore and Australia. While my office was the size of an expanded foot locker, his was considerably larger, but still only half the size of Sidney Wing's.

It was just as well I met him at the airport with Mercy B. Lord because he was clearly drunk, although admittedly still pleasant and not slurring his words or falling over. It was fortunate that Sidney, no doubt using his considerable *guanxi*, had organised for Dansford to pass through the airport without any of the usual checks and paperwork. His passport had been taken by an airline official as they landed and was returned to him as he entered the airport building. By some mysterious Chinese sleight of hand his luggage appeared on the baggage carousel before anyone else's, and in no time flat we had him walking towards the parking lot. Fortuitously, the exceedingly long flight from New York via Los Angeles and Honolulu landed mid-afternoon, and the plan was to take him directly to Raffles, where he could bunk down early for a good night's sleep.

It was apparent at once that he was a nice guy. The first thing he said after shaking our hands in the arrivals area was, 'I would take it most kindly if you folks always address me as Dansford.'

As we were walking to the Buick he looked around vaguely and said, 'Hey, what's the smell?'

'It's the smell of Singapore,' I explained. 'Very distinctive.'

'It's mostly rancid cooking oil, smoke and the open drains in some of the outlying *kampongs*. Add the tropical heat, rotting vegetation, mildew and, of course, the polluted river and it's . . . Well, as Simon says, it's distinctive,' Mercy B. Lord added, cleverly establishing her authority as his guide, if not at the same time enhancing his opinion of the city.

Dansford grinned. 'It isn't the way they described it to me in the States, honey. Tropical paradise, palm-fringed beaches . . . I guess you get the picture.' He fanned the air in front of his nose and declared, 'I think I need a drink. What's the time here in Singapore?'

I glanced at my watch as we reached the car. The driver, Mohammed, a short, fat Malay, stood with the back door open. 'Just after three-thirty.'

Dansford's expression brightened. 'Say, that's practically the cocktail hour, Simon. It would give me great pleasure to buy you both a martini.' He turned to face the airport building. 'Is there a bar here at the airport?'

Quick as a flash, Mercy B. Lord said, 'The martinis are famous at the Long Bar at Raffles, sir.'

Good girl! It would get us away from the airport, linked forever in my mind to my dramatic loss of face. The last thing we needed after my own pathetic entrance into the country was a drunken public scene with the new chief executive of Samuel Oswald Wing Asia, who'd been extended every courtesy and privilege on arriving. I decided I would encourage Mercy B. Lord to go home and I would stay with Dansford Drocker, fervently hoping that the flight from LA had taken its toll and he'd opt for an early night.

If you live with an alcoholic all your life, as I had with my dad, you develop an instinct for spotting other alcoholics. I knew within minutes of meeting him that Drocker had a drinking problem and that his grog-laden breath wasn't simply a case of one or two too many to kill the boredom of a long plane trip. He held himself together well, as my father usually did, with a particular deportment that's easy to recognise but difficult to describe: it has a rigidity and deliberateness that's unmistakeable to the practised eye. My father, who had remarkably few illusions about his fondness for the bottle, referred to himself as a practised drunk. This is what I saw in Dansford Drocker and my heart sank. My first three months going it alone against the Wing brothers had been tough. In my mind I'd already imagined us as collaborators – Dansford Drocker and Simon Koo ranged against the Three Wing Circus. Of all the things I didn't need, it was a lush to partner me in the boardroom.

We were to learn that Drocker's drinking problem needed constant attention from noon onwards. He attended to it diligently by never returning from lunch. In fact he would become the Singaporean version of a legend in his own lunchtime. If ever there was a match of environment to man, it was Dansford Drocker and the mysterious, accommodating and indulgent East.

But I'm getting ahead of myself.

After visiting the agency the morning after his arrival to meet the three Wings, he was, as I had been, handed over to the care of Mercy B. Lord. They had spent the first day together, or rather the two hours left of the morning, looking for an apartment, but Dansford Drocker was indifferent to his future residence and more interested in returning to Raffles for a pre-luncheon drink. Fortunately, Mercy B. Lord had tossed up between two penthouses for me, and now she showed him the second. They'd spent a cursory five minutes looking at it before he told her he'd take it. 'Go ahead and furnish it, honey, and send the bill to Mr Wing at the agency.' Then Dansford changed tack and asked, 'When do the bars open?'

She'd called me at the agency, explaining what had happened then saying anxiously, 'Simon, I know nothing about him. How can I choose his furniture?'

'Well, my guess is he's an alcoholic, or giving a damn good imitation of one. When you left us – after we'd returned from the airport – he drank solidly till one in the morning, when he finally toppled over. God knows how much he consumed on the plane, but he had at least nine hours of steady drinking. When he finally passed out I had to carry him upstairs to bed from the Long Bar.' I laughed. 'I hoicked him up over my shoulder, but his hands were almost dragging on the floor behind me and his toes were dangling above the carpet in front of me. He must be well over six foot, and I'm only about five foot eight.'

'What's him being an alcoholic got to do with choosing furniture?' she asked, clearly not amused by my graphic description.

'Well, drunks don't notice stuff like furniture, so just choose anything.'

'Simon, that's not very helpful!'

While finding apartments was part of her job description, furnishing them wasn't. Foreign men coming to Singapore to work were, in most cases, followed shortly afterwards by their wives, who took over the task of nest-making. But it was difficult to refuse our new American chief executive, who, like me, was a bachelor.

Mercy B. Lord had kindly agreed to supervise the furnishing of my flat, including soft furnishings, linen, towels, kitchen utensils and all the paraphernalia required to make an empty space seem like home, and she was anxious to help Dansford as much as possible. The Beatrice Fong Agency required her to attempt to please her clients in every way that didn't involve lying on her back. She told me that when a client put the hard word on her she would smile sweetly and say, 'Thank you, sir. I'm afraid that is not an item in my job description. If it is a service you require, the agency will supply an escort for 250 US dollars a night. Her excellent and strictly confidential services will then be billed to your account as a banquet for important government officials. We will even issue a receipt from the China Doll Restaurant.'

'A fictitious restaurant, very funny, clever too,' I remarked when she'd told me how she neatly sidestepped a client's amorous approach.

'No, a real one. It belongs to Beatrice and Sidney Wing.'

'You're kidding!'

'No, really, it's very nice. It's where the client meets his escort. That way he pays for an outrageously expensive dinner as well.'

Ronnie had mentioned those two, Beatrice and Sidney, in the same breath the first time we'd had lunch at the Town Club, when he'd warned me it was hands off Mercy B. Lord. Perhaps this appropriately named restaurant was the connection. I wondered if they also shared the commission from the escort's fee.

'Hmm . . . sounds interesting. Shall we dine at the China Doll some evening?' I'd teased.

'No!' Mercy B. Lord had said, not amused. 'All the high-class whores go there!'

When we'd been looking for furniture we'd visited several Chinese carpentry shops and I'd picked out more or less what I liked, on the 'keep it simple' principle. 'Perhaps you could do for Dansford what you did for me,' I suggested tentatively.

'It's not the same, Simon. With you it was an adventure. I loved it and you taught me so much.'

Clearly the search for Dansford Drocker's furniture was not going to be as much fun as ours had been. As I mentioned earlier, I have some knowledge of antique furniture, and I'd enjoyed explaining to Mercy B. Lord the mix of modern and period furniture I'd envisaged for the flat. Here we were in a place where you could have anything you wanted, or a pretty close copy anyway. All you needed to do was show the Chinese or Malay cabinet-makers a picture and they'd make what you required, and do it beautifully.

'Okay, so here's what you do. We've chosen the stuff for my place, so just tell them to double up on the order. I don't care and he won't know. Simple.'

'You sure?' Mercy B. Lord sounded doubtful.

'Sweetheart, it's just a pad where he'll fall into bed in the early hours, probably with his shoes on.'

If I'd solved one problem, Dansford Drocker was able to provide several more. 'He doesn't want to be shown around Singapore. He's only interested in the location of drinking places – "watering holes", he calls them.' Mercy B. Lord sounded exasperated. 'He's not like you, Simon. I don't know what to do. Beatrice will still want our agency fee and she'll blame me. Besides, I have to do a report on him for her and Mr Wing.'

I was jolted by this last remark but managed to keep my voice calm. 'I'll talk to Ronnie and get back to you. In the meantime, double up on the furniture, then use the next eight days to find him a damn good housekeeper who doesn't mind his drinking. In return for a commensurate rise in her salary, she can clean up after him and get him going in the morning.'

'I hope you're right, Simon.'

'Don't worry, I am. My dad's an alcoholic. They need someone to mind them constantly. We've had a lady called Dolly Maloney, who refers to herself as "The Very Well-Paid Maid". Her husband was a hopeless alcoholic who died when he fell off a platform in front of a train. She claims that she loves the job, but it may be the pay and the security.' I laughed. 'She also says she has a recurring nightmare in which my dad decides to go to AA.'

I spoke to Ronnie about Mercy B. Lord's problem and he took over the familiarisation work with Dansford Drocker. I would have to get a lot closer to Mercy B. Lord before I could ask her about the report she wrote on each of her clients, what she included, in how much detail, and, more importantly, why she'd been asked to write such reports. It was clever espionage: a pretty and charming young woman sufficiently intelligent to write a detailed report on any person with whom Sidney Wing was going to be associated. After two weeks in the company of someone who is astute but only asks apparently normal questions, anyone would give away a fair bit about themselves. It was very Chinese and also, I was beginning to realise, very Sidney Wing. The Chinese cherish any information they have obtained secretly about you, stuff they might later use to their advantage. Come to think of it, I suppose we all do.

Now the job of escorting Dansford was in Ronnie's hands. Whether or not he wrote a report, the task of accompanying Dansford soon proved too difficult even for a talented elbow man like Ronnie. After three days of pretty solid drinking from mid-morning to midnight and often beyond, Ronnie gave up and brought his chief executive in to the agency to start work.

Ronnie would later confess to me that once Sidney had ascertained that Dansford Drocker was a benign drunk and, even when inebriated, didn't disparage his work or his Chinese partners, he was secretly delighted. His American director would be a cinch to control and wouldn't be snooping around or asking awkward questions. It would be business as usual. Moreover, the Yank was unlikely to be interested in the creative process, so I would be isolated, on my Pat Malone.

But he was wrong in at least one respect: despite the damage the grog was doing to it, Dansford Drocker had a good mind and was exceedingly conscientious about those international brands he'd brought with him from New York and was required to service. Pepsi-Cola, Colgate-Palmolive, Goodyear Rubber & Tire Company and Wild Turkey Bourbon were a formidable and, in advertising terms, demanding line-up, all of them clients that required expertise of one kind or another.

I hesitate to tell the unfortunate story of what happened to Dansford the first time we went to Bugis Street on the obligatory night out on the town, but thankfully he managed to get into trouble all on his own so neither Ronnie nor I was implicated. Before I go on, perhaps a few details about the common set-up in a girlie bar are in order, but first, a description of the notorious Bugis Street and its environs. The street was in the heart of *Xiao Po* (Little Slope), the red-light district where, between Victoria Street West and Queen Street, the serious drinking with the visiting *ang mo*, the term used for Westerners, took place.

The night would begin respectably enough, usually at Bill Bailey's, a bar and grill said once to have been owned by the original Bill Bailey, although there's nothing to suggest this was true. Because I'm a nut about times and dates, I worked out that when 'Bill Bailey', the song, was composed by Hughie Cannon in 1902, the Singaporean Bill Bailey would have been about thirteen years old. Nobody seems to know with certainty when the bar opened but its original name was Bill Bailey's Coconut Grove Bar, although for as long as anyone could remember, it had been referred to as Bill Bailey's.

Nevertheless, Bill Bailey's was the top spot in Singapore for a feed of Shanghai eels, shredded and cooked in a thick peppery sauce. Ronnie insisted that it was a dish guaranteed to set you up for a long evening of drinking, the oily eels miraculously warding off drunkenness by a couple of hours. In other words, the stop at Bill Bailey's was an essential prelude to the long night that lay ahead.

Then it was off to Bugis Street, where we were initially accosted not by girls but by young boys, some of whom looked no older than eight, each carrying a noughts-and-crosses board. For a dollar they would challenge you to a game.

'I've got to have a go,' I said. 'I'm pretty good at this – we played it sometimes at school. I was the acknowledged champ,' I boasted, fishing out a dollar and nodding to a small kid who had approached with a challenge.

'Don't waste your time, Simon,' Ronnie laughed, 'No *ang mo* in history has ever won at tic-tac-toe.'

'There's always a first time,' I said, with immoderate self-confidence. I was good at board games, from chess to silly little noughts and crosses, and I prided myself on not often losing.

Ronnie turned to Dansford. 'It's not every day you meet a true sucker. I'm putting ten bucks on the kid and I suggest you do the same.' Both produced their money and the kid said something to Ronnie. 'He wants to do the same,' Ronnie laughed and nodded to the kid, who promptly produced ten crumpled dollar notes, counting them carefully before placing them beside the two ten-dollar notes on the pavement table outside a bar. 'We'll have to buy a drink. If you lose, you pay for them as well as the kid's Coca-Cola,' Ronnie said. 'He works this patch with the permission of the bar owner.'

Three games of tic-tac-toe later, much to the amusement of the other two, I'd lost ninety Singapore bucks and the cost of the drinks.

'Never mind, Simon, the kid is probably his family's sole supporter,' Ronnie consoled me with a laugh.

As we moved along, the street seemed to overflow with beautiful young girls collected from the far corners of Asia – Vietnamese, Thais, Cambodians, Indians, Sinhalese, Laotians, Nepalese and, of course, Chinese. They stood outside the neon-lit bars touting for customers, most wearing the smallest possible bikinis, their slender figures gyrating and grinding or even playfully humping a telephone pole or colourful pavement umbrella still open despite the hour. It was a human smorgasbord impossible for any red-blooded young male to ignore, or as Dansford exclaimed, 'Hey, hey, hey, yeah, man, maybe they didn't graduate from Vassar but they sure got everything a gentleman could possibly need for his delectation.'

It was a predictable reaction and I recall thinking much the same thing the first time Ronnie brought me there. It was blatant exploitation of poor and unfortunate village girls with no other prospects but selling their bodies and was therefore reprehensible and inexcusable. But this was Asia, so it wasn't in the least sleazy. The girls giggled and competed with each other in a lighthearted way and seemed to possess an instinct for recognising a first-timer.

'Hello, handsome man,' one would call out.

'You come my bar, darling?' another would cry.

With one or two exceptions, the girlie bars were much of a muchness. You stepped from the neon glitter of the street through a canvas curtain into a place named Jungle Jim's, or the Beachcomber, Bangles or Texas Cowboy, the most improbable being a bar called Christmas Carol's. There were simply dozens of these places. An attractive girl would pull back the curtain that covered the doorway and say, 'Welcome, handsome man. Come, I show. Inside you can have evee-thing you want.' Then, after touching her crotch, she would draw her forefinger slowly up towards her navel. 'Girls very beautiful, very tight, she will make very happy for you special tonight.'

Inside, the music would be very loud and on a stage in the background would be a dozen or more girls gyrating round metal poles to the beat of the music, some topless, others in tiny bikinis, all eyeing the customers. When one caught your eye she would hook her thumb into the top of her skimpy bikini bottom and pull it down so that you caught a split-second glimpse of what was on offer, whereupon the *mama-san* would emerge. She was invariably an older, plainer woman and usually well known to Ronnie, whom she would greet like a long-lost brother. 'Too long no see, Ronnie!' she would shout above the music. 'Where you been, hey? You bring nice friend. For sure they have good time! I have new girl, very beautiful all for you friend; Cambodia, also Vietnam, you will see.'

I'm paraphrasing, of course, but the *mama-sans* and the welcoming dialogue were more or less interchangeable and Ronnie knew them all by name: Rosie, Dolly, Suzie, Dorothy, May, and the one at Texas Cowboy who was called Holy Mother Mary. They were hard women who ran the girlie bars along strict lines. There was a barman serving drinks at a bar that seated a dozen or so girls and their *ang mo* clients: soldiers, sailors, tourists in shorts and Hawaiian shirts, and businessmen in lightweight safari suits that were almost the expat uniform.

I recall one exchange with a *mama-san* on my initial visit to Bugis Street. Ronnie had introduced me. 'Dolly, this is my friend Simon from Australia.'

Dolly was overweight, very short and almost as broad as me, and she looked as though she could pack a mean punch. 'Ah, Australia! I like Australia man, very kind, very nice. You have kangaroo . . . Hop-hop, very funny, you lucky man have such kangaroo, big, strong, maybe like you. I also have girl she can hop-hop for you, Simon, she very beautiful hop-hop girl.'

The procurement procedure was the same at every bar: if you selected a girl for a short time or for the night, you paid a bar fine. It was one of two standard amounts you paid to the bar for the time your 'new girlfriend' would be absent. There was no sense in pointing out that this was illogical, given the purpose of the girlie bar. You were also expected to buy her 'lady drinks' – either cold tea or a watered-down version of whatever she requested, which cost three times what you paid for your beer or Scotch. No girl would allow you, on pain of death from her *mama-san*, to leave without buying her at least two, but usually three drinks. 'I must know you, darling. You tell me. What you name? Where you come from. We have happy time. You buy drink for me. We have happy talk.' Drinks at the bar were a highly profitable sideline both for the bar and the girl, who received half of the cost of every lady drink she could get out of a customer.

The local punters who knew the ropes negotiated the fee for the girl's sexual favours, or 'further activity', as it was euphemistically sometimes called by expats, but the tourists, sailors and visiting business types foolish enough to go into a girlie bar alone paid whatever the girl could extract over and above the usual price.

In my case, and again with Dansford, Ronnie warned us not to get too carried away. 'We'll have a few drinks, check out the chicks, but leave any serious decision until last, until we get to the Nite Cap in Victoria Street West. Their girls are the ones who set the standard. Besides, the transvestites come into the street at 11 p.m. You won't want to miss them because you're otherwise occupied.'

With Dansford in tow, we hit the Nite Cap just before eleven o'clock. While I suspected, and still do, that Ronnie got 'squeeze' from Aunty May, the *mama-san*, he was correct about the girls. We'd ended up here the night of the Town Club lunch, and while we'd seen some lovely young creatures along the way, these Nite Cap girls were something else again. This was where Ronnie's Suzie Wong, Moi Moi, worked, but on that particular night he hadn't sought her services, as we were involved in a 'last man standing wins' competition, my bloody stupid attempt to prove I could take him on drink for drink after having behaved like a bit of a moralising arsehole at the Town Club.

By the time the three of us arrived at the Nite Cap, Dansford was pretty drunk. Knowing we would be accompanying him on his first Bugis Street girlie bar soiree, Ronnie hadn't gone out to lunch, and I never drank during the day, my first on this particular evening having been after the kid had beaten me at tic-tac-toe. Dansford, however, had been drinking since lunchtime.

Aunty May met us, accompanied by three truly pretty girls. Two of them – Veronica and Moi Moi – were known to Ronnie and me; the third was introduced as Swallow and was obviously intended for Dansford.

I'd already done my share of client entertaining with Veronica and Moi Moi over the months I'd been in Singapore, and had taken Ronnie's advice and picked Veronica as my permanent late-night minder. She was paid regardless of whether we slept together. I had discovered, as Ronnie had suggested, that a good massage, a cup of hot green tea and a couple of hours' kip with your pretty minder on the alert for your guest was much the best way to deal with the client's night of adventure.

Dansford, ever dapper, declared that Swallow was a splendid choice but, alas, he needed to go to the john urgently. Remarkably polite as he was, he bowed, and I caught him by the back of his collar just in time to stop him crashing to the floor. Drawing himself up to his full height and leaning slightly backwards with just the hint of a sway, he excused himself to Swallow and asked Ronnie for directions.

'You have to go out the front, turn right then right again and into the lane beside the building and it's there at the back, a white door with a big "M" painted on it. Would you like me to show you?' Ronnie volunteered.

'No, pal, I'll find it,' Dansford declared with the stubbornness of the inebriated, then turning to his girl again he said, 'Now you stay right there, honey. Dansford Drocker will be back 'fore you know it. Ronnie, you see she has any damn thing she wants t'drink. Now don't you fly away, honey baby. Dansford's got big eyes for his little Swallow!' With these immortal words he left and did not return. He was as drunk as a lord but still managed to string his sentences together, whereas I would have been a mumbling fool.

After twenty or so minutes I became worried. 'Should we go and look for him? He may have passed out in the toilet,' I suggested.

'I'll go,' Ronnie said. 'I should have insisted on going with him.'

Ten minutes or so later he returned. 'No sign of him.'

'Shit! What now? We better go and look for him.'

'No point,' Ronnie replied. 'No one on the street will tell you if they saw him.'

'Huh? Why not?'

'A drunk is good for business. They won't hurt him but they'll take his money – just his money, nothing else. If anything else is taken, the cops get really nasty.'

'C'mon, Ronnie, we've got to do something,' I said, my agitation showing.

Ronnie spoke quietly to Swallow, and she left and returned shortly with Aunty May. After Ronnie explained the situation, she nodded and said, 'I send.'

She murmured something to Veronica, who kissed me on the cheek and said, 'I be back, Simon,' then she turned and made her way to the door.

'She go find, she good.' Aunty May waited with us. A short time later Veronica returned.

'He go with Destiny,' she said, smiling.

'Oh my God!' Ronnie exclaimed.

'What? What's wrong?' I asked, concerned.

'No, no, Dansford's quite safe. He'll take him back to Raffles.'

'He?'

Ronnie laughed, whereupon the girls and Aunty May all giggled. 'Destiny is the most beautiful transvestite in Singapore,' he explained.

'Oh, Jesus, what now?' I said. 'He's pissed – will he know?'

Ronnie shook his head. 'Probably not. They're very clever. He'll claim he has his period but has other ways to please. The main thing is he'll take his fee for . . .' he chuckled, 'whatever, then put Dansford in a taxi back to Raffles. Destiny has a reputation to uphold.'

'Ronnie, we don't say a word about this to anyone, you hear? Promise me, mate.'

Ronnie sighed. 'Of course, but Dansford probably will. If he doesn't catch on, he may brag he had the prettiest girl in Singapore. Believe me, Destiny is gorgeous. We can only hope he is too drunk to recall his name, otherwise everyone will know.'

'If he brings it up with either of us, what do we do?'

'We tell him discreetly. Let's hope he doesn't do it in the company of others. Destiny is known throughout Singapore. Some of his . . . er, conquests have been notable visitors.'

It was several months later that Dansford raised the subject. 'You know, Simon, I was pretty smashed, but that first night we went out together and I lost my way coming back from the john, I met the prettiest gal I've ever seen.'

'Oh?' I said cautiously.

'Yeah, but that's the thing. She had her period, but, man o' man, she still gave me the best sex I've ever had.' He grinned. 'I have no idea of the various ways and means – I wish I could recall them – but it was a complete education without her even performing the main event.'

I forced a knowing grin. 'Do you remember her name?'

'No, that's just it, I don't,' he said regretfully. 'But, damn, she was good.'

'Did you pick her up on the street?'

'Well, yeah, I suppose I did.'

'Probably a good thing then. When they say they have their period, it's usually because they may have . . . you know . . . something else.'

'Damn, I never thought of that,' Dansford said.

'If you see her again, mate, best to keep your distance,' I advised.

As if to confirm that he would henceforth keep to the straight and narrow, Dansford married his Chinese housekeeper, a plain-faced, pockmarked Cantonese woman with all the low expectations of men her station in life had afforded her.

He asked me to be the sole witness to the registry-office wedding and of course I agreed, but only after we'd had a bit of a talk.

He was the scion of an old and notable Boston Irish-Catholic family and I couldn't see a Chinese peasant woman being welcomed by them when his contract expired and he returned home. He was in his mid-forties, and if the grog didn't get him, he'd be an excellent ad man. 'Dansford, have you thought this out? What about your family back home? I mean, what about when you return?' I asked.

'Simon, good of you to care, but America the brave is no place for the timid. Unlike MacArthur, I shall not return. Bill Bailey can't go home.'

The subject was never brought up again.

When it came to signing the marriage register, Dansford's Chinese wife turned out to be illiterate, so her thumbprint appeared on the marriage certificate together with her Chinese name, which translated as Wing. Dansford named her Chicken Wing and insisted that it appear on the certificate, although he was careful never to let the Wing brothers hear her name.

It says something for Dansford Drocker that he married her even though he could have had Chicken Wing provide all the same services without doing so. She could never appear as his wife in Singaporean social circles, and if he informed his Boston family that he'd married an illiterate, heathen Chinese woman, which seemed unlikely, I can't imagine they would have been happy. But to his credit he insisted that as Chicken Wing did more than could be expected of any servant, she should, as he put it, 'have the dubious honour' of being his wife. When it was inappropriate to refer to her as Chicken Wing, he would simply say, 'My good and excellent wife'.

Chicken Wing put him to bed when he arrived home, usually well past midnight, then got him to work punctually by 9 a.m. looking starched and perfectly presented or, as we might say in Australia, bright-eyed and bushy-tailed. She never complained and may even have regarded herself as being in a fortunate position, with plenty of time to herself, money to spend and no meals to cook – he couldn't face breakfast and was never home for lunch or dinner, even on weekends. I must say, I never once heard him complain of a hangover, although I have no doubt that almost any part of the inside of Dansford wasn't a nice place to be first thing in the morning.

Despite taking Chicken Wing as his wife, Dansford remained

quintessentially American. The only concession he made to the local culture was to learn Singlish, the local patois, and this was only because Chicken Wing spoke very poor English. He made no attempt, or very little anyway, to understand the local scene, dismissing the differences between cultures as inconsequential. 'Chinese are just folk, like everyone else. Not so different to us. Like everyone they hanker after the miracle of the American way. We'll give it to them straight, no tonic or soda water, straight Kentucky bourbon. No need to fuck with perfection.' Dansford Drocker sincerely believed that the American way was several notches above anything else civilisation had to offer, and if he liked a layout or a campaign, he complimented it in one of two ways: it was either 'straight Kentucky bourbon' or 'spam from Uncle Sam'.

Dansford's theory may have been correct for Pepsi-Cola or Wild Turkey, where the product's American qualities were the attraction, but it didn't apply to all things emanating from the fifty states of the union. The perfect example of this was the Texas Oil Company, for which we were invited to pitch, already long established in the Asian market and not emblematic of New York.

Texas Oil was my first opportunity to win a big local account with my own creative pitch, working with Dansford Drocker as the account supervisor. If we won, Dansford would be responsible for all the advertising for Texas Oil.

The local Texas Oil chief, Michael Johns, invited us to present our credentials just two weeks after Dansford arrived. He specified that we make the pitch in three days' time and to front up at the Texas fuel refinery for a briefing the following morning.

Johns was a large, lumbering Texan beginning to go to fat, an ex-marine who wore a Stetson and cowboy boots and who when dressing formally added a silver tie toggle, a fawn, twill-work tasselled shirt and steer-horn silver belt buckle. He was now, after three marriages, a bachelor and was known to have an eye for the ladies, not only in expat society, where they called him Big Loud Mike, but also in the girlie bars, where he was predictably known as Cowboy Tex. This all came to us via Ronnie, who knew everyone and informed us the Texan boss of Texas Oil didn't like being called Michael Johns but much preferred his nickname or simply 'BLM'. When in his cups, which was fairly often, he was known to lament, 'Man cain't change his name. The goddamn name my pappy and mama give me ain't good, man! When them two names're throw'd together like that – Michael Johns – they sound like some goddamned limey faggot.'

Dansford and I turned up to be told that Texas Oil had experienced a drastic 18 per cent downturn in sales, due to Caltex entering the market with an additive named Boron that they advertised at the pumps with a picture of a rocket taking off. Consequently, the Chinese thought of it as some kind of rocket fuel, and all the other petrol brands were taking a hiding.

Texas Oil had been placing their American advertising with a local Chinese agency that simply translated the American slogan into Chinese. When I had it retranslated I discovered it was a pretty bland statement – *Makes car go better*. The Caltex rocket on the petrol pump was much more effective. Everyone could understand it and the slogan translated as *Rocket power for your engine*.

The problem was that we had no chance of coming up with an in-depth creative approach in two days. I'd told Dansford, 'I don't want to screw this up. If it's possible, we should attempt to get the account without doing a creative pitch, then take our time to do a proper job.'

Dansford nodded but then said, 'Don't like our chances. He'll want to see something, Simon.'

Big Loud Mike completed his brief and looked directly at Dansford. 'We're losing more than the local currency; we're bleeding fucking US dollars. Show me something I can use – Thursday at the latest.'

'Tex, I regret we can't help you,' Dansford replied, to my surprise.

'Hey, what sort of a cockamamie answer is that?' Big Loud Mike replied. 'I got a decent budget. We ain't no penny-ante Chinese account!'

'Getting back your market share won't be easy – we have to do it right,' Dansford said, then turned to me. 'How much time, Simon?'

'Two weeks.'

'Jesus! That's the best y'all can do, before —'

'Before what?' Dansford asked.

'Before we get something at the gas stations that'll blow those Caltex cocksuckers away, man!'

'I can present a proposed campaign to you in two weeks. If you approve it, then realistically we'll need a month to six weeks to produce it and get it on the road, sir,' I replied, now convinced we'd *really* blown it but knowing it was an honest answer, even if Sidney Wing would have strongly disapproved. His view was 'Promise them anything to get the account, then try to sort out the mess later' – the theory being that the client, having hired you, will be reluctant to fire you and eventually you'll reach some kind of solution. It occasionally worked but it bred distrust and resentment and more often than not was a recipe for disaster.

Big Loud Mike wanted something fast, and when you're chasing lost market share, fast is never a good idea. This was, I knew, my big chance. Michael Johns ran all of Asia and if I could pull this off, it would be a feather in my cap. It would also show New York we were able to generate worthwhile local business. If I fucked up a campaign that would run in several countries simultaneously, my career in Asia would be over. But I took a chance that he was desperate and would give me the minimum time I needed – that way my destiny was in my own hands.

Two weeks was barely sufficient to come up with the initial idea. Even if he approved it lock, stock and barrel, it would be bloody near impossible to produce final copy, radio ads, layouts and point-of-sale at the service stations, as well as twenty-four-sheet posters, in a mere six weeks. For the point-of-sale and press ads there was only a Chinese calligrapher and myself, with Ronnie helping out on the production. I'd be going day and night and then some.

'Mr Koo, they got my balls on the fucking chopping block. They ain't happy in Houston and y'all better know what you're talking about or before I'm back pumping gas in Dallas, ever-body in America gonna know y'all fucked up big-time! Before I say yes, you gotta oblige me with sumpthin' to give me some con-fee-dence!'

Dansford calmly assured him that we would be happy to oblige him but what was it that he suggested we do?

'Well, maybe I just come in, meet some-a the key people and have a mosey around, see what ideas you got. What say eight o'clock day after tomorrow?'

Dansford sat quietly for a moment then looked Michael Johns in the eye. 'No, I can't do that.'

Big Loud Mike was obviously not accustomed to being denied. 'Why the hell not, Mr Drocker? What the fuck's up wid you guys?'

Dansford hesitated, then said with a big smile, 'Because I don't stop puking until nine.'

The agency visit was organised for 10.30 a.m. two days later.

Once we were in the taxi going back to the agency I asked, 'Dansford, what are we going to do, mate? No way I can have anything half-decent ready in two days. When he comes in he's going to expect something, anything – a poster, point-of-sale, something with a slogan that points to an ongoing advertising theme . . .'

'He's a Texan and believes in the American way. That's what we'll give him,' Dansford replied calmly.

'Jesus, Dansford, they've lost 18 per cent of their market and they're in Shit Street. They've used the American campaign and it isn't working. What's more, this proposed visit and talk to the staff is pretty bloody funny. Talk to whom? Sidney Wing, grinning like a hungry goanna, exaggerating his American drawl and suggesting a round of golf at his club sometime soon, and Johnny "Dracula" Wing, both greeting Big Loud Mike with a handshake that has all the strength of an over-ripe banana. Ronnie's okay, but as for the rest of the staff, they're almost all Chinese and could qualify as paid mourners at a misanthrope's funeral. The whole place smells of shit and when I complained to Sidney yesterday, he called it "a slight sewage overflow that doesn't require attention"!'

'We'll think of something, Simon. We'll have him in to the agency for a chat and then, as one American to another . . . I'll take him out to lunch.'

My heart sank. 'Dansford, do you think that's such a good idea?'

'Bourbon. He's a bourbon man. Can't mistake a bourbon man. It's written on his face. Take my word for it, this is going to be "spam from Uncle Sam".'

I looked doubtfully at him. 'And, er, taking him out to lunch is . . . going to give him confidence in us?'

'Sure, "straight Kentucky bourbon", I can tell instinctively.'

It wasn't yet noon and Dansford was unquestionably sober. Besides, he was the agency's chief executive and had the final say, so I was forced to accept his decision. 'We'll need Ronnie when we get back to the agency. Will you send him round to my office?' he concluded.

I'd known Dansford Drocker for only two weeks but his after-lunch disappearances were clearly a habit. I was suddenly *really* worried. It was obviously a crazy decision to take Big Loud Mike out after the agency visit to a lunch that might well go on until midnight and beyond, that is, if the big Texan didn't abandon Dansford on the way to oblivion – Dansford that night and us the next day. There evidently wasn't going to be a pitch for the Texas Oil account and I'd be implicated as part of the team that had taken the brief and blown it. If Sidney wanted to shoot me down in the eyes of New York, he was going to have all the ammo he needed. *Simon, baby, you're history!*

In the three and a half months I'd been in the job, I'd been getting a hard time from the two senior Wings. It was nothing you could confront them with, but almost everything I suggested for their long-held pre-merger accounts was rejected. There were several things I could have done to greatly improve the ads they were running, but all my efforts were to no avail. I could never get to talk directly to the Chinese clients they controlled, and they would invariably return from seeing a client to say my new layout and copy had been rejected. I doubt very much that my work was even taken out of its folio.

Now, with Dansford's crazy lunch idea, it was all over. I might as well throw in the towel and slink back to Australia. Try to forget the most desirable and beautiful woman I'd ever met, because she too was out of bounds, untouchable.

I was feeling pathetically sorry for myself. In fact, since arriving I hadn't made the slightest dent in the agency's creative product; my total impact was a big fat zero. *If the blokes in Sydney could see you now – some Fortune Cookie!* In my thoroughly morose state, I thought that Mercy B. Lord probably wouldn't agree to return to Australia with me if I asked her, and the White Australia Policy probably wouldn't permit her to enter as my intended bride anyway. *Fucking drunken Yank!*

Ronnie returned from Dansford's office with a smile the size of a slice of watermelon. 'Action stations, Simon! At last, at last! Hallelujah! At last! An idea bigger than fucking Texas!'

'What, Dansford on the town with Big Loud Mike? Jesus, you can't be serious, Ronnie?'

He looked at me astonished. 'What, you don't agree? It's fucking brilliant, man!'

'What is?'

'The twenty girls!'

'What twenty girls?'

'Sorry, Simon, can't hang about. I'm off to get the T-shirts printed and the hotpants made . . . Shit, where am I going to get twenty pairs of red high heels?' With that he was gone. I had never seen Ronnie more excited.

The afternoon prior to the Texas Oil visit, our receptionist, Alice Ho, and any plain girls (which was almost all of them), plus anyone over the age of about twenty-five, were told they'd been given the following morning off and were not to come in until after lunch. In their places the following morning were twenty ravishing and well-stacked girls all wearing skin-tight red hotpants, white T-shirts and red patent-leather shoes with five-inch heels. Their over-stretched T-shirts carried the red Texas Oil logo on the back and on the front the message: 'Texas Declares War on Boron'.

There were two girls waiting in the hotel car park to welcome Big

Loud Mike and escort him across the road to the agency. A particularly gorgeous girl sat in reception and gave him a knee-trembling smile of welcome. In fact, wherever he turned or went in the agency over the next three hours, a glorious-looking young woman smiled beguilingly at him, some playfully thrusting their bosoms out to emphasise the slogan.

It all seemed to go rather well. We had even distributed Air Wick in an attempt to mask the smell of the latrines. Nevertheless, I watched with a sinking feeling as Dansford and Big Loud Mike, seemingly happy and laughing, departed for lunch.

As for the lunch that followed, Ronnie found them with their arms around each other, singing 'The Yellow Rose of Texas' in Bill Bailey's Bar at one o'clock the following morning. He paid the exorbitant drinks bill and organised a couple of taxis to take them home.

The next day we were told we'd been awarded the Texas Oil account. Moreover, Big Loud Mike and Dansford Drocker became great mates and regular drinking buddies, eventually forming the 6B Club, a charitable organisation for expats who were fond of a drink, to raise money to rescue street kids. The six Bs stood for the Brotherhood of Bourbon Boozers at Bill Bailey's Bar, the watering hole where they usually finished a night's carousing. As Dansford had predicted, the American way had triumphed. All that was required now was an Asian way to sell petrol.

I came up with a concept that required them to rename their petrol – or gasoline, as Michael Johns called it. It was to be known as Texas Tiger. The slogan was simple enough: 'Texas Tiger puts the roar into your engine'. The petrol pumps were to be painted in tiger stripes with a tiger's face in full roar at the centre of each. The pump hose was made to resemble the stripes on a tiger's tail. As the nozzle was lifted from the bracket at the side of the petrol pump, it would trigger a deep growl and, of course, all the radio commercials and later the television ads ended with the slogan and a tiger's roar.

Ronnie Wing hated the concept. 'It's bullshit, Simon. The Chinese won't buy it. The tiger is a sacred symbol, and you're insulting them.'

After having worked with him for months I understood that he was an unusual individual. He had an uncommon characteristic, which was that his opinion on matters of effective advertising was always wrong – not occasionally wrong but *invariably* wrong. He was the perfect barometer. If he liked an advertising idea – in his words, ran it up the flagpole and saluted it, and was convinced it would work – this meant it would fail and should immediately be scrapped.

'Sorry, mate, Dansford likes it. We're going ahead with it,' I replied.

'Well, just remember who told you,' he replied, greatly miffed.

The new Texas Tiger petrol was launched with a street procession down Orchard Road during the lunch hour with twenty convertibles painted in tiger stripes, each carrying one of the girls who had greeted Big Loud Mike on his visit to the agency. Now, though, they wore skin-tight tiger outfits, complete with ears and whiskers and tiger tails, and stood on the bonnets of the cars, their feet gripped by two leather sleeves fixed to the bonnet so they wouldn't fall or lose their balance. These sleeves were painted to resemble tiger paws. The parade drew a massive crowd, estimated at fifty thousand. As Dansford later remarked, the launch got away to a roaring start.

In Asia the tiger is, of course, the king of beasts and represents, among other things, fearlessness and wrath. In myth it is equal to the dragon in importance. Ronnie was adamant that it wouldn't work and claimed the Chinese would object to it being used as a brand symbol for petrol, but I had to take the chance.

I'm happy to say that over the next six months Texas Tiger, the petrol that put the roar into your engine, regained and increased market share in every Asian market. Even today the Chinese fondly refer to it as tiger piss and it remains a leading brand. I guess you could say that in advertising terms I was a made man, but from that point on, a very busy one as well.

Dansford worked hard every morning on the plans for an ad campaign for one or another of our major American accounts. This invariably involved us working together, but when he went AWOL at lunchtime I was left to do the creative work and a fair bit besides.

I would never have been able to cope with five major accounts had it not been for Pepsi-Cola, for which we used the spam-from-Uncle-Sam approach and reran the same ad campaign translated into the local language. I was doing the work of two, perhaps even three creative groups in Australia.

After Dansford had been in Singapore for about six months, Colgate-Palmolive asked us to do a market survey for a new liquid laundry detergent, a product that could be used without a washing machine. I had been particularly keen on a laundry detergent for hand-washing, which was as cheap as, but better than, the blue soap bars local women commonly used to do their washing, and which were infused with lye or caustic soda. I hadn't forgotten a remark from Mercy B. Lord after my foolish question about the brand of washing powder most commonly used in machines in Singapore. 'You can tell by their hands. They use cheap lye-based soap and it burns their skin.' Mercy B. Lord had been amused by my question, but not at the physical price these poor washerwomen paid for their masters' and mistresses' clean laundry. *Amahs* did all the washing by hand, using a washboard or rock and the strong caustic soap.

This hand-washing detergent had been another one of my recommendations, but before accepting it and doing the necessary development, they required us to investigate the customer base and find out the likely reaction to proposed names, the product description and pricing, as well as the conditions in which the product would be used and all the usual information needed to launch a new product.

In any European or Western market this would have been a routine task for a market-research company but in the Asian market it was damn near impossible. For a start there was no such thing as a market-research company; secondly, the Chinese and the Malays, in fact most Asians, seldom answer a question honestly for fear of causing a loss of face. Instead they tend most often to give you the answer they believe you require or would most prefer. But there was another problem – personal opinions are regarded as dangerous because they can indicate intent, and it is always bad joss to tempt the gods with having plans before you have consulted them. A stranger asking questions and wanting your opinion could destroy your luck.

The request for the survey came directly from America and Dansford pointed out that this explanation wasn't what they wanted to hear back in the States.

'Dansford, what the hell are we going to do?' I asked.

'Simon, this is your baby, but let me assure you they're not going to take one step further in the labs in Milwaukee or the marketing department in New York until they get their market survey.'

'But I'm certain such a product will work. Even the name, "Big Lather", translates well into Chinese and Malay. We could test-market it here and then take it to the rest of Asia.'

'Simon, do I not recall you telling me that you're no friend of market research, that you thought it was mostly bullshit?'

'Yeah, true, if it's the kind we did for a new brand of cigarette in Australia. But a test market is different. Can't we persuade them to go straight to a test market?' I had some respect for that kind of research. A test market is where you test a new product on the potential user to see how it fares under working conditions, so you can iron out any product or marketing bugs it might have. Singapore, with almost two million people and four separate cultures, Chinese being the major one, was an ideal test market for greater South-East Asia.

'Absolutely not! They don't make a move without market research. Colgate-Palmolive doesn't believe in hunches, inspired guesswork, local expertise or opinions.' Dansford Drocker shrugged. 'You don't believe in market research, they do, so, hey, what the hell, make it up.'

'What, do a phoney research project? How the hell do we do that?'

'Easy. We have to write the submission and questionnaire, so why don't we print two thousand or so and fill them in ourselves? You get the answer you want and they're happy.'

'Jesus! You sure? What if they find out?'

'How?'

I thought for a moment. 'Mate, it's just the kind of thing Sidney Wing would like to tuck up his sleeve for possible future use against us.'

Dansford Drocker grinned. 'That son of a bitch will do anything for money. Let me see, printing the questionnaires, the salaries for a couple of dozen fictitious field-research personnel, travel, crunching the numbers, writing a recommendation – that ain't chicken feed. We'll have to bill the client, and all but an itty-bitty printing job goes into the agency's pocket.' He laughed uproariously. 'Sidney Wing is going to love it, son!'

It was the first time I'd heard him say anything derogatory about his Chinese partners. Dansford was right, Sidney knew nothing about market research, but loved the prospect of making money with virtually no outlay.

'There's only one problem,' Dansford said as he explained the idea to Sidney. 'We need an independent organisation, something with a letterhead.'

'No problem – Beatrice Fong Market Research Company,' Sidney volunteered.

'They have one?' I asked. It was curious that Mercy B. Lord hadn't mentioned it to me.

Sidney picked up the telephone. 'They have now. Tomorrow we will have stationery.' He turned to me. 'Just let me have the details and one of your fancy layouts and slogans, Simon. Ronnie will organise the rest through production.'

Dansford cleared his throat. 'Perhaps something more anonymous? New York knows about Beatrice Fong.' He looked directly at Sidney. 'If they were ever to find out, it could be awkward.'

'Yes, her name is not necessary,' Sidney replied, then looked directly at me. 'You're the creative one, Simon. Any ideas?'

I searched my mind for an acronym. 'South-East Asian Research Agency, SEARA?'

'Splendid,' Sidney said. 'What about a slogan?'

'I don't think research companies have slogans. Maybe a line under the company name, you know, *Researching the needs of the Asian market,* something dull like that?'

'Excellent!'

It wasn't particularly good, but what the hell – a research company that didn't do any research didn't need any research into the copy that went under the stationery masthead. 'What about registering the company?' I asked. 'It could take months. I mean, I can't put "Pty Ltd" on the masthead when the company doesn't officially exist. Wouldn't that be fraud?' I was trying to recall my long-forgotten economics studies.

Sidney gave me a look that could only be described as pitying. 'It will be done before the end of the week,' was all he said. Of course it would – his *guanxi* connections would see to it. There was a Chinese way of getting things done and there was a Western way. In matters such as this, the Chinese way was undoubtedly the better one.

Sidney had obviously seen the advantages of a merger with an American ad agency and, moreover, must have weighed up the consequences and decided there was more going for it than against it. But, as a general rule, inviting foreigners into the boardroom was not only dangerous, it went against every Chinese instinct. With Westerners came transparency, no more smoke and mirrors. No longer could a *tokay*, that is, the proprietor, keep two sets of books, one for the tax man and one for himself. The phoney research company would have given him renewed faith in the power of duplicity and was tailor-made to his Chinese way of thinking.

Like all Chinese businessmen, Sidney was a trader. Buy today, sell tomorrow and repeat the process ad infinitum. He patently didn't believe in building the integrity and personality of a brand in a market – what we call brand equity – so he would regard the Colgate research initiative as utter foolishness, which in fact it was, but for the reason I mentioned earlier, the almost pathological reluctance of the Chinese to give a straight answer that would truly reflect how they felt.

'We'll have to find someone to front our "independent" research company,' Dansford declared. 'Someone plausible, articulate and presentable, who can be trusted not to spill the beans, someone who can also be trained to do a token field survey.'

'That's going to involve some training. Is it really necessary?'

'We have to base our questions and the results on some local information – a small field project to determine how a local washerwoman thinks.'

'I will find someone,' Sidney said.

'Absolutely trustworthy, I suggest; someone we can quickly train in the language and procedure of market research, preferably female. She won't need to run the company, since there's nothing to run, but she will need to do the token survey. We'll take care of whatever number-crunching and office work there is here in the agency.' He turned to me. 'You've seen a fair bit of field research, Simon. What do you suggest?'

'Well, it was mostly in tobacco – cigarette advertising in Australia – but I expect the techniques don't change much. To make this look authentic a token field study should involve close to 200 legitimate interviews. In Australia that's a sample and allows you to "taste" the market before you go full steam ahead. We need someone who can go out into the kampongs and interview the Chinese amahs, the washerwomen, using the questionnaire we design, so we can then extrapolate the answers for the overall findings. This is not paperwork we can invent without having that first "taste" on which to base the final recommendations. Otherwise, any experienced market researcher in New York will pick the fraud.'

'How long will that take?' Sidney asked me.

'Three weeks would be my guess. We'd have to work with her to devise the questions she asks. That's why it's important to get someone who is not only intelligent and intuitive but who can also relate to the needs of potential customers – Singapore's washerwomen.'

Sidney looked doubtful. 'It would be unusual to have a woman do this interview work.'

'On the contrary, it's essential,' Dansford shot back. 'We're talking about a laundry product, Sidney. Who the fuck uses the product?

Women, right? They are the ones who will buy it, use it and decide whether they like it. A woman coordinating this research makes perfect sense. There has to be a bright young woman we can trust. New York and Milwaukee will buy that.'

Sidney nodded. 'We will find one. How old?'

I hardly dared think it, but Mercy B. Lord would be perfect. She was twenty, almost old enough to have taken a degree, personable, accustomed to dealing with foreigners, beautiful and intelligent and could be said to know the locals from the washboard up. She would be ideal to work with us on designing a questionnaire. Briefing her on how to front a research meeting, if that became essential, wouldn't be too hard. I thought of the countless research meetings with Wills where just such a young woman was involved. But if I suggested it, Sidney would be onto me in a flash. He was nobody's fool.

Then I heard Dansford say, 'Oh, not too old. Advertising market research is a young profession even in the States, and here it's non-existent. Let me see, someone in her early twenties, bright, can handle the client . . .' He smiled and looked at Sidney. 'It would help if she was sexy.'

I quickly did a layout for SEARA Pty Ltd, together with the slogan Ronnie assured me translated well into Chinese. I went along with it, even though it met with Ronnie's approval.

The slogan I'd created for the soap – *Easy on your hands, easy on the price* – was as close as I could get to the Chinese words in English. This time Ronnie was adamant it wouldn't work. Which was why I persisted with it.

When New York came back and asked why we hadn't emphasised the claim – 'More whiteness and brightness, the result: personal pride and reward' – I explained that to credit the detergent with the result, not the person doing the washing, would be considered a major loss of face for the Chinese user. It was a guess, but a fairly educated one. I had explained the concept to Mercy B. Lord and worked through it with her. This may not have been strictly kosher but she knew the market and the people from the street level up and spoke the various languages and the patois known as Singlish. Most importantly, she understood the Chinese taboos. But she had one other advantage: as a Catholic she wasn't locked in to the local superstitions – or, if you like, religious beliefs – and so could be more or less dispassionate. She also did the various translations from my English 'purchase proposition', that is, the information about the product you want the customer to retain – *Big Lather looks after your hands, helps you get great results, and because you use less and get more lather it costs less than soap.*

Advertising agencies very seldom invent the concept for a new product, and in Asia it had never been done before. If Big Lather proved to be successful, after the enormous success of Texas Tiger, I was well on my way to being a big wheel in Asian advertising, and in terms of Samuel Oswald Wing, untouchable. If Big Lather worked in the rest of Asia, it would eventually be worth hundreds of millions of dollars to Colgate-Palmolive. I would have not just a feather in my cap, but a floor-length Maori-style cloak made entirely of feathers. If it failed, I would be, as we rather crudely say in Australia, dead meat.

So there you go. I was doing something unethical, which, if it were discovered, would result in my instant dismissal. The concept of the laundry detergent was my idea; my judgment was on the line. If the product failed and it ever got out that we'd fudged the research, as always happens after a disaster, then I would be entirely to blame. I knew that under no circumstances whatsoever would I implicate Dansford, who had stuck his neck out to help me. You could bet London to a brick Sidney had his butt well and truly covered. I could hear him in my mind: he had, at my request as a director, located the Beatrice Fong Market Research Company and then taken no further interest, blah blah blah.

Looking back I can only think that when you're young you regard yourself as bullet-proof and disregard the consequences of failure. The Big Lather concept was radical. Instead of coming in a box, it came in a large tube, like toothpaste. You squeezed out about half an inch that would dissolve in cold water to produce enough liquid to wash a big garment. For instance, two squeezes would clean a double-bed sheet. Furthermore, a tube lasted as long as two bars of blue lye soap and was cheaper and easier on the hands. It was a big ask, and I learned later that the boffins in the lab in Milwaukee initially pronounced it impossible. But New York had the final say and the product-development marketing team liked it. Naturally, they weren't prepared to go ahead with the lab R&D without covering their arses with good market research.

However, as some sort of defence, excuse or justification, I reasoned that if the Western research model didn't suit the Asian mindset, it must be possible to develop one that did. This request from Colgate-Palmolive was the first from our international clients, but it wouldn't be the last. Whether or not I believed in market research wasn't the point.

Even before we'd completed the phoney research project, I had formulated a plan that I hadn't yet discussed with anyone. Over the last months I'd seen a fair bit of my mother's family and grown quite close to two of my second cousins, Peter and Henry Kwan, henceforth referred to simply as cousins for convenience. Peter, the elder, ran a very exclusive Chinese antique shop in Orchard Road that had been started by his grandfather on his mother's side in 1918, and Henry was associate professor of sociology at the Singapore Institute of Technology, neither of them electing to go into the family palm-oil business.

If we got away with the phoney or, if you like, unacceptably small research sample we planned, using a questionnaire that was mostly guesswork, my plan was to consult the family academic and see if it wasn't possible to build a research model to take to the population, 'in the field', so to speak, that was psychologically correct for Asian conditions and mindset.

However, this all depended on our pulling off the phoney research project and me keeping my job. If we got away with it, I would have the time to work on the real McCoy. In the meantime there was no point in thinking about it.

Of course, I could always have pulled out of the ersatz Colgate-Palmolive research. That was morally and ethically the correct thing to do, but all I can say is I didn't. I was convinced the Big Lather concept would work in a test market and I guess I allowed my personal vanity and need to succeed to overrule my conscience.

There was one further factor. Ronnie Wing hated the Big Lather concept. 'It's ridiculous, Simon, the Chinese won't buy it.'

'So, tell me, Ronnie, how many times have you done the family wash by hand?' I replied.

'What's that supposed to mean? I'm Chinese, I know.'

'Okay, but we're going with Big Lather regardless.'

'Remember who told you it was shit, Simon.'

'Yeah, mate. As I recall, you said that about the Tiger.'

'That was different,' he mumbled. 'It was the girls on the cars in the parade down Orchard Road that made that work for Texas Oil.'

It was pointless arguing. I had to believe that if Ronnie hated the idea of Big Lather, then it was spot-on.

I more or less salved my conscience by convincing myself that we'd do the 'taste' first; futile as it might be, it was better than nothing. If Big Lather went into limited production and failed in the test market, Colgate-Palmolive would be unlikely to smell a rat. After all, wasn't that the point of market research? To find out what works and what doesn't? Some seemingly great concepts had been known to fail in test markets in the West, even after the initial market research into the concepts had supported them. People, much as we'd like to think the opposite, are simply not predictable or, as I'd often suspected with the W.D. & H.O. Wills research back home, research simply asked the wrong questions. If Big Lather failed, then the client would be likely to put it down to market experience and with Lady Luck on my side no one would be any the wiser. I told myself this happened every day and that Big Lather might just prove to be another one of those products over which you fold your tent and move on.

You may imagine my surprise and delight when Mercy B. Lord called

me at the agency three days after we'd talked to Sidney to announce
that Beatrice Fong had decided to open a market-research company
called SEARA. 'Oh, Simon, I'm terribly nervous. I know nothing about
market research,' she cried. 'Beatrice says Sidney Wing has agreed I'll be
trained by you and Mr Drocker. Is that true?'

'Congratulations! We didn't know it was going to be you, but of
course I'm delighted.'

'Yes, but will I be able to understand you?'

'I haven't noticed you having a great deal of trouble understanding
me before now.'

'You know what I mean, Simon – the technical language, that sort
of thing.'

'You'll learn that soon enough. In truth we need you rather more
than you need us. You see we have to devise a questionnaire for
washerwomen, and really we don't have a clue, but you do. You're in
touch with the respondents.'

'See, "respondents", is that a technical term?'

I laughed. 'No, I should have said the common people, ordinary
people,' I corrected myself.

'And then?'

'Well, you go out into the field, the *kampongs*, and ask washerwomen
the questions we've devised between us, we crunch the numbers and we
use them in our report to Colgate-Palmolive.'

'Honestly, do you think I can do it?'

'On your ear – I mean, easily. When can you come in?'

'Tomorrow. I've been given three weeks off from my meet and greet.'

'That's not a lot. The first week will be spent devising, designing and
printing the questionnaire; the rest of the time you'll be out in the field.'

I made up my mind that Mercy B. Lord would never know the
dodgy nature of our research, that she'd only be exposed to correct
methodology, or as correct as Dansford and I could make it while never
having had any hands-on experience ourselves.

Working on Mercy B. Lord's training for the initial Colgate-

Palmolive research for Big Lather was highly enjoyable. After we'd reviewed what needed to be done, we decided we would need closer to six weeks if we were going to cover our arses. But Beatrice insisted that she could only spare her protégé for three weeks, which was the time we needed for Mercy B. Lord to go out into the marketplace and ask questions. The old bitch wouldn't budge, or that's what Sidney told us, so Mercy B. Lord volunteered to come to my flat at night to be trained. It was a rewarding but difficult time. I loved having her to myself but was falling more deeply in love with her, especially in the hours when I could gaze at her openly as she sat for the portrait I was painting of her.

After the wonderful night of the black cheongsam at Raffles, we'd been out to dinner perhaps once a fortnight, but there was no promise of a relationship and she kept me at arm's length – a chaste kiss at the end of the evening and that was it. The six weeks of training her in research techniques and language proved to be no different. I grew accustomed to watching the brake lights of a late-night taxi as it turned the corner to disappear finally into the darkness, her departing peck on the cheek exaggerated in my mind into a lingering lover's farewell.

To cut a long story short, Mercy B. Lord spent her first week helping us devise the questionnaire and the next two using it to do field research. She brought back eighty-two interviews that we used as the template for answering, in dozens of variations and combinations, the 2000 fake questionnaires. Once we'd crunched the numbers, surprise, surprise, they came out in favour of the name and product promise of Big Lather, clearly indicating it was worth doing the R&D then going to test market.

Our luck held. New York was delighted with the research and approved the R&D. We were going to go to test market with Big Lather. I'm ashamed to say that Jonas Bold called to tell me that the head of research in our New York office, who had personally done the presentation to Colgate-Palmolive, thought I ought to be congratulated for what was a beautifully designed piece of research, since my name was so clearly associated with organising and working with the independent research company. Jonas added that he (the research director) wanted me to know that the task of presenting so well-crafted a piece of work had been a pleasure, and that he looked forward to future projects.

It was obvious that for any future projects we couldn't simply continue with the scam. The time had come to put to Dansford my idea of creating a viable market-research model for Asia.

'Excellent suggestion. We'll get New York to back the project,' he said.

'But they think what we've done is terrific, that excellent research facilities already exist. They'll want to know why we should fix it if it ain't broke.'

'Ah, tell them that we weren't entirely satisfied with the Big Lather model and want the university to work on an ethnocentric or Asian model.'

'What, and then hand it over to SEARA – make it legit?'

'I guess that's the idea.'

'Dansford, I'd rather not. Sidney doesn't believe in research, and that way he'd end up owning the only legitimate research company in Singapore, with Beatrice Fong.'

'There's something very Chinese about that,' Dansford laughed.

'Yeah, but I don't believe I should contribute to making either of them richer than they already are. Besides, we'll have to create the organisation, train the people, get someone to run it, and finance it initially. I can't see Sidney agreeing to supply the money for something he doesn't believe will work. If we do it within the agency, it's a catch-22 anyway – it won't be seen as independent research.'

'So, what have you got in mind?'

'Well, for a start, let's simply look at it as building an Asian research model. By the way, I like the term *ethnocentric*; we'll use that – it sounds suitably academic. Forget about the research company that may eventually use any prototype model we evolve. My cousin, who's an associate professor of sociology at the Singapore Institute of Technology, has agreed to come on board but, of course, knows nothing about advertising. That would be my contribution.'

'For someone who earlier admitted to me that he had doubts about research, you've come a long way, Simon.'

I laughed. 'That was Australia and cigarettes. Quite different.' I sounded like Ronnie. 'I can clearly see the need to get to know the Asian market and mindset a lot better than we do. Anyway, I thought we should make it a university initiative.'

'Oh, now that's interesting.'

'The sociology department builds the model in conjunction with their new school of business, which then licenses it to us – or anyone else for that matter. That gives it the authority. Then, if Sidney or Beatrice Fong cares to take SEARA any further, they have only to make the decision to start a legitimate research company without getting the agency involved. What do you think?'

'I can see you've done a fair bit of thinking on your own, Simon. But have you thought that you won't be able to do your share of the work on agency time? Unless, of course, we sponsor it.'

'No chance, and when would I find the time during the day anyway? It will have to be at night, in my own time. My cousin, Dr Kwan, is prepared to do the same. He has his own reasons for doing so. The university need not be involved until much later. I don't think we need a sponsor, not yet anyway.'

'Well then, what can I say? Damned good initiative. It's also a big relief.' He grinned. 'Frankly, if Big Lather had failed and Colgate, as they usually do, had done a post-mortem, I'd hate to think what would have happened to my – our – prospects in Asia.'

'Dansford, I owe you big-time for having faith in me and taking a risk on my behalf when you could so easily have played it safe, covered your arse and said no to the project.'

'My absolute pleasure, dear boy. I'm of the firm opinion that we're here for a good time, not a long time. Covering your arse invariably leads to mental constipation. Big Lather is in R&D and soon it'll be in test market, so all's well that ends well. But, come to think of it, with you and Doc Kwan working on a genuine research model over the next few months, it may be a good idea for SEARA to quietly close. Go broke. That way we can begin with a clean slate. The good thing is that you're keeping it in the family, just you and Doc Kwan. Nobody else need know, if you see what I mean.'

He obviously meant the Wings – in particular, Sidney. 'Oh, yes, of course, but there's a possible catch. We need a third research partner, a field researcher to test, you know, hypotheses, various concepts. It's essential to the project. I thought perhaps Mercy B. Lord. She now has some experience and she's pretty bright. She's the obvious choice if she'll agree to do it in her own time – weekends, nights. Of course, I'd pay her . . .'

Dansford's reaction was unexpected. His head jerked and he was clearly taken aback. 'Oh!' It was an exclamation not a question.

'What? What's the problem?' I asked, surprised.

Dansford quickly regained his composure. 'Please don't take this the wrong way, Simon, but stay away from Mercy B. Lord.'

'But why? She's so obviously the right person to work with us.'

Dansford, now back in control, said quietly, 'Simon, I'm no expert on Chinese bosses and their employees, but from what little I've learned I don't think Beatrice Fong will see it that way.'

'Christ, Dansford, it's the girl's own decision. It's her free time! What's it got to do with Beatrice Fong?'

'I'm not sure that's entirely correct, Simon. The old lady seems to have a very firm and decidedly unhealthy hold over her, and Sidney as well.'

'Dansford, what are you trying to tell me? Is there something I should know?' I had the distinct feeling that he was warning me, as Ronnie had done that first day in the Town Club.

'No, I'm not *trying* to say anything, Simon. But it's pretty damned obvious. Those two, Sidney and Beatrice Fong, are thick as thieves. Sidney accepted that Mercy B. Lord should work on the phoney SEARA research. Now I'm to persuade him, them, to close down SEARA and you employ her to work on your new model?' He spread his hands. 'It doesn't look good.'

'They need never know. Anyway, let them keep SEARA. I'm sure if there's a problem, Mercy B. Lord will refuse my offer or agree to keep it in the family.'

'She's not in your family, son.'

'No. I should be so lucky. But she's trained to be discreet.' As I spoke my heart skipped a beat. I still hadn't confronted her admission, or slip of the tongue, about doing reports on her clients. I'd buried it, deciding they were just routine reports, perfectly normal.

'Hmm, I'm not too sure about that.'

'Mate, Mercy B. Lord is an employee of the Beatrice Fong Agency. She's not a part of anyone's *guanxi*. She's an orphan, for fuck's sake! She doesn't have to answer to anyone. If you think about it like that, no ties, no extended family obligations, she's perfect for the project!'

Dansford grinned. 'It's never a good idea to mix business with pleasure, Simon.'

'Who said I am?'

'You did, a moment ago. You said, "I should be so lucky." I know you're very fond of her. Not a good idea, old son.'

'There's nothing between us,' I protested, adding foolishly, 'I've never so much as laid a finger on her.' It was technically, if not emotionally, the truth. I admit, this time my heart was doing more than just skipping a beat. I could hear it boom-boom-booming.

'Simon, it seems to me that the fact that she's unconnected, has no support, no *guanxi*, allows people like Fong and Wing to prey on her. They'll make sure one way or another that she's dependent on them.'

'That's exactly my point. The culture doesn't allow talent alone to prosper. If she's trained in research, she's potentially a free and independent agent. That at least makes it worthwhile.'

I was suddenly furious and struggled to contain myself. Thank God for a bland, flat peasant face. I knew Dansford's logic was sound, but I felt it was bitterly unfair that Mercy B. Lord could be seen to have no rights, to always be a pawn in someone else's game, the orphan with nobody on her side. I had become convinced that her absence from Singapore each

Thursday night had something to do with Beatrice Fong – something unpleasant. Admittedly she'd said nothing, but it was in her eyes, her body language, where I saw something close to fear. I told myself that helping her had nothing to do with my falling in love. For better or worse, she had me on her side. I was not going to let her down, watch her drown, even if she'd never actually asked me to help her.

Dansford sighed. He could see I was determined to have Mercy B. Lord on our team. 'Well, as you said, she'll either agree or she won't. If she's reluctant, my advice, for what it's worth, is don't try to talk her into it.'

'She's not the type to be talked into anything,' I said, a little defensively. 'We need her. Besides, she should be encouraged, helped. Why should she be a prisoner to Beatrice Fong's needs? She has rights of her own.'

Dansford gave me a small smile. 'Simon, in my experience, we're all prisoners, one way or another, of someone else's needs.'

'Yeah, but I'd like to help. If she doesn't want my help, she's free to reject it.'

'Well, take it easy, won't you, Simon. Don't let your heart rule your head. As King Solomon says, and I quote: "There be three things which are too wonderful for me, yea, four which I know not: the way of an eagle in the air; the way of a serpent upon a rock; the way of a ship in the midst of the sea; and the way of a man with a maid."'

'From the Bible?' I said, surprised.

'Aye, my Irish Catholic childhood. I tried very hard to avoid the dogma, but some things stick. For instance, the noble concept of Christian charity.' He paused. 'It can often be an excuse to interfere unnecessarily or even perniciously.'

CHAPTER SEVEN

IT WAS EIGHT MONTHS since I'd first arrived in Singapore. Big Lather was in test market and I was no nearer to bedding Mercy B. Lord. As a result, I was beginning to develop a bit of a complex. I was happy to admit I was no Casanova, nor God's gift to womankind, but I'd served my apprenticeship between the sheets and more than one bunny had been complimentary and happy to return. I also knew that I was generally liked by the women I'd been fortunate enough to take to bed.

The irony was that here I was in Asia, where there were more women available than I'd had hot breakfasts, and the only one I really wanted didn't appear remotely interested. That's not to say we weren't friends – we got on like a house on fire. But that was it; we were affectionate friends or, as we'd say in Australia, great mates. Despite our declarations of love that night at my flat, which I still clung to with all the desperation of a drowning man, there had been no other expressions of feeling, and I was too nervous to press her to explain.

It was obvious Mercy B. Lord liked my company, and she often initiated a date. Sometimes I'd be in the agency working back and my phone would ring. A laughing voice would say at the other end, 'It's seven o'clock, Simon Koo, and I'm hungry. How would you like to take a beautiful woman to dinner?' Singapore had hundreds of hole-in-the-wall and street eateries, and she'd always choose one or another of these out-of-the-way local restaurants not frequented by expats or wealthy Chinese. We laughed a good deal, never quarrelled, though sometimes we argued – she was her own woman and not without opinions – but we always had a good time. There you go – even with all the right ingredients you can't make someone love you, I guess. King Solomon may have wondered at 'the way of a man with a maid', but it would take the wisdom of Solomon to fathom Mercy B. Lord.

It was all so bloody pathetic. This was Asia, after all, where sex was a commodity, not a sacred rite of passage dependent on a promise of everlasting love, although if Mercy B. Lord had required such an affirmation I'd gladly have given it to her. I admit I hungered for her body, but also her mind and soul. It was not simply lust.

Veronica from the Nite Cap girlie bar would have happily moved in with me to satisfy my every desire. I was potentially her ticket to freedom. While she sold her body and so was technically a whore, prostitute, bar girl, whatever, that was far from the way she regarded herself.

In fact, most women in girlie bars imagined that one day they'd be the sole partners of men who could take them away from a life dictated by poverty, and a lack of education, opportunity and *guanxi*. All their energy was directed not at pleasing the conventional or aberrant desires of their clients, but at winning some decent man and becoming his loving wife. Drunks don't generally require a lot of sophisticated technique or sexual acrobatics, for that matter. In the minds of these women, their only assets, other than their appearance, were their seductive arts, cultivated to please a man to whom such a woman would remain forever faithful. In Eastern terms, this had little or nothing to do with love. *Madame Butterfly* was a romantic Western tragedy, but no bar girl would ever be surprised by poor Butterfly's betrayal.

Marriage or even being a concubine was an arrangement that brought with it both privileges and obligations. Sex was one of the obligations. Being loved for your own sake was seldom seen as one of the likely privileges. You gave your partner everything he required as a man, and in return he gave you security, safety and respectability. He eventually grew old or preoccupied, and after you produced a clutch of kids you could generally rely on his desire fading a little. A man of one's own was the ultimate prize and you didn't need to be a whore to aspire to it. When you think of it, my own culture was not without similar examples.

Which brings me back to Mercy B. Lord, the orphan with no *guanxi*, who was being offered all she could possibly wish for and had everything to gain but refused to comply with accepted Asian societal rules. All right, she didn't know I was in line to inherit a fortune from my hugely rich family with *guanxi* bigger than she could ever have imagined. But, nonetheless, I was earning a good income and was not without prospects. Besides, I considered myself a kind, considerate, caring, generous person. I didn't drink to excess and we seemed to be very happy when we were together. Yet she constantly kept me at arm's length with two simple words – 'Not yet' – that were beginning to sound less like a promise than a rebuke.

Veronica, at the Nite Cap girlie bar, lavished a great deal of tender and loving attention on me and, while I paid for it, she was always generous and gave me far more than the sexual favours I paid for. I always tipped her generously, too, but even so I felt beholden. I'm ashamed to say that without her soft hands, tender mouth and compliant thighs I think I would have perished from loneliness and the ache of longing. Naturally, Veronica's hope and dream was that I'd take her away from the girlie bar and ensconce her in my flat, something that was not in the least unusual among the expat population. I felt sorry that I had to disappoint her.

I was genuinely fond of my little whore. To openly admit as much is to sound incredibly naïve (sniggers all round in the Cricket Club bar), but I accepted her right to aspire to a happy ending, and she always responded to my needs with more loving attention than I'd ever received from any woman before her. No bunny even came close. The brutal truth was that I was in love with Mercy B. Lord and Veronica was merely a paid substitute. Not nice, I know, but the truth.

I would sometimes imagine a scene where I took Veronica home to Australia to meet a mortified Chairman Meow – history, in effect, repeating itself. Veronica would be my twentieth-century Little Sparrow, my imported peasant bride, but Thai instead of Chinese. Then I'd smile to myself. I wasn't at all sure that Mercy B. Lord, despite her looks and demeanour, would fill my mum with any less horror, once she knew of her origins. My mother wanted an educated middle-class Chinese girl from a well-connected Singaporean family for me, who wanted sufficient offspring to guarantee at least two healthy male children to begin the 're-orienting' of the Koo family.

Of course, I refused to admit, as Dansford had suggested, that my being in love with Mercy B. Lord was what was influencing me to choose her to partner Dr Kwan and myself in the research project. She was obviously the best choice, having worked with and gained experience on Big Lather. Dansford had witnessed this himself and so his reluctance to agree was totally unexpected and therefore all the more surprising. Perhaps he was trying to keep things in the agency on an even keel, knowing that Sidney and Johnny weren't going out of their way to be pleasant to me. Who knows?

However, I did at least try to do the right thing. Instead of approaching Mercy B. Lord myself to ask if she'd work with us on the research model, I asked my cousin, in his capacity as associate professor, to interview her. Then, if he thought she was a likely third partner, he was to offer her the job, stressing the fact that it was a totally confidential project and had nothing to do with Samuel Oswald Wing, where only Dansford Drocker, who was sworn to secrecy, was aware of it. Finally, he had been told to inform her that the work involved late nights after a full day's work and that the salary was equal to what she earned with the Beatrice Fong Agency. I even instructed Dr Kwan that if, after interviewing Mercy B. Lord, he thought one of his sociology students who needed the income would be better for the task, he was at liberty to make the decision either way. I admit I took the precaution of telling him what an excellent job Mercy B. Lord had done with the Big

Lather field research, but I swear I put no pressure whatsoever on him. I reasoned that if Dr Henry Kwan chose her and she agreed, then who could possibly argue?

As far as I knew, my cousin wasn't aware of my feelings for Mercy B. Lord. On the several visits I'd made to my local extended family I'd never suggested she accompany me. I was only too aware that her stunning looks and outgoing personality would have resulted in a phone call to Chairman Meow in Australia ten minutes after we'd departed.

Henry interviewed Mercy B. Lord and called me to say she was ideal for the project and had agreed to be a part of it. She was adamant that she didn't want a salary. He stressed that the confidentiality of the project was of paramount importance to her, too. Apparently she'd loved doing the previous research and would jump at the opportunity to learn more.

'She can't make it on a Thursday night, otherwise she's free,' he said, then added, 'She strikes me as being very bright. I only wish some of my sociology students were as intelligent. Fortunately, she is familiar with every demographic of Singaporean society. Nobody in my faculty or among my students can boast such a connection to the common people. She's a real find, Simon,' he concluded.

Naturally, I was delighted and felt myself entirely vindicated. It had been a professional decision and Mercy B. Lord had been under no pressure to accept. In fact, she had been given every opportunity to refuse.

The six months that followed were both agony and ecstasy. While our discussions would occasionally take place in a cheap restaurant (cooking at home in Singapore being a needless exercise), we worked mostly from the flat. Mercy B. Lord would take a rickshaw or a taxi and pick up our dinner on the way. Having her so close, often late at night, nearly drove me crackers. On only two occasions, when it was well past midnight, had I suggested she stay the night. However, she'd repeated the same dreaded words: 'Not yet' – two words that were slowly driving me crazy. It wasn't only the refusal, it was the promise in those words. Perhaps I was being ingenuous, but it was the way she said it, her eyes full of what seemed to be genuine longing and the glint of tears. Either Mercy B. Lord was the world's best actress, or whatever it was that prevented her was sufficiently fraught with consequences to overcome any desire she may have had for me. Or perhaps, as Chairman Meow would say when we reached a wrong conclusion as kids, 'Simon, you're confusing dust motes with fairies.'

Mercy B. Lord was not only beautiful, she was also dead sexy, so prior to our nightly meetings I'd taken to wearing a jockstrap, otherwise known as an athletic support. In this way I hoped my erections, firmly constrained by an elasticised cotton cup and belt, wouldn't show. I suffered constantly from agonising post-erection pains in the scrotum, commonly referred to as 'lover's balls', sometimes so severe that I felt as if I was bandy-legged. I'd then have to take myself off to the shower, though not the proverbial 'cold shower', to masturbate to relieve the pain.

But even this wasn't always sufficient to calm the badly battered ball-bearings, and it was to Veronica that I went to seek relief after I put Mercy B. Lord into a taxi. I make no bones about the fact that I'm a man and therefore probably an insensitive creature, but I was invariably greeted warmly, which somehow helped. I was always stone-cold sober, and it was usually past midnight when I arrived and paid for the obligatory round of drinks, the accepted entry fee. Veronica would then escort me to a back room, referred to as a jig-a-jig room, for obvious reasons. I don't know how or where she was trained, maybe in Thailand, but she would fit me with a condom, then allow me to have my urgent way with her and afterwards apply various oils to the offending area and gently massage it. Lastly she would serve me a cup of steaming green tea before calling a taxi to take me home. It may sound crass, but in this way sweet little Veronica made the constant longing for Mercy B. Lord almost bearable, and miraculously I would wake up in the morning without pain. Can you sublimate your desire for one woman by taking another? I'm not sure, but then men are pretty basic creatures.

But, of course, all good things, as well as all bad things, come to an end. One late night in October, a year and one month after I'd arrived in Singapore, we put the finishing touches to our grand ethnocentric research model. I should have bought a bottle of champagne but I'd organised a celebration dinner on the Saturday night at the Goodwood Park Hotel, one of the best eateries in town. It was late and we were happy, but also a little let down, as one often is at the prospect of something ending that has absorbed your attention for a long time and resulted in great camaraderie.

I turned to my cousin. 'Dr Kwan, we owe you big-time, mate.'

He laughed. 'And me you, Simon. If I don't get a full professorship out of the paper I present to my university peers, then my *guanxi* isn't working. I'm off. It's almost midnight and I need some sleep. I've got student exam papers to mark all weekend, but I'll see you Saturday night at the celebration.'

I waited until he'd left then turned to Mercy B. Lord. 'You too, kid. Your knowledge of the streets and the *kampongs* was invaluable. You've made an enormous contribution. Thank you. If this works, as I know it will, I feel sure something big will come of it. Saturday night we're drinking French champagne again. Do you think you could wear your black cheongsam?'

'Oh, Simon, of course!' She clapped her hands, laughing. 'I've seen a pair of even higher heels at Robinsons. They're lipstick-red for good luck. Now I have an excuse to buy them!'

'May I be permitted to buy them for you?' I asked, adding quickly, 'you know, as a thankyou for the effort you've put into the research project?'

'No!'

'But I'd really like to. You'll please me by wearing the black cheongsam, so let me please you in return.'

'Simon, it's not professional! Dr Kwan said we were equal partners, that my name would appear on his paper for the university.'

'It's not meant to be professional,' I protested. 'It's a simple thankyou. For God's sake, you've given up months of your free time without any compensation. You refused to be paid for your time. Mercy B. Lord, we, Henry and I, owe you a great deal more than a lousy pair of red shoes!'

'Simon, you owe me nothing. I've been working with Beatrice Fong since I was sixteen – it's all I've ever known.' She looked at me. 'When you've done the same thing for five years, meet, greet and be sweet —'

'You do a whole heap more than that, Mercy B. Lord,' I interjected.

'Hold on, let me finish, Simon . . . you begin to think that's all you can do. That first research project, I mean, the part that was . . .' She paused, searching for a word.

'Legit?'

'Yes, legitimate . . . made me realise that perhaps I *could* do something else. Being nice for a living has its limits. But then I thought, well, it's only an extension of what I know, meeting people and making them feel at ease, but instead of answering their questions I asked them my own. So it wasn't really much of a test, much of a change.'

'There was a lot more to it than that. You did brilliantly. We based the entire report on what you gave us.'

Mercy B. Lord ignored this obvious compliment. 'But working with you and Dr Kwan over the past six months has made me realise that maybe I have the capacity to do something more intellectually challenging one day.' She looked down, hesitating. 'Something that didn't depend on me being just . . . you know . . . attractive and personable.' She looked up. 'That's what you've given me and it's more than enough thanks.'

I will never know how I resisted sweeping her into my arms and kissing her and telling her over and over how I loved and admired her. But all I said was, 'Dr Kwan says you're very bright, that you'd beat the pants off his best students.'

'Simon!' Mercy B. Lord exclaimed in mock shock. 'I have no intention of removing his best students' pants!' Then she giggled.

I grinned. 'Although I'm sure every one of his male students would be delighted if you did.'

She gave me a mischievous smile. 'Simon, if I was going to remove any male's pants, they'd be yours.'

'Yeah, but "not yet",' I replied softly, the easy, rather silly bantering suddenly over. 'Come, sweetheart, it's late. We'd better call your taxi.'

'Oh no, Simon.' She lifted her handbag from the chair where it rested and, reaching in, produced a toothbrush. 'There's a new pair of panties in there as well. I got both when I went out to pick up dinner.'

I was too dumbstruck to react. 'But you just said—?'

'Well, make up your mind. Our project is over. Don't you want me to stay tonight?'

Like a bloody idiot, I said, 'Mercy B. Lord, are you sure?'

She lowered her eyes and in a voice not much above a whisper declared, 'No, Simon, I'm not sure. I've tried so very hard not to.' She looked up at me, her eyes brimming. 'But I've made the terrible mistake of falling in love with you.'

Everything is perfect in the imagination – two lovers slipping into each other's arms, the touch of perfumed skin, the slow quickening of the breath, the gasp, the cry then the sigh of a first wet, smooth entry, the daring agony of withdrawal to delay the coming of the ultimate moment. Then the tenderness of mouths meeting and tongues touching, exploring breasts and nipples taut with desire, the questing tongue finding, enjoying, cultivating a slow and wonderful excitement before coming together once more. Then the urgent thrusting, and the sheer bliss of a woman's urgent cries as she abandons herself to a carnal, primitive, all-consuming and glorious excitement that is the perfection of a simultaneous climax. So much for imagination.

If I have described it clumsily without the foreplay, the words of tenderness, the promise of fulfilment to come that most women love to hear, it is because in my imagination I see pictures that stimulate, arouse and heat the blood. Perhaps this is why, as an artist who thinks in images,

I find it difficult to translate them into words, even though words are so much a part of making love. Sometimes tender, sometimes raunchy, they include the passionate promise of things to come, the small ecstasies that are going to be performed if her lover is as good as his urgent, salacious promises. To describe these murmured words as 'dirty' is an altogether puritan and offensive notion that denies the erotic vocabulary and part of the variety and pleasure of lovemaking.

I still have great difficulty describing that night, finally making love to someone I'd imagined making love to countless times. I recalled that first week in Singapore when I had lusted after her, consumed by blatant carnal desire. But by the second week my feelings had changed, and for the first time in my life I felt something different. When she lightly brushed my cheek with her lips, although the kiss was not intended to be provocative, nonetheless it sent a frisson down my spine and set off a small explosion in my gut and then directly below it. But even so, I had begun to imagine what it might be like to have Mercy B. Lord as a permanent part of my life. My feelings had grown from that point until I now wanted all of her: her sidelong glances; her giggles; her frowning concentration; those spontaneous touches; her complex female mind; her surprising clarity of thought when, for example, she put herself in the shoes of the women in the *kampongs*; her confidence in her own beauty and desirability; and her humility and compassion when she talked to the *amahs*, the Chinese washerwomen in their white blouses and black pyjama trousers. I loved the way she walked and stretched; her clean, pink mouth when she yawned after a long night's work, touching her lips after the yawn had passed.

Perhaps that's why I foolishly and insensitively asked if she was sure about her resolve to stay with me. I had long since realised that Mercy B. Lord was not reluctant to make love or to give up her virginity. Her fear sprang from something else, even, perhaps, someone else. Whether Mercy B. Lord came to me as a virgin or with the past of a promiscuous woman wasn't of the least concern to me. She wasn't a trophy or a challenge and never had been. Now I had triggered the fear that for so long had been expressed in those two words, 'not yet'. She still held the new toothbrush in its cellophane wrapper, but now her head was bowed and a single tear moved slowly down her left cheek. I stepped closer and kissed her lightly on the forehead, then cupping the back of her head in both my hands I raised her head and kissed her on the mouth. Her lips parted and she gave a small gasp at the touch of my tongue but then she joined in like a hungry child. She had made no attempt to hold me, but suddenly she pulled her mouth from my own. 'Undress me, Simon, everything. I want to be naked.' She said this softly yet boldly, as if it were an instruction, albeit a loving one. 'I want to kiss you when I'm naked.'

She was wearing a light yellow and red floral summer dress with short puffy sleeves and a wide skirt to just above her knees, and on her feet were a pair of simple open leather sandals from which protruded bright-red varnished toenails. She wore little make-up apart from mascara to frame her dark eyes and light green eye shadow on her lids. I undid the half-dozen mother-of-pearl buttons below her neckline. 'Close your eyes and I'll tell you when to open them,' I said. I slipped her dress over her head and smoothed her hair back into place. She stood in her bra and panties, a prettiness of skimpy white lace, and I realised that the idea of staying with me wasn't a spontaneous decision brought on by the euphoria of having completed the project with the possibility of regrets in the morning. 'Keep them shut now, no cheating!' I laughed. I then turned her around slowly so that her back faced me and undid her bra strap and removed her bra, turning her back to face me. 'No peeping, darling.' It was the first time I had used the endearment and it sounded gloriously possessive. Her breasts were small – about the size of an upturned teacup – firm and pointing slightly upwards. I kissed them, taking each nipple momentarily between my lips so that she gave a small gasp. 'More, much more later,' I murmured, then slid to my knees and undid her sandal straps and removed them. Then slowly, gently, I pulled down her panties until they reached her ankles and she could step out of them.

'Can I open them now?' Mercy B. Lord asked.

'No, keep them shut just a few more moments.' I buried my face in her dark loveliness and kissed her Venus mound then slid my tongue down and deeper, searching for her core. Another gasp, this one louder, as my tongue found the place where her vulva parted, then a small whimper. The softness of her warm pubic V was enormously exciting and I felt the straining hardness within my trousers. Then, rising, I faced her and gently grasped her shoulders. 'You may open your eyes now. I have seen you and tasted you, Mercy B. Lord, and you are perfect: very beautiful and absolutely delicious.'

She opened her eyes and smiled. 'Thank you, Simon.' She raised her arms and cupped her breasts. Ridiculously, she still held the toothbrush, which had somehow broken through the top of its cellophane wrapper and was pressed against her breast. 'But my breasts are too small.'

Later I would ask myself why every woman is unhappy with some part of her anatomy. Now I said, 'They're lovely, perfect, but scrubbing them with a toothbrush won't make them any bigger.'

'Oh, I should clean my teeth!' she cried. 'They always – I mean, in Barbara Cartland books – they clean their teeth before . . . going to bed.'

'You've been reading the wrong books,' I laughed, removing the toothbrush and placing it on the coffee table. Then, taking her by the hand, I led her to the bedroom.

I switched on the bedside lamp and pulled back the covers. 'Hop in, darling.' She climbed into bed and pulled the sheet up to her neck. 'I am now going to reveal what is laughingly known as my body. I don't expect you'll be impressed,' I joked in an effort to put her at ease.

Mercy B. Lord giggled. 'I can barely wait, darling.' It was the first time she had used the endearment, so commonplace but in this context so wonderful. Then there was a sudden look of consternation. 'Simon, I'm not on the pill.'

'Lucky my dad gave me a lecture on the birds and the bees,' I said with a grin, telling her the story as I started to peel off my clothes. I'd been fourteen, around the age that puberty strikes a young bloke like a sledgehammer. I suppose my mum had instructed my sisters, but it was Dad who called me into his study. I don't remember very much of what he told me, something about the various things you could catch if you weren't careful. But then he handed me a packet containing a condom. 'Always carry one of these in your wallet, son. Replace it every month if it hasn't been used.'

Shocked, I blurted, 'Dad, I'm only fourteen!'

'A man never knows when he's going to get lucky, son,' he'd replied. Now I looked down at Mercy B. Lord and was relieved to see she was grinning. 'And tonight I got lucky, exceedingly, wonderfully, terrifically lucky. And I always took my dad's advice.' I reached into my back pocket and withdrew my wallet, opened it and removed a condom. 'Mercy B. Lord, would you do me the enormous honour?'

'Oh, Simon,' she said, shocked and surprised, 'I don't know how.' Then she started to giggle.

'On the scale of difficulty it probably rates as a one, just up from zero,' I joked.

Mercy B. Lord took the small packet between forefinger and thumb. 'Oh, look, it's in something squishy!'

'Lubrication. You pay extra for that. I'll have you know I'm no cheapskate,' I laughed. Then I said, 'I too have a confession.'

'Oh?'

'I'm wearing a jockstrap.'

'A what?'

'An athletic support.'

'Oh, Simon, there is something wrong? You are hurt?' she cried, concerned.

Somewhat sheepishly, but eventually much to her delight, I explained how she was responsible. 'Then I shall remove it and —' she held up the small condom packet, 'hopefully put this on.' I removed my shoes and socks, dropped my trousers and quickly stepped out of my underpants. My shirt covered the jockstrap, which was already struggling to restrain my urgent need to break free.

Mercy B. Lord leapt from the bed – God, she was beautiful – dropped to her knees and, to my surprise, held the condom packet between her lips as she lifted my shirt. 'Hold,' she said, handing me the ends of my shirt. Then she removed the jockstrap with the predictable result. All that constrained longing became a hugely distinct possibility. 'Oh, Simon!' she said with a gasp. 'Is that all for me?' Then, suddenly serious and biting her bottom lip in concentration, she opened the small packet and carefully slipped the condom in place. 'Isn't your daddy a clever man?' she said, rising to her feet. Suddenly she let out a mischievous giggle and pointed at my left breast pocket. 'Oh, Simon, your shirt! I hadn't noticed before.'

'My shirt?' I asked, glancing down. It was a new one, unlike any of those purchased in Australia. This one had short sleeves and, as was the custom for expats, was custom-made and carried the owner's initials on the left-hand breast pocket. This was no doubt an affectation to show that the shirt was tailor-made. Rather than have my initials, I had asked that mine be in Chinese calligraphy and read 'Fortune Cookie'. I admit I was rather proud of the difference, a sort of private joke, a bit of a send-up, because most expats sported at least three initials. The Chinese tailor questioned me closely about the word 'cookie' and I explained it was a small, round, delicious cake with a saying or a wish inside. 'It very expensive, yes?' he'd asked. 'No, very cheap,' I'd replied. I must say, he did a nice job of the three shirts I ordered.

But as I reached the last button, Mercy B. Lord, having great difficulty restraining herself, asked, 'Do you know what the calligraphy on your shirt says, Simon?'

'Yes, Fortune Cookie – my nickname in Australia. It's meant to be a bit of a joke.'

'It says, "Very cheap, small, round, delicious wish cake"!' She giggled again. 'Are you going to let me taste it and make a wish, sir?'

Whereupon we both broke up, consumed with giggles. 'Certainly. If you're a good girl, and relax and do exactly as I say, the result will be simply delicious and everything you wished for,' I finally managed. 'Back into bed, beautiful. Let the fun begin.'

It had all gone so well but now I had to deliver, and my most ardent hope was that I wasn't overstating what was to come. I knew enough to know that what worked for one woman might not work for another; that, unlike men, women had complex needs and desires. In the case of Mercy B. Lord, it was an overdeveloped desire to please, which undid all my earlier efforts. 'You must show me, Simon. I *must* make you happy.' She was clearly a neophyte, eager and willing enough, but awkward and distracted by her desire to please me. 'I want to do what you like. Please show me.' In her present frame of mind it was clearly going to be difficult or impossible to arouse her; her own desire would be squandered in an attempt to satisfy me.

'Sit up, darling.'

Mercy B. Lord, looking anxious, did as she was told, sitting on her heels, the sheet covering the lower part of her body. 'What have I done wrong, Simon?' she cried.

'Mercy B. Lord, I have wanted you countless times, made love to you in my imagination. You are even more beautiful than I ever imagined, but . . .'

She gasped in dismay and brought her hands up to cover her mouth. 'Oh, Simon, I don't know what to do!' she wailed.

I kissed her lightly on the forehead. 'Well, then, it's fortunate that one of us does.'

'You said "but" . . . but what? You're disappointed – I know it!'

'No, of course not, *but* there are two rules you simply must obey.'

'There are?'

'Yes. The first is you have to allow a man to make love to you – to please you. That's rule number one.'

'But I *must* please *you!*'

'Later! That comes later.' I assumed a stern expression. 'You are not permitted to worry about pleasing me, and doing so is really very simple. When the time comes, you'll know.'

'We're supposed to please each other?'

'Darling, I am already pleased. Very, very, very pleased. And don't worry. If we get this right, as I know we shall, I will be even more pleased. But there's another rule, rule number two. You have to tell me what pleases you and guide me around your body. Sometimes a quarter of an inch, even much less, makes all the difference – with my finger, my mouth . . . my penis. Will you promise?' I was immensely grateful to the Australian bunnies who had generously educated and directed me in the matter of their sexual tastes.

'But, Simon, I don't know. It only happened once when I was fourteen, with a boy at school. Afterwards I bled. I thought the blood was a punishment from God for sinning! I said a thousand Hail Marys but I didn't go to the priest, to confession. I thought I'd probably go to hell!' She smiled.

'There's often a little blood when your hymen breaks, darling – it's a small membrane at the entrance to your vagina – it's perfectly natural. Now, if you relax and take the pleasure as it comes, it will be a lovely experience, I promise.'

All the bunnies I'd bedded in Australia had been experienced, and, as I said before, I was grateful for their instructions on how to please them most. I had no idea how long it might take to win the confidence of a neophyte, and it was a good hour before Mercy B. Lord was sufficiently relaxed again to enjoy my caresses. I smiled when I recalled my florid fantasies, but the reality was much more powerful. I had explored her delicious body and finally elicited a tentative response. With a little more exploring she became moist and fully responsive, crying out joyously when we discovered an erogenous zone that was her particular turn-on. Then, quite suddenly, her breathing quickened and she gasped, 'Now! Please, please, now, Simon!'

I entered her and her pelvis came alive. She moaned and cried out in our urgent, compulsive, blinding, wonderful act of lovemaking as we climaxed simultaneously. We had achieved the near impossible in our first coupling. Then, a little later, I used my tongue a second time for her exclusive delight and she was able to surrender to her own pleasure.

Afterwards, as I held her in my arms, she said, 'Simon, did Dr Kwan really say, you know, that I was bright?'

'Yes, more than once, darling.'

She snuggled even closer. 'In that case you may buy me the red shoes.' She sighed and promptly fell asleep in my arms and my joy was beyond imagining. Even so, I found myself doing my habitual mental arithmetic: it was Tuesday 30th May 1967, that is 3 + 0 = 3. 1+ 9 +6 + 7 = 23. 23+3 = 26. 2+6 = 8! Yippee! Eight is the luckiest number for the Chinese. The numbers hadn't let me down.

The following morning Mercy B. Lord left the flat, saying she had a client in from Germany and so couldn't see me again until Friday as Beatrice had agreed she'd have dinner with him on the Wednesday. 'Oh, Simon, it's going to be awful not seeing you until Friday evening.'

'Will you think about moving in . . . permanently?'

She looked at me, then down at her feet. 'Simon, I can't. Please don't ask me to explain. I simply can't, that's all.'

'You mean what happened last night was a one-night stand?' I said, failing to disguise the hurt in my voice.

She looked up, alarmed. 'I didn't say that. It was lovely, but we have to be discreet, that's all.'

'You mean Beatrice?'

'I can't answer that,' she said, now close to tears. 'Simon, we mustn't be seen being lovey-dovey in public, only as friends.'

This was the moment where I could have persisted. But one look into her pleading eyes and I let it pass. Besides, 'lovey-dovey' was such a quaint old-fashioned term. 'I will do no more than politely guide you by the elbow on Saturday when they show us to our table,' I promised. Then, in an attempt to lighten the mood I put on an upper-class English accent. 'I will henceforth demonstrate no more than those public gestures expected of a gentleman, my dear.'

'No, you're *not* allowed to pinch my bottom in public, Simon!' she laughed.

We had invited Dansford Drocker to join our celebration, as he had always been supportive of the research project. When questions had arisen that we couldn't answer, he'd contacted New York for advice. In fact, he'd been an enormous help while remaining absolutely discreet.

I had deliberately chosen Saturday night in the hope that Dansford would arrive at the Goodwood Park Hotel relatively sober. He was pretty incorrigible most nights, but on Fridays, given that he wasn't required to come into work the next day, he was usually particularly outrageous.

Dansford wasn't a destructive drunk or one who abused people. He stayed happy and didn't fall about, throw up in public or disgrace himself in any other way. In fact, his capacity for holding his grog was astonishing and I have never met anyone who could match him. It was just that you didn't know what to expect from him next. His pranks, performed on the spur of the moment, were becoming the stuff of legend.

He had an excellent voice and could sing opera and popular ballads, both sentimental and current, play the alto saxophone in a brilliant imitation of Jimmy Dorsey, was a truly good jazz pianist, knew and sang all the Frank Sinatra hits remarkably well, was a good stand-up comic, could conduct a band or take over an orchestra, and in a dozen ways disrupt a restaurant, a boring cocktail party, government reception or dull concert to the joy of almost everyone present. But all of this and more occurred *only* if he was intoxicated. Sober, Dansford was a softly spoken, modest, well-bred, Harvard-educated Bostonian and a gentleman to his bootstraps.

Dansford's Friday nights in particular produced gems for the anecdote-collectors. Early Saturday evenings offered the best chance of him behaving more or less decorously. He would have spent most of the day at home, alternately sleeping and throwing up from the climax to the week's outrageous behaviour. Up until about 10 p.m. on Saturdays he was tolerably good . . . well, good by his own remarkable standards of bad.

However, it must be said that he was generally popular with expats, with the exception of a few old fuddy-duddies. As a general rule, most of them had left for a nightcap at home well before Dansford attained his outrageous zenith.

He was also greatly loved in the various bars around town, where he was a generous tipper and big spender. In fact, the proprietor of Bill Bailey's bought an alto sax and installed a piano just for Dansford to play, an investment they claimed paid off handsomely, as every drunk in town seemed to make a point of ending the evening's revelry there in the hope of catching a Dansford Drocker spontaneous late-night shindig. He always opened, perhaps as a tribute to his host, with the ballad 'Won't You Come Home, Bill Bailey', which he sang in the turn-of-the-century manner in which it was first composed.

Admittedly, drunks are not, generally speaking, a discerning lot, but many a drunken sailor in their home ports all over the world insisted that they'd never heard better jazz or boogie-woogie played on the piano or alto saxophone than very late at night by a drunken American at Bill Bailey's in Singapore.

When I invited Dansford to our celebration dinner he'd insisted that he pay for the drinks – wine, in particular, was very expensive at the time. 'Simon, my friend, I'll be drinking most of what we'll consume, so it's only fair that the evening's libations are my shout. We shall have French champagne. Then we shall have wine. Others will watch enviously as the four of us dine.'

I'd accepted his gracious offer knowing it was pointless arguing: Dansford Drocker didn't tolerate anyone paying for his self-indulgence – that is, unless they were rich Chinese or high government officials, the former because they would otherwise lose face and the government wallahs because they took more from him in taxes than they returned in tangible benefits.

I don't know why it is, but a woman who has recently made love to a man for the first time holds herself somewhat differently. Mercy B. Lord was just as stunning as formerly in the black cheongsam – she still wore no jewellery, her hair was done in the same Vidal Sassoon five-point style – but she was subtly different, and it was more than just the outrageously high red patent-leather heels. Whereas she was a breathtakingly beautiful woman before, she now seemed to have gained a confidence and sexuality that made women look and men dream. Most would have concluded that she must be a famous model and that the short, thickset guy with her could only be her manager, because she belonged on the arm of someone like Marlon Brando. People like me didn't pull women like her unless they were obscenely rich.

Henry Kwan arrived early and alone, straight from marking student papers. Day dress was the just-about-universal white short-sleeved shirt, tie and cotton slacks in various subdued tones of buff, fawn or light khaki. As a concession to the occasion he'd added a light khaki cotton jacket. On semi-formal occasions such as dinner at the Goodwood Park Hotel, one of the best eateries in Singapore, men pretty well wore what they pleased, provided it included a tie. Some didn't even bother to wear a jacket. But the women were expected to be dressed 'to the nines', supposedly to please their blokes, although Mercy B. Lord once told me that dressing up had nothing whatsoever to do with men.

I wore a new pair of slacks and a light blue long-sleeved shirt from Australia, having given up the Mickey Mouse and psychedelic ties for plain colours. Tonight I was wearing a red tie Mercy B. Lord had purchased at Robinsons at the same time as she'd bought her splendid shoes. 'It's almost the same red, Simon,' she'd laughed and kissed me on the cheek. 'People will know I belong to you, darling.' How nice the single word 'darling' sounds when it's newly minted. In Australia, wearing an outrageous tie was a matter of being seen to be different. Here, the three-lettered monogrammed shirt pocket was the way expats differentiated themselves. I guess it was meant to convey, though to whom I'm not sure, that you knew your way around and were not some gawky tourist. I'd given my three offending shirts to the *amah* who came in daily to clean the flat and do the laundry. Nobody, unless they're short, fat and outrageously camp, wants to be known as a very cheap, small, round, delicious wish cake!

No more ostentatious gear for you, mate, I'd told myself, pulling on my new pair of strides. But then it suddenly struck me that the trousers I was wearing had been purchased from a trendy menswear boutique in Orchard Road, a part of town that was beginning to dress up a bit itself.

The shop, owned by the husband of Jasmine Koh, Singapore's top model, was named the Purple Zip, and the only difference between the other trousers sold in a town renowned for its good Chinese and Indian tailors and my new pants was that they came off the rack and featured a purple zipper in the fly. Additionally, they came in a fancy purple shopping bag that carried the shop's name and slogan, *The only way to fly*. The other difference was that the factory-made strides I'd bought cost roughly three times as much as a pair of tailor-made slacks of identical or superior cotton. In other words, I'd fallen for a coloured zip nobody but me would ever see, and then only when I sat on the toilet with my trousers around my knees. If I regarded people who wore monogrammed shirt pockets as wankers, then what did a purple fly zipper on a pair off-the-rack daks make me?

Anyway, Mercy B. Lord seemed happy with the way I looked after I'd added a cotton two-button (there I go again) navy jacket. It was enough to make me worthy of my stunning companion.

We found Dr Kwan waiting at the bar drinking a beer. Dansford invariably arrived late and I'd warned my cousin that we'd have to have a drink for half an hour or so, then we'd ask to be shown to our table. Waiting any longer for Dansford was pointless.

Mercy B. Lord had taken a taxi to the flat, kept it waiting and we'd taken it on to the hotel. This time her entrance caused only a sudden hush. The dining room was less intimate than on the previous occasion at Raffles, and the patrons, already half-pissed from Saturday-afternoon cocktails, were more talkative. I sensed Mercy B. Lord's sigh of relief that this time there would be no clapping or crying out.

To our surprise, we'd hardly seated ourselves at the bar when Dansford arrived. He wore a beautifully tailored grey lounge suit, Brooks Brothers button-down shirt and a blue Macclesfield silk tie (sorry, I can't help myself), his usual silk knee-high hose and, to add a supposedly casual touch, black Gucci loafers. While he admitted to having stopped off at Bill Bailey's for a drink or two (read six or seven), by his standards he was practically sober.

'Champagne! A bottle! Cristal!' he shouted out to the barman even before he'd greeted us.

'Steady on, mate!' I cautioned. Cristal was, I knew, horrendously expensive.

'Hello, everyone. Glad you haven't ordered your drinks,' Dansford said. Then, turning to me, 'No, Simon, we *must* begin with champagne!'

The head waiter, which is what he was called at the Goodwood Park, was an Irishman, the only non-Chinese or Indian in the place – always the traditional waiters in Singapore's better establishments. He was passing the bar at that moment and stopped when he heard Dansford's order. Immediately he took over from the surprised Indian barman. 'Excellent choice, sir. We have a bottle on ice. Shall I serve it at your table?'

I subsequently got to know him quite well. His name was Denmeade, Owen Denmeade, and he was a one-time ship's purser on P&O. He admitted to me later that the only reason they had a bottle of Cristal both in stock and cold was in case Long Me Saw, the older brother of the famous Asian movie impresario Long Long Saw, dropped in with a couple of movie stars on his arm.

Dansford's extravagant lifestyle obviously cost him more than his no doubt liberal chief executive's salary and must have been topped up with a private income. I wondered if he was a latter-day remittance man whose family paid him to stay away.

Unfortunately, our table wasn't that far from the bar and Dansford's directive to the barman must have been heard by most of the nearby diners, because a number of eyes followed us and, alas, were destined to stay on us and increase in number as the evening progressed. When the head waiter popped the cork, not in the usual discreet manner but with a loud bang as it issued from the bottle of Cristal and hit the ceiling, there was a round of applause. Furthermore, the presence of a stunning-looking woman in a black cheongsam and the hope that Dansford would come up with something probably made for compulsive viewing. We toasted the research project and then I made a little speech congratulating the inestimable Dr Kwan on his tireless and brilliant efforts and insights. I added a few well-chosen, though carefully neutral words of congratulations and thanks to Mercy B. Lord, ending with a thankyou to Dansford for his cooperation. It seemed like a hopeful start to the evening.

Unfortunately, my hopes were not realised and most of the fun that night was had at our expense by the rest of the diners. I'd been lulled by Dansford's timely arrival into thinking that everything was hunky-dory, but I'd underestimated the number of drinks he'd consumed; the champagne proved to be the tipping point. We'd each drunk a glass while I made my little speech of appreciation, and Dansford had downed three before we'd even decided to consult the menu.

At least on this occasion the waiters were attentive. Dansford was famous for punishing what he regarded as a lack of attention in busy restaurants by rising from his chair and walking to the entrance to the kitchen, where he'd lie flat on the floor and block the path of any waiter coming or going. When they'd stop in bemusement at the crazy American prone in front of them, he would demand Denmeade attend his table and his guests immediately.

But now Denmeade himself hovered.

'And what is the most expensive wine you have?' Dansford asked in a voice loud enough to be heard by at least half the diners in the room.

'Why, the 1956 Nuits-Saint-Georges, Mr Drocker,' Denmeade said in a carrying voice, enjoying the moment, the two Irishmen immediately en garde.

I groaned inwardly and Henry, a light drinker who had left half his glass of champagne, looked thoroughly nervous. He was by nature a quiet and conservative man.

'And how many bottles do you have left?' Dansford demanded, raising his voice so that the entire restaurant grew suddenly deathly quiet and expectant.

'Four, sir,' Denmeade replied, clearly not wishing to have the establishment's wine cellar seen as overly miserly.

'Ah, then bring them all!'

Losing his composure, the head waiter hesitated. 'All? You mean . . . *all* four bottles, sir?'

'Certainly!'

Denmeade gave an obsequious bow and departed, totally defeated. I looked over at Mercy B. Lord, my right eyebrow arched. The entire restaurant was hushed and you could hear the rattle of cooking paraphernalia coming from the kitchen. But she hadn't lost her composure and smiled brilliantly back at me. Dr Kwan cleared his throat. 'I need to go to the men's room,' he announced in a voice barely above a whisper.

Owen Denmeade personally escorted the waiter pushing the service caddy upon which stood the four bottles of Nuits-Saint-Georges. He seemed to have regained his composure somewhat. 'I haven't wiped them clean from the cellar rack, Mr Drocker. Perhaps you'd like to choose the bottle you desire?'

Enjoying the moment, Dansford pitched his voice in the direction of the silent diners, as the food on their plates slowly cooled. 'Open them all, please.'

'But, Mr Drocker —'

'Just do as I say.'

I remember thinking, *Shit! This isn't happening!*

The audience, because that was what it had become, watched as all four bottles were opened. Never mind the champagne cork popping, there was a distinctive murmur at each squeak and plop of the corks. I noticed that the hotel manager had appeared and that the entire kitchen staff had entered and stood at the doorway to watch. Dansford then picked up each dusty bottle, examined it and brought it to his nose. Then, choosing one, he asked the very nervous waiter to pour a splash into a glass. The waiter lifted the bottle but his hand was shaking, so Denmeade took it from him and poured a liberal splash of crimson into the glass.

By this time it seemed there was no way we could be further

embarrassed. No doubt the wine would be suitable and the diners could all go back to eating and, with the entertainment finally over, we could order dinner and the night would proceed more or less as planned, though I was growing concerned that Henry hadn't returned to the table.

Dansford rose from his chair and, playing to his audience, brought the glass to his lips. You could have heard a pin drop. He took a mouthful, gargled in the appropriate manner, then suddenly his eyes grew wide and he hurriedly placed the glass on the table and began to claw at his throat, sinking to his knees as he choked, eyes popping.

There was consternation. Several women cried out, and the hotel manager came running, no doubt thinking that not only was the hotel's most expensive wine off but that they'd somehow poisoned an important patron.

Dansford rose to his feet and resumed his seat just as the concerned and solicitous manager reached him. Then, leaning back in his chair, Dansford indicated the bottle and announced, 'That is a beautiful wine. You may pour it.' He waited until all our glasses had been filled, rose and extended his glass in a toast to the audience. To thunderous applause from the diners, he said, 'Thank you, you have been most patient and shall be rewarded.'

Resuming his seat he said quietly, 'Not a bit hungry, but I feel a severe bout of piano-playing coming on. Will you excuse me?' Instructing the waiter to bring two of the bottles, he made his way to the piano on the bandstand. His opening number was 'Won't You Come Home, Bill Bailey', which he sang with great gusto, thumping it out on the piano in just the manner it was meant to be performed.

There are some who were in the restaurant that night who years later claimed it was undoubtedly the best concert they had ever attended. Mercy B. Lord and I left at midnight, having shared a bottle of Nuits-Saint-Georges and having sent the remaining bottle over to Dansford, who was still at the piano, playing and singing the ballads from George Gershwin's folk opera *Porgy and Bess*. Henry never returned. The last we saw of him was when he left for the men's room at the start of the evening. Later he told me he'd escaped by fleeing through the kitchen. Once outside, he'd run half a mile before he'd stopped to hail a taxi.

If Mercy B. Lord was my first great stroke of luck, the second was to occur a month after Dansford Drocker had further enhanced his reputation as the most outrageous and entertaining drunk in the highly competitive boozy environment of Singapore. I met Elma Kelly. It was on a Friday, mid-morning, and I'd been to see and approve the colour separations for a Texas Tiger twenty-four-sheet poster. As it was close to the printer's, I stopped off at my cousin Peter Kwan's gallery in Orchard Road. I was in the process of admiring a green-glazed pottery vase when a booming voice announced her presence. 'Stand to attention at once!' barked a female version of a British regimental sergeant major.

I turned to see a very large and formidable-looking woman bearing down on me. I don't usually bow to the demands of strangers unless a uniform denotes their authority or makes some kind of sense of their demand. 'Attention? Why, madam?'

'Quiet! Two minutes!' she barked, tapping the face of her wristwatch and coming to rigid attention herself, her arms, great hams, clamped against a vast, tent-like hibiscus-patterned muu-muu. Her face was partly disguised by owl-like horn-rimmed spectacles and further concealed by a very wide-brimmed floppy white cotton sunhat. The muu-muu almost reached the ground, brushing two enormous feet in plain leather sandals from which unvarnished toenails protruded.

I dutifully came to attention. What the hell, two minutes, why not? I was curious. She must have been six-foot-something and around sixteen stone. Then I remembered. *Shit! It's Armistice Day!* The building had fallen silent and even the traffic noise on Orchard Road seemed to drop a decibel or two. The monstrously large woman stood in front of me, breathing heavily, her eyes tightly shut.

Then, when the outside traffic noise seemed to suddenly increase and I guess the two minutes had elapsed, she opened her eyes, glanced at her watch for confirmation and pointed to the green-glazed vase I'd been inspecting before her commanding arrival. 'The dynasty?' she demanded.

'I'm sorry, I don't know, madam. You'll have to ask Mr Kwan. I'm still learning about Chinese antiques. Oh, and thank you for drawing my attention to the day, and the time. Very careless of me.'

'It's Han Dynasty.' She squinted down at me, ignoring my apology. 'You look decidedly Chinese, but your accent . . . Australian, are you?'

'Yes, madam, afraid so.'

'That's three apologies in as many sentences. No need to apologise, young man. Your frightful accent is not your fault – sins of the fathers, convicts, dreadful mix-up. Liverpudlian, Glaswegian, Mancunian, Cockney, Geordie, Irish and dozens of other local country bumpkin patois – poor hapless convict fellows hardly understood each other, so it's not surprising they came up with such a terrible hotchpotch of an accent. Your lot have the nerve to refer to it as the Queen's English.'

She really had a decidedly forbidding presence. 'Are you a linguist, madam?' I asked.

Again she ignored my question. 'Who are you, young man?'

'Simon Koo, madam. Peter . . . er, Mr Kwan is my cousin on my mother's side.'

'Interesting. There is no resemblance. You must take after your father.'

'Not at all – he doesn't look Chinese.'

'My name is Elma Kelly, how do you do? You're a chunk of a lad. No fat, though. Good peasant stock, solidly rooted to the earth. Li blood, I'd say from looking at you, eh?'

'I'm fourth-generation Australian and a throwback to my great-great-grandmother. My three sisters look Caucasian,' I added, perhaps a tad defensively.

'Fourth-generation? Ah, I see, the gold rush, eh? New Yellow Gold Mountain.'

She certainly had a quick mind and knew her history. I was to learn there wasn't a great deal she didn't know about the Chinese. 'Are you the Mrs Kelly who runs Cathay Advertising? Head office in Hong Kong, I think?' I was taking a punt in an attempt to reclaim some control over the conversation.

'Miss – never daft enough to add a permanent man to my life. Silly business, marriage – mostly quarrels and compromise. Had a sailor-boy once, nice chap. Only saw him once in a while; good arrangement – serviced me well, ha ha. I was much younger then. Died . . . torpedoed in the war.' She looked at me as if with dawning comprehension. 'Ah, I've put a face to a name. I know who you are. Wing Brothers, eh? Sly Sidney, Awful Johnny and Cheerful Ronnie! Damned clever move getting the Americans to buy in. Frightful trio, know absolutely nothing about advertising.' She threw back her head and chortled. 'You have the misfortune to be the creative director appointed by the Americans, no doubt in an attempt to make some sort of sense out of the chaos, out of the three ding-a-lings. Sidney hasn't a creative bone in his body and only thinks about making money. Johnny is a morose and thoroughly nasty fellow who does all his brother's dirty work, and Ronnie, number-three son, is a delightful chap with plenty of brains and character, but, alas, lacks the intestinal fortitude to stick up for himself. He's also rather too fond of the bottle, though that's probably Sidney's fault for making him entertain foreigners. Besides, it's hardly unique in this part of the world, where the right elbow is kept constantly bent and busy. The whole place runs on a wing and a prayer, sorry – ha ha – couldn't resist the pun.' She paused to snatch a quick breath. 'But, my dear boy, just how are you managing in what's commonly known in advertising circles as the Three Wing Circus?'

Whatever else, Elma Kelly knew her competition. I tried to grin. 'With some difficulty,' I replied, then building on her circus analogy added, 'Sometimes I sense I'm the clown, but mostly the animal trainer. Attempting to put a Chinese creative team together isn't easy. I can't say I've made much progress, and I've been here over a year.'

She seemed to appreciate the honesty of my reply and glanced at her watch. 'It's five past eleven, the sun is not nearly past the yardarm and I never drink until sunset anyway, but do you fancy a spot of tiffin, Simon?' Then without waiting for an answer she added, 'I think you probably need an introduction to Chinese thinking, oriental *Winguistics*,' failing to resist another even worse pun. 'Excellent Peranakan restaurant around the corner, quite clean, spicy though. Do you tolerate spicy food?'

'Yes, but it depends on the amount of chilli.' I'd skipped breakfast and the invitation – lunch with the redoubtable Elma Kelly – was not one to be passed up.

I suppose, strictly speaking, she represented the competition but it seemed there was nothing I could tell her about the three Wings, and of course I wasn't going to mention the pseudo research for Big Lather or the new Asian research model we had recently completed. I happily accepted Elma's invitation to tiffin. 'Thank you. I can't get over the food in Singapore – the variety and quality is astonishing.'

'Good. I'm sure you'll enjoy it. But mark my words, Simon, there will come a time when you crave sausages, peas, gravy and mash, and when you do, the Tangle Inn here in Tanglin Road is just the place – shepherd's pie, English cheeses, even bacon and eggs – run by a grumpy Englishwoman. My countrymen can be unpleasant, and she's one such, almost as big as I am, packed tight with bile, watches her customers from a large peacock-tail wicker chair – quite bizarre, my dear. Now come along, Simon.' She hesitated as if making a decision. 'We won't invite Peter. Much too early for him, and besides, he has a fussy appetite. Too much garlic doesn't agree with him. Did you know Sidney Wing buys from him? As do I.' She brought her forefinger up to touch the side of her nose in a decidedly unladylike manner. 'Say no more, it might only confuse matters, eh? Peter is a loyal soul, but he *is* Chinese and we don't know how well he knows the notorious Sidney or how much he spends on stuff to impress his chronically censorious ancestors, do we? The Chinese rate people in terms of money, not character. That's lesson one.'

If this was intended to be confidential, it failed because her booming voice carried to Peter and anyone else in the building. I was to learn that Elma Kelly only spoke at full volume in a sort of glottal bark.

Once outside she walked to the edge of the pavement, put two fingers in her mouth and let out a piercing whistle, a sound bullet that cut through the steady din of the Orchard Road traffic and found its mark. She raised her free arm, two fingers extended, and within moments two rickshaws moved towards us. 'It's only a short ride,' she volunteered.

Both rickshaw men were scrawny and barefoot, each wearing just a pair of sweat-stained khaki shorts, their ribs showing clearly under their sun-blackened skin. I don't suppose you put on a lot of weight pulling people around the streets. The scrawnier of the two gave Elma an almost toothless grin and indicated his rickshaw, then said something in what I took to be Malay or Singlish – although he spoke too fast for me. He grinned broadly again, showing a mouthful of red gum and a single yellow tooth I'd missed the first time round. 'He wants double the fare,' she laughed, and nodded to her man then said, 'Don't pay your fellow more than twenty cents. He'll make a show of looking disappointed, but it's only around the corner and if I wasn't quite such a behemoth we'd walk it in a couple of minutes.'

Peranakan cuisine has reputedly absorbed influences from all the major cultures in Singapore – Chinese, Malaysian, Indian and Indonesian – and then made up its own mind. Tiffin is an Indian word for a light meal, although Elma Kelly ordered enough to feed a medium-sized hungry family. There was no menu in evidence. 'No point in consulting you, dear boy, you'll just have to trust me. Not the kind of restaurant where they have menus, or tablecloths.' She rattled off all the dishes she required to the kowtowing proprietor, and when she finished I asked her to explain what she'd ordered.

'I can't imagine why you would want to know. You'll be gone in a couple of years. You're on a contract, I take it?'

'Yes, three years,' I laughed. 'If I make it. It's been a bit over a year and it feels that long already.'

'Pity – we could use you right now, though it doesn't pay to break a contract. Did you know we're part-owned by an Australian agency?'

'No, I had no idea,' I said, surprised.

'Yes, well, George Patterson Advertising, one of your bigger shows, what. We don't make a big splash about it. Most of my accounts are British and they might not take too kindly to colonial interference, in particular a brash lot like the Australians. Bill Farnsworth, the chairman, leaves me pretty much to my own devices but he's proved very useful. I like the Australians, despite your appalling accent. Good chap, Farnsworth, cultured too, patron of your art gallery and owns an original Gainsborough; has a definite neurosis about socks.'

'Socks, you mean foot-type socks?'

'Foot-type socks! Yes, socks, the woollen and cotton kind. He insists they must be worn to just below the knee.'

'You mean when wearing shorts?'

'No, no, that's British army and navy. Under long trousers. He insists every male employee must wear them in this manner.'

I glanced momentarily downwards, thinking about the grey cotton ankle-hugging socks I was wearing. 'But why? And here, in this heat?'

'Gentlemen don't wear short socks, he insists. So when he comes out, I purchase twenty-four pairs of long hose from Lane Hancock for the male staff. Our Chinese employees think I'm completely daft or that they're some sort of good-luck charm. Bill's Chinese name is "Big Boss Long Sock".'

The first dish arrived and I asked Elma what it was called. 'You won't remember the names of the dishes – much too complex. Takes a lifetime of dedicated eating. Well, then, no more shop talk. Shall we relax and enjoy the food?'

'It's not about just remembering food names,' I insisted. 'I've tasted a good deal of local food and can probably recall the names of most of the dishes. The agency gave me a delightful and very pretty guide for two weeks when I arrived. We went everywhere and ate off bicycle carts, street stalls, tiny hole-in-the-wall family eateries and on river and harbour *sampans*. It was marvellous. It's just that I want to remember *this* particular meal. You're the first person I've met in the local advertising scene who is not in my own agency. Dates, times, places are important to me, especially those associated with particular circumstances and people. I want to be able to recall the conversation and the food we were eating when it took place.'

'You really are a strange boy, Simon. But be warned, I shall test you at the conclusion of the meal.' Then she surprised me by saying, 'You were most fortunate to have the services of the delightful Miss Mercy B. Lord. Lovely gal. I've tried several times to employ her, but she won't leave Beatrice Fong. Can't imagine why, my dear.' Her right eyebrow rose above the black horn-rim of her owl-eye spectacles. 'Now, there's a particularly nasty piece of work. Execrable old woman!'

I would have loved to know more about the so-called execrable Beatrice Fong but realised I'd give the game away if I asked questions. Elma Kelly was much too smart not to pick up on my feelings for Mercy B. Lord, who'd warned me not to make them public.

We started with what Elma described as savouries, *cincalok*, a dip of salt-preserved fresh shrimps, if that doesn't sound like a contradiction, as well as *keropok udang*, prawn crackers. This was followed by soup, *bakwan kepiting*, crab and pork meatballs in a light broth – absolutely delicious. Elma then got down to the serious business of working her way through the main dishes: *curry kepala*, fish-head curry; *sotong sambal asam*, squid fried in a spicy paste with tamarind sauce; *udang ketak sambal*, slipper lobster in spicy paste; beef *rendang*, beef simmered in fresh coconut milk and spices; and finally *ayam betawi*, fried chicken smothered in an Indonesian-style spicy paste. All the mains were accompanied by a large bowl of steaming sticky rice and a constantly replenished pot of green tea.

While the portions were not large, they nevertheless amounted to a small banquet. I managed a bite or two of just about everything at Elma's insistence, while she managed to polish off most of the food we'd ordered, which was certainly enough for four people. She ate quickly and seemed to barely chew, and I was somewhat surprised when the *bakwan kepiting* arrived and she simply raised her bowl in both hands, upended it and chug-a-lugged the broth and the meatballs. It was all over in less than a minute. 'Ah, splendid! River crab, not farmed,' was all she said before reaching hungrily for the next dish.

She may have sensed my amazement at her voracious appetite because she said, 'I won't eat on the aeroplane back to Hong Kong tomorrow evening. The food is disgusting. The airlines, the lot of them, should be prosecuted – better still, lined up and shot – for positively poisoning their passengers! Worst thing is we have all their accounts.'

I wasn't quite sure what she meant. Was it that this was her last meal until she arrived back in Hong Kong a day and a half later? It hardly seemed possible, but if so, she was making sure she wouldn't starve in the interim.

Thankfully, when we'd hoed through all the food, she summarily dismissed dessert. 'Mostly glutinous rice or tapioca, much too sweet. They use palm sugar. No, my dear, I shall end with one more small dish that is a decided favourite of mine – *ayam buah keluak*. Stewed chicken with black nuts, though I don't suppose you'll care for it – the nuts are an acquired taste.'

Buah keluak, I was to learn, is the fruit of the *kepayang* tree that grows wild in Indonesia and Malaysia. It is roughly the size and shape of a rugby ball, and the nuts are not unlike chestnuts in appearance. They are soaked for days then pounded into an oily black paste with spices added. Elma seemed to relish this apparent delicacy most. I had a small portion and found the taste peculiar and not at all to my liking, almost gagging on my first and only mouthful.

'Simon, you'll know you've become a Peranakan, a true Singaporean, when you grow to love this delicacy,' she assured me.

'But you're from Hong Kong,' I pointed out.

'Ah, but I enjoy honorary Peranakan status,' she insisted. 'Lee Kuan Yew offered me the keys to the city when he came to power. We, Cathay Advertising, helped with his political advertising campaign.' She suddenly chortled, the shaking of her great breasts and thighs causing the dishes on the table to rattle. '"No thanks, Prime Minister," I told him. "Some other time, perhaps, when Singapore city isn't such an awful dump! I have an image to maintain! Give me a few years, Elma," he said. Shouldn't be surprised if he succeeds. Things are beginning to change already. They had a fire in one of the Malay *kampongs* last month, nobody hurt,' she laughed. 'It is always a great relief to be told where and when an accidental fire is about to occur. With the ash still warm, the foundations for a public high-rise housing project are dug and the cement poured. A strong man, Lee. Doesn't brook too much opposition from the trade unions and communists.' Elma then added, 'It was the luckiest day of his political life when those Mecca-mad Muslims in Malaysia kicked him out of the Federation. Terrified Lee and the Chinese would end up running the show.' She chuckled. 'They probably got that bit right.' I was to learn that Elma had strong opinions, which she expressed using all the riches of the English language. She had a large vocabulary and liked alliteration.

Elma continued talking and I mostly listened. Some of what she said I had already heard from Ronnie and Mercy B. Lord, but this was, to say the least, an education in a lunch hour. 'What do you know about *guanxi?*' she'd asked almost before we'd sat down.

'You mean the Chinese way of doing business? Squeeze and inter-family relationships? A little from Ronnie Wing and Mercy B. Lord, and what I've observed over the past year. There's a lot to know and I sometimes feel like a babe in the woods.'

'Well, then, let me try to explain it. In the crudest terms, it's "I scratch your back and you scratch mine", but of course it's more complicated than that. If you hope to work in a largely Chinese business community or with government in a place such as Singapore, you must understand *guanxi* or you won't get very far.'

'How did the British Colonial Service manage when they were here? Didn't they – the local Chinese – have to toe the line?'

Elma laughed. 'My dear Simon, the system is tailor-made for us Brits. Besides, we made the rules. *Guanxi* is not all that different from our old boys' network – Whitehall has been practising it for generations, though the Chinese version is vastly more complex and isn't simply dependent on Eton and Harrow, Oxford and Cambridge. Nowhere in the world does the phrase "It's all about who you know" have more relevance than in Asia, and among the Chinese in particular. It's not only who you know but also how the other person perceives his or her obligations towards you. The more favours you do for someone, the more obligations they have to you and, of course, vice versa.'

'I see. So what happens when you're pitching against another agency? I mean, when the client is not happy with, say, my agency's work and asks you to pitch for his business?'

'Under the Chinese system of *guanxi*, that's simply not possible.'

I grinned. 'So there's no point in pitching for one of your accounts, Miss Kelly?'

She smiled. 'Not unless you want to waste a lot of time, money and effort. Pitching is a Western idea, one that's simply incomprehensible to the Chinese.'

'You mean you've never lost a Chinese account because the client thought your advertising wasn't up to scratch?'

'I should jolly well hope not!' Elma said, plainly confounded by such an idea. 'Nor for any other reason. We are very careful to work within the client's orbit of influence – that is, as a part of his *guanxi*.'

'But the British or international accounts you hold – surely they become vulnerable once in a while? A new product or marketing manager, a managing director wanting to make his mark or a client disagreement, I mean – that sort of thing is common enough in our business. Your advertising agency is an easy mark when things go wrong, isn't it?'

'Absolutely not! In our case that's for other reasons, though not all that different from *guanxi*.' Elma Kelly didn't explain further.

'I guess I have a fair bit to learn,' I admitted.

'Simon, in all of Asia, when dealing with, say, a government department, where approval for some action is required, people with the right connections, with *guanxi*, can get around almost any official regulation with comparative impunity. What can be accomplished in a day or two using *guanxi* can literally take months without it. Why do you think Samuel Oswald bought into Wing Brothers Advertising?'

'Well, that's easy enough to understand. Some of the American clients from our New York office are being encouraged by Lee Kuan Yew's PAP Party to see Singapore as a gateway to the South-East Asian markets for consumer goods, offering all kinds of incentives to set up factories and distribution centres.' I was aware she would know all this, but I didn't want to appear entirely stupid or naïve. 'After your own agency, Wing Brothers is the biggest, and New York wanted someone on the ground to service the advertising needs of their clients. I guess they also bought the Wing Brothers' clients as part of the package.'

'Absolute piffle, stuff and nonsense! Wing Brothers' assets and profit potential in terms of existing advertising accounts were pretty negligible. Sidney Wing wouldn't be stupid enough to show a profit, other than in the set of books he'd prepared specially for the Americans. What he sold them, at a considerable price, and what they bought – remarkably perspicacious of them, by the way – was the Wing brothers' and in particular Sidney Wing's *guanxi*.'

'Do you think the Americans would have understood that?' I asked doubtfully, thinking of Dansford Drocker and his spam-from-Uncle-Sam mentality.

Elma shrugged. 'Perhaps you're right, but they've learnt a few lessons from the Vietnam War, where *guanxi* undoubtedly plays a part. Anyway, Sidney Wing's connections are the only thing of real worth they will receive for their investment.'

I sighed. 'Like I said, there's a lot to learn. How long will all this take? I've been here over a year and I still don't understand the culture.'

She leaned back in her chair. 'Of course you don't. It takes several lifetimes, I'm afraid. I don't fully understand it and I don't think anyone in the West does or ever will. Just know with absolute certainty that nothing is what it seems to be or is said to be. Don't look for logical explanations. *Guanxi* in the big, rich Chinese families can go back ten generations. Often something that doesn't make sense to you and me is repayment for what happened fifty or a hundred years ago. I am fortunate: almost all my clients are British companies and, in addition,

I am careful to hire my local staff, mostly Chinese, within the major invisible *guanxi* networks both in government and private business.'

'I'm not sure I understand. Do all Chinese families have these elaborate interconnections based on *guanxi*? How do the poor ever get a start?'

Elma Kelly smiled ruefully. 'With the Chinese it's always family. They don't believe in giving strangers, particularly poor strangers, a helping hand. Hiring a poor artist would be counterproductive. The poor are expected to drag themselves up by their bootstraps. That is, if they own a pair of boots in the first instance. Regrettably, I've learned only to hire the children of the powerful families.'

'But what if a talented artist or copywriter comes from a poor family?'

'Too bad – he or she doesn't get the job. Talent without connections will always be passed over for perhaps a very mediocre artist from a big *guanxi* family or association. He or occasionally she will prove infinitely more useful and profitable in the long run.'

'What about Miss Mercy B. Lord? You wanted to hire her. I don't suppose she has much *guanxi*?'

'Yes, strange that, but she seems to have been included in Beatrice Fong's vast circle of influence. Never could understand how that might have come about. Very unusual.'

'What? Her being included?'

'Yes. Mark my words, there is something very peculiar going on with her. That old shrew has never been known to make a charitable gesture in her miserable life. Furthermore, that delightful young gal has, by Chinese notions, very bad mixed blood – mother raped by a Japanese soldier – *and* she's a child of the Church of Rome.'

Again I couldn't let on I knew about the circumstances of Mercy B. Lord's birth. There was also nothing I dared say about her association with Beatrice Fong either. Instead I shook my head. 'It doesn't seem fair – I mean, to the poor.'

'Fair isn't a word the Chinese recognise, Simon.'

'Christ! No wonder I'm having such a bad time trying to put together a pool of talent. I tried to run several small ads in Chinese newspapers and magazines calling for applications for positions as artists and writers, but Johnny Wing flatly refused to place them. Sidney called me into his office and wanted to know why I was wasting the agency's money.'

Elma smiled. 'Well, now you know why. Sidney Wing has a very big circle; his *guanxi* goes back four generations to China. He's also very rich, and in Chinese terms that means powerful. You are going to have to find another way, my boy. I'll help you if I can. Just tell me what you want. Hong Kong may be a better place to look.'

It was a hugely generous offer. I was later to learn, though not from Elma, that she had been a prisoner-of-war when the Japanese occupied Hong Kong, having refused to be evacuated with the British and other European women. She'd pointed out that she had a degree in science and volunteered to be the expert in case of a gas attack by the Japanese. She'd ended up being interned along with all the expatriate business elite, the local heads of the great trading houses, banks and government institutions.

Elma, it seems, was a large and formidable person even then, someone who didn't take crap from anyone, including the Japanese guards, mostly Koreans and Taiwanese, whom she managed to intimidate, remonstrating in no uncertain terms when they acted harshly towards her fellow prisoners, both male and female. Elma showed no fear of them and thought nothing of marching in to see the Japanese commandant to lodge a complaint against a cruel or unjust guard. In order not to lose face in front of this formidable woman, and because he also despised the Koreans and Taiwanese, he usually took note of her demands. Elma was not the only virago amongst the prisoners. She was partnered in the cantankerous stakes by another formidable woman, who went back to Australia, where she is known simply as Andrea and is a well-known radio personality. They saved many prisoners from severe beatings and, some claimed more than one life in the process.

By the end of the war Elma was a heroine among the British prisoners, and upon assuming their former important positions they called her to a meeting. 'Elma, we owe you. What is it we can do for you?' they asked.

Elma, who prior to the war worked for a fairly small and rickety advertising concern, very cleverly nominated advertising as her future career. The Governor of Hong Kong, Sir Mark Aitchison Young, himself a prisoner under the Japanese, was present at the meeting and is claimed to have made her a proposition. 'Elma, we shall give you a test. We have no telephone directory and it's pure hell trying to contact anyone in Hong Kong. Do you think you can make us a new directory in three months?'

Elma had no idea what might be involved or even how to go about the task, but she replied, 'Certainly! Will the post office cover my expenses?'

'Of course, my dear.'

'Then they shall be my first account,' she announced.

The governor is said to have turned to the business nabobs, now restored to their former positions, and said, 'Gentlemen, with success must come reward. Will you pledge your future advertising to Elma, should she be successful with the new telephone directory?'

There was all-round agreement and Elma set to work. The telephone directory was duly delivered with a week to spare, and in one stroke Elma gained, virtually in perpetuity, all the important British accounts wherever they operated in South-East Asia. She had effortlessly created Cathay Advertising, the biggest regional Asian advertising network, without ever having to pitch for a single piece of business. In every meaning of the word she had achieved her own *guanxi*, or the British version anyway, to which she'd sensibly added the Chinese equivalent when she employed the sons and daughters of the rich local Chinese who were important in both government and business. It was well known, in Hong Kong in particular, though also in Singapore, Thailand and the other Asian countries with British industries, that pitching for an account held by Cathay Advertising was, as she'd warned me, a waste of time and money.

We parted after I attempted to pay and Elma wouldn't hear of it. 'Oh, Simon, a timely warning: if a Chinese invites you to lunch or anywhere else that involves payment, never, under any circumstances, offer to pay.

He will lose enormous face because, in effect, you're suggesting he can't afford to treat you.'

'Miss Kelly, thank you. I can't say how much I enjoyed our lunch, and I am honoured to have met you.'

Elma Kelly smiled her acknowledgment then paused momentarily before asking, 'Simon, you said you could remember the name of every dish? So let me hear it, my boy.'

I knew it was some sort of important test, one that was somehow going to affect the future. Chairman Meow's advice to us as children had always been that boasting begins where wisdom ends, and I'd always been cautious about claiming to do more than I could. Fortunately, I have a mind not only for times and dates but also for details.

'Right, we started with *cincalok*, then *keropok udang*, prawn crackers, then the soup *bakwan kepiting* . . .' I recited the names of all the dishes that followed, ending with *ayam buah keluak*, the strange-tasting fermented fruit of the wild *kepayang* tree.

'Good boy, Simon. I thought I was going to have to call your bluff. How interested are you in Chinese antiquities?'

I explained my fascination with furniture and antiques, and how I didn't want the responsibility of owning pieces as a serious collector but still wanted to learn about the subject. 'It's the who, what, why and where, the details that fascinate me. One day perhaps I'll own a few choice pieces, but only if their stories are unique. Chinese antiquities appear to be much more complex in their personal significance than do European ones. I think I could well become very interested.'

'Well, you're not exactly a Simple Simon, are you?' Elma Kelly observed.

It was a nice compliment. 'Thank you, Miss Kelly,' I said for a second time. 'I sincerely hope we meet again soon.' I didn't want to gush but I had truly enjoyed her company.

She appeared to be thinking. 'Look here, lad. I come to my Singapore agency from Hong Kong every first Friday of the month and stay until the Saturday evening flight back to Hong Kong. If this arrangement suits you, I will see you at the Kwan Gallery on the first Saturday every month at twelve o'clock sharp. Now don't be late. We'll enjoy a bite together and catch up.'

She looked me in the eye. 'You're a greenhorn and have lots to learn, Simon. Singapore can be a dangerous place for amateurs.' Whereupon she whistled up a passing taxi and worked her huge body into the back seat to arrive finally with a thud that rocked the small yellow and white Ambassador cab so that its springs squeaked in protest.

Crimson-faced from the effort, she leaned out the window. 'When next we meet you may call me Elma and it will be your turn to pay for tiffin.' Then, quite unexpectedly, she boomed, 'Oh, and congratulations on your work with the Texas Tiger campaign. Regrettably, it's first rate. I should know – we have the Shell account!'

Then, turning to the driver, she commanded, 'Onwards, my good man!' The small engine revved furiously then, with a groan of protest, the taxi pulled slowly away from the curb. I watched as it turned into the busy Orchard Road traffic.

I could have hugged myself. Apart from Mercy B. Lord, Miss Elma Kelly was the first piece of real luck that had happened since my coming to Singapore. I had somebody on my side to show me how to take on the two older Wing brothers. This enormous, charismatic, switched-on, extremely kind, larger-than-life woman was offering me her knowledge, experience and good mind, as well as her very broad shoulders to lean on.

I checked the time as the taxi pulled away. It was precisely five minutes past one on Armistice Day, that is the 11th of November 1967. I did the mathematics in my head: five minutes past one, that's sixty-five minutes past noon, $6 + 5 = 11$, that's two people meeting. Miss Elma Kelly and me. Furthermore, we'd met at the eleventh minute of the eleventh hour when she'd stood me to attention. My obsession with the times and dates when important things happened in my life was working. I grinned to myself. And I had the temerity to think the Chinese were whacko!

CHAPTER EIGHT

DESPITE THE FACT THAT I still lacked a creative department with the necessary skills to compete successfully, we'd achieved a fair bit. I was essentially an art director, and although I liked words, my skills were primarily visual. I had never thought of myself as a copywriter, but this was Asia and you simply pitched in where necessary, whether the job involved words or pictures. We now had half a dozen big American international accounts as well as Texas Tiger, and I was buzzing around like a blue-arse fly, barely able to cope.

I'd managed to hire a young Chinese calligrapher who showed some promise as a copywriter. He was brought in to replace Zi Gee Ha, the ancient calligrapher who had worked with the Wing brothers since the inception of their agency and had long since lost any zest for the business of selling – if, in fact, he'd possessed any in the first place. Already in his eighties, he spent most of the day with his head on his arms, asleep at his desk. He was finally permitted to retire after over forty years' service, and while Sidney was vehement he receive no pension, Dansford got New York to approve a pathetically small sum of money that allowed him to buy the rented house in an outlying *kampong* where he lived with his daughter and grandchildren.

The new copywriter, William Wong, was a university graduate

recommended by the newly appointed Professor Kwan, his appointment having nothing whatsoever to do with our research program. He came from a good family (*guanxi*) and, surprisingly, spoke Hokkien and Cantonese as well as Malay, Singlish and of course English. He also produced beautiful Chinese characters.

He was a cheeky, fast-talking, gum-chewing, 22-year-old hepcat with all the latest Stateside (his word) jargon, who loved chocolate, wore his hair as long as he could and was desperately trying to grow Elvis sideburns on his perfectly smooth face. He was also wonderfully enthusiastic and surprisingly ingenuous for someone who had taken his bachelor's degree in sociology. Nevertheless, he believed himself to be 'switched on' and 'with it, man', which kept the usually timid production staff amused.

We dubbed him 'Willy Wonka', after the character in the children's book *Charlie and the Chocolate Factory* by Roald Dahl, which had recently come out in Singapore, a sobriquet he loved and even used when answering the phone. If you called him Willy or Willy Wong he'd pull you up. 'It's Willy Wonka, please. Every male has a willy and there are more Wongs in China than there are Wrights in England.' It was a favourite joke.

He proved to be a good sounding board, and his translations were a lot closer to what I was trying to say than those of nodding, smiling, toothless old Zi Gee Ha, who, I felt sure, hadn't the foggiest notion what I was talking about, despite my rapidly improving Cantonese. With Mercy B. Lord's coaching, I was almost completely fluent in street-level Cantonese, spoke Singlish passably well and had a few useful words of Malay. There may well be some truth to the old adage that the best way to learn a new language is in bed with a beautiful woman. It was certainly true of my experience with Mercy B. Lord, who had a touch of Chairman Meow about her. She wouldn't go to bed with me unless I had mastered twenty new words in any of the local languages she'd chosen and was able to use them in a sensible sentence. I can guarantee that the old carrot and stick works. I carried either a Malay, Cantonese or Singlish dictionary around with me every day, allocating two days for each, and grabbed a new word whenever I had a chance, mostly in taxis where I could practise with the driver. Maybe it isn't a very romantic notion but, I can assure you, it proved highly effective. Eventually, I could make love in a mixture of four languages, sometimes – mid-thrust – reducing Mercy B. Lord to tears of laughter.

And then Sidney Wing brought us our first Japanese account, gained on the golf course while playing with Hercules Sun, the Singapore agent for Citizen Watches. Sun informed Sidney that the Japanese wanted to use television to sell their product and, despite the fact that no advertising agency in Singapore or Hong Kong had ever filmed, cut or edited a local television commercial, Sidney readily agreed. Hercules Sun demanded a price and a deadline for a sixty-second commercial on the spot, and Sidney, undaunted by his total ignorance of the costs involved, simply quoted the first figure that came into his head and the first date, working on the principle that you first secured the client and then worked out a way to keep him.

Back at the agency he was ebullient. He called me to his office, indicating the chrome-and-yellow-leather chair. 'Well, Mr Big Shot Creative Director, I have a job for you,' he announced.

As I'd never had a layout accepted for any of Sidney's Chinese accounts, I'd long since given up trying to impress him. 'Sidney, we're pretty busy at the moment. I'm not sure I have the time to do another unsuccessful layout for one of your Chinese accounts.'

'Not Chinese, Simon,' he said beaming.

'Oh?'

'Japanese.'

'You're kidding! Japanese? Who? What?'

'Citizen Watches,' he replied, grinning like a Cheshire cat.

'Jesus! How? That's big-time. And without a pitch?'

'Of course,' he replied smugly. 'There's more. I've agreed to make them a TV commercial.'

'And you want a script for the station announcer to read?'

'No. Hercules Sun wants a proper commercial like the American ones, sixty seconds.'

'What?' I began to laugh. 'You're joking, of course.'

'No. Budget and deadline all settled.'

My heart sank. 'Sidney, we've . . . Nobody's made a TV commercial in Singapore. How can you agree to a budget or deadline? That's ridiculous!'

Sidney shrugged. 'It was necessary.' He fixed me with a stern look. 'If you don't deliver, I'll have to assume that you are deliberately undermining my authority.'

'Oh? Tell me the budget,' I replied, feeling the first small hint of pique.

'2000 dollars.'

'That's US dollars, of course.'

'No, local, Singapore dollars.'

'Sidney, that's bloody ridiculous! I couldn't hire a 35-millimetre movie camera and operator for that! That is, if there was one for hire in the first place.'

Sidney let rip with one of his St Vitus giggles. 'Your problem, Simon – I've given my word.'

'And I'm stuck with it?' I could feel myself growing angry.

Another giggle. 'You've got two weeks.'

'Sorry, Sidney. I can't do it. Not for the money. Even if it was sufficient – and it's at least ten or fifteen grand short of the barest minimum – I couldn't meet the deadline. You'll have to go with a live spot by the station announcer.'

'Johnny has already bought the time, sixteen sixty-second spots on STV starting two weeks from today.'

'In that case you'll have to tell him to cancel it.'

'No!' He thumped the desk with his fist. 'You will do as I say!'

'Please don't do that, mate. I'm not one of your kowtowing lackeys.' I was getting pretty pissed off but was still in control, just. 'Sidney, you can't get blood out of a stone. It's too little money. It's too little time. We have no camera, no production facilities. It takes a week just to process film in Hong Kong. I know, because I looked into it for Texas Tiger, but the logistics and lack of facilities made it impossible. Two grand in Singapore dollars probably won't even buy a late-afternoon station presenter to flog the watch on camera.'

Sidney banged his fist on the desk again. 'No! No live on camera! A regular TV commercial like Pepsi-Cola from America!'

'Sidney, that's absurd. An American commercial would cost at least 40 000 Singapore dollars.'

'You fuck up on this and we get no more Japanese accounts. I assure you, Hercules Sun will see to that! And you may be sure I will let New York know who is responsible!'

I sighed, my patience running out. 'Sidney, there's nothing to fuck up. We *can't* do it.'

'Simon, you listen to me! I'm not going back to Hercules Sun.'

'Why? You'll lose face, is that it?'

It was the wrong thing to say. He completely lost control and spat, 'Don't you fuck with me, Simon! You sabotage me on this and I'll terminate your contract!'

All the frustrations of the past months came flooding in. Sidney Wing threatening me was the last straw. I laughed sardonically. *'You'll* terminate my contract? I tell you what I'll do. I'll personally roll it up and shove it up your scrawny arse!' Shaking with anger, I rose to leave.

Sidney jumped from his swivel chair, gripping the edge of his desk, his knuckles white. His entire body was consumed by rage as he roared, 'Do as I say, Simon Koo, or I promise in the name of my ancestors that you'll never see your girlfriend again!'

A voice inside me said, *That's enough, Simon! Stop! Stop right now!* But I couldn't restrain myself. 'Screw you, Sidney!' Furious beyond belief, I walked to the door.

I had almost reached it when he barked, 'Stop!'

I turned, still shaking.

'Get on with it, no more money, no more time.'

For years afterwards I told myself that was the moment when I should have packed my bags and left. But Sidney Wing had pressed exactly the right button. Mercy B. Lord meant too much to me; I wasn't game enough to take him on, to call his bluff. Piss-weak, I suppose. She still disappeared every Thursday without explanation, and my frequent attempts to get her to come clean always ended in tears. The last time, she'd begged me tearfully, 'Please, Simon, no more questions or you'll lose me!' Now I knew that the bastard was onto us (silly of me to think he wasn't) and that he had some sort of power over her, enough to make good his threat to take her away from me. Sidney Wing was a bully, but not the type to lose his temper easily. He was imperious, secretive and sly by nature, more the slow-drip-of-acid type than the fire-and-brimstone type, the stab in the back rather than the punch in the face. He believed in keeping everyone disconcerted while he remained cool, aloof and superior.

For instance, he used a lack of even the smallest courtesies to discomfit people: he never returned the morning greeting of a member of his staff and treated them all like dirt. He expected them to kowtow and, of course, to a man and a woman, they did, fearing for their jobs. His entire life had been conducted in this imperious manner until he sold to the gwai-lo, the Americans. Then Dansford and I, the drunk and the half-caste, both street dirt in his estimation, were appointed, and he deeply resented our familiarity and easygoing egalitarian attitudes. On more than one occasion he'd instructed us, via Ronnie, to 'demand more respect', and Ronnie had duly explained that treating staff as equals was 'not the Chinese way'.

For our part, we'd been careful not to invade his turf, to leave him with his Chinese clients and his 'squeeze' and get on with the American part of the business. Initially, I'd tried to improve the look of his Chinese clients' advertising, until Dansford pointed out that hell would have to freeze over before one of my new and improved layouts would be accepted or even shown to Sidney's clients. We'd also noted that his spontaneous St Vitus giggle occurred most often in our presence and, while he appeared not to notice it, I was convinced he realised it was a nervous affliction beyond his control.

Now I'd had the temerity to challenge his hitherto unchallenged authority. He'd secured our first Japanese account. So what if the deal had been made Chinese-style, on the golf course, at the club or over the banquet table, in this case with an almost impossible promise. He'd nevertheless triumphed. His aim was to show us that he was an effective force in getting new business. I had now been given the task of cleaning up the mess. This was, after all, how he always conducted his life.

Sidney must have known that terminating my contract was an idle threat. He'd have to go through New York and Dansford would certainly intervene. Besides, he'd been generous enough to let New York know that both Big Lather, a great success in the test market and about to be launched throughout Asia, as well as Texas Tiger, which had more than recovered the company's lost Asian market share, were both essentially my initiatives. And New York knew Colgate-Palmolive, which stood to make tens of millions of dollars in a vast new market with Big Lather, would no doubt have demanded an explanation if their Mr Lather disappeared.

Not that I would have been unduly concerned about being dismissed. Elma Kelly had begged me to join Cathay once my contract was up. Moreover, I had another project tucked into my back pocket. While Professor Kwan and the school of business had a good working research model ready to go, they hadn't sold it yet, and it was time to do something about that. I was fed up to the back teeth with the Three Wing Circus and would have been glad of an opportunity to pack it in. It was only pride and my signature on a contract that held me. But when I'd calmed down sufficiently I realised that Sidney's threat to remove Mercy B. Lord from my life, spoken in the sacred name of his ancestors, was real and not bombast. I was suddenly very scared, and not just for me but for Mercy B. Lord, who had nobody to protect her, no *guanxi*.

I knew instinctively that Sidney would regret losing his temper and threatening me, if only because it would put me on the alert and turn dislike into loathing. Secret knowledge is power, and he'd blown it in a fit of temper. He'd used too big a stick to beat me over the head. It had been unnecessary. In the end, something would have been worked out. If it wasn't and Hercules Sun was adamant, it wouldn't be the end of the world. New York would recognise that I'd acted professionally. What had started as a storm in a teacup was now a force-ten gale.

I left his office and stormed downstairs to the production department and into my office, but it was no sanctuary – the top half of the walls were glass and there was no door. I decided I had to get out, go home. The threat to remove Mercy B. Lord from my life was really worrying me. I needed to be alone to think. Colgate was bringing out a new toothpaste that claimed to harden tooth enamel and I needed to 'Sinofy' the American copy so that it could be translated into Mandarin. I threw the notes into my leather folder, telling myself I'd work at home but knowing I'd probably be too upset to do so.

There was a sharp rap on the glass and I looked up to see Willy Wonka standing at my door and tapping the face of his watch with his forefinger. 'You ready, Simon?' he asked.

'Not now, mate, please.'

Willy Wonka looked surprised. 'But we're going to lunch, remember?'

'Not today, mate. I can't.'

'But it's all arranged, Simon,' he said, clearly disappointed. Willy Wonka's disappointed face was something to see. The Chinese are pretty good at hiding their emotions but he was an exception, wearing them like they were sergeants' stripes on his sleeve. 'My aunt Daisy's restaurant, True Blue, remember? She's cooked specially. *Udang galah goreng sambal* – lobster fried in spicy paste. I told her I was bringing my boss. She went to the markets early this morning to get fresh lobster.'

Now I remembered. Willy Wonka had mentioned the name of the restaurant in passing and at the time I'd asked, surprised, 'True Blue? An Australian restaurant?'

'No,' he'd replied. 'Aunty Daisy is a Christian and she named it after St Francis of Assisi.' When I looked blank, he explained that followers of St Francis wore blue, and that Aunty Daisy, who wasn't his real aunty, had been the Wong family cook when he was growing up. After twenty years in their service, his family had rewarded her with the means to open her own Peranakan restaurant. He'd subsequently invited me to lunch and today was the day.

'I'm not good company today, mate,' I warned.

'Think lobster, boss. Her spicy sauce is the best!'

Unable to find a cab, we took separate rickshaws, a good thing because it allowed me time to calm down. I paid the rickshaw man double because, in the stinking heat of midsummer, it was a fair distance to the restaurant in an old shop-house in the Peranakan enclave of Katong.

There was no air-conditioning and, despite the efforts of an ailing ceiling fan in the centre of the room directly above our table, it was stinking hot. The small room had six tables, all of them occupied, which I took to be a testimony to Aunty Daisy's modest prices and good cooking. Willy Wonka ordered two Tiger beers from the solitary waiter, an elderly Malay in slippers who snuffled as he shuffled. His cheeks were covered in white stubble and he'd obviously lost most of his teeth because his chin almost touched the end of his nose.

'Make sure they're cold,' I said in my limited Malay. If he heard me he made no sign other than a sniff.

'Table fridge,' Willy Wonka said.

I was impressed. It was very rare for a restaurant that catered for locals to be able to afford a fridge. That was also the reason you knew the food was always fresh. No proprietor who hoped to stay open for long could afford to serve pork, fish or any food that might go off in the appalling heat unless it was very fresh. But the downside was that beer was invariably served warm, or, if you occasionally got lucky and were early to lunch, a few bottles would have been left in the ice that had accompanied the fish from market.

'A table fridge – that's pretty posh.'

Willy Wonka laughed. 'No, it's one of my dad's inventions. We've got a big box freezer at home in the garage and my dad loves Aunty Daisy's cooking and drops in for lunch twice a week, but he doesn't like warm beer, so he invented the table fridge. He makes one the night before he comes and Aunty Daisy sends a kitchen hand up to get it from our place an hour before he comes for lunch. He made one last night specially for us today.'

I felt ashamed. I'd been churlish and self-indulgent and very nearly cancelled lunch. It was obvious Willy Wonka had gone to a lot of trouble in anticipation.

Old Shuffle 'n' Snuffle arrived shortly afterwards carrying a deep aluminium roasting dish with a handle at each end, the shoulders and spouts of two bottles of Tiger beer protruding above the rim.

'Ah, the table fridge! Check this out, buddy,' Willy Wonka exclaimed.

We watched as the old bloke placed the dish at the centre of the table, and I saw that it contained a solid block of ice, the bottles resting in two holes in the ice block so they could easily be lifted out. In addition, two more holes in the ice contained two frosted beer glasses.

'Neat, hey?'

'Very damn clever and, like all good ideas, dead bloody simple,' I noted.

The old waiter shuffled in again with two more beers, which he placed in the holes vacated by the glasses; then, when we'd finished the original bottles, two more arrived. In this manner you could theoretically drink cold beer all afternoon, or for as long as it took for the ice to melt.

Willy Wonka wasn't the silent type, and I was grateful for the fact that he could talk the hind leg off a donkey and proceeded to do so as Aunty Daisy plied us with savouries that would have sent Elma Kelly into raptures. But, apart from making the effort to congratulate Aunty Daisy after each of these, I contributed little more than a series of grunts to the tirade about Lee Kuan Yew's latest ruling on long hair and hippies who smoked funny cigarettes. A taxi driver had been made an example of and jailed for thirty days for throwing a cigarette butt on the pavement, and this also produced an indignant tirade. But finally my garrulous Chinese copywriter and host could bear it no longer. 'What's wrong, Simon?' he asked.

'Huh? Oh, nothing. Bad day. Got a bee in my bonnet, that's all.'

'Bullshit.'

'Oh, just a bit of a contretemps with the chairman.'

'Simon, it's more serious than that, isn't it? In Production they say you are the only one not afraid of Sidney Wing and that he doesn't like it. He wants people to be afraid of him. You've had a row, haven't you?'

Of course I couldn't tell him about the threat to Mercy B. Lord. 'Mate, he's brought in a new account, Citizen Watches. Wants us to make a TV commercial. Trouble is —'

'Yeah? Shit, hey!' Willy Wonka exclaimed, clearly excited, my reason for the row with Sidney Wing quite forgotten at the prospect of a TV commercial. 'Have you ever made one . . . I mean, a TV commercial?'

'Yeah, a few back home, mostly for cigarettes.' I grinned. 'All real deep and meaningful groundbreaking stuff,' I said, sending myself up. But the irony was lost on him. 'Would you like an example? A blow by blow?' I offered. I wasn't anxious to talk about the row with Sidney Wing and I hoped this would act as a diversion.

Willy Wonka nodded vigorously. 'Yeah, man! You can do all that stuff?'

I began hamming up a typical Wills TV spot, one I'd worked on for Escort Filter Tipped. 'Location: cliff top, late afternoon,' I began. 'Music over then under. Open on long shot: male smoker meets pretty female smoker. Sound effects: gulls overhead, crash of waves. Cut to two shot medium close-up.' I paused to explain. 'That means both of them from the waist up. He offers her an Escort Filter Tipped. Cut to close-up of pack and girl's hand.' I grinned. 'She withdraws a fag. Cut back to medium close-up as he lights her cigarette using expensive lighter. Voiceover: *"The flavour is filtered to bring you the smooth Virginia tobacco taste."* Cut to close-up of her face: she inhales, looks up, exhales. *"Will you be my Escort?"* she asks, small grin. Cut to two shot: he exhales, smiles down at her. Cut to long shot: they walk arm in arm towards the edge of the cliff. Dissolve to silhouette of couple standing on edge of cliff, brilliant sunset background. Sound effects: gull calls, waves crashing on the shore below. Voiceover: *"Enjoy the true smoking satisfaction of new Escort Filter*

Tipped." Dissolve to close-up of pack against sunset with slogan: "Smooth Virginia Tobacco Taste".'

Willy Wonka looked deeply impressed, although he probably didn't understand it all. 'Wow! Shit, hey, Simon. You did that?' he exclaimed. 'We could do that again, man!' He thought for a moment. 'Only this time he gives her a Citizen watch. "Will you be a Citizen?" he asks.' Willy Wonka looked pleased with himself. Then, misty-eyed, he went on, 'Enjoy the timeless gift of beautiful time. Citizen Watches.'

I realised that my irony had been completely wasted. 'Mate, those cigarette commercials were absolute unadulterated crap.'

Willy Wonka looked at me uneasily, not quite believing he'd heard me correctly. 'Yeah?'

'Yeah, no-expense-spared total shit.'

'But we are going to make one, aren't we? The first TV commercial in Singapore?' he asked anxiously.

'Mate, the budget Sidney's agreed to wouldn't hire a cameraman for a day. That's if we could even find one in Singapore with a 35-millimetre movie camera. Or a studio to build a set, let alone lights, crew, make-up, talent, wardrobe.' I shrugged. 'And we couldn't make it in time anyway. It takes a week just to process the film at the lab in Hong Kong.'

'But in your cigarette commercial you did it all outside. Couldn't we do the same?' Willy Wonka said hopefully, neatly inserting himself into any production crew he thought might eventuate.

'What, do it on location? No, mate, take my word for it, that's even more expensive. Not a chance.'

'So what are you going to do?'

'Dunno. Sidney's demanded that I make it. That's what the row was all about. He doesn't want to go back to Hercules Sun, the Citizen agent, and tell him he got it all wrong, that he was talking through his arse.'

'Did you say Hercules Sun? My dad says he's Triads, a nasty piece of work.'

'Yeah? All the more reason, I suppose, why Sidney isn't willing to eat crow.'

'Crow not good to eat, huh? What's it mean?'

'Humiliate himself, lose face.'

'I know a guy with a camera, Simon.'

'What, Kodak home movies?'

'No, a big one.'

'But 35-millimetre?'

'I think so.'

'Probably 16-millimetre. Some keen amateurs have them.'

'No, I don't think so. He's not an amateur. Sometimes he does stuff for the BBC, when something big happens here.'

Aunty Daisy arrived at that moment with the lobster in spicy sauce. There was much ado about the dish and the usual congratulations for the beaming ex-family cook, who looked to be in her sixties, then a question from me, followed by her explanation about how the spicy sauce was prepared. Aunty Daisy left with an instruction to us to eat the lobster while it was hot because the sauce lost some of its flavour when it congealed. We opened the second two bottles of beer from the ice-block table fridge and got stuck in. As a cook Aunty Daisy was every bit as good as she was cracked up to be. I made up my mind to bring Elma to True Blue, but I'd wait until the heat wasn't so severe.

And then, halfway through the lobster, an idea hit me. The block of ice! Trying to conceal my excitement, I turned to Willy Wonka and enquired, 'This cameraman – how well do you know him?'

'He took the pictures for my sister's wedding.'

'Movie?'

'No, colour photographs. They were damned good.'

My heart sank. 'He's a wedding photographer?'

'Yeah, he has a studio.'

'I thought you said he worked for the BBC.'

'Yeah, but only on the side; he does weddings to make a living.'

'Do you know him well?'

'Well, yeah, I suppose, sort of . . . he does all the big weddings.'

It wasn't sounding good. 'What's his name?'

'Harry "Three Thumbs" Poon.'

'You're kidding! How'd he get the name? Is he clumsy?'

'No, he was born with three thumbs. He has two on his left hand.'

'And he has a big movie camera?'

'Yeah, that's right.'

'When can we meet him?'

'I'll have to call home and get his number from my mum.'

'Can you do that now?'

'Now? This moment?'

'Yes, I think I've got a great idea.'

'For a TV commercial?'

'Yes, of course.'

'Can I help?'

'You already have, Willy Wonka, more than you can ever possibly know.'

'Don't eat my lobster while I'm gone,' he laughed, rising from the table.

'Tell him we don't have a lot of money.'

'We'll have to buy him a big lunch, Simon.'

'Naturally. Tell him swallows-nest soup and Swatow tea.'

Willy Wonka laughed again. 'He's a married man, Simon!'

Swatow tea was a very expensive brew served in a tiny cup to the guest of honour at the conclusion of a banquet. No Chinese business deal takes place without its attendant banquet, and feasting is the very first move in a business deal. 'Eat first, do business later' is the Chinese mercantile mantra – that way you get to eat even if the deal isn't closed. It could be a simple lunch at the bottom rung of the business ladder or a veritable banquet at the top. Budget permitting, or if the deal were sufficiently important, the elaborate meal would be followed up with the complimentary services of a lady of the night, not at a girlie bar, but a private assignation in one's hotel room, where she would be waiting wearing little more than a set of false eyelashes, tiny spangled G-string and possibly thigh-high boots. Ronnie had explained to me that Sidney favoured using the services of a woman who called herself Sabina Fong, and who boasted having had one of the very first breast implants in Singapore. Her grapefruit-sized, unyielding mammaries were thought to be beyond the wildest dreams of the clients Ronnie was attempting to impress. The tiny cup of Swatow tea at the conclusion of a banquet was intended to equip the drinker with a hard-on that couldn't be discouraged with a stout stick.

Needless to say, the luncheon we invited Harry 'Three Thumbs' Poon to share with us as a prelude to engaging him and his camera didn't run to such Elysian heights. He'd never attempted to film a commercial with his early 35-millimetre camera, having hitherto only used it to point at riot mobs, police brutality, dockside fires and the like. He'd never filmed anything in close-up and couldn't guarantee sharp focus. He knew nothing about lighting but I guessed I could manage that. But he was enthusiastic and cheap as chips, and besides, he was all there was.

The idea was so simple it was scary. Simple-sounding ideas have a nasty habit of turning out to be very complicated. I planned to freeze the watch in a block of ice overnight, then, with the camera locked, chip open the block with a hammer and cold chisel, remove the watch to show that it was still working, then dump it into a glass saucepan of boiling water and remove it to show it was still keeping perfect time. All of this in sixty seconds without any cutaways, just one continuous shot, the whole demonstration taking place in front of the viewer's eyes. The Citizen watch was aptly named 'Hero', so the voiceover would simply state: '*No extremes of temperature can possibly stop the Citizen Hero. It's never too cold, never too hot for a Citizen watch.*'

Willy Wonka offered the use of his dad's garage freezer and we shot the entire commercial in the kitchen of his home: Harry 'Three Thumbs' Poon on camera, Willy Wonka chipping the block of ice and removing the watch, holding it close to the camera to show the sweep of the second hand, then dumping it into the steaming glass saucepan of boiling water and removing it exactly fifteen seconds later. Sounds simple, but it wasn't; it was all timed to the split-second. I did the lighting and whatever direction was involved. Finally, we used Dansford's mellifluous American tones for the voiceover.

Sometimes the gods smile benignly. We had no idea whether the watches would actually survive the extremes of temperature, whether the ice blocks would be sufficiently clear to reveal the sweep of the second hand through the ice and whether the glass saucepan and boiling water would be similarly translucent. We'd encased three Hero watches in ice blocks and all came out of the freezer almost as clear as glass. The first one didn't chip open quickly enough, but the second did. The watch under the ice could clearly be seen to be working, and it kept working while it was bubbling in the glass saucepan. We made it on budget and on deadline, including the film processing and sound mixing at the Saw Bros facilities in Hong Kong, which cost a little more than half the budget.

The commercial was a huge success and the entire Singapore stock of Citizen watches sold out in a week. The same happened in Hong Kong. I did a full-page newspaper ad in the *Straits Times*: the top third a photograph of the Citizen Hero embedded in the ice block, the middle third with it boiling in the glass saucepan, and the bottom third mostly white space with the words

We can do the same for you

Samuel Oswald Wing Advertising – Singapore

The agency's phone rang hot for days and we were flooded with potential new clients wanting TV commercials made by the agency with the proven sales record. On a hunch that this was the start of something very big, I offered to buy a 75 per cent share of Harry 'Three Thumbs' Poon's wedding photography business, which he happily accepted. We then registered the name 'Three Thumbs Films' and I offered Willy Wonka a 24 per cent share, on the proviso that he go to Australia or the US to be trained in film. I'd persuaded the board of Samuel Oswald

Brickman to let him join the TV production department for a year's training. I told Dansford that I'd pay for his airfare and board. But he'd insisted the agency pay and contacted New York, explaining that it was in the interests of the fledgling local TV commercial facility. They agreed and, much to Sidney Wing's chagrin, we were required to meet his costs. His family happily supported the plan, having never seen the value in a sociology degree. They were relieved to think that the exaggerated sense of social justice that had motivated Willy Wonka originally was finally out of his system. This left me with 51 per cent – in other words, a controlling interest, something the importance of which Chairman Meow had hammered into us as teenagers. 'In business, sooner or later there is disharmony. Always own the final vote. Even if it is only 1 per cent more shares than all the rest put together, it is still enough.'

The Citizen Hero TV commercial won the first Asian Advertising Award for television and a Clio in America as the world's best commercial in the watch and jewellery category. Needless to say, Sidney Wing flew to America to collect the award at the spectacular black-tie awards night in New York, accompanied by the president and senior vice presidents from the New York office. Jonas Bold had been among them and phoned a day later to say that you couldn't have wiped the smile off Sidney Wing's face with a blunt axe, and that our beloved chairman had modestly claimed he'd done everything himself, from having the idea, through production on a shoestring budget to the final product. Furthermore, the only time my name was mentioned was when Wing stated that I had been violently opposed to making the ad in the first place.

Having passed the halfway mark of my contract I didn't give a continental. Locally, my contribution was well known and, I admit, the commercial and the awards it won didn't do my reputation any harm. Sidney Wing, of course, never thanked me for saving his arse, or for anything else for that matter. When I met Hercules Sun his first words to me were, 'So you're the guy who told Sidney Wing my television commercial couldn't be done, eh? Damned good thing he didn't listen to you, Mr Koo. I'm not sure I want you working on my advertising account.'

I kept quiet, my silence being the price I happily paid for keeping Mercy B. Lord safe. I comforted myself that revenge is a dish best served cold and that I could wait, though until when and for what, I had no idea. It was one of my father's sayings, although I never witnessed him putting it into action.

The only hitch in all these carefully laid plans concerned poor Willy Wonka. Flushed with the success of his newly minted film career and with a giant-killing first TV commercial under his belt, he'd declared himself crazy about film. He was waiting for a special temporary working visa to be arranged for him by my former chairman, Charles Brickman, when he received a conscription notice to join the fledgling Singapore Army. One of the most unlikely soldiers Singapore's armed forces were ever likely to encounter was dragged kicking and screaming from the agency into the arms of the unsuspecting military. No doubt they hoped to make a man of him. All I knew was that I'd lost a very good young man who might not suit the military template but was a one-off well worth cultivating in any society. While the long hair had to go, I ardently hoped that the essential Willy Wonka would remain unscathed over the two years of compulsory military service.

With Willy Wonka's departure I was stretched to breaking point. We replaced him with Sarah Ping, a shy and retiring widow in her forties with two teenage children, who'd worked since the age of eighteen in the government translation office. She was diligent, translated well in all the required languages and was always polite. She showed no interest in advertising or selling and worked nine to five and no more. I desperately needed an English copywriter but Sidney simply wouldn't pay for anyone from Hong Kong or Australia. I'd always put in a fairly long day but it was now stretching into twelve and even, on occasions, sixteen hours at the agency and then most nights I was taking work home. While Mercy B. Lord was patient and loving, I could sense she was getting thoroughly pissed off, and we'd had a couple of rows that had been essentially my fault.

Then, at one of our regular monthly Singapore luncheons, aware of my urgent need, Elma Kelly recommended Mrs Sidebottom, the wife of a civil construction engineer who was being transferred from Hong Kong to Singapore. In Elma's forthright manner, her recommendation came with a warning: 'She has a pathological fear of the dentist, my dear. You don't want to get too close – simply frightful breath. She could buckle a brass spittoon at twenty paces! Ha ha! Useful gal, though. Once worked for Marks & Spencer in London and we used her for retail advertising for Lane Crawford, a department-store client.' Elma paused. 'Absolutely no hesitation in recommending her to you, Simon. Damned hard worker. She won't tell you, but she was in Intelligence during the war, Bletchley Park gal. Best to have her working from home. Poor woman's an insomniac, and she's very self-conscious about her teeth.'

I confess I looked somewhat sceptical. 'Sorry, Elma, but if her teeth are so bad, why doesn't she have them all out? Fix her breath as well!'

'I told you, fear of the dentist, nothing the poor dear can do about it, so be sure not to let her anywhere near your clients.'

'Does Mrs Sidebottom have a first name?' I asked.

Elma's head jerked backwards. 'I say, how very curious. It never occurred to me to ask. I mean, what can you possibly add to a name like Sidebottom? Topsy? Ha, ha, Topsy Sidebottom, not bad, what?'

I was desperate for help, bad breath notwithstanding. We were about to pitch for the Singapore Tourist Promotion Board, and while you can do a fair bit with pictures and headlines, I needed an English-language copywriter for the ads, brochures and direct response shots (ads with coupons) – what is known in the lingo as 'body copy'. I discussed the matter with Dansford, who approved, and the following day I phoned Mrs Sidebottom and suggested we meet for lunch at Raffles.

'Oh, hello, Mr Koo. Elma Kelly said you might be calling. Raffles? Lovely.' Her voice was beautifully modulated, whereas, I can't say why, I'd expected it to be broad and probably cockney. To me, Sidebottom just didn't sound like a posh name. On the other hand, it wasn't unusual back then for lower-middle-class English people sent out to the colonies to fly the flag for Mother England to return home with an acquired accent several rungs up the social ladder from the accent they'd had when they'd left Blighty.

Mrs Sidebottom, pointed out to me by the concierge, was waiting in the foyer when I arrived. She didn't react when I approached. No doubt she wasn't expecting a short, solid, ugly Chinese bloke after hearing my Australian accent on the phone.

'Mrs Sidebottom?'

'Yes,' she replied tentatively.

I stretched out my hand, smiling. 'Simon Koo.'

To my surprise she ignored my outstretched hand and scrambled to her feet. A half-sucked peppermint dropped from her mouth as she said, 'Oh, oh, I do beg your pardon. You're not at all what I expected.' Then, hurriedly taking my hand in both her own, she shook it vigorously. 'How do you do, Mr Koo.'

'Simon. Please call me Simon,' I replied, smiling despite the first blast of toxic breath. Elma Kelly's warning was no exaggeration. Sending a peppermint into the attack was like aiming a slingshot at an elephant.

Not only had I misjudged Mrs Sidebottom's class, but I'd also imagined a big, broad woman with the breast of a pouter pigeon and the backside of a Zulu maiden. Instead she was diminutive, almost wraithlike, and viewed side-on appeared to have no bottom whatsoever.

Mrs Sidebottom looked to be in her late forties or early fifties, heavily powdered, so that her small oval face appeared abnormally white against the blood-red lipstick that coloured her little cupid's bow mouth, its twin peaks painted in rather too generously. As if all this wasn't sufficiently disconcerting, she possessed a pair of the most beautiful, innocent baby blues, two large, starkly brilliant, crystalline marbles against a chalk-white background, without even a dab of softening eye shadow. Hers was a face that belonged to a pantomime fairy, where such astonishing eyes would prove utterly compelling to an audience of excited children. Now they seemed to lock onto mine, holding me transfixed, so that her appalling breath kept arriving in waves.

'Simon it shall henceforth be,' she said, adding, 'and you must call me

Sylvia, although you probably won't. Even Cecil, my husband, calls me Mrs Sidebottom. I almost didn't marry him because of his surname, but, alas, it seems once it became attached to have become an organic part of me. I'm so looking forward to the Tiffin Room. I've heard so much about it.'

'I've requested a table as far as possible from the serving table so we can talk,' I replied, delighted to swing out of her breathing range as we walked down the polished wooden corridor towards the famous curry restaurant. I'd taken the precaution when booking to explain to the clerk that our luncheon was to double as a business meeting. 'We'll put you in the alcove,' she'd replied obligingly. 'It has a nice view of the garden, sir. That way you'll be neither seen nor heard.'

We were shown to our table at the far end of the dining room near a big bay window that looked out onto a pleasant garden. While it meant we had to weave our way past most of the other diners to get our curry, the garden gave a sense of being more private. The drinks waiter appeared. 'What's it to be?' I asked, guessing it would be gin and tonic.

'Oh, lovely, G and T, please.' She looked up at the waiter. 'I say, do you have Tanqueray?'

'Of course, madam.'

'And a Tiger beer,' I added.

After the waiter departed Mrs Sidebottom smiled. 'It's my little test. Never quite right if they don't have the right gin.'

'There is a right and a wrong gin? I mean, among the better brands?' I asked.

'Well, of course, dear boy, it's the angelica, juniper and coriander. Splendid mystery, don't you think?'

I could see we were about to embark on one of those nonsensical bouts of verbal shadow-boxing, conversational skirmishes that the English are particularly adept at mounting, designed to size up one's opponent and at the same time fill the silence when two strangers meet. And so I said, in what I hoped was an urbane manner, 'I confess I've not spent a lot of time thinking about the mystery of gin beyond knowing juniper berries are somehow involved.' Then I added with a grin, 'Had I been asked, I would have guessed that Angelica was the name of a saint, or perhaps an Irish nun, certainly not an ingredient in gin.'

'Terribly important to know what goes into things. Half the joy of tasting is the guessing game. Why do you think gin is favoured more by women than by men?'

'The angelica?'

'Well done, Simon. By the way, it's particularly pronounced in Tanqueray.'

Sometimes you know you're about to hear someone else's fascinating fact that has you reaching to open the garbage bin we all keep in a corner of our minds for stuff we know we're never, ever going to need to think about. I just knew this was one such moment, but then thankfully a diversion arrived in the form of the waiter with our drinks.

Mrs Sidebottom remained mute while the waiter placed the drinks in front of each of us. He left and I looked up into those twin cerulean lakes, raised my beer and said, in what I hoped was a gallant voice, 'Cheers, and welcome to the team. I hope this is the start of a long and happy partnership.' I grinned, affecting a boyish modesty. 'I always feel as if I'm cheating when I write copy, that the half-decent layout I'm capable of rendering definitely deserves much better.' The moment arrived to clink glasses but I'd been too busy composing my *bon mot* to see that Mrs Sidebottom's G and T remained where the waiter had placed it.

'Flatulence,' she pronounced.

I wasn't sure I'd heard correctly. Lowering my glass, I said, 'Pardon?'

'Menstrual problems . . . pre-menstrual symptoms, painful menstruation . . .' then, 'menopause.'

'I'm not really sure . . .?'

'My dear Simon,' she picked up her glass, 'to angelica! It's why women prefer gin.'

With information overload about the efficacy of the herb angelica for problems unique to women – flatulence aside – we touched glasses. While of course I was familiar with the word, I don't think I'd ever used 'menopause' in a sentence, or even silently to myself. The several menstrual-related words seemed to me a strange prelude to a toast immediately preceding lunch, although it was obvious this thought hadn't occurred to Mrs Sidebottom.

Neither the angelica, coriander or juniper in the gin did much to quell her breath. Nevertheless, I soon discovered that Mrs Sidebottom was a very pleasant woman, and after I'd outlined the new business pitch for the Tourist Promotion Board, she seemed to know at once what I required in a copywriter and readily agreed to come on board.

'I'm afraid you'll have to work from home, though. The agency is pretty noisy and we don't have a spare office,' I said, finally adding, 'You could share mine but it's tiny and very noisy.'

She looked genuinely relieved. 'Oh, splendid! I like to work in my own time. But I shall come into the agency to meet your account director, Mr Drocker.'

'That could be awkward.' I said quickly. 'You see, Dansford is only available for meetings in the morning.' I assumed a look of regret. 'I'm afraid it's an agency rule.'

Mrs Sidebottom smiled, not a pretty sight. Her teeth were in a frightful state. 'In that case I shall attempt to get a good night's rest so as to be bright and chirpy.'

'Really, there's no need,' I said firmly, imagining the effect of Mrs Sidebottom's breath on Dansford's delicate state each morning. 'I can brief you at your home and bring the layouts around.'

'That's very sweet, Simon. We're not settled in yet – frightful mess at home. Most happy to come in. Cecil will wake me before he leaves. Besides, one likes to get an impression of an agency and its people. No, no, I absolutely insist.'

I decided that one visit might be endurable, provided I warned Dansford not to get too close.

She'd finished her G and T by the time we'd been through all the details. 'Another Tanqueray?' I asked.

'Oh no, one at lunch and another at sundown is sufficient unto the day.' She smiled. 'Now, what about these splendid curries? How exciting!'

'It's self-service, I'm afraid.'

'Oh, lovely, no fuss or having to decide immediately.'

The tiffin table contained sixteen different curries each in a stainless-steel serving dish resting on a stand under which burned a small flame. When we arrived, several people were serving themselves, swinging the lids back and sniffing at the curries before making their choice. But as we drew closer I could see those nearest hesitating momentarily. They had obviously caught a whiff of the miasma surrounding us. All glanced at me, their thoughts obvious: *Dreadful pong – must be the ugly-looking Chinese bloke.*

Mrs Sidebottom stood next to a big guy with a pronounced beer gut who was bending over to sniff at a chicken vindaloo. She leant forward to share the aroma, and the big bloke suddenly pulled back in alarm. Pointing to the curry, he hissed, 'Jesus! Don't touch that one, lady!' I obviously wasn't the only Australian in the room.

Nearly two hours later, lunch was beginning to feel like an eternity. Mrs Sidebottom insisted on tasting all sixteen curries, half a serving spoon of each together with a teaspoon of rice and a different condiment. Each serving was placed on a clean plate, and as she finished each curry she wrote its name in a tiny spiral-bound pad, ripped out the page and placed it on the plate, carefully avoiding the curry-stained portion. Placing the second plate on top of the first, then rising to return to the tiffin table, she said, 'Now, you won't let the waiter clear away my precious plates while I'm gone, will you, Simon?'

She was a careful, if not to say downright slow eater and would take four or five minutes to savour the small portion on her plate, commenting on its flavour, aroma and texture. I found myself bobbing up and down like a yo-yo every time she rose to fetch yet another curry. 'Do sit, dear,' she'd repeat each time, although I found this impossible. She rose from the table with such eagerness that the other diners were beginning to take notice, the big Aussie bloke who'd cautioned her at the tiffin table now openly chuckling each time she passed his table. I wondered whether I was witnessing some sort of record: the diner who tasted every curry on offer.

Halfway through, she looked up from her umpteenth plate, leaned forward and grasped my hand, her bony birdlike claw as small as a child's. Her incredible arctic-blue eyes held me transfixed. 'Oh, Simon, thank you, this is such fun!' The blast of bad air that hit me full in the face very nearly caused my lunch to return, but she spoke with such enthusiasm that it was impossible to be upset.

The spent plates, each garnished with a note, were stacked between us on the table, so that I found myself wishing that the pile would rise high enough to create a bulwark against her toxic breath. She returned with plate fourteen, the chicken vindaloo, tasted it cautiously and pronounced it delicious: 'Piquant. Nice creamy texture. Whatever can that silly man have been thinking?'

Finally, when curry number sixteen was just a yellow stain on the plate, she leaned back in her chair. 'I do so like to remember the flavour, work out the herbs and spices in each.'

I pointed to the stack of plates. 'Well, you certainly seem to have enjoyed them,' I said somewhat lamely, thinking we were going to still be there when the supper guests arrived.

'Oh, just a few more details, Simon. The real trick is getting the various flavours firmly into your head. I've made my notes but need a quick review – I hope you don't mind?'

What could I say? 'No, of course not,' I mumbled.

Then she called a waiter and asked for a large jug of water, sixteen sherry glasses and three fresh damask table napkins. When these eventually arrived she asked me to fill each sherry glass roughly half full. Then, with her notepad open beside her and starting with the top plate, she ran her forefinger through the smudge of curry left on it and brought it to her mouth, then dipped her finger into a sherry glass containing clean water, rinsed and then dried it on a napkin and checked its note against her previous notation, sometimes adding a comment or simply ticking what she'd previously written, piling the plates to one side and the notes to the other. She'd reached curry plate number twelve when the manager arrived.

'Madam, is there something wrong?' he asked.

Mrs Sidebottom looked up. 'No, no, not in the least! Splendid lunch.'

'Am I permitted to ask what you are doing, madam?' the manager persisted. By this time the maître d' had joined us.

Fortunately, the sixteen curries seemed to have somewhat quelled the immediate impact of Mrs Sidebottom's breath. 'Why, of course you may. I write for the food page of the *Guardian* and also an occasional gourmet column for the *New Yorker* magazine.' She looked up at him meaningfully. 'With so many Americans arriving in Singapore, I feel certain they'll accept my piece. After all, today's remarkable tiffin will give me,' she chuckled, 'a great deal of food for thought.'

Both men, beaming, excused themselves, backing away, apologising for the intrusion and promising a warm welcome at any time in the future madam would care to call.

At the culmination of the meal, and with the notes and notebook returned to Mrs Sidebottom's handbag, I rose wearily and excused myself in order to pay for what seemed to have been the longest lunch of my life.

'There is no charge, sir,' the smiling cashier said. 'We do hope to see you and madam back in the Tiffin Room soon. Oh, and the manager asks if you would care for a glass of champagne in the library?'

'Awfully nice of him, but I really have to get back to work. But please give him my thanks,' I replied, smiling weakly, grateful that Mrs Sidebottom was sufficiently distant not to hear my desperate excuse. I was truly beginning to think the bloody luncheon was never going to come to an end.

The doorman, at my request, whistled for two taxis. As I opened the back door of the first to allow Mrs Sidebottom to enter, she asked, 'I trust you were not required to pay, Simon?'

'Well, no, as a matter of fact, they wouldn't hear of it. Interesting. I had no idea that you were a food writer.'

Mrs Sidebottom, now seated, threw back her head and laughed, sending a blast of noxious breath towards the hapless driver. 'Never written a word about food in my life, dear boy. Oh, except once the cooking instructions on the back of a can of spaghetti in tomato sauce. Not really my thing, food – can't fry an egg.' She chuckled. 'Happily, dining out with my notepad and pen works every time. I haven't paid for lunch in years. Couldn't possibly allow you to do so – ruin my perfect record!'

With its tyres crunching on the gravelled driveway, the taxi moved off, the driver with one hand on the steering wheel and the other fanning his nose.

'See you at the agency, 9.30 sharp, day after tomorrow!' I called after her. A hand waved behind the rear window in acknowledgement. 'Elma Kelly, who in God's name have you sent me?' I cried aloud as I climbed into the rear seat of the second cab, once again free to breath God's fresh air, or at least the sweltering, stifling fug that passed for air in Singapore.

On the day Mrs Sidebottom was due to visit the agency, Dansford arrived, as usual, precisely at 9 a.m. He looked frail, his face sporting several fresh shaving nicks, and his thick, brick-coloured hair still wet from the shower he'd taken after his stomach had performed its usual series of morning evacuations. Though immaculately laundered and freshly groomed by Chicken Wing, he was nevertheless in no fit condition to be confronted with Mrs Sidebottom's breath.

I'd warned him and suggested he remain seated behind his desk while we sat at the coffee table some ten feet away. 'Dansford, for goodness sake, don't get up and greet her. I'll knock twice to allow you to grab the telephone and then when we enter you can smile and indicate the telephone has your attention, then point to the coffee table. For God's sake, don't leave your desk.'

'Pretty damned rude, don't you think?' he'd replied.

I looked at him sternly. 'Mate, take my advice, okay?'

But of course he did no such thing. I met Mrs Sidebottom in the foyer at nine-fifteen, where I caught just a whiff in passing of Listerine mouthwash fighting a losing battle with the bad breath. The germ-killing gargle had as much hope as a tot hammering its fists against the back of an angry gorilla.

I knocked twice then opened the door slowly, expecting Dansford to be engaged on the phone, but he rose from behind his desk and came forward to meet us, hand outstretched. The first whiff was sufficient to wipe the welcoming smile from his pale face, the second produced an involuntary movement – his left hand shooting up to cover his nose and mouth – then, bent almost double, stomach heaving, he mumbled something through his fingers and bolted for the door. He later told me he'd retched into the executive toilet bowl, then decided he lacked the courage to return and fled into Sidney Wing's office.

I apologised to Mrs Sidebottom more or less honestly. 'Big night last night. Dansford had a whiskey client from Tennessee who wanted to see the sights, Bugis Street and . . . well, the bright lights of Singapore,' I explained.

Mrs Sidebottom nodded knowingly. 'No explanation necessary, Simon. My Cecil found himself often enough in Wan Chai for the same reasons – oh, the Wan Chai district is Hong Kong's equivalent of Bugis and Victoria streets.'

I showed her the layouts for the Tourist Board pitch and briefed her on the copy I needed. By the time I'd completed this task Dansford still hadn't reappeared. After I'd apologised again for his absence, we did a brief tour of the agency. Fortuitously, Sidney was in America, Johnny out somewhere and Ronnie had not arrived. I then sent the agency messenger boy out to hail a taxi to take Mrs Sidebottom home. Needless to say, she was henceforth briefed by phone.

I have often wondered why a misplaced sense of good manners, or a lack of courage, or an excess of kindness prevents us from telling someone, in the nicest possible terms, that they have a bodily odour or some other socially disadvantageous problem that, with some attention, might be overcome. But we don't. It's especially difficult with someone who has social pretentions or is genuinely posh. I mean, how would you tell the Queen she had bad breath? I admit, I'm just as much a coward as everyone else.

I wondered about Cecil, though. Surely, as her husband, he'd say something to her? But then again, if you were born with the name Sidebottom and your parents chose to compound it with a name like Cecil and you took to calling your nearest and dearest Mrs Sidebottom, you probably had enough problems. Come to think of it, Simon Koo isn't exactly a presidential name either. If, as seemed increasingly remote, Mercy B. Lord agreed to marry me, she'd become Mercy B. Koo! A bad pun on 'thank you' in French.

If I appear to have emphasised Mrs Sidebottom's weaknesses, then let me hasten to say that she was pleasant and easy to work with and did a great job of the Tourist Promotion Board copy. Furthermore, inspired by her retail experience (as a girl she'd been an assistant to a senior window dresser at Harrods), she suggested the giant panels or screens that, without a doubt, were one of the major contributions to our winning the business.

Three weeks before the pitch, Sidney Wing returned from America and, after hearing from Johnny about the proposed presentation and the giant screens, called an emergency meeting where he objected vehemently to the expense.

'You're crazy, Dansford. You won't win a government account by spending money on wooden panels with pictures,' he insisted.

Dansford remained calm. 'I agree, Sidney, but we're not spending money on wooden panels with pictures, as you so nicely put it – we're spending money on a *great* idea.'

'Who says?' Johnny could be relied upon to support his older brother.

'Well, I do,' I said.

Sidney laughed. 'Oh, surprise, surprise!'

'It won't work, Simon,' Ronnie joined the debate. 'It's not the Chinese way.'

'Oh? And what is that?' Dansford asked.

Sidney exploded with one of his St Vitus giggles. 'I'm surprised I need to tell you after all this time.'

'Are you going to say it's *guanxi*?' I suggested.

'Well, well, well – Simon, the expert on Chinese ways,' Sidney said.

Ronnie, ever the peacemaker, said quietly, 'Simon, it won't work. Listen to Sidney.'

'Go ahead, Sidney, tell us why,' Dansford said.

'I must lead this team. It's government business. I have contacts. It was I who brought in Citizen Watches, now a big account. I didn't spend money on expensive panels! All this creative bullshit! I made a cheap commercial and look what happened. It's not what you know . . .' he left us to complete the sentence.

'The Citizen commercial was a great creative idea that belongs wholly to Simon,' Dansford said firmly.

Sidney banged his fist on his desk. 'Mine! My account!' he shouted like a recalcitrant child. 'We will do it my way!'

Dansford remained calm. 'That's not what your prime minister seems to be saying. He has abolished "squeeze" in government; it is a punishable offence.'

'He cannot, you cannot. It is tradition. It will always be the way!' Sidney insisted.

'Or, for that matter, the impression we got from the brief by Tan Sri Long Me Saw, the chairman, and Molly Ong, the marketing director,' Dansford offered.

'Ha, they are only puppets!' Johnny growled.

'With the greatest respect, you don't know the system and I do!' Sidney spat.

Ronnie, attempting to calm things down, said, 'The accepted etiquette . . . er . . . protocol . . .'

'I need to consult people. There are things I must do. You are spending *our* money, wasting our money! These panels are just rubbish!'

'And bribing a member or members of the government is the right way?' I asked. It was getting very heated and decidedly personal, two systems ranged against each other. Smoke and mirrors versus a good idea and transparency – at least, that's the way I saw it at the time.

'A banquet held for a minister, with the courtesies that follow, is the

Chinese way. There's nothing wrong with that,' Ronnie protested.

Dansford sighed, finally losing patience. 'Not the goddamned Chinese way again!'

'This is bad rice,' Johnny scowled. 'You *must* listen to us.'

'Well, no, Johnny. I don't think so. We're going Spam for Uncle Sam.'

Sidney Wing now completely lost his cool. 'I will call New York!' he announced angrily.

Dansford's jaw jutted. 'As you wish, Sidney. While you're at it, remind them again how you did all the work on Citizen Watches. But we'll still be going ahead with the panels. Oh, and we won't be needing you at the presentation.'

Sidney, furious, called New York after we'd left, and pointed out to Arthur Grinds (he who grinds slowly but exceedingly fine) – Senior Vice President International – that it was impossible to win a government account without inside influence and that he, Sidney, should be put in charge of the pitch, given his success with the Citizen campaign, despite the miniscule budget. He urged New York to veto the wasteful expense on the panels at once.

This resulted in a call from New York to Dansford demanding he explain himself, which he did, sticking his neck way out for the cost involved and insisting we go with the panels. It was a brave decision, as the panels were Mrs Sidebottom's idea and he could have dropped them without upsetting anyone except me, and I wouldn't be there forever. The entire presentation was visual, so without the panels we had only a theme and slogan, but we needed to show how it could be made to work.

We made three revolving screens, each thirty feet high and ten feet wide. Then we produced separate narrow photographic panels with full-colour images printed on them by a local silkscreen company. These were clipped onto the basic panels so they could be easily removed and replaced with other scenes. The printers had baulked at our request at first. No Singaporean or Hong Kong silkscreen company had ever made one-off posters this large and kept them in focus at close quarters. Simple enough today but in the late 1960s it was a major breakthrough.

We chose the town hall as the venue for our presentation, as it was the only building with both a stage and ceiling sufficiently high to accommodate the panels. On the big day a dozen government people plus the Singapore Tourist Promotion Board chairman and marketing director were present. We'd decided on twin presenters, Dansford and myself, speaking from separate podiums with microphones at either side of the town-hall stage, the three giant screens set up between us, side-on, so that only their outer edges faced the audience. Using microphones for so small an audience was a tad melodramatic, but we hoped the big sound would add to the impact of our presentation.

Dansford, sober as a judge, having not touched a drop for two days, began the presentation, and even if his hands were a bit shaky, his voice was, as always, commanding.

'We are indeed fortunate to have all the attractions any tourist could want – great shopping, exotic sights, Muslim, Hindu and Chinese temples and mosques, a magnificent harbour and great beaches,' he began. This obviously went down well, with smiles all round. The music began and the first giant screen slowly swivelled from profile to en face, showing the aspects of Singapore he'd just mentioned. This brought spontaneous applause from the small audience, who I could see were delighted that it wasn't going to be the usual boring presentation.

I gave them enough time to take in the screen and to allow the music to fade. 'But!' I exclaimed, the word punched from the microphone and left hanging in the air. Chinese music began and the second screen swung round to show an aerial shot of Hong Kong. 'Hong Kong has better shopping and a better harbour.'

The first screen kept rotating until its back faced the audience, displaying a series of magnificent temples as the music changed to a well-known Malay folk song. 'Malaya has better temples,' Dansford added.

The second screen now rotated to reveal Thailand's beaches and the soundtrack changed to the tinkling tones of traditional Thai music. 'And Thailand has better beaches,' I concluded.

'So what have *we* to offer?' Dansford asked. The music rose to a crescendo as the last screen slowly turned to face the audience. On it were dozens of smiling faces, adults and children, representing the ethnic mixture that was Singapore – Chinese, Malay, Indian, Indonesian, Eurasian, European, along with the slogan:

SINGAPORE
THE MAGIC OF PEOPLE!

It was all over, red rover. The theme fitted perfectly with Lee Kuan Yew's vision of a multicultural society. We went on to say that good tourism is based on the experience of different cultures and exciting new food, and we had both in abundance. The last screen rotated to reveal hundreds of images of ethnic foods, both raw and cooked, clearly more variety than all the other nearby tourist destinations could provide. We then suggested that the tourist campaign be both international and intra-national, the former showing the cosmopolitan nature of the island and the latter designed to encourage the shopkeepers, hotel employees, taxi drivers, rickshaw owners and the general population to participate in the campaign by making tourists feel welcome and happy.

Lastly we suggested that, with a little care, we could make Singapore the only green city in Asia, where trees and green spaces and people could coexist, unlike the crowded, ugly slums of Hong Kong or the putrid *klongs* of Thailand. We called this 'The Greening of Singapore', and it was this suggestion, apparently, that delighted the prime minister.

While all this was happening, a dozen helpers were working quietly behind the screens to remove the first set of images from the thin panels and replace them with new ones. A hundred-strong children's choir, representing all the ethnic groups in Singapore and clad in red shorts and white shirts emblazoned with the Singapore flag, assembled barefoot on the stage and sang the national anthem, as all the panels rotated so that they completely dominated the town-hall stage. Above the heads of the choir the giant words were repeated:

SINGAPORE
THE MAGIC OF PEOPLE!

After the anxiety of the presentation came the euphoria of the backslapping and congratulations from the chairman, Tan Sri Long Me Saw. 'Well done,' he said, 'but also lucky, eh? What would have happened if the electrics had failed?'

'Ah, no electrics,' I explained, 'we did it all with the magic of people. All the screens were moved by hand. There's an old Australian saying: always take the spoon out of the sink before you turn on the tap. We couldn't take a chance with an electrical fault.'

Long Me Saw gave me a hard look. 'I'm a film man and I know back-up is essential. The "just in case" factor is the most important in any production. I won't forget that you understand this, Simon.' He waved at the stage with the screens and slogan still in place. 'Not only a *big* thinker but also a careful one. Well done.'

It felt good.

We would later learn that the panels and the manner in which we'd used them were a major element in blowing the opposition's presentations out of the water. Every agency in Singapore had pitched, including two recently arrived heavies, Leo Burnett and J. Walter Thompson, who a year previously had entered the Asian market and hadn't stopped banging their drums, as well, of course, as Elma Kelly's Cathay Advertising. But we won!

Mrs Sidebottom deserved much of the credit for this. Dansford sent her a case of champagne, a gesture that caused Sidney to have such a conniption that the Three Wing Circus didn't speak to us for a week. But even before the case of French champagne, the relationship had deteriorated. Sidney Wing had been denied the opportunity to big-note himself in front of some of the government's most powerful people. He'd been swanking for the past five months about the Citizen Watch award, won by his own glorious efforts, and it had become a bit of a joke in the industry, especially since my part in it had become well known and I'd maintained a decorous silence. Elma Kelly had personally spread the word, although I'd told her it didn't matter. 'Iniquitous, Simon! Positively iniquitous! I shall personally see he doesn't get away with it.'

We had won the Tourist Promotion Board account without Sidney Wing's influence, his *guanxi*, and as a result he'd lost a good deal of face – or, perhaps more importantly, he *believed* he had. With the Chinese, perception is everything and in this regard they can be their own worst enemies.

The relationship between East and West in the agency, while never good, was now beyond repair. Even Ronnie, whom we'd always relied on as go-between, was no longer his good-humoured and cooperative self, no doubt due to Sidney's instructions. In my last months at the agency I was determined to set up the Tourist Promotion Board campaign, after which I knew I had several decisions to make, not the least of them being about my relationship with Mercy B. Lord.

I don't suppose, when you consider what else was happening in the world during the sixties, that winning an advertising contract to put a city or island on the tourist map amounts to very much. But the emergence of Singapore as an unexpected force in South-East Asia was particularly significant at the time and it was important that this be seen to be happening. The world in the late sixties was an exceedingly unhappy place, especially in Asia.

Perhaps a small explanation is appropriate.

The Cuban missile crisis in October 1962 had shown the world just how easy it would be for a nuclear war to engulf us all, and the fact that now President Lyndon B. Johnson had escalated the Vietnam War meant more Americans and Vietnamese were dying than ever. Nixon began secretly bombing Cambodia, after bombing the Ho Chi Minh Trail, which ran through Laos and Cambodia. Lots of people were extremely nervous.

Both China and the Soviet Union supported the Viet Cong. Would there be another Cuban missile crisis? This time it might easily end in a series of mushroom clouds above Washington, New York, Moscow and Beijing. Both sides had the nuclear capacity to blow the world to smithereens, and both sides had nuclear submarines carrying warheads capable of doing enormous harm. The ones that scared the daylights out of everyone were the fifty or so American and Russian nuclear submarines prowling around below the surface of the world's oceans. Each carried sufficient warheads to wipe out one of fifty cities. They were positioned so that the missiles, erupting out of innocent-seeming seas, could hit an enemy city anywhere on the globe within half an hour.

Nearer to home – in fact, next door – Indonesia was almost as steeped in blood as Vietnam. The Indonesian army under Major General Suharto was responsible for the gruesome and merciless killing of half a million of its own citizens in a blood-soaked purge of the Indonesian Communist Party, as well as anyone else who attracted his attention, mainly wealthy Chinese.

The wealthy Chinese in Singapore, invariably supporters of Lee Kuan Yew's PAP government, were happy to see the Indonesian communists crushed, but were deeply disconcerted when the Indonesian army almost eliminated the large ethnic Chinese merchant class, by definition largely non-communist, a move undoubtedly motivated by racism and greed. At least 100 000 Chinese Indonesian citizens were slaughtered and buried in mass graves. Not surprisingly, the local Chinese had a deep and abiding fear that the Indonesians would join up with their co-religious Muslim cousins in Malaya and decide to invade little Singapore, sandwiched between them.

While this may or may not have been a realistic fear, it was one Lee Kuan Yew was quick to exploit. He initiated universal and compulsory conscription for all males at eighteen. Unofficially the government excluded those of the Muslim faith. Draft dodgers in Singapore faced an indefinite jail sentence, unlike their brothers in the US.

In Hong Kong the old China hands had never seen the Chinese

communists so belligerent. They felt that at any time they would be swamped under a screaming horde rushing in to kill every last stinking *gwai-lo*.

The Chinese, having already digested Tibet, clashed with the Indians in 1962 and again in 1967 along their long mountainous border, and Beijing was once more issuing threats to 'resolve' the dispute and seize even more of India's territory, having occupied part of Kashmir since the 1950s. All the while, the Indians and Pakistanis were picking at the open wounds left from the partition of India in 1947, which had cost up to a million lives. Now the dispute over Kashmir looked increasingly as if it would lead to war.

In 1962 Burma, seized by a clutch of army generals led by the half-insane Ne Win, was well on the way to reducing the rich little nation to beggary.

Outside Singapore, much of Asia seemed to be going to hell in a handbasket, and communism, despite the annihilation of the Indonesian communists, seemed a real threat. Lee Kuan Yew and his PAP government, while pathologically opposed to communism, needed to demonstrate the advantages of Western capitalism, making his city and his state an example of the virtues of an alternative system without having to resort to the murder of its citizens. The government wanted green space, gardens and decent housing for its multicultural society – a secure place run by Asians for Asians – so that people could continue to live together in harmony. Given the times, it made perfect political sense, even if it wasn't quite as perfect and harmonious as it seemed.

There were those among us – myself included, I like to think – who, in retrospect, didn't much care for the draconian and autocratic way Singapore was run by a government without any truly effective opposition. But as a state it couldn't be faulted for its social-welfare programs, and there was no significant bloodshed, although there was plenty of bombast and, lamentably, opposition members of parliament were jailed, the communist furphy being used as an excuse. With the Asian world in turmoil and with Indonesia next door, it wasn't hard to see why the Singapore government wanted its youth to undergo military training.

As expats, we chose to ignore the darker side of Singapore. We joked about Lee Kuan Yew's idiosyncratic laws that banned long hair for men, chewing gum and carelessly discarded cigarette butts. These were rules with which we could happily live. We didn't inject heroin, so the death penalty for the possession of even a small amount of the drug didn't affect us. We soon gave up chewing gum and told ourselves it was much too hot to wear your hair down to your shoulders.

If 'accidental' fires were razing slum dwellings in the *kampongs* and destroying traditional Malay village life, modern high-rise tenements for workers were taking their place. Improved sanitation was well overdue. Freedom of speech was a nice idea but it didn't put food on the table, and we all knew trade unions were self-seeking and riotous organisations. Nobody was willing to point out the essentially anti-democratic nature of the PAP government, least of all those expats, myself among them, who were happy to comply with even the more draconian, as well as bizarre, of Lee's dictates in order to prosper.

Nobody wanted communism, and Muslims were not like us – the promise of forty virgins waiting in paradise said it all. So why not go with the flow? Singapore saw itself as the Asian equivalent of Israel, and 'The enemy on either side of us' became the mantra of a people who saw the restrictions imposed on them as necessary if they were to enjoy a peaceful and prosperous environment. And none of this affected us directly. The law of convenient compromise ruled the day, although if, on a whim, Lee Kuan Yew had decided to ban alcohol, and he was quite capable of such a thing, then I dare say the island state would have seen a mass exodus of Westerners and the international trade he had so assiduously courted would have ground to a juddering halt. But the prime minister was sufficiently sagacious to realise we needed each other. So all was well in the city state where visitors could experience . . . well, of course, the magic of people.

Getting back to things of less earth-shattering import, winning the

Singapore Tourist Promotion Board business was our first truly big local account, won against other international agencies. The three competing foreign agencies now knew we were no longer the Three Wing Circus and had to be considered genuine contenders in any future pitch for new business. The Citizen commercial had shaken them up somewhat, but this was the very first government publicity account won purely on merit. Not only did it mean a big budget but also tremendous prestige for the agency. It made an unequivocal statement to the Chinese business community that the ancient practice of 'squeeze' in the business of the state was over. The Sidney Wings were henceforth rendered ineffective. A conviction of bribery or favour-mongering now carried a prison sentence for both parties.

I greatly looked forward to my next luncheon with Elma, where I could thank her for recommending Mrs Sidebottom to us. Finally, we'd stuck it right up Sidney Wing's arse with the big government win. Childish as this may seem, it felt *real* good.

But then Dansford had the idea of holding a reception two days after the win to introduce the Tourist Promotion Board to the agency. He had not had a drink for days, stopping forty-eight hours before the presentation and remaining sober afterwards in anticipation of the reception that was to take place at the poolside at Cuscaden House Hotel. At 11 a.m. on the day of the party, which was due to start at 6 p.m., I went into his office to question him about some small detail and arrived just in time to see him clearing his desk. Dansford was meticulous and always left his desk spotless.

'Oh,' he said, 'about to call you, Simon. Just off to the Town Club for a "settler".'

My heart sank. 'Mate, please, it's been almost a week. You've been bloody magnificent and as a consequence we've landed the biggest and most prestigious account in Singapore. No grog until you get to the reception tonight – you promised.'

Dansford looked hurt. 'Buddy, would I let you down?'

'Well, yes, you would,' I carped. 'But please, Dansford, you fuck this up and Sidney Wing will have you by the short and curlies. We lose this account on the last turn and the phone to New York will run red hot. He's thoroughly pissed off about the presentation. He and Johnny are only attending because he'll lose face if he refuses. Half the bloody government will be there. There's even been mention the big guy may attend. As MD you run the show, and you need to be sober as a judge, mate.'

'Simon, I give you my word.'

I shook my head. 'Let me come with you. Remember the bank?'

'That won't happen again. The bank owner was a horse's arse!'

The incident had occurred some months previously. The owner of a small Singapore bank, one of Sidney Wing's accounts, threw a cocktail party to celebrate its twenty-fifth anniversary and Dansford had arrived pretty smashed, whereupon the owner, a pompous Chinese, had taken him to task in front of the assembled guests. To everyone's amazement and horror, Dansford replied to this dressing-down by directing at him a string of extremely explicit Cantonese expletives. He must have learned them from Chicken Wing, because it was well known he'd made no effort to learn any of the local languages, not even a few essential words of Singlish. The upshot was that we were fired on the spot and Sidney lost a great deal of face in the process. The bank incident, as it was referred to, was yet another double underlined entry in the Wing payback ledger.

Dansford looked annoyed. 'Buddy, I don't need a nursemaid! It's a settler, that's all. I don't want to get the shakes at the cocktail party.' I remained silent, hoping he'd come to his senses. 'I tell you what, if I break my pledge I'll dye my hair pink,' he promised.

'Mate, you can dye it all the colours of the rainbow; if you fuck up and arrive drunk we'll blow the account before I've had time to render the first layout.'

'Steady on, Simon. I'm going for a settler, calm my nerves, that's all.' He extended his hands and I had to admit they were shaking. 'See!'

'Dansford, your hands shake every morning – nothing unusual about that.'

He glanced at his watch. 'Not this bad at eleven o'clock. Imagine what I'll be like this evening. A settler, that's all.'

I would have insisted on playing nursemaid, but I had to check the colour separation for a Marlboro poster at the printers. Lee Kuan Yew, on one of his whims, had three days previously banned cigarette advertising on TV, effective immediately, and there'd been a rush on poster sites and production. I remembered to call Mercy B. Lord to ask her to pick up my suit from the cleaners and told her I'd be home by five to change for the cocktail party.

'What's the matter, darling? You sound worried.'

'Yeah, well, get ready for anything to happen tonight. Dansford's gone to the Town Club for, as he puts it, a "settler".'

'Oh dear, what now?'

'He promises he'll dye his hair pink if he isn't sober at the party,' I laughed.

Five o'clock came and Sidney, Johnny, Ronnie, Mercy B. Lord and I were waiting around the pool at the Cuscaden House Hotel. The cocktail party was on the third floor and guests arrived in a lift that opened up to reveal the pool and garden area. This enabled us to greet each of them in person as they stepped out of the lift. All was perfection: French champagne in silver ice buckets, canapés on silver platters covered with white damask napkins to prevent them from drying out in the late afternoon sun, Indian waiters in white gloves, starched white jackets, black pants and polished shoes standing to rigid attention. A baby grand, no doubt intended by the hotel to lend a sense of elegance to the poolside venue, stood under a red and white striped canvas awning with huge displays of orchids on either side of it. The venue, fit for a maharaja, was in readiness to receive the minister for tourism and eighteen assorted bureaucrats and politicians, as well as Long Me Saw and Molly Ong, our new bosses. The only one missing was Dansford Drocker, Managing Director, Senior Vice President of Samuel Oswald Wing Advertising and host of the cocktail party.

Mercy B. Lord had been initially reluctant to come because Sidney would be present but she'd eventually agreed. While this sounds like a small victory, it wasn't. It was the first time we'd been to a formal agency occasion, or for that matter any other official occasion, together, and I was anxious for it all to go off smoothly, especially with Sidney in attendance. By 6 p.m., when the first of the guests started to arrive, there was still no sign of Dansford. Most of the male guests, all dressed identically in white, the uniform of Lee Kuan Yew's senior government officials, had come directly from work so there were no spouses in attendance. The guests of honour were, of course, Tan Sri Long Me Saw and Molly Ong, unless the PM showed up.

As the first guests emerged from the lift I glanced at Sidney Wing, hoping that, as chairman, he would take over the role of host. It was an opportunity for him to gain lost ground and get one up on Dansford and me. But instead he gave me one of his Ming the Merciless looks and stood back. Ignoring the scowling Johnny, I glanced at Ronnie, but he simply shrugged and looked helpless. He was obviously under instructions from Sidney not to be his usual ebullient self or to get involved with the welcoming proceedings, thereby adding to my embarrassment. But it wasn't a complete disaster; I'd played host at garden parties in our Vaucluse home often enough when Chairman Meow pronounced my dad unfit for duty, so I knew what to do.

With Mercy B. Lord beside me and with the first guests approaching, I muttered out of the corner of my mouth, 'C'mon, kid, best smile. We've got to do this together.'

Taking my hand, she pressed it and smiled. 'Meet and greet is my business, darling.'

It was soon obvious that my partner was a big hit, although I was a bit nervous about Molly Ong's arrival. Molly had been appointed marketing manager of the Tourist Promotion Board, more for her Miss Singapore looks and status than for any business acumen she might have possessed, and I didn't know how she'd react to any serious competition in the looks department. In her mid-twenties, she was a stunner, but Mercy B. Lord was every bit as gorgeous. To add to the duo of beauties, Long Me Saw appeared with a surprise guest, the ex-wife of Indonesia's President Sukarno. Dewi, every bit as beautiful as the other two women, was being groomed by the Saw cinema empire for movie stardom. Molly and Mercy B. Lord thankfully hit it off immediately, while Dewi remained attached to our new client's arm.

Six-thirty came and went, then seven, with the cocktail party due to end around eight. Sidney was smirking and I was panicking, not by this time because of Dansford's absence, but because of his possible appearance when all was running rather well. Only a handful of people, those who'd been at the original pitch in the town hall, had asked about his whereabouts and then only in a cursory or polite manner. Three stunningly beautiful women were sufficient distraction. In the immortal words of the now fortunately absent Dansford on the visit of the Texas Oil boss to the agency, 'Simon, with all those foxy chicks, advertising ideas are irrelevant.' This was especially true at the cocktail party, because Molly Ong and Mercy B. Lord joined forces and made it their business to charm the champagne-fuelled male guests. As well, Dewi, not for one moment releasing the arm of her ebullient escort, turned out to be a very pleasant match for the movie mogul and chairman of the Tourist Promotion Board.

To use a clutch of metaphors, our ship of fate sailed on through a tranquil evening sea without an apparent cloud in the sky. Even the torpedo-armed Wing submarine had found a gaggle of government servants they wanted to impress and seemed temporarily disarmed.

But then, at seven-fifteen, the lift doors swung open and out stepped Dansford, dressed in a cowboy outfit complete with tooled leather cowboy boots, shouting, 'Yeehaa!' and firing two Colt cap guns in the air above his head. What's more, his hair was dyed bright pink.

A shocked silence fell as everyone turned to face the lift. I confess I was momentarily speechless and then I heard Mercy B. Lord laugh and cry out, 'Dansford, you're late. Delayed at the hairdressers, I fear.' A gale of laughter followed as Mercy B. Lord hurried up to Dansford and took him by the arm. Turning, she announced, 'Ladies and gentlemen, Mr Dansford

Drocker, who you can see is feeling decidedly in the pink after winning your tourism account. She turned to the smiling Dansford, who, though drunk, had enough nous to realise he was being rescued. 'Now, Dansford, because of your delay at the hairdressers it's a little late, so why don't you just wave "howdy" to everyone, and then get straight down to the entertainment.'

'Oh, well done!' I heard Molly Ong exclaim in admiration. 'That girl has a lot of class.'

'Yeehaa!' Dansford yelled and fired off the toy six-guns before holstering them. 'Howdy, folks!' he yelled, then allowed Mercy B. Lord to lead him to the baby grand, grabbing a bottle of champagne from a surprised waiter on the way.

She seated him and Dansford, taking a quick slug, placed the champagne bottle beside the piano stool and prepared to play. 'Go, cowboy!' Mercy B. Lord cried, laughing.

Stomping a cowboy boot to the beat of the music, Dansford launched into 'Yellow Rose of Texas' and followed this with a medley from the musical *Annie Get Your Gun*, delivering all the lyrics in a light operatic voice. How Dansford could perform at such a high level when drunk was truly remarkable. All this was met with wild applause and it was obvious the party was going to be an even greater success.

Molly Ong, a little tipsy on champagne, then asked Dansford if he knew the music to *West Side Story* and came to stand at the piano as Dansford launched into a medley. When he reached Leonard Bernstein's lovely 'I Feel Pretty', she accompanied him in a very pleasant contralto voice that had everyone gathering around the piano. The song could have been written for Molly. She was pretty – more than pretty – and in a way the city had given her its key.

I glanced over at Mercy B. Lord and decided that she, too, deserved the key to the city for her quick thinking and grace.

'Bravo! Bravo!' Long Me Saw called, clapping loudly. 'Champagne, beautiful women and good music – perfect! I can see our tourist program is in excellent hands!'

With the exception of Sidney and Johnny, everyone seemed to think

Dansford's hilarious arrival was the best part of the evening. The pink-haired cowboy had been a big hit and, as usual, his additions had proved to be so much more than his subtractions. The final comment came from Dewi Sukarno. 'I rike Mr Dansford – he very funny man and good music also!'

Later, back at the flat, I hugged Mercy B. Lord then kissed her. 'Darling, that was remarkable, the quickest piece of thinking I've ever witnessed. You saved the show single-handedly. It was poised on the brink of disaster.'

Mercy B. laughed. 'You're quite wrong, Simon, it was all arranged.'

'What?' I asked surprised, 'Dansford arriving late and drunk?'

'No, just the plan in case he did. Remember the night of our celebration when we'd completed the research project and he ordered those bottles of horrendously expensive French wine?'

'Yes, of course, how could I forget?'

'Well, when you called at lunchtime to ask me to pick up your suit from the cleaners, you told me Dansford had gone to the Town Club for a "settler" and how worried you were. Then you joked about him promising to dye his hair pink. Well, I called the hotel and asked them to move the baby grand to the side of the pool. If Dansford was going to arrive drunk, which seemed highly likely, our only chance was a repeat of what happened at the Goodwood Park Hotel when he entertained the diners at the piano.' She shrugged. 'Luckily, it worked.'

'You said something quietly to him when you ran forward and took his arm, didn't you?'

Mercy B. Lord laughed. 'I'm not sure I can tell you.'

'Go on.'

'Well, I told him, "Dansford, you fuck this up, then Sidney Wing wins and Simon loses and I lose Simon!"'

I swept her into my arms and, bending her backwards, leaned down and kissed her deeply, then swung her upright and gazed into her dark eyes. 'Mercy B. Lord, will you marry me?' I begged.

'Simon, I've never used that word before!' she exclaimed.

'Well done! That practically makes you Australian, but that's *not* what I asked you,' I insisted.

'Darling, I've had much too much champagne.' She giggled then added, 'But right at this very moment, I'd rather like to go to bed with the man I love and adore!' She took me by the hand. 'Come with me, Simon Koo.'

CHAPTER NINE

AFTER WE WON THE Singapore Tourist Promotion Board account, I couldn't wait to have lunch with Elma Kelly – mostly, I admit, to bask in the glory of winning the account against her own agency and the other big outfits. Of course, I would be modest, call it luck, thank her for her congratulations and point out that these things, as she well knew, are often capricious decisions and that it had been our day, that's all. But she'd know she'd been beaten fair and square, having expected, with her connections, to win. I admit it was all pretty pumped-up little-boy stuff but the ad business is very competitive and she was a formidable opponent. What with Sidney Wing's opposition to the panels, I felt I was entitled to bask, although Elma deserved my thanks for recommending Mrs Sidebottom, who'd come up with the idea of the screens in the first place.

It was Elma's turn to pay and since she was 'dying for a curry' and nothing else would do, she elected to go to the Tiffin Room at Raffles. In the taxi on the way, much to her amusement, I told her the story of the Sidebottom free-lunch scam.

Arriving at Raffles it was obvious that Elma was regarded as something akin to visiting royalty, and there was much hurrying and scurrying and best-tabling and napkin-flapping.

'Champagne, my man!' she boomed the moment we were seated. 'The boy has excelled and must be duly rewarded.'

'Elma, a cold beer will do nicely,' I protested.

'Nonsense, a fitting drink for a splendid win. Those government chappies are never easy and the minister is an old fuddy-duddy not known for bold decisions. We went conservative, unaware that they'd appointed Long Me Saw and Molly Ong to the board. Silly, we should have checked. Must remind myself to give someone in the office here a kick in the bottom. Those two certainly add some much needed pep.'

'Bit of luck, really. We didn't know either of them. I guess Long Me Saw has sat in on a few presentations in the movie business, but I tell you what, I was impressed with Molly Ong.'

'Good gal, did a splendid job as Miss Singapore.' The champagne arrived and Elma lifted her glass. 'Here's to the Three Wing Circus and its new creative ringmaster. You've certainly got your act together. Well done, Simon.'

We clinked our glasses. 'Thanks, Elma, but I have to be honest. Sidney and Ronnie, and Johnny of course, tried their best to prevent the pitch we made. Sidney insisting it was all about influence – *guanxi*, I guess. He kicked up a terrible fuss about the cost of the moving photographic panels, which by the way were Mrs Sidebottom's idea, so the real credit goes to her and of course to you for recommending her.'

'Ah, the Baba, they need to be dragged kicking and screaming into the new Singapore.'

'Baba?'

'Old Chinese families, the ruling class here in Singapore. They're all interconnected and can't get it into their heads that Lee Kuan Yew, whose family is also Baba, has largely outlawed all the old-school-tie stuff in government, preferring brains to connections. It's a lesson we're all learning, and while I enjoy the British equivalent in Hong Kong, as you've just demonstrated with the Tourist Board, *guanxi* doesn't play the part it formerly did with the Singapore government chappies.' She paused to take a sip of champagne. 'Having said that, don't ever underestimate the power of the Baba. They go back a long way in Singapore's history and they're accustomed to getting their own way, as you've seen often enough with Sidney.'

'I'm beginning to learn that,' I said. 'Ronnie once told me about his family and how he happens to belong to the Town Club.'

Elma looked at me, her right eyebrow slightly arched, a look I'd come to know heralded disapproval or suspicion. 'Oh, really? Pray tell?'

'Well, it seems his great-grandfather, William, the name he eventually gave himself – I can't remember if Ronnie told me his Chinese name – arrived in Malaya from China penniless and worked as a labourer in a tin mine. He must have saved a few bob – Ronnie didn't say – but in 1880 he came to Singapore and married a Chinese girl. Then, later – how much later, again I can't say – he purchased the machinery to make an airtight double-sealed tin can. To cut a long story short, he opened a small canning factory, mainly for vegetables purchased from the Chinese and Malay market gardeners, and made a pretty good living victualling merchant ships. Then the First World War gave him his big break. He bought land, indentured his own coolies as farm labourers to grow vegetables, and added pork 'n' beans, bully beef and Irish stew to his line of veggies and exported them to Britain for the troops in Europe. Not only did he make a fortune but at the end of the war a grateful colonial administration awarded him an OBE and the local Brits allowed him to join the "whites only" Town Club.' I laughed. 'The latter, according to Ronnie, is regarded by the family as the greater of the two honours, with family membership now in its third generation.'

Elma laughed. 'Ah, selective perception, one of the greatest of human foibles – the ability we all have to tell ourselves only the convenient truth.'

'You mean that's not the whole story?' I asked.

'Why don't we get our curry and then I'll elaborate on the Wings – William and his wife, in particular.'

Seated again with our plates piled high – Elma always had a good appetite and I was a bit of a curry man myself – she started by saying, 'As you will have gathered, Simon, the Chinese do their homework; they like to know as much about each other as they can, especially if they know something about you that you don't know they know – they regard this as a powerful weapon to hold in reserve.'

I nodded. 'Yes, my mother warned me before coming to Singapore to tell as little about myself and my family's circumstances as possible.'

'Well, she was right. But as the saying goes, "When in China, do as the Chinese do." After the war, when we decided to expand from Hong Kong and open an agency here in Singapore, my internment as a prisoner of war and my years of experience before the war had taught me to do due diligence, to know both my man and my opposition.' She paused and looked at me, smiling. 'Something I clearly neglected to do with the Tourist Board pitch. Singapore's a small place and the people have long memories. My British colonial referrals from Hong Kong were good, so getting to view the local records was easy enough. The Wing Brothers agency was one of the bigger outfits, and as it involved a Baba family, I went to work on them first, then eventually the other wealthy Chinese families.'

'Aha, and what are you saying – that there's more to it than the tinned veggies?'

'As I said, Ronnie's guilty of selective amnesia, though aren't we all. William Wing married a woman who came to Singapore to work as a prostitute.'

'Oh, I see!' I exclaimed.

'No, no, don't get me wrong. There isn't a Baba family in Singapore that doesn't have a fearful lot to hide. She, William's wife, was a very enterprising, some may even say, remarkable woman.' Elma said. 'She rose from her back, so to speak, and eventually owned several brothels and opium dens – the two things tended to go together at the time. And again, though perhaps not the sort of thing one talked about, both opium smoking and prostitution were perfectly legal. All I'm saying is that drugs and whores are where the money came from to buy the machinery for the cannery.'

'And so they became respectable.'

'Good lord, no! The Chinese don't give up a profitable business to become respectable. Besides, respectability as we in the West regard it is a fairly recent notion among orientals. William's wife continued to run her side of the business, and when she died not long after the Great War her younger sister took over. She too married and, as the Chinese say, the bitter rice continued: she had a daughter who took over and ran the show right up to the Japanese invasion. The Japanese banned the use of opium and closed down the brothels, except for the "comfort houses" for their own troops. The Japanese are not fools and they were suspicious of places like brothels, where information could be passed on, particularly to the communists fighting them in the jungles of Malaya.'

'Elma, are you saying that opium – in other words, heroin in a different form – wasn't banned until the Japs invaded?'

'Quite right.' Elma leaned back in her chair. 'I say, this bubbly's lovely. We shall have a second bottle, and with it what say a little more curry tiffin and a history lesson? It's a subject I'm particularly fond of: South-East Asia, and of course China – you can't keep China out of anything. Know your history and things become a lot clearer.' She raised her hand to summon a waiter and then ordered another bottle of Bollinger. We rose to go to the curry table and on the way she asked, 'Simon, what do you know about the Opium Wars?'

'I confess, not a lot. A couple of stoushes between Britain and China over the importation of opium, wasn't it?'

Elma sighed, helping herself to a fresh plate and beginning to add rice and chicken vindaloo. 'It beats me how you young people can come to a foreign place and think you can operate effectively without knowing any background, any history.' Selecting a variety of raitas, the tasty accompaniments for curry, she asked, 'Hong Kong? What do you know about Hong Kong, Simon?'

'Well, it's rented from the Chinese, isn't it?'

'Well, yes, leased. But why?'

'I haven't the foggiest. Ninety-nine years, wasn't it? Was it because of the war?' I could tell by the schoolmarm tone of voice she'd adopted that I was in for a long afternoon. Still, Elma Kelly was almost always worth listening to and never tedious. Besides, she was perfectly correct – I knew bugger-all about British colonial history in Asia.

'Good guess. The first Opium War in 1842 at the Treaty of Nanking.'

We returned to the table where the waiter stood. He popped the cork and poured the champagne. Elma raised her glass. 'To history and all its abracadabra – all the magic and the mystery it reveals,' she said.

I grinned rather ashamedly. 'You're perfectly right, Elma, I simply haven't done my homework. You remind me of a saying my dad sometimes used when one of us kids was passing high-minded judgements on someone we didn't much like: "You only truly know a person when you know the cause of the scars they carry." Then he'd add, "While you may dress and heal the wounds you can't eliminate the scars." I guess it's the same with countries.' I looked directly at Elma. 'I stand suitably reprimanded."

Just the stuff Elma had told me about the Wing family, the bit Ronnie hadn't spoken about, brought them into sharper focus. When I came to think of it, Ah Koo and Little Sparrow's story allowed me to understand, to place myself on the firmament, with a little more certainty.

'Well then, where was I?' Elma asked.

'Hong Kong, and before that the Opium Wars,' I reminded her.

'Yes, well, opium, the root of all the evil that was to follow. Opium, as you probably know, is the juice of the poppy.'

'*Papaver somniferum*, the sleep-bringing poppy,' I said quickly.

'That's very clever, Simon!' Elma exclaimed, surprised.

I grinned. 'Not really. Still life in art school. We had to paint a vase of flowers in the seventeenth-century Dutch baroque style, tulips, peonies, roses, carnations, poppies, all very Maria van Oosterwyck, a famous painter of the time. As a joke I painted a vase of opium poppies to see if anyone would catch on. I remember I had to go to the Mitchell Library to get the botanical reference. I called it "Sleeping Beauties" but no one caught on or questioned the name. Artists often give their works weird names so nobody questions them.' I laughed. 'I seem to recall I got a distinction and my mum had the painting framed. It's probably still hanging in a guest bathroom at home.'

'Well, then, you'll be aware that it's also the source of heroin and codeine. But do you know where it was first grown commercially for export?'

'India? The British East India Company, wasn't it?' I resigned myself to Miss Kelly the schoolmistress.

'Yes indeed, the most powerful trading organisation at that time in the world and the surrogate British government in this part of Asia. They owned the land, grew the opium poppy, bled it, packaged it and shipped it to the port of Canton. That is until China banned it, which left us in a bit of a pickle. The British couldn't be seen to be exporting opium to a sovereign state without permission.'

'Hence the Opium Wars?'

'Yes, eventually, but not quite then. We simply found another way: we auctioned the annual opium crop to foreign shipping merchants, mostly sea scum, including Chinese traders. They smuggled it through Canton, bribing corrupt officials. In this way we Brits appeared to keep our hands clean. Ha ha. In reality we were up to our ears in the business of drug trafficking.'

'But why – I mean, what was the big deal? A few opium addicts in China, so what?'

Elma looked directly at me. 'A few opium addicts, you say? By the time the Qing empire in China banned it, twelve million Chinese had become hopelessly addicted to opium. And the big deal was that by the mid-nineteenth century, opium profits largely greased the wheels of trade, or played some important part in the commerce of the entire Western world. By 1840 Britain was the major drug-trafficking criminal organisation in the world.'

'Hang on a mo! That's the equivalent of the whole Australian population. You did say twelve million addicts? I had no idea! Twelve million,' I repeated, shaking my head in disbelief.

'Well, it's the reason Singapore came to be created. The East India Company – read British Colonial Office – needed a port both where opium could be traded and where trading vessels leaving Calcutta for Canton could find safe harbour from pirates and other adventurers looking for opium hauls. They created an entrepot port with no taxes and soon they had most of the seagoing traffic passing through the Straits of Malacca. Protection and a free port, a halfway house for the drug trade – it made an irresistible combination. Singapore even started growing the opium poppy on the island. In fact the largest portion of Singapore's colonial government's income for most of the nineteenth century, almost half, came from locally grown and sold opium.'

'Sold to whom, the foreign trading vessels?'

'No, dear boy, you misunderstand – to the local population. Many of the wealthy Chinese merchants and even sea captains settled in the new port. They were the first of the Baba. They brought in Chinese coolies from China – the piglets, as the British called them – to do the labouring work in the thriving port, then build the roads for the growing port town and the tin mines, plantations and forests of Malaya, promising them they'd make their fortunes and return to their families and villages rich men after just a few years.'

'Ah, just like the gold rushes in California and Australia. That's how my great-great-grandfather Ah Koo came to Australia.' I could give a history lesson, too. 'He expected to make his fortune in the New Yellow Gold Mountain, but instead only made enough to buy a few scrubby acres in the bush and turn them into a market garden, from which he supplied fresh vegetables to the timber-getters who were cutting cedar in the forests. Eventually he sent back to China for a wife, Little Sparrow, my great-great-grandmother.'

'No such luck for most of the Singapore piglets,' Elma snorted. 'The Baba's indentured labourers had to pay them from their pitiful salaries for their boat fare, clothes, tools, rations and bug- and flea-infested accommodation, a process that took almost three years. The Baba bought the opium from the local colonial government and brought in whores and got their labourers hooked on local opium, garnisheeing their wages for the cost of both these activities and turning them into drug-addicted slave labour. This was the beginning of the profitable combination brothel and opium dens that at one stage kept almost the entire local population in thrall.'

'It makes William Wing's success sound commendable, almost heroic,' I remarked.

'Well, yes, there were a few who instead of succumbing saw opportunity. In William Wing's case, in whores and drugs, the two things Chinese men weren't prepared to do without.'

I grinned. 'Not only Chinese men, I dare say.'

'A great many died or wasted away from opium use but the Baba didn't care. After all, there was China with its endless supply of willing muscle and bone. Certainly very few ever returned home.' Elma paused. 'The local death rate from opium addiction was soon higher than in China, and by the mid-nineteenth century, with 20 000 Chinese coolies in Singapore, it was estimated that three-quarters were addicts, the highest addiction rate in the world.'

'Jesus, is that right?'

'This colony was founded and built on human suffering. We British were ultimately responsible for untold misery over a period of 130 years. Some historians insist Britain's opium trade to China and elsewhere is the greatest human catastrophe ever deliberately perpetrated on another people by a single European nation.' She'd finished her second plate and looked ready for a third. Elma was a big woman and took some filling up, a process she did quickly, scooping up great mouthfuls, unlike her friend Mrs Sidebottom. 'Wicked, wicked, wicked!' she exclaimed. Then, barely pausing for breath, 'What say a taste of the fish-head curry, Simon? Not authentic Indian, a local dish, but excellent nevertheless.'

'I'm about done, thanks, Elma.'

'Nonsense, Simon. I'm a big girl and you're a growing boy. All this talk improves the appetite. History is such a rewarding subject. Fish-head curry is mild, good for your stomach. Come on – I can't be seen scoffing on my own. Besides, we haven't done the Opium Wars.'

I'd first tasted the local fish-head curry with Elma, and then several more times with Mercy B. Lord. It was a particular favourite of hers when we ate at various cheap holes-in-the-wall, and here it was in posh old Raffles. 'Okay, you've got me, Elma. Fish-head sounds good for the Opium Wars, which were, I take it, a pretty fishy business.'

'Oh, bad, bad pun!' Elma cackled, then suddenly frowned. 'Simon, I trust I'm not being a perfect bore, am I? I do so love history and am apt to get a bit carried away. Ha ha, wouldn't be the first time my audience has turned glassy-eyed by the time the port was passed around.'

I assured her truthfully that I was fascinated. When read history can sometimes seem pretty turgid, but history told by a good raconteur who knows and is passionate about the subject can bring it to life. Elma was just such a raconteur.

'And not only by the Opium Wars, Elma. I was hoping you'd take me right up to the Japanese invasion. Like most Australians I know a bit about our own prisoners of war, the Burma Railway, Changi prison and all that, but it would be fascinating to hear it from the Chinese point of view.'

'Do my best,' she said, rising. 'As you know, I was involved in a contretemps with the Japanese in Honkers myself, so I wasn't on the spot. But for some of the Singapore people, particularly the Babas and those suspected of being involved with the Chinese communists, it got pretty ghastly.'

'Ah, yes, my mum talks about it. While she was in Australia during the war, some of her family were involved here, but managed to flee to a remote plantation in Malaya.'

'Do you mean they were communists?'

'I don't think so. They grew and processed palm oil.'

We'd reached the curry table. 'Oh, goody,' Elma exclaimed, 'fresh supplies!' She stooped and sniffed at the steaming fish heads. 'Ah, delicious!' She turned. 'Have we had this dish before at one of our lunches, Simon?'

'Yes, at our very first lunch. And I've had it with Mercy B. Lord several times.'

'Oh, but you must try it here. As I said, most of the curries here are Indian-inspired but this one, perhaps the spiciest and most tantalising of them all, is hybrid Indian, Chinese and Malay, a tribute to the local cuisine, and they do it particularly well here at Raffles.' She started helping herself. 'And don't forget the soft bun, will you, Simon?'

Mercy B. Lord had been the first to show me how to eat the sauce, the real delicacy of fish-head curry. You use a soft bun to wipe the plate clean, as you would a slice of bread to sop up the delicious gravy from the Sunday roast, but in Singapore it would not be considered the height of bad manners. The Chinese are far more tolerant regarding table manners – in fact, if the tablecloth is clean after a meal they take it to mean that it was not enjoyable, while a burp of satisfaction is a compliment to the host. But there was another reason for the use of the soft bun with fish-head curry: the sweetness of the white bread helps to soften the taste of the sharp, spicy sauce.

Seated at our table with our buns at the ready, Elma Kelly tucked into what was our third helping from the curry table. 'Now, where were we? Oh, yes, your family. I apologise, I didn't want to pry, Simon. I only asked because a lot of middle-class Straits-Chinese joined the communists after the Japanese invaded Manchuria in the thirties. Japan committed unspeakable atrocities against the Chinese, well before the Pacific War. The massacre of Nanking on the 13th of December 1937 alerted the world, of course.' When I looked blank she went on, 'For about six weeks Japanese soldiers pillaged the city and raped and murdered over 300 000 Chinese civilians, mostly women and children. By the way, among other atrocities, they used live Chinese men for bayonet practice in order to harden up young Japanese military recruits.'

I shuddered. 'The poor Chinese peasants seem to attract disaster from outsiders or from a warlord or the emperor or the government. Ah Koo, my great-great-grandfather, left China for the gold rush after his family and some twenty million other peasants lost their lives in the apocalyptic Taiping Rebellion led by Hong Xiuquan, a Christian convert of all things, who referred to himself as "The heavenly king and younger brother of Jesus".'

'Well, well, so you *do* know something of Chinese history, Simon.'

'Not really. That's family stuff, Elma. Only it seems that the poor bloody peasants always get the rough end of the pineapple.'

'Ah, yes, true, but it's often because of an attempt, albeit usually a disastrous one, by the Chinese peasant to get out from under the yoke of oppression. In the case of the Taiping Rebellion it was to escape from the persecution of the Qing dynasty. After a hundred or so years of oppression they put their hopes for emancipation in the hands of a raging lunatic.'

'Poor buggers don't ever seem to get it right,' I said.

'Right or wrong, it also accounts for the appeal of Mao's communists in the 1930s,' Elma replied. 'Not only was his a peasant army, a force with which they could identify, but it was also one willing to fight against the Japanese invasion. At the time, Chiang Kai-shek's Kuomintang government was fighting Mao's communists in the Chinese civil war and they were reluctant to split their forces and go against the murdering, all-conquering Japanese.'

'What are you saying? Chiang Kai-shek would rather have had the Japanese conquer China than allow Mao Tse Tung to get the upper hand?'

'I wouldn't be the first to accuse him,' Elma said. 'In fact, it wasn't until 1937, when both sides in the civil war agreed to cease hostilities and combine to fight against the Japanese, that the sons of Nippon were effectively opposed.'

'So eventually the communists and Kuomintang stopped fighting each other to fight a mutual enemy – seems a fairly obvious strategy.'

'Quite. The Chinese have a very strong sense of motherland, of nation,' Elma answered. 'They may have lived for five or six generations in another country but they still think of themselves as quintessentially Chinese with their first loyalties to their ancient motherland.'

While I was beginning to feel the effects of the champagne, Elma didn't seem in the least affected by the French bubbly. She went on to explain. 'It soon became clear that Mao's peasants were far more interested in fighting the Japanese and defending the homeland than in Chiang Kai-shek's Kuomintang army, so it's hardly surprising that the communist cause appealed to Singapore's working-class *and* middle-class Chinese. Their forebears were originally from peasant stock, so it made sense to join the communist party in support of their homeland.'

She paused. 'Remember, Simon, the Straits-Chinese middle class and working class had no reason whatsoever to love their British colonial masters, or the Baba, who between them had exploited them and then destroyed them with opium addiction over the previous hundred and more years. So being a member of the communist party or a communist trade-union member in Singapore was seen as a badge of honour, a sign of resistance against the oppressive colonial government and their English-aping rich Chinese Baba toadies, who were playing cricket and rugby and sending their sons to Oxford and Cambridge.'

I remembered that Chairman Meow's father, my maternal grandfather, had been sent to Cambridge to study organic chemistry. 'How did the Brits, the local government, feel about this? I mean, being a communist wasn't outlawed in Britain or anywhere else before the war, was it?'

'Ah! The exception was Singapore,' Elma said. 'The administration and the wealthy Baba families felt very threatened and cracked down on the movement and trade unionists. They wanted no part of a doctrine that put the common people first. This in turn forced the local communists and affiliated trade unions to go underground.' Elma raised her head from her plate and chuckled. 'Of course, the irony was that when the Japanese invaded Singapore, they, the communists, were the only well-organised underground movement. They fled into the jungles of Malaya and harassed the Japanese from there, becoming a highly effective partisan force. Your family may well have been among them in Malaya.'

'I'd love to think so, Elma, but it doesn't sound like my family. My mum's dad went to Cambridge. I think they were more concerned with saving their skins when the Japanese started murdering the wealthy Straits-Chinese.'

'Very perspicacious of them. The Japanese retribution on the local Chinese was a very nasty business, I can tell you.'

'Elma, can we go back a moment?' I asked. 'Singapore was thought by the Allies to be an impregnable fortress. Did the locals feel the same way?'

'Unquestionably yes. It was perhaps the one thing for which they were grateful to the British. They'd been nurtured from the cradle to believe Britain controlled the seven seas and Singapore was a veritable fortress against aggression from outside. After all, it was one of the original reasons for its founding. They believed they were safe and made almost no preparation for possible conquest by the Japanese. Singapore island was the citadel, so why, they asked themselves, leave it?'

'Is that why so many of the Baba were caught with their pants down and stayed put and didn't escape or go bush as my family did?'

'Well, of course, I wasn't here when the Japanese invaded, being, as I said previously, in a spot of bother of my own in Hong Kong, but I think I can probably answer you. I've spoken to a number of people who were here at the time and they all make the same point. They may have disliked the British, but to a man and woman they believed the propaganda about Fortress Singapore. In a word they felt safe, protected by British naval guns and 200 000 British and Commonwealth troops, many of which were Australian, incidentally. They believed the Brits when they said the Japanese couldn't possibly come through a neutral Thailand and march down the Malay Peninsula through the impenetrable jungle. They even believed that Japanese pilots couldn't fly at night because the entire Japanese population suffered poor night vision!'

I grinned. 'They were not alone in that – we believed the same propaganda crap in Australia.'

I knew what had happened to our forces. In the briefest terms, the

British expected the attempted Japanese invasion of Singapore to arrive by sea. Although the big guns could be turned and pointed inland towards Johor on the Malayan mainland, they were designed to fire at an approaching Japanese fleet and were only supplied with armour-piercing ammunition. This meant that they were largely useless against land targets. The massive shells, weighing a ton each, tended to bury themselves in the soft earth without exploding when they hit their targets.

Despite being told repeatedly that this wasn't possible, Singapore woke one day to find the Japanese had arrived via the back door. They'd marched and bicycled down the Malayan peninsula through the impenetrable jungle, capturing Malaya on the way, to arrive finally at the Johor Strait, the narrow stretch of water separating Singapore from the Malayan mainland. They crossed onto Singapore island to face largely ineffective resistance. Percival, the British general in charge, had convinced himself that they would choose some less obvious place to come ashore.

Another calamitous miscalculation by the British was that almost the entire water supply for the 'impregnable fortress' was carried by a pipeline running along the Johor causeway. All the Japanese had to do was turn off the tap. But the British saved them the trouble by blowing up the causeway, thus robbing the island of its main water supply. Percival does not go down in the annals of military history as a major thinker and tactician.

The Straits-Chinese population watched as the 'racially superior' and 'invincible' British forces, out-fought and out-thought by the Japanese, surrendered after a week. I hoped Elma Kelly would be able to give me some insight into local feelings round this time.

We'd completed the fish-head curry and polished our plates with the soft buns. Now, a little lightheaded from the champagne, I confessed myself full to bursting.

'Oh, but you must have a tiny space for dessert. The *gulab jamuns* are a house speciality,' Elma insisted.

Once again, compliments of Mercy B. Lord, I knew about these wickedly sweet balls of what amounted, as far as I was concerned, to eating large balls of sticky goo. 'No, really, thank you, I simply couldn't,' I protested. After the sharp, almost stingingly hot fish-head sauce, the idea of the sticky sweetmeat was revolting. Elma Kelly was proving she had a stomach of cast iron. 'A cup of tea will do me very nicely,' I said.

'Well, I have to say you're a big disappointment, Simon Koo! Not only in your lamentable knowledge of Asian history, but also in your appreciation of Indian delicacies.' She laughed, her right eyebrow raised in mock disapproval. Then she indicated the direction of the dessert table with a nod of her head. 'Would you mind terribly?'

'No, of course not, but I'm chockas.'

'A tick? Yet another appalling idiom, I take it?' she quipped, rising to fetch her dessert.

Returning shortly afterwards, she hoed into the plate of sweetmeat as if she hadn't eaten in days. Remarkable.

I ordered tea for both of us.

'I'll have chai masala,' Elma said.

'English, black for me,' I instructed.

'Now, yes, the locals, you wanted to know their reaction to the capitulation. I recall Jenny Choo, my media manager in our agency here, telling me of the day the Allies surrendered; how as a twelve-year-old with her mother she joined the people lining the streets at the command of the Japanese and watched in dismay as the numerically superior British Empire Forces were marched silently into shame-faced captivity. I recall her exact words: "Elma, the Japanese soldiers were in torn and ragged uniforms and they wore dirty rubber-soled canvas shoes. I remember the shoes in particular. They were designed with a weirdly separate space for the big toe that allowed it to move independently. We stood silent, not daring to even whisper, and all you could hear was the soft squelch of enemy rubber on the hot tarmac as they marched by, and then, in the distance, coming ever closer, the crunch of polished hobnailed boots worn by the men who were now prisoners, all in immaculate uniforms, brasses polished. None of them would look at us as they passed."'

'That's a pretty graphic description,' I volunteered.

Elma nodded. 'Indeed. But one thing became clear immediately. In one fell swoop the myth of white racial superiority was shattered and the unquestioned European domination of India and South-East Asia was over. The Japanese were the first so-called yellow race to call the white man's bluff. This lesson was not lost on the Chinese or the Straits-Chinese, even though the Japanese were their mortal enemies. Nor was the irony that the outlawed local communists were the only group that had any chance of mounting an effective resistance campaign against the Japanese.'

'And then, I'm told, all hell broke loose for many of the locals. I know many of them were beheaded, because the Australians who came back after the war told of going to work in prisoner-of-war gangs and seeing hundred of Chinese heads impaled on sharpened poles lining the streets. As you said, the Japanese had a terrible contempt for the Chinese.'

'Yes, of course, and although raping women and young girls was common among the enemy troops, it was not necessarily condoned by their superior officers. Almost any conquest throughout history results in spontaneous rape and pillage. In fact, the Japanese massacre of the Chinese in Singapore and Malaya was carefully planned before the occupation. They knew from their spies exactly who they needed to get rid of and the task was given to Lieutenant Colonel Masayuki Oishi of the dreaded *kempeitai*, the Japanese secret police. The Japanese are nothing if not thorough. The bloodbath that followed, which was mostly by public beheading, included the Baba; anyone thought to have supported the war against Japan in China; members of the Overseas Chinese Anti-Japanese Volunteer Army; all Hainanese – which would have meant all your Li relations, Simon – because they were automatically considered to be communists; men with tattoos, who were considered to be Triads; JPs and former Chinese civil servants, because they were seen to be British sympathisers; anyone, not only Chinese, who possessed a weapon; and several other groups I can't at the moment recall.' She took a deep breath and then sighed. 'Too much champagne.' Then she turned and directed the hovering waiter to pour more tea.

In fact her memory was quite remarkable. 'That's quite a list,' I said. 'The streets must have been running with blood. How many local Chinese perished? Does anyone know?'

'No, not precisely. Lee Kuan Yew once claimed it was 100 000, and while he's not a man to be contradicted, it's generally accepted to be around half that number. You hear about those who died in the death camps, or on the Burma Railway, but you rarely hear about the Straits-Chinese who lost their lives in the Japanese conquest of Singapore.'

I sighed. 'Yeah, I guess we conveniently forget the statistics that don't concern us. Another case of selective amnesia.'

Elma Kelly glanced down at her watch. 'Good lord! It's three o'clock. Bloody hell! I've got to be back at the agency for a meeting in fifteen minutes. Bill Farnsworth, Boss Long Socks, is flying in from Australia – never easy, will be sure to ask why we failed to win the Tourist Board account and then go through the budget. Have to be on my toes, what. Waiter!' she boomed. 'Get the Sikh chappie at the front to call me a taxi at once!' She stooped to pick up her handbag.

'Elma, allow me. It's been a most instructive lunch and I've loved it and come away a lot wiser. The least I can do. Besides, I owe Raffles for the Mrs Sidebottom con.'

'Thank you, Simon, jolly nice of you, must be off. Farnsworth is probably in the boardroom, tapping his watch.' She imitated a carping male voice, which for Elma meant softening her usual *basso profundo*. 'Elma, I've flown 4000 miles to be on time and you're the one who's late!' She left the Tiffin Room with all the grace of a battleship ploughing through a big sea.

'The Opium Wars! We didn't get to them!' I shouted after her.

'Britain's abiding shame! Next time, old boy!' she shouted back, and she was gone in a clatter of heavy footsteps.

PART TWO

Thursday Girl

PART TWO

CHAPTER TEN

HAD IT NOT BEEN for my love for Mercy B. Lord, which at times seemed to completely overwhelm my judgement, I guess I would have served out my contract with Samuel Oswald Wing and left the odious bully Sidney Wing and his misanthropic brother Johnny and the nice but inconsequential Ronnie and gone home to Australia. Ostensibly I'd have been a success, with Big Lather, Texas Tiger, Citizen watches and the Singapore Tourist Promotions Board to my credit, but if the truth be known, I'd have returned with my tail between my legs. I'd made the Wing brothers more money, and hadn't done too badly myself, thanks to my contract, and the Americans were happy enough, but I hadn't managed to establish a permanent, working creative department or even the real beginnings of one.

If I chose to remain in Singapore, I almost had sufficient money of my own to start two projects. The first was a market-research company that would use the methodology we'd developed with Henry, now Professor, Kwan, in which I hoped to eventually involve Mercy B. Lord. The other was to develop a film company with Harry 'Three Thumbs' Poon and Willy Wonka that would specialise in advertising commercials. There would be opportunities for both market research and TV commercials in all of neighbouring Asia – Malaysia, Indonesia, Hong Kong, Thailand, the Philippines and even Taiwan. All lacked decent film facilities and market-research organisations that truly understood and could interpret the Asian way of thinking. Both ideas would involve, in addition to my own money, a loan, though not a huge one, from my dad and Chairman Meow.

On the other hand, I could simply take up Elma Kelly's generous offer to join Cathay as creative director, and there attempt to influence the local advertising scene in the way I'd imagined I was going to do when I'd originally left Australia. This seemed unlikely, though. I'd had my fill of Asian advertising agencies, and while I had grown hugely fond of Elma, I could see she wouldn't be all that easy to work under. If I was going to stay, I resolved to work for myself.

Whatever I chose to do, it would thankfully be the end of my time at Samuel Oswald Wing, and while I'd miss some of my clients, I'd had more than enough of the Three Wing Circus. Of course, the very best decision would have been to call it quits in Singapore and head back home, but my love for Mercy B. Lord made me incapable of any sort of intelligent reasoning.

Dansford had long since guessed that I wouldn't require a renewal offer from New York, but I thought I should make it formal so that they could set about the process of appointing a new creative director when the time came. So I delivered a handwritten letter to him one morning only minutes after he'd arrived at work, starched and spruced up by Chicken Wing.

He sighed, wordlessly accepted the envelope and used it to indicate I should take a seat, then, without opening it, began to tap the corner of the envelope on the edge of his desk. I usually waited an hour or so in the morning before entering Dansford's office, to give him a chance to recover from the previous night, but I wanted to be rid of the resignation letter. Now, with only the tap-tap of the envelope breaking the silence, I saw that there were still faint traces of pink in his hair and that his features, clean-shaven with several razor nicks, were deathly pale from his early morning gastric ritual in which he rid his stomach of the results of the previous night's carousing. Dansford possessed an amazing ability to recover and by mid-morning he would be going full throttle. He'd usually done a good day's work by the time he escaped to lunch. But now, first thing, he looked vulnerable and a little beaten, even woebegone, as if life were steadily getting the better of him.

He lifted the envelope and said, 'The time has come, the walrus said . . .'

'. . . to talk of many things,' I added, smiling.

'Of shoes – and ships – and sealing wax . . .' Dansford continued, waiting for me to come in.

'Of cabbages – and kings . . .'

'And why the sea is boiling hot . . .'

'And whether pigs have wings,' I concluded.

Dansford sighed. 'I take it this is what I think it is?'

I nodded.

'Ah, Simon, I shall miss you so very much.'

'And I you, mate, but it was pretty inevitable.'

'Yes, I guess so. The Three Wing Circus is going to lose its main attraction. New York will not be at all pleased. Colgate-Palmolive will not be happy either. As you know, their entry into Asia with Big Lather has been spectacular and they rightly give you the credit.'

I laughed. 'The credit's not really all mine. Had you not decided to fake the market research, it would never have happened.'

'You've achieved a lot, Simon. The Tiger campaign put Texas Oil back into profit; the ice block sold a squillion Japanese watches; the big screens in the town hall gave us the tourism win.'

'Kind of you, Dansford, but you brought in the Texas Oil account with your Chinese chicks in hotpants and heels, which turned on Michael Johns, aka Big Loud Mike; Willy Wonka produced his dad's beer fridge at lunch to give me the watch idea, and Mrs Sidebottom came up with the screens. Besides, if you hadn't persisted with Sidney, he'd have put the kibosh on financing them.'

'Oh, Christ!'

'What?'

'Mrs Sidebottom. You just reminded me – she's had an accident! A call came through yesterday just as I was leaving for lunch. You were at the printers so the switch put it through to me.'

'Is it serious?'

'Can't say – it was her husband . . . Percy, isn't it?'

'Cecil.'

'Cecil, that's it. Said she was doing something for you but now couldn't.'

'That's okay. It was only brochure copy, it's not urgent.'

Dansford looked upset. 'Very careless of me. I should have left a note for you – damn stupid.'

'Don't worry, it'll be okay, but I'd better make a call.'

When I phoned her home, the maid answered and I asked her rapidly in Cantonese about her mistress. She answered in English and told me the madam was in hospital. 'And Mr Sidebottom?' I asked.

'Master, he also,' she replied.

'He was in the accident?'

'No. He go to see her, he stay by there, not come back. Also the night, he not come back, go work.'

I called the hospital but they wouldn't give any details except to confirm that she was there. 'Is there a ward phone?' *Of course there must be.* Not waiting for an answer, I said sharply, 'Put me through to Mr Sidebottom. It's very important.' I'd long since learned that with working-class Chinese, being assertive worked better than being polite. With the Baba, or wealthy, it was the opposite; everyone knew their place in the social structure. When I'd referred to Sidney Wing's contemptuous attitude to staff at one of my monthly lunches with Elma Kelly, she'd replied, 'My dear boy, haven't you understood yet? This is a tone-of-voice society.'

But my demanding tone didn't work this time. 'I'm very sorry, sir. We are not allowed to put a call through to the emergency unit on that floor,' came the reply.

'What floor is that?' I demanded.

The switch operator refused to be bullied. 'I'm sorry, sir,' came the reply. So now I knew Mrs Sidebottom must be in a pretty bad way.

Half an hour later I arrived at the Singapore General Hospital in Outram Road and entered the emergency reception area, where I waited until the lift opened and an orderly stepped in. I followed. 'The serious traffic accident ward,' I demanded in Cantonese and watched as the preoccupied orderly silently pressed the button for level three. But then my luck ran out. As I stepped from the lift, a large European nursing sister glanced up from writing at a desk directly facing the lift – no sign of the Chinese nurse I had hoped to bully. After a noticeable double-take, her incurious glance changed into a fully fledged imperious glare.

Fountain pen poised, she demanded, 'And who may you be?' It was a question asked without the courtesy of an added 'sir'. I was completely taken by surprise by this very large, well-corseted virago in white with her many-pointed starched veil, which, with her long pinched nose and sharp eyes, gave her the appearance of a bird of prey coming in to land. She looked as if she could take on Elma Kelly in an arm-wrestling contest and possibly win.

'Ah . . . er, Simon Koo,' I offered, too surprised and tongue-tied to add any further explanation.

'And what are you doing in my ward, Mr Koo?'

'Oh, yes, ah . . . Mrs Sidebottom . . . I've come to see Mrs Sidebottom.'

'Are you a doctor?'

'No, no, a friend . . . a concerned friend. I heard she's been in an accident and I'd like very much to see her . . . please?'

The ward sister, or matron, gave me a withering look. 'No! The patient is in a coma.'

Her refusal brooked no discussion and, ignoring me, she returned to her writing. I stood my ground, less out of stubbornness than from an inability to decide what to do next. She glanced up and jabbed her gold nib in the direction of the lift behind me. 'Press the down button!' she commanded.

'Mr Sidebottom . . . is he here? May I talk to him?'

'No, you may not!'

Keep your cool, Simon. A sign on the wall behind her read: *Strictly No Smoking*, the 'Strictly' printed in red. I recalled Mrs Sidebottom once mentioning that Cecil was a three-pack-a-day man. I'd wondered at the time whether tobacco smoke helped to lessen the effect of her halitosis. 'Will you please tell him I'll be waiting in reception downstairs?' I asked.

She gave an impatient cluck of her tongue. 'Would you be good enough to leave at once?'

I had been waiting less than twenty minutes when a bleary-eyed Cecil Sidebottom entered the hospital visitors' reception room. 'Simon, old chap, how very good of you to come!' he exclaimed, his hand extended in a welcoming gesture.

'I'm so sorry. I was at the printers all yesterday afternoon. I only got your message this morning. I would have come sooner.'

'Good of you to come,' he repeated. 'You're the nearest thing she has to a friend here. Can't tell you how chuffed she was with the French drop. Jolly decent.'

I immediately felt guilty. The champagne had been Dansford's idea. Apart from our initial curry tiffin lunch at Raffles, we hadn't socialised and had communicated by telephone; I'd sent her my layouts by taxi. I told myself I couldn't go through the spiral-bound notepad routine again, not to mention the halitosis. But, of course, I had been remiss and should have made the effort. Her copywriting for the Tourist Promotion Board had proved almost as invaluable as her suggestion to use the giant screens. 'How bad is she?' I asked tentatively.

He tapped a cigarette from a Camel soft pack and I waited as he lit up, took a puff and exhaled. Then, as if it had all been bottled up inside him, he burst out with, 'She's in a coma, a bit beaten about the face, both eyes black as a nig-nog's bottom, internal injuries, broken collarbone, cracked ribs, could be a lung puncture, breathing complications, tracheotomy. Otherwise she's fine; it'll take time, that's all.' He paused and sighed, seemingly grateful that he'd got it all off his chest. In the familiar manner of a heavy smoker – slightly stooped, chin on chest – he took a deep drag on his cigarette, its tip flaring noticeably, then almost immediately blew the smoke out in a steady stream and turned his head towards me, eyes blinking. When he spoke again his voice was calm. 'Simon, would you mind if we went outside . . . a rather tricky question's come up.'

He moved towards the door and I followed. 'What exactly happened?' I asked as we reached the front steps.

'Taxi. Driver swerved to avoid hitting a rickshaw, hit the gutter, vehicle spun almost precisely 360 degrees and sideswiped a telegraph pole. The driver was killed – his door took the impact and flattened him – top of his head missing, upper window frame caught him, acted like a can opener, brains everywhere.' It was a civil engineer's answer and a lot more than I needed to know.

'Poor bugger. Probably left a wife and kids behind.'

'No, no, much too old for that! Shouldn't have been allowed behind the wheel. Undoubtedly paid a bribe to keep his licence. Bloody disgrace, can't be trusted, shouldn't be allowed, sticky fingers, the temptation's too much for them.'

From the way he'd described his wife's black eyes, Cecil Sidebottom was an old-style colonial. There wasn't any point in suggesting that Lee's government had pretty well cleaned up corruption among minor officials, or that bribery carried a heavy penalty for both parties.

It was stinking hot outside and we'd reached the shade of a large banyan tree. Cecil Sidebottom killed the butt of his cigarette by dropping it to the ground and extinguishing it with a twist of his shoe. I wondered briefly if a butt being dropped in a public hospital's garden carried the same penalty as one being dropped on a city pavement. I was becoming conditioned to the new squeaky-clean Singapore and its profusion of petty laws. We like to think of ourselves as mavericks but my observation is that most people quite enjoy a set of rules, a bit of conspicuous law and order, providing always that it doesn't impinge on their lives or threaten their livelihood.

Bringing me outside in the heat when the reception area was air-conditioned seemed a strange thing to do, and I wondered what Cecil Sidebottom could possibly tell me that was meant for my ears only.

He lit a second cigarette. 'Tricky, very tricky,' he said again, squinting at me as the smoke from the cigarette curled around his head.

I wasn't sure how to respond. 'Anything I can do?'

'Yes. Be most obliged, Simon. Teeth.'

'Teeth?'

'Yes, the old girl's. You may not have noticed, but they're in rather bad shape.'

'Well . . . er . . . perhaps, yes.' There seemed nothing else to say.

'Oh, good, I thought perhaps you might advise? I can't ask her, she's unconscious.'

'Advise?' I was beginning to feel rather foolish, as if I'd missed something obvious.

'The doctor says they're badly infected and this could lead to complications. Very dicky position, what. He wants them removed . . . wants to remove them,' he corrected. 'She's always been very conscious of her teeth. Afraid . . .' He looked at me and shrugged, his expression an appeal for help. 'I'm not sure I know what to do.' The courage had gone from his voice.

I knew from what Elma Kelly had told me that Mrs Sidebottom was mortally afraid of undergoing dental work. 'She's afraid of the dentist?' It was an obvious but necessary question.

'Oh, yes, I see, you *do* understand,' he exclaimed, relieved. 'You see, I know she wouldn't agree.'

'If they're not removed, then what?'

'Possibly septicaemia.'

'Blood poisoning!' I felt a twinge of anger. 'Cecil, mate, you have no choice. Out! Out, while she's unconscious.'

'Yes, yes! You're right! Thank you!' he exclaimed, beaming. 'Oh, dear, I do feel so much better. Silly, silly, of course!'

Mrs Sidebottom remained in hospital for six weeks, so that her gums and other parts of her body could heal properly. I swamped her with Singapore orchids and visited on several occasions, during which our conversations would take place with her holding a book over her toothless mouth.

Once she'd recovered, we celebrated with a small dinner party in a private room at Raffles, with Mercy B. Lord acting as hostess. The guests were Dansford Drocker (Chicken Wing was invited, but declined); Peter and Professor Henry Kwan; Elma Kelly, who'd flown in from Hong Kong to be there; Willy Wonka, on weekend leave from the army; and, finally, Cecil and Mrs Sidebottom.

It was as if she'd undergone a transformation: Mrs Sidebottom looked decidedly different. Her incredible arctic-blue eyes now danced within a face no longer powdered into a matt, white, clown-like mask, her complexion was what is traditionally referred to as that of an English rose, and while her lipstick was still Rita Hayworth red, it didn't trespass beyond the boundaries of her lips. Best of all, she now wore a dazzling new smile, and her breath was peppermint-free and fresh as a field of summer daisies, except perhaps for the tiniest hint of gin suffused with angelica, coriander and juniper berry.

Between the main meal and dessert I had excused myself to go to the toilet and was just about to enter when I heard my name. I turned to see Cecil Sidebottom had followed me. 'Great men think alike,' he laughed as we went in. Standing side by side in front of the two urinals, he said, 'Simon, old chap, wasn't sure when I'd catch you alone again. Just wanted to thank you for restoring my bride to me. Damned decent of you.'

'Thanks, Cecil, but not necessary. I did nothing.'

'Oh, but you did, old boy! Could never have made the teeth decision on my own. Owe it all to you.'

'Well, thanks, but like I said, unnecessary.'

'We're spring chickens! She's lost twenty years, looks like the young gal I married.' To my surprise he began to cry.

'Oh, mate!' I said, shaking and zipping up quickly. I would have hugged him, but you can't hug a bloke who has his donger dangling from his strides. 'I'm glad it's all worked out.' It wasn't a lot of comfort, I know, but I wasn't sure what else to say.

'Damned stupid of me . . . apologise, all a bit much, that's all.' He sniffed and zipped up.

At the neutral washbasins I ventured a compliment. 'She looks great, Cecil. I'm glad it's over, and she seems completely recovered from the accident.'

'Not just that, old boy, we've recovered our lives. Couldn't have done it on my own. Needed your support. Bloody grateful.'

Chairman Meow had been invited to the dinner party, but when she'd heard it was in honour of Mrs Sidebottom and why, she'd declined, saying she wouldn't change her travel plans for a woman whose sole claim to fame was to have acquired a complete set of dentures, which she referred to – deliberately, I think – as false teeth. I must say I was relieved, as I wasn't at all sure it was the right time to present Mercy B. Lord.

After our first glorious night together we'd been jumping into bed at every opportunity, but afterwards she would always insist she had to go home. It felt wrong, immature, redolent of the shagging you did as a uni student when your girlfriend shared digs with several other students and you were what was known in the vernacular as a wombat – eats, roots and leaves. Only this time it was Mercy B. Lord who had to get dressed and take a cab home, often very late, and often when she had to be up to meet someone at the airport in the morning. I felt strangely guilty that I was the one able to stay and crawl back into a warm bed after I'd put her in a taxi and watched its red rear brake lights disappearing into the night.

With my own flat at home in Australia, it had been years since I'd either been a wombat or required my lover to leave after we'd made love. Here in Singapore I had a luxury flat where Mercy B. Lord would be totally at home, but she'd rejected it for reasons she wouldn't, or couldn't, explain.

I'd like to say I'd finally persuaded her to move in, but that was not the case. One evening she simply said, 'Well, then, I suppose you'd like me to move in with you, Simon?'

'You serious?' I asked, not sure she wasn't pulling my leg.

'There's one condition.'

'What?'

'Thursday night.'

'What about Thursday night?'

'You have to promise never to mention it.'

'You mean to someone else?'

'No, between us – you must *never* bring it up.'

'And that's all?'

She looked up, holding my gaze. 'If you do, I'll leave. Simple. No discussion.'

I nodded. 'Just one more question: is what you're doing on your night away safe?'

'What, are you asking if I'm in danger?'

'Yes.'

'Simon, I've never been threatened or assaulted, if that's what you mean.'

'Mercy B. Lord, I don't know what I mean – your life, your person, your wellbeing, your job . . . ?'

'I really think you should leave that to me. I've been a big girl for some time now.'

It wasn't the unequivocal answer I was hoping for, but there wasn't any more I could say without forcing her to tell me where she went on a Thursday and why. 'Okay,' I said, which was a pretty dumb rejoinder, but what else could I say? I was desperate to have her in my bed, my flat and my life.

So, with Mercy B. Lord living with me, I knew that on my mum's next visit I'd have to introduce her. This wasn't a problem from my side – it would be a delight and a privilege – but it meant answering a whole heap of questions from Chairman Meow and I didn't have the answers I knew she'd demand. Although she'd agreed to stay, Mercy B. Lord hadn't agreed to anything else.

Chairman Meow, like Elma Kelly, believed that blitzkrieg was the best method of dealing with most things. To carry the military analogy further, if Elma was a Sherman tank, my mum was a polished and perfectly presented cruise missile. Both brooked no opposition and both shared the absolute conviction that what they decided was correct for whomever they'd decided should be the recipient of their overweening attention.

Years of childhood practice with my mum was probably what allowed me to maintain the relationship I now enjoyed with Elma Kelly. The trick was to see such women for short and intense periods of time – Elma for lunch once a month, my mum for three days at a time every three months (evenings only) – and then to escape before either of them made a takeover bid on my life, with the singular purpose of correcting my clearly misdirected intentions. Any attempt to keep my mother out of Singapore for the three years of my contract would patently have been futile, however much I might have wished to try.

In Chairman Meow's mind, my coming to Singapore wasn't about forging an independent future for myself. Plainly, this was impossible. My independence was simply not a concept she could grasp – why would her son want to leave such a comfortable and superior nest? At best, she might have accepted that my time in Singapore was three years spent flapping my wings to strengthen them for when I finally needed to fly on behalf of the family's businesses or fortune. Her plans for me had always been crystal clear: I was to return to Australia, whereupon my father would retire and I'd take my rightful place as chairman – with her riding shotgun – *after* I'd acquired a Chinese wife sourced from a family with an excellent pedigree and possessing good *guanxi*.

Most fortuitously, her role as surrogate chairman of our various enterprises kept her busy. Mum had to be on sentry duty beside my father so that several designing uncles on the board couldn't get up to any mischief, which meant she couldn't spend prolonged periods away from head office. She'd come for a week, see me for the three allocated evenings and visit her relatives for the rest of the time, no doubt conspiring with them over my nuptial future. But then, thankfully, she always had to get back to Sydney.

I know this all sounds pretty ungrateful, but my mum, as you will have gathered, only knew one speed: foot flat to the floor – and frankly, three evenings in a row every three months was enough. Chairman Meow was clearly the boss of the family and everything that concerned its welfare, and she saw me as part of that, a big part. But, to mix my metaphors, she juggled a dozen or more balls in the air at any one time and clearly she was intellectually superior to the rest of the extended family. With a veritable family empire to run, there was never much time for small talk.

Under her ultimate direction the older companies had been hugely successful and several new ones had come into being. One of them in particular, White Lotus Funerals, an offshoot of the original Blue Lotus Funerals, was now a hugely successful all-female funeral parlour chain, headed by a cousin who had graduated with honours in law.

My father, whom doubtless my uncles privately dismissed as a feckless drunk, was smart enough to realise that my mum as chairman was head and shoulders above him or any other male family member. He didn't regard her having her role as surrogate chairman as a dereliction of his responsibilities. On the contrary, he considered that by abdicating in her favour, he was, in fact, exercising those responsibilities effectively.

I recall one of the very few occasions when he'd been unexpectedly frank about my mother. This occurred when I was in my final year of Commerce at uni. We were returning from Leichhardt Oval around sunset on a Saturday afternoon, and I was driving. He was pretty pissed and somewhat morose. The Balmain Tigers, his beloved rugby league team, had been trounced by their mortal enemy, the South Sydney Rabbitohs. Possibly to avoid talking about the game, he started to talk about company affairs and my mother's involvement in the business. He'd always appeared to accept that I wanted to be an artist and that I was only doing my Commerce degree to be a dutiful son. On this occasion, I concluded he'd had a bad week at work and, what with the Tigers losing and putting paid to their premiership chances, was simply letting off steam. But then when I thought he had finally finished what I foolishly regarded as a bit of a whinge, he suddenly said, 'Don't you worry, son, she'll get you. Nothing more certain.'

This statement, from someone who had always encouraged me to be myself and whom I'd come to regard as an ally against my mum, came as a huge shock. Even pissed, my dad was seldom if ever indiscreet. He fell silent for a couple of changes of traffic lights, his tie pulled down and his chin tucked deeply into his loosened collar. I kept my eyes on the road directly ahead, the engine of the Rolls Silver Cloud purring. Finally, my heart recovered its rhythm and I hoped he'd dozed off. But as we passed the stadium at Rushcutters Bay and I was about to change gear to go up Edgecliff Hill, his head suddenly jerked up and he placed his hand on my arm. 'And when she does, take my advice, son: do it *her* way, *always* her way. You're a smart kid, Simon, but she's smarter than all of us put together. She's the fire-breathing dragon. As long as she's guarding the cave entrance you'll be fine.'

I'd previously advised Peter and Henry Kwan not to mention Mercy B. Lord to any of the other members of the family, and they'd been as good as their word. For the first eighteen months, whenever Chairman Meow arrived on a lightning visit, I prepared for the onslaught: a nightly interrogation that, after three repeats, left me exhausted. I'd protest that I was too busy at the agency and simply lacked the time to escort the carefully chosen 'possibles' selected for me by her female cousins, no doubt working on a very strict brief from you-know-who.

Chairman Meow had the ability to switch from a corporate persona with a mind like a steel trap to an injured and helpless uncomprehending mother. A typical confrontation might go like this.

'Simon, I can't believe you've remained celibate!'

'Mum, I've been awfully busy.'

'Why, at the flat above the garage you had girls almost every night. The cleaning lady was always finding frilly lace panties tucked under pillows or left in the bathroom.' An exaggeration, but one calculated both to flatter and accuse. Chairman Meow was in attack mode.

'Mum, I honestly haven't had time for a serious relationship,' I fibbed. Not entirely a lie, because Mercy B. Lord was still in her 'not yet' stage.

'Simon, don't treat me like a fool!'

Deep sigh, shrug. 'I'm flat-out at the agency. I honestly haven't got time to scratch my bum!'

'Don't be crude.'

'Okay, then . . . this is Singapore. I have an arrangement.'

'What? A prostitute? A Chinese prostitute! Lowborn Chinese women are ruthless! They'll stop at nothing!'

Not only lowborn Chinese women, I thought. 'It's not the same here. That's not how it's seen . . . regarded. It's a convenient —'

'Simon! Don't you tell me how it's regarded! She'll trap you – or give you something nasty. There's a VD strain coming out of Vietnam they can't cure!' Her carefully manicured fingers flew to her face as Chairman Meow turned back into my panic-stricken mother. 'Oh my God! Have you been to see a doctor?'

'Mum, she's not Chinese, she's Thai,' I replied foolishly.

'Thai? Bangkok! That's America's major base outside Vietnam. They use it for R&R. Simon, are you mad?' Chairman Meow was back.

I thought of kind, attentive Veronica at the Nite Cap, who had so often relieved my pain after Mercy B. Lord had denied me. 'Mum, she's a very nice person and, medically speaking, completely safe! I pay her for her services and there are no complications.'

Chairman Meow shook her head. 'I can't believe I'm hearing this, and from my own son. Medically safe – you know this for sure, of course? You've been to a doctor regularly after every . . .' she couldn't bring herself to say it. 'Have you?'

'Well, no, but I take all the proper precautions!' This wasn't the kind of conversation one has with one's mother, in either of her personas. I was getting pretty agitated myself.

'They deliberately put holes in those things!'

'Mum! I'm over thirty years old! I'm not stupid. I supply my own contraceptives.'

'And then don't see the doctor.'

'Okay, Mum, what am I supposed to do? All those precious little China dolls your cousins select for me – no doubt to your specific brief – are hardly going to allow me a test run in bed, are they?'

'Don't be crude, Simon! Of course not! They're well-bred young ladies!'

'So what then?'

'You choose one of them to marry, of course.'

'But what if I'm not ready to marry? Or have kids. What if I don't like any of them?'

'Tch! They're all nice girls. They come from good families. How could you not like them? Besides, it's high time you settled down.' She paused, then returning to the attack, she spat, 'I can't believe it, a Chinese peasant!'

'Thai.'

'The same, but worse!'

'Mum, you started this by saying you couldn't believe I was celibate. That implied you believed I wasn't. Then when I said I had an arrangement you had a conniption about lowborn Chinese women stopping at nothing. By the way, just for the books, may I remind you Little Sparrow was a lowborn Chinese woman?'

The words had hardly escaped my mouth when I realised it was the wrong thing to say. My mum might have been feeling emotional, but the Chairman Meow mind was always waiting in the wings, ready to spring the goof-trap. 'Ah! I'm glad you brought that up, Simon. Ah Koo went through all the correct channels. He sent a clear and very specific brief to the village elder, telling him exactly what he needed. Not looks, not material prospects, a good woman who was capable of giving him male children. Very sensible and traditional and, if I may say so, with a very successful outcome.'

'Yes, but can't you see, he made the decision himself.'

'Of course he didn't! The village elder made the decision, and he, very sensibly, accepted.'

'As I see it, Ah Koo didn't have a lot of choice. He couldn't exactly send her back, could he? He was forced to take what he got. But I'm not! And what about love?'

Chairman Meow sighed, or perhaps it was my mother – the emotional and the rational were both in evidence now. 'Love? What about it? Forget love, darling. Simon, can't you understand? We are one of Australia's richest families. You can have *anyone* you want. You're a prime catch. You can offer a lifetime of every indulgence any young woman could possibly imagine. You're not just a young man looking for a wife, settling for some girl he enjoys groping in bed, or . . . what's the expression? Oh yes, a young man sowing his wild oats. You did that in Australia and I said nothing. Do you think I didn't worry when I saw a female shape silhouetted against a lighted window in your flat? Listen to me, darling! You are heir to a vast fortune. You, with your sisters, will inherit the largest shareholding, 55 per cent of the Koo commercial empire. What am I supposed to do? Stand by while you catch an incurable strain of venereal disease from a Thai whore who says she loves you?'

'Mum, that's the whole point! I don't want you to play village elder. I won't marry a bar girl. I don't want someone who turns out to be a clever gold-digger. I simply want a girl who will fall in love with a reasonable guy with good prospects who makes a decent but not ridiculously big salary as the creative director of a Singapore advertising agency. I've started but haven't come close to completing a painting and it's been a long time, but eventually I hope to be an artist. And I don't want to be an artist living on his family's money. I can ultimately do the things I want to do right here, where Koo isn't a name that's picked out in diamonds on a tiara worn by a Chinese princess who's been minutely scrutinised and sanctioned by my mother!'

'The tiara, it would be too, too terribly gauche, darling.' Chairman Meow *and* my mum both laughed at the concept of the diamond tiara name badge.

I'm sure by now you get the idea of a fairly typical 'Chairman Meow and Mum' three-day blitzkrieg. But of course this all happened before Mercy B. Lord moved in.

So, with Mercy B. Lord living with me but at this stage committed to nothing further, I was faced with quite a different set of Chairman Meow problems, but more about that later.

Mercy B. Lord's presence in my life, and thankfully also in my bed, naturally spelled the end of my relationship with Veronica at the Nite Cap girlie bar. I guess I owed the little Thai bar girl nothing. I'd always paid the *mama-san* for her services and then given Veronica a generous personal tip before I left. I was aware of the usual warning to expats ending a relationship with a bar girl: don't fall into the trap of feeling sorry. When it's over, don't even say you're leaving, simply disappear into the night.

Bar girls who sold their sexual services were experts at putting the hard word on clients. They all had hard-luck stories: some of being sold into prostitution at the age of fourteen by their impoverished parents so that their families could own a small patch of arable land or build a house; some of being raped at thirteen and having to support a child; others of working for money to buy their brothers an education and so break the cycle of poverty.

The received wisdom amongst the men using the bar girls was that it was all a scam the girls would work on their sucker expat customers time after time. It was said that some of the better con girls owned property, and it was often claimed that several actually owned the girlie bars they worked in, selling their services while they were young and pretty and by doing so creating their own future or dowry for when they were older and could become *mama-sans* or housewives.

Frankly, I wouldn't have blamed them if all of this were true, but it wasn't. It wasn't even close to the truth. The truth was horrible. It had existed for a very long time and would continue as long as poverty and misery existed and women were powerless and valued only for the purse they carried between their legs. Sex trafficking brought about by poverty, misery and despair most often begins in rural areas. More than two-thirds of the world's countries are involved in some way in human trafficking, whether they are countries of origin, transit or destination. It is patently impossible for impoverished girls, most no more than twelve or fourteen, to have the means to obtain a passport and thereafter organise any sort of work for themselves in a foreign country. It is also obvious that the various governments involved turn a blind eye to sex trafficking – it would be easy enough to stop issuing passports or work permits to teenagers without very detailed checks. The trade depends on a permissive attitude from the very top down, and often corruption from the bottom up. In Singapore at the time, prostitution from girlie bars was against the law. This was easily overcome by having the client pay a bar fee so that he could take the girl to other premises, often next door, the fee representing only her drinks, hence a single beer or Scotch could cost as much as the girl's service fee. In theory, she was agreeing to have sex for nothing or whatever she could get from a drunk or generous client.

Sex traffickers are invariably criminal gangs (if Chinese, usually Triad) who seldom pay very much for their captives but instead simply promise to place a daughter in a good domestic job overseas where she will earn money to send home regularly. The recruiter then pays the cost of getting the girls to Singapore or any other location in the world and sells them to brothel and bar owners, recovering his expenses and making a large profit. The girls even come with a warranty. Not only does their new owner hold their passports but the sex-trafficking gangs also frequently supply the muscle to keep the girls in line or the drugs to keep them compliant. In this way the owner can't be accused of physical maltreatment, even though violence is ever-present in the life of a girl sold into prostitution.

The new owner adds various costs to the amount he has paid for a girl so that she must spend her first three or four years paying off this initial debt as well as returning him a handsome profit. If a bar girl or prostitute eventually repays her debt, she is still trapped, because she is only given a small allowance to live on while under contract and is unable to save money in the interim, thus lacking the means to return home. Her 'freedom' – the second stage of her life – doesn't mean her liberation. She's broke and knows no other lifestyle, possesses no life skills apart from pleasing men, and has often acquired a drug habit from her owner and now has to find a means to support it. In most Asian countries the usual drug of addiction was heroin; in the new Singapore the supply or possession of heroin carried a death sentence and so amphetamines were the drug most often used.

Most victims of sex trafficking are ignorant village girls, mostly teenagers without the education, contacts or strength to avoid the deliberate pitfalls placed in their way to keep them captive. In this second stage of their lives, when they are still young and pretty enough to attract men, they usually continue working as bar girls or prostitutes, often for the same owner who previously held their passports, particularly if they relied on him to feed their drug habit.

In Singapore there is almost inevitably a third stage, when they are too old and no longer useful in a bar or brothel popular with expats or the local rich: they find themselves on the street, compelled to work as poorly paid prostitutes in increasingly downmarket brothels, or, if they are really unlucky, gathered up by a pimp who feeds their drug habit in return for their services to perverts who demand unspeakable acts of cruelty and depravity.

The dream is always the return of the prodigal daughter, having saved enough to start a new life back in the village. But this is rare. I explain all this because many of us regard Asian sex as a common commodity for sale, which of course it is, just like anywhere else, but the difference is that so many of us secretly see it as involving worthless, even redundant, girls and women. These hapless village girls are somehow dismissed as human detritus. We have been conditioned to think, in the same way as the sex trafficker, that these young village girls are simply part of supply and demand, a commodity, a surplus in one area that is tradeable and highly desirable in another. It's an age-old business in which human traffickers export an ignorant labour force to foreign lands, cynically using false promises of sufficient reward to allow them to return home with the means to change their original circumstances. Only this time it's not young blokes with strong backs who labour in foreign fields, on farms or docks, roads or building sites, but young girls with supple thighs intended for the predilections of men. Worst of all, most of them have no say in their fates: it is slavery by another name.

While I paid for her services, Veronica would have received very little of the money I gave the owner of the girlie bar; only a small amount would have been deducted from her unconscionable debt. Of course, I could have walked away with a clear conscience, and while I don't want to appear holier than thou, nevertheless I felt I had reasons to be grateful. She had never taken me for granted or simply gone through the motions, but had always serviced me with concern or enthusiasm, good humour or care. Of course she hoped for rescue, but she never put any pressure on me. She accepted that she was there to meet my needs at whatever hour I appeared.

I was rarely intoxicated when I was with her so I got to know her almost as if she had been my personal concubine. That's not to suggest that she was exclusively reserved for me. Of course she had other customers to please, some of them the usual drunk, groping, lascivious *gwai-lo* men, although there were many others – I'd like to think of myself as one of them – who didn't abuse or take these girls for granted. Women like Veronica repaid sensitivity and kindness by making you feel as if you alone mattered. She never attempted to con me or exploit a hard-luck story. She came from a village in northern Thailand and accepted her family's right to sell her, a practice common enough in many villages in that part of Thailand. I'd asked her on one occasion how she saw the future, and to my surprise she seemed quite optimistic. 'Simon, I must not take bad things,' she brought her fingers to her mouth to imitate swallowing a pill and touched her head, shook it and assumed a cross-eyed, stupefied expression. 'Then I work hard, make mans happy, and I save tip they gives for me.' She giggled. 'One day, enough. I go home, marry, make baby.' It occurred to me that she couldn't have been much more than eighteen years old but seemed to be going on thirty.

To cut a long story short, I paid her debt to the Nite Cap. She'd been with the girlie bar three years and had only six or so months to go, so it wasn't that onerous. She'd saved, she told me, all the tips I'd given her and no doubt others she'd received, and to this I added a reasonable amount and bought her a cheap plane ticket and her bus fare from Bangkok to her village in the north. Altogether it was quite a large sum, but nothing I couldn't easily afford. Okay, I would possibly never know if she made it home or if I'd been nicely, politely conned. But if mine was a self-indulgent gesture, a bit of goody-two-shoeing, I nevertheless felt a whole heap better for it.

Sex for the gratification of the out-of-towner, not to mention the locals, has been around since Marco Polo discovered the mysterious Orient – probably longer – and while there is poverty, hopelessness, lack of opportunity and the concept of bitter rice (a belief that girls and women are worthless, or worse than worthless), the underworld predators who traffic in pubescent girls are going to continue their merciless trade.

So who could possibly blame the bar girls if they tried to con their clients? Chairman Meow, of course, was right to see them as manipulative and calculating – these are often the only skills of the powerless. Bar girls who have little experience of men other than those in various stages of inebriation and sexual arousal are and always will be alley cats who have taught themselves to purr like pampered pussies, rat-catchers hoping to stumble across a bowl of cream.

Veronica was free, or so I hoped, and with sufficient funds to allow her to purchase her own house and have enough left over for a dowry to attract a good man so she could marry happily and settle down to life as a village mother.

With the joy of having Mercy B. Lord share my life, things romantic should have settled down for Simon Koo, Fortune Cookie. But, alas, between the two women dominating my life, my adorable lover and a mother morphing into Chairman Meow, things were not always easy, and my remaining time with Samuel Oswald Wing in Singapore looked as if it might require fairly careful management.

Mercy B. Lord continued to disappear overnight every Thursday, and while I hated the notion that I didn't know where she was or what she was doing, we'd made a deal. I know it sounds piss-weak, but I was forced to compromise. Playing the heavy male archetype was pointless, and besides, I'd given my word. Everyone knows the conventional wisdom that love should be about being completely open, but I wonder how often it really is between couples. At least I knew about the forbidden area, so technically we were being open about being closed. I know it sounds dumb, an oxymoron, but my secret hope was that either she'd eventually let me know where and why she went or she'd simply not go there any longer.

In the meantime, whether weak or not, I'd given my word and would try very hard to keep it. The thought of losing Mercy B. Lord simply wasn't worth it, provided always that what she was doing was safe. And that was perhaps where I might finally slip up. I couldn't bear the thought of something happening to her, something I might be able to prevent. I clearly remembered Ronnie Wing's warning on my first day at the Town Club: if I tried to become involved with Mercy B. Lord I would be kicked out of Singapore so fast that I wouldn't even bounce. If he was right, then she was taking a chance being with me.

Of course I'd wanted her permanently in my life and equally for her to live with me. But after warning me not to persist after the first night we'd slept together, I hadn't tried to force the issue. I'd ignored Ronnie's caution but I hadn't forgotten it. It was Mercy B. Lord's decision to move in and I could only hope she knew what she was doing.

Thursday night was obviously a compromise she'd reached. Whether it was one in her own mind or with others – namely Beatrice Fong and the Wings – I couldn't say. I'd asked her if she was safe and all she'd said was that she was in control of the situation – not by any means a perfect answer but again it had left me with nowhere to go.

We'd been together for about three months and we'd fallen into a routine. I made good use of her Thursdays away – to be perfectly honest, it meant I could work back late without feeling guilty – and life was sweet. But then the phone rang one afternoon and Sidney's secretary said, 'Simon, Mr Johnny wants to see you in the chairman's office.'

I was aware that Sidney was in the States at the time and Johnny was nominally chairman in his absence, but this wasn't even a one-off event. In the time I'd been at the agency, he'd never summoned me in Sidney's absence, or at any other time, for that matter. He was a silent presence, even in the boardroom, except when Sidney needed his vote on something Dansford didn't care about. As I headed for his office I was mildly curious.

'Sit.' Johnny Wing simply didn't know how to be polite and had the manners of a pig.

I sat on one of the yellow Scandinavian chairs. 'What is it, Johnny?'

'The girl! She goes!' To my surprise, he brought his fist down hard on the desk.

'Eh? What girl?'

'The one you fuck! Gone!'

'I beg your pardon?'

'No more! She goes. Dangerous!'

'To whom – dangerous to whom?'

'You! Her also!' He was sitting bolt upright, with both fists clenched on the desk.

'Is this an order?' I was trying very hard to keep myself under control.

'Go to China Doll, pick for yourself, she free for one month!' he yelled.

'I don't want a China Doll whore,' I exclaimed. 'Besides, who the fuck do you think you are? You can't talk to me like this!'

Both fists slammed down on the desk again. 'She goes! No more talk. Go now. Finish!'

Johnny's spit-flecked monosyllabic expostulations seemed somehow dated. Unlike Sidney and Ronnie, he lacked an education. This was not quite Singlish, the local patois, but more like the street English the Chinese speak in Malaysia. Normally he spoke better than this. It was almost as if he were translating directly from Cantonese and speaking to me as he might to a member of his staff. I made no move and looked him in the eye. The bad portrait of Sidney behind him seemed to add to the threatening atmosphere. Johnny, who never wore a suit or tie but simply a white open-necked shirt, looked like some evil oriental military captain out of a Sydney Greenstreet movie. If it hadn't been so serious, it would have made an excellent parody, a funny skit for TV, although I was pretty steamed up and there was nothing funny about it. As the seconds ticked by and I held his eye, I was beginning to realise there was no possible rebuttal and it was I who was going to have to move. My dad would have simply got up and walked out. He'd have done so on Johnny's 'fuck' sentence. I'd left it too late to leave with any dignity.

The brain plays funny tricks and in my mind's eye I saw Mercy B. Lord on the night we had made love for the first time. She'd raised her hands and cupped her breasts and still held the toothbrush she'd bought, which had somehow broken through the top of its cellophane wrapper and pressed against one of her breasts. This was what he was threatening to take from me. My anger grew dark and explosive.

In two bounds I was around Sidney's desk and had grabbed Johnny by the shirtfront and lifted him bodily from the chair. I dragged him clear of the desk then hurled him across the room. His bum hit the carpet ten feet or so away. He skidded into the far wall and bumped his head hard against it, inches from the ancestors' cabinet, where he slumped, his chin resting on his chest. He had been too surprised even to yell out. I realised later that he'd beaten his fists against my arms and shoulders but at the time I'd felt nothing. Without a word I left the room, hoping I'd killed the bastard.

I remained in the agency, waiting for the repercussions and determined to face the consequences. Dansford was away on his usual extended lunch and Ronnie was entertaining a client and by this stage would probably be hitting the first of the drinking holes or girlie bars. If he was conscious, Johnny was in charge.

Nothing happened. No ambulance or paramedics bearing a stretcher appeared, no fuss and no call from Sidney's secretary; the agency seemed to function normally. Five o'clock came and the place emptied out. The receptionist, Alice Ho, knocked off at 5.30, so at 5.25 I walked up to her and asked casually, 'Mr Johnny left yet, Alice?'

Alice was a past mistress of the inscrutable demeanour but, even so, I sensed she had nothing to conceal. 'Always ten past five,' she exclaimed, eyes wide, as if she expected me to know. 'You want I call him in the morning for you, Mr Simon?' Then she added, 'Always ten past five.'

'No. Thanks, Alice.' Like a lot of the offices of Chinese head honchos, Sidney's was soundproofed. Snooping is a Chinese artform. Knowledge is power. Sidney's secretary couldn't have heard us. Her conversations with Sidney were always via the intercom. Obviously Johnny had recovered and whatever damage I'd done hadn't been permanent. He looked as if he had a thick skull. I'd replayed the events and imagined what might have happened if he'd crashed into the ancestors cabinet and smashed the priceless jade and porcelain or the fat Buddha. That may have been a better reason to kill me than whatever was behind his order to stay away from Mercy B. Lord: not just the value of the contents, but the anger and retribution of the ancestors, the permanent loss of good fortune, would have marked the end of me. *There must be a god in heaven*, I thought.

With the five o'clock rush still on, it took some time to find a taxi and it was nearly six o'clock before I arrived home, half an hour before Mercy B. Lord usually arrived. In Singapore, cooking your own dinner is a particular stupidity, unless you love to cook – it's the place where all the Asian cuisines meet for breakfast, lunch and dinner. She usually stopped off somewhere and ordered our dinner and brought it home with her in a tiffin box. I was sorry it wasn't a Thursday, which would have given me a day or so to recover. Frankly, I didn't know how to react to what had happened. There was obviously something about her I didn't know – her disappearances on Thursdays testified to this – and it didn't take a genius to work out that the Wings and Beatrice Fong were involved. Elma Kelly had called Beatrice a despicable creature, so she was obviously a nasty piece of work.

When there were no repercussions from me losing my temper and manhandling Johnny, I began to wonder if he might be bluffing, simply trying to frighten me; Ronnie first, with a lighter hand, and then, when I'd ignored that, Johnny with a two-fisted frontal attack. Then I realised that even though there had been no immediate repercussions for me, I might nevertheless have endangered Mercy B. Lord. Myself, too, I suppose. But I hadn't really stopped to think about that.

Despite my promise to her, this was an extenuating circumstance. As soon as she arrived we would have to talk – that much I knew. I couldn't ignore this; it wasn't going to go away. It was tricky, because I didn't know what I was up against and she did but wouldn't say – as my dad would advise, 'Simon, only a fool or a woman places a big bet without knowing the odds.' I asked myself what problems Mercy B. Lord and I could possibly create for the Wings that would make it worth their while to get rid of her or me or both of us. In my case they'd have some explaining to do and it would need to be worth jeopardising the relationship with New York. I'd achieved success for the Americans. Big Lather, in particular, looked like being a smash hit throughout South-East Asia. The Texas Tiger campaign had been a spectacular success, it was going worldwide and New York had picked up the account, giving us – me, in particular – the credit for the win. I knew the partnership with New York was important to Sidney, so my partnership with Mercy B. Lord would need to be a pretty big issue for him to risk disrupting it. I didn't even know if Johnny was acting independently.

Alternatively, it might simply be a case of the phoney Chinese-Australian getting in the way of a routine, albeit nefarious, business arrangement in which Mercy B. Lord was involved, and they were afraid she might spill the beans on the pillow. Whatever it was, I reasoned she couldn't be a big player because she appeared to receive little or no significant reward for what she did.

If Sidney had found a way to fire me that the Yanks would accept or could be forced to accept, I couldn't have given a shit. A bit ego-bruising perhaps, but I was thoroughly jack of the Wings, and as long as

Mercy B. Lord agreed to accompany me back to Australia, it would be a happily-ever-after ending.

All this stuff raced through my mind as I waited for my beloved to come home. They say the pheromones that make us fall in love finally wear off and are replaced by something more permanent, yet I couldn't imagine my feelings for Mercy B. Lord ever changing. The idea that she might come to harm or even die was beyond my comprehension. I was possibly being melodramatic, but this was Asia, and even in a civilised society like Singapore, taking a life to conceal a crime or to avoid trouble was common among the Triads. While my disappearance might cause problems, hers wouldn't. She had no relations, no important connections to speak of, apart from Beatrice and the Wings, nobody asking questions except an expat who was having an affair with just another pretty Chinese girl.

I had been plainly warned never to question her disappearances on Thursdays. But now, after Johnny's threat, I knew I must. If we had to catch a flight back to Australia the following day, it wasn't an issue. I had been given no reason for the order to give her up, but I knew there must be one. Unless she explained what was going on, there wasn't anything I could do to help her – help us. I decided not to tell her too much, so as not to alarm her unduly. My fear was that she would leave me in order to protect me. I'd tell her the Wings had asked me to stop seeing her, but had given no reasons, that I felt compromised. Then I'd beg her to explain what the hell was going on.

Mercy B. Lord arrived a few minutes after 6.30 p.m. carrying a tiffin box. She had a way of lighting up a room. It wasn't just for me; I'd heard others say the same. I guess it's a quality found with truly beautiful women. 'Peking duck tonight, very posh Chinese!' she cried as she came into the kitchen, smiling. She placed it on the counter and ran to embrace me.

'Lovely!' I said, trying to sound enthusiastic.

She stopped dead. 'What's wrong?' she asked.

'Let's eat. I'll tell you while we eat.'

We sat on stools at the kitchen counter while we ate and I told her about Ronnie's initial warning when I was new to Singapore, then gave her an edited version of that afternoon's exchange with Johnny. I concluded by saying, 'Darling, I don't know how serious this is, whether you're in danger, or I am, but I couldn't bear it if I was putting you at risk. Until I know what's involved there's nothing I can do, no plans I can make, no decision we can take. As I promised, I haven't questioned your disappearances on Thursdays but now I feel I must. Please understand things have changed suddenly and dramatically.'

Mercy B. Lord was silent for what seemed like minutes but was probably less than thirty seconds. 'Simon, I can handle this,' she said at last. 'There are certain rules, and as long as we don't break them we'll be safe.' It wasn't the answer I expected. There was nothing in her eyes that suggested she was unduly afraid.

'Rules? Whose rules? The Wings'? Beatrice Fong's? Who? How will I know if I'm breaking them if I don't know what they are?'

'Ah, but I know and I will be careful not to compromise you.'

'You knew you *might* be in danger if you stayed here, didn't you?'

She shrugged, tilted her head and gave me a beseeching look. 'I can't answer that. Just trust me, Simon.'

'I'm not sure I like that, your being the guardian of my safety. May I say, you're making it very bloody difficult, darling.'

'No, believe me, I'm making it *easy* for you, Simon.'

'Bloody hell! That's an answer? I'm supposed to walk around knowing I'm playing with dynamite but have no means of removing the fuse or knowing if it's already alight?'

Mercy B. Lord laughed, although she sounded closer to tears than merriment, and she had lost control of her voice. 'Simon, there's only one rule you need to know and obey. If you don't, I can't and won't be a part of your life. I resisted you for a very long time and it hasn't been easy.'

'You mean Thursdays? Bloody disappearing Thursdays!'

'Yes. You may *never* question me. If you want me, then that's the rule. If you break it, then you lose me.'

'Darling, it must be perfectly obvious that I love you. But you can't just pop off every Thursday with a "See ya later" and expect me never to question you. I know I said I wouldn't. Not now that I've been warned on two separate occasions. Sidney Wing is dangerous and Johnny is a fucking goon! I've heard Beatrice Fong described as a despicable creature. And you're somehow involved with them and I'm supposed to stand by and play dumb-fuck lover! Mercy B. Lord, can't you understand? I want to marry you! I want us to have children!'

Mercy B. Lord looked as shocked as if I'd slapped her face. 'Marry me?' she repeated in a shocked, incredulous voice, as if the idea had never occurred to her and was far from welcome. She shook her head. 'No, Simon, you've got this all *terribly* wrong!'

I ignored her, gulping down my anger but still too pumped-up to really listen or register surprise. 'My mum is paying one of her three-monthly visits to her prodigal son. I've told you before about her carry-on, her matchmaking me with Singapore's finest virgin daughters. I want you to meet her, darling. I want her to understand that I've found the love of my life.'

'No!' It came out like a hammer-blow on rock. She jumped from the kitchen stool and glared at me. 'Simon! How dare you!'

'What? You don't want to meet my mother? Have I got everything completely wrong?'

'Right both times!' If I'd expected Mercy B. Lord to break down and sob at this point, I would have been disappointed. She looked me directly in the eye, her expression resolute, her right eyebrow slightly raised. 'Well?'

This was someone I didn't know. Her reaction to the news, the warnings from Ronnie and Johnny, had been totally unexpected, but now there was a second, even greater surprise. Or was it all a part of the same Mercy B. Lord I didn't know? *Steady on, Simon, cool it! Start to listen. When you don't know what to say, stay silent* (my dad's advice). *Listen with your eyes as well as your ears.*

So much for the best laid plans of mice and men. In my mind I had set up the meeting between the two women in my life. I would warn

Chairman Meow not to mention the family money, not that she would have done so anyway. She'd initially be horrified at Mercy B. Lord's lack of background and connections, deeply suspicious of her beauty and, I dare say, her sexiness, but how could she fail to appreciate her and ultimately love her?

Now it seemed I'd got it all wrong. In my male arrogance I'd seen our living together as the prelude to marriage and spending the rest of our lives together, happily ever after. As I think I've said before, I'd warned my cousins Peter and Henry never to mention my family's financial circumstances, so this wasn't Mercy B. Lord playing hardball, putting up a sham resistance to keep me keen and then eventually appearing to make up her mind so everyone would know she was the genuine article. At least I was pretty confident she wasn't one of the gold-diggers who kept Chairman Meow permanently paranoid. But then, you never know what people know about you, especially the Chinese, who regard information as money in the bank or the single greatest advantage they possess over an opponent. If Mercy B. Lord was a gold-digger, then she was ready for a leading role on Broadway.

Belatedly, my survival instinct kicked in. I wasn't accustomed to being on the back foot, especially when I'd assumed that the outcome would be favourable. I'm usually fairly careful with speculation and don't assume I have any extra rights, but I'd never seen any problems on the horizon from Mercy B. Lord herself, who was nothing but loving. I had concentrated almost solely on overcoming the resistance to my marriage that I felt sure would come from Chairman Meow. Nothing, I'd told myself, was going to prevent me from marrying Mercy B. Lord.

I'd never asked anyone to marry me before and so I'd never had a knockback, and while I didn't have any tickets on myself and knew that my looks were pretty unprepossessing, I had no serious bad habits or addictions, wasn't difficult, didn't make unreasonable demands, worked hard and earned an above-average income. I also told myself that if Mercy B. Lord was not interested in me, then she wouldn't have agreed to stay with me in the first place.

However, I was also aware that wealth was the potential enemy of true love. From childhood my sisters and I had been warned repeatedly to watch out for what my father called the 'cheque-book sheilas'. Sometimes I thought I'd have to find and fall in love with someone whose family was as wealthy as my own to eliminate the money problem. In Australia that considerably limited the odds of finding someone suitable, which may have been another factor behind Chairman Meow's thinking. Now, just when I thought I'd beaten the odds and found the girl of my dreams, she refused to marry me, or even to meet my mum. She'd declined with admirable economy, just a few words. If there is meant to be a script for this sort of thing, clearly I'd lost my place.

Mercy B. Lord headed for our bedroom and I followed, knowing with certainty that I was about to lose the best thing that had ever happened to me. I tried to think clearly about the sequence of events over the past ten minutes. We'd started with the warning I'd received and she'd fielded that, but insisted on her rule about disappearing on Thursdays. I'd spat the dummy. She wouldn't budge. I'd declared my love, plans, our future and she'd gone ape-shit! How could I recover from this disaster? I was desperate.

'Okay, no meeting Mother and no marriage plans.' I sighed. 'May I think about your disappearances on Thursdays?'

'Of course.' Mercy B. Lord glanced down at her wristwatch. 'You've got twenty seconds, Simon.'

'Hey, wait on – your watch doesn't have a second hand.' It was an attempt at a joke, perhaps because I didn't really believe her.

She glanced up momentarily. 'Seventeen!'

'Hang on, this is ridiculous!'

'Twelve!'

'A moratorium?'

'Eight!'

'Can we at least —'

'Five!'

'Oh, shit! Can't we talk this over?'

'Zero! Your time's up, Simon.'

'What happens now?'

'I pack up and leave.'

'Ah, c'mon. What do you expect me to say? Am I so repulsive?'

It was a cheap shot but she was ready for it. 'Oh, I see. I make a habit of sleeping with repulsive men, do I? What does that say about me? That I'm just another Veronica?'

'I didn't mean it like that!'

I hated the whine in my voice. She'd taken me by surprise. I was unaware that she knew about the Thai bar girl, but I should have known better. Come to think of it, I was unaware of lots of things about this truly glorious, kind, generous and now surprisingly tough creature. But she certainly had my measure.

Mercy B. Lord had opened the door to the built-in wardrobe where she kept all her things and removed her suitcase from the top shelf. It was cheap but served its purpose. Had it been bespoke or designer luggage, it would have raised yet another question. When she'd arrived she had just the one large suitcase and none of the usual paraphernalia that I imagined went with a young woman moving house permanently. It should have alerted me to the fact that this was a trial run, but I'd been much too excited to think about it at the time. She'd volunteered to stay and I was simply over the moon at the prospect.

Now she was going, and all because I'd broken my word about Thursday. Shit, it was a bit rough. Surely, after Johnny's warning, I was entitled to say something? Surely that was the responsible thing to do? But now I realised that the control she'd shown upon hearing the news meant that she'd known all along what might happen. I'd broken my promise – in a sense I hadn't trusted her. It was bloody tough-minded, but she obviously wasn't going to make any exceptions. I simply couldn't be trusted. Now it looked as if the test run was coming to a regrettable end. This, I knew, was a lot more than a lover's tiff.

She started to plonk clothes into her suitcase and it was obvious, despite the defiant tilt of her chin, that she was upset. 'Plonking' wasn't her style. She was neat in her person and in everything she did.

'Mercy B. Lord, please don't leave. I'm sure we can work this out. I apologise, for everything.'

She paused, a pair of lacy black knickers in one hand, then she let me have it, without raising her voice, but in a steady, emphatic tone, and with each statement she furiously stuffed another item of clothing into the suitcase.

'Simon, I love you. God knows, I've been offered all sorts of inducements for sex, including work at the China Doll or as the concubine for some Chinese billionaire. Every time I meet a foreigner at the airport – French, German, American, English and now the Japanese – I can always be confident of one thing: within forty-eight hours he will be propositioning me. I told you about the German the night we had dinner at Raffles. He wasn't joking, nor was he an exception. Many of these foreign visitors own or run large international concerns. They don't care how much they have to pay – they work at the very top international rate in New York, Hamburg, London, Paris, and now, I suppose, Tokyo. They're spoilt little boys accustomed to winning, and the more exorbitant the price, the better it is for their egos.

'I'm half Chinese, and in this culture, the only one I know, money matters. I'd be lying if I said there weren't times when I was tempted. I think that even if I had been born into a good middle-class Chinese family, I would have yielded to temptation. The Chinese are ambivalent about these things, especially if you operate at the very top and command outrageous sums. But I was born a nobody, a half-caste, with no future, no education to speak of, no *guanxi*. Being a prostitute, a high-class whore, makes me no different from your Veronica. Worse! She is taking the only way out she knew. She may have had no choice. While I was expected to do the same, I didn't have to do it. I had a basic European education. If opening my legs was the only way, even if it was very profitable, then I would demonstrate to myself that you start as rubbish and end as rubbish.'

'Mercy B. Lord, you don't know how to be rubbish. It's not possible.'

I was anxious to steer her away from her background and the way she thought about herself. I'd been born with a silver spoon halfway down my throat, but with a face that looked as if it had been hit repeatedly with the back of a spade, so I knew all about those moments of self-doubt. I also hoped that if I could keep her talking I might think of a way to keep her here with me. 'And so you what? Started with Beatrice Fong? By the way, I can't deny Veronica, but I want you to know that since you and I have been together, that's all over.'

'Yes, I know. And yes, I started work in Beatrice's office at sixteen. She'd come to the orphanage the previous year and selected me, urging me to finish my schooling and paying the nuns to send me to typing and bookkeeping lessons after school. I matriculated at sixteen and won a scholarship to university.' She shrugged. 'That was the first time I was approached to go on the game. Working university vacations only. It was tempting and would have paid for my education. But in the end I took the Beatrice Fong Agency job.'

'Is that because you were brought up as a Catholic?' I will never know how I came to ask such a stupid and insensitive question.

She picked up a carved wooden box. 'You bastard!' she cried, and flung it at me with all her strength.

The box hit me square in the stomach and fell, landing on a corner so that the lid flew open and a piece of khaki fabric spilled out. I stooped quickly to recover it and saw that it was a man's short-sleeved shirt. I picked it up.

Mercy B. Lord gasped, then cried, 'Give that to me!' and snatched it from my hand. 'The box!' she demanded.

'Darling, how can I apologise?' I begged.

'You can't,' she said quietly, her sudden recovery remarkable under the circumstances. This was a girl who could hide her emotions, and I sensed that she was mortified by her sudden loss of control.

She spread the shirt out on the bed and smoothed it carefully. There seemed nothing unusual about it, except that the sleeve nearest me had been removed, hacked off with a sharp pair of scissors in a deliberate zigzag pattern, and on the right pocket was a round disc picked out in tiny needle holes like carefully unpicked embroidery. There are some things you just know for sure, and this was one of them. I dared not ask about or even comment on the severed sleeve. How long the shirt had been in the box, I couldn't say. She silently folded the shirt and laid it back in the cheap wooden box, closed it and placed it carefully in a corner of the suitcase as if she were apologising for having used it badly. Then, wordlessly, she reached under the pillow on the neatly made bed to retrieve her pretty cotton nightgown. I recalled that she hadn't arrived fully equipped with *femme fatale* lingerie. As far as I knew, she possessed one pair of black lacy panties and a sexy black bra that she'd laughingly told me she'd bought at Robinsons the afternoon she'd decided to seduce me. All her other stuff seemed to be what my sisters had worn every day, undies they called Cottontails and white cotton bras.

When she finally spoke, she did so quietly. 'Simon, I just want you to understand I came to you because I wanted to. Excluding the boy at school, you are the first.' She closed the suitcase with a click of the cheap tarnished locks. 'You don't own me and I don't want you to make plans for us. There are things in my life you don't know about and never will. I haven't made any demands except for one, and you've known it all along. The proviso has always been there – I'm away on Thursday until late afternoon Friday. If you can't accept that, and you obviously can't, then you can't have me.'

'But I have!' I protested pathetically. 'Up to now! It was just the warning, I —'

Mercy B. Lord cut me short. 'If I had agreed to be your wife, then, of course, that would be different. If I'd agreed to any plans that involve us, yes again, but I haven't. Now, if you'll please call me a taxi . . .'

The wardrobe door was open and the black cheongsam was all that was left hanging there, with the red patent-leather high-heeled shoes placed neatly beneath it. If the brain forms permanent images, then the black cheongsam and red shoes were one for me. They had, in combination, burned themselves into my subconscious mind. While there may have been fifty delightful ways I saw Mercy B. Lord in the abstract, this was the one that thrilled me the most, gave me a mental frisson I could conjure up at will.

I was conscious that this image wasn't necessarily a truth, an absolute. As an artist and an ad man, I knew that images could be misleading, and that the secret lay in stripping them back to observe what was underneath and gave them their power. But for the most part, the human mind doesn't work in this manner. It prefers to make pictures, and the sum of those pictures leads us to our beliefs. The Catholic Church has always known this. In order to avoid cultural chaos, we create visual stereotypes and infuse them with power. The black cheongsam on a young, slender oriental female sends all the right sexual messages to a male, particularly a Westernised male. With the red stilettos, two stereotypes join – the sexual mystery of the Orient coupled with the red high-heeled shoes that are pure *femme fatale* raunchy Hollywood – and create a Western fantasy.

This image wasn't all of Mercy B. Lord – in fact, she was only a very small part, but it was a part that brilliantly embodied a stereotypical fantasy, and I loved and cherished it. But now it was as if two important parts of the many parts of Mercy B. Lord I adored were deserting me. As if the gown and the shoes were about to step out and leave me forever.

I picked up her suitcase and silently left the bedroom with her following. Maybe I should have begged, objected, persisted or promised, but my instinct told me she wasn't going to change her mind, and that her survival depended on her leaving. Waiting for the lift and feeling pretty bloody shitty, I said, 'Hey, you left your gown and shoes.'

'You may keep them. I don't have any further use for them.' She sniffed back a tear and started to cry, then to howl. I'd never heard such despair, and knew it wasn't just about us. What I was hearing was a far greater sadness.

CHAPTER ELEVEN

———

OF COURSE I BEGGED unashamedly. I'd fucked up and lost my girl. Not to a worthy competitor, but to an unworthy self. I called Mercy B. Lord at the Beatrice Fong Agency every day but always received the same polite answer from the switch – 'Just one moment, sir' – then a thirty-second pause followed by the same reply: 'Miss Mercy B. Lord is not available at this time.' I knew it was pointless yelling down the phone but I often did long after I had heard the click of the receiver at the other end. As my tiny office had no ceiling and the glass panels would have exposed me to the silent ridicule of the production staff, and more importantly of Ronnie Wing, I would make these calls from home, taking a taxi there during my lunch break.

I sent Mercy B. Lord baskets of local orchids and roses, cards and, upon reflection, mawkish love letters written with what felt like my blood and tears, but that came from my heart and soul. Then I noticed that the splendid Noël Coward aspidistra in reception was missing and that a basket of Singapore orchids had taken its place. When I'd sent two dozen red hothouse roses, the following day the same numbers of red roses would appear, resplendent on the ornate stand. I questioned Alice Ho at reception. She had been with the Wings for twenty years and, like all switchboard operators, knew everything. But she was the classic inscrutable oriental and it was impossible to tell what she was thinking. With a face as bland as a boarding-house dinner plate, she claimed that the flowers were delivered addressed to the agency with no card or note accompanying them. Then, when summoned to Sidney Wing's office about an invoice, something that could have been done over the phone, I saw the aspidistra on a new stand next to the ancestors' cabinet. The message was clear. I stopped sending flowers, they stopped appearing in reception and the aspidistra duly reappeared in its rightful place. My letters were routinely returned bearing a post-office stamp that read *Not at this address*. While I didn't bundle and tie them with ribbon, I didn't throw them out either, keeping them in the drawer of my bedside table, all thirty of them, a testament to my pathetic love for Mercy B. Lord.

She had always forbidden me to visit the Beatrice Fong Agency and I knew that to do so now would be unproductive. In an attempt to hang on to the final threads of my tattered ego, I resisted what appeared to be my last resort: to sit watching her building from a tea-house across the road. I had sufficient pride, but only just, to resist playing the grieving and uncomprehending dog who visits at the same time every day the place its master routinely frequented before he died. I tell a lie – I went once and sat for an hour between five and six o'clock, but she didn't emerge, and I summoned sufficient dignity to leave the tea-house, dragging my shadow behind me like a sack of potatoes.

Stupidly, in an attempt to ameliorate the agony and conjure up the ecstasy, I removed the wardrobe door so that the first thing I saw as I awoke each morning was the black cheongsam and the red shoes. I'd sit on the bed cross-legged, sometimes holding my head in my hands and shaking it from side to side, telling myself to get a life, then I'd groan and go to the bathroom and clean my teeth without looking in the mirror. I imagined her with me under the shower as I soaped and serviced my desperate need for her. I told myself every morning that today would be better, but it wasn't.

Chairman Meow came and went and it was the usual shitfight. She even asked me one night, 'Simon, have you turned gay?'

I felt about as far from gay as it was possible to feel, but I replied, 'What do you mean?'

'Oh, it's a new expression I heard on the radio. It means are you . . . you know, a nancy boy?'

The time dragged by until, curiously, Ronnie invited me to lunch at the Town Club one Thursday. It wasn't the first time he'd done so, nevertheless we'd only been there on a couple of occasions. The last time had been after I'd explained fairly forcefully to Sidney that he couldn't begin to make a TV commercial for Citizen watches on the budget he'd agreed to with Hercules Sun. Ronnie had invited me to lunch in an attempt to persuade me to find a way. The loss of face to his brother would be extreme and unacceptable, and – to use an expression familiar to Australians – Sidney was between a rock and a hard place. He couldn't go back and admit his error, and he couldn't, or wouldn't, pay the difference out of agency funds. If I didn't somehow find a way to make the commercial, it would almost certainly destroy his brother's relationship with me. I recall thinking that the relationship wasn't much chop anyway; if it wasn't already in tatters, certainly the edges were decidedly ragged. I was also loath to share the beginnings of the idea I'd had for filming the commercial. Let them sweat.

'Ronnie, I can't squeeze blood out of a stone, mate. This has nothing whatsoever to do with relationships. I don't give a shit where the money comes from but I can't make a commercial on what Sidney's quoted. There's barely sufficient funds to buy film and pay for processing!'

'Simon, *please* understand, it's not about money!' Ronnie cried.

'It's a Chinese thing,' I said, a touch acerbically.

'Yes,' he replied, missing the irony in my voice.

'Okay, whatever you say, but *only* money can solve the problem.'

'No, you *must* find a way!' he'd insisted.

'What? Pay the difference myself?' I'd asked.

'Yes, if that is what it takes,' he'd replied.

Come to think of it, there was a precedent for my footing the bill. I'd insisted that Sidney do something about the state of the staff toilets, but this too had resulted in a stalemate and I had ended up personally paying for two fans to be installed after holes in the brick wall for the flue had been knocked in.

I'd arranged for this to be done secretly on a Sunday for both the male and the female toilets. It was the Sunday before Dansford was due to arrive and I didn't want him to walk into an agency that smelled of shit. While nothing was said and no one, as far as I knew, realised who'd paid for the fans, Ronnie informed me that his brother was furious. Several of the staff had thanked him when they'd come into work on Monday.

'Hey, wait on,' I'd said. 'He could have taken the credit. I don't care. Nobody knows who did it. I arranged it for a Sunday. There wasn't a soul in the office all day. The workmen had cleaned up and gone home before five o'clock.'

'This is Singapore, Simon. The whole goddamned staff knew before lunch on Monday,' Ronnie said, emphasising his American accent. 'Hell no! Serious loss of face, man!'

'What about the people who thanked him?'

'It's a Chinese thing. They knew it wasn't him.'

'What? They were sending him up?'

'Yeah, the Chinese way.'

'Well, bugger me,' I remember saying. But I quite liked the idea of the sycophantic staff having a giggle behind their hands at Sidney's expense.

However, despite this loss of face, the two toilets still couldn't cope, and there remained a semi-permanent miasma within sixty feet of them. I continued to pay for air freshener every week until I got smart and buried it as a taxi, bar or lunch expense.

So I knew that this luncheon invitation to Ronnie's club wasn't a casual or generous gesture on his part.

If British-inspired men's clubs have any value, it is that they never appear to change. There are no unpleasant surprises: the same people are always at the bar, the same smell of floor polish and brass- and silver-cleaner persists, the familiar starched linen and monogrammed cutlery lie on the dining-room tables. The menu is always neatly typed with its equally predictable 'daily special' inserted on the inside flap, usually some oxymoron such as 'Fresh smoked haddock flown directly from the UK'. The ambience of the dining room is unruffled, with the ceiling fans rotating at a level just below an unacceptable whir; lunch is always followed by the exodus to the afternoon lounge with its somnolent rustle of broadsheet newspapers and recumbent planter chairs and chalked wake-up times marked on the soles of stout brogues. Remarkably, even new staff members looked like their predecessors, the carefully obsequious Indian and Malay waiters. A British club is a male safe house and a solid tribute to the security of an unchanging and carefully tended world.

Ronnie ordered his very dry martini and a beer for me and we chatted about nothing in particular. I had a sense of what was coming and he, no doubt, was rehearsing the phrasing. He downed the first martini in three gulps and immediately called for a second. This one he sipped more slowly, and then a third followed, by which time I'd downed my lager and we went in to lunch.

At lunch he had red wine from a half-full bottle marked with his name. I abstained and had the waiter pour me a glass of water. Whatever was coming, I didn't want to hear it half-tanked. Ronnie toyed with his food, allowing the liquor to quell his anxiety, while I ate steadily, deliberately saying very little.

Then, pouring the last of the wine, he said, 'She won't be coming back, Simon.' Clearly, he'd decided to drop the preliminaries I know he would have been silently rehearsing.

'Oh? She told you?' There was no point in pretending.

'A message. I'm sorry to be the vulture man, Simon.' It wasn't an expression I knew and it could have been one of Ronnie's specials, but it sounded apt.

'You know this for sure?' I was attempting to keep my voice even.

'Believe me, Simon.'

'Nothing I can do?'

'Haven't you done enough already? You were warned.'

'Well, nobody's bounced me over the border so far.'

'Big Lather saved you, man. Count yourself lucky.'

'Lucky? This sounds like a conspiracy, rather than one individual's decision. Are you telling me —'

'I'm telling you nothing. Just that it's over.'

'And you're the messenger?'

'I told you that already, I'm the vulture man.'

'Delivering a message from big brother.'

'Simon, don't be ridiculous.'

'Yeah, right, as the vulture man once said, you can't knock two holes in a shithouse wall on a Sunday without everyone in Singapore knowing.'

Ronnie chuckled. 'Good one. Touché. I can see you're taking it on the chin, buddy.' He suddenly brightened. 'Hey, man, let's head over to the Nite Cap. The *mama-san* says she's got a new chick to replace Veronica; Vietnamese. Her name is Mai Khiem Ton – in English, Modesty. Must have come as a surprise, Veronica up and leaving, eh?'

'Yeah, yeah, of course!' I said with more than a touch of sarcasm. 'Thanks, Ronnie, but if you don't mind, I'll give the Nite Cap a miss. Heaps of work back at the agency.' The very fact that Ronnie knew the name of the new Vietnamese bar girl clearly indicated that meeting her was a set-up that would prove Mercy B. Lord had been simply a convenient sex object.

The weeks trundled by like a slow goods train but things didn't get any better. Mercy B. Lord and I had only been together for a few months but it might as well have been a lifetime. Whatever had happened before her was inconsequential, and everything that had happened since was as dark and miserable as dragging my potato-sack shadow behind me that day as I left the tea-house opposite the Beatrice Fong Agency, in other words, heavy going.

I hated coming home and worked late at the agency most nights, although the weekends were the worst. There is something quite wrong about going in to work on a Sunday that has nothing whatsoever to do with Christianity. Then one Sunday I picked up a brush and started to paint the portrait I'd started of Mercy B. Lord. She'd sat for me only three times and I'd done a dozen or so preliminary sketches, simply details of her hands, eyes, the tilt of her head, the angles of her body. Thinking there was plenty of time, I hadn't committed anything to canvas.

Now I prepared a life-size canvas and began to outline in paint her shape, and the slight tilt of her head when she would look at me as I approached her. It was a winsome look that never failed to touch my heart. I'd felt it perhaps most powerfully the night I'd walked into the reception area at Raffles and seen her in the black cheongsam seated in a peacock-tail wicker chair. This had been one of the defining moments of my life, a glorious vision I would never forget. I'd come from a forced inspection of my minuscule future office, convinced I'd made a huge mistake coming to Singapore when, seemingly in seconds, she'd changed everything.

It was arrogant on my part, but what I was going to attempt to do was to capture that moment, the sense of overwhelming feminine beauty that could create such a miraculous metamorphosis in a man. That Sunday morning I blocked out the basic planes, the shape of her face and hair and the lines of her body. I'd taken several colour photographs during those first three sittings so, at the very least, I had some whole-body references as well as the details in the sketches. The difference between a portrait that looks and feels natural and one that looks artificial or false can often be a matter of a few lines or a shift in perspective. In layman's terms, if the artist lacks the ability to draw really well, he won't be able to make up for this deficiency with paint. If you don't get the framework correct at the very beginning, it can be almost impossible to correct later in the painting, even if you're using oils. I was using acrylic, mainly so the paint would dry quickly, but also because it was something new.

I'd purchased a beautifully elaborate cane chair similar to the ones at Raffles, and Mercy B. Lord had wriggled into the black cheongsam and red high heels but remained fresh faced without make-up, and with perhaps only a casual brush run through her hair. While I loved her with a bit of this and that added to her eyes and lips, Mercy B. Lord was a beautiful woman even when she was completely unadorned, and I made a mental note to follow this full-length portrait with a head-and-shoulders study of her without a skerrick of make-up and with her hair in the disarray of morning.

The portrait progressed slowly over the next few weeks, and deliberately so, as I didn't want to complete it. On the other hand, neither did I want to overwork it, something every artist has to be careful to avoid. Gilding the lily can turn a decent painting into a cliché. You have to know when to stop.

Then, picking up the *Straits Times* one day, I saw an advertisement reminding artists that entries for the Hong Kong International Portraiture Prize being held by the Hong Kong City Hall Museum and Art Gallery had to be submitted within three weeks. Obviously, I'd missed the original announcement some four months previously. I decided on the spur of the moment to enter my portrait of Mercy B. Lord, thinking it might distract me from my self-absorbed misery. No, I lie – I told myself it was perhaps a way of bringing our affair to an end in my mind and eventually my heart, that by sending her image away I might begin to heal. It was almost like a funeral. By sending her image to Hong Kong, to what amounted to its final resting place, where it had no chance of winning – of being resurrected, as it were – I was, in effect, letting go of Mercy B. Lord. When it was returned to me, I hoped I would have the strength to be able to destroy it. Or that's what I thought, anyway. I'd just have time to complete the painting if I took a week off work, using some of my holiday entitlement. When the entry form arrived I filled it in, and in the place where it called for the name of the painting I wrote, 'Thursday Girl'. Bloody pathetic, really, but there you go – those were the two words that, in effect, had cooked my goose.

As always seems to happen, the very next day I was called into the office of the minister for tourism, who briefed me on seven large paintings he required, based on architectural sketches of proposed redevelopments that tourists might visit in future. He hadn't forgotten the presentation that had originally won us the account and wanted these painted panels to form a backdrop on the town-hall stage for a presentation of the 'Magic of People' at a travel convention for a hundred senior international travel agents, flown in at the government's expense, which would be held in a little over a fortnight. There was insufficient time but there was no refusing the minister, who had himself chosen the pen and ink architectural drawings we were required to bring to life.

It meant I could kiss my portrait goodbye. But then I got lucky. A freelance graphic artist, a young German bloke recently arrived in Singapore named Helmut Kraus, called me and asked if there was any work available. 'Grab a taxi and bring your portfolio,' I said. Maybe, just maybe, the gods would smile on me.

Helmut looked like a bit of a hippy, with a full blond beard and tawny hair down to his shoulders (the hair police hadn't yet caught up with him), but his portfolio was good, very good – well disciplined with just the right artistic and commercial graphic touch. He assured me he could do the job in a week but needed a space to work in, as he was living at the YMCA.

I couldn't quite believe my luck. With a solid week working late into the night I could almost complete the portrait, giving me the following week's nights to do the finishing touches and have it framed in time to get it onto the plane to Hong Kong the following Monday. I needed to be at work the week before the travel conference to put the final touches to the international advertising campaign we had prepared for the Singapore Tourist Promotion Board (Sidebottom copy with Koo art direction and TV). It was a huge feather in our cap – the first locally produced campaign to go both to Europe and the United States.

I rented a cheap room for Helmut in the hotel across the road from the agency and proceeded to brief him thoroughly, taking him carefully through the architectural sketches. His style suited the precise rendering of the buildings and I took particular care to stress the importance of the outdoor recreational spaces, where the architects had indicated trees and greenery.

'Fill the squares and spaces with people having a good time, eating and walking, and make sure there's a lot of natural-looking greenery,' I'd stressed.

'I do vun every day. Hey, man, it's cool job!'

I'd laughed. It was an expression that wasn't common in Singapore at the time. 'Cool is great! We want the scenes to have a nice cool feeling, like enjoying a gin sling on a lazy late afternoon, the feeling of cool shade and a soft breeze blowing in on a tropical evening.'

'Ja, ja,' he agreed, 'spring I know, also gin. This is special in Singapore . . . gin spring?'

'No, gin *sling* – it's a tropical drink known as a sun-downer, because you drink it mostly in the early evening when the sun's going down.' I was beginning to realise his English comprehension wasn't all that great and that I had been over-explaining. 'Helmut, just keep the pictures looking fresh, eh?'

'Like spring. Ja, ja, I do like spring!'

'Well, no, not exactly, this is the tropics. The seasons don't change all that much. Like I said, just keep the pictures looking fresh.'

While I wasn't in the agency for the next week, I took the precaution of inspecting the first painting, after instructing Helmut to call me at home when he'd completed it. He'd called me early on Monday evening. Although the one he'd chosen to do was largely architectural, it was one of the most difficult and he'd done an excellent job. He was fast, accurate and the colour was good. I'd taken him out for a quick meal, and with that, satisfied he was up to the task, I'd foolishly left him alone for the remainder of the week, something I wouldn't have done had I been working in my office.

He called me late Friday afternoon to say he'd completed the job, and I caught a taxi to the hotel, where I very nearly had a heart attack. While technically perfect, the paintings were full of trees and flowers from Europe, cold-climate deciduous varieties – oak, birch, beech, sycamore, plane trees and the like – and the squares featured daffodils and tulips and several pink or white flowering fruit trees. The pictures were ablaze with the spirit of an English spring. Not a strelitzia, palm, bougainvillea, poinsettia, frangipani or Singapore orchid to be seen. No tropical trees, no palms, no bamboo. He'd worked indoors and perhaps he'd been smoking funny cigarettes, because he certainly hadn't bothered to glance out of the hotel window. Furthermore, the drawing featured no Singaporeans, only Europeans; he even had a white bloke pulling a rickshaw.

I felt obliged to pay him – in theory he'd done what I'd asked him to do. Sidney complained bitterly, and if it hadn't been for the fact that it was government business, he'd have refused to hand over the money. However, it meant I had to work until 2 a.m. in my studio at home for the next five days to redo the panels. I wasn't as skilled as Helmut, and when I was through with them, they had a noticeable looseness about them. Compared to the original brief from the minister, a pretty straight up and down man who'd instructed me to bring the architect's precisely rendered drawings to life, they might have looked brash or just plain slapdash. I'd used brilliant exotic colour, even mixing in a little fluoro paint I'd obtained to draw the eye away from the variations in style. Upon seeing the panels Dansford declared them simply splendid – not the most reassuring compliment as he was a 'less is more' person and the Chinese, as a general rule, favour 'more is always better'.

I told myself I'd done my best in the time available, and it just couldn't be helped. I'd screwed it up with Herr Helmut Kraus and had to complete the new panels by Friday or, as it turned out, Saturday morning at 1 a.m. They had to be in place by that afternoon for the dress rehearsal for the conference that was to open, trumpets blaring, at 10 a.m. on Sunday.

If questioned, I was going to bullshit that I'd taken my inspiration from the new international art movement coming out of tropical South America that was taking the West by storm. I didn't have the time to find out which South American countries lay within the tropics but Brazil seemed like a good guess – Copacabana beach, bikini-clad brown bodies, the samba and all that jazz. As Sidney Wing's office décor attested, the Chinese think foreign is always better than local.

One of the first principles of advertising is that if you're going to bullshit, you may as well bullshit big. Inventing a trend that doesn't exist sometimes works because it makes the other party look and feel ill-informed and behind the times. To explain, every new trend with a chance of succeeding is taken up by about 7 per cent of people, known as 'early adopters'. If this group go for an idea, then it's worth building on, and if the product or idea is a good one, it will have a better than even chance of making it in the marketplace. The key words in my bullshit explanation were 'international', 'West' and 'by storm', as the conference delegates were mostly Westerners from America and Europe, and 'by storm' hinted at a certain excitement, which we'd been sufficiently hip to be aware of in Singapore. Or, as Herr Helmut Kraus might have put it, '*Bullshit uber alle!*'

I was required to attend the conference, where Dansford and I were to present the international ad campaign we'd designed. I was drop-down-dead tired but thought that if I skipped the cocktail party after the conference and grabbed a couple of hours' sleep, I'd have Sunday night into the following morning to complete Mercy B. Lord's portrait. It had to be dispatched to Hong Kong by mid-morning on Monday. This would be only just sufficient time for it to make the final deadline.

I shall never know how I got through that week, and when I finally crashed, it was for fourteen hours. I reckon I'd averaged no more than three hours' sleep per night all week, supplemented by a handful of half-hour naps. When the taxi arrived to take the portrait to the airport on Monday I was practically hallucinating. I'd used the hairdryer Mercy B. Lord had inadvertently left behind to dry the last of the paint, and then, just as I was preparing to wrap the canvas, I was seized by a need to alter the neckline. I'd worked very carefully on some gold thread that outlined the dragon that ran around the mandarin collar of her cheongsam, its head and tail meeting at a gold wooden toggle that held the collar together at the front. But now I altered it and painted a tiny gold chisel, the blade of which ran through the dragon's head. I cannot say why or how it worked, but the portrait suddenly came to life. It was as if I could hear Mercy B. Lord breathing.

Now I was running really late and the taxi had been waiting downstairs for forty minutes, as I desperately attempted to dry the fresh paint with the hairdryer. I wrapped the canvas in heavy cardboard and plastic bubble-wrap, hoping for the best. But of course I hadn't realised that the picture would be too big to fit into the cab, and so finally – and, I feared, calamitously – we had to strap it to the roof.

When I got there they'd run out of 'Fragile' stickers, and while I'd written 'Handle with Care – Fragile!' all over the plastic wrapping with a black magic marker, it didn't really stick. The luggage handlers couldn't read English anyway, and I realised that it was simply the look of the orange and black stickers that warned them something should be handled with care.

I hadn't even had time to have Mercy B. Lord's portrait framed, so its safe transit was going to depend on the stretchers, the flimsy wooden frame and the struts used to hold the canvas taut. One bad bang on a corner and it would completely collapse. I was exhausted, which added to my feeling of anticlimax and worthlessness, and while it wasn't yet noon, I went to the airport bar and had a stiff brandy, telling myself that painting Mercy B. Lord to help me get over her had been the paramount purpose and that the Hong Kong competition was merely incidental. Even if the painting arrived intact, it was an international competition and I probably wouldn't even make the *Salon des Refusés*. I took a taxi home and slept, like I said, for fourteen hours.

The following day at work Dansford told me the conference had been a great success. He'd attended the cocktail party and said that people had congratulated him on our ad campaign, and that lots of them, two in the presence of the tourism minister, had commented on the splendid murals. One was a UK travel agent, who offered to buy three of them, and an American delegate standing close by, on hearing him ask if they were for sale, wanted another two, which pleased the minister no end. They were, of course, presented to the delegates in question, because one was a senior director of Thomas Cook and the Yank was the New York agent for American Express. The remaining two ended up in the foyer of the Tourist Promotion Board building, with the first panel painted by Helmut Kraus – the architectural one I'd originally okayed – chosen by the minister for his office wall. As the Malay Muslims say, '*Allahu Akbar* – God is the greatest'. At least I'd got something right, or got away with it without using the bullshit explanation.

With Mercy B. Lord's picture missing from my studio, I realised that what I'd taken to be the first signs of my getting over her was merely the presence in my life of the portrait project. The concentration required to get it right, to attempt to capture that moment in Raffles, had made me feel almost as if she was with me during those nights and days I worked on it. I'd paint almost every night after getting home from work until very late, and I'd be dog-tired by the time I collapsed into bed, so that I didn't lie awake thinking, drowning in my own pathetic misery. Furthermore, my libido went into the painting and the physical ache for her wasn't nearly as bad.

But after I awoke from my giant sleep it all returned in spades. In the time that had passed while I painted, each month I'd send a large and expensive bunch of something with a note, not quite as desperately entreating as the previous ones but asking if we could meet somewhere, in this way begging for a response. But the flowers boomeranged back to the agency just as they had before. I couldn't believe three months had passed and Chairman Meow was due for another visit in a couple of weeks' time.

Then, two days before she was due and just as I was about to leave for work, the phone rang. It was Elma Kelly calling from Hong Kong. 'Congratulations, Simon!' Even over the phone her voice boomed.

'Good morning, Elma . . . What for?'

'You're famous, my boy!'

'Huh? Why?' I replied.

'You're on the front page of the *Morning Post*!'

'I beg your pardon?' I asked, momentarily mystified. But then I thought it might be an ad, part of our international Tourist Promotion

Board campaign. She'd know it was mine. Though it was unusual to get one on the front page of the *South China Morning Post*, if I was right, then Johnny Wing's media buying was definitely improving.

'You mean you haven't been told?'

'Elma, what are you talking about?'

'You've won, Simon! You've won the International Portraiture Prize for "Thursday Girl"! I'm *terribly, terribly* proud of you!'

'Oh, Jesus! What now?' I heard myself exclaim.

'Now? Why, dear boy, you're the toast of Hong Kong! Wouldn't be at all surprised if there's a street parade! It's the first time in thirty years of the competition that it's been won by an artist in the region. Jolly good thing you look Chinese, what! Ha, ha. We're all terribly thrilled. Why didn't you tell me?'

'It was just a whim. I didn't bother telling anyone. This is really very unexpected, Elma.' It wasn't an entirely truthful answer, but how could I explain that sending the painting to Hong Kong had been a metaphorical funeral of the heart? It wasn't something you could talk about.

'I'm calling from a phone box across the road from the gallery, waiting for it to open,' Elma continued. 'There's already a long queue forming. Dear, dear Simon, I am so proud of you . . . Must go and join the crush. Goodbye, dear boy!'

After Elma had rung off, all I could think of was that I hoped to Christ the news didn't reach Singapore. I would have compromised Mercy B. Lord in one fell swoop – far worse than simply questioning her whereabouts on Thursdays. I'd almost given up on ever seeing her again, but if there had still been a tiny chance, I'd have blown it forever when the news of the win got out locally. For a start, the Tourist Board people would immediately recognise her – Molly Ong and Long Me Saw and a host of others had met her – and they would be bound to want to make a fuss. So would the newspapers and magazines and possibly the television stations. A pretty girl – correction, a beautiful woman – especially one of your own, is always news. I realised I would have blown my chances big-time. We'd have to be seen and, no doubt, photographed together, and that was not only going to be awkward, but would look like a conspiracy on my part to bring us together again. 'Ouch!' I could feel myself blushing at the thought, at the same time as my heart beat faster at the possibility of seeing her again.

I'd almost convinced myself that a portrait win in an art competition in another country wasn't exactly world-shattering news to the people of Singapore, but on my way to work I stopped the taxi to pick up a copy of the *Straits Times*. The announcement might be buried somewhere in the back section of the newspaper. If so, if anyone approached me in the office, at least I'd know. I opened the neatly folded paper and there it was on the front page, the portrait taking up almost half the page. The headline read:

ASIAN ARTIST
WINS
INTERNATIONAL
PRIZE

Seeing Mercy B. Lord looking at me in miniature and out of context in the newspaper, I realised with a start that I really had captured that moment at Raffles. At the same instant I realised fully what I had done to her. *Shit! Shit! Shit! What now?*

The 'What now?' began to build on the horizon like a cumulonimbus cloud invading a clear blue sky. I arrived at the agency to find Alice Ho in a rare tizz. 'Mr Sidney wants you to go up right away,' she announced.

'Did he say why?' I asked, knowing she wouldn't know but trying to appear casual.

'He not happy, Simon,' she replied. 'You see newspaper? Also this morning radio!' She was obviously impressed and shot me a look that was as close to sympathetic as she ever got.

I knocked on Sidney's door. 'Come!' he called. I hated this imperious monosyllable and on past occasions I'd thanked him for his generous welcome, my sarcasm completely lost on him.

Alice Ho had, no doubt, alerted him, because as I entered I saw that he sat rigid with his stomach pressed against the edge of his desk, the *Straits Times* in front of him. He jabbed hard at the picture of Mercy B. Lord. 'What the fuck is this?' he barked.

I deliberately walked over to the side of the desk and looked down at his indignant finger resting on Mercy B. Lord's breast. Attempting to keep my voice normal, I said, 'Oh, that. What do you think?' as if anxious to hear his opinion of the likeness.

'Think?' he shouted. 'Think?' he repeated. 'How dare you!'

'I beg your pardon?' I said, my tone deliberately more surprised than defensive.

Sidney suddenly lost it completely. 'She's not yours to paint!' He clenched his fist and banged it down hard on the desk. 'She's mine, you hear? She's *my* property!' He banged the desk a second time, the corners of his mouth spit-flecked with anger.

'Oh? Your concubine? Your mistress?' My heart was now beating furiously and I knew that in moments I'd be hyperventilating, my anger overwhelming me.

Sidney Wing pointed to the door. 'Get out! Get out of my office!' he screamed.

I only just made it with dignity, closing his office door behind me and bending double to suck in air, then straightening to take a couple more deep breaths. I'd won the most important art competition in South-East Asia and I was up to my eyebrows in excrement.

This was only the beginning of a very long day. I got back to my glass cage, stopping on the way to greet several of the staff members, knowing that they'd all be aware of the news but afraid to react, conscious, as if by some kind of osmosis, that the chairman was angry. And so, in a very Chinese way, they pretended not to know a thing. I'd barely reached my desk when the phone went. It was Alice Ho again. 'Simon, people come.'

'People?'

'They from the newspaper, also others, they got television camera. Miss Karlene, she big shot on the television, Simon. They all, they ask they can see you? How I tell them?' I felt sure there were lots of switchboard operators in Singapore with perfect diction whom we could have hired, but Alice Ho had been with the Wings since the beginning and they trusted her implicitly. She wasn't afraid of anything or anyone, and even Sidney and Johnny greeted her when they came in. While her loyalties clearly lay with the Wings, she wasn't a bad old stick.

'Alice, please tell them I'll be there in ten minutes. Something urgent has come up. Thank them for their patience.'

'I think Miss Karlene this urgent, Simon.'

'Ten minutes, Alice.'

'I tell,' she replied with a sigh.

Even the implacable Alice Ho was thrown by a phalanx of reporters with cameras crowding into her reception area; the TV crew, in particular, would have freaked her out. Miss Karlene, a name that could have belonged to a Kings Cross transvestite stripper, was obviously well known. I admit I wasn't much looking forward to facing the press, but my most urgent and immediate task was to get a note of apology to Mercy B. Lord. I sat down to write it, knowing I had little or no time to think it out. But first I called Connie Song at Corona Flowers in Orchard Road.

'Connie, do you have a dozen yellow roses?' Yellow, because Chairman Meow, despite disastrously sending the pink roses to Charles Brickman, the chairman of the agency in Australia, had always maintained that yellow roses indicate friendship.

'No, Simon,' she said, recognising my voice, 'white, red or pink.'

White was for Chinese funerals, red meant romance, and pink wasn't quite right under the circumstances, but would have to do. 'The pink, then. Are they long-stemmed?'

'Yes, fresh off the plane from Taiwan, first flight in this morning.'

'I'll have a dozen. Can you do them up nicely but not lovey-dovey, and I'll send a messenger boy around to pick them up.' 'Lovey-dovey' was Connie's term for a wide pink silk shantung ribbon with a crimson silk heart, half the size of a female fist, attached. The flowers were nestled in white tissue and shiny chocolate-brown paper. All my previous floral entreaties had been sent with ribbon and heart attached, and while they never appeared on the boomeranged bunches in the foyer, I secretly wondered if Alice Ho had a reception desk drawer that held a collection of red hearts and a couple of hundred feet of pink silk shantung ribbon.

My dear Mercy B. Lord,

How can I possibly apologise? You will no doubt have seen this morning's newspaper and be justifiably angry. You must believe me when I say I never harboured the slightest hope that I would win. If, as I suspect, I have hurt or upset you, then I most humbly beg your forgiveness. That was never and could never be my intention.

Simon

It wasn't much of a note but I sealed it and yelled over the partition for Louis Fi, the young dispatch boy, whom I called Louie da Fly because he seemed always to be buzzing around, sticking his nose into other people's business. It was the name of a character from a famous Australian animated TV commercial for a popular brand of insecticide.

Louie da Fly appeared seemingly out of nowhere, as flies are wont to do. 'Yes, boss?'

I instructed him to pick up the roses and to deliver them along with the note to the Beatrice Fong Agency, urging him to hurry and handing him the money for a taxi, aware he would keep most of it and take a rickshaw instead.

Reluctantly, I went down to meet the press, who by this time filled the reception area and spilled outside, a veritable babble of reporters and photographers, as well as a television crew of a woman and two men. The TV guys, both tall and good-looking, were on camera and sound, and the woman – well put together, tall, blonde and athletic – was obviously the interviewer. She pushed her way forward, calling 'Mr Koo!', protected on either side by the TV cameraman with his heavy camera on his shoulder and the sound technician with boom and sound-sock, who was also wielding the camera tripod.

'Yes, good morning, ma'am.'

'Karlene Stein, *Karlene's People.* Congratulations! Well done!' Her voice was nicely modulated, with what was known as a mid-Atlantic accent – you couldn't quite place it, but it was much favoured by Australian broadcasters who hadn't yet come to terms with their own accent and generally thought the way we spoke was ill-suited to radio and television. The same went for TV commercials. The accent was phoney but everyone used it and nobody ever questioned it. That is, until an ad man named John Singleton used 'fair dinkum' voices in his commercials and the mid-Atlantic accent sank slowly beneath the waves and drowned.

'Thank you, Miss Stein. Please call me Simon.'

Karlene Stein extended her hand, gripped mine firmly and said as she released it, 'We'd like to do a five-minute interview for tonight's show, Simon.'

'Bit noisy,' I grinned, indicating the reporters with a nod.

To Alice Ho's and my astonishment, Karlene Stein stepped out of her court shoes and jumped up onto the reception desk. While the desk wasn't that high, it was a pretty impressive feat. 'Basketball,' she said, laughing down at me. Then, smiling broadly, she held up her hand and addressed the other reporters, her accent now clearly Australian. 'Righto, everyone, your attention, please!' Her leap onto the desk had brought everyone to instant silence and now she stood, bare-foot, legs apart, totally in command, with Alice Ho's round face framed between her tanned calf muscles. 'Just give me ten minutes and we're out of here. If you'll now please wait outside very quietly, I'll buy you all an ice-cream.' This brought a roar of laughter, and the reporters and photographers good-humouredly trooped out of reception to wait outside. Karlene Stein was obviously a woman of character and one who, I imagined, usually got her way. 'Please don't let me down, Simon.

I've now more or less promised they'll all get time with you,' she said, looking down at me.

I nodded. 'Do I get an ice-cream, Miss?' I noticed her toenails were painted bright pink.

'Of course, vanilla and chocolate,' she laughed. She wasn't just a pretty face. Hopping off the desk to land lightly on her toes, she accepted the microphone from the sound man, and I noted that the camera and tripod were now set up and the cameraman was ready to go. This was an efficient outfit. Alice Ho beamed at me; Karlene Stein had obviously won her heart.

Suddenly all business, Karlene Stein explained that she would do the background in the studio that evening and then go to this interview. 'Okay, I'll start by congratulating you and we'll take it from there.'

If I appeared to be enjoying this, I wasn't. But what could I do under the circumstances? I suppose I could have played the temperamental artist and told them all to go to buggery, but I wasn't the type to spit the dummy. It was Chairman Meow's conditioning, I guess. I could hear her now: 'Simon, everyone knows we're filthy rich. They expect us to be rude, to flaunt our wealth, so always be very polite.' Then she'd add, 'Not everyone can be rich, but we are all capable of good manners.' They were only doing their jobs and Sidney Wing had provided enough aggression in what, I was beginning to realise, was going to be a very long and tiring day.

Karlene lifted the microphone and began the interview. 'Mr Koo, firstly, my congratulations. You are the first Singaporean to win this very prestigious prize.' She smiled. 'How does it feel?' She pushed the hand-held microphone close to my mouth.

'Well, first of all, I'm Australian, and I guess I'm somewhat bemused.'

'Cut!' Karlene snapped. 'No, no, Simon, that's not what I want.'

'Oh, sorry,' I said.

She looked at me sternly. 'This is Singapore television for Singaporeans. Someone in our community has just been greatly honoured and he promptly gives away all the glory to another country? No, we simply can't have it.'

'Well, you're an Australian, aren't you?'

'Not on television! Here I'm Singapore's Karlene Stein. *Karlene's People* is local and loyal. The prime minister likes it that way and so do I. By the way, "bemused" is not a word I'd choose myself.'

'Well, what do you want me to say?' My first interview had got off to a bad start. Karlene Stein was no purring pussycat with an ego to stroke.

'Just say how proud you are, the usual blah, blah. Now, shall we begin again?' She nodded to the men on sound and camera. 'Mr Koo, firstly, my congratulations! You are the first Singaporean to win this very prestigious art prize.' She smiled. 'How does it feel?'

'Please call me Simon. How does it feel?' I smiled and shook my head. 'Very surprising. I haven't won an art prize since primary school.'

Karlene nodded her approval. 'And now the big one! The Hong Kong International Portraiture Prize is, I believe, the third biggest in the world. Only London and Venice are bigger.'

'Oh, I didn't know that.'

'Now, let's talk about your gorgeous model, the Thursday Girl. A Singapore girl, I take it – and, I must say, very beautiful.'

I grinned. 'Yes, true on both counts: born and raised here, stunning looks and, may I add, also very intelligent.'

She laughed. 'Just a typical local girl then.' Karlene Stein certainly knew which side her bread was buttered. I could almost hear the canned laughter.

'Yes, truly lovely.'

'And her name?'

The question was reasonable enough but nonetheless came as a surprise. I was conscious of wanting to protect Mercy B. Lord and now I was faced with a direct question that would expose her. I hesitated then said, 'This has all been very sudden and I haven't had an opportunity to talk to her. She may not wish to reveal her name.' I looked appealingly at Karlene. 'Would you mind if I left it for her to decide?'

'Ah, a real gentleman, of course not.' She smiled a TV smile. 'We'll just call her the Thursday Girl, shall we?' I sensed that Karlene wasn't happy and her next question sounded a tad sharp. 'Why have you named your portrait "Thursday Girl"? Is she a real person?'

'I beg you pardon?'

'Well, perhaps she is a composite of several women . . .'

Keep your cool, Simon. 'Ah, I can't think why anyone would do that. I'm an artist, I love women, but I love them just the way God made them: fat, thin, old, young, however they come. The way Thursday Girl came was how I painted her.' I spread my hands and shrugged. 'Simple. As for the name, again, simple enough, I first met her on a Thursday.'

'And just how did you two meet?'

If I was supposed to be a local Singaporean, I couldn't very well explain that she'd been my guide for my first two weeks here. 'Ah, we met through business,' I said. It was the best I could do.

'And it started from there?' Her question was obviously loaded, her eyebrow just slightly raised.

'Started? I asked her if I could paint her portrait, yes. We agreed to three sittings.' I paused. 'It was very kind of her to indulge me, to give me that much of her time.'

'And that is all there is to it?' Bang, the loaded pistol fired. 'You know, artist and model?' She smiled knowingly.

'I wish!' I exclaimed, pretending to laugh. 'Look at me! I'm not exactly God's gift to women and my subject is a particularly beautiful one. It was privilege enough just to be allowed to paint her.'

'Nicely put, and thank you, Simon Koo. Well, I do hope we all get to meet the mystery Thursday Girl on this program soon.' She laughed again. 'That would be a real Koo!' Canned laughter would follow that pun as sure as God made little apples. Karlene Stein was a true professional and it wasn't any surprise that *Karlene's People* ran in a prime-time slot: the half-hour leading up to the evening news. While there was only one camera and it was positioned on me throughout, I knew that they'd do close-up takes afterwards of her asking the same questions or showing her reactions to my answers. Karlene struck me as someone who liked the camera, and the camera, I imagined, would like her.

It took another hour to get the other interviews done and I was emotionally pretty whacked by the time they were all over. Alice handed me at least a dozen messages from calls that had come in asking me to make contact. 'Very happy day for me, Simon. I meet Miss Karlene!' she exclaimed.

I detoured to Dansford's office on the way back to my own, which, since the demise of my relationship with Mercy B. Lord, had been rechristened 'The Coffee Percolator' due to the number of cups of black coffee I'd taken to drinking.

Dansford leaned back in his chair as I entered. 'Well, what can I say? Do I congratulate you or what?'

'Don't,' I sighed, taking a seat.

'Awkward. Does she know? Of course she would. Has anyone contacted you?'

'Sidney read me the riot act and threw me out of his office.'

'Oh dear, that wasn't very smart of him.'

'Yeah, he practically imploded, banged his first on the table, both fists – "She's mine, you hear? She's *my* property!" he screamed at me.'

'Well, that certainly lets the cat out of the bag. Not very Chinese, eh? He must have been pretty mad.'

'Mad as a cut snake! What shall I do? Should I resign?'

'Hardly seems worth it, with so little time to go on your contract. What you did was careless, but that's strictly between you and her. Now that he's cooled down, he'll be furious with himself for handing you the advantage.'

'Advantage? Believe you me, I know I've been a complete idiot. It never occurred to me I could possibly win the bloody competition. Never entered my mind! It was just . . . you know, a deadline to work to . . . the Hong Kong thing, take my mind off . . . you know. Then, having to repaint the panels for the convention, I was pushing shit uphill with a broken stick and hardly had time to think.'

Dansford grinned. 'Very colourful metaphor. How'd you go with the press? In particular, Singapore's own Karlene Stein? She's no lightweight.'

'Okay, I think. At least I managed to keep Mercy B. Lord's name out of it.'

'She'll have it by tonight, Simon.'

'Yeah, but not from me.'

'I'll see what I can do.'

'Do? What, threaten them? They're our only TV station. As it is we have to beg for time.'

'You're right,' Dansford said, not explaining further.

I rose, sighed heavily and said, 'Well, I guess I'm just going to have to cop it sweet. My own fault entirely . . . Shit! Shit! Shit!' I was feeling decidedly sorry for myself again.

Dansford gave me a sympathetic smile. 'If it helps, know that I'm on your side, Simon. It might help to keep me in the loop. A friend in need and all that.'

'Thanks, mate, I appreciate it.'

It was almost midday when I got back to my office. I went through my phone messages: one from Mrs Sidebottom, the remainder from Hong Kong newspapers and magazines asking me to call urgently, and one from Chairman Meow, also from Hong Kong. I concluded that as she was due here in two days she'd stopped off for a bit of shopping, something she occasionally did. The last message was from Molly Ong, the ex-Miss Singapore and my client at the Tourist Promotion Board. I dialled the number and she answered herself.

'Hi, Molly. Simon returning your call. Sorry it took so long. It's been one of those days.'

'Simon, wonderful news! Congratulations. We're all terribly chuffed. How do you feel?'

I tried to sound normal. 'Weird. Not at all what I expected. It came as a shock, really.'

'A nice one, I hope.'

I laughed. 'I'm not sure. The place has been crawling with reporters all morning.'

'Oh, dear, I know what you mean. After I won the you-know-what,

I grew very weary of smiling, looking suitably modest and answering the same questions over and over again for months. That's the hardest part, making it seem as if you're hearing the question for the first time!' She laughed. 'I was actually quite pleased when I missed out on Miss Universe. Everyone here was happy that I'd entered, and it finally stopped the questions.' She paused then said, 'Simon, Long Me and I have been talking. I mean, this morning, on the phone. He's staying with Long Long Saw in Hong Kong and he saw this morning's *South China Morning Post*. We have an idea. A good one, I think.'

'What, for the Tourist Board?'

'Yes, of course.'

'Okay,' I said, hesitantly.

'It fits in perfectly with our slogan, "The Magic of People", but gives it a different slant. Not just waiters, bus boys, cheerful taxi drivers, boat people, rickshaw drivers, cooks, kids, friendly people but also glamour. Your winning picture being the inspiration.'

'Oh? How's that?'

'Well, what if every year the Tourist Promotion Board picks someone we name the Singapore Girl, a young Singaporean who is not only beautiful but also has brains, someone with enormous presence. Her job would be to travel all over the world, running seminars and acting as an ambassador representing Singapore tourism.'

My heart was beating faster almost from the first sentence. It was a great idea but I knew what was coming.

'We'd launch with your portrait of Mercy B. Lord, and she'd be our first Singapore Girl. The job would carry a good salary and afterwards, if she chooses, a career in tourism, maybe even a scholarship to study tourism at an American university. At the end of the year we'd have you, or some famous portrait painter, paint her picture. Even more publicity.' She paused, clearly excited. 'What do you think?'

It was only just past noon and now the day I'd been desperately attempting to hold together was finally blown to smithereens. Just then, Louie da Fly tapped on the glass, holding up an envelope. I nodded for him to come in and accepted it silently, then took a deep breath before answering Molly Ong.

'Molly, it's a great idea. I'd be lying if I said any different. Singapore Girl will make a great campaign, but . . .'

'You don't like it?' Molly cut in.

'No, no, like I said, it's a great idea. Spectacular. But I don't think Mercy B. Lord will agree.'

There was a silence at the other end that seemed to last an eternity. When Molly spoke at last she sounded shocked. 'Simon, I can't believe what I'm hearing. There can't be a young woman in Singapore who wouldn't give just about anything to do this – first-class air travel around the world anywhere and everywhere, and at the end of twelve months an education and a career! You can't be serious.'

It was time to come clean. 'We're not together any longer, Molly.'

'Oh, I'm sorry. You've broken up?'

'Yes.'

'Bad?'

'Not good.'

'Your fault?'

'It's complicated.'

'Simon, it's always complicated – she's a woman. May I talk to her?'

'Molly, it's been months.'

'And you haven't spoken?'

'No.'

'Hmm. But you don't mind if I do?'

'Of course not.'

'And if she agreed, you'd work with her?'

'Of course.'

'No bad blood?'

'Not from me.'

'Tell me, Simon, do you still love her? You two were gorgeous together.'

'Yes . . . with all my heart.'

'Ah! That makes it difficult,' Molly said.

After she'd hung up I put my elbows on the desk and clutched my head in disbelief. By winning the painting prize I'd created one almighty fuck-up. Then I realised I still had Louie da Fly's envelope in my hand. It looked familiar, and it was. My own note to Mercy B. Lord had been returned. I opened it.

My dear Mercy B. Lord,

How can I possibly apologise? You will no doubt have seen this morning's newspaper and be justifiably angry. You must believe me when I say I never harboured the slightest hope that I would win. If, as I suspect, I have hurt or upset you, then I most humbly beg your forgiveness. That was never and could never be my intention.

Simon

I started to laugh, not funny-ha-ha, but in spite of everything. At least it was a tangible response, the first in months. I called over to Louie da Fly, who came in. 'Louie da Fly, what happened to the pink roses?'

'She don't want, Simon. Give me back.'

'Right, and then?'

'My mother, I give my mother.'

I opened my hand and held it out towards the dispatch boy. 'Okay, hand it over, you little shit.'

He reached into his pocket, produced two one-dollar notes and placed them in my hand.

'And the rest!'

He dug into his trouser pocket again and produced another dollar. 'That's all, boss.'

'Louie da Fly, you're either insulting my intelligence or you're stupid. What's it to be?'

'Not stupid, boss.'

'Righto, hand over the rest.' He produced another two bucks. Louie da Fly didn't like anyone to think him stupid, even if it cost him money.

'Okay, but next time I expect more. They cost me twelve bucks. You sold them for half price.'

'Buyer's market, boss. No fucking time, must come back work!' he grinned.

'Yeah, yeah, sure.' I stuffed five bucks in my shirt pocket and handed him one.

He looked disdainfully down at the crumpled note in his hand. 'Maybe next time I give flower to my mum,' he said in disgust.

'Maybe next time I kick your arse. Now vamoose!'

Catching out Louie da Fly looked like being the only win of the day and it was, to say the least, a hollow victory. I looked down at my note with the one word, 'BASTARD!', scrawled across it. What was I thinking? It was another total defeat. The word itself was written by someone whose hand was shaking badly. Mercy B. Lord must have been very, very angry.

And I had yet to phone Chairman Meow. I decided to leave that pleasure for last. She was probably out shopping, anyway.

Louie da Fly was back again with the afternoon mail, a single letter for me. He seemed reluctant to leave, standing at the open door.

'What is it, Louie da Fly?'

'Why you send pretty flower to bad old lady, boss?'

'Old lady? What do you mean, mate?'

'Very old, two stick.' He hunched over almost double, pretending to be supporting himself on two walking sticks, his neck stretched out in the manner of an old crone. 'Very cross, shouting old lady.'

'You gave the roses to an old lady at the Beatrice Fong Agency?'

'Ja, ja, the switch for the telephone, she tell me wait. Then she take me, we go upstair into room same size like your. Also desk, but Chinese dragon leg and . . .'

'Carved?'

'Ja, ja, much carve, also chair, not carve.' He pointed to my swivel chair. 'New one like your. Room dark, only one light on desk, small one. She tell me wait, then comes old mother, very old, maybe 100 year, clop . . . clop . . . clop . . . clop . . . two stick, very, very slow.'

Louie da Fly obviously possessed a strong sense of the dramatic. 'Chinese?'

'Ja, ja, she sit very slow in chair. Much pain, I think. Old bone. Switch girl, she help and take her stick, she tell I must give flower and letter.'

I spoke Cantonese better than Louie da Fly spoke English, but he liked to show off and I usually indulged him. But this was an unexpected turn of events and I was suddenly impatient. Louie da Fly's English was tediously slow as he searched for words. He was from a poor Straits-Chinese family and had obviously attended a local Chinese-language school – the family was probably too poor for him to complete his education, but he was a bright kid. I was anxious to hear the rest as accurately as possible. 'Tell me in Cantonese,' I instructed.

Louie da Fly looked hurt. Nothing unusual in that – he was an actor from way back. 'My English, you don't like?'

'Louie da Fly, your English is very good but I'm in a hurry.'

He then told me in Cantonese how the old lady had taken out a magnifying glass and instructed the switchboard girl to open the envelope and then the note and place it in front of her, directly under the table lamp, where she read it carefully. She'd then called for a calligraphy brush and ink and slowly written *BASTARD!* across my note, whereupon she'd knocked the roses from the desk onto the carpet and turned slowly in the swivel chair, pointing to the fallen roses, her face now almost completely in shadow. Louie da Fly reverted to English. 'I can see much gold in tooths and the eyes, very shine,' he said. Then, speaking again in Cantonese, he explained that he'd picked up the roses while she instructed the switchboard girl to fold my note, replace it in the original envelope and hand it to him. '"Tell the one who sent this letter he is *chusheng!*" she spit.' Louie da Fly looked at me and asked once again in English, 'Why you send very bad old lady flower, boss?'

I sighed, pretty shaken by the whole description, but trying hard not to show my emotion in front of a kid of fifteen. *Chusheng* means 'animal', and telling someone they are born from an animal . . . Well, there are few worse insults in Chinese. I reached into my shirt pocket and fished out the five dollars I'd previously confiscated and added a further five from my wallet. 'Buy your mother some roses, kid,' I said in English.

He accepted the notes in the customary manner with both hands. 'Thank you, boss.' Then, ingenuously, he added, 'Maybe I tell lie before. Maybe my mum, she dead long time.'

I tried to grin. 'Scram! Beat it, kid!' I said, waving him away with a flick of the hand.

I didn't know whether to laugh with relief or cry from a mixture of frustration and dismay: relief because it was Beatrice Fong and not Mercy B. Lord who had scrawled the crude reply on my note; frustration because I was no nearer to reaching her; and dismay because she was obviously under the direction of or captive to others and may well have been all along. Patently, Beatrice Fong was involved and it seemed certain now that Sidney Wing was implicated. Whatever it was had been going on a long time. What could it be? Mercy B. Lord wasn't some compliant, weak-willed, dependent young female. She knew her own mind, was resourceful, even stubborn at times, and she certainly had a will of her own – she was nobody's fool. They, whoever 'they' might be, had something over her that was sufficiently powerful to control her life, something almost certainly to do with disappearing Thursday. The portrait win had obviously set the cat among the pigeons, which was putting it much too mildly if she was in danger. Then I realised that, for now at least, because of the publicity surrounding the prize, she was probably safe.

I had no doubt whatsoever that the press – in particular, Karlene Stein – would eventually find her. Molly Ong most certainly would. The Singapore Girl concept was hers, and it was a good one and fitted perfectly with the portrait award. There were people who claimed Molly got the job with the Tourist Promotion Board simply because she had been Miss Singapore, but they were wrong. She had a very good mind and her ideas were invariably sound. The Singapore Girl idea was extra good and she wasn't going to let it go in a hurry.

Sidney Wing would know that if Mercy B. Lord disappeared there would be a huge ruckus and the publicity would spread well beyond Singapore. It was just the kind of incident the PAP government tried to avoid, and they'd almost certainly become involved. Associated as she was bound to be with the winning portrait, Mercy B. Lord would automatically became a high-profile missing person, and that would wreak havoc on tourism in Singapore, quite apart from anything else.

At Dansford's pink hair cocktail party, Molly Ong had taken a particular shine to Mercy B. Lord, as had Long Me Saw, who reputedly knew a beautiful woman when he saw one. Even the minister had seemed captivated by her charm. Having initially endangered her with the portrait win, paradoxically I had probably now ensured her safety. Nonetheless, it didn't make things any better, knowing I had placed her in a very difficult position and compromised her privacy. Any hopes I'd hitherto harboured of having Mercy B. Lord back in my life were now well and truly gone. I felt a fool. I was a fool.

I opened the letter that had come in the mail. It was from the Hong Kong City Hall Museum and Art Gallery and was dated three days previously. Delivery was usually next day in the new Singapore, but these things happen, I guess. It announced my win and the prize of 5000 Hong Kong dollars. I only wished I could have been happy about this or given it to Mercy B. Lord. Additionally, the letter invited me to the awards dinner in two weeks' time – 'lounge suit preferred' – at which I had been allocated a table for eight personal guests as well as myself and my partner. Finally, it offered to pay for two air tickets from Singapore and overnight accommodation – a suite, compliments of the Peninsula Hotel, where the awards dinner was to take place. I couldn't help imagining how all this might have been different, with Mercy B. Lord on my arm in the black cheongsam and red patent-leather stilettos, the portrait brought to life.

I spent the remainder of the afternoon returning telephone messages from local and far-flung places in South-East Asia, even one from *The Age* in Melbourne, and I began to sympathise with Molly Ong on the subject of repetitious questions. Imagination is not a quality that appears to characterise many in the media. It was after five when I finally phoned Chairman Meow, who was staying at the Hong Kong Hilton. I expected her to be a bit cranky about waiting all day for my call. As a general rule, she didn't take kindly to waiting for anyone, unless she'd allowed for it in her plans. She was prompt in returning calls, either business or personal, and procrastination wasn't one of her faults. Moreover, unlike my dad, she'd never been wholly enthusiastic about my desire to become an artist, so I doubted she'd be thrilled by my win. Chairman Meow ran on one track when it came to her only son and, as far as she was concerned, that track led directly to the chairman's office. But I was quite wrong.

Hearing my voice, she went directly into rapture mode. 'Darling, congratulations, I'm thrilled!' she almost trilled. 'Wonderful, simply wonderful! Imagine! I'm here for a few days' shopping before coming over to see you, and I open the *South China Morning Post* at breakfast in my suite this morning and there you are! My son! My famous son!'

'Mum, it's not such a big deal,' I protested.

'No? Only the front page! Only the first Asian ever to win! What are you talking about? I picked up the phone and ordered the hotel limo to take me directly to the gallery. Not a big deal! There was a queue a hundred yards long waiting for it to open. Simon, your mother stood in a queue, can you imagine that? Not only a queue but also for half an hour! There's a banner stretched across the whole outside of the front of the building that reads "Simon Koo's Thursday Girl".

'Oh my God, and the girl! I stood transfixed for an hour. I looked into her eyes. I just stood there and looked. Simon, she's got everything we need! I can tell.'

I felt a sudden pain as my stomach muscles clenched. 'No *guanxi*, Mum.'

There was barely a pause. 'I don't care! I can tell she's the one! In my bones, my blood! And to think you've been hiding her from me all this time!'

'Mum, listen!' I pleaded.

'Simon, I'm catching the plane tomorrow. I know it's a day early, but I can't wait. I must meet this glorious creature!'

'Mum, listen, *please* listen – she's *not* mine.'

CHAPTER TWELVE

A TABLE FOR EIGHT guests for the awards night presented an immediate problem: I knew three strong women, Chairman Meow, Elma Kelly and Mrs Sidebottom. The latter, since she'd been fitted with dentures, was no longer a shrinking violet (the scam at Raffles should have alerted me), and had emerged as a garrulous and forceful character in her own right. With sweet breath and a constant smile, Mrs Sidebottom now attended the frequent Tourist Promotion Board meetings, which allowed me to be absent from time to time. Apart from writing excellent copy, she also contributed sound and original promotion ideas. The newly 'indentured' Sidebottom was no longer backward in coming forward and held her own in the company of Molly Ong and Long Me Saw, both forceful people not short of an opinion. Long Me Saw, who possessed a wicked sense of humour, privately referred to her as 'Full-frontal Sidebottom', while Molly Ong happily teamed up with her to demand that the woman's point of view be introduced into the tourism platform.

Somewhat unfortunately, she gave all the credit for the transformation of her life to me. While I insisted Cecil had been solely responsible and should be given the credit, he didn't help matters by maintaining that without my encouragement – in fact, he used the word 'permission' – he could not have made the decision on his own. Previously beholden to his wife, Cecil was now completely under the thumb of the diminutive Sylvia with the arctic-blue eyes.

I only mention this because Mrs Sidebottom had assumed the role of my surrogate mother. While all three of the older women in my life were very different, they all in their own ways exhibited strong proprietorial feelings towards me. My mum packed twice the punch as both Chairman Meow and my actual mother; then hard on her heels came the avuncular (why is there no female equivalent?), singular Elma Kelly, all guns blazing; and now the new Full-frontal Sidebottom had added herself to my growing list of mother figures. All expressed concern for my lovelorn state, Elma Kelly and Mrs Sidebottom because they knew of Mercy B. Lord's departure from my life, and Chairman Meow, aka Mum, because her matchmaking attempts had all been stymied. But now, consumed by the beautiful woman she had seen in the portrait, my mother seemed determined to secure her for her only son. All three believed they would be the one to ameliorate my unhappiness.

My immediate concern about the awards dinner was that all these women would come together for the first time at my table. Even worse, to the three forceful women would be added an inebriated Dansford, Cecil, the chain-smoking mouse, and possibly Long Me Saw and Molly Ong. Molly was not exactly a wallflower herself, while the movie mogul, now in his sixties, wasn't accustomed to taking a back seat even with presidents and royalty present. I took some comfort from the fact that he was very unlikely to attend.

If Long Me were to accept my personal invitation, his only possible reason would be a whimsical one. The Saw brothers were generous patrons of the arts in Hong Kong and elsewhere, and the committee would have sent them an invitation to sit at the governor's table. Nevertheless, it seemed only polite for me to invite him. If I had been truly Chinese, inviting him to be a guest at my table would have been seen as extremely dangerous. If he refused, as seemed certain, then I would lose enormous face. Conversely, if he accepted, I would gain in equal proportion. But the chances of his accepting were very small, and for most Chinese the risk of refusal would have been too great.

Money is in almost all cases the sole arbiter of social standing and importance amongst the Chinese, but there are a very few instances where, in addition to wealth, there exists undisputable status in its own right. If extreme wealth allows you to sit at the table of your peers, the status of *tai-pan* entitles you to be seated at its head. Only royalty, presidents or, in a British colony such as Hong Kong, the governor would take precedence.

The Saw brothers were both *tai-pans*, and although our family wealth, had they known about it, would probably have gained my dad a seat at the far end of the banquet table, the Saw brothers' influence in Asia and their *guanxi* were such that there would have to have been a very specific and additional reason apart from mere wealth for someone like Chairman Meow to be included in their social stratum.

The fact that Long Me Saw sat on the Singapore Tourist Promotion Board was a feather in the board's cap and not his own. His presence gave Singapore added importance in the world of entertainment and travel. The further fact that he took the role seriously and worked at it, rather than simply appending his illustrious family name to the letterhead, was an indication of his character. He certainly stood to gain nothing in influence or power and needed no favours from government.

The Long Me Saw I knew from board meetings was a nice bloke: he listened, was polite and his opinions on ad campaigns and promotions were always worth considering. But my presence in his life was purely coincidental and it would have been foolish to think otherwise. I was simply the creative ad guy who attended strategy meetings. I admit that while it was proper to invite him, given the already potent mixture at my table, I would have been hugely relieved if he refused, as seemed certain – never mind the loss of face. On the other hand, if he accepted, I feared my bowels mightn't be entirely trustworthy.

Molly Ong's very clever concept of the Singapore Girl, with Mercy B. Lord as the template for others to follow, may well have been discussed with or approved by Long Me, and he might just see his attendance at the awards night as Tourist Promotion Board business.

There were two other reasons, apart from the explosive mix of guests, for my anxiety at having Long Me Saw present on the big night. The first – bizarre as this may seem to a Westerner – was his concern about being kidnapped. Long Me Saw and his brother Long Long were paranoid about being kidnapped by the Black Society, a branch of the Triads who made kidnapping the very wealthy their criminal *raison d'être*. Kidnapping the very rich or their loved ones was a highly organised and professional criminal activity and by no means uncommon in Asia. The fear of the Black Society was ever-present in the minds of the Saws and other extremely rich families, and their paranoia was easy to understand. They and members of their families required protection around the clock. A favourite method of the Black Society was to kidnap a loved one and ask for a large sum of money. When this was paid, they'd push the envelope by refusing to release the hostage and would start sending bits and pieces through the mail – a finger, an ear, a nipple, male genitals, a nose, even an eye. Each mailing would up the ante until they were satisfied. If the family had been milked beyond its means or refused to pay up, they would find what was left of their loved one dumped on the front doorstep.

However, protection against a Triad kidnapping wasn't simply a matter of having an armed guard, or guards, present at all times, like a president or prime minister in the West. A Black Society Triad gang had to be made to understand that the retaliation would be greater than anything they themselves could engineer. The Saw brothers and their families would have been paying enormous amounts for a kung fu master or two of great standing and respect to discourage Triad gangs. The gangs would be aware that these masters had a huge, totally loyal and absolutely lethal following who wouldn't hesitate to go to war on their behalf. They, the Triads, would know that, should the master lift a finger, it would herald a slow and very nasty death for each and every member of the Black Society gang involved.

A kung fu master is not an all-guns-blazing, sudden-death, Hollywood-style terminator. In fact, he wouldn't use guns at all, and it was this that created the real fear. This particular martial art, while deadly in its own right, often involved a range of vicious hand weapons, the favourite being a meat cleaver, but also including swords, spears, knives and especially the *kuan dao* – a scimitar-like blade mounted on a long staff, which, when used by a kung fu master, can kill instantly or simply remove bit by bit the parts of an opponent.

The point I am making is that when either of the Saw brothers moved from home, it would be in the conspicuous presence of an acolyte with skills approaching those of a master, or at particularly vulnerable venues, the kung fu master himself. If any potential kidnappers dared to approach the *tai-pans* or members of their families, they could expect a swift and very nasty death. I envisaged one such guardian hovering by our table at the awards dinner. It wouldn't exactly add to the ambience.

The second and much less serious reason for my anxiety over including Long Me Saw on the guest list was his preoccupation with longevity. Added to the kung fu guard would be an attractive young woman he laughingly referred to as Miss Chew. She stood behind his chair as he ate, her only role being to supervise his mastication, tapping him on the shoulder when he'd reached one hundred chews, whereupon he was entitled to swallow.

The Saw brothers, both highly intelligent and sophisticated men, nevertheless possessed the Chinese obsession with longevity. What and how they ate was of great importance in ensuring a venerable old age. For instance, they would not eat Western food, but prized all manner of seafood, the rarer the better, cooked in the Chinese manner. Another important part of their diet was a special soup to boost or raise the ch'i by cleaning the blood. It was both medicinal and wholesome and consisted of various meats, particular vegetables in season, and very potent and rare herbs, as well as common herbs prescribed by a physician or from an ancient family recipe. Often, to aid particular organs or systems in the body, bo soup would contain exotic ingredients: cicadas and other insects, dried snake, scorpions, seahorses, fungi, minerals (in the old days pearls and jade would have been used for royalty), bears' bile and owls' eyes. Long Me's food preparation would be supervised by a chef who was a master of Chinese imperial cuisine, whose knowledge would cover all the exotics, some of which, while prized by the Chinese and only available to the very rich, were barely imaginable in the West. While I am not suggesting the Saw brothers ate these exotic dishes, because I would, quite simply, have no way of knowing, dishes that supposedly aided longevity contained such niceties as parts from tigers, swans, larks, bears' paws, live fish, clean blood and, most unimaginable of all, live monkey brains. This last dish was prepared by placing a live monkey in a tight-fitting box under the table with just the top of its shaven skull protruding through a round hole in the surface of the table. Its cranium was removed, sawn off by a skilled assistant as the monkey screamed, then the living brain was scooped out and eaten at blood temperature using a long-handled silver spoon designed for the purpose.

While there were doubtlessly other rituals the two brothers underwent to extend their lives, not all of them were bizarre. Special breathing regimens would be followed daily into old age and each mouthful of food chewed one hundred times. The Chinese believe that controlled breathing and reducing the effort required by the body to digest food places less strain on an ageing physique, in particular, the bowels. Sluggish bowels are commonly linked to cancer, and the Chinese believe heart attacks can be caused by the effort to pass solid excrement. Western doctors are well aware that a percentage of heart attacks occur on the toilet, no doubt from the same cause.

So you can see that, all in all, the awards dinner, fuelled with vintage French champagne and, should Long Me Saw accept, very good brandy, contained all the powder-keg ingredients for a major disaster. On top of this, Elma Kelly had declared that, because Hong Kong was her city, she more or less expected to take charge. I'd never seen Elma in full major-general mode, but I couldn't imagine her taking a backward step. Naturally, she knew all the directors of the art gallery as well as the main curator of the portrait exhibition. 'Splendid chappie, great fun, ha ha, shares a certain proclivity with Noël Coward, and I don't mean singing, playing the piano or writing risqué songs.'

The day of the press scrum that had begun with Elma's congratulatory telephone call had left me pretty much emotionally exhausted. I'd undergone twenty face-to-face interviews and I can't remember how many phone calls. Added to this was the Sidney Wing conniption and Beatrice Fong's response to my note of apology. I'd taken the last phone call around 5.30 p.m. then rushed home to catch *Karlene's People* on the box. Not because I wanted particularly to see the final version of the interview, but with a combination of hope and despair that she'd found Mercy B. Lord.

I admit I hungered for a glimpse of her and for the sound of her voice. After the desecrated note from the evil Beatrice Fong, I convinced myself that Mercy B. Lord had been prevented from receiving the numerous letters and flowers I'd sent, which had all boomeranged back. If she appeared on *Karlene's People*, at the very least I'd know she was safe.

I knew she'd be much too dignified and poised to appear indignant or upset in public because I hadn't sought her approval to enter the portrait in the competition. But I felt certain that I'd be able to read the true message, good or bad, in her dark eyes.

It was immediately obvious that the general tone of the TV program was self-congratulatory: Singapore patting itself on the back for producing a so-called local artist who'd won a major international art prize with a portrait of a Singapore woman of incomparable beauty. Mercy B. Lord would, I knew, sum up the situation in a flash and play her part with modesty in the carnival of self-satisfaction that followed.

So anxious had I become to see my beloved that I barely listened to Karlene Stein's introduction or even to her interview with me. I all but burst into tears of disappointment when Karlene finally concluded, 'We have tried, though without success, to find the whereabouts of the beautiful Singapore woman who was the model for Simon Koo's winning entry. The artist "claims" not to know her immediate whereabouts, nor will he give us her name without her permission.' Head to one side and with a sad little smile, she added, 'And so, we are no closer to solving the mystery and discovering the identity of the woman.' She paused, and raised one carefully outlined eyebrow while looking directly into the camera. 'Of course, there is always the chance that the winning portrait is a figment of the artist's imagination,' another slight hesitation to milk the moment, then Karlene Stein added, 'in which case it would be interesting to know if Mr Koo is entitled to this prestigious prize.' She effected a stern look of disapproval in a close-up to camera. 'If any of our viewers recognises the subject of the portrait —' The camera cut to my winning portrait, not the newspaper version but actual film, no doubt despatched on the afternoon plane from Hong Kong, 'and can identify this beautiful young woman, please call the station. I cannot emphasise enough how important it is to the reputation of our island to know that this Singapore girl – or Thursday Girl – actually exists.' Cut back to Karlene Stein looking serious, with the station phone number supered on the screen. 'In the meantime, we are all on tenterhooks.'

Seemingly only moments after the program ended, Chairman Meow called from Hong Kong, adding to what had been one of the most difficult days of my life. I will return to her phone call later. Needless to say, exhausted as I was, I didn't sleep much that night.

You may imagine my surprise when, the following morning, the *Straits Times* ran a small piece on their front page. Well, not so small – it was spread over two columns and was perhaps five inches deep, with a headline that couldn't be missed:

MISSING
SINGAPORE GIRL
WINNING PORTRAIT
MAY BE FAKE

It went on to say that an extensive search by the TV station had failed to establish the identity of the beautiful woman in the Australian artist's portrait, blah, blah, blah, suggesting that a woman of such exceptional 'movie-star' looks, if she were real, would be well known. It seemed that overnight I had lost my status as one of Singapore's own and as a con artist my Australian nationality had been restored. Karlene Stein had truly set the cat among the pigeons and, of course, Mercy B. Lord – and Beatrice Fong and Sidney Wing – would be certain to see the story.

It had been months since Mercy B. Lord left and she had disappeared as completely from my life as she apparently had from Singapore, if Karlene Stein was to be believed. I hadn't had a word from Mercy B. Lord herself, not even a rebuke by phone or a note in her handwriting. There had been only the boomeranging flowers, the apology note with the word *'Bastard!'* brush-scrawled across it by Beatrice Fong and, of course, the unopened letters returned with *'Not at this address'* stamped on them.

Suddenly the smouldering anxiety I had felt for her safety flared. I swallowed my pride and phoned Ronnie to inquire about her welfare, only to be told in a crisply modulated voice, 'Simon, she's safe and getting on with her life, and we'd thank you to kindly mind your own business. I think you've done enough, don't you?' His answer sounded rehearsed, not at all like the usual Ronnie, who was invariably polite, the exception among the Wing brothers. It seemed as if he'd been prepped for my call. I guess after Sidney's spit-flecked desk-thumping declaration – 'She's mine!' – there was little or no point in pretending they, the Wings, were not involved in Mercy B. Lord's life.

To put it mildly, I was up to my eyebrows in excrement. With the awards dinner less than a week away, my febrile imagination immediately identified yet another potential problem. The Fong–Wing alliance could send Mercy B. Lord out of the country for a week to cause me maximum embarrassment. This placed me between a rock and a hard place. I either copped the flak and caused a major ruckus with the Hong Kong Art Gallery people, and might even have to pass up the prize (the entry form had specified that all artists would need to be able to authenticate the identity of their living subject), or by revealing her name and whereabouts without her permission, betray Mercy B. Lord's trust. I wouldn't have minded if the Hong Kong people had decided to pull my portrait – there had to be a second placegetter. I was an ad man and knew it would be great publicity for the gallery; I could tell them exactly how to capitalise on the apparent disaster. My concern lay elsewhere. It was inevitable that Mercy B. Lord would eventually be recognised; the paper was right – she turned heads in the street. And when she was, she would be blamed for ruining the career of an up-and-coming artist, robbing him of the prize and future career opportunities. My only hope was that someone whose word could not be doubted would vouch for her authenticity and be able to prove she existed even if she had been hurriedly shipped out of the country.

I did the only thing I could think of and sent her one of the Hong Kong Art Gallery's elaborately printed invitations to the awards dinner, this time insisting Louie da Fly personally deliver it into her hands. First thing the next morning at the agency, I phoned Connie Song at Corona Flowers to order a corsage. She suggested a deep purple cymbidium orchid in a beribboned clear plastic box, but pointed out that they were specially flown in from Taiwan and the courier from the airport wouldn't arrive until mid-morning. She phoned back at ten-thirty to say the cymbidiums had arrived and I sent Louie da Fly to collect the one she'd suggested.

In retrospect, I realise the orchid was a pretty clumsy gesture but I wanted to indicate to Mercy B. Lord how anxious I was to have her come to the dinner, to have her share the glory, in fact, to be the centre of it all, as a beautiful woman ought to be. There was something wrong about an ugly Chinese-Australian peasant with the build of a tree stump and a face about as interesting as a dinner plate getting all the credit. Carefully duplicating the script used on the invitation, I added the words:

Airline ticket, black cheongsam, red shoes and single accommodation provided.

All horribly gauche, I admit, and I still blush to think of it, but I was hopelessly in love and my addled brain wasn't coping all that well.

Besides, all this unnecessary brouhaha had only served to sharpen my sense of personal loss.

If love is the act of falling, tumbling head over heels, then I had not only fallen in love but was somersaulting into a bottomless abyss where the adage that time heals all wounds didn't exist. I confess I was rendered stupid by love, even on occasion stupefied by it. I'd wake at 2 a.m. and pace the flat, mumbling tearfully, 'But I love you, I love you, I love you,' like a congenital idiot. I'd have to be careful not to say or think her name, for if I did, I'd get an almost instant erection, and I could no longer visit Veronica for relief.

I added the invitation to the boxed and ribboned corsage and handed it back to Louie da Fly, then gave him his taxi fare and two dollars for drink and sustenance at the tea-house across the road from the Beatrice Fong Agency. If he walked or took a rickshaw and spent only fifty cents on his food (the cost of a cheap meal), he would profit by about five dollars.

'Louie da Fly, this time don't go inside,' I said to him in Cantonese. 'Wait in the tea-house across the road until Miss Mercy B. Lord comes out or goes in, then give her the envelope and the flower. You understand, only give it to her, *nobody* else.' I hesitated, trying to keep my voice casual. 'Tell her to please phone me.'

'Yes, boss,' he replied in English. 'How much this one flower?'

'Ten dollars, and it's not for sale, you hear? If she's not there today, you go back tomorrow.' I pointed to the small glass tube with the rubber bung that contained the orchid stem. 'This flower will be perfect tomorrow. It can last all week.'

'I go back all week, boss? Maybe Mr Ronnie not so happy I don' come my work.'

'No, just today and tomorrow morning. Don't worry about Mr Ronnie. You have my permission to be away. If she doesn't come, you bring the flower back here to me.'

'I can give my sister, boss. She not dead yet.'

'Louie da Fly, you heard me. Bring the bloody flower back!'

'Yes, boss, ten dollar one flower. Last time twelve dollar twelve flower, maybe you can take it back to dat lady for flower shop and she can give money back? This pretty bad business. Look at stem! Last flower all got long stem, this one got no *bloody* stem!' he said, picking up with alacrity my previous use of the vernacular. While Louie da Fly spoke the four local ethnic languages fluently, he'd convinced himself that his pathway to a bright future lay in mastering the English language.

Since Mercy B. Lord had left me, I'd habitually worked back each night at the agency, dreading the prospect of returning to an empty flat and a bowl of lukewarm take-away noodles. Ronnie no longer asked me to help out with entertaining clients or even invited me to lunch, but Dansford, having left the office at lunchtime, would sometimes call after five, already well lubricated, and suggest meeting him at a girlie bar for a drink. 'Do you good, Simon. Lift you out of your misery. A few drinks and then get your rocks off. You'll be a new man, buddy.' Why is it that most men believe that the damage done to your heart by the loss of a girlfriend can be instantly repaired by getting drunk and getting laid, as Dansford would have put it?

While I knew Dansford was only trying to help, the last thing I needed was another woman. I missed Mercy B. Lord totally – in mind, spirit and body. It was just that the first two were internalised and the third was manifest, but together they represented a constant longing, an ache that had nothing whatsoever to do with sexual gratification.

It was only when I had been painting that my sense of loss seemed to fade a little. Mercy B. Lord's image, slowly emerging from the flat white canvas, gave me a sense of her returning to my life. No longer did I need the ice-cube therapy or pace the floor each night mumbling the same mournful endearments.

However, in the days that followed my sending the painting off to Hong Kong, I sank – crashed is a better word – into a deeper despair than ever. It was as if I'd now lost Mercy B. Lord all over again. Years later I would understand that in my mind and imagination I'd brought her to life. It was like feeling the presence of a phantom limb. In retrospect, I suppose it sounds pretty strange, but curiously, the comment most people made when they saw the painting was that it had enormous presence. In fact, of the sixty portraits by international artists accepted by the Hong Kong Art Gallery for exhibition, 'Thursday Girl' was described as the painting that most frequently caught the eye of visitors and drew them to it.

The Chinese have a penchant for renaming things, the names usually based on some physical quality the thing possesses. For instance, a new high-rise building in Hong Kong featuring hundreds of round windows was immediately referred to as the 'Building of a Thousand Arseholes'. A Guinness stout bottle featuring an Irish harp on the label has been known for over fifty years as the 'Broken Bicycle-wheel Beer'. My portrait was renamed by a Chinese journalist as 'The Princess with the Dragon Chisel', and by some form of oriental osmosis, within a couple of days everyone was calling it that and it bore this new name whenever it appeared in the Chinese press. Someone on the gallery staff soon called and asked if they, too, could use the Chinese name in their promotional material, saying they planned to have a second banner printed for the front of the building with the new name in Mandarin. I hurriedly agreed to the name change, thinking it might cause less trouble for Mercy B. Lord. I had no wish to remind her of the subject of our last, fateful discussion.

They'd also delicately referred to the suggestion made by Karlene Stein and the *Straits Times* that Mercy B. Lord didn't exist. While not quite knowing what to say, I fired a shot in the dark and assured them that she lived and breathed and would be identified soon enough. I reasoned that if the worst came to the worst, I would ask Molly Ong to verify Mercy B. Lord's existence and then cop whatever flak came my way. I daresay I could also have used Long Me Saw, but he constituted heavy artillery, almost like getting the prime minister to vouch for your character.

Involving Molly was a lousy solution, and no doubt Mercy B. Lord would think I had betrayed her, but it was the only way I could think of to avoid a major embarrassment for the gallery and also stop the press from speculating. After all, what had occurred wasn't the Hong Kong Art Gallery's fault, and having Mercy B. Lord's existence authenticated was the lesser of two unfortunate outcomes, if not for me then certainly for everyone else involved.

Naturally, for the umpteenth time I chastised myself for my impetuosity – no, that sounds too lenient – for my downright carelessness and thoughtlessness in entering the competition. While there was no possible excuse, it never entered my head that I'd win or even be exhibited. Even the prospect of making the *Salon des Refusés* only occurred to me fleetingly. But that's not the point, is it?

And then there was my mother. Who the hell would have thought she'd be in Hong Kong just when this was all happening? But then again, Chairman Meow seemed to have an instinct for being where the action was. It had not endeared her to most of my uncles; she seemed to have an uncanny knack of appearing at one or other of the little empires each of them ran on behalf of the family at exactly the wrong or right time, depending upon whose viewpoint you were taking.

As I mentioned earlier, she'd followed up her original excited mid-morning phone call with another that came just after Karlene Stein's program. For me it was the worst possible timing. What I didn't need was a Chairman Meow interrogation after Karlene Stein's asinine remarks on TV.

To my enormous relief, she announced in a voice filled with disappointment that she couldn't come to Singapore the following morning because my Uncle Colin, responsible for the company real-estate portfolio, was causing a ruckus about a building in the CBD, which he wanted to demolish to build a high-rise office tower. 'Can you imagine – no please or thank you – he had the nerve to tell your father that he had Whelan the Wrecker standing by and needed his signature on the contract to give him the go-ahead! Your father is very against it. The building is a Georgian masterpiece – Sydney sandstone – the first investment Little Sparrow ever made, apart from the restaurants and what-have-you. It's been in the family for sixty years! Your father has called an extraordinary board meeting and I'm afraid I have to be there. Your Uncle Colin can be rather stubborn and his judgement isn't always to be relied upon,' she concluded in Chairman Meow business code. Roughly translated outside the boardroom, that last statement would go something like this: 'Colin is a bumbling nincompoop, a philistine whose judgement can't under any circumstances be trusted!' There was an audible sigh from the Hong Kong end and then she concluded, 'Anyway, I'd better go.'

'Okay, Mum. Nice of you to call,' I mumbled, then waited, knowing that her farewells often took longer than her conversations.

'Never mind, darling. I'll be back on the afternoon flight on Thursday week and we'll fly to Hong Kong together on Saturday morning for the dinner in the evening. I am so looking forward to meeting your nice friends. Oh, and, Simon, you will be wearing black tie, won't you?'

'Mum! No. It's optional. I'm supposed to be an artist – it won't be expected,' I protested. 'I've got the suit you had made in Sydney.'

'You're also supposed to be a gentleman, darling. The two things are not mutually exclusive, unless you're one of those new hippies. Besides, it is expected. I shall be with you and that suit is well below par. I shall be wearing a beautiful Christian Dior gown I bought in Paris last season, which I have yet to wear. It's raw silk, with the bodice and hemline decorated with black Tahitian seed pearls. I think I've got a diamond dragon brooch somewhere – in the vault, I think – oh, and, darling, you will be sure to have a haircut, won't you?'

'Mum, this is "short back and sides" Singapore. And I don't possess a dinner suit.'

'There's plenty of time to have one made, dear. One of those clever overnight tailors in Orchard Road will make it for you – single-breasted is what everyone's wearing these days. You don't want to look like a young Bob Menzies. What about your gorgeous Thursday Girl? You quite neglected to tell me her name this morning.'

Whacko! Chairman Meow was back, her timing perfect. She'd slipped Mercy B. Lord into the conversation seemingly effortlessly. 'It's Mercy B. Lord.'

'Did I hear you correctly? Mercy's very nice, but Belord? That's not a Chinese name.'

'No, Mum, Mercy as in "to have mercy", "B" as in the initial, and "Lord" as in Jesus. Mercy B. Lord,' I repeated.

'Oh, how extraordinary! And that's her real name, Mercy B. Lord? But she is Chinese, isn't she?'

'Mum, she's an orphan, left on the steps of a Catholic orphanage. That's what the nun who discovered her exclaimed when she set eyes on the tiny swaddled bundle on the front steps – "Mercy be Lord!" – so that's how she was named. Simple, really. As I told you this morning, she has absolutely no *guanxi* whatsoever.'

'We'll talk about all that when I get there, darling. I'll see you on Thursday night.'

'Yes, Mum. Why don't you stay with me? Make a change from a hotel.'

'You mean you're on your own? I was rather hoping —'

'No, Mum, I told you this morning, she's not mine!' I replied sharply.

'Oh, did you? I must have missed that in all the excitement.'

'Yes, well . . .'

A moment's pause, then, 'Oh, and tell me about Little Sparrow's dragon chisel.'

'It was an afterthought, Mum, instead of a toggle. I added it at the very last moment.'

'Simon, I think you're fibbing. It was no afterthought, or if it was, it's a sign, a definite sign. Listen to me. I stood for an hour looking at your painting, looking into her eyes. That's not something you can paint if it isn't there.'

'What isn't there, Mum?'

'Simon, that beautiful young woman has Koo – I mean *you* – written all over her.'

'Mum, please, she's not mine. Please don't make any plans. They simply won't work,' I cried down the phone like a plaintive teenager.

'I daresay she'll wear the gown and shoes in the picture, but I thought I'd bring a set of diamond drop earrings, perfect with her lovely Sassoon helmet-style haircut.'

'Mum!'

'What, darling?'

'I told you – she's *not* mine! I don't even know if she'll attend!'

'Oh? But you *have* invited her?'

'Yes.'

'And?'

'I haven't heard from her.' Technically, it wasn't a fib.

'And you sent flowers, I hope?'

'Yes, Mum, I sent roses – they didn't have yellow, so I sent pink, a dozen.'

'Good boy.'

I breathed an inward sigh of relief. Fibbing to Chairman Meow was always dangerous. Beatrice Fong's brush-stroked 'BASTARD' across the middle of my letter of apology wasn't something you could explain to your mother. 'She's barely had time to reply,' I explained, having trouble keeping my voice steady.

There was another pause, then she said, 'Darling, you do know how proud I am. An artist who becomes the chairman of the board of a vast family conglomerate . . .' A titter came over the line from Hong Kong. 'Now, wouldn't that be something? Must go, darling, I'll call you from Australia and, yes, I'd love to stay with you.'

'Bye, Mum,' I said, exasperated, and waited. But this time I heard the click as she replaced the receiver.

I knew it was pointless telling Chairman Meow that Mercy B. Lord wasn't part of my life, but at least she'd dropped the subject when she realised I was becoming upset. Chairman Meow and Mother combined had swiftly changed the subject, and in the process reminded me, not too subtly, of the end game: Simon Koo, Chairman of the Board.

Very occasionally, the congruence between Chairman Meow and my mum increased. When this happened the decisions that resulted were forever chiselled in granite. The point I'm making is that both had made up their minds about Mercy B. Lord in a double-whammy decision and, like the Georgian building in the heart of Sydney's central business district, no metaphorical Whelan the Wrecker was going to be allowed to reduce it to rubble. The apparent Freudian slip of the tongue – 'That beautiful young woman has Koo – I mean, *you* – written all over her' – I knew with absolute certainty was no slip at all.

I clasped my head in my hands and shook it vigorously, gnashing my teeth and growling in frustration. Chairman Meow versus Beatrice Fong and the Wing Brothers would be an even and deadly contest. The fact that Mercy B. Lord or Simon Koo might want to be involved in this clash of the oriental Titans that was now almost certain to eventuate wouldn't occur to either Chinese faction. Simple: Australia and Singapore would soon officially be at war.

All this happened on what had been, for me, a very long day. Now I'd sent Louie da Fly to try to accost Mercy B. Lord as she entered or left the Beatrice Fong building. He'd left shortly before noon and hadn't returned by five, so I could only assume he'd missed seeing her and gone home to return to the task in the morning.

Because of yesterday's media circus, I'd done no work in the agency and we had a meeting with Michael Johns of Texas Oil the next day. They planned to launch a new type of oil onto the Asian market. It was purported to increase the efficiency of the engine in much less time than normal engine oil, by lubricating the moving parts almost instantly upon ignition. Big Loud Mike's idea for the copy was: *the engine is instantly sprayed with tiger piss*, which we were to translate cleverly into Chinese. Following the huge success of the Texas Tiger petrol campaign, he had practically become a legend back in Houston, Texas, and he now regarded himself as an expert on all matters relating to Chinese tigers and petroleum products.

I was required to design a new twenty-four-sheet poster for service stations and roadside sites featuring the new oil. The tiger piss idea sounded ludicrous, but because you can't easily read the oriental mind, we'd tried the name on a sample of forty truck owner-drivers and on the same number of taxi drivers in four Asian countries. Almost to a man, they'd burst out laughing when they heard it, shaking their heads at the absurdity of the idea and no doubt at the presumption of the *gwai-lo*.

The Chinese, in particular, always try to second-guess what answer you would prefer when you ask them a question, and may never tell you how they feel personally about the subject discussed, so this spontaneous outburst of mirth at Big Loud Mike's suggestion told us everything we needed to know: there are limitations even to the Chinese imagination, and the concept of tiger's piss for engine oil was going a tad too far.

The idea I'd settled on when designing the poster showed a tiger running fully stretched along a mountain road, with the immediate background scenery speed-blurred, and above it a dark brooding sky ripped asunder with a brilliant strip of lightning that ended on an illustration of the oil container. The caption read: 'Tiger lubrication – greased lightning for ultimate engine care'. While it was a little clumsy in English, it translated well into most Asian languages with the exception of Tagalog, the language spoken in most parts of the Philippines.

It was rendering rather well, the poster layout coming along nicely, and I'd lost all sense of time when I heard the night buzzer ringing in reception. I glanced at my watch; it was eight o'clock. I'd arrived at the agency at seven that morning and hadn't eaten all day. I glanced out of the window to see that it was already dark and a streetlight had come on in the distance.

Walking into reception, I switched on the light and was surprised to see Louie da Fly with his face pressed to the plate-glass front door, fist pounding for attention. I opened the door to the teenager, who panted excitedly, 'You come now, boss, quick time. I got also rickshaw!'

'Hey, whoa. Steady on, mate. What's going on?'

'You see, come, we go.'

'Hang on, Louie da Fly. Calm down. Tell me what all this is about.'

'I find Missy Mercy. She want to see you, boss. I got rickshaw. We go. She waiting for you.'

'Why didn't you bring her here?' I asked, surprised.

'No! Too danger. We go. She be there by Muslim temple.'

'Mosque?'

'Ja, ja, big one, boss! More big all church and temple in Singapore. We go *Kampong* Glam.'

He was talking about the Sultan mosque round the corner from Arab Street. Mercy B. Lord had taken me there as part of my orientation tour when I'd first arrived, and we'd discovered a Malay shop-house restaurant, where an old Muslim woman served and her even older husband, predictably named Mohammed Ismail, did the cooking under a single tiny electric bulb in the ceiling.

We'd returned several times after that, but neither husband nor wife appeared to recognise us. It wasn't one of those places where patrons were welcomed with a fuss, or welcomed at all. You sat, ordered, ate and paid. For all we knew, the old lady may have been snarling at us, so little could we see of her under her burqa, which covered her entire face apart from her eyes. But the attraction was the food, especially the curry. Mohammed Ismail made a wonderful chicken curry served with *raita*, a yoghurt and cucumber dip seasoned with coriander, and *roti jala*, a lacy flatbread sometimes referred to as net bread. While the curry was already cooked, he made the accompaniments as they were ordered and the service was as slow as the movement of their ancient slipper-clad feet.

The patrons were invariably young Malay labourers who, after a hard day's work, were happy to linger, many of them sleeping at a work site or on the floor, a dozen men in a cheap, poorly ventilated room, so the lack of service wasn't a problem for them. Needless to say, the curries, always three different kinds, were cheap as chips, though this was not the reason we went; the food was truly exceptional.

The tiny restaurant was situated down a small lane not far from Arab Street, and when Mercy B. Lord had asked Mohammed Ismail if the eatery had a name, he had let out a toothless cackle. 'The Ritz,' he said, repeating the name twice. The joke seemed out of place coming from the old cook, but when more closely questioned, he explained that the name came from two *ang mo* (Europeans) who had somehow stumbled on the place. Enjoying his curry, they had asked him the same question and he'd replied that it didn't have a name. They'd then suggested he name it The Ritz. 'What means this name?' he asked Mercy B. Lord. She'd replied that it meant it was a place with especially good food. She could have added 'and very poor lighting'. 'The Ritz' was perpetually in semi-darkness and it was absolutely perfect for a clandestine meeting.

I gave the rickshaw driver two dollars, the equivalent of the taxi fare, while Louie da Fly looked on, frowning in disapproval at my utterly profligate gesture. I invariably felt guilty taking a rickshaw. The poor bastard had, after all, pulled Louie da Fly from Beatrice Fong's to the agency and then, with the added burden of the chunky Chinaman, a fair distance across town on a hot humid night where the acrid atmosphere caused by forest fires in Indonesia was dangerous to breathe. He deserved taxi rates or even more. A taxi driver sat on his arse, his only physical exertion involving a hand on the horn, a foot on the pedal, and yelling abuse at other drivers and pedestrians. Besides, there was something decidedly un-Australian about another human pulling you, using the sweat of his brow, as if he were some poor dumb animal.

'I go home now, boss?' Louie da Fly asked, eyeing the rickshaw about to depart. 'I tell him two dollar you pay also for take me home?'

I handed the rickshaw driver another fifty cents. 'Go on, scram. And thanks, mate.'

When I entered the beaded door of the shadowy Ritz, it was just past eight-thirty and the labourers had already departed. The small room was empty but for a Muslim woman in a burqa sitting at a table in the corner, whom I took to be Mohammed Ismail's wife putting her feet up after a busy evening. My heart sank. Mercy B. Lord had obviously grown impatient and left. I almost sank to my knees in despair, but then the woman in the dark corner called out quietly, 'Simon, over here!'

I reckon my smile was wide as a slice of watermelon. Just three words – impossible to tell if they were happy, sad, angry or simply businesslike, but I hadn't heard her voice for months and didn't care. I wanted to dance up to her, suddenly transmogrified into Fred Astaire, from tree stump to top hat, white tie and tails, my arms extended as I swept her from the chair, the ugly hangings of black cotton she wore transformed into an elegant silk ball gown with skirts that flounced as we danced. I guess I lumbered rather than danced to her table, propped and tried to see if her eyes were friendly and welcoming, but the black headgear denied me any sign whatsoever. It was impossible to tell – the light wasn't great, and eyes alone are not the indicator they're always claimed to be.

'Mercy B. Lord, thank you, thank you for seeing me. I wanted to apolo—'

'It's nice to see you, Simon.' Her voice was slightly muffled by the mask of black muslin.

'I've missed you.' It was only at that moment that I saw the orchid. I mean, it was pinned over her heart for all the world to see but I'd been so intent on her eyes that I'd missed this magnificent splash of colour against her dark blouse. I pointed to the bloom. 'I hope you didn't think it presumptuous, which of course it was.'

'Simon, it's lovely.'

'May I sit?'

'Of course.'

My heart sank. Her tone was measured, not exactly the voice of a long-lost lover finding her beloved again. *Whatever happens, keep your head. Don't let it get emotional straightaway,* I urged myself.

'Have you eaten?' she asked.

'No, I'm starving. I haven't eaten all day.'

Mercy B. Lord laughed, the first tiny breakthrough. 'You need a good woman to care for you, Simon Koo.'

I winced visibly. 'I wish!'

'Well, you'll be happy to know your chicken curry is on the way, with the usual *raita* and net bread.' She laughed again softly. 'I'm afraid Mohammed Ismail thought he was through for the night. The old lady was washing dishes as I entered. I think "go slow" has assumed a new meaning in the kitchen of The Ritz.'

Her tone of voice was now sufficiently light for me to venture the next question. 'Have you converted to the Muslim faith, Mercy B. Lord? If you have, you'll have to change your name to Mercy B. Allah.'

Her eyes danced as she laughed once more. I'd broken through. Mercy B. Lord reached up and removed the part of the burqa covering her nose and chin, then pushed back the scarf resting on her forehead so that her entire face was revealed. I knew how pretty she was – no, how beautiful – but the sight of that gorgeous face still made me catch my breath. Swathed in black with only her face revealed, she looked like an oriental Madonna.

'Simon, just one thing.'

'What?'

'Did you tell Molly Ong to call me?'

'No, I didn't.'

'Are you sure?'

'Yes, certain.'

'Do you know why she called?'

'Yes, I have a fair idea.'

'Why?

'The Singapore Girl?'

'Simon, it sounds like one of your ideas.'

I attempted a laugh. 'Don't you ever say that in front of Molly. She'll think I appropriated the idea. No, honestly, it's all hers, 100 per cent. She . . . ah . . . saw the . . . er . . . thing in the paper and called me. I told her it was a great idea, but that's all.' I looked directly at Mercy B. Lord. 'And it is. She asked me if I'd seen you and I said no, there had been no contact, then she . . .'

'What?'

'She asked if you, that is, if she managed to persuade you . . . you know, on the idea, whether I would have trouble working with you.'

'And?'

I grinned. 'You can guess my answer. I assured her I'd be over the moon, doing handstands, double somersaults in the air, jumping over tall buildings in a single bound.'

I had hoped for a reaction, even a twitch of a smile, but instead she picked up her handbag, opened it and withdrew a piece of folded newspaper. Of course I knew instantly what it was – the moment of truth was upon me. 'Mercy B. Lord, I know it's pointless, too late and all that, but I am truly sorry! I never for one moment expected this to happen. It was just . . . well, painting you was a way of keeping you in my life each day . . . like you hadn't left. The competition was just something . . . a deadline that kept me, you know, painting.'

By this time she'd unfolded the newspaper and smoothed it out on the Laminex surface of the table. She stabbed at it with her finger, pinning her portrait so that I winced at the gesture. I waited for the expostulation to follow, averting my eyes and shaking my head in regret, willing myself to accept whatever she said, determined to offer no protest other than my regret at having humiliated her. But no explosion followed. Mercy B. Lord remained silent, her finger rigid, motionless, blood pooling above the nail, turning the tip a darker shade under the skin. Had it been a stiletto blade stabbed into her breast it couldn't have been more meaningful.

I can't say how long it was. In my mind the days and weeks and months since she'd left me passed in what was perhaps no more than an agonising half a minute in real time. Then, in a voice barely above a whisper, she said, 'Simon, have you any possible idea of the harm you've done?'

Sometimes you have to believe in a higher force. Just then, a slap-slap of slippers approached as Mrs Mohammed shuffled towards the table with our dinner on a large painted tin tray now scratched and worn. Placing the curry and *raita* on the table, she muttered something in Malay to Mercy B. Lord.

I waited until the old lady had departed and looked into Mercy B. Lord's eyes. I could see she was close to tears, while I was not far from them myself. 'Mercy B. Lord, I'm an arsehole.' She folded the newspaper clipping and returned it to her handbag, then started to silently serve me rice and chicken curry, tears now streaming down her cheeks. 'I've done the wrong thing,' I continued. 'I know that now. It was arrogant and thoughtless and entirely out of order.'

'Yes, it was all of those things, Simon,' she said, her eyes averted as she replaced the serving spoon.

'But there may be a way out of this mess,' I said quietly.

'Oh?'

'Karlene Stein's program and yesterday's *Straits Times* have both suggested that you may be a figment of my imagination.'

'Yes, I know. So?

'I'll withdraw the painting.'

'You'll what?'

'Admit it – that the portrait is phoney.'

'Oh, I see, and promptly create another media mess?'

'Yeah, possibly, but one that leaves you out of the equation.'

'How is that?'

'Well, I'll tell them that, technically speaking, it's a fake. That it's based on a guide who showed me around Singapore when I arrived almost three years ago. I asked her if she'd allow me to paint her portrait and she agreed.' I glanced up. 'Do you agree that's true so far?'

Mercy B. Lord nodded. 'Yes.'

'I then did half a dozen preliminary pencil sketches.'

'Yes again.'

'Then nothing more.'

Mercy B. Lord nodded again.

'Okay, then we eventually lost touch.'

'That's stretching things a bit.'

'Yeah, but not essentially untrue. Then, six months ago, two and a half years after we'd met, I set about painting her portrait pretty well from memory and contrary to the rules of the competition.'

'Is that true about the rules?'

'As it turns out, yes, although at the time I simply filled in the entry form and didn't bother reading the small print or even the larger print. My only ambition was to finish. I'm an art director – my life is ruled by deadlines. Not in my wildest dreams did I think the painting would get anywhere.' I grinned. 'The last prize I won for portraiture was in primary school, when I painted a picture of Miss Thomas, my teacher.'

'Do the rules state that you have to have the permission of your subject to exhibit?'

'Yes, as it turns out, the express permission, and it's the right of the gallery to authenticate the subject's existence.'

'And you are refusing to give her name?'

'Well, the gallery hasn't brought it up yet but, yes, on TV and in the interviews I did. I simply insisted it was – she was – to be referred to as the Thursday Girl.'

'And no one asked you why – why Thursday Girl?'

'Yes, of course. I told them it was the day I met you.' I paused to take a mouthful of chicken curry.

'Simon, you idiot, it was a Saturday!'

'Oops!'

'So far you're doing very well, I don't think. Still, I'd be surprised if anyone checked, so go on.'

'Well, from the perspective of the Hong Kong Art Gallery, it's beginning to look very much on the nose. With all this TV and newspaper speculation, it might appear that the woman in the portrait is a figment of the artist's imagination. The subject, if the artist is telling the truth, is, at best, based on a few hurried sketches in his notebook, and he hasn't seen her and refuses to name her without permission. It's all pretty bloody suss, wouldn't you say?'

'Until tonight.'

'Until tonight, what?'

'Well, I'm here.'

'Oh, so you're happy for me to announce to the world that you've been found?'

A sudden look of real fear crossed Mercy B. Lord's face. 'No!'

she cried. 'No, you can't! If they find out we're meeting, they'll . . .' She pulled herself up just in time and my heart skipped a beat. She'd confirmed she was in some sort of danger. But I knew instinctively this was the wrong time to pursue the matter.

'Well, there we go. So we didn't meet tonight.'

'But this is ridiculous. Your cousins Peter and Professor Kwan, Mrs Sidebottom, Long Me Saw and Molly Ong, the Wings, Dansford Drocker, Beatrice Fong, Elma Kelly, and I daresay there are others, have all seen us together. We lived together!'

'Hang on, I haven't denied that, but it doesn't change a thing. If anyone brings that up, I have simply respected your privacy. It doesn't alter the facts of the matter. As for those in the know, that's just it, see! Some, like the Wing brothers and Beatrice Fong, have reasons not to speak to anyone. My cousins will keep their mouths shut; so will Dansford and Mrs Sidebottom, and if Elma Kelly hears about it – well, I imagine she'll call me before she says anything. She's pretty sharp.'

'And what about Molly Ong and Long Me Saw? Oh, and the tourism minister? I was pretty alive and well as your partner at Dansford's pink-hair cocktail party!'

'Ah, that's the best part!'

Mercy B. Lord frowned and looked stern. 'What exactly do you mean by that, Simon?'

'Well, thinking laterally . . .'

'What's that mean?'

'It's from a book I've been reading by a guy named Edward de Bono. It means thinking outside the square, looking for a lateral rather than a conventional or direct solution to a problem. You know, something perfectly obvious when you see it, but nobody's thought to do it that way or in that manner before.'

'I'm not sure I understand . . .'

'Let me give you an example. A hotel chain, I forget which one, but they've got a hotel in Hong Kong and, anyway, the problem exists in all five-star hotels —'

'How do you know so much about five-star hotels?'

'Huh? Oh, my mum, she's an expert on finding the best hotels. Anyway, they were finding that they had to replace the very expensive carpet in the foyer lounges every two years, due to uneven wear as people came and went from the hotel. Now, you can imagine that to replace carpet in every hotel in a worldwide chain costs millions of dollars. So they called Dr de Bono in as a consultant and told him that if they could extend the life of the foyer carpets for, say, a further eighteen months, the savings would be enormous.'

'Why didn't they just use polished wood instead?' Mercy B. Lord suggested.

'Ah, not a bad idea, but that's a conventional solution and, dare I say, well within the square. Wooden floors are noisy, and because the foyers are where all the traffic is, it would immediately detract from the relaxed ambience and the appearance of luxury. Too clever by far, and the public are not stupid and clearly know a cost-cutting measure when they see it.'

Mercy B. Lord leaned over and touched my hand. 'Oh, it's so nice to be here, Simon. Just to talk. You always make me think, even if it is about five-star hotels.' My heart skipped several beats as she continued, 'I thought we might have a row. That you'd be angry with me.' She withdrew her hand as suddenly as she'd placed it on mine, as if she'd momentarily forgotten the circumstances of our meeting. She seemed to take a deep breath, although it was hard to tell under the ugly tentlike burqa. But when she spoke her voice was bright, as if she were forcing herself to stay calm and pleasant. 'Okay, smartypants, what did your clever Dr de Bono do?'

'It was simple really – he looked heavenwards.'

'He asked God?' Mercy B. Lord had an endearing tendency to take things too literally sometimes.

'No, the chandeliers. Most luxury hotels have those enormous fancy chandeliers. This chain was no exception. Edward de Bono simply suggested they change to bulbs with a lower wattage. This, in turn, added to the ambience of the foyers while effectively concealing the wear on the carpet, extending its life, as it turned out, for a further two years. Simple solution.' I leaned back. 'In a nutshell, that's lateral thinking.'

Mercy B. Lord smiled. 'That's very clever. And you've come up with one of these lateral ideas?'

'Well, yes, I think so. Bear with me a moment. I announce to the Hong Kong Art Gallery people that I've broken the rules and painted a woman pretty much from memory who I met three years ago, did so without her permission, and I refuse to give them her name unless she agrees.'

'And she can't be located,' Mercy B. Lord completed the sentence for me, implying that our meeting at The Ritz was off the record.

'Precisely, so they have no option but to withdraw the portrait and award the prize to the guy who came second, and that way you're off the hook.'

'Oh, Simon, what about you? That's simply awful. Your reputation as a painter will be ruined. The portrait is brilliant!' she cried.

I grinned. 'What reputation? It didn't exist before I won the bloody prize, so I'm just back to square one. It's not a big deal.'

'But you'll lose face! That's terrible.'

I grinned. 'I seem to be pretty good at that. No point stopping now. You rescued me at the airport, so I owe you one.' I paused. 'Mercy B. Lord, I truly beg your forgiveness – I've let you down terribly.'

She bit her bottom lip and took a deep breath, then tossed her head as if to change the subject. 'Go on, we'll get to that later.'

'Yes, well, with my tail between my legs I metaphorically slink back to Singapore with the portrait and cop the media flak.'

'Oh, Simon, is all this necessary, this personal disgrace? I sometimes think to hell with everybody.' She looked down at her hands. 'My life is fucked anyway. I should have the courage to go on Karlene Stein's program and tell everyone, let them see how brilliant you are and clear up the whole stupid mess!'

'And then what?'

Mercy B. Lord looked straight into my eyes. 'Does it matter?'

I reached over and held her hand. I'd never heard her use the 'f' word in that ugly way before. 'Darling, it matters more to me than anything else in my life. May I ask you a question?' I could sense that we were about to break down simultaneously and that I must avoid doing so at all costs. Her safety was paramount; nothing else mattered.

She averted her eyes. 'It depends on the question, Simon,' she said softly.

'Are you in danger? Physical danger?'

Mercy B. Lord was silent and her hand went to the orchid and touched it lightly. 'It's beautiful. I've never had a corsage before.'

'Please, you don't have to say anything, just nod or shake your head.'

Her eyes rose slowly to meet mine and she nodded. I sighed and nodded in turn. 'Right.'

'Please, Simon, no more questions.'

I told myself I must hold my nerve, keep my resolve. She'd answered my question; now was not the time to pursue the subject. I attempted to keep my voice calm as her eyes brimmed with tears. 'Okay, where was I? Oh, yes, the portrait is brought back to Singapore in disgrace.' I paused. 'But not entirely.'

'How is that?' Mercy B. Lord asked, clearly grateful for the release of tension.

I grinned and shrugged. 'I'm a dumb artist. Artists don't read the rules, everyone knows they're away with the fairies. Anyway, it's obvious to everyone that I love beautiful women.'

Mercy B. Lord grinned. 'So what now?'

'Well, naturally everyone wants to see it, the portrait, in the flesh, so to speak. Take a gander, see what all the fuss is about. So the Tourist Promotion Board borrows the portrait of a supposedly impossibly beautiful Singaporean woman, this figment of the fevered imagination of a disgraced artist, and displays it in the City Hall for public viewing.'

'And that gets you off the hook? You save face?' Mercy B. Lord was starting to look relieved.

'Maybe, although people love dirt more than anything.'

'But wouldn't that mean the Tourist Promotion Board encourages cheating? Hong Kong is going to howl!'

'Well, yes, of course. Normally they wouldn't have a bar of it. In fact, it will be important to castigate me publicly, show official disapproval and so on.'

'Simon, you've lost me, where from here?'

'Think laterally. The emotional trigger isn't a disgraced artist, who, by the way, is no longer from Singapore but is just an Australian con artist. The emotional trigger is that the media have speculated that the woman in the portrait is too beautiful to be real, to actually exist in the flesh.'

'Simon, if you're thinking what I'm thinking, the answer is no. I told you I can't, I simply can't make a sudden appearance, solve the whole messy business in a single stroke. I left you because I couldn't reveal a part of my life and I still can't. God knows I wish I could. Every bone in my body aches for you. Besides, I'm not beautiful, not like that. I saw your portrait on Karlene Stein's show and it's breathtaking.'

'Oh, but so are you!'

'Simon, don't talk nonsense, that's enough! No!' The strong-minded Mercy B. Lord was back.

'No, no, you've got it wrong. You don't have to make a public appearance, right the wrong, vindicate me – nothing like that, sweetheart.'

She ignored the endearment I'd slipped in. 'Go on then, Simon. I'm intrigued.'

'Well, Molly Ong, ex-Miss-Singapore, makes an announcement. They are going to conduct a competition to find the Singapore girl or girls who are, in their own particular ways, every bit as beautiful as the painting. The winning girl will promote tourism, and travel overseas as a travel ambassador. Entrants dress identically to the girl in the portrait, pose in the original peacock-tail chair for a photograph by Harry "Three Thumbs" Poon and a TV camera records each entrant's portrait. Then the day's entries are run on TV that night on *Karlene's People* and the shots printed the following day in a special supplement in the *Straits Times*, with viewers and readers voting for each day's winner, who gets a prize of some sort. At the end of a month, the public vote for seven to go into the semi-finals, then three into the finals.'

'Which by sheer coincidence is won by me?' Mercy B. Lord said, clearly appalled. 'Simon, that's cheating!'

'No, that's simply not true. You enter under precisely the same conditions as everyone else and the judging is all above board. Whoever becomes the Singapore Girl will have won fair and square.' I shrugged. 'If you lose, you're off the hook; if you win, you can be sure you've won on your own merits, and there's been no malarkey.'

'But I told her – that is, Molly Ong – that I couldn't come to the Hong Kong dinner or ever see you again.'

'Did she ask you why?'

'Yes, of course, but I told her it was a matter of face. Too many people would lose face. She's Chinese, she understood. "What about Simon? What about Simon's face, his reputation?" she asked, twisting the knife.'

'That's tough. Let me ask you a question.'

'I'm not sure, the last one was —'

'No, nothing like that,' I interrupted her. 'Mercy B. Lord, all things being equal, would you like the job she described, the role of Singapore Girl?'

'Oh, Simon, you must know I would. Any girl in Singapore would die for it.'

'But, as you said, for private reasons you can't accept her direct offer because of . . . well, we know why . . . past associations?'

'Yes.'

'But if you win, you're suddenly a high-profile identity and a public servant under state protection, which means you're safe. Secondly, I'm not directly involved, except as a professional, a creative director for the Tourist Promotions Board, a Samuel Oswald Wing account, and even that's only until my contract ends.' I grinned to reassure her. 'After that I become a disgraced painter of beautiful women. But there's just one catch – you have to win fair and square by public vote.'

'Molly Ong called this morning. I saw last night's TV program and that horrid insinuation in the *Straits Times* this morning. It was clear that if I didn't make myself known, you were going to be disgraced, when all you'd done was the honourable thing and refused to reveal my name.' Mercy B. Lord burst into sudden tears. In a plaintive voice she said, 'I told Molly when she mentioned you losing face that it was *your* problem, *not* mine, that you shouldn't have done what you did; you should have asked my permission. But that's so cruel! Oh, Simon, I'm so sorry.' She wept. 'I feel so guilty that I've betrayed you – that I've been the cause of your disgrace. It's such a brilliant portrait – you thoroughly deserved to win.' She looked up at me and sniffed, knuckling back her tears and then tossing her head and sniffing again. 'That's when I decided to see you tonight, to . . . to try and explain. My office upstairs looks out onto the street and I'd seen Louie da Fly sitting at a window of the tea-house across the road, watching for me to come out.'

'Whoa, steady on, girl. I brought this whole thing on myself, remember? You haven't betrayed me. On the contrary, I betrayed *you* by not seeking your permission to exhibit the painting. I won't have you feeling in the least guilty. I did the wrong thing and I have to cop it sweet, whatever the consequences of my action.'

'It just doesn't seem fair! But truly, Simon, there's nothing I can do to change it.' She looked me straight in the eye. 'It's not only for my own sake.' She paused, continuing to give me a meaningful look. 'You do understand, don't you, Simon?'

'You mean if we're seen together? Like this?'

She nodded and I recalled Ronnie's first warning nearly three years previously and then Sidney's furious 'She's mine!' I avoided asking the obvious next question and simply nodded back, knowing she wouldn't or couldn't elaborate. She was plainly implying that I too was in danger if we were seen together. It was an awkward situation – she was warning me but there was no possible reaction except to keep it light and play it down, hoping the nod would tell her I understood. 'Is that why you're wearing the burqa?' I asked. 'I must say, the world is a poorer place without your pretty face.'

'Oh, this,' she said, touching the scarf. 'I sometimes wear it when I travel.'

It was a tiny slip and I wondered if it was deliberate. Mercy B. Lord wasn't careless and was highly conditioned to be discreet. It was yet another question to be put aside for consideration later.

I had always known that she travelled beyond Singapore island on her Thursday absences. She'd get home at just after six on Friday, and it took almost exactly thirty minutes in the rush hour to get back from the airport. My enquiries had revealed that a plane from Hong Kong and another from Bangkok landed within five minutes of each other at around the right time on Friday afternoons. All the other flights were intercontinental or ones that had taken longer than six hours from takeoff. She only ever carried hand luggage, a small overnight bag and a briefcase, so she could walk straight out of the airport to a waiting Mohammed in the big, black Beatrice Fong Buick. The limo was another giveaway. If her Thursdays were spent locally, why would she use it? There was also something else. She'd bring the briefcase home on Wednesday night but it was never with her when she returned on Friday evening. While I worked back at the agency until around seven most nights, on Fridays I'd leave at five, pick up dinner on the way home – Peking duck, her favourite – set the table and, when she arrived, pour her a glass of white wine, wine being a new and, I must say, pleasant habit we'd acquired from Dansford.

On one such occasion just after we'd started to live together, I'd laughingly pointed out that she'd left her briefcase behind in the Buick. She smiled then said it was the office briefcase and Mohammed took it back with him on Fridays. She usually locked it in a drawer in her side of the wardrobe when she returned home from the office on a Wednesday evening, but once for a couple of minutes she'd left it on the kitchen bench while she went to the bathroom for the compulsory female wee before departure early Thursday morning. Despite having checked on those incoming Friday flights, I wasn't really much of a snoop, but I couldn't resist and picked up her briefcase and was surprised how heavy it was. I tapped the leather lid, then pressed against it and realised that the casing under it was definitely metal. I tried thumbing one of the very professional-looking combination locks, my heart beating surprisingly fast, ears pricked, listening for the toilet to flush, but the lock didn't budge. I shook it but there was no movement within. Whatever it contained was packed tight or was completely solid.

Mercy glanced up. 'Simon, I don't feel pretty. Not since . . .' Without completing the sentence, she changed the subject. 'I must say, Louie da Fly is persistent. I first noticed him around one o'clock and at six he was still waiting in the tea-house.' Mercy B. Lord laughed. 'I can't imagine how many cups of chai he must have consumed.'

'Don't worry, he's a born operator. He will have come to some sort of arrangement with the owner.'

'Well, naturally I guessed why he was there and also why he hadn't come upstairs to the office after the last incident with Beatrice. She told me gleefully what she'd done to your letter before returning it.' Mercy B. Lord looked at me, her pretty head to one side. 'I'm awfully sorry about that, Simon.'

'I can't say it wasn't a smack in the mouth.' I grinned. 'But I guess I'll recover.'

'When I decided to see you following Molly's call, I had to find a way of leaving the office without being noticed.'

'You mean you can't just walk out?'

'Well, no, not without Freda Chong – the switch girl – reporting my absence to Beatrice. Those two are thick as thieves and, knowing Beatrice, Freda's being paid off or threatened with dismissal if she doesn't monitor all my phone calls. When you called after we first parted, none of them were put through to me. She was instructed to simply wait a few moments then give you the answer you invariably got.'

My hands shot up. 'No more apologies or I'm going to break down and blub. I can't tell you how awful those first weeks were, with my boomerang flowers appearing in the agency foyer and my letters returned marked *Not at this address*.'

'Flowers? Letters? I had no idea, Simon. Please believe me, I was in a terrible emotional mess myself, and for the first month I was being followed wherever I went. Then, thank God, it seemed to stop.'

'That's when I finally gave up sending flowers and letters begging you to come back to me.'

'Oh, Simon, please don't think it hasn't been the same for me. These last months have been the hardest of my life. But after *Karlene's People* and the article in the *Times* I simply had to see you, but there's been a guy two doors down from the tea-house who hasn't moved all day. I was pretty sure I'd be followed.'

'Not much of an operator if he's that obvious,' I remarked.

'On the contrary, it's important that I see him following me. It's all a part of the warning not to stray in a certain direction. Anyhow, I keep this burqa in the office and, as you know, we have the top two floors – the ground floor is occupied by *Hizbul Muslimin*, the Pan-Malayan Islamic Party's Singapore office.'

'No, I didn't know that. Remember, I was under a certain young lady's explicit instructions never to visit her office.'

'Oh, of course, but you do understand there were reasons?'

'Yes, Ronnie Wing warned me.'

'Let's not speak of that,' she said quietly. 'Let me tell you about Freda Chong. She has this beehive hairdo plastered with enough lacquer to glue two buildings together, and wears much too much make-up, so she spends a good half hour in front of the toilet mirror preening before she leaves each evening. She has a night job working as the receptionist at the China Doll. I think she thinks she's Lily Ho, the Saw brothers' biggest movie star.'

I couldn't quite see where this was leading, but I said, 'Ah, the China Doll, yet another Beatrice Fong and Sidney Wing connection.'

Mercy B. Lord ignored this last remark. 'So, with Freda in the toilet, I switched on my office light so that anyone watching from the street would think I was working back late. Beatrice always closes her office door between six-thirty and seven to burn incense and pray at her personal shrine to *Tsai Shen Yeh*, the god of wealth, then, at precisely seven o'clock, Mohammed comes to pick her up. So I grabbed the burqa and slipped on a pair of flat shoes I wear when I have to do a lot of walking with a client, and snuck down the back stairs, stopping to fix the burqa to cover my head and face. Then I simply walked out through the *Hizbul Muslimin* front door.'

'Not just a pretty face, huh?' I grinned.

Mercy B. Lord smiled at the compliment. 'A covered face, more to the point. Then I crossed the street to confront a very surprised Louie da Fly, who, after recovering from the shock of being accosted by a strange Muslim woman, gave me your gorgeous orchid and very kind invitation to the Hong Kong dinner. I told him where I'd meet you and paid for his lunch and afternoon tea.'

'Cheeky bugger! I gave him money. I'll give him a good kick in the arse for that.'

'Then I went home, had something to eat and came on here to The Ritz to wait.'

I mimed clapping. 'Clever girl! By the way, what did Mrs Mohammed say to you when you revealed your face in front of me?'

Mercy B. Lord giggled. 'She said it was shameful for a Muslim woman to remove her burqa and show her face to an infidel. That the Prophet would be very angry.'

I'd been scoffing chicken curry throughout our conversation. While this may not seem an important detail, there had been a few times when I – we – had come close to breaking down, and there's nothing like eating as you talk to help you regain your self-control. But now, with the curry dish empty and only a few scraps of net bread left, Mohammed was banging pots and pans together in the kitchen to make it clear that it was time for us to leave. He'd probably stayed open an hour later than usual, and I guess after Mercy B. Lord's facial defrocking in front of the Chinese infidel, Mrs Mohammed wasn't all that enamoured of us either. The meal cost eighty cents, and even though I gave her a dollar and apologised in Cantonese for keeping them back, instructing her to keep the change, it wasn't sufficient to get a single word out of her; I could only imagine the curl of her lip behind her burqa.

'One final thing before we leave, Simon. Did you, I mean, have you discussed this Singapore Girl competition with Molly Ong?'

'No, I promise you, I haven't – at least, only superficially. I guessed you wouldn't come to the Hong Kong dinner and I understand why. I always knew I had Buckley's.'

'Buckley's?'

'An Australian expression – it means there's no chance of something happening. Anyway, I reckoned you'd also refuse her invitation to become the first Singapore Girl, based on my portrait. It's a damned good idea but under the circumstances it wasn't going to work. So I thought up the promotion. It was something Sidney Wing couldn't refuse as he has the tourism account, and if he did, the government could fire him or exert pressure. Besides, it was kosher, legit, and added to this is the fact that I'm leaving the agency. I'd be gone by the time the promotion runs. So I'm not a factor. No doubt he will secretly enjoy my public disgrace while fearing it might lead to them losing the tourist account, so such a promotion would reassure him.'

'And the competition wouldn't be rigged in my favour?' Mercy B. Lord asked once more.

'I can't guarantee that. It wouldn't be in my hands and, of course, there is an obvious bias; you *are* the portrait and that could affect the result. But it isn't a lookalike competition. There are three finalists, the three most beautiful girls according to the public's vote. The final decision will be made after interviewing all three. The interview will obviously involve factors other than looks, so, yes, there's an element of chance.' I shrugged. 'If you make the finals, well, what can I say? You're likely to top the interviews.' I hesitated. 'But even that's not absolutely guaranteed.'

Mercy B. Lord moved towards the street. 'We really should go, Simon.'

'I'll walk you to the mosque. You're sure to get a taxi from there.'

'No, I'll go out first – you just never know. The mosque isn't far and I can make my own way. Wait a couple of minutes or so, then walk in the opposite direction when you leave.'

Mercy B. Lord looked at me, then gave me a peck on the cheek and quickly adjusted her burqa so that only her eyes now showed. Reaching into her bag, she produced the small plastic box that had originally contained the orchid. Placing it on the table, she unpinned the magnificent bloom and replaced it in the box. 'I wish it would last forever,' she said softly. Then, without a further word, she turned and started to walk towards the door.

'Will you at least think about it? May I talk to Molly about the promotion?' I called after her.

'Yes,' she called back in a tearful voice.

I'd phrased the two questions carelessly, running them together. Yes, what? That I could call Molly or that she'd think about entering the promotion? 'May I see you again?' I called out once more. But there was no answer as Mercy B. Lord opened the door and disappeared into the night.

I waited three minutes with Mrs Mohammed hovering at the door, anxious to see the last of the infidel. Then I finally walked outside and turned in the opposite direction, the smoky air biting at my nostrils. One thing puzzled me. Mercy B. Lord hadn't once brought up the subject of Thursday.

CHAPTER THIRTEEN

AFTER WE PARTED, I was too excited to get much sleep. The last couple of days had been pretty full on, and the thought that I didn't have to deal with Chairman Meow for a week and a bit was a terrific relief. I wondered briefly how she'd cope with her son's status as disgraced artist, but I confess it wasn't one of the factors that kept me near sleepless. I spent the night hugging myself over what seemed to be the start of a reconciliation with the girl I loved, and tossing and turning in fear that she would decide not to come back to me.

While I wasn't sure we'd achieved a great deal, or that Mercy B. Lord would agree to be a part of the portrait promotion, should it eventuate, at least we'd taken the first step towards each other by meeting, and, most importantly, she'd initiated it. She'd admitted that she'd missed me perhaps almost as much as I'd missed her, though I didn't think that was possible. There had been an empty space inside me, a once sunlit room where the shutters were drawn and the door locked on memories that were slowly gathering dust. But now we'd laughed together and she'd cried a bit and there were moments when I'd been pretty choked up myself. Most significantly, the first hopeful steps had been taken, the first rattle of the key in the lock of the memory room had sounded, and I told myself, probably quite stupidly, that we were on the way to a shared life.

The thrill was in knowing she still cared, that it wasn't just old misery-guts carrying the pain of separation around with him.

When I was going through puberty, my mum and sisters would sigh as I slouched in to breakfast, with a good-morning grunt about the best I could manage. 'Oh dear, here comes old Mr Simon Sad Sack,' they'd say in unison. At the time I naturally resented them sending me up, wondering how I could possibly have been cursed with this Neanderthal family. But 'Simon Sad Sack' was a perfect description of my psyche in the months after Mercy B. Lord left – it was exactly as if I were dragging a hugely heavy sack of memories behind me.

We had a meeting with Texas Tiger mid-morning the next day and I hadn't quite completed the greased-lightning layout so I went in to work early. I intended calling Molly Ong just after nine to ask if she was free for lunch the following day. Molly liked to be seen at the city's best watering holes, although with my potential disgrace looming she might opt for a quieter venue or even decide she was busy, though that would have surprised me.

I called Molly, apologised for the short notice and asked if we could have lunch the next day.

'Oh, lovely, Simon, but I can't make it tomorrow. What about today?'

'Great. Where would you like to eat?'

She agreed to have lunch at the Goodwood Park Hotel. I then called Owen Denmeade, the maître d', and asked for a quiet table. We'd become quite good friends following Dansford's four-bottle vintage French wine fiasco and his subsequent drunken and very successful performance at the piano. 'Wine?' he asked, half-jokingly.

'Can't say. Molly Ong's with me.'

'Ah, a nice French chablis,' he said right off. 'I'll put a bottle of '65 Vaudésir Grand Cru on ice. A good blend of citrus, oak, peach, butter, lemon and nectarine.' He paused for the final verbal thrust. 'Nice tight acid structure.'

'C'mon, Owen, cut the bullshit.' I laughed. 'And isn't a bottle, even if it does have a tight acid structure, rather a lot for one lady at lunch? I'll be drinking beer. She'd probably rather have a couple of martinis.'

'Trust me, it won't be wasted, Simon,' he replied.

In the nearly three years I'd been in Singapore, the place had grown up fast. There seemed to be a kind of electricity in the air, and there was now barely a trace of the sleepy, colonial, far-flung corner of the empire that it had once been. The city state, however undemocratic the conduct of its PAP parliament, was working for the majority and there was a growing sophistication among its so-called cognoscenti, so that French wine at the luncheon table was becoming common and Owen, harking back to his days as head steward on P&O, was brushing up on what he referred to as his 'oenological frog patois', which roughly meant his knowledge of French vintages.

I'd been so busy on the layout, and the rickshaw dash with Louie da Fly to Arab Street, that I wasn't sure what had transpired on Karlene Stein's program the previous evening. My mind was so full of Mercy B. Lord that I'd neglected to stop the taxi on my way to work to pick up a copy of the *Straits Times* to see if there were any further developments in the teacup storm. Now I'd need to go straight from the Texas Oil office after the presentation to luncheon with Molly, which would mean I'd still be in the dark.

Dansford, after the initial news of my big win, obviously hadn't watched the subsequent drama unfolding on TV or read the paper, so he was oblivious to the phoney-portrait fuss. By six o'clock, when Karlene Stein came on the box, he'd have been well into the evening's carousing; he had admitted to me he'd only picked up the news of the win by seeing it on the box in a bar somewhere. Big Loud Mike would probably be unaware of it, too, no doubt regarding Karlene Stein as much too parochial.

The layout looked okay – in fact, it was rather good. I was becoming a dab hand at drawing and painting tigers, although I wasn't confident enough to do the final art. I'd give that to Alejandra Calatayud, a Mexican freelance artist who had married an American oil engineer, then divorced him but decided to stay in Singapore and revert to her maiden name. She had the knack of painting a tiger with a distinctly Asian feel. The trick was not to make the tiger too Chinese and so rob the Tiger product of its air of Western technology, but to add a subtle difference – it was more a matter of mood than line. She seemed to understand this and reached a perfect compromise between East and West. It was not something Big Loud Mike would notice, just me being pernickety.

Dansford had the job of telling Michael Johns his tiger piss idea was ratshit. Big Loud Mike was a bit of a sulker and didn't like to appear to be in the wrong, which meant I'd have to sell the new concept hard. At the end of the year he was due back in Houston, where he was slated for a promotion to head office. 'Just one more stripe on mah goddamn slope combat fatigues!' he'd say, adopting the ugly nickname for Asians that had become increasingly popular during the Vietnam War. I'd have to convince him that there'd be one more stripe if he took on 'Tiger lubrication – greased lightning for ultimate engine care'. I completed the layout with half an hour to spare, so I roughed out a variation on the running tiger idea – what is known in advertising as a 'back-pocket concept', a just-in-case-you-can't-sell-the-one-you-recommend. This one showed the same tiger simply outlined in pencil, with only the sky rendered in gouache and coloured chalk, this time featuring a blazing sunrise and the words 'Tiger Liquid Gold – your engine's best investment'. It needed a bit of work – the word 'lubrication' or 'oil' had to fit in somewhere, also 'fast action' or something similar – but gold was an obsession of the Chinese, their safety net when Lady Luck turned against them, and as a concept it had a half-reasonable chance of working. We'd been lucky with Texas Tiger but you learn not to be complacent; sooner or later, your opposition comes up with something, as I had done when Caltex ruled with their 'boron' rocket-fuel concept. All it takes is a promise from the competition that appeals to the consumer's imagination and suddenly you're dead in the water, a thoroughly drowned tiger.

The previous night's TV wasn't mentioned at the Texas Oil meeting, nor was there anything in the morning paper, but Dansford must have said something because Big Loud Mike congratulated me on my win – 'Hey, Simon, it don't come as a big surprise, man.' He pointed at the greased-lightning layout. 'Any guy who can paint a running tiger like that – be chickenfeed to paint a piece of slope *poontang*.'

I opened my mouth to give him a serve but Dansford quickly placed a cautionary finger to his lips so that all I could say was, 'Steady on, Mike.' It didn't surprise me that the local head of Texas Oil had been divorced three times. Later I would castigate myself for not having a proper go at him. Racism, the girlie-bar mentality, was common enough among expats, many of whom were hardly God's gift. The Australians were no better than most, and while there were notable exceptions, many expats were in Asia for all the wrong reasons. It was not uncommon for a local second-in-command to be more intelligent than the expat sent to run the show, and they were often left to do the job while the Western boss arrived late, lunched long and, if he returned, left early to entertain until late.

Though neither Dansford nor the Texas Oil boss let on at the mid-morning meeting, it was highly likely that Big Loud Mike had been with Dansford the previous night. Dansford had a dangerous habit of 'softening up' clients, as he called it, which involved taking them out on the town the night before making a big presentation, his theory being that the client would be too hung-over to be overly demanding the following morning.

Fortunately, Big Loud Mike liked the greased-lightning concept, and I met Molly in the foyer of the Goodwood Park Hotel at a few minutes past one, apologising for being late. If Molly Ong had any bad habits, I'd seen no evidence of them. She was always organised, on time and exceedingly pleasant. She knew her own mind and was nobody's fool. Giving her a place on the Tourist Promotion Board was a very intelligent move. Apart from more than pulling her weight, she had a knack for getting people to cooperate and could make two blowflies trapped together in a matchbox behave calmly. But she was no purring pussycat, and when roused had a way with verbal darts that seldom missed their mark. Her earlier training as Miss Singapore may have helped, but you got the feeling that Molly had always been like this, the pretty kid who owned the playground through a combination of charm and strength of character. She would have been more than a worthy fourth contender among the female heavyweights at the awards dinner, which was now unlikely to eventuate.

After speaking to Mercy B. Lord, I knew she wasn't going to come forward as Thursday Girl and that it was completely out of the question that she would attend the awards dinner. This meant Molly's idea of basing the Singapore Girl concept on the portrait wasn't going to work, so I was anxious to outline the idea I'd discussed with Mercy B. Lord, almost guaranteeing that everything about the beauty-plus-brains competition would be kosher and that she'd have to win selection fair and square. My primary purpose, of course, was to ensure Mercy B. Lord's safety.

I wanted to assure Molly that her original idea could still work and was too good to lose. But she didn't need to be told what the inevitable outcome would be, or that it would provide even greater opportunities for prolonged publicity. Perhaps it was cheating, but I told myself it was in a good cause, a win–win situation whichever way you looked at it. The general public would have had a lot of fun voting, Singapore's reputation for beautiful women would have been vindicated and the portrait belatedly recognised as genuine.

Owen seated us with a commendable fuss and Molly agreed she'd have wine. 'Perhaps a chilled white to accompany fish.'

'Excellent, Miss Ong. We have fresh brown trout, invariably nicer than the rainbow, in my humble opinion,' Owen smirked, flapping her starched damask napkin and carefully placing it on her lap with a triumphant sidelong glance at me. Then he suggested the '65 Vaudésir and unashamedly launched with aplomb into his previous ridiculous wine-buff description, though this time omitting the bit at the end about acid structure. Molly agreed it was a splendid choice. I ordered a Tiger beer in honour of the morning's successful Texas Oil meeting. Menus were opened and, in a surprisingly short time, the chilled wine appeared in its ice bucket.

'That was quick,' Molly said brightly.

'One always tries to anticipate in the hope that someone with exquisite taste will come to luncheon, Miss Ong. Very occasionally, one is rewarded,' the smarmy bastard replied.

'One is suitably impressed,' said Molly with a laugh, not taken in by the sycophantic spiel. Owen removed the bottle to a clatter of ice cubes, napkined it and poured.

'Nice tight acid structure,' I noted.

'Oh, you've tasted it, Simon?' Molly asked.

'No.' I glanced at Owen. 'One learns a bit from one's friends.'

We ordered our lunch, then clinked glasses. 'Thanks for agreeing to lunch, Molly. I know you're busy.'

Molly smiled. 'Now, let me guess – this is all about that dreadful busybody Karlene Stein and the piece in the paper, isn't it?'

'Well, yes, but not entirely. Actually it's about several things – three actually, all of them related.' I couldn't mention Mercy B. Lord's refusal to cooperate with Molly, because she'd warned me that no one must know of our clandestine meeting. I admit, I felt a bit of a fraud when I asked the first question. 'Have you called Mercy B. Lord, Molly?'

'Oh, yes, not long after I phoned you.'

'And?'

'Well, it was not an entirely successful outcome. I can't understand the girl. You told me, of course, that the two of you are no longer together, but it seems more than that. She doesn't strike me as someone who would do something like this out of revenge or spite.' Molly paused and looked at me. 'Simon, there was something about her voice. I think she's frightened.'

'What, of me?' I played dumb, just to be on the safe side.

'No, that's not the impression I got. But she's afraid of something, or someone.'

I held my breath, hoping she'd pursue this, but she went off on a tangent.

'She did say it was your fault for not asking her permission before you entered the painting in the competition. However, I got the distinct feeling that wasn't why she'd refused. Although, of course, you know the old adage, a woman scorned . . .' She paused as if thinking. 'But I really don't think so. She explained it was about "face" but wouldn't elaborate, wouldn't name names. Awkward, really. I think the Singapore Girl is a good idea, and we need someone like her, with looks and intelligence, someone who knows her way around important people. I'm convinced she'd do a great job.'

'Well, you may have to think of some other way to promote it,' I replied. 'Pity, though. I agree, she's ideal.'

'Simply appointing her to the job without the razzamatazz surrounding the portrait – that is, if she'll accept – isn't quite the same thing. The Singapore Girl would have made a lovely Tourist Board promotion. The idea was for Long Me and the minister to announce it the day after the awards dinner.'

'Well, with Mercy B. Lord's existence in doubt, Hong Kong may want to withdraw the prize. The entry stipulates the subject of the portrait must be real. I guess that could disqualify me.' I was softening her up nicely for plan B, the back-pocket concept.

Molly looked at me, surprised. 'Simon, you obviously didn't see *Karlene's People* last night.'

'No, I was working back at the agency, rendering a layout, and lost track of the time.'

'Well, an elderly nun named Sister Charity from the St Thomas Aquinas Catholic Mission Orphanage vouched for Mercy B. Lord's existence and delightfully explained how she got her name. Next to God validating her existence, it doesn't get any better. Of course the name and the story make her even *more* charismatic.' Molly took a sip of wine. 'No, Simon, the dinner is well and truly on. This morning's *South China Morning Post* features your friend Elma Kelly. She must have heard Karlene casting aspersions on your portrait and implying that the subject was possibly a figment of your imagination, and no doubt she'd also seen the article in the *Straits Times*. Anyhow, she's waded in and given Karlene a proper serve.' Molly giggled. 'Called her "The Television Trollop"! She also had a few well-chosen words to say about irresponsible journalism directed at "Singapore's leading morning newspaper", as she terms it. Then she vouched for Mercy B. Lord's existence, while also lauding your absolute integrity to the high heavens. I imagine that's all the reassurance the Hong Kong Art Gallery is likely to need.'

Lunch arrived – the brown trout for Molly and a rump steak with pepper sauce for me – and we waited until the waiter had left to talk more. 'Well,' I said, leaning back, 'that's good to know. I must admit it's a relief, but it doesn't solve your problem, does it?'

To be truthful, I wasn't sure it *was* a relief. I found myself suddenly experiencing twin emotions – as an artist, I was vindicated; as an ad man with a terrific idea for a promotion, I was defeated. But, much more importantly, it meant Mercy B. Lord wasn't yet safe. As the Singapore Girl, she would have had quasi-government protection backed by the promotional campaign. Both would have put real pressure on Beatrice Fong and Sidney Wing not to try anything untoward. Now, with none of this likely to happen, she remained isolated and in a parlous situation, one created entirely by me.

It suddenly struck me that if they decided Mercy B. Lord should go missing, there would never be a better time. In my mind I could hear Beatrice Fong explaining that she simply hadn't turned up at work, but that she was a big girl with no family to consider, so maybe she had decided to avoid the publicity. My mind ran on feverishly, imagining Beatrice Fong spilling the beans about our affair, which had ended badly, making things quite impossible for her. I could see the evil old bitch cackling to herself after her final querulous complaint that she'd been let down by her ungrateful employee, who had been shown nothing but kindness.

Molly carefully parted the flesh of the trout from its spine and lifted a delicate morsel, holding the fork halfway to her mouth. 'Yes, it makes things awkward. It's a promotion made in heaven and I was so sure she'd love the job. She's certainly made for it. Ten years ago I would have walked over hot coals for the same opportunity. It's more than an opportunity, it's a career.'

'Did you explain it to her?'

'Of course, but I got no reaction, other than that it was impossible for her to attend the dinner or even make herself known as the model for "Thursday Girl".'

'But she didn't say directly, "Molly, I don't want your job," not plainly like that?'

'No. Call it women's intuition, if you like, but, as I said, I got the distinct impression she wasn't free to decide for herself. So if she won't attend the awards dinner or agree to the proposal, there goes a fine idea.' Molly paused. 'But we need somebody like her, a beautiful young woman with brains, to promote tourism.' She took another mouthful of trout. 'By the way, Simon, I've been meaning to ask, why did you call your portrait "Thursday Girl"?'

'Oh, you know, a picture needs a title,' I laughed. 'Nothing important, really. We met on a Thursday – a rainy one, as I remember. This glamorous young creature met me at the airport. I was hugely chuffed, told myself whatever happened to me it couldn't be all bad.' It was a fib, of course, but, as Mercy B. Lord had noted, nobody was likely to check that I'd landed on a Saturday and within minutes had lost massive face with the Chinese-woman-and-baby incident. In fact, if Thursday hadn't meant what it did, I could well have named the portrait 'Saturday Girl'.

Molly smiled. 'Simon, you're a lousy liar. This is Singapore. It was a Saturday. By Sunday morning we all knew about the hilarious incident of the Chinese mother, the umbrella and the newcomer from Australia. It was one of the things that endeared you to me when you made your new business presentation for the tourism account.' She laughed. 'Sir Galahad comes to Singapore!'

'Oops!' I'd been caught out a second time. I could feel myself blushing. Chairman Meow and my sisters could always tell if I was fibbing as a kid. 'I keep forgetting Singapore is a very small place.' I laughed, a little shamefaced.

'Not just small, Simon, it's the so-called "upper-middles" who form a small but very nosy part of society. And then there's a government that likes to know who's in town and who they're dealing with. For instance, we probably know rather more about you than you think.'

'Oh? Why would that be? Not much to know – ad man and a bit of a painter, that's all, really.'

'Oh, Simon, you are so naïve,' Molly laughed again. 'As a matter of routine, the Tourist Promotion Board would have checked your background. The government doesn't like nasty surprises. If I know, then you may be sure others know as well. There is no such thing as going incognito on this island.'

'Oh, dear,' I said.

Molly threw back her head and laughed at my obvious embarrassment.

Eager to change the subject, I said, 'Molly, I've got an idea for a Singapore Girl promotion. It could still work and get you what you want.'

'Well, go on, then – let's have it, Simon.' She smiled.

I outlined the idea, modifying it on the run, suggesting an exhibition of the portrait in the town hall, with first prize being a big cheque and a portrait painted by me or some other painter. I was aware it lacked the zing of scandal: the disgraced artist, the idea that the portrait was a fiction and Singapore was being accused of lacking beauties to match the girl in the peacock-tail chair. It had lost a bit of its original motivation, its big idea – meeting the beauty challenge, finding the missing girl and so vindicating the nation, which was what is known in the ad business as its 'drive'.

Molly was too nice to dismiss it out of hand. 'I can see how well it might have worked,' she said. 'How do we get you back to being a disgraced artist, Simon?' she teased. Then she let me down gently. 'I'm still not convinced that Mercy B. Lord would enter, but I'm glad you told me. Don't lose that promotion. There's something in the pipeline that I can't speak about yet, but it could be useful. I especially like the idea of the public voting – it gives it a wonderful sense of community involvement.'

'Yeah, you're right. No guarantee she'll enter and, I agree, the promotion has lost its drive.'

'If only I knew what or who Mercy B. Lord fears. What it is that prevents her attending the dinner or sharing in the glory of your portrait. She struck me as a happy, outgoing sort of girl when we met at the cocktail party, someone who might enjoy a little of the limelight. She must be seriously frightened to pass up an opportunity like this.'

'You could try Beatrice Fong and Sidney Wing,' I said, attempting to sound offhand.

'Really?' Molly said, not missing a beat.

'Well, it would be a damn good start. I confess I've never met the old crone personally, but there's no doubt the two are in cahoots and that Mercy B. Lord is somehow involved.'

Molly grinned. 'Aha! Are you sure, Simon?'

I nodded.

She paused, thinking. Then, with her head to one side and her eyes narrowed, she said, 'And it wouldn't affect you if we took a closer look at the two of them?'

'No, I'm leaving the agency anyway. Oh shit! I shouldn't have said that. Dansford was going to announce it after the Hong Kong dinner.'

Molly was already well into her third glass of wine, the ever-hovering Denmeade waiting to fill it the moment it reached the halfway mark. 'Leaving? Oh, Simon, don't say that! You're the major reason we're with Samuel Oswald Wing.'

'Thanks, Molly. I've enjoyed every minute with you and Long Me. Learned a heap from both of you as well. But my contract expires soon and the three senior Chinese elements in the agency don't want it renewed, and I confess I feel the same. I've had enough of the Three

Wing Circus, although the Yanks are pushing for me to stay another six months to put the new Colgate-Palmolive campaign to bed. It's really unnecessary – all the work has been done. It's just that those big international accounts are paranoid something will go wrong in a foreign market. After Big Lather, they're convinced I have the magic touch.'

'Oh, but you *do!* Right from day one, your new business presentation was miles ahead of the others.'

'Thanks, Molly, but the presentation for your account was largely Mrs Sidebottom's idea, with only a soupçon of Dansford and myself mixed in.' I smiled, I hoped, enigmatically. 'Everything comes to an end. You're in good hands with Dansford, and the Yanks are bound to send a crackerjack creative director to replace me.'

'Simon, Singapore needs expats like you. Don't leave us. You guys open the windows and let in a breath of fresh air. Not every expat, but certainly the good ones. Singapore is a small and somewhat incestuous island with everyone —'

'Molly, I'm leaving the agency, *not* Singapore. I have one or two things – opportunities – I'd like to explore.'

'I'm delighted to hear that, Simon. Though I shall miss working with you,' Molly replied graciously, then she stopped dead. It was as if a momentous thought had suddenly occurred to her, the proverbial light bulb flashing on above her head. She leaned back and drained her glass as if the action were an exclamation mark. 'The girl is right! It's all about face! The Achilles heel of the Chinese!'

I laughed. 'That's a mixed metaphor from opposite ends of the body, but what's all this about face?'

'We need to do a little digging to uncover the past,' Molly cried. 'So simple when you know whom to target.'

I watched as Owen Denmeade filled her wine glass with a barely concealed look of triumph; the level in the bottle was well below the halfway mark. He placed it in the ice bucket and asked me if I cared for another beer. I nodded, hoping to hell Molly hadn't had too much wine to think straight.

She was absorbed in thought, absently bringing the newly filled glass to her lips then replacing it on the table. 'Yes . . . yes, that's it,' she said as if to herself, a smile on her very pretty face. 'Should be enough time to dig a small mountain of dirt. God bless the British colonial archivists – they made a habit of keeping records of the notable, culpable, good, bad and indictable people in the past. Wing and Fong . . .'

'Sounds like a Chinese brass band,' I quipped.

'Maybe it's time to bang the big bass drum and see what we shake out,' Molly replied. If she was stonkered, it wasn't affecting her wits.

The following Monday I arrived in the agency to be told by Alice Ho that Mr Sidney had left for America. A little later, apropos of nothing, Ronnie told me, keeping a very bland expression, that Sidney had gone to visit his golf course in Florida, where he was constructing a state-of-the-art retirement village for golf-o-holics (a Ronnie word).

Then, just before 10 a.m., Alice called from reception to say a courier had delivered an envelope she thought I might want right away. She gave me a knowing look as she handed it to me. 'Maybe good news, Simon?' she said as I recognised the handwriting on the envelope. I didn't kid myself that Alice was unaware of all the salient details concerning Mercy B. Lord, but she was letting me know I could now count on her silence.

The enclosed note, also in Mercy B. Lord's handwriting, said:

Miss Otis no longer regrets she cannot attend and would be delighted to accept your kind invitation to dinner in Hong Kong.

Miss Mercy B. Lord.

P.S. Kindly send the cheongsam and shoes.

The miraculous Molly Ong worked fast. I called to thank her. 'Molly, I'm hugely impressed. Mercy B. Lord has accepted!'

Molly giggled like a naughty schoolgirl. 'Simon, this is Singapore. The past has its chin resting on the shoulders of the present – that is, when it concerns the old Singapore Chinese families.'

'Well, you certainly lost no time doing the pick and shovel work.'

She laughed. 'It never got to pick and shovel, Simon. With a little help from my friends in the government archives, digging the dirt wasn't hard work. In both cases I simply had to scuff the ground once or twice with the toe of my shoe.'

'Have you contacted Mercy B. Lord?' I asked.

'Yes, of course, a couple of hours after the minister made a phone call to each of the evil empires.'

'So you know Mercy B. Lord has accepted the invitation to the awards dinner?'

'Yes, but she told me she wanted to answer your invitation formally.'

'And the Singapore Girl?'

'That too.'

I'm sure Molly must have heard my sigh of relief. 'Does this mean Mercy B. Lord no longer has anything to fear from you-know-who?'

'Well, for the time being, but once she becomes the Singapore Girl she'll be hard to touch.' Molly paused, then said, 'There's a hitch, though, and I think you may be able to help, Simon. She insists she has to be free on Thursdays until Friday evening.' Molly seemed to take a breath because the tone of her voice changed markedly. This was now a Molly who demanded answers. 'Simon, last time I asked, you fibbed shamelessly in an attempt to protect Mercy B. Lord. I've done my part, now you have to do yours; it's time to come clean. Why is your portrait named "Thursday Girl"?'

'Molly, you have to believe me. I simply don't know what the hell happens on those days. It nearly drove me crazy and ultimately caused our break-up. Whatever it is, it's pretty bloody serious and involves Sidney Wing, maybe all three Wing Brothers, and Beatrice Fong. She simply won't say and she won't budge.'

There was a silence at the other end, then, 'And that's all?'

'I'm pretty sure she travels overseas.'

'Overnight?'

'Yes.'

'Well, that shouldn't be too hard to check. Anything else?'

'She carries a reinforced briefcase. It looks normal enough from the outside but when you tap it, the interior is obviously a metal box. The two combination locks are not for decoration.'

'I take it you don't know what's inside.'

'Haven't a clue, except that it doesn't rattle.'

'Right, we'll check customs. Anything else?'

'No, I don't think so . . . Oh, yes, she never brought the briefcase back to the flat on her return. Claimed she'd leave it with Mohammed, Beatrice Fong's chauffeur, who returned it to the office.'

'The briefcase – was it always the same one?'

'Yes, I'm pretty sure it was. I think she was telling the truth about it, the point being that she's never lied about anything. She just clams up, doesn't answer questions.'

'So it seems she's a regular courier, delivering something to someone somewhere. We'll soon know the somewhere but not the what or the who.'

I didn't reply. Was I risking everything by telling Molly this?

'Think, Simon. Is there anything else you can remember?'

'She sometimes carries a burqa.'

'As a disguise?'

'I suppose. Honestly, Molly, I don't know any more. I lost her because it was driving me nuts, but I tell you what, provided I know she's safe, if she'd come back to me, I'd never broach the subject again.'

'Simon, those kinds of secret arrangements always end badly, like one partner having a secret lover. Sooner or later the relationship falls apart.'

I gave a rueful laugh. 'I'd happily take my chances to have her for five days of the week.' It sounded as if Molly, a magnificent-looking woman in her mid-thirties and still single, knew what she was talking about.

'Oh, Simon, you do truly love her, don't you?'

'I don't want to see her hurt. I know she wouldn't willingly be part of anything bad.'

'But you feel she's in real danger? I must say, I agree. Those two are both nasty pieces of work.'

'But clever,' I added. 'Also very careful. I think finding out where Mercy B. Lord disappears to on a Thursday, and why, may require a bit more than scuffing your toe in the dirt.'

'Never know what you can find if you use the sharp end of a stiletto heel,' Molly replied.

After putting down the phone I called Connie Song at Corona Flowers and ordered a dozen red roses, telling her that I'd pick them up in a couple of hours. Then I took a taxi to Robinsons, the department store, and asked if I could buy a box big enough to carry a pair of shoes and a dress, with sufficient tissue paper to wrap them in. I'd had the cheongsam dry-cleaned in one of my sadder examples of magical thinking – if I keep the dress fresh, perhaps . . . Robinsons were kind enough to give me the box and paper and I then bought a yard of wide dusty pink grosgrain ribbon. I know it sounds a bit sissy, but I'm an art director and a painter, and appearances matter. Besides, delivering Mercy B. Lord's gorgeous gear in a brown paper shopping bag was not on.

I knew there were several goldsmiths, mostly Indian, in Raffles Place, just down from the department store. I soon located one, an old Indian man with a three-day growth of white stubble. He was sitting outside his shop, touting. 'Beautiful signet ring for lovely gentleman, sir. Eighteen carat, going very, very cheap today!' he said as I approached.

'Do you manufacture on the premises?' I asked.

'Of course. We are making for you special. Maybe initials? Or diamonds, ruby also. Opal, topaz, amethyst too soft, but I can do emerald, or zircon semi-precious . . . first-class good one from Ceylon. Also, number-one workshop. In Singapore you cannot have better. Branches in India.' He rose to his feet and, with a sweep of his arm, indicated the doorway. 'You come inside, please, sir. We are at your service always and most definitely.'

The shop smelled of incense and marigolds, and once inside I asked him for a small piece of paper. With my ballpoint I designed a chisel brooch or pin about the size of the toggle fastening the dragon's tail and head on the mandarin collar of the cheongsam. Then I drew the flip side to indicate the brooch pin. 'Can you make this for me?' I asked, handing him the slip of paper.

The old guy examined my design, then called out in what I took to be Hindi. Moments later, a younger guy wearing a soft leather apron and leather slip-on sandals came through the beaded curtains separating the back of the shop from the front.

'Number-one goldsmith, Calcutta-trained, also my son, at your humble service, sir.' The old bloke handed him the drawing and they were soon locked in a rapid conversation. Finally the old bloke turned to me. 'He can make it.' He paused, shaking his head. 'But not cheap – very complicated.

I gave him the eternal bargainer's sigh. 'How much in eighteen-carat gold?'

He brought his hands to his cheeks in alarm. 'My goodness gracious me! We are thinking always fourteen carat! Eighteen carat, that is fish of another kettle!' He turned and spoke rapidly to the goldsmith, then turned back to me. 'His children will go hungry, but we are making in eighteen carat the cost of fourteen carat, that is our pleasure, sir.'

'Hey, wait on, you didn't give me the cost of the fourteen carat.'

He smiled, revealing gummy gaps punctuated by half a dozen brown teeth stained with betel nut. 'This is your most lucky day, sir. You are getting a nice and excellent bargain, definitely and absolutely!' The goldsmith, looking down at his sandalled feet, nodded sagely.

'May I enquire what this definite and absolute bargain might be?'

'Eighteen carat for fourteen carat and no questions asked.' He took a breath, 'Just for you, sir, 150 Singapore dollars.

I attempted to gulp convincingly. 'You must be joking!'

The old guy completely ignored my protest. He pointed to the goldsmith. 'He must make special mould, pour gold, cut, polish; big, big, very, very delicate job. When must you have this masterpiece, sir?'

'In three days, Friday morning at the latest. The handle must be wood – persimmon, if you can find some.'

'What is this wood, sir? We are now carpenters? Goldsmith then abracadabra, we are becoming all at once carpenters? I beg your pardon, sir, but wood?'

'Well, you can save on some of the gold.'

'That observation you are making is true and not true. Where am I finding this persimmon wood in three days?'

'Any good Chinese cabinet maker.' I held up my pinkie. 'You need a piece no bigger than the size of the first joint, even less. Ask for the heartwood.' I pulled out my wallet, withdrew five bucks and handed it to him. 'This will cover your taxi fare and the cost of the wood. You've saved the gold you'd use for the handle and that should easily pay for the labour that goes into the handle.'

Clasping his hands to his face once again, he slowly walked twice around his silent son. Then he stopped and threw up his hands, 'Three days! *Oi-oi-eh!* Now also carpentry we are needing.' Then he launched a volley of incomprehensible words at the goldsmith, who had remained silent, staring down at the polished cement floor. Finally, the old bloke turned back to me. 'You are getting very lucky, sir. He, my son, say, this one time *only*, no surcharge for urgent job, normally two weeks, now only three days and carpentry also required. You are saving thirty Singapore dollar all at once together.'

'So am I to understand, then, that the final price is a hundred and twenty dollars and you'll have it ready by Thursday? Friday morning at the absolute latest?'

The old man grinned his sticky brown grin. 'You are very, very good at bargainings, sir. I am taking my hat off. But with surcharge for three nights and days 'round-clock workings and mouldings and pourings, and cuttings, and polishings, and altogether strivings and also carpentry,' he took a hurried breath, 'normally thirty Singapore dollars surcharge, total price 180 dollars.' He paused to allow this sum of money to register. Then, head to one side, hands wide in a gesture of generosity, he said with a smile, 'Now, surcharge we are very, very generously dropping, so you are getting a special once-in-lifetimes bargain.' He brought his head back to an even keel and folded his arms, letting me know that he'd run out of patience. 'Only 150 Singapore dollars, twenty per cent deposit on acceptance of quotings, all work personally guaranteed and certified most excellent and definitely first class, delivered by three-day miracle from Patel & Son, Calcutta-trained goldsmith!'

I knew when I was beaten but managed to get them to throw in a small presentation box covered in black leather (probably free anyway), and I left feeling thoroughly bamboozled, without the foggiest idea if the chisel was a fair price or not. However, I was dead certain it wasn't a bargain.

Returning home, I placed the tissue paper carefully inside the box, then wrapped it around the cheongsam and shoes and took a taxi to the florist, where Connie Song had the roses ready. She also just happened to have a purple and white cymbidium orchid and I opened the box and placed it on top of the tissue. I admit it was probably excessive.

Connie then offered to wrap the box in her gorgeous, shiny chocolate-coloured paper before tying the ribbon.

'No, no, I'm already going too far with the orchid. These are just clothes being returned. Maybe just one of your terrific bows with the ribbon I bought, just to make sure the lid is secure,' I suggested.

'This nice ribbon, but too expensive for florist. People they don't want to pay. I tie beautiful for you, Mr Simon.'

I returned to the agency, where Alice Ho, seeing the roses, jokingly cried, 'For me, Simon?' I guess after all those months of having her reception area adorned with my boomeranged flowers, the aspidistra, now resting on its former plinth, didn't quite measure up.

I had practically achieved immortality in Alice's eyes after the Karlene Stein interview, when her own personal reception desk had featured in the background, and later there'd been a reverse-angle cut where Alice's face, almost in focus, had appeared in the background. Alice Ho, a powerful ally to have, was now most definitely on my side.

I called Louie da Fly into my office. 'Okay, mate, now here's the drill,' I began.

He pointed at the roses. 'Hey, boss, what bloody going on? Long stem? This much better, and red one also. What in box?'

'Mind your own business, Louie da Fly. Now, listen to me carefully.'

He looked at me sympathetically. 'This no good business, boss. Always you pay, long stem, no stem, nothing happen. Maybe last time near Muslim temple, something happen, eh?'

'Maybe when you're grown up you'll understand, mate. Will you shut up and listen to me?'

'I grow up, already three,' he said in a hurt voice, holding up three fingers. 'Three womens, and I don't pay. Also no flower.'

'Louie da Fly, I don't need to know about your love life. Here's three bucks for the taxi, and don't think I don't know the fare is only a dollar fifty.'

'I take rickshaw, thirty-five cent. Sank you, boss.'

'Now, listen.' I pointed to the box and the roses. 'They go to Miss Mercy B. Lord, nobody else, you understand? Not the girl at the switchboard or the old lady. Don't take any crap. If she's not there, then wait in the tea-house. If you sat where you sat the day before yesterday, her office window will be directly opposite on the first storey, so if you get thrown out of the office, before you sit down to wait in the tea-house, stand on the street under the window and yell out. It's worth a try, anyway.'

'What I say for yelling, boss?'

'Say, "Louie da Fly has flowers for pretty lady!" That'll do.'

'Air-condish, boss.'

'What's that supposed to mean?'

'Window close, air-condish, no hear me, boss.'

'Ferchrissake! Just see that she gets them personally,' I yelled.

'Yes, boss. Why you not say first time?'

'Remind me to fire you when you get back, will ya?'

'Too vallabil employ, boss.'

'G'arn, scram!'

'Okay, I go, quick quick for bloody sure, boss.' Louie da Fly had become fixated on the great Australian adjective, convinced that peppering his speech with it gave his English added veracity.

Louie da Fly returned an hour later without reporting to me but instead went straight back to work. The little bugger knew I could see him, wrapping stereos in newspaper and then tying them with coarse twine for delivery to the various Chinese newspapers, from my office.

You may be wondering why I didn't pull rank with the production staff. Being a director, I had the power to fire on a whim without bothering to give an explanation. The PAP government had little time for unions and, metaphorically speaking, they'd pulled out their teeth, nails and toenails, leaving them with no voice and a very tenuous grip on industrial welfare, limping along, going nowhere. The left-wing leadership had been locked up in 1963 during 'Operation Cold Storage', and six years later still languished in jail. The PAP government enforced a law inherited from their former colonial masters that allowed indefinite detention; somehow, they hadn't got around to abolishing it.

But for your average worker, there were swings and roundabouts. While the new government kept wages low and annual holidays short, they made up for this with a calendar peppered with public holidays – fifteen, plus two bank holidays – and they'd instituted a pension scheme and were building decent housing complete with excellent sanitisation almost as fast as it took to bake bricks and mix cement. No longer, as in British colonial times, could you smell the stench of Singapore from five miles out to sea. Affordable apartment blocks for workers were beginning to rise all over the island. There was no doubt that the average Singaporean was a lot better off than ever before.

However, strikes were illegal, and at the clerk and general factotum level there had never been much protection. You owned your business, owed your employees nothing but their wages and were free to hire and fire pretty much at will. When they grew too old to be effective you showed them the door.

But that was precisely the point. The agency before the Yanks bought in was totally autocratic. In fact, even after, very little had changed at the staff level. Sidney and Johnny ruled through fear. Ronnie, while still demanding a measure of kowtowing, was on slightly more familiar terms with staff. It was the Chinese way, but it wasn't mine or, for that matter, Dansford's. This egalitarian attitude, far from pleasing the older members of staff, totally disconcerted them. They simply didn't understand the new practice of the *gwai-lo* who treated staff with respect. In fact, they seemed to silently resent the familiarity. Most people don't like change, but the Chinese working class abhors it, even fears it. For centuries, change has only brought disaster with it. They are past masters of adaptation, making the system work, no matter how draconian. As Dansford once remarked, 'They just don't dig it. There has to be a catch, but they can't figure it out.' I recall him shaking his head. 'The irony is that, unable to understand our motives, they become even more mindlessly eager to please.'

It was only with the young guys, the Willy Wonkas and Louie da Flys, that you could get the concept across that a harmonious office atmosphere with *chi feng shui* – positive energy, as Willy Wonka had once translated it – created a better working environment.

But every once in a while you were forced to pull rank and jerk one of the kids into line. I guess that goes for anywhere. Even Willy Wonka, before he disappeared into the army, would occasionally need to be straightened out. I must say, the army had changed him, though I wasn't sure if it was for the better. He'd visited us when on leave. The old Willy Wonka in one of his father's oversized suits, excitedly jumping about, hands flying every which way as he talked, now stood more or less at attention and gave polite answers to questions. His short army-style crew cut and scrawny frame in a neat khaki uniform made him look vulnerable and a little disconcerted. The 'polished brasses, shiny boots' neatness imposed by the army, rather than lending him authority, gave him instead the appearance of a young cockerel that had lost most of its feathers in an unfortunate scrap with a large and domineering rooster. The delightful qualities the old Willy Wonka had possessed now seemed to have been starched and ironed out of him. The one good thing was that he hadn't entirely wasted his time in the service of his country. After his basic training, he'd applied for and been accepted into the military film unit, making up for his disappointment at not being sent to Australia for film training. On the basis of his experience on the Citizen watch campaign, no doubt vastly exaggerated, he'd earned a single stripe as a lance corporal. I wasn't at all sure that he was capable of carrying the crushing weight of responsibility thrust upon him by this lowest possible form of military authority. When eventually he completed his time in the military, we still had plans, along with Harry 'Three Thumbs' Poon, to develop a film studio. My hope was that Willy hadn't lost his spark or his wonderful enthusiasm for the business of life.

I walked over to the door of my office, opened it and yelled out, 'Louie da Fly – at the double!' Much to the amusement of the production staff, he jumped in fright, dropping the metal stereo he was wrapping and sending it clattering across the floor. Then, without stopping to retrieve it, he came running.

With the errant dispatch boy standing to rigid attention in my office, I enquired, 'Well? What happened?'

'Ribbon fall off, boss.' He pronounced it somewhere between 'libbon' and 'ribbon'.

'Ribbon? What ribbon?'

'For box, boss.'

'You little bastard! You opened the bloody box!'

'Fall off from my hand, that box, from rickshaw, ribbon fall off. Inside come outside. Why you buy more rubbish no stem flower, boss?'

'Don't give me that bullshit! You took a peek!'

'What peek, boss?'

'Jesus! Looked! You looked. You opened the box.'

'Only little bit, boss.'

'You little shit!'

Louie da Fly's eyes widened and he looked decidedly hurt. 'Not shit, boss . . . very vallabil employ.'

I had the distinct feeling that if I stayed around long enough, I'd end up working for Louie da Fly. 'Did you tie it up again?'

'Very beautiful, boss.'

'Yeah, I can imagine. So what happened? Did you give the roses and the box to Miss Mercy B. Lord personally?'

'Ja, ja, of course! No crap!' Louie da Fly looked at me quizzically. 'What happen, boss? Last time switch-bor lady with big hair on top and old lady no teeths, they take flower. Now, Missy Mercy B. Lord, she come take flower himself.'

'Herself.'

'Yeah, big smiles for me . . . Very happy.'

'Did she say anything? Ask you to wait?'

'She say ribbon on box very pretty.'

'You know, Louie da Fly, I really ought to give some serious thought to firing you.' I sighed, but couldn't hold back a grin. 'She said no such bloody thing.'

'Boss, how much you pay this ribbon?'

'Never mind. Miss Mercy B. Lord said nothing to you?'

'Ja, ja, she say she call telephone tonight.'

'What time?'

'She say to tell usual, boss. I not know what means this, usual.'

'Ferchrissake, Louie da Fly! Why didn't you tell me?'

'Maybe big surprise, boss. Maybe pick up telephone, you got Missy you loves.'

'Big surprise, my arse. When were you going to tell me?'

'Maybe one hours, boss. Stereo for Chinese newspaper very urgent, I very vallabil wrapping boy.'

I anticipated Mercy B. Lord would call me at the flat around seven o'clock, the time I usually got back from the agency when we were together. I stopped off and bought supper for two, her favourite Peking duck with a serving of rice and one of bok choy. Yeah, I know, *in my dreams* she was going to agree to come to dinner in the flat. Sure enough, punctual as mosquitoes after sundown, the phone rang at one minute past seven.

I grabbed it and forced my voice to sound casual. 'Hello?'

'Simon, it's Mercy B. Lord.'

'Hello, Mercy B. Lord, lovely to hear your voice again. Louie da Fly said you'd be ringing me.' I was trying to sound urbane, to keep my voice pleased but casual, but I could feel my heart beating faster. Just the sound of her voice set it thumping nineteen to the dozen.

'Thank you for the roses, Simon.' She giggled. 'The red roses, and the gorgeous orchid. I now have two, one on either side of my bed.'

'But only one person in bed between them when there should be two,' I quipped, thinking the wicked giggle was permission to banter a little.

'Now, Simon, I have several serious questions, so behave yourself!' It was said lightly but was nevertheless a reproof, a caution to keep my head pulled well in. It wasn't the first time her manner had changed within a single sentence, lightness turning to firmness. It reminded me of Chairman Meow. My dad called it 'whipped cream' – first the cream, then the whipping.

'Right,' I said, chastened.

'Simon, what did you do?'

'Me? Well, nothing, really. I had lunch with Molly Ong.'

'Yes, she told me. But what happened?'

'Molly may want you to be the Singapore Girl, but she also *really* likes you. She knew we'd broken up.'

'Oh?'

'I told her the first time she phoned, when she rang to congratulate me on the win and wanted to talk to you as well. I guess about the idea for the Singapore Girl promotion . . . maybe offer you the new job.'

'Simon, that's not the question I asked.'

'Yeah, okay, you ask what happened at lunch. Well, I admit we discussed the situation, the portrait, the predicament I'd placed you in —'

'Then you talked about Beatrice, Sidney and me?' she interrupted.

There was no point in lying. I wouldn't get away with it. 'Yes.'

'Yes what?'

'Yes, we talked about . . . you know, your . . . unavailability two days a week. She said with the Singapore Girl job there was probably lots of travel involved – you know, tourism business, all over the world. Molly wanted to know why I named your painting the way I did.' I was trying desperately to avoid using the word 'Thursday'.

'And what did you tell her?'

'Nothing. What could I tell her? I still don't know myself,' I protested.

'But you mentioned Beatrice?'

'Yes?'

'And the Wings . . . Sidney?'

'Yeah,' I said again, somewhat defensively. I was beginning to feel decidedly uncomfortable. 'Mercy B. Lord, I've fucked up big-time with the portrait and placed you in an invidious situation, probably a dangerous situation. The Singapore Girl is a way out, and Beatrice and Sidney are obviously making it impossible for you to accept.'

'You know that for sure, do you, Simon?'

I winced inwardly but persisted. 'Yes, I think I do. You said yourself that you'd love the job.'

'And Molly Ong wanted me for it . . . so you put two and two together?'

'Yeah, I admit I dobbed them in. After you said they'd put a tail on you and you were afraid, you know, the burqa . . . Then at the Ritz you said your life was fucked.' I paused. 'Mercy B. Lord, I'm truly sorry, but I love you and I want you back in my life and I don't want you to get hurt and I don't want your life to be fucked!' It all just poured out of me.

'Have you eaten?' she asked suddenly, the whip of the tongue gone and the cream back.

'No. I bought Peking duck, with rice and bok choy for two. Actually, I was hoping . . .'

'Yum! Turn on the oven – I'll be there in fifteen minutes.'

Perhaps when you're in love, you read signs into everything. I opened the door to Mercy B. Lord not much more than fifteen minutes later, having turned on the oven as instructed. She was wearing jeans and a white shirt with leather open-toed sandals, nothing sexy. It was the shirt that carried the telltale sign: she'd left just one button beyond modesty unbuttoned, and while she wasn't big in front, she was a B-cup, which was pretty big for an Asian woman, and I could see she wasn't wearing a bra. She also wore no make-up – another sign – and I confess I wondered whether she carried a spare pair of panties and a toothbrush in her bag. I'd slipped a jockstrap on when she suggested coming over for dinner. That part wasn't wishful thinking. I knew precisely what would happen the moment I laid eyes on her. No other fully dressed woman had ever had that effect on me. No, that's probably not true – sexy is sexy – but I didn't walk around with a hard-on the way I often did after a glimpse of her in the morning – a sideways glance at almost any time would do it. Bent over the kitchen bench preparing breakfast or dinner; reaching up to open the curtains; coming out of the bathroom barefoot, wrapped in a white terry-towelling gown with a turbaned towel on her head; in a Chinese grocery shop examining lychees, picking the plump, fleshy ones – anything would set me off. The one-eyed snake simply couldn't be trusted and seemed to have a mind of its own where she was concerned. People say that carnal desire shouldn't be confused with true love, but I couldn't separate the strands that made up the whole of my loving her. I was completely, totally, in love, and making love to Mercy B. Lord was a fundamental part of the entire gorgeous whole, and my feelings hadn't diminished in any way in the months we'd been apart. Now, as she stood in the doorway with the light falling obliquely on her face, I had trouble breathing.

'Come in, sweetheart,' I said softly. 'Sweetheart' is a cautious endearment that can swing from casual to meaningful, and I waited for her body language to tell me if it was the first step in a reconciliation or whether I'd overstepped the mark.

Mercy B. Lord hesitated only a moment, then rushed forward and grabbed me by the shoulders. If I hadn't been a tree stump, she would have bowled me over as she planted a kiss on my mouth, forcing my lips open with her tongue, then moving deeply inside.

They say reconciliations are among the best moments in lovemaking, perhaps because there is a second agenda. As you make love, you confront the agony of separation and exchange it for the ecstasy of renewal, until you finally rise and rise and explode, and crash exhausted. You have scrubbed all the hurt and anxiety and the dark corners of recrimination clean, and you end up with an empty space you can proceed to repaint and decorate. There may well be an equally important role for talking in reconciliation, two lovers regaining the closeness they've lost, making promises and sharing expectations, then solemnly signing the bottom line of a contract for future behaviour. But until the emotional spring cleaning is complete, there is no real platform for getting together again. Maybe there is a more lyrical and romantic way of putting it, a better analogy, but to me separation is an abandoned space that was once an intimate room. That is why there is such a feeling of emptiness when it happens. The shutters are pulled down on a dark place gathering emotional dust. Until the heart is satisfied, the head can make little sense of things. By morning light, Mercy B. Lord and the human tree stump had scrubbed the room we'd re-entered four glorious times, and fresh air and sunlight now streamed through the brightly polished windows.

We showered together and then I percolated coffee while Mercy B. Lord, wearing my terry-towelling dressing-gown, hair not yet blow-dried and Sassooned, drank a cup of hot water – a Chinese dietary habit that probably makes a lot of sense – then made scrambled eggs and toast. Barely a word other than morning pleasantries had escaped through our frequent smiles – a love requited; silence – content and happy.

Of course, I knew we had a lot to talk about. Obviously, things had changed or she wouldn't be with me now, but even though I was anxious to know what had transpired, there seemed no point in trying to push it. The woman I loved would tell me in her own good time, or perhaps not at all. Maybe it sounds weak but what I'd said to Molly I meant: I was willing to have her back on almost any terms, with no questions asked.

Then she changed into fresh panties she'd taken from her handbag, a bra that came from the same source, her jeans and one of my shirts that could comfortably contain two of her. I dressed for work, though I'd considered calling the agency to say I wouldn't be in after asking Mercy B. Lord if she could take the day off. But, turning off the hairdryer she'd left behind when we'd parted, she said, 'Darling, I have to go home and change and then open the office. At eleven I'm meeting the president of a Pittsburgh steel company, who is flying in unannounced to take a look around and doesn't want to be bothered with the usual government meeting and greeting contingent. I have to arrange a limo. Mohammed is in Kuala Lumpur with Beatrice.'

'Kuala Lumpur?' I asked. She'd told me once that Beatrice arrived at the office at six every morning to pray at her shrine and to make international phone calls, and never went anywhere in public. Mercy B. Lord opening the office was therefore a rare occurence.

'Beatrice has gone to KL to check on various business interests,' she explained.

'Isn't that unusual?' I asked.

Mercy B. Lord laughed. 'You're digging, aren't you, Simon?'

'No, no,' I returned hastily. 'It's just that you told me she gets to work early and never leaves the office.'

She walked up to me, eyes shining. 'And for two weeks!'

'Does that mean what I think it means?'

'If you'll have me?' she laughed.

My heart suddenly sank. 'Oh, shit!'

'What?'

'My mum's coming on Thursday to stay the two nights before the dinner. God, how stupid!'

Mercy B. Lord suddenly looked uncertain. 'You don't want me to meet her?' she said in a hurt voice.

I grabbed her and hugged her. 'You mean you will?' I cried excitedly.

Mercy B. Lord pulled back slightly and looked up at me. 'Oh, Simon, what if she hates me?'

I laughed. 'No chance of that. She told me over the phone that she'd stood for an hour looking at your portrait, looking into your eyes, then she said, "That's not something you can paint if it isn't there."'

'If what isn't there?' Mercy B. Lord asked.

'That's what I said. Then she said, "Simon, that beautiful young woman has Koo – I mean *you* – written all over her."' I kissed Mercy B. Lord. 'I know my mother. It wasn't a slip of the tongue. She is going to be the second-most excited member of the Koo family to know you.'

Mercy B. Lord pushed out of my embrace then, eyes averted, said, 'Please, Simon, let's not look beyond the awards dinner. I just don't know what's going to happen. Beatrice has never been away before. It's all very strange.'

Steady, Simon, don't react. 'I'll book you a seat on the plane. We can all go to Hong Kong together.' Then, trying to remain casual, I said, 'By the way, Sidney left for the States on Sunday or perhaps Monday – I'm not sure which – but Ronnie made a point of telling me, even though I hadn't asked.'

'Simon, are you sure you don't know any more than that?'

'Scout's honour. Molly only intimated that a couple of phone calls had been made.'

'By her?'

'I don't know. But I shouldn't think so. She's well connected but she isn't heavy duty.'

'Who then?'

'Mercy B. Lord, now you're the one who's digging. I simply don't know, I promise you.'

'But you named Beatrice and Sidney?'

'Yes, but I told you that last night.'

'Simon, listen to me. You have to call Molly and tell her to get whoever called to make a second phone call to Beatrice or to Sidney to say you're protected.'

'Huh? You can't mean that!'

'Oh, but I do. You must! Either that or hire a kung fu master from Hong Kong, like the *tai-pans*.'

I burst out laughing. 'Come on, you can't be serious. I couldn't possibly do either of those things.' But I recalled Molly's remark about Singapore's upper-middles being a nosy lot and I wondered momentarily whether Mercy B. Lord had heard anything about my family.

Her eyes suddenly welled. 'Then I must. I shall call Molly,' she choked. 'Simon, you have no idea who you're dealing with.'

'Hire a kung fu master for protection? It'd cost a fortune. But come on . . . *really?*'

Mercy B. Lord was back in control. 'Yes, and of course you couldn't afford it, so call Molly.'

'Hey, wait on. If being the Singapore Girl protects you, surely the portrait, you know, all the publicity from the win, should protect me?'

'In the short run, yes,' she replied, 'but the Chinese have long memories.'

'What could possibly be the point?'

'Face.'

'Face? I know it's important, but c'mon . . .'

'Important? Simon, when will you understand – it's *everything!*'

'Can I think about it?'

Mercy B. Lord glanced at her wristwatch. 'I've got to be going.'

'Wait, I'll call a taxi.'

'No, I'll get one on the street.' She kissed me, a nice kiss, if a little hurried, moved to the door then propped. 'Simon, you said your mother's arriving on Thursday?'

'Yeah, that's right.'

Mercy B. Lord tossed her head. 'Don't book me a ticket. I'll see you both in Kowloon, the Peninsula Hotel, Friday evening. See you tonight, darling. Maybe we can have dinner somewhere.'

On Thursday, she'd be gone as usual and would meet us in Hong Kong on Friday. Mercy B. Lord was letting me know that, in this one respect, nothing had changed.

CHAPTER FOURTEEN

HOW DO I EVEN begin to talk about the awards dinner? Four feisty females – five with Mercy B. Lord. Chairman Meow, Mrs Sidebottom, Molly and Elma were all primed to enjoy themselves, although possibly all were a tad wary, too, as women of character sometimes are when suddenly mixed together. To this coterie were added four males: Long Me Saw, who could bring a room to instant and obedient silence merely by clearing his throat, Dansford Drocker, whose exuberance and unpredictability made him a figure not easily ignored, and while the power of these two men was somewhat counterbalanced by Cecil Sidebottom and myself, the sum was still a potentially explosive mix.

It was probably a combination no sensible or sensitive host would have thought to bring together at one table, but then, of course, I was thinking like a man and naturally got it all wrong. While men immediately sniff and circle each other to establish who is top dog, women seem able to cooperate and conjoin, absorbing, matching, surmising and deciding, all somehow simultaneously. I watched in amazement as they began this process. While all this happened as if by some form of osmosis, we four men waited for each to assume their preordained roles.

Seemingly within minutes, the women began to share quite intimate details and to decide that they were well matched, settling down to enjoy the evening and each other's company. While I have no doubt that they may have passed the odd remark about each other at home, they seemed to really enjoy the opportunity to compare notes with women they regarded as their equals. Chairman Meow, as used to commanding respect as Elma, clearly recognised at once that this wasn't a group she could hope to dominate, and quickly relaxed and enjoyed being Phyllis Koo, the artist's mother and an intelligent woman in her own right.

We, the males, having sniffed and circled as a matter of form, immediately assumed our roles. Long Me was, by wealth, importance and social standing, top dog; Dansford was resident wit or clown; Cecil was the Mr Nobody every male group requires; and I, for the duration of the evening anyway, was the boy hero. We would all be expected to play our parts accordingly, but our first joint activity was to get stuck into the grog as a sign of mutual acceptance.

Top dog Long Me Saw hadn't brought his eponymous mastication minder, Miss Chew, which meant he wasn't going to eat but would instead drink brandy all evening. A bottle of Hennessy XO cognac and a brandy balloon had been placed beside his place card at the table. However, he'd arrived accompanied by two black-suited, very dangerous-looking Chinese minders walking three steps behind him. One of them had a dragon's head tattooed on the back of his left hand, its body and tail disappearing into the cuff of his jacket. Both men, while no taller than me, possessed physiques that made mine look positively puny. At the cocktail party they positioned themselves so that they could see anyone approaching, and later, at dinner in the ballroom, they stood at what I presumed was within kung fu striking distance of Long Me's chair, just in case some Triad gang happened to stroll into the Peninsula ballroom with hostages on their minds. Our two unarmed combat goons were not alone: the ballroom contained several black-suited lookalikes obviously on duty for some of the other wealthy members of the Chinese community. The interesting thing was that nobody seemed to take any notice.

Dansford had arrived in full dinner suit but without shoes. This wasn't because Chicken Wing had neglected to pack them but because he'd left home fully dressed, lest he lose his portmanteau. Losing this ancient leather bag was not an infrequent occurrence, but because it was such an old-fashioned and distinctive piece of crocodile-skin luggage, it somehow always turned up again, though often days after his return to Singapore. He referred to it fondly as ABTATS, a mnemonic for 'A Bag Too Awful To Steal'. In the very likely event that he would leave his portmanteau of evening clothes behind in a bar somewhere, Chicken Wing knew to dress him for an event that involved travel, the awards dinner being a perfect example.

Predictably, on his way to the airport Dansford had stopped off at Bill Bailey's for a steadier, no doubt topped up several times on the flight to Hong Kong, then, upon arrival, he'd paid a flying visit to the bar at Kai Tak Airport. Finally, he'd taken one of the famous Peninsula Hotel's 'Lollysy Loisy', the Chinese pronunciation for the several Rolls-Royce Phantoms the hotel sent to meet guests. However, approximately a mile from the hotel, the Rolls got stuck in traffic coming in to Tsim Sha Tsui, so he'd abandoned it, deciding to walk the remainder of the way to sober up. Within a block he discovered that his new evening shoes pinched him badly, so he'd dropped them into a rubbish bin to arrive finally with his black silk hose worn through and both his big toes exposed. The Rolls arrived at precisely the same time as Dansford limped into the driveway of the Pen, as the hotel was fondly known. He tipped the chauffeur, who handed a bellboy his precious ABTATS, then sat on the top step leading to the front doors. Much to the chagrin of the rigid chief bellman, an impressive display of service medals the only colour on his immaculate white uniform, Dansford proceeded to remove his socks. With the socks held in his left hand and his right hand flat on the marble step to steady himself, he got to his feet, but then momentarily lost his balance and quickly reached out to grab the bellman's arm. Misjudging the distance, he grabbed a handful of medals, which, fortunately, but for two that clattered to the steps, held tight to the bellman's chest, allowing Dansford to regain his balance.

Naturally, this required a gratuity, so Dansford slapped the warm socks into the doorman's white-gloved hand and reached for his wallet, handing the speechless and dishevelled chief bellman a mollifyingly large note in exchange for the return of his worn hosiery. He then deposited the socks in the hotel umbrella stand and proceeded to march through the swing doors, across the vast hotel foyer into the cocktail party. Seemingly unconcerned, he approached me, arms flung wide. 'Say, Simon, this is bigger than the fourth of July,' he pronounced happily. 'Ah, waiter!' he called then, as the man came over, lifted a glass of champagne from his tray.

'Dansford, what happened?' I asked, pointing to his naked feet.

'Blisters, severe, agonising, couldn't walk, either this or no show, couldn't possibly miss your moment of glory, old buddy.'

'But what about the hotel car?'

'Stuck.'

'What, the Rolls broke down?'

'In traffic, walked.'

You could usually tell how far gone Dansford was by his speech. He never seemed to slur his words and was quite capable of conducting a conversation even when completely stonkered. The one way you knew he'd had a few was by his truncated sentences. He'd answer in single words or short, clipped phrases, never rudely, but perhaps, conscious of being drunk, he concentrated on being precise. On the occasions I'd had too much to drink, I usually had some trouble recalling the details of the previous night when I woke up the following morning. Dansford, on the other hand, remembered everything, chapter and verse. You couldn't claim inebriation sharpened his mind – it was pretty sharp anyway – but unlike most of ours, his seemed to remain reasonably clear, which gave him a distinct advantage in avoiding the *in vino veritas* moments we've all been guilty of during the course of a heavy night's drinking. Dansford, sober as a judge or gone with the wind, never gave anything away.

The evening began with cocktails in the foyer leading into the ballroom, where anyone who was anyone in Hong Kong – Brits and wealthy Chinese – mingled in a twittering and chattering of elegant evening-gowned women and dinner-suited men. The occasion presented two opportunities for the glitterati: to be seen as patrons of the arts, and to visit the new Hong Kong Museum of Art, recently opened by the governor.

There is something to be said for British aplomb. Unbeknownst to me, the governor, Sir David Clive Crosbie Trench, knew Dansford and came over to us, pumping his hand and warmly welcoming him, completely ignoring the fact that he wore no shoes. Dansford introduced me and Sir David offered his congratulations, then added very kindly, 'Simon, the committee is particularly pleased that the winner's subject is an Asian, and such a very beautiful gal. Alas, the winner is usually some craggy old crone or doddering chap, the conventional belief being that such subjects have more character etched into their faces and are more challenging.' He smiled. 'Absolute poppycock, if you ask me. A glorious-looking woman seems to be a far greater challenge than half a hundred wrinkles, a tuft of white hair and weepy bloodshot eyes.'

Later, after the governor had left, I questioned Dansford. 'Well, that was a surprise. How do you know each other?' I asked.

He laughed, deftly lifting another glass of champagne from the tray of a passing waiter. 'Surprised he remembered. Goes back a ways – 1949 Joint Services Command and Staff College in England. I was seconded from the US army. Communications course. Regular guy. Good soldier. Likes a glass or two of scotch and honky tonk music. Hank Williams "Lovesick Blues".' It was all he said and I knew it would be pointless asking him anything more. Drunk or sober, Dansford seldom talked about his past, and when he did it was cryptic and revealed little or nothing, particularly about himself. He had a prodigious memory, being able to recall facts as he'd just demonstrated. It was not the first time I'd speculated about why Dansford wouldn't or couldn't return to the States, and what the hell he was doing in London in the US army four years after the war. I knew I'd almost certainly never know the answer.

Cecil Sidebottom, the third, almost invisible male at the table, said very little and fidgeted constantly with the starched wing collar of his evening shirt. It was obviously too tight, and every minute or so he inserted his forefinger down beside his Adam's apple and cleared his throat. The rasping glottal sounds were to be his major contribution to the conversation until much later in the evening, when, sufficiently pissed, he allowed me to convince him to remove the stud and loosen the offending collar. It sprang open as if grateful for the release and, held by the stud at the back of his neck, a glossy wingtip rested on either shoulder. Mrs Sidebottom's pursed lips whenever she glanced at him didn't augur well for later, when they were alone in their hotel room. A Sidebottom did not let down the side.

Sylvia Sidebottom, flashing her new teeth, had greeted me with 'Lovely, lovely, Simon. We'd never have been invited to a posh do like this when we lived in Hong Kong. Just a notch or two above our reach.'

'Mine too,' I confessed.

'Oh, I can't believe that. Your mother seems completely at home,' which was, of course, an accurate observation. Chairman Meow hadn't taken a backward step, and, while dressed in the best possible taste, she was a highly noticeable shimmer among the glitterati.

Thus, at the artist's table at the grand start to the evening were: Mesdames Battle Cruiser Kelly, the diminutive Full-frontal Flashing Fanged Sidebottom, the Elegant Chairman Meow *aka* Mum, and the pretty one-time Miss Singapore – Molly the Ong-trepreneur, as Long Me Saw had appropriately dubbed her. Of the men, one was drinking brandy on an empty stomach, one was pissed and barefoot, and one was slowly choking to death but staving off his premature demise with ice and water as a lubricant. This left two potential non-combatants, Mercy B. Lord and myself. Except that she was missing from the action.

Chairman Meow had arrived on the afternoon plane from Australia on the pre-ordained Thursday, and by the time we left for Hong Kong on Saturday morning, a tailor in Orchard Road had delivered a single-breasted evening suit with all the trimmings; two dress shirts, both with starched fronts, one of them with detachable wing-tipped collar, the other with a normal turn-down collar; two bow ties, one tied, the other not; hose and patent-leather evening shoes. She'd also brought a set of my dad's tiny gold-nugget shirt studs and cufflinks, and just in case I objected to wearing so ostentatious a display, she'd handed them to me with the comment, 'A gift from your dad. Count yourself lucky, Simon. I had to stop him from giving you the de Beer's specials, the ones set with diamonds with matching cufflinks and signet ring.'

Hong Kong Chinese women of wealth are seldom overweight and even in their sixties carry few wrinkles. The majority are among the best-dressed, most sophisticated and good-looking guests it is possible to gather en masse under one roof. Discounting for a moment the heavyweights in body, mind or spirit, like Elma Kelly, the governor's wife, Lady Trench, and a clutch of the other top British colonial civil service wives – all, with few exceptions, less than resplendent in weary satin evening dresses – the foyer contained a turnout far worthier than any I was entitled to expect. But it was meat and drink for Chairman Meow's naturally competitive nature and very much to her liking.

She wore the Dior gown she'd previously described on the phone and flashed more diamond points than a gang of kids carrying sparklers on Guy Fawkes night. If I'd managed to conceal our extreme wealth from everyone since coming to Singapore, my cover was finally and irretrievably blown. This was one slim, elegant, attractive and sophisticated woman, and the number of carats she wore would not be lost on the audience, most of whom assessed their social equals, inferiors or betters by the outward display of their wealth. The fact that the *tai-pan* Long Me Saw sat at our table would, according to Elma Kelly, undoubtedly add to her credit as a woman of influence and become an instant passport to acceptance. Elma had called me aside. 'My dear boy, you have been hopelessly trumped by your mater. This is Hong Kong and I'm afraid the mysterious Phyllis Koo who speaks Cantonese with an Australian accent is going to be the centre of speculation all night.' She drew her head back as if examining me in an entirely new light.

'I say, Simon! How on earth did you manage to conceal all this from us? Particularly the Chinese mandarins, who keep a close eye on the wealthy, wherever they originate.'

I laughed. 'One look at me should answer your question, Elma. The first time I entered Sidney Wing's office, he said to Johnny in Cantonese, assuming I wouldn't understand, "He looks like a Chinese peasant," to which Johnny replied, "And that's the way we'll treat him!"'

Elma laughed. 'More fool them. Well done, Simon. No spoilt little rich boy, eh? You've taken the Wings on the chin, served out your time and now you can tell them to sod off! I can't tell you how pleased I am we are friends. Your lack of presumption is what attracted me to you in the first instance, but had I known your family background I would probably have avoided you. How foolish, but one is always rather wary of people one believes were raised with the proverbial silver spoon stuck halfway down their oesophagus. I count myself fortunate not to have made so gauche a mistake.'

It was quite the nicest compliment. Elma then went on to say, 'The press is being allowed in for the official unveiling, and it wouldn't surprise me if your dear mama doesn't upstage us all. That canary diamond dragon brooch she's wearing simply defies description. But I can see she's not simply *la grande dame* but a woman of real spunk as well.' She smiled. 'After all, she raised you, dear boy. I shall enjoy getting to know her.'

With my cover blown, it at once became obvious that the 1969 Hong Kong Museum of Art International Portraiture Prize wasn't going to some impoverished painter taking his first step out of an impecunious lifestyle. Alas, there had been so much media speculation since the morning Elma had called to congratulate me that I was pretty worn down by all the kerfuffle, not to mention by the Mercy B. Lord difficulties that had ensued, so that little personal excitement remained for me. My most ardent wish would have been to rise from the table when I was called to the podium to receive the prize and turn to Mercy B. Lord seated beside me, taking her hand and lifting her to her feet. Then we'd walk onto the stage together. I'd rehearsed the scene in my head a dozen times. Her surprise, perhaps reluctance, the little assertive tug it might take. Now that fantasy only added to my disquiet: I'd submitted the painting without Mercy B. Lord's approval, I'd embarrassed her and compromised her, and it looked as if Chairman Meow would steal the limelight that rightly belonged to my beloved, who should have been the centre of attention and who wasn't even present.

When we'd arrived at the Peninsula on Saturday morning, instead of Mercy B. Lord waiting for us, having arrived earlier, we found a note in our suite addressed to me recording an earlier telephone call from her. I had immediately become concerned. The neatly typed note was obviously dictated over the phone and contained no endearments:

> Dear Simon,
>
> I have been unavoidably delayed on business, but hope to be in Hong Kong in time for the awards dinner.
>
> Mercy B. Lord

It didn't sound a bit like Mercy B. Lord. I hadn't told my mum about our reconciliation, wanting to save the surprise for when they met face-to-face, so when she questioned me about the note I replied that it was excellent news. Mercy B. Lord had sent a message to say she hoped to be at the awards dinner and to keep a place for her at the table.

'Oh, Simon, how lovely. I shall greatly look forward to meeting her. I brought the diamond pendants just in case.'

'Mum, promise not to fuss, I told you . . .'

'Yes, yes, dear, I know you two are not together. I've had several days to get over that particular disappointment. But she's a beautiful woman, she honoured you by allowing you to paint her, and she deserves to wear diamonds, if only for one glorious and forever to be remembered evening.'

'Mum, I'm not at all sure she'll agree. She may not even be able to make it to the dinner.' I waved the note. 'It says she'll try to be there.'

'But why, my dear? What could possibly be sufficiently important to keep her away? Surely for a young woman this is an occasion that could well be the most important she'll ever experience? One she'll recall in her dotage.'

'Mum, I can't answer that. The note – and it's only a telephone message – says that she's delayed on business. I simply have no idea where she is or why.' I smiled. 'Let's just hope she gets here.' I moved over to a wastepaper basket situated under a genuine (or, if not, a bloody good imitation) antique Louis XV–XVI transition writing desk. Tearing the note into tiny pieces, I dropped them into the basket.

'Mum, all I know is that once a week she travels beyond Singapore. I don't know where or why, but she's obviously been delayed and has very courteously let me know.' So far I'd navigated around the note without having to fib. Looking Chairman Meow aka Mum in the eye required a pristine conscience or I'd register on her PSS – Prime Suspect Sniffometer, as we'd called it as kids.

The dinner part of the evening was all but over, with only the presentation to come. On our table it had been a rowdy affair, and it was apparent that the four women had taken a great deal of pleasure in gathering intimate details about each other that, had they been males, might have taken months or years to accumulate. At any given time, two conversations were taking place at once. Women have an extraordinary knack of listening to two disparate conversations simultaneously and partaking of each, dipping in and out without losing the drift of either. In the hour it took to serve and finish dinner, the list of topics discussed by the women was, in no particular order, as follows: hippies, long hair, beards, sideburns (everyone agreed they looked awful, neither one thing nor the other), ghastly bellbottom pants, tie-dyed shirts, marijuana and LSD. They then moved on to husbands, sport, dancing, quilting, recipes, cooking, diet, animals, servants, lemon juice for cleaning jewellery, fashion, make-up (face powder was on the way out), the end of the beehive hairdo, dressmakers, mothers who had once darned socks, children, and youth going to hell in a hand-basket. What was interesting was that Elma and Molly were single, and Mrs Sidebottom confessed that she and Cecil had tried but failed to have children, although the way she said it suggested that the trying was in fact *very trying* and after a while they hadn't really bothered. Only Phyllis Koo could claim any experience of parenthood. But they'd still discussed in an animated way all these topics, and if they could not draw on personal experience, they had observed friends or relations. The conversation seemed to serve as a means of establishing backgrounds, states of mind, experience and points of view, and functioned as the introduction to a deeper dialogue. Nor did I sense that any one item was more important than another – that is, until they reached the subject of men, whereupon the level of animation increased noticeably.

Conjugal bliss received short shrift. Elma's sailor boy bobbed up and then disappeared under the waves, and while there was no comment on Cecil's efforts, Mrs Sidebottom's sniff at the very mention of male contributions to life said it all. Molly Ong claimed that, while she'd known 'a few' men in her time, she could only remember enjoying, present company excepted, two in particular: a Frenchman and an Italian, but she didn't elaborate. Chairman Meow admitted she'd enjoyed making kids but said very little more about my dad's contribution to her nocturnal activities. There then followed a discussion about the pill and how the present generation of young women would be a lot better adjusted now that they possessed the ability to train their male partners as to their needs without the spectre of marriage or the fear of pregnancy. Elma, predictably, had the last say on the topic. 'Splendid idea, lots of jolly good bonking before marriage makes Susan a wiser and happier gal, what.'

By far the most interesting topic turned out to be the inadequacy, incompetency and downright stupidity of men outside the bedroom. There were numerous examples given of all three characteristics but the interesting part was hearing the basis for them. This discussion was the only one that interested the men at the table, and despite Long Me's cognac bottle reaching the halfway point, he, in particular, seemed fascinated by this rarely expressed female point of view. It was a revelation few males could ever have heard, and was possibly due to the champagne the femmes were steadily imbibing.

Elma told of being a prisoner of war and how, as a woman, she could make demands on the Japanese commandant that the British male prisoners were either too frightened, too proud or too racist to make or even consider making.

Mrs Sidebottom described how women were able to break the German and Italian secret codes simply by understanding how the male brain worked. As she pointed out, it wasn't a very sophisticated process and she could never understand why the Germans, Italians and Japanese hadn't employed women to create their codes.

Molly talked about the beauty pageant industry and how the men in charge treated the girls like bovine creatures and toys, pretty dolls. 'In bed by nine unless in bed with them' was how she wittily put it. How they, the male minders, were constantly being hoodwinked, sometimes unknowingly dancing with their charges, who, with a change of make-up and a blonde wig, could dance away the night in the same nightclub until two in the morning.

But it was Chairman Meow who stole the show on this topic, when she explained the principles behind negotiating with men in the boardroom, pointing out that all men by their very nature are competitive animals and so likely to disagree on just about anything. By listening to every point of view and taking from it what was cogent, then reformulating it into a policy of her own that she could then get her husband to deliver, she'd almost always get her own way. 'It's like panning for gold – you have to discard a lot of male rubbish while trying not to damage their egos in the process.' She'd concluded by saying, 'With men it's always about "face" gained through innovation; with women it's always about "about face", doing it by looking first at the result you want to achieve and then working backwards to implement it.' According to Chairman Meow, women understand that originality is almost always dangerous in business. It is far better to find a successful example that has worked previously and then improve on it than to rush ahead with some male-inspired brainwave. At the conclusion of her speech, Long Me Saw invited her to sit on the board of Golden Future Films, the movie company he ran with his brother Long Long Saw.

While all this was going on, and excluding the discussion involving the inadequacies of men in general, the four men at the table discussed the 1968 Ashes tour, and the qualities of Hennessy XO cognac and why it was the brand most wealthy Chinese preferred. Long Me expanded on this at some length and, I confess, told us more than I personally needed to know about brandy. For instance, did you know that the best cognac is made from a blend of over forty *eaux de vies* (the product of the second distillation of wine) from various regions of Cognac in France? The wine itself tastes awful, but when boiled and distilled and given a few years of age in French *Limousin* oak, the end product is spectacular. XO (Extra Old), the cognac Long Me was drinking, must be at least six years old and is usually matured for fifteen years. We also discussed why golf was becoming increasingly popular among the wealthy Japanese and Chinese businessmen, and Dansford, who even when drunk was seldom boring, for once bored us – or me, anyway – to the bootstraps with a long diatribe on why baseball and not cricket suits the American psyche, although, come to think of it, he had to sit through what was for him equally tedious stuff about cricket.

I guess I may well have been more interested in the men's conversation had I not been distracted. Throughout dinner I kept an eye on the entrance to the ballroom in the vain hope that Mercy B. Lord might suddenly appear in her black cheongsam and red shoes. The idea of walking up to the stage to receive my award from the governor was beginning to fill me with dread. One fundamental question was beginning to preoccupy me: if Mercy B. Lord was missing and didn't turn up and if she hadn't returned home when I got back to Singapore, how was I to find her? Where would I begin to look? I'd barely touched the food on my plate and had drunk only a solitary beer, yet my stomach was churning and I felt ill with anxiety.

I glanced up at the stage for the umpteenth time, my hand going to my jacket pocket to feel the tiny leather case that held the gold chisel. Patel & Son had done a splendid job and the result was exquisite. My portrait had been suspended on two wires that dropped some fifty feet from the ceiling and then concealed behind a beautiful screen comprising four frames or sections, each representing a season. The section nearest our table represented autumn – a painting of migrating cranes flying high above an autumnal Chinese landscape that was far superior to anything I could ever hope to paint. When they removed the screen to reveal my portrait, this visual feast would, paradoxically, become at once a famine. I wondered if anyone in the audience would sense the irony. I cringed inwardly at the thought of standing beside my painting while the flashlights popped and the television cameras rolled, and thereafter making a short speech expressing my gratitude, while all I could think about was the whereabouts of the living subject of that misbegotten picture.

My imagination was beginning to run riot. With Beatrice Fong in KL and Sidney in Florida, what better time was there for Mercy B. Lord to appear to have absconded while, in truth, she'd been captured and held against her will? The note had been too offhand, too deliberate. The very least she would have done was to have ended it with a simple endearment . . . *love, missing you,* even *looking forward to being there,* not just the unadorned 'Mercy B. Lord'. After listening to the women's conversation around the table, I became convinced the note had been composed and delivered by a man.

The dreaded moment finally arrived and the chief curator climbed the steps to the stage. A murmur of excitement rose from the guests as the ballroom doors opened to welcome the media, a contingent of some twenty people armed to the teeth with Nagra reel-to-reel recorders strapped over their shoulders, microphones in hand, and cameras and

TV film cameras. Karlene Stein, with cameraman and sound guy in tow, was there, as well as a camera crew using 35-millimetre film and bearing the Saw movie empire logo, Golden Future Films.

I knew that Molly would have responded to my invitation whether it had been business-related or not, but it was unlikely Long Me Saw would have done so. Nevertheless, he could easily have left the whole thing to the very capable Molly Ong, so his agreeing to come was a personal compliment, one of which Chairman Meow could never have imagined her son worthy. But, to be truthful, when all was said and done, he'd essentially come for the sake of Singapore. Mercy B. Lord's presence and her association with the portrait was to be a grand kick-start to a very big promotion, and he, as well as Molly, would want lots of footage for the publicity to launch the Singapore Girl. Both Molly and Long Me had hinted that there was something else of importance in the pipeline that would involve the promotion.

It was clear that an immediate crisis loomed. With Mercy B. Lord missing, the Singapore Girl concept and the promotion depending on it would not happen. The television crew he'd arranged, probably at personal expense, would be wasted, and he needn't have been present. Long Me Saw wasn't the sort of man you disappointed. Monday at the agency promised to be a rough ride. Long Me had every right to be furious about Mercy B. Lord's absence. Molly Ong would have egg on her face as well.

I glanced at them both in turn, but neither seemed unduly worried. I'd mentioned the note to Molly at the cocktail party, warning her it looked as if Mercy B. Lord would be arriving late, but she seemed unperturbed. 'Oh, I'm sure it will be fine, Simon.' I remember thinking I hadn't the courage to explain that Mercy B. Lord might not appear at all. I was packing it, big-time! There seemed to be trouble on all sides, but the idea that something might have happened to my beloved was the worst of the looming disasters.

The slightly effete curator Elma had mentioned on a previous occasion, acting as the master of ceremonies, made a speech that now, in my rising anxiety, I barely heard. He then called on the governor to award the prize. Sir David Trench now stood at the podium acknowledging the crowd's applause. *Shit, shit, shit – concentrate, Simon! He's going to call you up at any moment. Smile!*

The governor of Hong Kong made a short witty speech about the views he'd earlier expressed to me on beauty versus craggy character, much to the delight of the dinner guests, then added that all daughters should be painted at twenty-one and not, as usually happens, when they are perhaps past the first flush of beauty, while all men should be painted at the age of forty before they lose the capacity to attract the interest of a twenty-one-year-old woman. (Laughter.) He then drew everyone's attention to the splendid new facilities for the arts and called me to the stage. I looked over at a beaming Chairman Meow and I think she was about to burst with pride as the entire room applauded. Elma, Mrs Sidebottom and Molly seemed just as pleased for me.

I cast one last wishful glance at the ballroom door in the hope that a miracle would occur and Mercy B. Lord would appear as if by magic, then arranged my mouth into a fixed smile (more a rictus than a smile) and tried to prepare myself for what was to come. The applause ended as I reached the podium and stood beside Sir David Trench, with my back to the beautiful Chinese screen that concealed my own inadequate effort.

'Ladies and gentlemen, as governor of Hong Kong and chairman of the Arts Council, it gives me great pleasure to welcome Singapore artist Mr Simon Koo to the stage to receive his gold medal and cheque as the winner of the 1969 Hong Kong International Portraiture Prize,' the governor announced, then he nodded in the direction of the bandstand. A sustained drum roll began as the beautiful Chinese screen somehow folded into a single piece and lifted off the stage and was pulled up into the ceiling. How this was done I shall never know, so great was my shock. My portrait hung suspended no more than a foot above the stage, and next to it was a peacock-tail chair identical to the one I'd painted. Seated motionless within it was Mercy B. Lord, wearing the black cheongsam and red shoes, mirroring the pose of the portrait.

The guests started to yell and clap and leap to their feet, and the media rushed forward as I stood like a stunned mullet, sudden tears welling then running willy-nilly down my face. The orchestra struck up a fanfare of some sort as Mercy B. Lord rose slowly and walked towards me, smiling and with her arms outstretched. There must have been at least 300 people in the ballroom, all cheering, but I was oblivious to the cameras, flashlights, the media, the guests, and even Sir David, as I took her into my arms and kissed her.

I don't remember much about the rest of the presentation. Sir David handed me a medal and an envelope, and I gave a short, sniffingly tearful speech, no doubt making a perfect fool of myself, although people would later say it was enormously moving – not the speech, but the tears and sniffs and my obvious love for Mercy B. Lord.

What followed was a media scrum where questions were hurled at us from all sides, microphones were shoved into our faces, and cameras rolled. I tried to field the questions, while Mercy B. Lord just smiled graciously, answering in monosyllables – that is, until the Saw Golden Future camera crew approached, whereupon she was suddenly animated, answering questions as one soon to be known as the Singapore Girl might be expected to do. Molly had picked the right girl. Mercy B. Lord was tailor-made for the role. For *Karlene's People*, she fielded some difficult questions and some very personal ones, and was far more gracious than I would have been in the same situation. The press then scattered and headed for the various dignitaries, my table with Long Me Saw being a prime target. Someone must have alerted the reporters to the mysterious artist's mother. Protesting her embarrassment (ha ha), Chairman Meow was soon surrounded by reporters and camera crews.

When Mercy B. Lord and the boy hero finally made it back to the table, Chairman Meow aka Mum burst into tears. She stood and embraced Mercy B. Lord, clasping her to her bosom, and in between the blubs she kept repeating, 'Oh, oh . . . You came from behind Little Sparrow's screen!' which made no sense to anyone but me. She was, of course, referring to the time Little Sparrow sat behind the screen during the banquet to recount Ah Koo's dream to the Triad Dragon Master in Sydney, nearly a hundred years previously.

Three bottles of vintage Cristal miraculously appeared on the table with nine clean champagne glasses, and Dansford lost no time popping the corks. Then, to everyone's surprise, Long Me Saw got to his feet, a tribute to his constitution, as the bottle of cognac was now two-thirds empty. He'd been fairly quiet for most of the evening but now, with everyone's glasses charged, he stood and said, 'I should like to propose a toast.' Then, lifting his glass, he continued: 'Here's to great beauty, and to those who have the gift to translate it onto canvas so that the gift remains forever young and wonderful. Simon and Mercy B. Lord, we wish you both a long and happy life.' Male cheers and female tears followed, and Cecil declared he hadn't been as moved since the completion of his first all-steel bridge.

But the evening proved far from over. The orchestra was waiting for the governor's party to depart when Dansford suddenly upped and crossed the ballroom on his bare feet, sat down at the Steinway and began to play and sing. He opened with 'Lovesick Blues', the honky tonk number by Hank Williams. The governor remained seated, which meant the guests were obliged to do the same. The orchestra happily joined Dansford while he performed what was a truly varied and amazing repertoire, from honky tonk to comic opera, including, for the benefit of the Brits, 'The Major-General's Song' from *The Pirates of Penzance*. Judging by the ovation after each number, remaining for the impromptu concert hadn't proved to be an inconvenience for the guests.

An hour later the governor's party left, but not before Sir David had come over to the bandstand microphone to congratulate Dansford, noting that he'd seldom enjoyed an official engagement as much and offering to buy him a pair of shoes out of the government house maintenance budget – 'I'll put it down as "Running Repairs",' he said, to much laughter. Dansford Drocker had pulled it off once again. The guests left smiling, obviously having very much enjoyed his spontaneous performance.

With Mercy B. Lord at my side, my life seemed complete. In fact, I couldn't recall any time when I had been so happy, elated, content or wonderfully at peace with myself. It also allowed me now to do something I'd planned all along. Much to the joy of 'she of the signs and portents', the inestimable Chairman Meow, who'd finally stopped sniffling over the screen incident or coincidence, depending on how you looked at it, I gave the tiny box containing the gold chisel to Mercy B. Lord. Then I handed her my winner's cheque. 'Mercy B. Lord, this is yours to give to Sister Charity at the St Thomas Aquinas Catholic Mission Orphanage with my sincere thanks for nurturing and raising the single most beautiful woman I shall ever have the joy of knowing.' Tears flowed from all the women, with even Elma allowing a tear or two to escape.

I can't say it had been an easy evening, though it had certainly been a momentous one, and later Mercy B. Lord, realising what I had been through, apologised in the nicest possible way by waiting until Chairman Meow was asleep in our three-bedroom suite, then tapping softly on my door. In bed, she explained how Molly and Long Me Saw had arranged to meet her to discuss the needs of the promotion, both having arrived on the flight before the one we'd taken. 'Simon, they promised they'd let you know, but Long Me Saw insisted that he wanted the surprise to be caught on camera, so he didn't want me to leave a note for you. He promised he'd leave one himself.' She looked up at me solemnly. 'Darling, I'm so sorry, it's all my fault. Knowing how you would feel, I should have had the courage to insist you were told I'd arrived in Hong Kong!'

I hugged her to me, forgiving her instantly. 'I can think of nobody in Singapore except for Lee Kuan Yew who would be sufficiently game to go against Long Me Saw's wishes.'

We made love and fell asleep in each other's arms, and, somewhat to our mutual embarrassment, were awakened by the sun streaming through the curtains and a beaming Chairman Meow aka Mum standing over us holding a tray bearing a teapot, milk, sugar and two cups. 'I'm about to order breakfast, my dears. What do you fancy?' she asked, with a would-be mother-in-law smile I'd never seen her wear before.

Chairman Meow returned to Australia and Mercy B. Lord and I returned to Singapore. The Hong Kong Sunday papers did a special Sunday supplement on the awards dinner, the *South China Morning Post* declaring 'The Barefoot Maestro's Concert' a wonderfully fitting end to a momentous evening. The paper's art critic also commended the chief curator for his brilliantly subtle and innovative example of living contemporary art – 'Naked Feet in Evening Dress'. There was also a special insert about the guests, featuring at the centre the portrait with the living subject posed beside it. It would be used in all the regional newspapers for the next week, and even made the *Sydney Morning Herald* and *The Age* in Australia, and eventually *Tatler* and *The Times* in the UK.

Karlene's People devoted the entire Monday-night show to the awards dinner and asked me for a live interview, but I'd had enough of KS and her entire carry-on, as well as being the centre of attention, so I declined. Molly, sensing the opportunity to get Mercy B. Lord great exposure on nationwide TV before the announcement, couldn't let the opportunity slip. She'd decided, for obvious reasons, to appoint her initial Singapore Girl without the competition, although she intended to have one a year later to select the next girl. The grand finale of the show (the tear jerker and Molly's idea) was Mercy B. Lord presenting the portrait prize cheque to Sister Charity for the St Thomas Aquinas Catholic Mission Orphanage.

I must say, we both thought this somewhat on the nose, or as Chairman Meow might have remarked, 'lacking in good taste'. But there's the rub. As an ad man, had the same thing happened to someone else, I wouldn't have hesitated to take the opportunity, pretty well regardless of any of the personal feelings of the participants. This was 'what's good for the goose is good for the gander' stuff. I hated to admit it, but this was top-notch thinking. It ticked all the boxes and possessed all the ingredients for prime-time TV – the orphan who had grown up to be a stunningly beautiful young woman, the grizzled old Irish nun who had found her on the doorstep and named her in that wonderful exclamatory way, the artist who fell in love and painted her to win an international prize for her portrait and then gave her his winner's cheque, which she gave to the orphanage as a token of her gratitude to the nuns who had raised her.

While we both realised it could be seen as publicity-seeking self-glorification and therefore in poor taste, I'd been well and truly hoist with my own petard. All I could do was refuse to be involved personally. In fact, all I wanted to do was find a quiet place to hide away from the limelight. While beautiful women belong in front of a camera, tree stumps don't.

Of course the presentation of the cheque to Sister Charity turned out to be a tremendous tear-jerker, one of those seminal TV moments people recall months or years later. Overnight, Mercy B. Lord became the toast of Singapore. Karlene Stein had a moment in the international spotlight, and the Hong Kong International Portraiture Prize received brief coverage on the weekly BBC art show. Some weeks later, we received, care of the Tourist Promotion Board, a letter on Vatican letterhead personally thanking us for our donation.

If it did nothing else, the media flurry placed Singapore in the minds of millions and clearly demonstrated the enormous emerging power of television. The 'Ong-trepreneur' was perfectly set up for the launch of her Singapore Girl promotion and Molly consolidated herself as a publicist of extraordinary ability. If the whole thing was in doubtful taste, one really good thing did come out of it. Mercy B. Lord was, by virtue of her immediate fame, someone the Fong and Wing conglomerate couldn't just expunge without some very severe repercussions in very high places. Singapore wasn't a country where you shat on your own doorstep and hoped you could get away with it. Both Fong and Wing, I felt sure, had much too much to lose to contemplate doing her any personal mischief.

I returned to work the Monday after the awards dinner, but only to wind up my accounts and prepare to hand over to my replacement. Sidney Wing had returned from Florida and Beatrice Fong from Kuala Lumpur, and Mercy B. Lord went back to work, but simply to wind up her job with the Beatrice Fong Agency before taking on the role of the Singapore Girl. She would become the new face of Singapore, a young woman who would promote tourism and business conventions for a year.

Mercy B. Lord, whether defying Beatrice Fong and Sidney Wing I can't say, moved in with me permanently, transferring her possessions to my flat the day we returned to Singapore. But, alas, despite the prospect of her new job, she insisted Thursdays remain sacrosanct. Quite how Molly Ong would arrange her schedule I didn't know, but she was obviously prepared to work around those two days. Clearly Molly was very impressed with her choice of Singapore Girl, and the publicity and enormous public approbation following Mercy B. Lord's appointment probably made it worth allowing her to take two days away from her duties each week. Through Molly's government-backed inquiries, I now knew Mercy B. Lord flew to Thailand each week, however, inquiries about the contents of the briefcase were less successful. The minister in charge of customs and excise simply informed her that the information was officially unavailable.

In a quiet moment at the awards dinner Molly had told me, 'Simon, I daren't take it any further. This is not a matter of corruption in high places – it's something more than that. The warning was very explicit. I was hauled up in front of the minister and told in no uncertain terms to keep my nose clean. I daren't make any further inquiries.'

I was now more than a little confused. What in the name of Christ was going on? Was the woman I loved someone I didn't even know, concealing a secret life I could never be part of? Suspicion is ghastly. It erodes confidence, trust and belief while giving rise to nefarious speculation. Mercy B. Lord had never lied to me, but had instead simply forbade any questions. There had been no denials, no confrontations, no explanations, simply silence. I was effectively shut out of everything for two days a week – nearly a third of her life. I loved her with every fibre of my being, I wanted her forever, but how could I accept these conditions? Plainly it was impossible and she must have known this. Why then did she continue to say she loved me? Why had she now ostensibly defied

Beatrice Fong and Sidney Wing and moved in with me, but still insisted on keeping Thursdays sacrosanct? Perhaps I should have kept her at arm's length, told her that unless she came clean it was all over, but I loved her too much. And I had become convinced that whatever she was involved in as a courier, it wasn't a decision she could make herself. The only thing that could be said about the entire ghastly scenario was that she obviously wasn't with me for the financial gain. She now knew about my family's great wealth, and yet even that made no impression on her determination to control her own life. I had on only one occasion suggested that we might one day be married. She hadn't objected or explained but had simply ignored the suggestion and taken me to bed. I had long since learned that Mercy B. Lord was a very strong-minded woman, but this silent refusal to budge was clearly non-negotiable.

Suspicion takes one into dark corners, and I began to wonder if there was some other agenda going on, if Mercy B. Lord was part of a conspiracy involving me. Perhaps my family's wealth had been known all along and I'd deluded myself that, until recently, I'd been incognito, just some shit-kicking creative director with a bit of ambition spending time in Asia, trying to build his career. Which was true enough. What was it Elma had said? 'The Chinese mandarins keep a close eye on the wealthy, wherever they originate.'

I told myself I was a weak shit, that I ought to take the initiative and confront her, ask for a reason and be prepared to end the relationship if I didn't get one. I told myself I'd let it go on a little longer, postponing the confrontation for a while before I took the bull by the horns. I confess, my heart completely overpowered my willpower. I simply loved her too much.

There was no one I could talk to. Chairman Meow was besotted with Mercy B. Lord, but if I told her about Thursdays and my suspicions, she'd immediately conclude they were correct and the shit would hit the fan in a big way – or, worse, she'd make it impossible for us to stay together. Chairman Meow on the warpath on behalf of her son and heir didn't bear thinking about.

I couldn't confide any further in Molly, who had her own agenda concerning Mercy B. Lord. Besides, she'd received an official warning to let the matter drop.

Neither was Dansford a likely shoulder to cry on. He had to work with the Wings, and while I knew there was no love lost between him and the three brothers, I didn't want to compromise him any further. He'd married Chicken Wing and built up a lifestyle he couldn't have maintained anywhere outside of Asia. Furthermore, as far as I could speculate, he intended to remain in Singapore permanently, or at least until the grog finally caught up with him.

Two days after the tremendous publicity around and excitement of the announcement of Mercy B. Lord as the first Singapore Girl, Beatrice Fong, while praying at her office shrine at the end of the day, suffered a massive heart attack. Mohammed, waiting in the Buick outside the office, became concerned when the old woman was late. Beatrice Fong never deviated from her routine. Not daring to enter her office or even call out, he phoned Mercy B. Lord, who had only just arrived home from a Tourist Promotion Board briefing. We immediately took a taxi to the Beatrice Fong Agency, where Mercy B. Lord hesitated in the foyer. 'Oh, Simon, I know it's stupid, but I feel . . .'

'Don't worry, darling,' I said. 'Most people are troubled by the sight of the dead. If that's what's happened, well, I'll be here with you.' Chairman Meow had insisted that once I was an adult I understand the family funeral business, and so my sisters and I were exposed to the deceased on several occasions. I put my arm round Mercy B. Lord's shoulder and we went in together.

The old crone lay dead on the carpet in front of the shrine, the incense she'd lit before the statue of *Tsai Shen Yeh*, the god of wealth, still burning alongside a large luscious peach she would have been offering as a sacrifice. Even in death, she had piercing black eyes, undimmed by age.

I stooped and closed them. Then I waited a moment while Mercy B. Lord paid her silent respects.

Outside, she sent Mohammed to fetch Beatrice Fong's physician, Dr Foy, a man in his early eighties who had attended her for half a century. Although she distrusted the Chinese banks, the old woman was ambivalent about medical matters and had chosen a young doctor who practised both Chinese and Western medicine. They'd grown old together.

While we waited for the old man to arrive, we sat in the foyer, where Mercy B. Lord explained that Beatrice Fong had long since made provisions and arrangements for her funeral and had charged her with carrying out the arrangements.

Mercy B. Lord hadn't reacted in any way to the old crone's death and this seemed surprising to me. She wasn't an unemotional person and had reason to be grateful to Beatrice Fong.

'Darling, are you okay?' I asked carefully.

She nodded. 'It wasn't as bad as it could have been, seeing her like that. In fact, it was the first time I didn't feel slightly apprehensive in her presence. She started briefing me on her death five years ago. Every Monday morning she'd call me in to her office. Tonight is almost an anticlimax. I'm so completely brainwashed I daren't mourn her until I've done my job, followed her wishes to the letter. Right now I don't know what to think. She was an enormously irascible old lady; it wasn't always easy.' She paused. 'Of course, she may have changed her previous arrangements, but I'm not sure she'd have had time.'

'Why would she do that?' I asked.

Mercy B. Lord was silent, her eyes averted. 'Simon, when I resigned and told her I was going to be the Singapore Girl, we had a dreadful row. If she'd survived, you can be sure she'd have blamed her heart attack on me. We'd already had a row when I told her I wanted to attend the dinner in Hong Kong and to accept the offer to be the Singapore Girl. Then we had another about my moving in with you. The first row was the day after we had dinner at the Ritz.'

'Why didn't you tell me, darling?'

Mercy B. Lord shrugged. 'You had enough on your mind. Besides, it was what I had expected. The old lady has always thought she owned me, and when I came the very first time to be with you, she was furious and barely spoke to me, sending me messages and directions through the switch. That's how Beehive Freda became her new office servant and intimate.'

'But she didn't fire you?'

Mercy B. Lord looked surprised. 'No, she couldn't do that.'

I knew not to question her further, other than to say, 'And you didn't . . .'

'Resign?'

'Yes.'

'No.'

'And when you returned? That first time?'

Mercy B. Lord smiled. 'As the prodigal daughter, it wasn't easy. She isolated me. I didn't know about your letters and flowers. At the orphanage, when we did something wrong the nuns isolated us; we were "sent to Coventry", to use their expression. Beatrice sent me to the Chinese equivalent. But first she told me that if I ever saw you again, she would see to it that a great harm came to you.'

'Is that why you warned me? You do know Ronnie warned me just after I arrived? He said my arse wouldn't bounce until I landed beyond the Singapore border if I had anything to do with you.'

'Oh, Simon, all those months I thought you hated me!'

I grabbed her and held her tight. 'Darling Mercy B. Lord, I love you! I was devastated. I told you that before, how I'd painted your portrait to convince myself I hadn't lost you completely. And then, when the weeks and months passed and it seemed you were never coming back, and Ronnie told me that you wanted nothing further to do with me, I thought that sending the painting away, entering it in a competition I could never hope to win, would allow me to finally say goodbye to you. It was a final act, like a funeral. You know, after the burial, while you may never be the same again, eventually you have to recover and get on with your life. When the painting won and I sent you the letter of apology and it came back mutilated with the word 'Bastard', and Louie da Fly told me what had transpired, I realised that it wasn't you but Beatrice who had intercepted all my flowers and letters. I decided that if I could just reach you, there might still be a tiny chance of . . . well, reconciliation. So I used the invitation, in the hope I might get it to you personally. I told myself that if you rejected me yourself, I'd know you didn't love me and that there was no further hope. Molly Ong had phoned me with her idea of the Singapore Girl and I realised that it was a great opportunity but one that you might just reject because of our past. I didn't want that to happen, to deny you the opportunity because of what had gone on between us. Then when I didn't or couldn't give Karlene Stein your name and suddenly they were saying you didn't exist . . .' I stopped. 'Well, you know the rest.' Like survivors from a disaster, we told and retold the story of our ordeal to reassure ourselves that we were, at last, safe.

'Oh, Simon, because of the reason for our parting, I told myself I wasn't allowed to love you. That it wouldn't work. That I *must* stop. But I couldn't. It wouldn't go away. It just wouldn't. I'd never been in love before. I'd never even been loved. I didn't know what to expect, how to behave. All I knew was the orphanage, and then Beatrice, who took me out at fifteen and gave me a home. That was seven years ago. I think she honestly believed she owned me.'

'You lived with her?'

'Yes.'

'Oh, I see. She sort of adopted you? Became your surrogate parent . . . er, grandparent?'

'No, it wasn't quite like that. As I said, I think she honestly believed she owned me. I was her personal property. I was given a room in her mansion, at the back. Not in the servants quarters, although I always used the back entrance. But she didn't say I had to, Simon,' she added quickly, 'use the back entrance, I mean; I just did, and she never invited me to use the front. After the girls' dormitory in the orphanage, having a room all to myself was an unbelievable luxury, almost as good as being loved.'

'And she never showed you any affection?'

Mercy B. Lord looked surprised. 'I keep forgetting you never met her. Beatrice Fong wasn't capable of affection, Simon. It just wasn't something she felt. She loved money, not people.' Mercy B. Lord pointed to the door of the dead woman's office. 'She died worshipping it. Instead of affection, she trained me in money matters. It's not something I talk about, but I can read a balance sheet upside down, prepare a profit and loss sheet and an investment brief on my ear. It was the closest she got to showing me she cared, teaching me how to do my financial homework, how to handle numbers, calculate the value of an investment in terms of return. She believed people existed to be used. According to her, there are only two kinds of people: those who make money and those who labour to make it for them.'

'But, having trained you, she never allowed you the capital to make any money of your own?'

'No, she didn't believe in handouts. If I couldn't make it starting from scratch, she wasn't interested. The training came first – that was her gift to me – the nearest she came to affection. She was giving me the key. I had to find the lock that opened the door to creating wealth myself. By falling in love with you I betrayed her. I had made the wrong choice – love instead of money. You had, in effect, destroyed her creation before she was ready to let me go, and she wasn't a forgiving woman. She believed her time had been wasted. The Singapore Girl was the final straw. I was to become a glad-handing beauty queen. She thought you had completely corrupted me, or that's what Sidney Wing told her, backed up by his vile brother Johnny. They told her it was a conspiracy between you and Molly Ong.'

'Yeah, that figures. What about Sidney? Was he a part of your apprenticeship? He was pretty bloody proprietorial about you.'

'If any of them, it was Johnny who had most to do with me. But it was strictly business. I was a connection in a business relationship.

Beatrice never got close enough to anyone for sentiment to enter into a relationship. But if she trusted any of the Wing brothers, it was Johnny. Having said that, she was a woman wholly and completely concerned with money. Everyone had a specific part to play. She had no morals, no scruples. "Money doesn't have a conscience," she once told me. It seems they've been business partners a long time. "Sidney the numbers man (he always had to be watched), Johnny the fixer, Ronnie the girlie man," was how she'd occasionally refer to them. It certainly wasn't affection that held them. No, correction, she obviously had a soft spot for Johnny Wing. But it started long before I came on the scene, so I don't know how it all came about.'

'And you never thought, in all that time, of leaving the job or her home? I mean, you're clever, capable, well trained and intelligent. Getting another job wouldn't have been hard. For instance, I'd have killed to have someone like you as an account executive in the agency, and you have already proved you would make a wonderful market researcher. You just told me you're well trained in financial matters, in business. Any of these skills would have given you a career and earned you more than your present salary.'

'Simon, a single Chinese girl without family, without *guanxi*, doesn't live alone, unless she's a whore. Now, under the PAP government, it's a little easier to be a single woman, but not before. Besides, when it began I was fifteen, an orphan, accustomed to rigid unbending discipline.' She shrugged. 'If Beatrice threw me out, I had nowhere to go except back to the orphanage. They would have let me go at sixteen anyway. She didn't beat me, she gave me a small room at the back of her mansion, the food from her kitchen was good and plentiful, and she clothed me until I earned enough to buy my own clothes. I was being trained at her expense and I loved learning. If she wasn't kind or loving, well, I didn't expect her to be.' She looked directly at me. 'There is precious little kindness and love in a Catholic orphanage. Irish nuns, ours, anyway, usually came from impoverished slum families with drunken fathers and abused mothers worn out from the effects of poverty and childbirth.

There were always too many mouths to feed, and their excess daughters, those who couldn't catch a man by sixteen, were given to the church to become brides of Christ, placed in a convent to be trained in the basics and sent to the ends of the earth, never to see their families again. Many of them are harsh, bitter, ignorant women who have no concept of being loved or of loving, except for the love you are told you're constantly receiving but never actually feel coming from Mary, the holy mother of God. As a child I thought love was learning your catechism off by heart.'

I'd never heard Mercy B. Lord talk like this before. 'But . . . but, darling, what about Sister Charity? You know, finding you on the doorstep, all that tear-jerking stuff on *Karlene's People*, the TV, the cheque you gave her? I mean . . . was that all pretend?'

Mercy B. Lord's eyes welled with tears. 'Sister Charity is no different. It's not their fault. They don't know any better and they learn to show the outside world an entirely different face. It's part of their training, the compassionate and caring front that some nuns adopt as a secular mask. Of course it can't be true of all nuns, but my lot were poor women from the slums of Ireland who often lacked even a rudimentary education and who were sent to alien places like Singapore because they couldn't or wouldn't complain. They had to be tough to survive and I assure you they were. Oh, Simon, I wasn't being a hypocrite. What you did was the loveliest thing anyone has ever done for me. You paid off my obligation, you set me free. How can I ever repay you for that?'

'Darling, you already have. You defied the old woman and we're together. She's dead now and can't harm you. By the way, who is going to tell the Wing brothers?'

'I'll send Mohammed around after he takes the doctor home. I'll give him a note. He can go there from the doctor's house. Johnny lives in the same area. After the doctor's issued a death certificate, we'll call an ambulance to take Beatrice home.'

'You don't think you should call Sidney now?'

'No, Simon, this is women's business. I'll get the doctor to lay her out and then I'll take her home and prepare her properly, in a dignified manner. She's Chinese and "face" still counts. She must look suitably dignified when the priests and funeral people come to cleanse her body and dress her and ready her for the rituals to come. All I can do tonight is prepare the front door for them to enter in the morning. The house is full of images of the various gods as well as several mirrors. I must cover the statues and have the servants remove the mirrors before anyone arrives.'

'Why the mirrors?'

'If you see a reflection of the coffin or the deceased in a mirror, it means you will have a death in the family. The ambulance men won't take her into the house unless the mirrors are removed beforehand. I must also hang a white cloth over the front doorway, with a gong to the right, and white lanterns around the outside of the house.'

I nodded my head towards the closed door behind which Beatrice Fong lay dead. 'I was expecting to have to comfort you but you haven't shed a single tear. How do you feel?'

Mercy B. Lord looked directly at me. 'It is a sign of respect, Simon. I am a Christian. If I followed Chinese practices I would, as a matter of ritual, have started to wail at the top of my lungs when I discovered her. But she wouldn't expect it from me. We've discussed it. She wants everything done by the experts, priests and professional funeral organisers and, because she has no family, by professional mourners. In Chinese funerals there are strict rituals; every step for the mourners and the participants is preordained. She has left her instructions and has forbidden me to mourn for her. I was not brought up in any of the Chinese faiths – I'm not a Taoist or a Buddhist – and she doesn't want anything to go wrong, to intrude.'

'Personal emotion is an intrusion?' I asked, trying to keep the surprise out of my voice.

'In her case, yes, very much so. She wanted to think that she had made me in her own image. She would often say, "Child, I would not mourn publicly at your funeral and I do not wish you to do so at mine. Cry for a lost business opportunity, nothing else." If I am to obey her instructions, then all I can do is prepare her house for the morning when the priest and organisers arrive, then place a notice in all the Chinese newspapers and the *Straits Times*. That's my job done. For the rest I must follow her instructions. These are in a vault in the main branch of Barclays Bank and I will retrieve them in the morning. She would often repeat, "You will see that all is done correctly, but you must not become involved."'

The old Chinese doctor arrived, a small elderly man with his grey hair parted in the middle and plastered down with Brilliantine. He was dressed in an old-fashioned black linen suit, complete with waistcoat and looped watch chain, white shirt with starched detachable collar and black tie. His shoes were twenties-style, pointy and high-gloss black, and he appeared somewhat myopic in his gold-rimmed glasses. He bowed deeply and offered his felicitations, adding in Cantonese, 'She has waited a very long time before going to her ancestors, a long life worthy of respect. They have waited impatiently to welcome her. She will make a venerable ancestor. It is most appropriate.'

Quite what was appropriate wasn't clear, and as she appeared to have no family, it was hard to see whose venerable ancestor Beatrice might become.

'Dr Foy, do you know her age?' Mercy B. Lord asked.

Dr Foy nodded. 'She has been in my care for fifty years. She is a venerable and most worthy eighty-one years of age.'

Unable to help myself, I quickly calculated that she would have been born in 1888, and so was of the same generation as the children of Ah Koo and Little Sparrow – my great-grandparents' generation.

Dr Foy indicated the office door and said to Mercy B. Lord, 'You have checked her pulse?'

She nodded. 'I also held a mirror to her mouth. There was no breath.'

The old doctor gave a curt nod. 'We will go in now, please.'

An hour later, Mercy B. Lord had written a note to Johnny Wing for Mohammed to deliver after he took the doctor home. Then she'd left me to wait for the ambulance, handing me an envelope with the death certificate Dr Foy had issued and the address of the Beatrice Fong mansion. I was to give it to them to bring along with the body.

'Simon, ask them to wait if I'm not there. Tell them I will reward them. I need to drop in to Chinatown to get the white cloth, gong, paper lanterns and so on to prepare the house. I suggest you go home after the ambulance has left.' She showed me how to lock the doors to the Beatrice Fong Agency, then added that she wouldn't be home because she would be required to sit with the corpse until morning to guard the old woman from evil spirits. She'd call me at the ad agency after she'd gone to the bank to fetch her instructions. She'd have to wait at the house for the funeral director and the priests to arrive so she could brief them. 'I daresay it will be sometime in the afternoon, but I'll call as soon as I'm free, Simon.'

The following day was my second-last at the agency and I had a fair bit of tidying up to do. While Sidney had been back from the States for three days, he hadn't spoken to me, but Ronnie came into my office first thing to say they wanted to have drinks with the staff at the grotty hotel over the road on my last evening, but that he, Johnny and Sidney couldn't be there because they would be attending the funeral of Beatrice Fong, who had died overnight. He looked at me quizzically. 'But of course you knew that, didn't you?'

I ignored his question. 'Mate, I'd be happy if you didn't have a farewell bash for me. I'll say my goodbyes to the staff individually.'

'You will lose face, Simon.'

I laughed. 'Well, I lost it coming in, why not going out?'

'As you wish. Maybe we could have a drink somewhere after you've left?'

'Yeah, sure.' Ronnie couldn't help wanting to be the good guy.

'Simon, you've done a hell of a job.'

I laughed again. 'I guess Sidney and Johnny wouldn't agree. By the way, I've worked out my share of the profits due to me for the last year. According to my contract, I will need to be paid before I leave tomorrow.' I pulled open the drawer, picked up an envelope and handed it to him. 'Would you see Sidney gets this, please? It's been counter-signed by Dansford.' I'd made the Wing brothers more money, kept the Americans happy enough, and as per the profit-sharing clause of my contract, I hadn't done too badly myself. I'd have enough to be able to look around, and I knew there were three readymade business choices.

'I don't know about tomorrow, Simon, the funeral . . .'

'Perhaps he can prepare the cheque today?'

'I'll see what I can do. But you know what Sidney's like with money. He'll want to do the maths.'

'Oh, it's been checked and endorsed by New York. Arthur Grimes has signed it as well.'

Ronnie laughed. 'Well, I can see you've learned something useful from us, Simon.'

'Yeah, to cover my arse with both hands.'

'Ah, then they won't be free to accept a cheque today,' he quipped. 'Sorry, Simon, a director's bonus cheque has to be signed by all the other directors and Johnny is away on private business today.' He shrugged. 'Stateside rule, buddy. This time you can't blame Sidney.' He gave me a smug smile then turned to go. 'We'll have that drink soon. Maybe one evening at the Nite Cap? Lots of new girls . . .'

'Thanks, but no thanks – all my evenings are taken up.'

'What, indefinitely?' A slight pause, then, 'What about a Thursday night?'

That crack brought me very close to jumping from my chair and smacking him in the teeth, but I managed somehow to keep my voice calm while the anger rose in my chest. 'Sorry, mate. Thursday night I paint.' I attempted a self-deprecating grin, shaking my head. 'I'm trying, though I don't know how successfully, to do justice to a head-and-shoulders portrait of a very beautiful woman. As for future Thursdays, it could be that Mercy B. Lord might like to come to Australia for a holiday – an extended holiday – you just never know, do you?' This last bit was pure invention but it had the right effect.

The invariably polite Ronnie suddenly lost his cool. 'Simon, you were warned on your second day in Singapore to keep your fucking hands off her. Beatrice Fong may be dead but I would be very careful if I were you. That old woman can bite back from the grave!' He turned and left, slamming the door of my pathetic little glass and plywood office so that it positively vibrated.

I spent the remainder of the morning briefing Dansford on the outstanding creative work, then in a meeting with the production staff, giving them last-minute instructions for the Big Lather point-of-sale material for the launch in the Philippines. The new creative director, this time a guy from the States, had been delayed a month on family matters, so I couldn't brief him face-to-face. I had written a long report, a sort of 'what to do when the shit hits the fan' list, together with a list of suppliers and production facilities, trustworthy and otherwise, in Singapore.

At noon Dansford and I caught a cab to Texas Oil to present the results of the test market for Texas Tiger 'Greased Lightning' engine lubricating oil. Alejandra Calatayud, the finished artist, had done a sensational job of the tiger illustrations, and the test-market results, based almost entirely on her display posters, indicated we had another potential winner on our hands.

As the Texan cowboy who rode the Asian tiger, Michael Johns was credited with making Texas Oil the number-one petrol brand in every South-East Asian country except Burma, where Shell still ruled. With the likely success of the new engine lubricant, he was going back to Houston in an even bigger blaze of glory.

He'd invited us to a double farewell lunch, for my departure from the agency and his in a month. He was returning to Houston to be briefed for his next assignment, running Texas Oil in South America. 'Say, Simon, you wouldn't like a job in South America, would you?' he'd joked on more than one occasion.

Dansford and Big Loud Mike got stuck into the martinis, and we all had large barbecued steaks and a monster potato baked in foil and garnished with fresh cream and chives, the Texas Oil boss's favourite meal. Things were beginning to kick along very nicely for the two of them, and I could see a very late night coming up and knew I must find an excuse to leave after nursing two beers. Mercy B. Lord would have been up all night sitting beside the corpse of the ancient crone, guarding it from evil spirits, then working her butt off all day, first visiting the bank then making the funeral arrangements. What she didn't need was her lover arriving home after midnight pissed.

I was beginning to formulate an appropriate excuse to get away when, thankfully, the waiter came over with a note for me from a printer, asking me to come in urgently to check the four-colour proofs of the new Texas Tiger service-station driveway posters. We'd inadvertently mixed a dark purple shade into the sky, and as purple can fade badly in direct sunlight, they wanted me to okay it before they pressed the button for the print run. Errors are expensive and printers always like to cover their arses. Big Loud Mike insisted I stay, but I explained what might happen if the printer got it wrong and he finally relented.

'I guess that's the professionalism we pay you for, buddy. I want you to know I'm mighty grateful.' He glanced over at a hovering waiter, then nodded to him. The waiter returned shortly afterwards carrying a large hatbox, which he placed on the table. Michael Johns removed the lid and produced a new Stetson, which he presented to me. 'That there Stetson is guaranteed genuine and from the original factory in Garland, Texas, son,' he announced proudly. Then, dipping back into the box, he withdrew a silver belt buckle he'd had made in the western style, with the traditional steer horn motif replaced by a roaring tiger's head with ruby eyes. 'Simon, buddy, what can I say? You came when we were in the shit, losing market share to those bastards from Caltex Boron. Oh man, you dealt me four aces and the joker with Texas Tiger – the gasoline that makes your engine roar. It was an unbeatable hand and I got to be a big hero in Houston.' He pointed to the hat. 'That there Stetson is a token of my personal esteem.

But, my good buddy, while I get all the glory, you are the true "Tiger" hero.' He held up the silver buckle. 'I have the honour of appointing you the first recipient of the Grand Order of the Texas Tiger Buckle!' He handed it to me. 'Mah friend, on behalf of the Texas Oil Company, we thank you from the bottom of our hearts. Come to Houston, Texas, and we gonna have the mayor give you a goddamn street parade!'

I left the two of them to play on, grateful for the printer's call. Michael Johns pissed could be very forceful and I didn't want to embarrass Dansford by insisting I depart, although I suspected they were both, after an afternoon of martinis, rapidly approaching the 'impossible to embarrass' stage.

While it was a considerate and generous gesture and an unexpected surprise, a Stetson on a Chinese tree stump isn't a good look and everyone at the printers nearly pissed themselves when I arrived wearing it. As Dansford had originally landed the Texas Oil account with his bevy of Chinese dolly birds in hot pants, I decided he deserved the hat for his contribution. Mercy B. Lord and I had just seen the new film *Butch Cassidy and the Sundance Kid*. In colouring and even in appearance, Dansford vaguely resembled Robert Redford, and on the notorious day of the pink-hair cocktail party he'd appeared wearing a cowboy outfit and fake Stetson, and the toy hat had looked great on him. Dansford, slim, tall and angular, was the perfect 'Howdy, pardner' cowboy type.

I arrived back in the agency from the printers just before five to find a near hysterical Alice Ho in reception. 'Simon, you call Miss Mercy, urgent, urgent. She cry on phone when you not be here!'

I tried to stay calm. 'Where is she? Beatrice Fong's house?'

'Ja, ja, dead lady house.'

'Do you have the address?' I was kicking myself that I hadn't looked inside the envelope Mercy B. Lord had given me for the ambulance drivers.

'I not suppose, Simon. Mr Johnny, he say no give to you.'

'Alice, ferchrissake, she's alone in the house . . . with a dead woman!'

Alice scribbled the address, handing it to me. 'You not say I give, Simon. I call for you now?'

'Yes, please.' I was trying to remain calm, but Alice must have sensed my concern. 'And don't worry, I could have got the address from Mercy B. Lord.'

'I don't know what is she crying. She not say to me. You run-run your office, Simon.'

I picked up the phone that started ringing moments after I got to my office. 'What's wrong, darling?' I asked anxiously.

'Oh, Simon!' Mercy B. Lord cried, and began to sob.

'Darling! What is it? Please!' But the pathetic crying continued. Then she finally gulped my name again, followed by a fresh outburst of tears. 'Take it easy, sweetheart! Are you hurt? Are you okay?'

A pathetic little 'yes' followed, then a sniff and more tears.

I'd phrased it badly. 'What, hurt?'

'No, okay,' she sniffed.

'Safe?'

'Yes,' she sniffed again.

'Now take a deep breath. Go on, please do as I say.'

There was a silence punctuated by three or four sniffs, followed by a pathetic little wail. 'Sorry!' Another sniff.

'Now, relax. I'm coming over right away, I'll be there in twenty minutes.'

'No! You mustn't!'

'What? Why?'

'Simon, Beatrice's lawyer phoned an hour ago.' More sobs.

'Darling, I'll be there soon.'

'No!' she screamed.

It was my turn to be alarmed. 'What is it! Mercy B. Lord, please tell me!'

'Beatrice has left me her entire estate!' She started to howl again.

'Darling, don't cry. That's marvellous news!'

'No!' Mercy B. Lord wailed. 'It isn't!'

'Why? What is it?'

'Johnny Wing is the executor and her proviso is that I never see you again. She wants me to marry . . .'

'But, but . . .' There was a pause then a muffled sound – anger, surprise, dismay – it could have been any of these, and later I would attempt to read meaning into it. But then she spoke again, and this time her voice sounded strong and deliberate, even cold. 'Simon, this changes everything. I can't ever see you again!'

I heard a gasp, then the rattle-clunk sound of the receiver being replaced.

CHAPTER FIFTEEN

———————

THE PRONOUNCED THUMP OF the receiver being replaced at Mercy B. Lord's end left me utterly bewildered. I leapt from my chair and ran through the production department and into reception, then out onto the street. Alice Ho, taken by surprise, shouted after me, 'Simon, where you go? Not so hurry! What happen? You come back?'

If I'd had to wait for a taxi I may have given myself time to think, but one pulled up in front of me to drop off a woman, and I barely allowed her time to scramble out before I jumped into the back seat. Then, furious, I had to wait for her to pay the cab driver, which she was attempting to do while hugging four shopping bags, groping blindly for her purse somewhere within a voluminous handbag. 'Get going, I'll pay her fare!' I shouted. But the elderly cabbie stubbornly waited to be paid before calmly turning around to inquire, 'Where you go?' I shouted the address in Katong that Alice Ho had given me and told him I'd double the fare if he hurried.

'No, no, cannot! I get fine,' he said, moving into the stream of traffic. 'I cannot. Police, they make trouble for me.' He chuckled. 'Licence gone kaput!' I wanted to kill the silly old bastard.

I was becoming increasingly rattled. Nothing whatsoever made sense and so my mind lobbed another component into the Mercy B. Lord mystery mixture – the all-too-human paranoia. Was there some deep, dark conspiracy behind all this? Could it possibly concern my family? Had I stupidly assumed that I'd been accepted at face value, a young Chinese-Australian creative director in an Asian advertising agency trying to make a career for himself, when really 'they' knew all along that I came from one of the five wealthiest families in Australia and the only one with a Chinese background? Hadn't Elma Kelly expressed surprise upon meeting Chairman Meow that our family's circumstances were unknown in Hong Kong? Hadn't she remarked that the mandarins kept their eyes on the wealthy Chinese worldwide? And what about Long Me's constant fear of being kidnapped? This prospect, far from being a sign of paranoia, was evidently a very real concern for the extremely wealthy. I was a mental and emotional mess, and certainly no closer to having any answers.

We finally arrived in Katong. Judging from the relatively traffic-free roads and large walled villas and mansions, it was an old and wealthy area. I flung a handful of Singapore dollars into the driver's lap, then raced across the road to the gates of what I supposed was now Mercy B. Lord's house, only to come to an abrupt halt. The tall wrought-iron gates were heavily chained and padlocked. I could clearly see the front of the house about thirty yards down a gravelled driveway, where, on a wide semi-circular apron at the top of the front steps, five men dressed in white were crouched, playing some sort of dice game. I concluded these were the men charged with staying awake to frighten off evil spirits to prevent them from entering the house. Chinese funeral tradition required them to gamble in order to stay alert. I shouted to get their attention and when one looked up, I beckoned urgently to him. Two of the men broke away from the game and sauntered up the drive to confront me. From their casual demeanour it was obvious they didn't think themselves in any way subservient. They were not unlike myself in build, the same short, square, peasant type, their bare legs and arms heavily tattooed. One was blind in one eye, his entire left eyeball a dirty white colour.

'Let me in,' I demanded in Cantonese.

'What your name?' the one with only one good eye demanded.

'Ah Koo,' I replied. 'You tell the missy Si-mon Koo.' I repeated both syllables. 'Si-mon.'

'You wait, I ask,' he instructed in a not overly friendly voice, then he moved away without the usual acquiescent nod of the head or the one pace backwards before turning to go.

My initial bewilderment, then paranoia, was turning into anger. I tried to stop it, but anger and self-justification are close partners. I didn't deserve this treatment. After all I'd been through, to be simply dismissed, albeit at the end of a weepy phone call, seemed unjust. I wanted an explanation; I told myself that's why I'd come. I was owed that much at least. Mercy B. Lord had never mentioned that money was important to her. Was that because all along she was conning me? *They* were conning me, setting me up? I could feel the anger rising, a slow, hot thing in my chest. I knew I must stay calm, but fuck it, I couldn't. I was turning into some sort of avenging angel and now, instead of wanting an explanation, I visualised myself rushing to confront Mercy B. Lord, marching up to the front door, shouldering it open and storming into the house, ignoring Beatrice Fong's wizened corpse while yelling out for Mercy B. Lord to come and get what was coming to her. Nobody was going to humiliate me like this. I had switched from anxiety and bewilderment to self-righteous anger.

However, brought up short by the gates, I realised that it was highly likely Mercy B. Lord would deny me entry. There was not a lot I could do from the wrong side of an eight-foot-high wrought-iron barrier. Even if I attempted to climb over the top, the five gambling guards were obviously capable of seeing off more than mere spirits. If they all resembled the two brutes I'd addressed, they were probably members of a gang – their tattoos were the giveaway – and by definition they'd be decidedly nasty types.

The mansion was impressive in the old style, a Victorian bungalow with a surrounding verandah of the kind built on the sub-continent for senior British civil servants. A high wall of quarried sandstone with most of the crumbling cement joints cushioned with moss appeared to surround the entire property. Tall palms fringed a gravelled driveway, which was bordered with pink and red cannas and led to the wide semi-circular front steps. What I could see of the mansion and grounds suggested old money of the settled British kind. Unlike the homes of most wealthy Chinese, no attempt was made by wealthy British colonials to impress the outside world. It was a big, solid, silent and permanent-looking house in a simple garden of clipped lawn and severely pruned shrubs. Two large white paper lanterns hung from either side of the front door with a gong on the right-hand side, as well as two broad strips of white cloth that dropped from the lintel to the verandah floor, on which there appeared to be Chinese calligraphy.

I was kept waiting for at least fifteen minutes and, inevitably, my anger began to cool, to be replaced once more by bewilderment. The thought of rushing in and yelling at her was, I realised, nonsense, entirely counterproductive. The unreasoning anger I felt still sat like a hard congealed ball somewhere between my chest and my stomach. Now I began to slowly take control, to work through the physical reaction and to make some sense of what was going on in my head, thereby attempting to overcome the rage and panic or whatever had taken hold of me and brought me to the point where I was standing with both hands white-knuckling two decorative circles in the gates' design.

I knew that, come what may, I could never physically harm Mercy B. Lord, or, for that matter, any female. My brain was simply not wired that way. I loved her despite everything, but perhaps confronting her and hearing her motives might help me to walk away. I couldn't bear the thought but knew I might have to accept the idea of losing her forever. I tried to see it her way. The orphan who had never known love or even kindness as a child, then the young adult who had been trained by Beatrice Fong to think that money alone was the true meaning of life, the girl who, I'd always thought, didn't believe this and truly loved me. But perhaps I was wrong. Could it be that she actually didn't *know* what love was? If you've never experienced the warmth and security of a mother's love, or later the euphoria of having someone in your life who makes your pulse race every time you look at them, the sheer joy of loving, then maybe you learn to fake it? Had it all passed her by? Was she emotionally destitute? Perhaps she wasn't just an orphan in the physical sense, but also in spirit, unable to trust an emotion over which she didn't have absolute control.

Then again, perhaps my previous suspicion that I was being deliberately conned made some sense. Out of the blue, there'd been the big turn-around when the old bitch carked it and left her God knows how much money. Now she didn't have to go ahead with her plans. Obviously she had sufficient cash to allow her to tell me to bugger off in quick time. She didn't have to pretend to love me any longer, or make love to an ugly bloke with a build like a tree stump, just because he was rich!

As more minutes disappeared, so did any chance of my being allowed into the house to confront Mercy B. Lord and ask her for an explanation of whatever had transpired when we met. I was mentally preparing to leave, knowing it was pointless waiting, when to my surprise the gambler with the bung eye returned. I waited for him to tell me to bugger off, but instead he produced a key and proceeded to unlock the gate, explaining that the priests and the funeral people were in the front part of the house with the corpse and that we must go around to the back to meet the missy. He let me in, then chained and locked the gate behind me.

We left the driveway and turned right onto a red-brick path with the house on our left, crossing a lawn edged with shrubs so severely clipped that they must never have been allowed to blossom – a remorseless pruning, as if Beatrice Fong had been determined to punish the plants for their variety and vigour.

A tropical garden virtually creates itself and can be a gloriously colourful exotic environment all year round. Apart from the pink and red cannas, there seemed to be no colour other than the various shades of cowering greenery. This was a garden dedicated to uniform neatness and order, a silent place unvisited by birds, bees or butterflies.

Now that I was about to confront Mercy B. Lord, I began to have doubts. What if she was simply amusedly dismissive of our shared past? What if she enjoyed making a fool of me? I had always seen her as a strong woman with a mind of her own. Now she might well mock me, laughingly admit to her true motives all along. I'd be sent away with my tail between my legs, even more humiliated. I had been easily and willingly conned, a soft touch who had to restrain his puppy-panting eagerness by wearing a jockstrap. The poor little rich boy who had everything he could possibly want, except the knowledge that he could make it on his own without his darling mummy designing his life for him. The worst part was that this was not entirely untrue, for while I appeared to have done okay in the agency – the billing had quadrupled and not all of it had simply been business handed to us from the States – in my own opinion, I'd failed.

Sidney Wing had put every financial obstacle in my path to prevent me building a sustainable and skilled creative department. Everyone we used, the prime example being Mrs Sidebottom, was freelance talent and, furthermore, I had to prove I could cover their fees before I hired them. I had no permanent staff, no back-up and no facilities. I'd made absolutely no impact on the organisation, other than to make the Wing brothers richer and to satisfy the creative needs of clients in America wishing to expand in South-East Asia. In fact, apart from my own creative efforts, aided by the loyal support of Dansford (at least between nine and noon), I'd achieved bugger-all. The poor bastard coming from America to replace me would have to begin building a creative department from scratch. In fact, I'd been so fucking inadequate that when the ventilation system I had paid for in the toilets had broken down two years later, I'd been unable to persuade Sidney to pay to have it repaired. 'I didn't think it was necessary in the first place, Simon. Why then should I pay for it to be fixed?' he'd declared.

'Because the entire agency downstairs smells of shit!' I'd protested.

'Oh? This is my concern?'

'I would have thought so,' I'd answered, somewhat tight lipped.

He shrugged. 'We have the directors toilet upstairs. It doesn't stink. I can't smell the toilets downstairs.'

'So you don't care?'

'No.'

It was almost funny to think that the only thing the staff would possibly remember about me was that I'd eliminated the smell of shit from the agency. In the end it was I who paid for the repairs to the ventilation, and this would, to the Chinese way of thinking, have emphasised to the staff my weakness and Sidney's dominance – he was top dog in the hierarchy and they all owed him respect.

We had reached the rear of the big old house where the path led to a stout wooden door set into a high brick wall, which looked to be part of a traditional walled compound that served as the servants quarters. In fact, it was probably the entrance Mercy B. Lord said she had always used to get into the house.

The leader of the gamblers reached out to slide aside the cover of a peephole. Seeing his hand flat against the door I noticed that its entire back carried a red, blue and green tattoo of a giant tarantula spider, with a single hairy leg running up the back of each finger and his thumb. He brought his good eye to the peephole to peer into the courtyard. Seemingly satisfied, he rapped firmly on the door. It opened inwards and he stepped aside to let me pass through. Whoever opened the door was hidden behind it, and I had only just enough time to see that two of the gamblers now stood a yard or so away directly in front of the open gate; the third had obviously opened it. They had their legs planted, their arms held lightly away from their sides, and were clearly there to confront me. I hesitated, ready to turn back, when a powerful kick to my spine propelled me forward to sprawl at their feet, whereupon they began to kick the living crap out of me. I attempted to rise to my knees, but a fierce kick to the ribs sent me tumbling over. I curled into a foetal ball facing the back of the house, my knees pulled up to my stomach, my arms wrapped about my head in an attempt to protect it from their furious feet. Judging by the rapidity of the kicks and the grunts that followed them, all of the five men were putting in the boot. It was less than two or three seconds before a brutal kick to the base of my skull rendered me unconscious, but in those few moments I saw Johnny Wing standing at a window of the big house, arms folded across his chest, looking directly down at me.

I came to as I was being lifted onto a gurney in the forecourt of the accident and emergency department of the Outram Road Hospital. I had been brought there by ambulance and was later told I had been discovered in an alley in Chinatown and that the police had been informed. The hospital lights were on and it was obviously well after sunset. As it turned out, the beating I had taken could have been a lot worse. According to the physician who examined me, the blow that knocked me unconscious could well have broken my spine and left me paralysed. Five of my ribs were broken. It would take weeks for my face to lose its swelling, and as long for my black and almost completely closed eyes to return to normal. My broken nose, at present lost somewhere in the centre of the inglorious mess laughingly known as my face, would not reappear for weeks. Other than that, it was only a matter of bruises, though they seemed to cover almost every inch of my body, including my private parts. In other words, while I wasn't going to die or become a cripple, and nothing was broken except a few ribs, everything hurt like hell. The evil spirit-chasers hired for the funeral arrangements had certainly kicked the daylights out of any demons that might have been lurking within me. At the same time, the Wings had clearly indicated that it was payback time for ignoring their warnings to keep away from their pretty little courier.

The doctor must have prescribed morphine for the pain and something to knock me out, because it was dawn when I surfaced to face the world – not a kindly place, under the circumstances. The painkiller had worn off and every bone in my body felt as though it was broken. I am ashamed to say that on this dawning of a new day I could bear no more and I completely broke down, my emotions overwhelming me, so that I blubbed like a child, my swollen throbbing face buried in the pillow to muffle my sobs. How long I lay weeping I'm not sure, but because of my broken ribs, every sob was excruciating. It was the pain in combination with my self-indulgent tears that eventually seemed to clear my thoughts. Or so I imagined. I was to learn that pain also plays tricks on the mind.

Black-eyed, barely able to see, swollen and bruised, I tried to pull myself together, to take stock and to attempt to think rationally about what had happened. I had clearly acted foolishly and had paid the price. In a curious way, the severe beating had brought me to my senses. It was my punishment for loving Mercy B. Lord, one that Ronnie Wing had first promised almost three years ago to the day. I couldn't say that I hadn't been warned.

Now, as I listened to the first of the birdsong, the quark of the ubiquitous Asian crow and the persistent double note of the indigenous koel in the hospital garden, I tried to gather my wits. This time I would attempt to be a little more analytical and less introspective and self-pitying. Blaming Mercy B. Lord for ruining my life was a cop-out. If she'd been behind the beating with Johnny Wing, then surely I was better off knowing it? Facing up to reality?

I had become convinced she was beholden to Beatrice and the Wings and I'd wanted to protect her from them, somehow weaken the hold they appeared to have over her. The research model I'd evolved with my professor cousin and Dansford was intended to ultimately get her away from the evil nexus. In my mind I had seen her running a market-research organisation I would help her build once I had quit the agency. I would also build a film studio together with Willie Wonka and Harry 'Three Thumbs' Poon. Mercy B. Lord would run the research outfit and Willie and Three Thumbs the film studio, and I – well, I wasn't entirely sure yet, but I'd do something complementary, begin a small communications conglomerate, ancillary services to marketing and advertising. Then along came Molly Ong's concept of the Singapore

Girl and it provided Mercy B. Lord with immediate protection, the assurance that Fong and Wing wouldn't risk harming her because of the possible consequences to themselves.

However, I now realised that her acting as courier for the Fong–Wing enterprise was something she willingly accepted as part of her training for the future. I was forced to acknowledge that she might have known all along that she would take over the Beatrice Fong Agency in the future. Now that this future had finally arrived, Mercy B. Lord would simply maintain the links between the evil empires of Beatrice Fong and the Wings. Despite everything, I knew that I could never love anyone as much as I'd loved her – alas, still loved her. How stupid is that!

The night sister came in on her final rounds and refilled my drip, adding a fresh charge of glorious pain relief that I concluded must be morphine, as it had the immediate effect of relieving the pain and once again changing my mindset. I now saw that I'd been quite wrong. If my previous attempt at a reasoned and logical explanation was correct, then why had Mercy B. Lord bothered to enter my life in the first place? She would have been far better steering well clear, brushing off my early advances. Her future was, after all, assured. Moreover, if she had never experienced love, why would she have submitted to it so willingly? If her destiny lay somewhere other than in a permanent relationship with me, she would have been crazy to place it in jeopardy.

And what about the portrait? Having left me and then at first rejected Molly Ong's offer to be the Singapore Girl, why then had she changed her mind and agreed to appear at the awards dinner and afterwards celebrate our loving reconciliation in the suite at the Peninsula, even agreeing to move back into the flat when we returned to Singapore?

I was forced to conclude that her rejection, on more than one occasion, of my pathetic offer of a permanent relationship was the only real clue to the situation.

I'd been through all the variations and permutations of everything without getting any closer to the truth than I had been moments after hearing the dreadful finality of the phone receiver clunking down. I'd been nearly beaten to death attempting, unsuccessfully, to discover some kind of plausible explanation. Nothing made sense. I'd carefully examined my angry emotional reactions, but the cold, calculating, logical analysis had more holes than a kitchen colander. I still couldn't convince myself that any of it explained what had happened to shatter the future I'd imagined sharing with Mercy B. Lord.

Throughout all this I kept hearing her anguished voice and her choked-back tears, then her cold dismissal and the unexpected and sudden clunk of the receiver being replaced. Almost immediately there followed the image of Johnny Wing at the window looking down at me a second or two before I lapsed into unconsciousness from the beating. While it was entirely possible to arbitrarily connect the thought with the image – her anguish and cold dismissal over the phone with Johnny's face at the window – there was no possible way of knowing whether they belonged together.

Johnny was the executor of the old crone's will and so had a perfect right to be in Beatrice Fong's home. Ronnie had mentioned that he was away from the agency for the day and couldn't sign my cheque. Furthermore, I had no way of knowing whether he was entitled to withhold Mercy B. Lord's inheritance if she continued to stay with me, or if this might, as I'd previously speculated, be simply a convenient invention by Mercy B. Lord.

The only fact I could be certain about was that I had been warned to stay away from Mercy B. Lord. The beating I'd received had almost assuredly been instigated by the vile Johnny Wing, but not necessarily *only* as a warning to stay away from her. It would also have been an unexpected but opportune payback for my assaulting him in Sidney's office.

But then again, I was forced to conclude he wasn't alone in the house. While I hadn't seen her witness my beating, it was difficult to believe Mercy B. Lord would have been unaware of it taking place in the courtyard. Frankly, having looked at it from every possible angle, nothing seemed to make sense. I still didn't know what I thought about the whole immense fuck-up, all of which I was forced to admit I had personally initiated by turning up uninvited at the gate.

With the night shift concluding and the day shift coming on, the ward radio was turned on, ostensibly to get the seven o'clock news. What I didn't know was that it remained on all day, blaring out popular songs. Ironically, the first of them after the morning news was Nat King Cole singing 'Love is a Many Splendored Thing'. While I don't remember the whole song, the lyrics I clearly recall on that grim, tropical and far from 'splendored' morning claimed that love turned a man into a king.

There are times in everyone's life when a distant unheralded storm causes dry riverbeds to fill then to merge in a confluence that brims then overflows and floods, taking everything with it – when a love seemingly tranquil and benign turns unexpectedly into a fiercely destructive force. 'Love is a Many Splendored Thing', a hit song when I was in my late teens, doesn't mention that the act of loving somebody may suddenly become an utterly miserable, confusing, bewildering, maddening, saddening betrayal.

Amusingly, though I wasn't laughing at the time, to further diminish the prospects of everything being bright and beautiful, the day sister in charge was the corseted, big-bosomed, stiffly starched and veiled virago who had sent me packing when I'd attempted to con my way into the ward to see Mrs Sidebottom after her accident. Fortuitously, my face was such a mess that it was doubtful my mum would have recognised me, and in the unlikely event that the sister had remembered I was called Koo, it is a very common Chinese surname. She'd only glanced at the clipboard at the foot of my bed. 'I say, we have been in the wars, haven't we, Mr Koo!' Then, turning to the ward nurse, 'Nurse, see that the patient gets his painkiller every four hours.' And back to me. 'Time will mend you, Mr Koo, but we'll try to make it pass as comfortably as possible under the circumstances.'

'What about visitors, sister?' I asked, in a pathetic attempt at a joke against myself, purely for my own benefit.

'Family?'

'No, not in Singapore, sister.'

The prospect of my mum's family traipsing in to see me, having first overheated to melting point the international telephone cable to Chairman Meow in Sydney, was too horrible to think about. I could imagine my mum impatiently pacing the carpet in the Qantas first-class lounge at Mascot ready to wing her panic-stricken way across the ocean to be at my side. Should she get the tiniest inkling of what had transpired, she would turn into a vociferous avenging angel. Chairman Meow on the warpath in defence of her only son and heir was beyond imagining.

'Then I'm afraid not, for the first three days,' Sister Virago announced. 'You're not going to die, but nonetheless we need to monitor your progress carefully. Visitors clustered around a hospital bed are not helpful to my staff. This is an accident and emergency ward where getting better has nothing to do with grapes, chocolates and idle chatter.' She paused. 'You'll need to save all your energy, anyway, because you can expect a visit from the police, Mr Koo. They found you and have alerted us that they will need to interview you. You have been assaulted and they will want our medical report as well. I don't want you overexcited by unnecessary visitors.'

I nodded. There was no point in arguing. I guessed I'd figure out how to get a message to Dansford at the agency after nine o'clock. 'Thank you, sister.'

With this, the hospital ship HMS *Virago* steamed off on her way to the next hapless victim, some poor bastard with his head swathed in bandages and both legs and feet heavily boarded, bandaged and hoisted high above him by a contraption on pulleys involving steel wire and two leather loops in which his heels rested. At least he wouldn't need to face a police interview, as his entire face was wrapped like an Egyptian mummy's with a tube stuck in a hole in the bandage so he could be more or less fed, and above it just the tip of his nose and nostrils showing to allow him to breathe.

Despite the calming influence of the morphine coursing through my system, I felt mildly panicked. I would obviously need to come up with a plausible story for the police that didn't implicate Johnny Wing or, more importantly, Mercy B. Lord. I'd clearly been dumped somewhere after the beating. I may look Chinese but inscrutable just isn't me. Lies require practice and I had been brought up with the world's best lie detector for a mother. It is claimed that a child up to the age of five is incapable of lying; the brain is not yet sufficiently formed to understand duplicity. With Chairman Meow in charge, when our brains finally acquired the capacity to tell fibs, she saw to it that it never evolved beyond the most fundamental level, at which they were easy to detect. Poor kids in disadvantaged families often need to tell untruths just to survive. Silver-spooners like myself and my sisters never had cause to acquire cunning or deception skills to protect us from adults.

I decided I would have to come up with a very simple story to tell the police, one I could stick to despite interrogation, a lie with only fundamental details that were easily repeated. A robbery and mugging in an alley where there were no witnesses and where I'd been knocked unconscious and remembered nothing more until I woke up as they were lifting me onto a gurney outside the accident and emergency department. Something simple.

See what I mean? Already there were more holes in my story than in a slice of Swiss cheese. Finding a lonely alley with no witnesses in the middle of rush hour in Singapore was well nigh impossible. What was I doing in the alley anyway? Why was my wallet still in my possession with a fair amount of cash in it? Why did the five men who had confronted me and knocked me unconscious with the first blow continue to beat me up when, with superior numbers in an empty alley, they could have simply removed my wallet from my back trouser pocket and left? Or not even landed the initial blow. With five of them standing around me I wouldn't have thought to resist and so they could have demanded my money and sauntered off. I was even failing the interview I was conducting with myself.

Breakfast came and went untouched. While the only part of me that hadn't been injured was my jaw and mouth, I wasn't in the least hungry.

Then, to my complete surprise, despite Sister Virago's ban on visitors, Dansford and Chicken Wing arrived late in the morning. Her presence was particularly curious – she never went anywhere with him and I'd only met her on two or three occasions at his flat, when she'd done a lot of obsequious bowing and nodding in near silence.

'Dansford! How on earth did you know I was here? How'd you get in? I've been told no visitors allowed!' I exclaimed. Then, glancing at Chicken Wing, I quickly added, 'Good morning. This is a surprise.'

Chicken Wing smiled and nodded. Obviously she'd learned a fair bit of English since being with Dansford. Then, without even greeting me, he said, 'Simon, not another word until we get you out of this shit-hole.'

'What, the hospital?'

'Afraid not, old son, just the ward – can't have you in here. Need to talk.' He'd barely completed this last sentence when two orderlies arrived pushing a gurney. Ten minutes later I was ensconced in a small private room overlooking a rose garden and a rather splendid poinciana in the background, the shady umbrella-shaped tree that looks magnificent when it flowers.

Dansford drew up two chairs, one on either side of the bed, and they both sat. 'Now, that's better. Good morning, Simon, though I imagine it's anything but. We apologise for barging in without first checking on your condition but we've rather a lot to talk about. First, though, tell us, are you up to talking, old son?'

He'd emphasised the 'we' and the 'us' and I looked somewhat quizzically at Chicken Wing, who I was aware spoke, at best, only rudimentary English.

Chicken Wing grinned. 'G'day, Simon,' she said with a marked Australian accent.

'Oh!' I exclaimed, taken aback.

She threw back her head and laughed. 'Canberra high school, then uni, ANU, where I took a degree in international law and Asian studies – my dad was in the diplomatic corps.'

'Oh, Jesus!' I distinctly recalled begging Dansford in English while she was present in the room not to be a bloody fool about marrying her. My already bruised and battered plum-coloured face was probably incapable of flushing a deeper shade of red. 'I think I owe you an apology,' I said sheepishly.

Chicken Wing laughed again. 'I remember. You begged Dansford not to marry me. It was really very funny at the time, but then again, perfect! Perfect cover.'

'Cover?'

'Chicken Wing is a senior undercover operative in the Singapore Police Force Drug Enforcement Unit.'

'Go on!' I exclaimed, looking incredulously at Chicken Wing. 'But . . . but I distinctly remember when Mercy B. Lord hired you to be Dansford's housemaid.'

'Yes, very fortuitous,' Chicken Wing said. 'In fact, if I may say so, rather well planned.'

I looked at them in turn. 'But then you two promptly got married.'

'Again, excellent cover,' Chicken Wing said.

'You mean you're not?'

'Married?' Dansford said. 'Yes, of course we are. But it didn't happen all that suddenly. I'd known Hilda a good while before we married. We first met in Washington.'

I glanced at Chicken Wing. 'Hilda? Do I call you that in future?'

She dropped her gaze and said almost shyly, 'If, as I sincerely hope, we are to become close friends, then yes, I'd like that.' Meeting my eyes, she went on, 'But I'm afraid today is rather more official, Simon.'

I glanced quickly at Dansford for an explanation and he looked at me a little sheepishly. 'Simon, old son, I'm afraid this isn't, that is, we are not just friends visiting, anxious though we are to know how you're feeling. I've already called several times to check that you're okay.

Detective Sergeant Wing is here to interview you in regard to what happened yesterday.'

I nodded. 'Yes, the ward sister said the police had been informed, would be coming around. But this is nonetheless a bit of a surprise . . . no, a helluva big surprise! Dansford, you said "we" a moment ago. Then before that you said the two of you had met in Washington? Hilda . . . er, Detective Sergeant Wing, your wife, turns out to be a police officer? What the hell's going on?'

Dansford grinned. 'I guess we need to fill you in, Simon.'

'What are you saying, Dansford? That you're not what you seem? Not an ad man?'

'Ah, *always* an ad man, Simon, pre- and post-war. But I spent the war in special operations, South Pacific, Japan, then after that the Korean War, then back to Madison Avenue. But Vietnam came along and the CIA got tangled up in the Asian opium trade, so I got hauled back to Capitol Hill to work for the DEA. I'm an undercover agent for the Drug Enforcement Agency in Washington.'

I tucked away the bit about the CIA. While it sounded pretty bizarre, my immediate need was to know more about Dansford's double life.

'You know, I always felt there was something different about you, mate. The last occasion was in Hong Kong. Your knowing the governor well enough for him to ignore the fact that you weren't wearing shoes and socks. Then remarkably remembering his favourite honky tonk number, "Lovesick Blues", sung by Hank Williams. That takes a special kind of mind. Then on one occasion I saw you at the airport when I'd gone to meet my mother flying in from Oz. You were supposed to be at the usual long lunch, but you were carrying ABTATS, your awful crocodile-skin bag, and were about to board a plane for Bangkok. I checked the flight afterwards, just to be sure. And there have been other times as well. For example, when we were doing the market-research project with Professor Kwan, you would sometimes come up with an insight into the Asian psyche that Henry would later tell me was remarkable. I recall on one occasion he simply shook his head. "Simon, I'm a trained sociologist; these are observations a layman wouldn't, couldn't possibly make," he maintained.'

'Harvard, Centre for East-Asian Studies, advanced psychology,' Dansford replied with a grin. 'That's either very perspicacious of you, Simon, or I'm losing my touch. But to continue, six months before I joined Samuel Oswald Wing, Hilda and I met at a combined special-operations briefing in the US. The briefing was on the alarming escalation of heroin addiction among American forces in Vietnam. The Singapore government had agreed to mount a joint operation with Washington.' He glanced fondly over at Chicken, now Hilda Wing. 'Hilda was one of the operatives they sent over for the briefing. The only pretty one.' He smiled. 'Even if I sound biased, she's a remarkably talented police officer, despite the fact that she obviously lacks judgement when it comes to men. I think I asked her to marry me two weeks into the Washington briefing.'

'And I was foolish enough to say yes,' Hilda grinned, then cleared her throat, her expression suddenly businesslike. 'Simon, I imagine all this will have come as a bit of surprise to you. Besides, you're not well and you've taken a bad hiding. There are reasons why we can't wait a few days to conduct this interview. We need rather urgently to talk to you about what happened, as well as brief you on several matters, then ask you a few questions. Your answers will be very important. Do you feel up to it now? We could let you rest for an hour or so and then come back.'

The effect of the morphine was slowly wearing off and I knew that before long I would begin to feel like shit. I wasn't at all sure I could focus for too much longer. All this was pretty new and there was more of the same to come. While Mercy B. Lord, the recently deceased Beatrice Fong or the Wing brothers hadn't been mentioned, one didn't have to be a genius to know what was coming. This was about crime, major crime – drugs, kidnapping, perhaps even murder. I could feel the anxiety rising in me, a dark, thick, steadily expanding substance in my gut. In

Singapore crimes like that almost certainly meant the death sentence, and what if Mercy B. Lord was involved? I couldn't bring myself to phrase the next thought. The Singapore government made no exceptions for a pretty neck.

'It's been over four hours since I was given a painkiller, Detective Sergeant Wing. Perhaps if they give me another shot of whatever they're dosing me with, I'll be right,' I suggested.

Detective Chicken Wing (the name that came most readily to my mind) rose from her chair. 'I'll find someone who can help,' she said, leaving the room.

'Dansford, what the fuck is going on?' I exclaimed.

'Sorry, Simon, but you came close to screwing up a three-year undercover operation. May still have,' he said, suddenly tight lipped.

'How?' I demanded, confused.

'By storming the fucking Bastille last night! Your ridiculous exercise in gate-rattling.'

Before I could reply, Detective Chicken Wing re-entered the room, followed by the hospital ship HMS *Virago* with an ampoule, the contents of which she drew up into a syringe. She fixed a tourniquet to my upper arm and injected into a vein in the crook of my elbow. Everything was done silently with lips drawn tight.

'Thank you, sister,' I said.

She grunted and left but then stopped at the door and addressed Dansford. 'You mustn't overtax Mr Koo. He's far from well and I don't want him upset.' She was gone before Dansford could reply.

After she'd departed, Dansford, now calm again, said, 'Simon, take it easy with that stuff. Make that the last time. Better to endure the pain in the long run, son.'

I nodded. 'Yeah, I've guessed what it was. I promise.' I grinned so that he'd know I'd calmed down, too. 'It works too well not to be addictive.'

'You got it in one,' he replied.

Detective Chicken Wing resumed her seat. 'Simon, this interview is not being recorded – in other words, it's not for the record. But I must urge you to answer the questions as accurately as you can. I, we, appreciate that you have divided loyalties and so you should be aware that we know exactly what happened.'

I frowned, bemused. 'That's hardly possible. How?'

'Alice, initially.'

'Alice Ho, the receptionist?'

'Yes. When you returned from the printer after Mercy B. Lord had been calling frantically since mid-afternoon, she got her on the phone for you and, like all good switchboard operators, sensing a crisis, listened in to your conversation. She saw you run out for a taxi, and it was pretty obvious where you were going. She knew Johnny Wing was at Beatrice Fong's house because he'd called earlier in the afternoon to tell Sidney he was on his way to the house. She feared the worst, so she called me.'

'Why did she call you? Did she know you're a police officer?'

'No, of course not! It's an arrangement Dansford and I have. When he's out entertaining, he calls me when he leaves one place to go to another. It's standard procedure. That way I usually have some idea where he is. Alice Ho knows if it's really urgent and she has to find Dansford to call me.'

'But Alice has been with the Wings for yonks. Her first loyalty is to them. As you said, if she knew Johnny was at Beatrice Fong's home, why wouldn't she have called to warn him I was coming over?'

'That's precisely why she called me, to alert Dansford. Johnny Wing is generally disliked and Alice Ho is no different from the rest of the staff. She, more than most, knows he's a nasty piece of work.'

'Alice knows there's no love lost between you and Johnny, Simon,' Dansford said.

I turned to Detective Chicken Wing. 'And Alice told you all this?'

'No, not at first, but she was pretty upset. It wasn't too hard, woman to woman. It's my job, after all.'

Dansford cut in. 'Evidently, she greatly admires you, Simon. Paying for the toilet ventilation out of your own pocket, freeing the agency from the smell of shit. Then you personally introduced her to Karlene Stein.'

Detective Chicken Wing laughed. 'Yes, the ventilation. She couldn't get over someone doing that, defying Sidney Wing, and paying to have it done out of his own pocket and not telling anyone, not making a fuss, caring about the welfare of the staff. She also told me how you'd formally introduced her to Miss Karlene, as if she, Alice Ho, was a very important person to whom the TV star was privileged to be introduced.'

'Well, I'll be damned! You could have fooled me. I've always assumed the staff regarded the ventilation brouhaha with Sidney as a great loss of face on my part.'

'On the contrary, Simon, they admire you. But the Chinese are funny – they like to hedge their bets. They see Sidney as the hand that feeds them. Anyway, Alice Ho was very concerned about your safety. Fortunately, we already had the Beatrice Fong house under police surveillance.'

At once curious, I glanced in turn at both of them. 'Why was that?'

'Ah, when Beatrice Fong's doctor notified police headquarters of her death, they called me almost immediately,' Detective Chicken Wing explained. 'You see, Beatrice Fong, despite her age, was the major player in an international drug operation. It was her original network that even today is critical to the success of the operation. With her gone, a major reshuffle has to take place in the leadership. It's just the opportunity we've been waiting for.'

'The next twenty-four hours, certainly the next few days, are critical,' Dansford said. 'Perhaps we shouldn't be telling you this, but Hilda and I discussed our options. We can do one of two things: arrest you and keep you in custody until it's over, or trust you not to go near Mercy B. Lord or to try in any way to contact her. Having known you as a partner for close to three years, I vouched for the second option.'

'Do you think she's involved?'

'Well, you know she is, Simon,' he said, a tad sternly.

'Yes, Thursdays, but how deeply?'

'I think that's the very point. Until yesterday, when she inherited, it may have been only marginally – we simply don't know. But now, with the old lady's death, everything changes and she certainly appears to be very much in charge at the moment.'

Then, before I could explain that the old crone had made her responsible for the funeral arrangements, Detective Chicken Wing said, 'An hour after her death was reported we had the house under plainclothes surveillance, front and back. We observed Mercy B. Lord arrive by taxi, unlock the gate and leave it unlocked for the ambulance to arrive fifteen minutes later. After the ambulance left, Mercy B. Lord walked up and chained and locked the gate.'

'Oh, I don't think that's suspicious,' I said, defending her. 'She told me Beatrice Fong had briefed her on the funeral arrangements. She was to go to Barclays Bank to get her instructions.' I turned to Dansford. 'Look, mate, I'm becoming very bloody confused. Obviously you've been watching Beatrice Fong, the Wing brothers and, it seems, Mercy B. Lord, for a long time.'

'Well, yes, they are why I came to Singapore, but of course the DEA had an eye on them for some time before that.'

'You said something about the CIA? Did I hear that correctly?'

'That's classified, it was a slip.'

'A deliberate one?'

'Yes.'

'Oh, I see,' which, of course, I didn't.

'Simon, it's complicated. May I leave that for later, perhaps? There are more urgent matters we have to talk about.'

I nodded. 'Just one thing. Are you ostensibly mounting an operation against the CIA? In effect, against yourself – USA versus USA?'

Dansford looked directly at me. 'It's complicated, but yes, in a manner of speaking, you could say that.'

Detective Chicken Wing then said quickly, 'Simon, I know it's a lot to take in when you're not well, but there's a bit more to come – a few direct questions, some background, one or two things you should know if Mercy B. Lord tries to contact you. To begin with, what do you know about Thursdays?'

'Not a great deal, I'm afraid. Mercy B. Lord is involved as a courier who leaves Singapore and goes to Thailand every Thursday.'

'Oh, and how do you know she goes to Thailand?'

'Molly Ong checked her flight records with the airline, and I'd made an educated guess after checking the airport for suitable flights.'

She glanced quickly at Dansford. 'Molly Ong – how much does she know?'

'Well, presumably only what I know. That Mercy B. Lord takes a briefcase to Thailand every Thursday.'

'Do you know what's in the briefcase?' she asked me.

'No. Molly tried to find out, but got hauled over the coals by a government minister – the minister for customs and excise, I think.'

'Why was it necessary for her to know what the briefcase contained?'

'She was doing research into Mercy B. Lord's potential to be the Singapore Girl. It was a chance to exploit . . . er, take advantage of the publicity surrounding my portrait win. The appointment of the Singapore Girl, who is intended to be an ambassador, required overseas travel, and her being away every Thursday potentially posed problems. I had to tell her Mercy B. Lord and I were no longer together. I think, I can't remember, I told her it was the reason we were no longer together.'

'I see. So she, Molly, and presumably you, didn't know what the briefcase contained?'

'And do you think that's all Molly Ong knows?' Detective Chicken Wing asked before I could answer Dansford.

'Who's first? Okay, Dansford. No, I didn't know what was in the briefcase.' I now glanced at Detective Chicken Wing. 'If Molly knew more, she didn't say . . . Well, not to me, anyway. But it wasn't hard to guess. It was metal lined, perhaps lead lined, locked with two very professional combination locks – it was almost certainly money. But what I didn't know was why she was carting money to Thailand every week.'

'Do you think Mercy B. Lord knew what was in the briefcase? Did she ever say anything to you?'

'The answer to the first question is: I don't know; to the second: no. She isn't a fool. If I can venture a guess about the contents, then so could she. But why are you asking? You obviously know the answer.'

'Yes, Simon, but it's necessary that you do as well, so you don't decide to rescue a maiden in distress. Mercy B. Lord isn't quite the person you or even she thinks she is, or until yesterday *may* have thought she was.' He paused, then announced, 'She's Beatrice Fong's granddaughter.'

'Oh, c'mon, you're joking!' I was totally taken aback. It was like being hit on the back of the head with a cosh.

Detective Chicken Wing then explained. 'We Chinese are obsessed with family. Beatrice Fong's granddaughter was her only hope of dynastic continuity. Besides, the wealthy Chinese don't as a rule leave everything they own to an employee or servant in gratitude, even for a lifetime of service. Especially as Mercy B. Lord would hardly qualify in that regard. She's only twenty-three, having been in Beatrice Fong's employ for seven years, a very short time by Chinese standards. It is very unlikely – in fact impossible, when you know something about Beatrice Fong – to believe the money was left to Mercy B. Lord because she'd been a loyal mule for the crime cartel.'

'Hang on – Mercy B. Lord is an orphan. She was left on the steps of an orphanage at two months. Brought up by the nuns. Her father was a Japanese soldier. She said her mother had to leave Singapore because of the stigma and couldn't keep her baby. Are you suggesting that Beatrice Fong is – was – her grandmother and that she allowed her to be brought up in an orphanage?' I turned to Detective Chicken Wing. 'You just said the Chinese are nuts about family!'

Dansford interrupted. 'Simon, you need to know the background. In fact you already know some of it, as I recall you telling me after your lunch with Elma Kelly. It begins with the first Wing, the patriarch, William. You know his story – he married the madam of a whorehouse and opium den, which financed his canning operation. She died owning three combined brothels and opium dens, then a sister came across from China and took over. Well, without going into too much detail, she married a customer, an opium addict who died shortly after she gave birth to a daughter in 1878, who was, of course, Beatrice. When her mother died, Beatrice, schooled early and well in the business, took over the three combined brothels and opium dens. She evidently ran the business very well: her brothels were clean, the girls regularly checked for disease, and the drugs – opium, that is – handled discreetly. As a result, she received the blessing of the British authorities when she wanted to expand. The Brits, as you know, never banned opium and additionally saw brothels as a necessity in a major shipping port. In other words, provided always she kept her place neat and discreetly tucked away in the general fabric of Singapore society, she was allowed to prosper, which she did – hugely, it would seem, as she ended with fifteen establishments.'

Dansford grinned. 'As an aside, while doing the research we came across a rather apt euphemism. In those days Singapore brothels were referred to by merchant seamen as "poke and smokes". With fifteen establishments, Beatrice was the biggest madam in town and her girls were reputed to be the choicest. She had a reputation to maintain and had become a major supplier of young girls. I guess Beatrice was, in her own profession, an entrepreneur. Anyway, she decided to go into the female flesh trade herself and soon became a major procurer from China and other Asian countries, mostly Thailand, Cambodia and Burma, countries she personally visited regularly to buy her raw product, if you'll excuse the term. It seems she also expanded the business beyond Singapore, selling girls to brothels in Europe and the Middle East as well as to surrounding Asian countries, first training them in her Singapore establishments in the niceties of pleasing a male, and then, as we say in the ad business, selling the value-added product at a premium.'

Dansford paused again. 'In our research we found a mention of Noël Coward, who in the 1930s paid a visit to Singapore, where he gave a concert during which he performed a song about the pleasures of drink and its consequences. The song contained the lyrics "fond fruit of the vine", but to get a laugh from the Singapore audience, he cleverly adapted them to include a reference to Beatrice Fong's trained concubines: "Fong Fruit – oh, divine!"

'Well, not allowing any moss to grow on the rock-hard Beatrice Fong, she soon realised that what works in the flesh business also works with drugs. In Burma she got involved in paying the peasant farmers to grow opium poppies. Again, she expanded this business beyond the needs of Singapore to other buyers, mainly in Asia, but also in Europe and the UK, where heroin was being used increasingly among the wealthy during the twenties. She even set up the first heroin lab in Burma – in fact, the first in Asia. By the mid-thirties she was already an international operator, one of the biggest, if not *the* biggest, in drugs and the female slave trade.' Dansford paused. 'I guess you're beginning to get the idea, Simon.'

All I could do was nod and add rather lamely, 'Bloody hell!'

Dansford continued. 'Anyhow, to backtrack a bit, in 1927 Beatrice married a Chinese named Samson Fong. She was thirty-nine and, as Hilda says, progeny and continuity of the family line are very important and her safe childbearing years were coming to a close. It seems Mr Fong was simply a means to an end, and soon after her daughter was born he disappeared from the scene, never to be heard from again. Beatrice named her child Lotus Blossom.'

I laughed. 'A touch of irony there! The lotus is the symbol of purity, although it has its roots in the muck. What happened to the daughter?' I grinned. 'She didn't put her in an orphanage, did she?'

'No, nothing like that. Perfectly normal childhood, if growing up as Beatrice Fong's daughter could be said to be normal. The daughter was fifteen when the Japanese invaded Singapore.'

'So, what happened to her?'

'Beatrice Fong?'

'Yes, but especially her daughter.'

At this point the hospital ship HMS *Virago* came steaming into the room. 'That's quite enough. My patient has to rest now,' Sister Virago announced. 'You may return after lunch. After 2 p.m., thank you!' The 'thank you' was said sharply and was clipped at the end so that it came out as a single word – *'Than-queue!'*

Dansford hesitated, glancing at Detective Chicken Wing, who nodded. 'If we return shortly after two, will that be okay, Simon?'

'Yes, sure. You've left me a fair bit to think about.'

'Come on, hop along now, you two,' Sister Virago said impatiently. I wondered briefly what it might take to scare her.

My mind was racing but I admit I was actually quite pleased that I'd be left alone for a couple of hours. I needed to think. But then a Chinese nurse entered with a glass of water and a pill. 'You sleep maybe little bit, sister say.'

I suddenly realised I was bloody exhausted. I pointed to the pill. 'How long will I sleep?'

'How long you want?' she replied.

'Two hours.'

She nodded vigorously. 'Ja, ja, you take.' I realised she hadn't a clue, but I took the sleeping pill anyway and woke up at one-thirty with my lunch tray at my bedside, two ham sandwiches and tomato soup grown cold. The morphine was wearing off and I was in a lot of discomfort, which is probably why I woke up. Despite the pain, I was hungry, so I drank the cold soup and ate the sandwiches, leaving the crusts as the extra chewing hurt. I left the cup of cold milky tea, but I felt a little better after eating. I wondered how I was going to get through the afternoon with Dansford and Detective Chicken Wing without the aid of morphine. I rang the bell beside the bed and when the same Chinese nurse arrived I asked her where the toilet was.

'No, no, I bring, you stay bed. What you want – wee-wee? Poo-poo?'

'I want to wash my face,' I told her.

'I do for you,' she said, and returned with a bowl of warm water and a facecloth and insisted on doing the job herself. I tried not to wince too often but her touch wasn't exactly delicate. At the end she said, 'You want inject? I tell sister.'

I thought, *Just one more shot of morphine won't hurt.* 'No! No more injections!' I told her. 'You got a codeine tablet?'

She nodded and smiled. 'No want inject. Very strong man, Mr Simon.'

But she was wrong. I was beginning to fall apart mentally. I realised all the implications of the inheritance for Mercy B. Lord and the shit she was in. This was Singapore where major crimes meant the death sentence, and they were not going to make an exception for her lovely neck.

Dansford and Detective Chicken Wing returned just on two o'clock, and after the usual pleasantries Dansford explained that Detective Chicken Wing was going to relate the remainder of Beatrice Fong's background. 'Simon, Hilda's done the painstaking stuff, Singapore under the Japanese. Most of this information comes from interviewing domestic staff and the now middle-aged prostitutes and, well, anyone at the time who knew anything. The Chinese are acute observers and listeners. The saying "The walls have ears" must have been invented to describe the Chinese servant class. They are also walking memory banks and their eyes miss nothing. So, while she can't vouch for every tiny detail, we've pretty sure we've got the Beatrice Fong wartime information correct.'

I should warn you that what follows sounds dramatic, but there is no reason not to believe it. In the end everything fits perfectly and Detective Chicken Wing did a fantastic job.

'Simon, your last question before we left this morning was what happened to Lotus Blossom, Beatrice Fong's daughter. I think it may be better to hear the whole story, as that's the only way I can really answer the question satisfactorily. I'll tell it as quickly as possible but stop me if you have a question.

'However, before I deal with the war, the story takes a curious twist that will eventually assume importance. The Wings, still very remotely related, reappear in the picture nearly a hundred years after William Wing married Beatrice's aunt. Johnny Wing at eighteen falls in love with the fifteen-year-old Lotus Blossom just before the fall of Singapore. Beatrice agrees that it is an appropriate match and that they may one day be betrothed but must wait until both are older. But, of course, the Japanese arrive just two months later, and Johnny escapes into the jungle, as did a great many young Singaporean men, to join the communist guerrillas to fight against the new enemy. This communist movement was mostly home-grown and grew up as a protest both against the British and what the Japanese were doing in China. The British authorities banned the movement and so it went underground, and when the Japanese invaded, the communists were a readymade guerrilla force.

'Anyway, Beatrice Fong was a very wealthy woman when the war broke out – some say the wealthiest woman in Asia. But before the Japanese invasion of Singapore, she too had been caught up in the "impregnable fortress" myth. Curious, that. She would have been well aware of the Japanese coming through Thailand and then down the Malayan peninsula. But she had prospered under the British and was an anglophile or, at least, believed Britain was invincible on this island, and she was caught napping. Virtually all her assets, including a large amount of silver and gold bullion in the main vault of Barclays Bank, fell to the Japanese, who, additionally, closed all the brothels except three, which they reserved as comfort houses for their troops. They also banned opium.

'The comfort houses were under the direction of a Japanese captain named Kazuhiro Takahashi, who charged Beatrice with choosing the best of the young prostitutes to fill the three brothels, the prettiest going to the House of the Swallows, as they named the officers' brothel. After this they appointed Beatrice to oversee the three houses. "Manage" is probably the correct word because they imported several Japanese *mama-sans* to educate the girls in the needs of the Japanese troops in two of the establishments and three retired geisha to train the young prostitutes in the sometimes peculiar sexual needs of the officers in the House of the Swallows.

'Beatrice was back in business, and while she had lost everything, she had permission from Captain Kazuhiro Takahashi to keep her daughter from being forced into prostitution. She'd also avoided the summary execution she might have expected as a drug dealer. Furthermore, unlike most of the population, there was rice in the bowl and so she could be said to have landed on her feet.

'All went well until Lotus Blossom was approaching eighteen, when Captain Kazuhiro Takahashi decided to take her as his concubine. There was no possibility of refusal if Beatrice hoped to stay alive.

'Then, on the 6th of August 1945, the atom bomb fell on Hiroshima, and three days later a second fell on Nagasaki. When the Japanese emperor announced the surrender, the Japanese troops in South-East Asia were taken by surprise. In the chaotic days that followed, and before the allies arrived in Singapore, Johnny Wing, along with other former city boys, came out of the jungle and slipped back in among the population to harass the suddenly disorganised and demoralised Japanese.

'Beatrice was duly informed by Captain Takahashi that the brothels were to be closed down and the prostitutes given their freedom. When she had completed this task, he would come to inspect the premises. He instructed her that he wished at the same time to pay a final visit to Lotus Blossom. It seems Beatrice must have known Johnny was back in town, because she sent him a message telling him of the intended visit. We can only surmise that Johnny knew what had happened to Lotus Blossom.

'Kazuhiro Takahashi, despite having taken Lotus Blossom as his concubine, had in the past behaved with dignity and always taken the necessary precautions, but this day he arrived an hour early and clearly drunk, accompanied by two guards who searched the vacant premises. Beatrice had wisely cautioned Johnny not to arrive until after the Japanese officer. The guards, having searched the premises, were told to wait outside. Beatrice then invited the captain to a beautifully prepared meal she had set up in the suite used by staff officers of senior rank, where a saddened Lotus Blossom would be happy to attend to all his needs. The idea was that she would serve him and, as she had done often in the past, relax him with warm sake and then remove what garments were necessary. At this stage Lotus Blossom would excuse herself to prepare —' Detective Chicken Wing glanced up at me, then said, 'for you know what.'

I grinned, giving her the word: 'Seduction'.

'No, for murder,' she corrected me. She had told the story quickly without missing a beat and now continued in the same manner. 'We don't know exactly what happened. There are various versions, probably all wrong. Only Lotus Blossom would know for sure. But it would seem that Captain Takahashi was pretty drunk and upset by recent events in Japan and wasn't interested in any of the usual preliminaries. While this is pure conjecture, we have it from a servant that the food and drink weren't touched. It seems that, shortly after entering the suite, Kazuhiro Takahashi simply had his way with Lotus Blossom, virtually or actually raping her.

'Whether it was Johnny Wing or Beatrice or Lotus Blossom herself we may never know, but Captain Kazuhiro Takahashi's shirtless body, his face smashed beyond recognition, was discovered, along with those of the two guards, in a ditch at the opposite end of the city the following day. The shirts of all three men had been removed, so that their unit couldn't be identified by means of the embroidered insignia on the pocket, but there must have been some identifying features on the bodies.'

Dansford now interjected for the first time, explaining. 'In those last days, facial disfigurement and the removal of the shirt and anything that might identify the body were common enough as the communist guerrillas went about settling scores.'

Detective Chicken Wing, a bit impatient and anxious not to lose her momentum, glanced at Dansford meaningfully as if to say 'butt out', then continued. 'According to an amah I interviewed nearly three years ago, who at the time worked for Beatrice, by the 12th of September, when the official surrender ceremony took place at the City Hall, presided over by Lord Louis Mountbatten, Lotus Blossom had missed her monthly.

It was soon apparent she was pregnant and in May 1946 a female child was born.'

'Jesus. Mercy B. Lord!'

Dansford grinned. 'You got it, Simon.'

Detective Chicken Wing sighed impatiently. Her explanation of what happened was textbook police verbal reportage. She'd accomplished a remarkable piece of research and she clearly wanted to finish recounting it without a hitch. 'With the war finally over, the indefatigable Beatrice Fong started all over again by re-opening the three brothels. It was a very different Singapore and she was acutely aware of the intense stigma associated with the circumstances surrounding her daughter's infant – not only a bastard child but also that of a Japanese soldier and the despised enemy. She decided to put the child in the recently re-opened Catholic orphanage. She swaddled the tiny infant in Captain Takahashi's shirt – with the sleeve removed – as a means of identification. She obviously hoped the nuns would keep the shirt as the infant's only possession on arrival, a crude baby blanket. She then took her daughter to Burma, where she renewed her contacts with the hill tribes, who trusted her, knowing they would protect the girl.'

'You mean she willingly abandoned her granddaughter and then banished her daughter?'

'Simon, those were not easy times and Beatrice Fong was beginning all over again from scratch. She was a tough, resilient woman, and while she had worked out a role for her daughter, she may have been ambivalent about what she regarded as a bastard and possibly mongrel girl child. Lotus Blossom was still a young woman capable of having many more children. Besides, Beatrice Fong could keep an eye on the child in the orphanage, which we know she did.'

'Do you think Mercy B. Lord knew any of this?'

'We think it very unlikely,' Detective Chicken Wing replied. 'Beatrice Fong was a woman who was fanatically secretive. It's taken three years to work all this out and we still don't know everything. But it's highly unlikely she would have confided in Mercy B. Lord while she was alive. After all, it would appear the inheritance came as a complete surprise to her.' She paused. 'But there again, she may now know some or all of it. The old woman may have left a written record among her personal papers in the bank deposit box. We just don't know.'

'So what are you saying? That, until yesterday, Mercy B. Lord didn't know the whereabouts of her mother or that Beatrice Fong was her grandmother? Do you know what happened to Lotus Blossom?'

'Oh yes, we know, and so does Mercy B. Lord.'

'What? I don't understand. Did you say she knows her mother?'

'She definitely knows who her mother is. In fact she visits her every Thursday in northern Thailand. What she doesn't know, or probably didn't know until yesterday when she inherited her grandmother's fortune, is that Beatrice Fong is her mother's mother and her own grandmother.'

'Christ, this gets more and more bizarre by the minute. But hang on, how?'

'How what?'

'How does she know, without knowing Beatrice Fong is her grandmother, that this woman she meets in Thailand is in fact her mother?'

Detective Chicken Wing laughed. 'You'd make a good detective, Simon. Of course, we asked ourselves the same question. But the answer, we concluded, was staring us in the face. It could only be the sleeve.'

'Ah, exactly,' I exclaimed, 'the missing sleeve on the Japanese captain's shirt. I've seen the shirt and she guards it like a precious relic.'

'Yes, well, either Lotus Blossom sent it to Beatrice from Burma or, as seems more likely, the old lady kept it herself all these years and told Mercy B. Lord it had been sent by the woman making enquiries about her whereabouts. It would have been simple enough for Beatrice to invent a story about a woman contacting the orphanage and asking the nuns about the girl who had been abandoned as a baby, wrapped in a khaki shirt. Then, by means of matching the sleeve and shirt, she would have been able to prove she was Mercy B. Lord's natural mother. In any event, there is no doubt Mercy B. Lord accepts that Lotus Blossom is her mother.'

'Incidentally, while this would have happened before we mounted the operation, it couldn't have worked out any better for us,' Dansford interrupted.

'Absolutely!' Detective Chicken Wing continued. 'Naturally, we put a tail on Mercy B. Lord in the hope that she would lead us to others involved in the crime cartel. Her routine was fairly simple – she'd arrive at Don Muang airport in Bangkok, which, by the way, is a major logistical base for the US air force in Thailand. Here she was met by corrupt officials, her passport stamped, and without ever going through customs or immigration she was driven across the airport to an American compound, where an unmarked Piper Aztec twin-engine light plane was waiting to take her north. Two hours later she'd land at a small airport near the town of Wiang Phrao near the Thai–Burma border. She'd be met by a car that would transfer her to the same small Chinese hotel in town, where she'd meet a good-looking Chinese woman who appeared to be in her forties.

'They'd have lunch together, and exchange identical briefcases, full for empty, then they'd spend the rest of the day and the night together at the hotel, where a set of rooms had been built, we were to learn, to accommodate members of the cartel when in town. We know this because we've had the premises bugged for two years and have two undercover agents working as hotel staff. The hotel was, of course, owned by Beatrice Fong. The restaurant makes it seem respectable, not that security was much of a concern. This is a drug town, almost solely reliant on the heroin and opium trade from across the border, and is protected by corrupt senior members of the Thai army and police force and others in local and national government. Finally, it has the blessing of the CIA.

'We imagine it was the reason why she never questioned the task she'd been given. It gave her weekly access to her mother, something she could never have afforded on her salary.'

It explained a lot. Quite obviously Mercy B. Lord had been controlled by the threat of not being allowed to see her mother again if she revealed the nature of her weekly task to anyone. To someone reared as an orphan, it must have seemed miraculous to find her mother and, more importantly, to learn that she was accepted and no doubt loved. She would have quickly grown to love the woman in Burma, which must have been incentive enough to keep her mouth shut, even with me. It certainly explained why she absolutely refused to give up her Thursday assignations, even if it meant leaving me because of it.

I turned to Dansford. 'My next question is an obvious one: how and why are the CIA involved?'

He laughed. 'Been waiting for you to ask, Simon. It is, of course, the sole reason I'm in Singapore and at the heart of everything. I'll attempt to make it short and sweet. When Mao's communists defeated the American-backed forces of Chiang Kai-shek, some of the remnants of the defeated armies escaped into northern Burma.

'Around 10 000 of them, under a General Li Mi, set up there and ran what's called the Shan States as their own territory. This part of Burma is hill and jungle country where the local tribes have always resisted the control of the Burmese government in Rangoon. They now found they had a potentially powerful ally. Many of the Shan tribesman joined General Li Mi and together they set up a quasi state that posed a problem for the new communist government in southern China, just across the border.

'Naturally, the Americans saw the advantage of continuing to lend support to Li Mi's forces by supplying them with arms, military hardware and medical supplies, which we did by air drops and, in the early days, flying into the heavily fortified air base at Mong Pa-liao in northern Burma. We even supported an invasion of Yunnan Province in southern China.'

'C'mon, that's absurd! What? They expected to bring down the Chinese government?'

'Ah, Simon, there's no accounting for some of the curious logic of a nation with a rabid paranoia about communism. It has warped our foreign policy. At the time, the CIA convinced Washington that the Chinese people would rise up against their communist oppressors and join the free world. When they didn't, we settled for becoming the covert allies of General Li Mi's troops, who had escaped into Burma, equipping them so they could make occasional incursions into southern China to satisfy our secret commitment.'

'And your government is still supporting them?'

'Simon, we're locked in a permanent war with communism. For a long time our experts believed, truly believed, the Chinese would sweep down through Burma and invade northern Thailand and Vietnam. It was felt the best thing we could do was use these anti-communists in Burma as our border guards. We've even recruited some of them to fight as mercenaries against the communists in Laos.'

'But hang on, mate. These blokes controlled the opium trade. Surely the US government – any government in the free world, for that matter – couldn't support that? I mean, how can that make any sense?'

'Simon, as far as Washington and the Pentagon are concerned, there's no room for idealism in this war against communism. The prevailing mantra is "Whatever it takes". Nobody admits America is involved with the ex-Chiang Kai-shek forces in Burma. You won't find US soldiers or US planes anywhere near there. It's all done through front companies like Air America. The CIA also supports a whole network inside the Thai police and army. For many years the CIA's main ally in Thailand was a General Phao, the commander of the Thai police, and he was the main connection in Thailand for the drug producers. It's people like him who run things in Bangkok. So you see, we can throw up our hands and deny direct US involvement.'

'Even though blind Freddy knows it's happening?'

'Well, I don't know this blind Freddy of yours, Simon, but I get what you mean. It's an open secret. So open, in fact, that the *New York Times* has run articles alleging US involvement in protecting the drug trade. It's all vigorously denied, of course. And the justification is always that

Chiang Kia-shek's exiled troops in Burma are useful allies in the fight against communism. So we simply pretend we don't know what else they're involved in.'

'But didn't Burma boot out Chiang Kai-shek's troops?'

'Things didn't all go strictly to plan. The Chinese government finally got together with the Burmese and drove most of our little friends out of Burma. But then several thousand settled in northern Thailand around Chiang Mai. That's where the opium was going anyhow. People such as Beatrice and the Wings stayed and re-organised the Shan tribesmen, the hill people, who continued to grow opium. The CIA and the Thai generals supplied the arms, the logistics and the political protection for these tribal warlords and their troops. The money that came from the opium trade kept everyone happy and paid the salaries of the troops, who, in turn, provided security for the growers and the mule convoys that carried the opium out of Burma into northern Thailand. The Chinese force kicked out of Burma simply set up their heroin labs in northern Thailand, protected by the Thai police and army, who then provided transport of the refined heroin to Bangkok for shipment to Hong Kong, Singapore and the rest of the world. Additionally, American-owned planes and pilots were flying heroin into Vietnam, Cambodia and Laos. In Vietnam, in particular, the demand began to grow steeply.'

'Christ, what a mess. It can't make you terribly proud . . .' I mumbled.

'No, but we're not the only ones, or the first. What the CIA is doing is exactly what the French were doing in their old territories, including South Vietnam. They used the profits of the opium trade to pay mercenary tribal groups to fight the communists. Simon, war and politics always shit on morality. There's another factor to consider too. While corrupt Thai officials are benefitting hugely from the drug trade, this is incidental to the fact that the Thai government will never close down the Burma operations because the ex-Chiang Kai-shek troops are the main security force protecting them along the Burmese border.'

'Well, if all this is true, as it obviously is, why are your mob, the DEA, going in against the CIA?'

'Ah, because we've totally miscalculated the effect of the drug trade on the Vietnam War. We've now got hundreds of thousands of addicts in America, many of them ex-GIs who got turned on to cheap heroin in South Vietnam and are still using. When they get repatriated they take their problem home with them. Heroin use is exploding in our cities. We've finally realised we've created a nightmare for ourselves. So long as the product was going to European or Asian addicts, it was less important than stopping the communists. Now it's a primary factor in stopping us.'

'In other words, you've shot yourselves in the foot.'

'If Hilda will excuse the French, you could say we've succeeded in fucking ourselves up the ass.' Dansford leaned back in his chair. 'That's all the background you need to know, which brings us right back to Beatrice Fong in 1945, who had resumed her operation trading in young girls and drugs. This is when the Wing reconnection grew into a business proposition.'

'I was beginning to wonder where the connection was. Johnny Wing's involvement earlier sounded like pretty hairy stuff. Obviously the teenage romance with the banished Lotus Blossom didn't continue, but the old bird, Beatrice, must have stayed close to him or she wouldn't have made him executor of her will, would she? Then there's Sidney and possibly even Ronnie. How do they fit into the picture?'

Dansford laughed. 'How indeed, Simon! It is, of course, the reason I'm here. As to how Johnny and Sidney got involved, it was simply a matter of money. Beatrice Fong and Johnny were fellow conspirators in the murder of the Japanese Captain Kazuhiro Takahashi and the two guards. Not that they could be indicted for murder, but taken together with Johnny's teenage love affair with Lotus Blossom, they became natural allies. When Beatrice started all over again, she needed money and help. Johnny was given the job of restarting the sex-slave trade, and Sidney, just back from sitting out the war at university in America, was persuaded by Johnny to meet Beatrice.

'Now, Sidney, who was already in America when the Japanese attacked Pearl Harbor, had taken the Japanese seriously and persuaded his father to move all his money to America, where he invested in US bonds and other secure assets. Napoleon Wing, the father, died of a heart attack during the Japanese occupation, and as the eldest son, Sidney inherited a now even larger fortune while based in America. Sidney, after talking to Beatrice, knew a good thing when he saw one and the Fong–Wing syndicate was born in July 1946.' Dansford grinned. 'Drugs and sex have always been a good combination, and rock 'n' roll was soon to arrive on the music scene.

'With Wing money, Beatrice returned to Burma with Lotus Blossom, who no doubt had been forced by her mother to "deposit" her tiny infant in the orphanage. The Shan tribesmen welcomed Beatrice back, and Lotus Blossom, now nineteen, was left in residence to re-establish opium growing in the areas where they had worked before.

'Three years later, when General Li Mi crossed the border with his troops, the Fong–Wing drug cartel was well underway, having bought a lot more land and encouraged the peasant farmers to grow opium poppies. While this wasn't as huge as it would eventually become, Beatrice had re-opened all her distribution channels. She supplied girls to brothels and bars worldwide and re-established the heroin-processing lab. She welcomed General Li Mi's incursion into northern Burma. She had the knowhow, the distribution and the trust of the hill people, and together they would in years to come control ninety per cent of the opium trade out of Burma. Since then they've grown the business from around forty tons of raw opium a year to over 400 tons.

'If it was an alliance forged in hell, it was a strong one, with the added advantage of having the United States as a covert ally. Sidney bought land in Florida, where he created a golf course and kept in contact with the CIA. It was sweet, it was neat and it was safe, a nice tidy operation. Then, in the early sixties, the US involvement in the Vietnam War escalated and the inevitable trickle of heroin to US troops began.

'The trickle of heroin going into South Vietnam became the Niagara Falls, and the Wings and Fongs thrived and continue to do so. The Drug Enforcement Agency – in other words, my lot in Washington – started to get alarmed. Once the heroin is shipped from Thailand to Singapore and Hong Kong for worldwide distribution, we are dealing with the Fong and Wing network. The heroin money received worldwide is sent back to several Singapore banks, where it is laundered, and a small portion of it, about two million US dollars, is what Mercy B. Lord carries each week to be used by Lotus Blossom to pay the corrupt Thai police, army and assorted officials.'

'Jesus, that's big-time!'

'Yessir,' said Dansford gravely. 'They've got the product, they have the money and the distribution system, bars all over the world where they'd built their contacts in the sex trade, as well as the girlie bars and brothels in Vietnam. They know who to bribe, and finally they have the covert endorsement of the CIA itself.'

'So, there you are, Simon,' Detective Chicken Wing interjected. 'Now you know what we're up against. We've already told you more than anyone outside the operatives knows and, of course, one or two government people. We can't tell you more for your own safety. With Beatrice Fong's fatal heart attack, everything changed overnight. Okay, we knew the old lady was going to die sooner rather than later, but we hoped to have the whole thing wrapped up before this happened. And, yes, of course we have and always have had contingency plans. But we didn't know or factor in the inheritance. Not only that, but Mercy B. Lord now controls the Beatrice Fong Agency. In the larger sense, together with Lotus Blossom's share, this is fifty per cent of the Fong and Wing drug organisation. She is now a big player – *the* big player.'

Dansford nodded. 'If Sidney and Johnny intend to take over the operation in Singapore, they have to sort out several things in a hurry. Not the least of these is Mercy B. Lord's future involvement in the organisation. They can't eliminate her, as there is Lotus Blossom to contend with, who, in her own right, is hugely wealthy and can't be easily dismissed because she controls the Burma and Thai side of the operation and is consequently very powerful, perhaps even more so than the Wings.

'The fact is that they've got to reorganise quickly and bring all the important operators worldwide up-to-date with the new arrangements.' He paused. 'But, of course, we don't know how Mercy B. Lord is going to react. That's the big question. Overnight she has become potentially one of the most powerful criminals in the world, and Sidney will no doubt emphasise when he's briefing her that, apart from her inheritance, she is now one of the richest women in Asia.'

I was beginning to shit myself. Mercy B. Lord was trapped, caught between a rock and a hard place. If she refused to be a part of the criminal cartel, the Wings would no doubt dispose of her. Lotus Blossom couldn't really do much to protect her from Burma – and besides, it could easily be made to look like an accident. And would Lotus Blossom came to the aid of her daughter and put the entire operation at risk? It wasn't a case of a mother's love prevailing at any cost. Mercy B. Lord was a once-a-week nominal daughter she'd never known as a child and was only getting to know now as an adult. Then again, if Mercy B. Lord agreed to take over from Beatrice, she was also doomed. She would be executed along with all the others. I knew I had to find some way to warn her.

I turned to Detective Chicken Wing. 'You've suggested, and I'm certain, that Mercy B. Lord knows little or nothing about the drug cartel run by Beatrice Fong and has only acted as a courier because of the opportunity it affords her to see her mother in Thailand each week. Is she not about to be caught up in something for which she can't possibly be responsible?'

Detective Chicken Wing was too much of a professional to look over at Dansford but it wasn't hard to figure out what they were thinking. Then she said, 'Simon, if it turns out to be an operation where the Singapore police are involved, then the local members of the drug cartel may be imprisoned here or possibly flown to America. I simply don't know. Hitherto, Mercy B. Lord appears to have simply been used as a mule to carry money, though money from the sale of drugs and who knows what, or who, else. She may argue that she couldn't have known this. It may work in her favour if she isn't implicated in any other criminal activity subsequent to her inheritance.'

It wasn't an answer, but then again it was. Hilda was demonstrating that her law degree hadn't been wasted. Dansford remained silent then said, 'Before we came this afternoon, we were informed that Sidney had arrived at the Beatrice Fong residence, ostensibly to pay his respects to the dead, but this is unlikely to have been his real motive.'

I nodded. 'When is the funeral?' I was aware that he was trying to divert me from the possible execution of Mercy B. Lord.

'Tomorrow morning.'

'Will they – all three Wings and Mercy B. Lord – be allowed to attend?'

'Yes, of course, it's business as usual.' Dansford then added, 'Simon, we cannot tell you anything more.' He looked directly at me, his expression sterner than I had ever seen it. This was a different Dansford Drocker from the merrymaking late-afternoon drunk. 'The entire reason we are here is to alert you to the gravity of this investigation, so that you won't under *any* circumstances, as you previously attempted to do, contact Mercy B. Lord. We don't know which way she will jump and we cannot, in any event, influence her. She's either voluntarily ensconced with Johnny Wing in the Beatrice Fong residence or she's not being allowed out until the funeral. Short of raiding the premises, we couldn't get to her even if we wanted to.'

'Oh, but you could!' I protested. 'You could have the funeral director or someone going into the premises to attend to the body, slip her a note to explain that she's in danger.'

Dansford sighed. 'Simon, you must know we couldn't and wouldn't do that. There are nearly 200 operatives worldwide and countless police waiting to close in on the cartel. By alerting Mercy B. Lord, we could effectively jeopardise the entire operation, and we cannot allow that to happen.' He glanced at Detective Chicken Wing and nodded almost imperceptibly.

She rose from her chair. 'Simon Koo, I must inform you that you are under arrest,' she said calmly, then added, 'You will be taken from here and placed in immediate detention.'

Dansford shrugged. 'Sorry, Simon, that's how the cookie crumbles.'

CHAPTER SIXTEEN

———

SO BEGAN THE WORST fortnight of my life. I was in a bungalow. Planes were coming in to land, their engine noise bruising the air; I could hear the distant stutter of kettle drums; a brass band; occasional marching feet and shouted commands; sirens once in a while. I was forced to conclude that I was near or within a military base close to an airport. But there were policemen, not military personnel, at the front door, back door and the gate, two with dogs – tongue-lolling Alsatians – patrolling what appeared to be large grounds surrounded by a high wall. While it wasn't a jail, I knew I was just as incarcerated as if I'd been locked up in Changi Prison. I was being prevented from causing further trouble. I'd have liked to go for a walk around the grounds to get a sense of the place, which I was permitted to do with a policeman accompanying me, but on the third day after my beating every muscle still hurt and I was as stiff as a board, my every step tentative. Just getting about the house was painful. Bending made me gasp, which in turn sent sharp, stabbing pains through my ribs. Even turning of my neck was pure agony. There was no mirror in the bathroom so I couldn't take a squiz at the damage to what has always been laughingly known as my face and that now, I daresay, was beyond being a laughing matter. But at least my eyes were beginning to open up.

The house contained all the bare essentials. It looked as if it may have been furnished by a Caucasian bulldozer driver in a hurry, who had pointed to stuff in a furniture shop and hastily scribbled an address for delivery. The general feeling was that this was temporary accommodation, ugly and solid as a house brick and not meant to be comfortable or accommodating. If not strictly punishment, it was distinctly reproving, a house designed for solitary male confinement, a hangover from British colonial days, with the only hint of Asia being the teak window shutters. There was one curious exception, though: instead of the iron cot and coir pallet you might expect in the bedroom, there was a double bed with a half-decent mattress. It may have been that in cases of prolonged incarceration, inmates were allowed a female visitor. The bed was certainly a curious addition to this subtopia.

The kitchen had utensils for one: one dinner plate, side plate, cup, saucer, teaspoon, soup bowl, knife, fork, dessertspoon – you'd be stuffed if you dropped and broke something – and a handful of assorted kitchen gadgets: cheese grater, egg flip, tongs, wooden spoon, can opener, all built to last but not to impress. The pantry was no gourmet's delight, either. It contained rows and rows of tins: soup – vegetable, tomato, mulligatawny and pea – baked beans, asparagus, potatoes (didn't know you could can potatoes), tomatoes, Irish stew, something named pork-belly fricassee (yuck!), sliced pineapple, peaches, chicken noodles in packets (just add hot water). The inventory included a large jar of Nescafé, tea bags, sugar, rice, salt, pepper, sliced white loaf, marmalade and peanut butter. It had the general air of underground bunker food, stored in case the atom bomb was dropped. I reached for a can of butter beans and couldn't believe my no doubt plum-coloured swollen eyes. The line at the bottom of the label read: *Enjoy fine dining from the Wing Canning Company*. I checked all the cans, and six of them had this dreaded injunction. I put them aside; I'd definitely be giving them a miss. Sidney had sold the family canning business to the Campbell Soup Company some years previously, and rumour had it that there was an ongoing lawsuit involving misrepresentation. Still, it was a nasty coincidence. Under the benches were two pots, one big, one small, an electric kettle and a frying pan. Butter, eggs and milk were in the fridge. I wasn't going to starve, but in a city where a tiffin box can contain some of the best grub in the world, piping hot and available within walking distance from almost anywhere, what can you say? Perhaps one of the cops would oblige.

You'll have to forgive all this mental sewage swilling through my head. I was worried sick, sore, angry, sorry for myself, but most of all ashamed that I could do nothing to help the person I loved more than anyone in the world. In fact, not to put too fine a point on things, I was bloody terrified.

I know it sounds pretty immature and I wasn't exactly a teenager, but I was very close to losing it completely. The pantry audit was one way of trying to calm my mind. Furniture and the designs on the tea towels would be next (one of them sported a picture of Donald Duck). There was nothing to read, and I had only one tiny spiral notepad and a cheap ballpoint; otherwise, there was nothing with which I could attempt to write down my codeine-induced semi-delusions. Hospital ship Virago had given me an entire bottle and I'd stupidly taken more than I should have, thinking it might block out my panicked thoughts. All it eventually did was block my arse. By the end of the week the act of going to the toilet was a distant memory.

I constantly tried to tell myself to buck up, pull myself together, but all I could see was Mercy B. Lord being hanged. My fevered imagination would take control and I seemed incapable of stepping outside this waking vision. In my mind's eye I would see Mercy B. Lord, her beautiful hair hacked off and her head roughly shaved, wearing a shapeless white garment of crumpled flannel, similar to an old lady's nightdress, that hung to her ankles, leaving exposed the hangman's territory: her slender neck and pretty shoulders. Even with her head almost bald she was beautiful.

She was standing on the scrubbed grey planks of a platform about eight feet from the ground, at the far end of a large rectangular room, the walls of which were painted an unpleasant creamy yellow, with white tiles reaching up to about five feet from the floor, which was raw cement, smooth, very clean and smelling of strong disinfectant. It was the kind of room you clean with a hose and a stiff broom, and as the thought occurred to me, I visualised a brass tap with its handle carefully polished on one of the walls. A single high-voltage spotlight, the shape and size of an old-fashioned chamber pot, was directed at the platform. The sharp white light flattened out what little detail there was in the room and gave Mercy B. Lord's shapeless garment a kind of blurry electric outline, so that all I could see in perfect focus were her naked feet, shoulders, neck and head. A large moth flew too close to the light and simply disintegrated in a sharp fizzle, one moment flying and the next nothing. Mercy B. Lord was going to be hanged and the electrocuted moth was a terrible precursor.

She stood at the very centre of the trapdoor. Usually her toenails were painted a cherry red but now the old varnish was chipped and broken, and a piece of flesh-coloured sticking plaster was wrapped around the two smallest toes on her left foot. Her hands were cuffed behind her back and a broad leather strap with a highly polished brass buckle pinioned her shapeless gown to her calves. I realised with horror that the strap was to prevent the skirt from flying up as she plunged through the trapdoor, a bizarre bureaucratic detail to preserve her modesty in her final seconds of life. The leather belt was stained dark with the sweat of the dead and the eight holes were worn with use. Prison guards referred to it as the 'death strap' and polished the brass buckle weekly as a matter of prideful duty. Its secondary use was so that Mercy B. Lord couldn't brace her feet against the sides of the trapdoor as it sprang open. The rope with the noose that would snap her beautiful, fragile neck like a dry twig looked insubstantial, ribbon-like, in the blinding white light as it hung suspended, lazily looped once around a hook in the ceiling. The noose at its end hung about eight inches above Mercy B. Lord's cropped head, ready for the hangman to unfold it from the hook and drop it over her head so that she would smell the newness of the pre-stretched hemp rope. It was carefully pre-stretched to remove the rope's elasticity so as to increase the shock as the rope snapped tight, breaking her neck.

Now, this wasn't a dream from which I would wake gasping and crying out, ghastly as that might be. It was a conscious thought-vision that came into my mind the moment I stopped doing something like auditing the pantry or counting the number of wooden parquetry blocks that made up the living-room floor. It terrified me, and yet I was powerless to stop it. I would shuffle around like an old man, losing count, then starting all over again, trying to force my mind onto something else before it allowed the pontificating priest to enter the room, mount the steps and deliver the last rites, watched by a frail and wizened Sister Charity from the St Thomas Aquinas Catholic Mission Orphanage, who was seated on a peacock-tail wicker chair. When I failed, the hangman would place a hood over Mercy B. Lord's beautiful head, and his smooth, brown hand would trip the lever that released the trapdoor, allowing her body to fall through the dark square, the hemp rope twisting and jerking frantically from the ugly steel hook in the ceiling. Then the terrible, terrible afterthought: Mercy B. Lord never took her accusing eyes from my face and never spoke a single word.

I now realise I was close to going crazy. I had barely slept, existing on a diet of instant coffee and codeine. On the morning of the fifth day I composed a note using all the pages on the tiny spiral pad, requesting that a policemen visit my flat and bring me a large canvas I'd prepared to paint the vista from my flat window of the river and the port. It was to be a large rectangular painting, eight feet long by five feet wide, intended to prove that I wasn't simply a portrait painter. But, apart from preparing the enormous canvas, I hadn't yet started it. In my note I asked them to bring all the brushes and the tubes of acrylic paint, the two large easels – in fact, everything in my studio, including the rags used to clean the brushes. It was a desperate last effort to prevent myself breaking down completely, and I handed the police officer the keys to my flat and asked him to give the note to his senior officer.

It was a long shot and I expected my request to be ignored, but in the late afternoon a police patrol van arrived with everything I had requested, together with my keys. The only thing they forgot to bring were the glass jars I used for cleaning the brushes. I emptied half a dozen cans I thought the guard dogs might eat, selecting all the Wing brands and the pork-belly fricassee, which the dogs seemed to particularly enjoy. The cops had even brought the gear I painted in, a pair of khaki shorts and a blue cotton shirt with the sleeves ripped out, both splattered with paint. The two garments were like the return of something familiar to my life. I should mention that the clothes I was wearing when I'd been beaten were completely ruined, and I had been led from the hospital in a pair of institutional pyjamas. In the house were two new white shirts, two pairs of underpants and a pair of khaki trousers with a belt. The pair of new sandshoes were two sizes too small so I simply went around barefoot, and the trousers were too small around the waist, so I was obliged to leave the zip undone and my white Y-fronts visible, the strides held up by the belt.

After several hours of reasonable sleep for the first time since I'd left hospital, I spent the sixth day since my beating preparing to paint. For the next week or so I ate cold stuff out of cans, slept only a few hours at a time, started to kick the codeine (the bottle was now empty) and painted as if my life depended on it, which in fact I had come to believe it did.

I had no news from outside. My police guards – pleasant enough young men under the direction of a somewhat irascible sergeant – kept largely to themselves, were polite when spoken to but not forthcoming. So I painted from dawn till dusk, ate something straight from the can then collapsed for no more than four hours before starting again. Totally obsessed, not daring to think, I painted Mercy B. Lord's execution as I'd seen it in my mind, painted the moment just before the hangman placed the hood over her head. The priest bore Dansford's face; Sister Charity, in her nun's habit and veils, I seated in a peacock-tail wicker chair, her wizened face sharp-eyed and grinning, as I remembered it from *Karlene's People* when she'd received the prize money from Mercy B. Lord. I allowed myself to change one detail of the hangman. I left the hood off and painted him in profile, giving him two faces like a Janus. The face nearest Mercy B. Lord was Johnny Wing's. The one at the back of his head was that of Sidney Wing.

The clarity of my demented mind was truly astonishing. I could see every minute detail. This was to be my last canvas, my final painting. My mind was in such a state that I believed that when I received the actual news that Mercy B. Lord was to be executed, I would take my own life.

On the extreme left and right of the painting I blocked in small frames, each about five inches square, eleven on the right, top to bottom, and on the left just four, centred. In the frames on the right I painted the portraits of the people who had played an important part, or whom I had loved or respected while I was in Singapore, and on the left those whom I had grown to loathe. Again I allowed myself one exception – Little Sparrow was the first portrait on the right, her face recalled from the ancient daguerreotype taken of Ah Koo's family; then below her was Chairman Meow, Dansford Drocker, Elma Kelly, Mrs Sidebottom, Molly Ong, Alice Ho, Long Me Saw, Willy Wonka, Louie da Fly and finally my little Thai bar girl, Veronica. On the left of the canvas I painted the two Wing brothers full-face, Sidney and Johnny, followed by Ronnie, then finally Beatrice Fong as I had seen her, her eyes still piercing even in death. I had some trouble deciding where to put Detective Chicken Wing. Unlike Dansford, who, despite his undercover role, I had grown to love, I barely knew Chicken Wing and couldn't decide how she fitted into the painting – she obviously didn't belong on either side of the canvas. I solved this problem by doing a tiny miniature of her face on one of the moth's wings as it flew towards the deadly light.

I can't explain the weird clarity of my mind, day after day, while I painted. It has never returned to the same extent, and it was doubly weird because obviously I wasn't thinking clearly, although I was seeing those faces down to the smallest detail and I painted them without the slightest hesitation. As it transpired, I also painted them with uncanny accuracy, right down to a dark mole on the left side of Beatrice Fong's nose. The only other thing I managed to do while I painted was to open a can of something every once in a while and gobble it down without recalling minutes afterwards what I'd eaten, using my lone fork or spoon, and each morning I'd manage a shower. There was no shaving gear and I could feel stubble on my chin, the only place, apart from my mouth, that hadn't received a kick.

On the fourteenth day of my incarceration – no, in fact the fifteenth – painting was completed, and I immediately began to weep, crawling into bed in the foetal position without undressing. I must have ultimately fallen asleep from utter exhaustion because I woke howling with the bedroom light still on. It was as if an invisible hand had struck me across the mouth, so that I actually cried out from the dream that had wakened me so violently. I glanced at my watch. I had been asleep for perhaps an hour.

In the dream I had been shown an alteration I was utterly compelled to make to the painting. I had not the slightest doubt that I had missed an essential component. I returned at once to the canvas and quickly removed Johnny's face and the top half of his head from the eyebrows up, and began to paint furiously, exploding the head in a bullet-shattered mess so that blood and brains and fragments of skull flew into the air above and to the side of Mercy B. Lord's shaven scalp, a split-second away from splattering her beautiful head and shoulders. I knew at that moment that I had gone mad. Bent over and clutching my stomach I crawled into bed and once more curled into a foetal ball. I continued to blub until I fell into what must have been a near coma.

Then a dream followed, and while it was beautiful, it was too terrible for words. A dead Mercy B. Lord was lying naked, cuddled into me. I started to bawl, really bawl, totally panic-stricken, battling to come out of the dream and seemingly unable to do so.

'Simon, Simon! It's me, Mercy B. Lord!' the dead woman said, sitting up with a start. She grabbed me and smothered me with kisses. 'Darling, I've come back.' Then she started to cry and we held each other so tightly that my broken ribs finally made me realise that she was actually there. I could have happily endured ten times the pain to know she was safe. 'Will you marry me, Simon, please?' she whispered, and for a moment I thought I must be dreaming again.

I held her at arm's length, still unsure that she was really there, that this wasn't yet another dream, a pleasant one after the horror of the previous nightmare. I brought my hand up to touch her face, felt her hair – it hadn't been hacked off. 'It's you, *really* you!' Then I started to sob again.

'You haven't answered my question,' she said gently.

'Yes, please, today,' I sniffed.

'No, we have to wait until you're beautiful again, darling. I'm going to wear your mother's diamond pendants and we're going to do it properly – a big white wedding!' She threw back her beautiful head and laughed. 'If you'll excuse my French, I'm going to become Mercy B. Koo, thank you very much!'

I managed to stop making a fool of myself, wiping my eyes on the edge of the sheet while laughing at her corny pun, and at the same time feeling things stirring below the sheet. Then I saw that I was naked – she must have removed my painting clothes while I was asleep or comatose. No jockstrap in the world could have contained me then, and when we made love this time, I swear, I didn't even feel my broken ribs.

Afterwards, as Mercy B. Lord lay in my arms, I said, 'Darling, I was convinced they'd executed you.'

'Oh, Simon, I saw the painting, the marvellous, ghastly, wonderful, frightening, beautiful painting!'

It seemed I had slept for nineteen hours and it was now just after eight at night. Mercy B. Lord had arrived at eight that morning, bringing my clothes from the flat. She made us both an omelette, and after we'd eaten she touched my face lightly. 'Simon, you must believe I had nothing to do with this. It was Johnny who grabbed the phone and banged down the receiver. What I said, you know, about never seeing you again, was to protect you. The will stipulated that I marry Johnny to inherit. It came out later that he knew all about it. The stupid man realised that I'd never agree under normal circumstances, but thought that the money would persuade me. After he'd slammed down the receiver I went totally berserk, and those terrible men came in and restrained me and I was locked in the room with Beatrice's body. It's in the centre of the house and has no windows, so evil spirits can't get in. I couldn't see or hear a thing. I had no idea what happened to you until Dansford told me after the raid.'

'Ah, that's over, is it? What happened? You have a bloody lot of explaining to do, my girl.'

'Oh, Simon, I know! All the time we've known each other I couldn't breathe a word!'

'About what – Thursdays?'

'Yes. I believe Dansford and Hilda have briefed you on all that, but not fully on my part. For the past two and a half years I've been a double-agent, working with Dansford.'

'But, but, if they'd found out – Beatrice, Sidney, Johnny – they'd have killed you.'

'It was a terribly difficult situation. I couldn't let you know the truth. The operation was top-secret and if there was a leak of any kind, it might have all blown up.'

'And you could have been killed!'

'Yes.'

'So then why? Why did you agree? Once you knew the truth you could simply have walked away. We could have gone back to Australia.'

Mercy B. Lord ignored this. 'It was Johnny and Beatrice more than anything who persuaded me to agree to help. Johnny, I learned, ran the sex-slave business; Beatrice, of course, ran both! The heroin was awful but I didn't know much about drugs; the other, the trade in human flesh, was, in my eyes, far worse. I'd never liked Johnny but now I loathed him. When I heard the details of what I had been supporting I had no choice but to join Dansford.'

'But before that, you must have realised you were carrying money to your mother every week?'

'Yes, of course, but I guess I was naïve or I just didn't want to know. Beatrice explained that it was to pay oil workers in Burma, that she and Sidney and Johnny owned several concessions to drill for oil, and my mother, Lotus Blossom, was the manager. I was so thrilled at the prospect of having her in my life, and until Dansford and Detective Sergeant Wing told me, I didn't realise how much money was in the briefcase. And until the lawyer told me, I had no idea Beatrice was my grandmother.' Mercy B. Lord looked down at her hands. 'I guess I've got a lot to live down.'

'Nonsense, we don't choose out forebears. What you did was terribly brave. You've redeemed yourself a thousand times. The raid was obviously a success or you wouldn't be here. Tell me what happened.'

'Simon, I'm supposed to call Dansford and Hilda, er . . . Detective Sergeant Wing, but it's too late now to find a phone, and besides, you know what Dansford's like by this time of night. He wants to debrief you himself. In fact he insisted. While I may give you details about myself, I can't, that is, I'm forbidden to tell you more. The raid is classified top-secret and there's another side of Dansford Drocker you don't want to cross. Did you know he was a major in the Second World War and promoted to lieutenant colonel in Korea? Which is about as high as it gets for an operational intelligence officer, apparently.'

I laughed. 'I now realise I know very little about Dansford Drocker.'

'Including how he spends his afternoons,' Mercy B. Lord said. 'Though he can be pretty wild, some of them were spent in a back-room communications office at Bill Bailey's bar preparing to clean up the Asian drug cartel, while others . . .' She paused. 'No, I'm not sure I'm allowed. I'll let him tell you himself.'

'Well, I'll be buggered! But if I have to wait for Dansford to debrief me, will you answer just two questions?'

'I'll try.'

'Johnny, as I understand it, wasn't involved in the drug side but ran the sex-slave business, so he can't be indicted for drugs. Is that right?'

Mercy B. Lord looked down at her hands. 'I really don't know. Johnny is dead.'

It was said in such a manner that my first thought was that Mercy B. Lord had murdered him. 'Dead! How?'

'Shot. Dansford will tell you when he comes. Simon, I *really* can't, I'm not allowed to say any more.'

'But you were not personally responsible for —?'

'Johnny's death? No, no such luck.'

'The second question is about Sidney.'

'Arrested.'

'And Ronnie?'

'That's three questions. Ronnie got off scot-free – he wasn't involved. He owns the Nite Cap and five other girlie bars. Johnny supplied the girls, but it's not a crime to have girls under contract. All the other bars get their girls from the same source; that business hasn't been closed yet.'

There was a fourth obvious question, about what happened to Lotus Blossom, but I wasn't going to ask it then. I could sense that Mercy B. Lord had had enough. 'Darling, shall we have a shower?' I suggested. 'I'm afraid I've got nothing to wear. The duds they gave me are too small, so are the sandshoes, and my Y-fronts show through the fly and certainly need a wash, but at least I'll be clean. Can you stay the night?'

Mercy B. Lord grinned. 'Well, now that you ask, I can stay every night for the rest of my life, if you wish. But I've got a better idea. The shower is good, and I've brought your clothes from the flat. Detective Sergeant Wing has signed you out and you're free to go – there's not a policeman in sight. By the way, one of them asked me to thank you for the dog food. What did he mean by that?'

'Pork-belly fricassee.'

'Sounds disgusting.'

'Not to police dogs.'

'I don't understand.'

I pointed to the pantry shelves, where a vast array of tinned food stood rank upon rank like the Duke of Wellington's army facing Napoleon at Waterloo. I seemed not to have made even the smallest dent. 'Never mind, I'll tell you later. I never want to see anything that requires a tin opener again in my life.'

Mercy B. Lord laughed. 'I promise, Simon. So, here's a suggestion, but only if you feel up to it. You've just had nineteen hours' sleep so you probably don't want to go to bed for a while . . . even with me. While you're still not the prettiest man in town, you'll soon be your old self. Do you think your various bruises and bumps could handle a night out on the town, then a late dinner before we go home? I'll organise for your painting and your gear to come home tomorrow. We can sleep in, and I've booked a private room at the Goodwood Park for lunch. Owen Denmeade, the maître d', says he has a couple of French wines that will knock Dansford's socks off. Dansford and Hilda will debrief you officially over lunch.'

I hadn't asked her about the Beatrice Fong inheritance for two reasons. The first was that it was none of my business, and the second was that I couldn't have cared if she'd declared herself mine in rags and tatters.

The following day I felt great. I even managed a shave, but still looked like a bit of a walking nightmare, with yellow bruises around my eyes and nose. But the swelling was all but down and the rest of my body was much the same, with yellowing patches like those on a marmalade tabby, but mostly they didn't hurt any longer, and it was apparent when I took a cautious deep breath that my ribs were beginning to knit. By the way, I was to learn that the five thugs who had given me the beating had been arrested. And also that Beatrice Fong's funeral, with no expense spared, went off without a hitch and she was sent to the hereafter with sufficient paper money and token goods and services to be welcomed with open arms by her waiting ancestors.

She was one of Singapore's worst, but it's almost as if there has to be a fixed percentage of the good and the bad in life – the evil component, the psychopaths and born wrongdoers at one extreme, and those who are born to be good, the saints of every religion, at the other. Between the two, the rest of humankind arrays itself. The gravitational pull of these two extremes is what decides whether, generally speaking, the world is in good or bad moral shape, at war or at peace with itself.

Beatrice Fong was fundamentally bad, and she used those who were willing to compromise their moral integrity for whatever reason, some simply to put food on the table, others to own mansions, yachts or, in

Sidney's case, a golf course in Florida. She came and she went unnoticed, except that she left nothing but misery and chaos as her legacy. She wouldn't even be posthumously vilified. Winding up international drug cartels embarrasses too many governments so the aftermath is invariably silence. She simply went unpunished, unnoticed and unmourned, getting away with unmitigated evil.

Owen Denmeade greeted us, exuding the usual bonhomie. I could see he was momentarily taken aback by my face, but he was far too professional to comment. He led us through the restaurant to a small private dining room where Dansford and Detective Sergeant Hilda Wing were already ensconced, Dansford on his second martini, the empty first martini glass still on the table. He'd obviously ordered two simultaneously. Detective Chicken Wing, as she would always be to me, was drinking a bloody Mary through a straw, a fair indication that it was simply tomato juice.

Dansford jumped from his seat and embraced and kissed Mercy B. Lord, who, in turn, bent to kiss Hilda on the cheek. I didn't respond in a similar manner, merely shaking her by the hand. I mean, can one really kiss a detective sergeant?

Dansford then turned to me. 'Well, Simon, what can I say?'

'As little as possible that concerns me directly over the past fortnight.' I grinned.

'Buddy, you're sure looking a whole lot better than when last we parted.'

'As I recall, it wasn't much of a parting. Did you have to use handcuffs? I was so beaten up I could barely walk. Escape was clearly not an option unless I crawled away.'

'That was my fault, Simon, and I apologise,' Detective Chicken Wing said. 'It's standard procedure when prisoners are moved from Outram Road Hospital. You see Sister Elkington, that's the senior sister who hustled us out on the morning of our visit —'

'Oh, you mean hospital ship Virago?' I interjected.

This got a bit of a laugh all round, then Detective Chicken Wing continued, 'Well, her husband, the incorruptible Georgie "Pug-face" Elkington, one of the few senior British police officers to keep his post after the Brits handed over, is an assistant commissioner of police, and if we didn't manacle you when you left the hospital under arrest, it would have got straight back to him over his toast and marmalade next morning, whereupon disciplinary charges would have been duly laid.' She laughed. 'His opening address to a group of young police officers is often: "Absolute nincompoops, the lot of you!"'

With the small talk over, we ordered lunch, and Owen Denmeade returned and extolled the virtues of the French wine. Dansford instructed him to bring three bottles and to open them, then at his suggestion we ordered both entrées and mains together, with Owen still hovering. 'Will you kindly bring the bell on the bar as well?' Dansford requested.

'The bar bell?' Owen asked, surprised.

'Ah, Monsieur Maître d' Denmeade, I intend to use it to summon a waiter, should we require one. After we've been served, would you and your staff kindly allow us a little privacy?' The exquisitely polite Dansford was plainly preparing to get down to business, and I sensed the return of the man who had looked me in the eye, shrugged and said, 'Sorry, Simon, that's how the cookie crumbles.' Now he addressed me. 'Simon, I guess it's largely up to me to debrief you.' He looked first at Mercy B. Lord, then at Detective Chicken Wing, and directed his next sentence to them. 'You may both correct me and add any details as you wish.' Then he turned back to me. 'Simon, I don't have to tell you that what is said here remains in this room. This was a covert operation. While it's all over, bar the tidying-up of bank accounts, money and formal convictions among those governments involved – America, Singapore and Thailand in the main – it remains a top-secret operation. I emphasise that none of this will ever appear in the world's press. The DEA and the CIA are in agreement. In fact, without their help this operation would not have been possible because they were responsible for the logistics.'

'Hang on, aren't they the enemy? I mean, the opposition?' I asked, somewhat confused.

'Ah, the politics of political expediency, my friend. In the past few months a lot has changed. President Nixon has been elected with a plan to win the war. He doesn't want any sideshows, no awkward accusations about the US government's involvement with heroin. The anti-drug lobby in Washington is growing increasingly vociferous, and the human damage heroin addiction is causing in our cities is becoming very apparent.

'The justification the CIA has used all along – that they were supporting the forces that were stopping the Chinese communists from invading South-East Asia and coming to the aid of North Vietnam – has been blown out of the water. The domino theory is pure bunkum, Pentagon- and CIA-inspired crap. The Chinese have been fighting a series of pitched battles against the Russians along the Ussuri River that forms the Sino–Russian border. We're no longer fighting world communism as a unified force. In fact, the Chinese hate the Russians and the North Vietnamese probably more than they hate us.'

'What? The CIA have been told to pull their heads in?'

'Very graphic, Simon, but yes, and there are several more compelling reasons I'll go into later for this sudden change in policy. However, this mood swing from Washington and the death of Beatrice Fong couldn't have been more perfectly timed.'

'But didn't you say her death threw a spanner in the works for the DEA?'

He glanced at Mercy B. Lord. 'We were trying to protect our mole. But it was actually ideal, in fact, heaven-sent. All the stars were aligned correctly; the CIA were willing to cooperate with the DEA but were instructed by Washington to let us run the show.

'Well, as you know, power always expands to fill a vacuum. Beatrice Fong had pulled all the strings for a long time, playing off the different interests to keep the entire operation running smoothly. In this respect she was a genius, and besides, she had ruled for so long she knew where all the bodies were buried. Her death destabilised a very complex web of interlocking interests.' He nodded towards Mercy B. Lord. 'Moreover, our mole here completely lacked the experience to take over, and so it fell to Sidney Wing to do so.' Dansford turned to her. 'Do you want to say anything, to comment?' he asked.

'Well, only to say that after the funeral, Sidney and Johnny sat me down and explained the whole situation to me. I had to pretend to be shocked – in fact, mortified. Sidney then asked if I wanted to continue.' Mercy B. Lord paused. 'No, that's not quite how he put it. The inference was that I was implicated as a drug courier, and whether I liked it or not I was obliged to stay involved. I then asked him what might happen if I didn't. That was when Johnny laughed and said, "You're going to marry me and help with the girl business." Sidney then said there wasn't any "if" – once in, the only way out was the way Beatrice had just left. He told me that he was taking over Beatrice's share of the business and that I would be working for him in the immediate future. "Don't worry," Johnny said in an amused voice. "After we're married, it's all in the family anyway."'

'Jesus, talk about a rock and a hard place!' I exclaimed.

Mercy B. Lord laughed. 'My grandmother may have been an evil old woman but she wasn't a stupid one. In the bank vault was the proverbial little black book with enough in it to put a rope, several ropes, around Sidney Wing's neck. I described just one entry and told him there were at least fifty more. If anything happened to me, it would go directly to the police, I told him.' She gave a short laugh, then looked at Detective Sergeant Chicken Wing. 'In fact, it already had.'

'Nice one,' I said.

She continued. 'Well, he turned to Johnny and said, "She's got the strength." Then he said to me, "We'll train you. I'll do the heroin part and Johnny here the women business." So then I said there was just one more thing. "What?" Sidney asked. "Simple, I don't marry Johnny and I keep the inheritance or —" "Or what?" he asked. "Little black book," I replied. I'd rather die than marry that cruel bastard! "I think we begin to understand each other," Sidney said. Then to Johnny, who was speechless with fury, he said, "You hear that? Business all done. Sorry, Johnny. Welcome aboard, Mercy B. Lord."'

'Christ, darling, bravo! But weren't you scared?'

'Of course, I was terrified. When it was over I went into the bathroom and threw up.'

Dansford took over again, giving Mercy B. Lord a fondly benevolent look. 'If I had my way she'd be getting the medal of honour for bravery under intense enemy fire.' He paused, lifting the first bottle of wine, checked our glasses, which we'd barely touched, then filled his own with the last of the bottle. He'd already had two glasses, but was such a skilled alcoholic that he'd managed to do almost all the talking and still down two glasses of wine virtually unnoticed. 'Well, we had our Mata Hari still in place and undetected, so were in a position to know Sidney's takeover plans.

'Now it was up to Sidney to prove to the various elements in the mix that he had the strength, determination and the knowhow to take over from Beatrice Fong and bring them all together in one place to ensure consensus and continuity. In fact, to his credit, he came up with a damn good plan, and fortunately for us he went to his old friends, the CIA, to help with the logistics required to implement it.

'The point was that any such meeting needed to be on neutral ground. No one was willing to come to Singapore or Hong Kong. Having the meeting up north, up in the border area in Thailand, controlled by the warlords with their private armies, was much too risky. The warlords were increasingly disgruntled anyhow – they grew the opium to meet the exploding demand, delivered it across the Burma–Thai border to be refined by the Chinese, and so they had come to realise that the Thai military, the police, government officials and politicians were receiving most of the profits. In other words, the situation was likely to become very unstable without the old woman's iron fist. As it was, things were very close to exploding.

'Sidney demonstrated his leadership by arranging to have the meeting on a large oil tanker in international waters beyond the three-mile limit near Bangkok port. It would arouse no suspicion – the size and draft of the oil tanker prevented it from docking, requiring it to discharge its cargo into smaller tankers, so it had every reason to be where it was. It was also, conveniently, one of the vessels whose crew was involved in drug-smuggling for the cartel. Now all Sidney had to do was to get all the big boys and the two big girls on board.'

I glanced quickly at Mercy B. Lord. The other woman referred to was obviously her mother, Lotus Blossom. She ignored my look, keeping her eyes fixed on Dansford, who, surprise, surprise, had almost emptied his glass once more. 'Well, Sidney went to his old friends. As far as he was concerned, the only honest broker was his Florida connection, the CIA. He asked if they could arrange air transport – an unmarked Chinook helicopter – with one of its front companies such as Air America, who flew out of the CIA compound at Don Muang International Airport.

'Well, of course the CIA agreed and duly informed us. Then Sidney arranged, through the usual corrupt Thai officials, for the big operators in the cartel to fly into Bangkok and to the compound in light aircraft owned by the drug cartel. Then, as Mercy B. Lord has so often done, they avoided customs, boarded the unmarked Chinook helicopter and were flown out to the tanker. Air America was to log the helicopter trips as short test flights to avoid suspicion. The plan was that the Chinook would fly out, land on the tanker's deck, disembark passengers and return to the compound. After the meeting the Chinook would return, and they would all then disperse the way they had arrived, with no trace of their ever having been on the tanker. It was neat, safe and earned Sidney a lot of respect and trust from his cartel peers.'

Dansford topped up our glasses with the second bottle and refilled his own, then looked up at the ceiling. 'There has to be a God in heaven. Sidney's arrangements were better than anything we could possibly have hoped for. Not only were they meeting on a tanker, but to prevent any problems or disagreements turning nasty, no arms were allowed and every cartel member had to agree to be frisked before climbing aboard the helicopter. We planned to simply board the returning Chinook with a heavily armed raiding party and take them all into custody.'

He nodded at his wife. 'This is where Hilda comes in.'

Detective Chicken Wing surprised me by directing a question at me. 'Simon, will you allow me to begin by defending my husband's afternoon routine?'

'It's well past redemption, Detective Sergeant,' I grinned.

She smiled, then, typical of a police investigator, asked yet another question. 'Did you realise you were temporarily accommodated on a military base?'

'Well, yes. I heard a brass band, sirens once or twice, shouting and marching feet on another occasion, and Mercy B. Lord told me after her surprise visit.'

'Well, it's where Dansford spent a great many afternoons training a special squad along the lines of the special weapons and tactics group known in the US as a SWAT team, using men from the Singapore armed-forces commando formation, together with an elite Singapore police drug squad. In all we trained fifty police and defence force staff, sufficient to form a cadre. We only took twenty to Thailand, because we included eight Thai police, specially trained operatives, plus Dansford and myself, thirty or so being the troop capacity of a Chinook.'

Perhaps the several glasses of wine and a couple of martinis were beginning to have an effect, because Dansford somewhat rudely interrupted his wife. 'Just one problem remained: Hilda had to figure out a way to get twenty heavily armed Singapore commandos plus her drug squad component into a foreign country. It was a diplomatic initiative practically without precedent.'

Detective Chicken Wing gave him a dirty look. He was using his familial status to interrupt what was officially her story. She took up where she'd left off. 'Dansford could, theoretically, go through the American ambassador to Thailand and have him make the arrangements, but there was always the problem of a leak. Not all Thai government officials or politicians are corrupt – in fact, far from it – but we didn't know who the bad eggs were. The Thai authorities are coming under increasing international pressure to cooperate. Heroin addiction is a huge problem in the West and even the UN is asking awkward questions. But having a foreign, highly armed and dangerous commando force land at their airport was tantamount to an invasion. Even though the actual raid was to take place in international waters, no government, no matter how friendly, will tolerate that kind of interference in their security or domestic affairs.'

Dansford disgraced himself by interjecting once again. 'We had the perfect setup, a battle location made in heaven against an unarmed opponent, and we couldn't organise the transport logistics.'

Detective Chicken Wing shot him another meaningful look and I wondered what would happen when they got home. She was no shrinking violet. 'Well, *guanxi* finally solved the problem,' she said. 'My Singapore family is directly related to our prime minister, and through my division commander I was able to see the great man himself. I briefed him and he simply picked up the phone and called Prince Bhisatej Rajani of Thailand, who recently started what is known as the Royal Project Foundation. This is a special initiative designed to teach the Thai border hill tribes how to grow sustainable crops and so wean them off the cultivation of opium.

'An hour after our prime minister made the call, and while I sat outside his office close to panic, the reply came back and his secretary escorted me back into the PM's office, where he told me we had a top-secret all-clear to enter Thailand.' Detective Chicken Wing paused. 'The prime minister then stabbed his forefinger at me. "Just one thing, Detective Sergeant!" "Yes, sir?" I replied. "For God's sake, for the sake of Singapore and my government, don't screw up this operation!" "No, sir," I replied in a tiny voice I hardly recognised as my own, then, shaking like a leaf, I mumbled my thanks and turned to leave. As I reached the door, he called out, "Good luck, Hilda! Give the bastards hell!"'

Dansford, as usual showing remarkable ability to hold his grog, now said, 'Well, there's not really much more to say. We landed on deck and in ten minutes had the biggest combined arrest of the principals of any drug cartel ever. Effectively we got everyone, or everyone at the top. The only one who got away was the biggest of them all, but she's permanently shut in a box underground.' He turned to Detective Chicken Wing and raised his glass. 'I'd like to propose a toast to Detective Inspector Hilda Wing of the Singapore Drug Squad.'

We all congratulated the new detective inspector and then Dansford rang the bell. Moments later a waiter appeared and we ordered dessert – in my case, trifle, my absolute favourite pudding in the world. And then I made my big mistake. 'And Johnny, how did he die?' I asked.

Absolute silence followed and then Mercy B. Lord started to weep and shake. I grabbed her and held her tight. 'Oh, what did I say?' I asked, looking for an explanation, hugely distressed. But my beloved simply continued to wail, and Dansford and Hilda remained silent, looking down into their wine glasses. 'What did I say? What's wrong?' I asked, upset at my terrible gaffe.

Mercy B. Lord pulled free, attempting to gain control of her emotions. 'Tell him, Dansford,' she choked, reaching for her napkin to wipe her tears. But then they started afresh and stopped again, as if a memory kept bumping into her consciousness then receding just as quickly.

'Are you sure?' Dansford asked her.

Mercy B. Lord nodded and came back into my arms.

'It was the one mistake we made,' he began. 'We foolishly underestimated Sidney Wing. He had sent Johnny out to the oil tanker by motorboat earlier in the day. Johnny wasn't in the drug cartel so couldn't be present. Having frisked all those attending the meeting, Sidney knew they were all unarmed. He had Johnny already positioned on board, armed with a Browning automatic in case something unforeseen went wrong at the meeting. He was hidden from sight and positioned to observe the proceedings long before the Chinook arrived bringing the members of the cartel.

'Well, as I said, we arrived in the returning Chinook and, remarkably, with only a warning shot fired, we arrested and manacled them all, including Mercy B. Lord and, of course, Lotus Blossom, which was necessary to protect the safety of our mole. We were leading all Sidney's dubious guests out to the waiting Chinook, where five heavily armed police officers waited to take over from the army and escort them back to Bangkok and from there on to Singapore. This would henceforth be a police operation under Detective Sergeant Wing's command. Then Johnny suddenly appeared, seemingly from nowhere, and grabbed Mercy B. Lord from the rear, putting his pistol to her head. "Stop!" he yelled, "or she dies!"' Dansford glanced at Mercy B. Lord, then said quietly, 'This is one of the many reasons why you should get the medal of honour, my dear.' He continued. 'With a pistol to the back of her head, she said in a calm voice, "Johnny, go ahead, shoot. We're all of us dead anyway." Johnny shoved the Browning further into the base of her neck and howled like a dog. "Beatrice promised I could have you! You're mine, you hear? You die first, you whore!" Then the sniper's bullet entered the back of his head . . .' Dansford couldn't bring himself to complete the sentence.

'How did you know, Simon?' Mercy B. Lord howled. 'It happened just like in your painting!'

Oh, God, how I loved this woman.

EPILOGUE

Singapore and Sydney, Australia 1990–91

IF I'VE MANAGED TO hold your interest thus far, then you may be interested in the twenty years that followed. Pretty uneventful, I'm afraid, but lovely, with Chairman Meow more or less reconciled to the fact that Mercy B. Lord and I decided to live in Singapore, until two years ago, or, if you like, at arm's length from Mercy B. Koo's mother-in-law. Given her unshakeable faith in the power of Little Sparrow's dream, she had every confidence that Mercy B. Lord and I would prosper and be happy, but nevertheless she would have preferred to have us within her sphere of influence. Well before our wedding, Chairman Meow had taken her soon-to-be daughter-in-law aside and recounted the dream, before going on to analyse its meaning.

'You are the infant in the dream, my dear, Beatrice Fong is the old crone, and the cord connecting you is the secret family relationship, you see.' Poor trapped Mercy B. Lord was far too polite to do more than nod and smile as my mother continued. 'The three lotus blossoms in the dream are, I believe, the three lives of Lotus Blossom – Johnny Wing's teenage promise of betrothal is the first, the rape by the Japanese captain and the birth of her child is the second, and the banishment to Burma and the drug cartel is the third. The fat wooden dragon, the traditional Chinese symbol of prosperity, as you know, is the wealth

570

accumulated from heroin, and the chisel through its heart is the fact that all the prosperity came to nothing because the money was ultimately confiscated.'

Mercy B. Lord then asked, perhaps only to be polite, 'The gold chisel – the fact that it stabbed the fat dragon and ended the wealth accumulated from drugs – do you think it's symbolically the work of the infant in the dream?'

It was all heading into La-La Land and so I interjected. 'Mum, give us a break, for God's sake!' I protested. 'You can make anything mean something if you try hard enough.'

'Oh, you think so, Simon?' Chairman Meow said, plainly piqued by my interruption.

'Of course. Look, let me show you,' I said. 'Mercy B. Lord was born on the 1st of May 1946. So, let's do the numbers, shall we? Fifth month, that's 5, first day, that's 1, so 5+1= 6.' I scribbled it down. 'Now add 1+9+4+6 = 20, add the 6 = 26, and hey presto, 2+6 = 8. There you go, the number-eight gold chisel and also the luckiest number for the Chinese.' I gave her a sardonic grin, complete with slightly raised right eyebrow. 'See what I mean?'

Chairman Meow paused for a moment. 'Simon, that's brilliant!' She clapped her hands together. 'Why, of course! How stupid of me. It becomes immediately obvious! Simon, you knew all along, didn't you? That's why you painted the chisel into Mercy B. Lord's portrait.' She looked at me. 'Now, don't you deny it, Simon,' she remonstrated. 'Just like you deny being the yellow-beaked bird. Anyone with a nose on her face can see the gold chisel is directly associated with the baby, and that both cannot be anything other than Mercy B. Lord.'

'Oh, that simple, is it?'

'Well, yes, as a matter of fact it is.'

'Okay, if I'm the yellow-beaked bird, who are the other birds, the ones that cleaned the baby's body? And the electric blue snake, who or what is the snake?'

'Why, all your friends in Singapore are the birds.' She spread her elegant manicured hands, 'I would have thought the snake was obvious – Johnny Wing, of course!'

'Okay, so who is Sidney?'

Chairman Meow was not the least fazed by the question. 'Yes, I must admit he doesn't feature directly, but he's got something to do with the large box,' she said confidently.

I sighed. 'Christ, Mum. I don't believe what I'm hearing. How can one of the smartest women in Australia be so deluded? So consumed by ignorance and superstition? All those tenuous connections you make with Little Sparrow's dream are crap. Like I just showed you with the numbers, you can make almost anything symbolise anything else if you're prepared to shut down the part of your brain that tells you it's clearly all a load of codswallop!'

'Simon, you shouldn't talk to your mother like that!' Mercy B. Lord said reprovingly. 'Besides, who's to say your mother isn't right?'

I turned on her. 'I am! It's arrant nonsense, if that's a more polite way of putting it.'

'Oh, is that so!' Mercy B. Lord exclaimed. 'Then kindly explain the painting with the shattered head? You didn't know what happened on board the oil tanker, you didn't know how Johnny died, but you painted it exactly as it happened!'

'Oh, Christ, not you as well!' I said, shaking my head in disbelief.

'Thank you,' Chairman Meow said, smiling smugly at Mercy B. Lord. 'Sometimes that son of mine is just a little too big for his boots. You'll have to watch that in him, my dear,' she warned.

So, there you go, humans seem geared to signs and portents and have been since time out of mind. Commonsense has nothing to do with it and few things in this world are wrought by logic alone.

Needless to say, Chairman Meow took over the wedding arrangements. She flew Mercy B. Lord to Paris to buy a wedding gown, and with diamond pendants dangling, Mercy B. Lord married me at St Mary's Catholic Cathedral, with Archbishop Gilroy presiding, in the early summer of 1970. No doubt this was agreed after a generous donation to some worthy church-related cause. The Catholic faith was chosen in deference to Mercy B. Lord, who was not all that fussed, but unlike my own iconoclastic family, she had at least some religion in her past.

I'm telling a fib. That's not *exactly* why we were married at St Mary's. The truth is that the alternative to a church wedding was the marriage registry office, directly across the road from the cathedral in an office with mullioned windows in Queen's Square. Chairman Meow was damned if she was going to waste a magnificent raw-silk Paris original wedding gown encrusted with God knows how many seed pearls on a clerk in a stuffy government office with only two witnesses present. Huge stained-glass windows, an impressive high altar, incense swirling, Latin chants, choirboys singing, towering naves and arches, and the archbishop in his splendid vestments pontificating were the absolute minimum requirement.

A huge marquee was erected in the grounds of the Vaucluse house, and every employee of the considerable Koo business empire – funeral, restaurant and property-investment arms – was invited to attend the church service and reception afterwards, catered for by three of our Little Swallow restaurants with two additional chefs flown in from Singapore.

Over a thousand guests attended from all over Australia and beyond: from Singapore, Dansford, who gave Mercy B. Lord away; Hilda; Long Me Saw; Molly Ong (now head of the Tourist Promotion Board); Mrs Sidebottom and Cecil; Willy Wonka; Louie da Fly (by the way, we made him my best man); Alice Ho; Harry 'Three Thumbs' Poon; Owen Denmeade; and of course my numerous Singapore relatives. From Hong Kong came the inestimable Elma Kelly. Then, from my former advertising agency in Sydney, Odette, from the switchboard; Charles Brickman, the chairman; and Ross Quinlivan, the creative director. From America, Jonas Bold and his glorious long-legged Bondi blonde bombshell wife, Sue Chipchase. In fact, there were so many guests that we were forced to book the entire first-class and business-class sections on a Qantas jet to bring them and my personal friends to Australia.

Chairman Meow aka Mum had waited a long time for her son and heir to be hitched to a Chinese maiden, and she wasn't going to allow a careless moment to intrude in the organisation of his wedding ceremony.

We honeymooned at Lord Howe Island, staying at Pinetrees – not posh, just a really nice traditional homestead – but it was wonderful to be completely away from the madding crowd. We now have two daughters, Charity and Faith, to complement their mother's name, and a son, James.

That's enough about us for the time being. Let me bring you up to date with events after the successful raid on the drug cartel. Sidney Wing was executed in Singapore jail in June 1970, and all the other members of the criminal cartel eventually followed him. Ronnie sold his share in the agency back to Samuel Oswald. He also sold the Nite Cap and his other girlie-bar interests in Singapore and moved to Bangkok, where he owned several more bars in Patpong Road and the area most favoured by US troops on R&R from Vietnam, New Petchburi Road. After the Vietnam War was over, he bought two 'night clubs' – read high-class brothels.

If you're wondering what happened to Lotus Blossom, she avoided the hangman's rope and lives in Taiwan, where she owns a string of French perfume boutiques she has aptly named after her daughter, Mercy B. Koo Perfumes. She never faced drug charges and got off scot-free because of a deal between Mercy B. Lord and the DEA via Dansford.

When, after learning the true nature of the Fong and Wing partnership, she'd agreed to be Dansford's mole, she had made only one request: that if the DEA were successful in bringing down the drug cartel, her mother would be allowed to go free. It was an early example of her ability to plan well ahead.

Dansford kept his word and Lotus Blossom was allowed to settle in Taipei. As he explained to me, 'Simon, politics is the art of compromise – exceptions are *always* the rule.' Now, here's a curious twist. Lotus Blossom was nominally a vastly wealthy woman. But, like all the other cartel bigwigs, she was stripped of all her assets; her money and property were confiscated by the various states, Thailand, Singapore and America, so that she was effectively dead broke. That is, until Johnny Wing's will was read. He'd left his entire fortune, a sum of twenty million US dollars, to his boyhood sweetheart. But, as Mercy B. Lord would say of her mother's acquired fortune, 'All the perfume in the world can't disguise the stench of that malevolent bastard.'

Beatrice Fong's estate was also confiscated, with only her residence in Katong, originally left to her by her mother, coming to Mercy B. Lord. We sold it (too many bad memories) and, together with my bonus cheque from the agency, financed the two businesses we were to start.

Sadly, our dear and wonderful Dansford Drocker, who took over the management of the now Wingless Samuel Oswald Advertising agency, died of obvious causes in 1978 – both lighted ends of the same candle had finally met and burnt out. He had requested that he have a very simple burial. 'Don't let a priest anywhere near me, Simon, unless he's drunk and Irish. It's been a great life, buddy; we don't want it spoilt by making false promises to God on my death bed.' I organised a plain granite headstone to be made and sent from Australia, on which I caused to be inscribed:

Dansford Metford Drocker
1924–1978
He lived life to its fullest
then
died happily, of everything.
R.I.P.

Elma Kelly sold her share of Cathay Advertising to Bill 'Long Socks' Farnsworth, who could now claim to own in his own right an international organisation. He then sold his now multinational agency to Ted Bates Advertising in New York, at a considerable profit. Elma never forgave him, not for the pass-on profit he'd made, but simply for outsmarting her, because she could as easily have bought Farnsworth's

Australian organisation, George Patterson, and made the same deal with New York herself. 'Simon, my dear, his convict ancestors probably pinched that Gainsborough he owns. Haw, haw, haw! Can't trust a man who's always punctual and orders steak and chips to eat alone in a Singapore hotel room, can you?'

Now, perhaps a little about us – that is, Mercy B. Koo and yours truly. Well, very briefly, Mercy B. Lord for the first six months, then Mercy B. Koo for the next six, became the first Singapore girl, a very successful concept that has continued ever since. Then, despite Dansford asking me to stay in what was now simply Samuel Oswald Advertising, I decided I'd had my fill of working for someone else, so I declined. The tourism minister then called me into his office and asked me if I was willing to start my own advertising agency, saying that the government was thinking of cutting its partnership with Malaysian Airlines and starting Singapore International Airlines, based around customer service and the concept of the Singapore Girl, adding that they would like me to do the advertising. It was attractive – more than that, it was a truly great offer and I was sorely tempted – but finally we decided we'd develop the two ancillary businesses we'd more or less planned all along: market research and commercial film. The airline account eventually went to a terrific young Australian ad man named Ian Batey, who consequently did an absolutely splendid job.

Mercy B. Koo developed the first truly Asian market-research organisation, which grew to be the biggest in Asia (still is). With Willy Wonka and Harry 'Three Thumbs' Poon, we developed a film studio that, I'm glad to say, has prospered mightily. Not that I can take the credit for either organisation. Mercy B. Koo was initially the exceptional financial manager, and Willy and Harry are both highly talented film men. I'll never know how she did it. Somehow we financed both businesses without borrowing from my dad and Chairman Meow. After ten years we were moderately well off, and Mercy B. Koo was becoming bored and wanted to stretch her business wings.

Enter the ever-vigilant and opportunist Chairman Meow, and

soon we shared a funeral business, under my wife's direction, with the Australian family company. The two women worked together and it wasn't all that long before they were opening up Blue Lotus Funerals in Hong Kong, Taipei, Bangkok and Manila. In the mid-eighties, Mercy B. Koo was spending a week every month in Sydney on business involving the deadly female duo.

As for me, I'd opted out of business altogether by the late seventies and was beginning to earn a reputation as an artist. It all started to happen when the Tate Gallery in London bought the painting of Mercy B. Lord's execution. In fact, that was what I'd named it: 'The Execution of Mercy B. Lord'. This brought to light the Hong Kong Museum and Art Gallery's purchase of what was now named 'Woman in a Peacock-tail Chair'. *The Guardian* wrote a bit of a story saying nice things about both paintings, devoting a page to them. It was picked up and reprinted by the *South China Morning Post*, and for the next week long queues formed at the Tate as well as in Hong Kong. Several commissions followed and now that's what I do. I paint and have been fortunate enough to have my work exhibited in several major galleries around the world.

The irony is that Chairman Meow is my biggest supporter, and the reason for this is her business partner and fellow entrepreneur, Mercy B. Koo. Which brings me just about to the end of my story.

Two years ago we moved back to Sydney with the kids. Both Charity (Masters degree) and Faith are attending Macquarie University, and James is doing his last two years at Cranbrook. But they are not the reason for our return. The schools and universities in Singapore are absolutely first-class.

The reason is that Mercy B. Lord had to learn the business from the Australian side of Koo International Pty Ltd. On the 2nd of January 1991, Chairman Meow, now a sprightly seventy-six, and my dad, a rather battered seventy-seven, retired. And guess who is to be the new chairman? Not surrogate, but your *actual* chairman, no ifs or buts. You got it in one, the glorious, wonderful, should-have-won-the-US-medal-of-honour-for-bravery Mercy B. Koo, née the mighty and still incredibly beautiful Mercy B. Lord! I've ordered a black cheongsam and red stilettos for her to wear on the day the board appoints her.

Oh, by the way, talking about chairmen, Louie da Fly is the new managing director *and* chairman of Samuel Oswald Advertising, Singapore. He has proved to be a 'very vallabil employ'.

ACKNOWLEDGEMENTS

———————

This is the twentieth book I've written over the past twenty-one years, and when I think about the effort it's taken I am immediately aware that I have needed a large support cast, people who have volunteered information, know-how and help, invariably giving selflessly of their knowledge and expertise. So, I decided to go through my other books to see just how large this supporting cast, to whom I am abidingly grateful, has become. The number is, to my mind, staggering –1017, at least the teaching faculty of a small university. They are the people who have helped me to become a recognised novelist.

I am told that it is unfashionable to include acknowledgements in works of fiction. Why is that? How can this be? Who possesses such arrogance? Without the knowledge and help of others, we fiction writers would be rendered almost mute. We ride piggyback on the life experiences and stories of others and then claim the approbation and rewards. The limp-wristed cliché by lazy literary critics 'an original work of fiction' is seldom true. We storytellers are dependent on the collective lives and experiences of others. We beg, borrow and steal shamelessly.

It is with gratitude and humility that I thank you all for your help, even such as comes to me mute but no less appreciated. Writing is a lonely job and so it's nice to have the presence of several writer companions who don't feel the need to talk. On my desk, designed long and in a U shape for the very purpose, rest the baskets of three of our four cats. Alas, Ophelia, the kitten, is illiterate. I sometimes wonder what's going to happen to our next generation of young felines who no longer read books. Princess Cardamon is onto her fifth book that she claims to have mostly written herself, with a smidgin of help from me; Mushka, the bush cat, her fourth; and Pirate, who blew into our safe harbour one cold winter's night, his very first, and the jury is still out as to whether he's going to make it as a writer.

All, with the exception of Cardamon who comes from a long line of Burmese royalty, just dropped by, liked the sniff of the place and decided to stay. RSCPA-acquired Timmy the dog of dogs lies at my feet. He's not much of a writer but he's good for an opinion, an excellent barking-board with a finely tuned snore.

I usually work ten or twelve hours, six days a week. Except to occasionally tap-dance on my keyboard to remind me that cats have to eat or to go outside to do what a cat needs to do, or when Timmy is taken for his daily walk, the purr and bark elements seldom leave my desk. So there you go, thank you for your collective good company and help.

And now to the mortals who helped variously and with enormous generosity.

My beloved partner, Christine Gee, takes the brunt of the book I'm writing. It's never easy being the general factotum in a writer's life. She takes care of the myriad details, feeds me, comforts me, listens, acts as a second researcher, suggests, protects and comments, all with unerring patience, intelligence and love, so that my needs often crowd out those of her own. I thank her with all my heart, and, in addition, for her selfless dedication and encouragement. I'm quite sure I couldn't do what I do without her.

Good editors are charged with the task of making books sing and words dance. When some of the notes are flat and the words clumsy, this is usually due to a pedantic or over-precious writer. Nan McNab is my editor, and, yes, she is almost always correct in her comments, which, in turn, can be very bloody annoying. Nevertheless I cherish her and thank her enormously for her talent, patience and dedication. Editing a writer as each chapter evolves while not knowing how a story ends must be very frustrating. But she invariably adds more than the sum of this author's ability.

Anne Rogan, my managing editor at Penguin, is less front-of-house, but an invaluable contributor to the book in more ways than I truly understand. Along with Bob Sessions, my publisher, she rides shotgun on every chapter, and I am truly grateful for their insights, experience, forthright opinions and honesty. While writers work in the foreground it is those who labour with them at the rear who add greatly to the end result. The sheer knowledge and perspicacity of Bob Sessions are gifts to any writer. I am most fortunate to have him as my publisher. I must add thanks to Julie Gibbs who, while not my publisher, has always taken an interest in what I do, and I invariably benefit from her involvement.

Bruce Gee, my researcher, must be and is a constant and utterly dependable resource. When I turn on the word tap he has to be ready with a bucket of knowledge to mix with the flow. I like to think that my fiction evolves within the facts of history or contemporary life down to the smallest detail. In my experience the actual facts are usually better than the ones you invent and, besides, the reader has the right to know that you are taking the care to be accurate with your incidental information. Bruce, who digs, suggests and constantly checks, is a rare and talented searcher of truth and plays an essential part in my books. Thank you, mate, we appear to have done it again.

Alex Hamill, good friend and true, first suggested the idea for this book to me and gave me helpful advice throughout, as well as several incidents to incorporate in the story. In fact without his input it would be a much slimmer and less interesting volume. Thanks, mate, I'm truly grateful.

Geoff and Phyllis Pike helped greatly with things Chinese, Hong Kong and in other ways. Thank you for generously giving of your time and knowledge.

To Professor Carl A. Trocki, Professor of Asian Studies at Queensland University of Technology, my gratitude for his references to sources, and personal and professional advice given at a critical stage of this book. Also, for allowing me to quote from his own book, *Singapore: Wealth, Power and the Culture of Control*.

Christine Lenton, my P.A., who has for the past thirteen years kept the world at bay while I write, and attends to the endless detail that seems to be a part of my public life. I simply cannot imagine what I would do without her.

What follows in alphabetical order are those others who helped in various ways: John Adamson, Yasuko Ando, John Atkin, Carole Baird, Ian Batey (Asian Branding – a great way to fly), Debra Calderbank, Phil Clegg, Russell and Barbara Coburn, Adam Courtenay, Brett Courtenay, Tony Crosby, Michael Dean, Tony Freeman, Alida Haskins, Jodie Iliani, Irwin Light, Nima Price, Debbie Tobin, Duncan Thomas, Wang Kangning, Wang Tai-Peng, and, by no means least, our cherished friends in Singapore, who provided knowledge and generosity of spirit.

Margaret Gee suggested the title and I thank her.

Finally those people who labour in the temple of publishing, all those at Penguin who in one way or another contributed to the final book. I thank you all for your personal contribution to *Fortune Cookie*: Vicky Axiotis, Sally Bateman (publicity is everything), Peter Blake (without retail sales, I'm dead!), Deb Brash, Nicole Brown, Gabrielle Coyne, CEO (the boss of bosses), Carol George, Chris Grierson, Lisa and Ron Eady, Anyez Lindop (my personal tour minder and publicity finder), Gordon McKenzie, Cameron Midson, Jordan Ormandy-Neale, Kim Noble, Tony Palmer, Adrian Potts, Sarina Rowell, Dan Ruffino (good luck, Dan), Louise Ryan (ditto Blakey comment), Andre Sawenko, SharleneVinall and Julian Welch.

Finally, there are the charities this book will help to support, and that allow Christine Gee and me to give back, something we value highly and which we regard as both an honour and a privilege: The Australian Himalayan Foundation, The Thin Green Line Foundation, Gene & Cell Trust, The Bookend Trust, The Taronga Conservation Society Australia, Sane Australia, Voiceless and Room to Read.